FOREWORD

Herb Alf has given us *Petals of Fire*, an authentic epic, drawn from his own experiences as a bomber pilot and prisoner of war and from further research. That's the dry, journalistic nutshell. However, if we stop there, indicating that we hold in our hands a mere "war novel," we cheat the reader.

We need to know that the novel has been seasoned and aged with more than a half century of mulling, writing, researching, talking, mourning, thinking, and rewriting. We need to know that the author has explored every cavity of his psyche, every dark and heroic place, every kind of human interaction, and that he has criss-crossed the globe to find answers to vital questions.

The novel's central characters are an air force colonel and three B-17 crew members who find themselves entangled in the massive machinery of World War II. In flying their ordered bombing missions, they fly into tons of flak that are walls of death thrown into the sky by the Germans and they battle fanatic enemy fighters. We are with them in the air and on the ground—fighting and loving, fleeing and surrendering, celebrating and dying—murdering, looting, singing, and playing. But the story demands that we reach beyond the experiences of men who put on a uniform and go off to war.

Woven together in this timeless story are the relations between men and women, their needs and emotions heightened by the furnace of war. In differing ways, the nurturing of the women is a decisive influence in the midst of the carnage. Nurse Randi Scott works to heal human relations as well as the wounded. Sister Johanna, a nurse in a prison hospital, helps a wounded soldier keep alive his spiritual connection with a Gypsy saint. Kristen, accused of being a Nazi general's mistress, shows us the power of ennobling art, lifting life-affirming inspiration with Chopin's *Fantasia in F minor*. Paula, a German woman raped by a Gestapo lieutenant and caught under the bombers as they bomb her home city, fathoms the ultimate insanity: the systematic killing of people by people who do not wish to kill them. . . . Sam O'Brien, a bombardier who sometimes displays disquieting softness, says, "Men are mostly killers, women are the life-givers."

Still, we acknowledge the novel's masculine motifs. As flyers are shot down we enter prisoner of war camps with them and join them on the death row of forced marches. Here the story's broadest scope of human emotions and values are encountered. Being powerless under a force that has no limits, . . . the patriot, the pacifist, the militarist, the mystic, the idealist, and the collaborator must accommodate their differences and band into "combines" to survive. With cold, hunger, and the closeness of death their constant companions, we experience their confrontations and increasing inter-connectedness. In the poignant drama of people locked into a boxcar on a journey to the unknown, the circumstance of all humanity is mirrored. Their journey is everyone's journey.

Petals of Fire gives us gritty truth infused with passages of awe-inspiring, poetic realism. A train hurtles through the dark, pulling boxcars crammed with what nurse Randi calls "human debris." In one boxcar, amidst the stench of the living and the dying, while a lightning storm encloses the anguish, a German guard sings from the Catholic mass "Libera for the Dead." In another scene, two prisoners escape and spend a night by the open fire of a band of gypsies under the spell of music and a stunning girl's dance with fire.

The war itself becomes a main character, battering everyone in its relentless currents. The substance of each character lies in the decisions he or she must make within this turbulence. These choices become the wondrously complex fabric of this intricately woven tapestry. Combining history, psychology, and philosophy, the author probes themes of universal importance to humanity with hold-onto-your-seat suspense. The story raises timeless questions and leaves us pondering for answers. On a literal level it asks: Why was the air force diverted from its promise of victory without the D-Day invasion?

Here is a story that can make us laugh or cry, as life can, for the story's roots are hooked into the universe and bridged to the human heart.

—*Terry Johnson*
January, 2000

Library of Congress No. 00-190054

ISBN: 0-9678140-0-6

PETALS OF FIRE

—By Herb Alf—

A Millennium Memorial 2000 limited 1st edition
in bonded leather. The first 2000 volumes are serial numbered.

945 Herb Alf

Published by Millennium Memorial Trust, Inc.
A Singing River Book

Dedicated to the many I knew whose daring generosity outreached their human limits and who still fire inspiration for deeds beyond self service.

A MEMORIAL TO AIR FORCE PIONEERS RETURNED PRISONERS OF WAR AND FLYERS STILL MISSING IN ACTION

Starting as a personal journal, this writing is now vaster in scope from years of study, interaction, thinking, writing, and rewriting. Specific credit is due my wife, Sylvia, as my editorial partner, Terry Johnson, as a copy editor, and Joan Chaffee as a critical reviewer. Many others deserve credit. If you are not here mentioned, I honor you no less.

—Herb Alf

PART I

The War

PETALS OF FIRE

THE WAR: CHAPTER ONE

0735 HOURS, 29 JANUARY, ENROUTE TO THE 100TH BOMB GROUP, ENGLAND: Braced into wine-velvet cushions of a first class train compartment, the U.S. Air Force eagle Colonel Dean Raymond held the attention of a one-star general and a two-star general seated across from him. Colonel Dean Raymond had just arrived from Washington, D.C., as an inspector general to investigate *Factors Delaying the Bombing Program of the Combined Bomber Offensive.* His authority was feared sufficiently to bring about this high-ranking reception.

A policy war was raging in England between ground-war and air-war commanders and between English and United States policy-makers up to Churchill himself. The different warring factions each wanted to win the inspector general's favor.

The two-star general had known Dean Raymond for almost twenty years—an ace card he now played: "I brought some words to refresh your memory, Dean, of a goddamn day you and I will never forget, 'My trial before this court-martial is the culmination of the efforts of the General Staff of the Army and the General Board of the Navy to deprecate the value of air power and keep it in an auxiliary position, which absolutely compromises our whole system of national defense.'"

"Billy Mitchell's words of his court-martial! You strike a nerve, General," Dean reacted with braced shoulders. "I was only a 2nd lieutenant back then in 1926, but I was there. The war he started has never ended. So you came prepared to remind me how long you've been with me in the Billy Mitchell fight! Your point is scored, General, but I've been sent here to focus on our failures not our good intentions."

The one-star general came alive with, "I hope you're here as a second Billy Mitchell who is going to make asses out of the ground-army generals trying to control us. Every day the weather is keeping us grounded, they're handing out

3

more bullshit about our pinpoint bombing plan to win the war not working like we promised."

Dean, allowing himself to again drift back to the infamous Billy Mitchell court-martial, said, "I didn't have rank enough to rate a chair, but I was there. Our hero sky general was already fighting the admirals and ground-generals to win us power in the sky back in World War One."

The one-star general came back with, "Piss on our history. We need you now to be a Billy Mitchell martyr noisy enough to save our plan to win this war from the sky!"

The two-star general interceded with his eyes on his fellow general, "Before you plead for Raymond to be a martyr, you should know more about why he is still only a colonel. Get the secret briefing on why our mystery colonel Raymond here was selected to be our inspector general."

Dean replied, "May we change the subject? Did you get my request of a meeting schedule today that will give me a chance to see my son? He's assigned to the 100th."

"Request granted, Colonel. I've been waiting for an I.G. like you to get here."

Dean kept to himself that a meeting with his "white angel" nurse sweetheart of his days in the Philippines was also in his plans for the day.

29 JANUARY, NISSEN HUT 23, DAISY MAY AIRFIELD, ENGLAND: Here twenty-eight beds were occupied by B-17 bomber pilots, co-pilots, bombardiers, and navigators of seven crews of the 100th Bomb Group. Here the mattresses did not have contours shaped by many months under the same slumberer. In bed 17, nineteen-year-old 2nd Lieutenant Tom Raymond was awake, thinking of the coming day. He had arrived only hours before and was scheduled to fly as the co-pilot of Captain Brewster Pierce's crew. He listened to the moaning and whining of the 128 bomber engines being punished under test strain, and he heard the wail of a winter storm. From the sounds of the night he read an ominous message.

The Hut 23 flyers were part of 800-plus bomber crews Alerted for dawn takeoff. A massive winter storm moving down from the Arctic made it seem impossible that the bombers could actually take off, get into formation, penetrate enemy territory, and, finally bomb a designated target. Yet, the commanding general was continuing the Alert to get the Eighth Air Force airborne at dawn.

From thirty-two revetments, horseshoe-shaped earth embankments along the field perimeter, work lights glowed through blowing snow. In each of these revetments—protection against all but a direct bomb hit—a ground crew was meticulously readying its Flying Fortress for the mission.

Lying awake, Tom Raymond pondered how he came to be here. *The Group Commander said he was giving me a break by taking me out of my crew I trained with, putting me on a strange crew with a lot of combat experience. Why me? Because of my dad? The special treatment makes me suspicious. This night started a long time ago on my dad's lap in a giant cockpit filled with dials and levers. I decided then that I wanted to be a pilot, but tonight, in the big war, I wonder why. Don't ask why, Dad says, when there are no answers. We are ants in a cathedral . . . but he still is always leading out to learn why. Why? . . . Mom's less complicated. She's sure to have a letter on the way.*

Reminding himself that take-off time was nearing, he tried to get some sleep. *I'll be replacing Buck's co-pilot who got killed. . . . Buck's crew came back from Bordeaux on two engines, and another time came back with a broken wing, but they've always got back . . . so far.*

Hearing the bomber engines roaring in test of their ability to lift a belly full of bombs, he suddenly realized that he was already locked into the war, and he felt very much alone.

29 JANUARY, AT THE MISSION BRIEFING: Buck Pierce, Sam O'Brien, and Walter Plank arrived together. Although Walt flew as a lead bombardier with another crew, he spent a lot of time with Buck and his red-headed bombardier Sam O'Brien from south side Chicago.

The target map of Europe at the front of the briefing hut was hidden behind a curtain. This map held a red ribbon leading from England to the secret target of the day. This ribbon could indicate fourteen hours over enemy territory or a brief "milk run" to the French coast with return in time for lunch.

Captain Brewster "Buck" Pierce said with a chuckle, "I hope the target's near Switzerland. I'd like the temptation of heading for neutral territory and sitting out the war with a Swiss milkmaid in each arm."

Sam was still certain that the storm would force the mission to be scrubbed. He felt confident that in a few hours he would be with his intriguing Sandra amour in London.

The curtain came back. The red ribbon did not mark a milk run. Groans rose from the crews. The Group Operations Officer announced, "Today, our target will be Frankfurt on the Main River. Take off is at 0735 hours. No use in kidding ourselves about the weather. We're hoping it will quit snowing enough to give us some visibility for take off. With your bomb and gas load as heavy as it is, you're going to need all your power to get airborne before you run out of runway. Try to aim right when you let loose the horses then pour on the coal and ride it out. The pilot who jockeys his throttles while he's looking for the runway will never make that mistake again." Nervous laughter ran across the room.

The Group Commander took the floor; he was scheduled to fly the Lead ship next to the Pathfinder ship. "We'll be taking off into cloud cover that goes up thousands of feet. That means we'll be doing individual climbs. There'll be a hell of a lot of airplanes crossing course to get upstairs. We will have the risk of collision, but that's unavoidable. Once we rendezvous, I want all of our thirty-two ships in tight formation at all times. We've been having a lot of losses and we're being talked about as a hard luck group—the Bloody 100th—but starting today we're going to earn the reputation of being a good luck group.

"Today we will have a Pathfinder ship from Alconbury. This means we can bomb through the clouds with our newly-developed "magic eye" the Pathfinder carries. This "eye" can see through clouds, but it is only accurate enough to find a city. It can't locate a pinpoint target like a factory. If the sky over Frankfurt is clear, we will bomb the factory specified for our Group. If the overcast holds, we will stay in our broader Wing formation and release a bomb every three hundred feet for dispersal over the area of the city."

Buck mumbled to Sam, "In other words, we'll fertilize the city free-style."

The Group Chaplain rose and announced, "The Mass for the blessing of the crews of this mission will be held in the armament warehouse immediately following the briefing."

The Group Intelligence Officer went to the stage and spoke officiously, "Gentlemen, I would remind you as I have in the past, if you are shot down and captured, remember: give the enemy only your name, rank, and serial number. I thank you, and good luck."

Buck mumbled again, "The ground-grippers sure are generous with their good luck when they're sending us out to the killing while they stay behind drinking coffee."

The Group Operations Officer standing at the front of the room raised his watch to eye level. The gesture took on the appearance of a priest raising his hand in benediction. The congregated officers lifted their watch arms in response. An air of religious respect was struck for the precision technology, the clock-tick divinity, that would prevail when hundreds of bombers would take to the air, climb to mission altitude, rendezvous into combat formation, invade the enemy sky, and at the place and time locked into the running clock of war, drop thousands of tons of bombs. The Operations Officer now spoke in a tone of reverence, "Let us synchronize our watches . . . Counting the remaining seconds: Five. Four. Three. Two. One. Hack." All watches of the hundreds of heavy-bomber crews in England being briefed for this mission at this time now ran as one clock of war.

BY THE POT BELLIED STOVE OF HUT 23:
> There are things you cannot understand
> Until you have shared a last cigar
> With a friend
> Before taking off into the sky
> Where one of you is going to die.

As he finished reading, Lieutenant Marks said to his friend Buck Pierce, "I found it in my drawer. My sisters are keeping a scrapbook. I ought to send them that poem."

Marks was the pilot of another crew. While their crews were readying the guns, ammunition, escape kits, and other combat gear, Buck and Marks were resting their feet on the rail of the Hut 23 stove and smoking panatela cigars.

After a stretch of quiet, with each in his own world, Marks said, "We're a close family. If it weren't for my sisters I wouldn't be here. I'm the only boy out of six kids. It was up to me to be the soldier."

Buck said, "Back on the ranch I used to sit by the stove like this with my chair leaned back, even in summer, reading a *Street and Smith* western magazine. One time Dad knocked the chair out from under me to get me to go out and weed the corn. Working to keep the weeds from taking over, you learn that the world doesn't come right on its own. You've got to put down your story-reading and go out and do some killing sometimes. Our religion is against war . . . but there was corn needing weeding, I figured. Still, I should have stayed on the ranch . . . my folks wanted me to stay."

AT THE *BARE LASS* REVETMENT: Buck searched the morning twilight and connected with the art work on his B-17, *BARE LASS*, inscribed on a bolt of lightning thrust across a naked woman. He had come to love this airplane more each time it brought them back from the war. "Baby, come through today," he mumbled. Then he pulled back the canvas of the hut that stood in the revetment and entered the warm interior.

"Hi, Captain," the crew sergeant greeted. "Help yourself to some coffee. It's freezing outside. We've been working in this mother-fucking weather all night. We should have got in another Number 3, but we had to quit for lack of time."

"How did the old Number 3 check out?"

"Rough, but still running."

Buck changed the subject. There was no point in worrying the crew. He knew the Number 3 engine should have been changed. His eyes fell upon the new co-pilot standing in a corner, his arms loaded with escape kits.

Tom regarded the hefty, six-foot-two-inch captain. The Group Operations Officer had told him that the day Buck lost his co-pilot he came in on three engines with no rudder or elevator controls, and he landed with his automatic pilot. *Is this that hot-shot pilot?* "Good morning, Captain Pierce," he said solemnly.

"Tom Raymond? Good morning. Not that I know what's good about it. You can drop the captain crap. On the *Bare Lass* I'm Buck. We're all one rank to the flak. Pass around the escape kits. Where were you at the pilot's briefing?"

"I didn't know there was one, sir. I was in such a hurry I must not have heard. I had to check out a lot of equipment, sir."

"I understand. It's been a rough morning for you. Did you get everything?"

"I hope so, sir." He had been told that Buck is tough but that he's the kind of tough you want when you need him.

"I see Supply gave you a chest-pack chute," Buck observed. "I've seen co-pilots out in space without a chance to snap on a chest-pack. After this mission I'll get you a back-pack chute if you want one. I won't take no from Supply."

"I didn't have much time—"

"You'd better have everything, because once we start taxiing and ships are rolling behind us and in front of us there'll be no way to go but on to the target—or to Switzerland. We've got a load of goddamn bombs in our belly to haul to some unlucky people, and not getting the bombs there is called 'aborting,' which is like a crime here. So we had better get our ass in gear. The talk among pilots is that your dad coming as inspector general has got our brass scared. We're figuring that's why we're taking off in this goddamn snow storm."

A few minutes later, Buck maneuvered the *Bare Lass* into the single file of thirty-two four-engine bombers crawling along the taxi strip toward the runway. He looked over to Tom and asked, "Where is your oxygen mask? Don't worry. 'Pilot to crew: Somebody bring up the spare oxygen mask for our co-pilot.'"

ABOARD THE LEAD SHIP, *LUCKY LADY*: Captain Walter Plank, in the nose compartment beside his top-secret Norden bombsight, was absorbing the full-power vibration of the engines under final run-up test. Underneath his flight suit, he was wearing two pairs of long-johns, an olive drab uniform, and a sweater. His layered dress for high altitude flying resulted from the experience of his twenty-two missions. The magic twenty-five that meant release to go home was only three missions away. But three missions were an eternity of fighters and flak. *God, let this one be easy—and after this, give me two more easy ones and I'll be back home with Cathy and our baby.* Falling snow was blowing across the runway. The lights marking the edges of the runway were visible for less than a hundred yards. The pilots would soon be searching for these vital lights while traveling a hundred miles an hour.

On the flight deck above Walt, the Group Lead pilot adjusted his oxygen mask, snapped it fast, and counted the remaining seconds to take-off time: Five. Four. Three. Two. One. 0735—Fire-brilliance of an orange-yellow flare arced upward through the snow as the code order for the mission to commence. The engines of the *Lucky Lady* roared as throttles were thrust to the firewall to put the horses to their maximum manifold pressure.

"Brakes off," the pilot ordered.

The co-pilot responded: "Brakes off. Tail wheel locked . . . Light off . . . Heading 321 . . ."

The ship shuddered with the beating of its forty-eight-hundred horses. Life hung on the lift of these engines. As the speed reached ninety, a flurry of snow made visibility zero. The pilot could not see the runway, but he had no choice other than to continue maximum power.

In the nose, Walt studied the terrain just ahead. He saw a runway edge-marker light pass between the wheels, telling him that the ship was straying from the runway. He expected death at any moment. . . . Then he heard the grinding of the electrical mechanism that cranked the wheels into the ship's body, and he felt the over-taxed airfoil shudder that told him the pilots above were trying to force the overloaded Fortress to leave the ground. Finally, he sensed the shift to positive lift. The *Lucky Lady* was airborne.

At this moment hundreds of ships from different air bases were lifting into the blinding storm. Ships on a collision course would be closing in at more than three hundred miles an hour. In each of the bellies of these blind monsters was a cargo of three tons of TNT and ten young men—barely not boys—few over twenty-one years old.

"God, be kind. Please, God, be kind," Walt whispered. Oh, how he had come to fear and hate this blind flying! After twenty-two missions . . . *I can't take this anymore. Maybe the forecast is wrong—we could break through to clear sky at any minute,* he lied to himself. He checked his watch again. Only a minute had passed.

Suddenly another bomber closed in, missing them by what seemed inches. The *Lucky Lady* pitched and rolled as it crossed through the prop wash. Then all was the same as a few seconds earlier—as if nothing had happened.

An hour of this before I can hope for clear sky! Walt clutched his bombsight and eyed the navigator beside him who was calculating his part of the complex maneuvers to rendezvous the Squadrons, then Groups, then Wings, then Divisions, which would be the invading Task Force today. *It would be a lot easier if I had something to do.* Their eyes met. *I wonder if he knows how scared I am?* A bright light flashed at 9:00 o'clock low and then waned as a lingering glow. Walt read the flash as news that a crew of the 100th had not made it off the ground.

AT 100TH BOMB GROUP HEADQUARTERS: The Deputy Group Commander informed Colonel Raymond, "We sent your son on the mission today."

"You what? He just arrived. Replacement crews are to get pre-combat indoctrination and flight training."

"We had a co-pilot vacancy on a seasoned crew. Your son is lucky. Casualties are highest with green crews on their first five missions."

"But putting a green co-pilot into combat was no problem for you. Right?"

"He's with a good pilot. Buck Pierce has a damn good record for getting in and back from tough targets."

"Who is Buck Pierce?"

"The First Pilot he's flying with, sir, Captain Brewster Pierce."

"How did you decide that Lieutenant Raymond would be the one to fly without further training? Did you draw lots? I don't like the smell of this. Who wrote his transfer orders?"

"It wasn't me, sir. The orders came from higher up. I'm getting in over my head here. I'd refer you to our Group Commander, but he's flying today."

"What is the estimated time of return?" Colonel Raymond asked.

"1518 hours, sir."

"We have strange orders coming from someone in high command. I'm going to look into this." Raymond reformed his plans. "When Lieutenant Raymond gets back, inform him that his father will return to see him this evening."

IN THE *BARE LASS* : Tom's sixty hours of B-17 flying time had been acquired in two months. After three weeks away from the cockpit, he was unsure of how well he could fly this four-engine bomber.

"Take over," Buck suddenly ordered as he focused on the instrument readings.

Tom jerked rigid as he put his hands and feet to the wheel and rudder pedals that gave him the ship to pilot through the tangle of clouds and bombers.

In the nose, separated from the cockpit, Sam O'Brien sat by his bombsight, unheedful of the sky. His mind had escaped to Scotland and arriving buddies singing the Roosevelt words: no American soldier will ever set foot on foreign soil. He could see the little railroad cars—the children begging for gum—the pubs—the girls—and then London . . . dark-haired Sandra discovered at Grosvenor House—*or had she discovered him?* What a beautiful ass she had. To watch her move was music . . . violins . . . harps . . . chimes . . .

Buck took the wheel again. His most immediate concern was the airspeed indicator. The needle was oscillating too violently to be read. He was flying blind without his airspeed, but he still had the gyro to tell him when his ship was diving, climbing, or turning. The intensity of his concentration had beads of sweat forming on his brow as he scanned the many instruments.

Tom had turned on the pitot-tube heater to thaw out any ice that could be causing the air-speed problem. He scanned the readings of all four engines in search of further trouble. He began checking the readings of carburetor heat that he had turned on to protect the engines from icing. His eyes roved across the manifold pressure, propeller rpm, and cylinder head temperatures of each of the four engines. He was particularly uneasy about Number 3. Buck had told him it would need special watching. He was too busy to fear what might be ahead in his first war flight, too busy to feel himself a stranger.

"Buck to Crew: You guys that can see backwards, keep a sharp eye for our 100th ships with the D mark. Navigator, if you decide we're lost, sing out and we'll tuck in with any Group we find."

"Radio to Pilot: Group assembly altitude will be five thousand feet higher than originally ordered."

"Roger, Radio. Let's hope it's clearer up there."

Buck climbed the *Bare Lass* up to 16,500 feet.

"Left Waist to Pilot: Just spotted a Group at our altitude, seven o'clock, but they went into the clouds again. Can't see a thing now."

"Roger."

According to Weather, at 16,500 there was supposed to be clear sky for several thousand feet between cloud layers. Instead, there was a cloud-packed sky. The *Bare Lass* now passed into the clouds again. Buck banked the ship slightly and eased back on the throttles as a tactic to allow the Group seen behind them to over-run him. This invited collision, but his combat experience had him accept this danger rather than the hazard of being discovered out of formation by enemy fighters. Life now hung on a deadly judgment game that played one danger against another.

Lacking his air-speed indicator, Buck judged his speed by the tension of his wheel and rudder controls. He kept himself ready to dump the stick forward and give full throttle at the first tail-shuddering sign of a stall.

"They're chewing up our ass. Pour on the coal!" came the tail gunner's shrill voice.

Buck jammed the throttles forward as bombers over-ran him. Three ships, stacked upward, passed underneath. Three more slid by a few feet above. Two more bombers passed over. The letter on each tail was D.

Buck slid down to a squadron now racing away from him. With engines at full emergency power, a setting that orders said should not be held for more than five minutes, he raced to catch the three-ship element he had been ordered to lead. There he slid into the slot to the left and below and back some few dozen feet from Musser's ship. Then he snapped his oxygen mask free to talk to his co-pilot without the interphone that carried his talk to all the crew: "Musser took the Element Lead 'cause we hadn't shown up. Since he's above and to the right, you can see him better from your side. So you take over. I'll worry about the engines. Keep her tucked in goddamn close so the fighters won't pick us as a soft spot. It's crazy to try to fly formation in these clouds, but hang in tight. The *krauts* like to hide in the clouds and then stab into us, so don't loosen up."

"Pilot to Crew: Who has a sure count on the ships in our Group?"

"Bombardier to Pilot: Marks' Lead Squadron spot is the only place I still see empty."

For an instant, Buck saw Marks puffing on his cigar while he read the poem about going into the sky to die. Then he was back with the *Bare Lass*, hemmed in to the left, back, and bottom by the Low Squadron which was properly stacked up and close in. To the right were the other ships of the *Bare Lass* element and ahead were the ships of the Group Lead element. There was no room for error.

Tom noticed that the cylinder head temperatures of Number 3 and Number 4 engines had passed the red danger line. With mechanistic habit of his training discipline he eased back on the throttles. The ship fell back a hundred feet.

Buck yelled, "What the hell is going on?" as he jammed the throttles full forward.

"We were exceeding the performance capability, sir."

Tom's reduction of engine-power was pan-caking the *Bare Lass* onto a ship just below. Buck overrode Tom's control to wrench the ship upward. The near collision disorganized the Low Squadron. A ship pulled up directly forward, not a hundred feet ahead. The *Bare Lass* hit the full force of this ship's prop wash. Previous to this moment, Tom had remained calm, keeping the discipline of constantly scanning the cockpit instruments. He had just noted that the ball of his oxygen intake meter was standing still when it should be moving up and down with his breathing. He now ignored the oxygen problem to throw his weight into the controls to help Buck. Together they fought to keep the rolling, pitching forces of the prop wash from taking control of the ship. Finally they sliced through to calm sky.

Tom felt dizzy. Vaguely he guessed why. He turned the emergency dial that supplied a pure, constant flow of oxygen. The cockpit came back into focus. He heard Buck's voice on the interphone, "Rich up the fuel to cool Number 4. That bastard engine is going to deliver whether it wants to or not." Then Buck leaned close, with his oxygen mask unsnapped, for a private message: "Screw your book-reading performance capabilities. We're going to catch up with our formation and stay with it and blow up with it if it comes to that. You chicken out again and I'll piss in your ear. I'm the head chicken here."

They were nearing the Wing assembly line. The other Groups that made up the Wing had already reached the assembly radio-beacon. The 100th Lead now increased its speed in a race to get where it needed to be for a tight ninety-six ship Wing formation. Tom, again flying the ship from his co-pilot seat, put the engines to full emergency power and held them there.

Buck sweated the ability of his engines to continue to deliver the power needed. Number 4 cylinder head temperature was still over the red line—now running rough. With fuel enriched, the other engines held to the red line. In spite of grim expectations, Number 3 had leveled into rough but steady delivery. Number 1 and Number 2 were roaring smoothly. For eleven more minutes all engines were kept at full emergency power. All the while, the air-speed indicator was still flopping about.

The 100th sped on with engines taking their punishment and still delivering until the tight Wing formation was achieved. The Wing convened into the Division Assembly line to take its slot in the 3rd Division invading force. Then the 3rd Division turned onto the course on which it was ordered to spearhead the 800 four-engine-bomber Task Force to Frankfurt.

As the mission continued its invasion of enemy sky, Tom raced, skidded, and slipped the *Bare Lass* as needed to keep into tight formation. His determination and skill were so remarkable for a green co-pilot that Buck once gave him a thumbs up sign of approval. Tom was completely absorbed in the challenge of keeping fifty feet below, fifty feet to the right, and at a fifty-foot diagonal from Musser's ship.

1002 HOURS, 29 JANUARY, IN THE *BARE LASS* COCKPIT AT 24,000 FEET: For the past hour the Frankfurt-bound air force had been in a soup of giant churning clouds causing wing, propeller, and windshield icing. The *Bare Lass* now entered a giant chamber of sky within the storm clouds and saw a formation of bombers ahead. Tom Raymond again had the engines at full emergency power to keep up with the speed the task force was traveling. Number 4 was again above the red line and was running rougher, but the engines were refusing to die.

In quick succession some twenty blotches of black flak burst ahead.

"Waist Gunners to Pilot: We're throwing out chaff."

Chaff was the name of the aluminum strands that children of the bombed called "angel's hair." It was fine aluminum strands floated into the sky to misdirect the radar of the cannon-fire.

Bursts of flak popped ahead every few seconds. One burst was very close. Buck guessed that it had not done damage, but he took over the controls, to feel for any variations in how the ship was handling.

Tom, relieved from the controls, watched the flak bursting. *This is what it's like in the air war Dad talked about.*

"Oxygen check," Buck ordered. This was a routine through which he could learn if any of his crew had been hit by the flak.

"Tail: 270 pounds. Okay."

"Left Waist: 270 pounds. Okay."

"Right Waist: 250 pounds. Okay."

"Ball Turret: 250 pounds. Okay."

"Radio: 300 pounds. Okay."

"Top Turret: 250 pounds. Okay."

"Pilot and Co-pilot: 300 and 270 pounds. Okay."

"Navigator: 250. Okay."

"Bombardier: 270. Okay. We caught a sliver in the nose. It tore about an inch hole in the Plexiglas, that's all."

"Roger." Buck was deeply conscious of his responsibility for the lives of this crew. *This ship has got to hold together. Once we level off we'll be okay.*

"Tail Gunner to Crew: Unidentified fighters straight behind us at our altitude: I mean at six o'clock level. They're circling toward three o'clock level."

"Pilot to Crew: Anybody that points his nose at us is an enemy."

"Navigator to Crew: Our fighter escort was scheduled to rendezvous with us here. I think it's them."

Number 2 began to whine. It was the unmistakable whine of a run-away prop. Buck guessed that the fifty-below-zero weather must have jelled the oil in the dome. He began to exercise the prop control and throttle, alternating the pitch back and forth, in an attempt to bring the pro-peller under control.

Sam called up, "Number 2's spouting oil from the cowl flap slot, on the inside, just under the wing."

"Bad?"

"Buck, this oil is sizzling on the exhaust."

"Feather Number 2," Buck ordered, and he and Tom started the coordinated procedure of shutting down the engine. The Number 2 propeller came to the standstill intended to cut down on drag. The Division was flying too fast for the *Bare Lass* to keep up with a dead engine. This meant aborting. Buck peeled off and moved down and away from the forma-tion quickly to save the combat unity of the Group.

"What's our position, Navigator?"

"Seventy-five miles from the English Channel."

"We're homebound!" Buck lowered the engine settings. He could not take the chance of losing another engine. Two engines would not keep a bomb-loaded B-17 airborne. The engine-sound that had been a pounding of steel hammers at the intolerable maximum setting now relaxed into the oil-cushioned cylinder-throb of the thirty-six hundred remaining horses.

"Pilot to Bombardier."

"Go ahead, Buck."

"Figure out what we're going to do with the goddamn bombs. We need to lose weight."

"Top Turret to Crew: I saw a fighter at 10 o'clock high. German—ME-110. He came out of the clouds and went right back in again."

Buck headed for cloud cover as his best protection. Without the air-speed indicator, he relied on the artificial horizon for the instrument flying in the clouds—until he dis-covered he could not put the ship into enough turn to tilt the register bar. He checked the vacuum pump that powered the artificial horizon gyro and discovered that Tom had failed to switch the vacuum pump to another engine when he shut down Number 2. To make matters worse, the vacuum trans-fer switch had frozen. *This is it; we'll never get through this.*

He gave the control of the ship to Tom and began to labor with the vacuum transfer switch.

Tom—overwhelmed . . . *no air-speed indicator, no artificial horizon, and only three engines . . . Like this, I'm supposed to fly blind? Which way is up? I've got to get out of the clouds before we stall and spin. Which way is out? Better just hold the controls steady while Buck works to get the artificial horizon going.*

Buck finally got the vacuum pump over to Number 3, then he took control again. Both he and Tom knew it would take several minutes for the gyro to right itself. The altimeter showed the ship losing altitude at five-hundred-feet-per-minute. Was he in a downward spiral? He knew he could not trust seat-of-your-pants flying in this predicament. Flying history was filled with names of the dead who had been caught in precisely this trap. The bombs would have to stay until he got out of the clouds. Or should he try to salvo? At that moment the ship emerged into clear sky.

He leveled off and called, "Pilot to Bombardier: I'm for dumping the bombs here."

"We're still over France. Headquarters would fry us. We'll have to wait 'til we're over the Channel."

"Wilco, to Sam the bird man."

The *Bare Lass* was near a French town named Abbeville where enemy fighters known as the "Abbeville boys" were famous for coming up to pay their deadly respects. Now one of the Abbeville boys who had spotted the lone *Bare Lass* dove down in a head-on attack. His guns spit out 20-mm explosive shells. One shell hit near the ball turret. Another shell came down slantwise into Tom's side of the cockpit and exploded as it entered, leaving Tom with a bit of hair on the back of his scalp and a piece of lower lip on his jaw.

The attack was over before the *Bare Lass* gunners could open fire. Now all was quiet again save for the laboring of the three remaining engines.

Buck, hit by fragments of the exploded shell, had cuts on his neck and a gash on the side of his face. Splinters of metal had driven into his right hand. His oxygen mask had been torn from his face. He was slumped over the wheel, stunned by the concussion.

The top turret gunner, standing just behind the cockpit, had been hurled against the back of his turret. With blurred vision he surveyed the blood-spattered wreckage of the cockpit. "This is it," he told himself, and he began to disconnect for bail-out. But before he could unsnap his connections, his interphone came alive with, "Pilot to Clair. Come here."

He hurried to Buck and opened Buck's emergency oxygen valve until he managed to re-attach his oxygen mask. Then he got a pair of pliers to work what was left of the engine controls. Buck, using the pliers, pulled the ship level and headed for cloud cover to hide from the Abbeville boys. Clair pulled Tom's blood-soaked corpse up to the turret area and took the co-pilot position.

"Oxygen check," Buck ordered.

All positions reported "Okay" except the ball turret, who reported a shell sliver in his right foot but nothing to take him away from his machine guns.

"Pilot 230, Co-Pilot 210. Okay," Buck lied into the interphone for the non-existent co-pilot. There would be time for truth later.

Buck hung to the bottom of a cloud layer and began evasive action to escape flak as he saw the French coast that offered hope that the *Bare Lass* would get back to England.

"Flak, 10 o'clock, low," the Ball Turret reported.

"Bomb bay doors open," Buck ordered.

"That's no navy ship shooting at us. That's coastal flak. We're still over France, Buck. We can't dump our bombs here," Sam protested.

"Do you see any houses under us?"

"It's barren, very bleak, Buck."

"I say we're over the sea. Hit your button. We need to lose weight."

"Bombs away," Sam announced.

Buck felt the ship lift as it lost its tonnage of explosive cargo. *Yeah. We just had a big, fat abortion.*

The *Bare Lass* flew on, dropping altitude gradually as it

started across the Channel to England with Number 2 dead and the remaining three engines falteringly delivering crucial power. At ten thousand feet Buck snapped free his oxygen mask and got out of the seat he had held since taxi time. "Can you fly her alone for a minute, Clair?" he asked the top turret gunner in Tom's seat.

"I think so."

Buck left the cockpit and lifted an oil can from under Tom's body. After four and a half hours of machine discipline he allowed himself the relief of urination. Forty minutes later they reached the 100th base. The storm had lifted enough to see the runway. Buck made a straight-in approach. Clair shot up a red flare to signal "wounded aboard." Then he desperately plier-forced the damaged engine controls to help Buck ease the *Bare Lass* down to where the wheels finally kissed the runway. When the wheels stopped rolling, Buck and Joe, the ball turret gunner, got into the ambulance that was a hearse for Tom.

On the way to the hospital the driver told Buck, "Marks blew up on take-off. He ran out of runway."

Buck listened but said nothing: *Until you have smoked a last cigar . . . he didn't make it up to the sky to die. Whoever wrote that poem is probably dead, too.*

Sam O'Brien got the crew to Interrogation. It was a short session.

"Anything to report, Lieutenant O'Brien?" the Intelligence Officer asked.

Sam downed his double shot of bourbon that was the routine jolt supplied to loosen tongues for interrogation. "Nothing important for you. We aborted. The medics have our casualty report." He knew that Intelligence was not interested in the personal drama of every crew's day.

The clock on the wall before Sam stood at 1153. Sam noted that in twenty minutes the Group would be starting on the bomb run, flying straight and level into the Frankfurt flak barrage, hoping to live through the gamble with suicide.

1153 HOURS, 29 JANUARY, 5 MILES ABOVE FRANKFURT:
Expansive peace prevailed above an endless sea of clouds.
What might have seemed from afar to be migrating geese
were heavy bombers arriving from the west in precise pro-
cession many miles long. The bombers were flying in a
seemingly endless column of ninety-ship Wing clusters.
Each Wing cluster was precisely stacked into a V composed
of a Lead Group of thirty-two bombers with a flanking
Group of thirty-two bombers to the right and another such
Group to the left. The intention was to have insufficient sky
between aircraft for an enemy fighter to penetrate the formation. The Groups were also stacked into V configuration.
A Lead Squadron of nine ships was flanked by a Low
Squadron of nine ships and a High Squadron of fourteen
ships. The squadrons flew as three-ship elements, stacked
either higher or lower than the element before them, to
avoid the prop wash and provide maximum fire-power. In
keeping with the master formation strategy, one of the element
ships flew a few feet higher than the element lead and the
other a few feet lower.

The total combat formation, if an awesome aesthetic
achievement, was yet more awesome as a defense weapon.
Each bomber bristled with fifty-caliber machine guns in its
nose, tail, top, bottom, right side, and left side. Each Wing
was a geometric masterpiece that could bring nearly a thousand machine guns to bear upon an attacking fighter. This
fire-power was one of the keys to success in daylight, precision bombing that was rejected as impossible by the English.
But the system was vulnerable. Some bombers would strag-
gle, some collide, and some be shot down by flak or by clever
fighters attacking out of the sun or out of the clouds.

The masterpiece plan, to win victory through specific
destruction of an enemy's ability to make war, required clear
sky. Nevertheless, the force approaching Frankfurt today,
by precise count, 817 bombers, was advancing above the
clouds in a train one hundred miles long. The cloud cover
denied the chance to do pin-point bombing. Today's mission
marked a policy change forced by complex command politics.

Today at the IP, the initial point, where the target run would start, the Wing formations would remain intact for city-wide bomb dispersal. The aim would be five thousand city blocks of obliteration of the city of Frankfurt. For this purpose the Lead Wing now opened the bomb bay doors.

1213 HOURS, 29 JANUARY, ABOARD THE LEAD SHIP, *LUCKY LADY*: From the nose of the *Lucky Lady*, Captain Walter Plank looked out to the Pathfinder ship that was flying beside him. He looked out to the three-foot metal eye that protruded from its underbelly. He saw this bulbous mechanical eye as a threat to him personally. His status as an officer hinged upon his skill with the Norden bombsight. Not the pilot, only the bombardier, carried a "bombsight pass" to get the secret bombsight from its steel vault for each mission. It was the accuracy of the Norden sight that was key to the idea of winning war by destroying an enemy's ability to make war. *This machine eye flying next to me is putting history backward by taking my job. If it's so magic, why is our formation a mile wide and why are we scattering our bombs? If this is Frankfurt, where is the flak? Why am I bitching? Two more missions after today I'll be going home.*

"Pilot to Bombardier: There's our Pathfinder smoke marker. Toggle every three hundred feet."

"Wilco. bombs away—one at a time, every three hundred feet."

"Jesus Christ!" the Command Pilot cried. "We're sure in the flak now!"

Thousands of black blots of a box barrage suddenly filled the sky to all sides of the bombers. The black blots blossomed from arriving steel exploding with cherry centers and firing slivers of steel in all directions. The blockade of shellfire declared certain death ahead. But the mission was committed to fly through this sky, straight and level, to get its bombs on target. The good luck of the first Wing to bomb today was that the flak had not begun before their "bombs away."

"Bombardier to Pilot: Bomb bay doors closing."

"Roger. Bomb bay doors closing."

The *Lucky Lady* began a curving dive, picking up air speed, changing altitude and direction to take the Wing it was leading out of the flak.

Walt pulled down on his steel flak helmet, crouched behind the steel plate of the nose turret, and tucked as much of himself as possible under his armored flak vest. *God! It's everywhere!*

A volley of four shells burst within fifty feet of the nose.

"Pilot to Navigator: We were briefed to turn left but there's more flak there. Do I need to turn left?"

"Navigator to Pilot: It's too late now, since you've already turned right."

Walt agonized: *Why this arguing!*

Another shell exploded forty feet away, its core briefly scarlet. Walt held his breath for ten empty seconds. Another shell fired scarlet straight ahead—more breathless seconds, waiting, then WHOOM—with a six-inch split through the aluminum wall of the nose.

Walt grabbed his right knee where the leg of his flying suit was ripped and blood-spattered. He tested his ability to still move the knee. *Should I report the hit? Not yet. Not until we're out of this flak.*

WHOOM—debris scattered all through the nose.

The interphone was quiet. White smoke swept into the nose from the hatchway that led to the escape door. He saw bombers pass by that he knew should be following. The ship arced downward. Then it rolled level. Then it went into a steep climb. Suddenly it shuddered. Then it rolled into a steep right dive. They were out of the flak now. The interphone was still quiet. The ship twisted, rolled, and went into a dive. The cloud layer below loomed closer.

Why doesn't the pilot tell us what's happening?

The smoke burst into flame.

This is it. I've got to get out of here.

The navigator beside him was shouting into the interphone, "Navigator to Pilot! Navigator to Pilot! Acknowledge! Acknowledge!"

Walt shoved him and screamed, "We gotta get out of

here! This is our life!"

The navigator blurted, "What's happening?"

Walt yanked the emergency cord that released his flak vest and exposed the rings for attaching his parachute. He snapped on his chest-pack. He attached his oxygen bail-out bottle—but he was trapped in the burning ship.

The *Lucky Lady* arced upward into a loop. Flames pierced into the nose compartment. Walt and the navigator crossed their arms over their faces and backed away from the heat—crowding against the Plexiglas of the nose. Walt screamed to the navigator again, "This is your life!" Then the *Lucky Lady* exploded. Debris and flames of gasoline and burning magnesium spewed outward.

Afterwards there was nothing but bomber debris . . . and one parachute floating earthward. Below there was the rumble of exploding bombs, but where Captain Walter Plank hung from his parachute the sky was quiet as he descended into the crimson clouds of the world of the bombed.

1238 HOURS, 29 JANUARY, FRANKFURT: Walt was becoming aware of being in a field, limping. *My eyes? My hands? I'm burning! I'm on the ground. My knee? I got hit. I remember now. Trapped in the fire!*

How did he get here? His vision was blurred, but he thought he made out patches of snow and shadowy forms of people coming toward him. Then he heard voices.

"Help!" he called.

The people did not answer.

"Help me!"

The people circled him, but they did not come near him.

He sat down and closed his eyes. He was again in the flames. *I've got to get out of here! This is your life!* He opened his eyes. *Where am I? What happened?*

He put his fingers to his eyes—he jerked away. The slight touch told him that his hands and eyes were burned. *That's why the terrible pain.*

The people were twenty feet from him. Two held pitch-forks, and one held a long gun pointed at him. *It's like I'm an animal and they're afraid of me.*

He looked at his hands that were red, puffed, and blistered. He looked at his flying suit—ripped and shredded. His right pants leg was soaked with blood.

"Help me!"

Nothing happened. Then it came to him that he was in Germany. He traced back to his childhood language with his foster parents and their German church in Nebraska.

"Bitte Hilfe!"

He heard talk too garbled to understand. The tallest person came forward. A woman. She pointed a pitchfork at him. He understood her say in German, "You are a Terrorflieger!"

"Ich bin Amerikaner."

Silence. The woman towered over him as he sat on the ground looking up to her. He reached toward her. She was wearing a blue and white dress. He saw her as his foster mother in her blue and white dress.

She set her pitchfork into a lunging stance.

"Ich bin Christian!" Walt called.

The woman spit at him. In slow German speech that he understood totally, she said, "You dare make a move and I will stick this fork through you."

Other people closed in with weapons pointed at him.

A squat man in a fur collar rasped, "Kill him. If he escapes, he'll come back to bomb us again."

An old man with no weapon said, "Make him tell where his silk parachute is. My granddaughter wants to be married in a white silk dress."

Then he blacked out. When his vision returned two men were raising him to his feet. They were wearing shiny helmets, as shiny as mirrors of steel. They led him to a farm at the edge of the field. They took him through the back door of the house and into a kitchen with a large stove and a large wooden table. They placed him in a chair with armrests. The armrests allowed him to hold his hands out to where they would not touch anything.

Shouts carried into the room. Someone pounded on the outside door. A man went out. He came back with a soldier in a gray uniform who barked orders at the other people in the kitchen. All left but one man and one woman. Speaking in German, the woman said, "What a day it's been. This is the second invasion of our home. This morning an SS Obersturmführer came and investigated us as black marketers."

The soldier in gray came back and bandaged Walt's leg where a two-inch chunk of flesh was torn out, and he applied white jelly to Walt's burning face and hands. Then in a sharp voice he instructed what Walt's memory of German interpreted as, "Don't give this gangster who murders women and children any of your food. If you are kind to him he will think you are not loyal to Hitler."

Walt tried hard to remember the language he had used with his foster parents. "How bad is it with me?" he asked the soldier.

"Too good. You deserve to be dead," the soldier threw out as he left.

Walt examined his hands more closely. His finger with his wedding ring had swollen flesh encasing the ring. His other hand was so swollen and blistered that he could barely see the Gypsy ring that he wore as a good luck charm from his English girlfriend. Only the diamond chips were visible.

"Nobody will get these rings off now," the man said.

This is my punishment for wearing Marg's ring. When I stopped seeing her, I should have given back her ring, but she wanted me to keep wearing it to keep safe.

A wail of sirens carried into the room. The tones seemed lower than the English sirens. They sounded a lonely, unearthly, misery.

Later another soldier came, talked to the people, then went away again. Walt's pain knotted into despair. His eyes had swollen shut. In his trauma he moaned and twisted in the wooden chair. The man came over and said in German Walt understood, "The soldiers say we should keep you here until a street is cleared to get you to Oberursel. This is a black day. Loving Jesus, when will the misery end for us? For you the war is over."

"Please, do you have medicine for pain?" Walt asked.

The woman gave him some pills, but they made no difference.

After a while he felt a spoon on his lips. "Do not think that I am not loyal to our Führer. I am only feeding you some broth from the ham the Gestapo threw into our pig garbage today. Feeding you pig food can certainly not be forbidden. You need strength. Hold yourself together young soldier. You will live through this and be back with your family. I have two sons on the Russian Front. God knows where they are tonight."

Bomb-burst reverberation sounded sporadically from the city. Walt found himself mumbling "bombs away" as he remembered that only a few hours ago he had toggled the time bombs that were now exploding.

After a while there was a shuffle of other people entering. Walt heard the strained voice of the old man who had asked for the parachute. Another voice screamed words too fast for Walt to understand, but he made out, ". . . silk from murderers . . . while our city burns . . . parachute silk for a wedding . . . criminal black marketers—finally, Heil Hitler . . . Heil Hitler . . . Heil Hitler," as the feet shuffled from the kitchen.

He had gained control of his moaning and was quiet now, but the pain still tortured him. *How bad is it with me? Will I get something for the pain? The enemy has me. This is what they are like. Cathy will hear that our ship exploded. She'll think I'm dead. It's a miracle. I'm alive. What will they do with me?*

Would this day never end? With eyes swollen shut, he finally asked if it was night.

The woman who had fed him soup said, "Hold on. It is still only four in the afternoon. I will put my own salve on your burns. Maybe it will help ease your pain."

He was finally told that it was night. The time bombs kept exploding as thunder reminding him that he was from the other world that had dropped them.

The woman again spoke to him, "Hold on. Hold yourself together until morning. Tomorrow will be better for you."

1748 HOURS, 29 JANUARY, ENGLAND, ENROUTE TO THE 100TH BOMB GROUP: Colonel Raymond's driver was making an emergency stop at a roadside pub. The Colonel was returning from Leigh-Mallory Headquarters at Stanmore where he had gathered more data in his investigation of the *Combined Bomber Offensive.* While he waited in his staff car, he worked at phrasing tomorrow's dispatch to Washington.

" . . . since the English cannot defend themselves in day-light, they are bombing at night with low target accuracy. They have developed the 'Key Point Rating' for ranking German cities for de-housing of civilians. It gives them big targets. On the other hand, with our daylight capability and with our fighter-escort range increasing, we can strike with pin-point accuracy deep in Germany. Nevertheless, on 29 January we made a city-wide raid that was a waste of our resources. I am seeking to clarify whether we Americans, too, are now beginning a policy of 'dehousing,' or plainly put, population extermination. Has our plan to win the war by destroying strategic targets like Oil targets been abandoned?"

To the driver, returning, Dean asked, "What took so long?"

"I'm sorry, sir. It must have been the fish I ate."

"Are you all right now?"

"I'll make it now. We're almost there."

"Let's hurry. I'm going to see my son. He's flown his first combat today, and I've never yet seen him wearing 'wings.'"

Raymond re-centered into his thoughts as they raced toward the base. *Did Washington send me to England mainly to get my nose dirtied by crap I wasn't admitting existed? Our warring factions should recognize that our production lines are already rolling out thousands of bombers to win the war our way. Doesn't everyone realize that it would be dis-astrous to switch our plan now to population bombing? That was Hitler's mistake in England. Will we never learn?*

He reviewed the summation he realized could get him court-martialed: *Churchill claims that Hitler's bombing of London civil-ians boosted the English will to fight. If that is true, are we now trying to boost the will of Germans to fight? Churchill has forced us into a game of revenge? We theorize that Hitler's switch from bombing Royal Air Force bases to bombing English cities saved*

England from German invasion, yet we are being forced to repeat Hitler's mistake. Here I am in 1944, again in Billy Mitchell's battle for wise use of air power, and again controlled, instead, by politics and bureaucracy. General Mitchell spoke for our air force today when he said on his death bed: The American people will regret the day I was crucified by politics and bureaucracy.

Dean began to think of seeing Tom, and afterwards Captain Randi Scott, of his romantic days in the Philippines two years ago. He recalled her black, flowing hair and her thighs cradling him in the warm fragrant nights of the tropics.

His staff car wheeled into the airfield. His driver received directions and hurried on to Hut 23. Sounds of celebration carried from the barrel-shaped barracks. "Pass the bottle this way, Joe . . . I'm going to get myself a queen. . . . I'm going to celebrate in bed."

Standing in the entrance-way a skinny lieutenant looking no more than sixteen displayed a disconnected grin and swimming eyes. He wore a khaki shortcoat that was too large for him, and he had a camera slung over his shoulder. Discerning the eagles on the uniform approaching, he struggled a salute. The Colonel noted gold letters inscribing "Tom" on the camera case, and he identified this camera as a gift he had given Tom for high school graduation. "You must be a friend of Tom's," he greeted as he pointed to the camera.

"This is my camera, sir. I am Tom."

"Smarten up soldier. I'm Tom's father."

"I'm sorry, sir. I didn't steal it. I just took it, so the Supply guys wouldn't steal it when they pick up his stuff."

Inside the barracks someone started to sing "Roll Me Over in the Clover."

"Our crew is celebrating 'cause we finished our missions. I am sorry about Tom. He was flying with—"

"Where is Tom?" Raymond abruptly interrupted.

"I was really going to send it to you, sir. We combat crews take the stuff, 'cause when Supply comes, we never know how much they'll send home."

The skinny lieutenant had unfastened the camera and was reaching out to Colonel Raymond.

Colonel Raymond took in the countenance of this boy with glazed eyes holding his son's camera out to him, and he got the message. With West Point poise he turned into the entrance-way of Hut 23 and asked in a voice loud enough to bring the barracks quiet, "Where is bed 17?"

"To the left, sir," said the skinny lieutenant, still holding out the camera as he followed.

Colonel Raymond strode down the aisle until he was stopped by the words, "Here, sir. It's in kind of a mess. It's an unlucky bed, sir."

The Colonel took in a ransacked dresser next to a neatly made bed scattered with a 2nd lieutenant's uniforms and a tunic with pilot's "wings" on the breast. The silence was awesome as he turned and strode back to the entrance-way and kept walking until he was again at his jeep.

"Start driving," he ordered.

"Where to?"

"Away."

Before the driver had gone a hundred yards the Colonel corrected, "Take me to Group Headquarters."

The Deputy Commander was still on duty. The long hours of airfield responsibility and the loss of the Group Commander in the *Lucky Lady* had unnerved him, yet he asked, "Would you like a scotch? I hope I explained adequately this morning why we assigned your son to an experienced crew. Sergeant, close the door." He drew out a fifth of scotch. "I need a good stiff drink. Have one with me, Colonel."

"No, thank you."

"I won't insist, but there are times when a man needs a good stiff drink, Colonel."

"I said, no."

"Our Group was shaken up today. Light losses, but for one thing, our command ship went down. We lost our Group Commander."

"And what else happened? Get on with it."

"We had some other losses, too. I was hoping the chaplain could be here. I am—"

"I know. My son didn't make it back. Was he killed, or

is he just missing? I came here for a full report."

"I don't know much about it. There was a fighter attack. Captain Buck Pierce will be able to tell you more about it."

"What do you mean?"

The Deputy Commander hesitated. He did not want to describe the condition of the body. "He was killed instantly," he finally said. "A 20-mm exploded in the cockpit."

Then to change the subject he went on. "I've been thinking about your question this morning about how soon he was put into combat."

"Why? Because he was my son? It's too late for appropriate orders for him. I'll leave it at that, for now, but be sure that there will be a court-martial if it's called for."

"Would you like to talk to his pilot, Buck—Brewster Pierce? He's in the hospital."

"How badly is he injured?"

"I don't know. I've been swamped. I've got to get the Group ready for another mission tomorrow."

Colonel Raymond faced the Deputy Commander wordlessly for a long while. Then he said, "I won't see anyone today."

"And the chaplain? Do you wish to talk to him? He came by earlier. He was saying that with you here a service could be especially arranged. Perhaps we could have—"

The Colonel interrupted, "You keep the chaplain away from my son. I need time. I'll be back tomorrow."

Dean Raymond returned to his car. He peeled off a handful of English pounds and gave them to the driver.

"Get yourself back to Norfolk House."

Alone. Driving. Dean turned his car up a narrow cobblestone lane and sped through the twilight. The snow was melting. Under the evening winter light that filtered through an overcast, the rolling terrain composed a gray canvas. The hedgerows, the winding lanes, the bicycles, the stone walls, the footpaths, the thatched roofs, the canals, the houses, and the roadside inns, all seemed desolate. He had faced death before with his mother, father, and a brother. But it was not like losing Tom. This left him weak and trembling.

2010 HOURS, 29 JANUARY, ALCONBURY, ENGLAND: Above Colonel Raymond were sky-probing shafts of light that the British Air Defense was thrusting into the night. As he stepped from his car, he looked out to the radiant shafts lacing a web through the darkness to trap a target in their rays. Then he went into the officers' club where he expected that Randi would be waiting for him.

As he approached, Randi regarded his military carriage and his wide-set brown eyes. She felt that she had grown old in the two years since their romance of the Philippines, but he looked the same except for a paler cast to his complexion. As he lifted his flight hat, a few strands of his straight brown hair fell out of place. With a smooth hand motion that was a mannerism she fondly recalled, he stroked the errant hair back into place. She was drawn by the unreachable in this man.

"You haven't changed, Dean."

"I'm sorry I'm late."

"I knew you would have a good reason. I ordered a double scotch for you while I was waiting and sipped two myself to while the time."

"Thanks, but I'm on the wagon," he said, still standing across the table from her.

Here is my angel nurse with her beautiful, long black hair. I'm not going to tell her about Tom tonight. He went to her chair.

She saw in his eyes that he knew about Tom just as she did. She rose and reached for him. Her palms pressed against his temples as she looked into his eyes and said, "I wasn't sure that you knew. I thought I might be breaking the news to you. I was on duty when they brought him in. He died instantly, Dean. He couldn't have known what happened." She embraced him. They held on to each other tightly.

He said, "I'm not good company tonight."

"What can I do?" she asked.

"I need, I guess, some time alone . . . to come to grips—

"Where will you go?"

"It was his first mission."

33

"You don't have to talk, Dean, but let me stay with you."

"I've called his mother. She was with her sister. I was relieved by that. . . . Perhaps, Randi, it would be good to have you with me for a while."

They went to the Black Swan Inn where a deep, quiet hall was dominated by a fireplace so large that it had a stone bench on the hearth inside. Flames reached skyward into the blackness of the chimney, dwarfing them as they sat facing each other. A waiter in a scarlet coat moved back and forth before the sky-reaching flames. A vein of steam rose from a copper kettle swung over the fire.

"I'm going to have a cognac. Will you join me?" Dean asked.

"I thought you were on the wagon."

"The more I think about it, the less important it is to impose a teetotaler's world upon myself tonight because I'm here as an inspector general."

"Is the inspector general's work something you can talk about?"

"It's mostly secret, but critical . . . two cognacs."

The waiter in scarlet apologized, "I'm sorry, the war—you know. We don't have cognac."

"What do you have?"

"We have brandy and scotch. It is a good scotch—hard to find."

"Put a bottle of scotch in my room and serve us a snifter of brandy here. Make that a bottle of brandy here."

Flames filled the silence while they waited. Finally Dean said, "As a man who drank with discipline all of my life, it is disgusting to no longer be sure of my discipline. I want to drink tonight, and when I want to stop, I am going to stop."

"Are you sorry you brought me with you?"

He smiled to her and pressed her hand before saying, "No. You help."

The waiter returned. Dean studied the flame-glow of the fireplace capriciously flaring on the globe of his brandy glass. "I suppose you know that the pilot was hit, too, but lived through it to bring the ship home. He's in your hospital. Have you talked to him?"

"No. I haven't talked to him."

"They split Tom from the crew he trained with. He arrived yesterday, and today they already had him flying. I'm not making any assumptions, but there are questions that need to be answered. I need to visit with his pilot. I can't bring Tom back, but I can get a court-martial on his behalf if it is warranted. Randi, would you look up Captain Pierce at the hospital, and let me know when he's well enough to see me?"

"Captain Pierce?"

"That's the pilot's full name. Captain Brewster Pierce."

"Sure. I'll do that for you."

"I would like you to know how it was with Tom and me, what he was to me," Dean continued, "but tonight I can't talk about it. If I hadn't been a military pilot he'd be alive. He wanted Wings because I brought the love of flying to him. That's my curse tonight."

"Talk about something else. You must be able to tell me something about why you're in England as an inspector general."

"I'd like to talk about that, but I can't. However, what the Eighth Air Force did today is no secret to the Germans. The mission today was a waste of lives, not only Tom's—he is only one of many who were living yesterday, but not today."

"Will you be flying combat?"

"I want to. I've got to learn the difference between theory and practice. There's no easy way to do that. I've got to get into it all the way," Dean said. Then he grew silent.

Randi waited for him to continue. She wondered if she should say something to draw him from his inner world. Then he began to talk again.

"Since the German bombing of England, the English version of air warfare has become an eye-for-an-eye-strategy. Our American air power was developed to win with strategy that's neater and quicker."

Randi responded, "Seeing how the Germans have bombed civilians here, I can appreciate how the English feel."

"Hitler, the house painter, no professional soldier, gave the order to bomb civilians. Militarily, it's a waste of air power capability."

Randi said, "The Germans have earned what they're getting."

"You're thinking in moral terms. A professional soldier fights to win, not to punish."

With diligent attention he refilled the brandy glasses.

"To hell with war," he toasted.

"I'll drink to that."

Returning her glass to the table, she said, "I'll tell you about me. What do you want to hear? How I escaped from the Islands? I came within a hair's breath of still being there right now as a prisoner."

"What happened?"

"A gallant pilot named Nicholai came in with a PBY and flew us out. Imagine a hero with a rescue ship full of nurses. Some of us got carried away. I almost married the man."

"You're joking."

"I'm not, Dean. It was dumb. In the Far East I still had my head in the clouds. If I ever think of marriage again, it will be back home on the High Plains to raise a family."

"I'm glad you still have a dream for when the war is over."

"Getting through the war is my challenge. The world of casualties is defeating me, Dean. Our times together have been more your world than mine. I'd like to be back there again, away from hospital thoughts."

"You've always been unforgettably special to me. I hope you will keep on being who you are."

"Dean with his head in the clouds. You haven't changed."

"Oh?"

"Have you changed?" she asked.

"My career has been held together by dreams of what air power could do. These are days of crisis for me. Tom's death is a final blow." He rotated his glass and watched the flow of the brandy along the rim and the flare of the fireplace on the globe as it turned. "The world should be run by women. Men even mess up running a war."

Randi reached over and pressed his free hand tightly between hers, saying, "Look at me, Dean."

He looked into her eyes. She locked to his vision, smiling, as she said, "I know you're not talking about how you are hurting. Yes, Tom's gone, but . . ." She was having trouble finding the words she wanted to say. He spoke from a world so removed from hers that she felt intimidated. ". . . I don't know what to say. I've got no advice, but I'm hurting with you."

He smiled, in spite of everything, and she saw in his smile her old friend of the Philippines. But she saw, too, the weight of despair burdening his smile, and she realized how much he needed her tonight.

"I wish we could escape to old Manila tonight," she said. "Every mission brings in more young guys for us to work magic on. It's tearing me apart."

Dean said, "You're still the angel nurse."

"Dean, I've lost my wings. I try to blot out my mind, but there's always tomorrow. Tomorrow you can fight to win the war. All I can do is nurse more casualties."

"Tomorrow, I can pull myself together and go fight the British."

"The British? How them?"

"At what level? Churchill is direct. At Leigh-Mallory Headquarters the British use such methods as assigning higher ranking officers to the staff than we Americans have. That's how they outrank us in decision-making."

"Blame the brutality of Coventry and the other bomb rubble of this island, Dean."

"The British demand action—our strategy demands patience—waiting for clear skies. It's ironic that my son was killed on their kind of mission. I'm asking myself who is to blame. Perhaps the problem is a diabolic force of the cosmos. I'm not making sense. I wish I had spent more time with Tom. It's so sudden—let me take you home, Randi."

"There's still some brandy in the bottle. Let's go up to your room and sit by the fire without talking."

"I've got plans for the brandy."

"And they exclude me?"

"I'd better take you to your quarters."

"I'm tired of being your goddamn angel! I know you want to take me home and then drink until you pass out. What good will that do?"

Dean's eyes were again on the flames flaring on his brandy glass. "There's a poem about the Battle of Blenheim. An old man with his grandchildren by his side looks out to the battlefield and tells them of the great battle that was fought there, and one of his grandkids asks, 'But what good came of it at last?' and the poem goes, 'Why that I cannot tell,' said he, 'but t'was a famous victory.'"

"You're drifting into morbid melancholy. I don't want you to be alone."

"I don't prefer to exclude you. I just don't want to put you through what this night is to me."

"What are you going to do?"

"There is still some brandy. I presume that I have a bottle of scotch by my bed. When I get around to it, I'll sleep. And in the morning, I will go see Tom. I've got to see him."

"With me with you. I won't give you up for scotch and brandy."

"Empty bottles leave me no regrets."

"No? My empty bottles are leaving me regrets."

"For Christ's sake, why are you badgering me, Randi?"

"Because you're more than Tom's father. You're one hell of a good man who must be on a hell of an important assignment that you need to be back to in the morning, but I'm not going to badger you. Take me home."

They moved past the curtains that shielded the light from the English blackout. The night had turned clear. The moon was down. There was only starlight. It was cold. They started driving. The car's blackout lights barely afforded vision, but Dean drove fast.

A wailing of sirens sounded. Dean turned off the thin rays of the blackout lights and pulled the car to the side of the road to wait out the raid. The blackness of the shrub-shrouded road engulfed them, isolating them. Searchlights stabbed the sky far to the right, and Randi said, "It looks like London is in for trouble."

"I've never been in a city being bombed, and I've never flown a bombing mission. I've got to live it myself to know what I'm asking of others."

The sirens quieted, and then the drone of an airplane sounded nearby.

"I'm nervous. It would be safer to take cover in the ditch," Randi said as she hurriedly got out of the car.

"They can't see us, and they're not after us anyway," Dean said, but he followed her to a rock wall beside the road. They sat down close to each other with their backs resting against the wall and their eyes in the sky. "You must have suffered some rough times before you got rescued."

"Yes, in several ways. At Little Bagio we had few medical supplies and lots of malaria, hepatitis, gangrene . . . you name it. Before Bataan fell on April 9th they took us nurses across to Corregidor on a launch. The shelling got worse and worse and the bombers came in at will above fourteen thousand feet where our guns couldn't reach them. We lived in the tunnels packed together with our patients in the foul air."

She shifted closer to Dean. "I was lucky. One evening late in April two PBYs came in on what was like a suicide mission. While the Japs were celebrating the Emperor's birthday, the PBYs slipped out with thirteen nurses. I was one of them. It was hair raising. Our pilot, that was Nicholai, flew out seven of us, and the other PBY took out six. We flew all night and landed on Lake Lanao on Mindanao. The Japs were already on Mindanao, closing in on the lake. We refueled and then Nicholai couldn't get the plane off the lake. We dumped all our belongings to lose weight and finally we got airborne. The other plane got a pontoon damaged by a submerged log. The crew took the nurses off while they repaired the pontoon. Meanwhile, the Japs moved in and captured the nurses. The PBY took off without them. Some other nurses got out by submarine, but I can't forget those who are still prisoners, if they're still alive. We were so close, packed together in the tunnels, nursing the wounded under endless attack. Why was I among the lucky who got saved? Part of me is still with them. I feel like I owe somebody. I don't feel free like the Randi you knew."

The searchlights went out. With the moon down, only the embers of starlight brightened the vast emptiness of night. All was still but for a distant rumble in the direction of London.

They didn't talk for a while and then Randi said, "When I'm out in the English countryside on a night like this I feel like I'm in a storybook."

"I want to hear more, but I'm a poor listener tonight. I hope you never go through what I'm feeling tonight."

"You don't know what I'm feeling, Dean."

The sirens began the long, constant wail that meant All Clear. Randi and Dean still sat close together with their backs against the wall, keeping the spell of their intimate isolation in the vast night.

"My dear Randi, you're so—how should I say it—Christ awfully good to be with."

She brought her lips to his in a tender kiss.

He said, "I can't believe Tom's dead . . . I know it . . . but I don't believe it."

"I'm going back with you," she said. "I'll take my own room, and in the morning I'll wake you for a new day."

They drove back to the Black Swan. In the night quiet before the entrance Dean said again, "I'm going to see him in the morning. I've got to touch him to know for myself."

Dean went to his room alone and sank into a soft chair next to the scotch and a bottle of water. He saw that the innkeeper had placed two glasses on the bedstand.

"War, love and death," the Colonel spoke with a sigh to the empty room. "We should have three glasses."

A fire burned in the fireplace, but the room was still chilly. A gray eiderdown lay on the bed like a cloud. He poured himself a scotch without bothering with the water. He took a long drink. Then he took off his top coat, blouse, and shoes and stretched out on the eiderdown. His body sank into the down cloud. He positioned himself near to the whiskey, and he let his eyes rove the intricate world of the flaming hearth. *I wish I could have been with Katherine when she got the news.*

Though they had not been close in recent years, he wished that he could be with her tonight. In his feelings of sympathy for her, he decided to arrange for a Catholic funeral, though he himself was agnostic. *The priests can have him. Katherine will feel better that way. How he lived is what counted, and he was among the few. The priests can take him to their make-believe heaven. People want magic . . . chemical magic from their doctors . . . fake worlds from their movies . . . holy brutalities from their Hitlers. Only a few are brave enough to stand alone in the puzzle of life. Tom had that courage. To be among the few, that's what counts. Whatever reward life holds will not be known to people who lack guts. I'm thinking that, and as of this minute I feel gutless. Where is Tom now? Mystery! With the will that holds the stars in place? Where is he? He can't be just nowhere.*

With his arms hugging a pillow, Dean fell asleep.

Sometime later he woke. The fire was gray embers. He turned out the lights, opened the blackout shutters, and looked out to the embers of stars glowing in the cosmic hearth. *What am I doing here in this expanse of night blinking my eyes back to the blinking stars? What is one life to the will that moves the stars? Why try? Why did Tom have to die? I remember Tom waking up once when he was afraid and making his way to our bed. What do you do when you are grown and there are no parents to go to?*

He closed the blackout shutters and turned the light back on to have another scotch.

Chemical magic. Easy way out.

He picked up the scotch bottle and rolled the amber fluid along the inside of the bottle. *To flow or not to flow? . . . Death is an option. Easy way out. Pathetic man climbing a two-foot ladder to reach Heaven. Tonight my ladder is whiskey and it's not enough. Tom, what ladder did I offer you? Flying? Your ultimate escape?*

41

He could not endure being alone longer. He had to get out of the room. Out. Where?

He put on his tie and uniform and opened the door leaving in panic to get away from his thoughts, to reach the escape of the military order of his life. Where to go?

He descended the stairway that led to the giant fireplace of the dining room. In contrast to the warm atmosphere of a few hours before, an emptiness prevailed here now. He saw the tables made up mechanically perfect for the customers of the new day. Then he saw Randi tucked up on the stone warming-bench within the giant fireplace. She was holding her bare feet near the glowing coals.

"The fire went out in my room," she said. "I felt cold and creepy."

"You're a goddamn good sight for whatever time of the night it is," he said. "I used to remember you gliding along a hospital ward in white, but from now on I'll see you here, curled up on this bench, warming your toes on the coals."

"Come and join me."

Dean moved beside her on the stonework.

"I listened by your door. It was so quiet that I decided not to disturb you," she said.

"I was thinking. Thinking too goddamn much. I had to get out."

Randi shared, "I've been dreaming that I was a Gypsy and you were asleep in our wagon, and in the morning we were going to hitch up our horses and move south. We were going to leave all the world of bombers and hospital beds forever behind us and live traveling down the road, free on our way to a better place."

"What I was thinking took me into a trap in which there were only two ways out. I chose the way of putting my uniform back on and coming out to where I am."

"I'm glad you did."

He felt her cheek come to rest on his chest. He breathed in the fragrance of her hair. He ran his fingers through the soft, black strands. "You're my rescue tonight," he said.

They climbed the stairway to his room. Dean opened the

door. As she entered, she said, "It's chilly. I'll stir the embers and put more coal on the fire. We can warm ourselves sleeping next to each other."

"I'll help you fix the fire. Then we'll have a warm-up scotch."

"We don't need the scotch," she smiled.

They tucked themselves under the eiderdown and lay close together in warm contact. Randi wrapped her arms around Dean, pulling his chest tightly to her. "I want to hug you so tight that we'll never come apart," she said . . . and she shivered. "I'm not shivering 'cause I'm cold. I'm shivering because I feel warm and loving and helpless. I wish I could help you, but I don't know how."

Dean wiped her tears as she sobbed . . . and then he, too, began to sob.

This quieted Randi, and she began to comfort him with kisses. "I have no words to help. All I have are kisses . . . but tomorrow you are going to get up stronger than ever. That's an order from your fallen angel nurse."

They lay in each other's arms and fell asleep, escaped, until the new day dawned.

THE WAR: CHAPTER TWO

RETURNING TO 0735 HOURS, 29 JANUARY 1944, FRANKFURT, GERMANY: Paula Schmidt's mission was a criminal plan to acquire food. Now it was threatened by an SS Obersturmführer, the lieutenant rank of the dreaded Gestapo. To avoid discovery, she had risen at sunrise and was hurriedly drinking her burnt-barley coffee in her cellar, bomb-shelter residence. She wanted to get away before the Gestapo stranger, who had arrived yesterday, came to the cellar as he said he would for a morning walk with her.

Her free time was precious since her job at the Post Office consumed fifty-six to eighty hours a week. She lost two more hours each day in the Moselstrasse Volkskueche soup line where she ate to give her five-year-old son Karl more of her ration. In addition, she had to walk to the Hauptbahnhof for water brought in by train from Limburg. She had labored all week to save time for today.

All week she had prayed for stormy weather that would keep the bombers away. As she now looked up through her cellar window, she thanked God for the dark clouds blanketing the sky. Little Karl, still cuddled in the warmth of his blankets, took advantage of the height of his board bed to reach for her neck.

"Mama, take me with you."

Paula put down her coffee and hugged him. "I wish I could, my brave son. Someday I will take you for a long ride on a train, but not today."

"Take him so I can go up and clean our apartment," Tante Hilda begged.

"Up five flights when you can barely walk?" She loved this old aunt crippled by a phosphorous bomb, yet hated being forced to live with her as caretaker for Karl while her husband served as a Luftwaffe prison guard.

"Good morning, Frau Schmidt. I come for the morning walk I promised you yesterday," she heard from the landing above.

She looked up to the invasion of black leather uniform starkly framed in the doorway by the sunrise light.

"Herr Obersturmführer, excuse me. I am in a hurry to catch a train."

"Then I will walk to the station with you."

"No, ah, ja," she fumbled. "Of course, I am going to walk to the station."

She went upstairs where he waited in the cold morning air. With their breaths trailing vapor, they took a direction toward the Haupt-Gueter-Bahnhof. As they walked, they occasionally reached out from their separate worlds with attempts at conversation. Paula was becoming desperate to be rid of him. *Why is he so insistent about walking with me? He will certainly ask me why I am going to the country. God, please take his interest in another direction.*

"How long will you be in Frankfurt, Herr Obersturmführer?" she asked as an opening to possible escape by promising him a walk at another time.

"On travel orders, I do not reveal time tables," he said. "I come from secret duty on the East Front and I am going to a higher position at Dachau with the Economic and Administrative Branch."

"You are indeed a prestigious officer. If you are here tomorrow, I will walk with you. I have plans for today. This is my only day off. I have no train ticket, so I'm going out on a cargo train and taking the water train back."

"You are rambling, Paula Schmidt. Simply said, you wish to escape the war by going to the country. What gives you the right to such a luxury? Only a few days ago I came home to learn that the gangster bombers have taken the life of my wife, yet I carry on. Good Germans persevere."

Paula could find no response. They walked on in silence. She decided that her best chance now was to board the train in spite of his reprimand. Still trying to take his interest in another direction, she said, "There are many places to visit in Frankfurt. Katharinenkirche is easy to find. It would be a good walk for you."

They were already at the station. *Please God, let me get away from him.*

45

"Churches have no interest for me." They were nearing the cargo train with its engine steamed up for departure. He continued, "I am going with you. I want to know what in the country so entices a woman whose husband is away serving his Fatherland."

Paula quickly calculated that she would go out to her usual stop, but she would only walk, using the excuse that she needed to get out to the open fields to know that everything in the whole world was not coming apart.

When the train departed, Paula and her unwanted escort were on it. She was perched on a stack of crates of an open gondola. He was standing close to her. She met his gaze with cold firmness to tell him she would not be prey of his SS eagles.

1002 HOURS, 29 JANUARY, FRANKFURT, GERMANY: Paula Schmidt and the SS Obersturmführer Herman Mehlhoff were crossing an open field. To avoid discovery of the farm she had intended to visit, Paula had turned in the opposite direction upon leaving the train. What she had started as a black market venture was now an effort to undo any suspicion of her intentions. She faltered, "I find new hope out here. I feel the life that will be coming back to the barren land with the springtime. You must be overwhelmed by the tragic news about your wife—"

"We will not speak of that. Tell me more about yourself. You need not pretend to me to be out here because you see the springtime in the land."

"I don't know. My mind gets muddled lately. I wish I were as strong as you. Being out here helps me feel that all the world is not coming apart."

"You have already told me that. I do not believe that you are so weak. We will turn around now. I prefer to walk toward the farmhouse. I may understand what you feel better than you think. You are too intent to be on a holiday. I think you are a woman who knows where you can get food forbidden by your ration card, and you would like to indulge in forbidden pleasure."

"I am a mother concerned for my child," Paula blurted. "I am no criminal."

"A good German woman would not be out here. You are lucky that I came with you. I will clear up your confusion on this trip so thoroughly that you will have no more need to visit the country. When we get to the farm house, I will be in charge."

"I have no plans to go to any farm house. I just—"

"You do receive one hundred grams of fat and fifteen hundred grams of bread each week, like other women?"

"Yes, I receive the same ration as other women."

"Then what brings you out here, Frau Schmidt? Explain that," he interrupted.

"I have, uh, already explained."

"We will see," Obersturmführer Mehlhoff said. He approached the front door of the farm house and knocked loudly. Paula trailed behind him, unable to get away from the morning that was moving beyond her control.

"Praise God. What can I do for you?" an unkempt rustic with wrinkled leathery skin spoke in tones tense with deference for the SS black leather coat before him. Herman Mehlhoff clicked his heels and shot out, "Heil Hitler!"

The trapped farmer shuffled his feet and trembled, "Heil Hitler!"

"We have a report that you are doing business here at our Führer's expense."

"There must be some mistake, esteemed officer."

The Obersturmführer pushed past the disheveled farmer and strutted into the home.

Paula was too distraught to look left or right. She followed with her eyes on Mehlhoff's neck.

They entered a warm kitchen filled with the yeasty aroma of fresh baked bread. A woman, packing loaves of bread into a storage box beside the stove frantically wiped her hands on her apron as she reacted to the black leather intruder. Ignoring her, Mehlhoff went directly to a wooden table holding two empty glasses. He lifted one of the glasses to his nostrils.

"Cognac," he said.

Surveying the room, he continued, "So, you keep your bread in the box other Germans use for wood. In what unsuspecting place do you keep your cognac?"

The farmer, following close behind Paula, fumbled, "Please, sir, we are poor farm folk. We will give you anything you want. Do not arrest us. Do you want ham? We have a beautiful smoked ham that is all yours if you will do us the honor to receive it. Martha, bring some of your good bread, and some butter and cheese for our guests."

"Shut up! I am not beholden to your hospitality. I order you to show me all your illegal goods. Start with the cognac. I want to see everything. How many people live here?"

"Only my wife and I live here, sir. We have two sons serving our Führer in Russia. Our deepest—"

"Bring out your goods. The cognac first."

The farmer and his wife looked at each other in terror. "My wife and I will do exactly as you say, Herr Obersturmführer," the farmer said.

"Ja. We are loyal to our Führer," the wife said.

The farmer bent over and pulled back a throw rug. Beneath the rug was a board that he shifted sideways enough to be able to lift up a section of floor. The open door revealed a larder containing several bottles, three hams, a box of sausage, a crock of butter, and three brown paper packages.

"The detestable black market," Mehlhoff sneered. He reached down and lifted out a bottle that he recognized from his service in France. "This is a very fine cognac," he said as he moved the bottle to the table.

"Now, businessman farmer, open your next larder."

"This is all we have, esteemed officer. It is all yours as you wish. Please believe me, we have only put away a little extra and our relatives have brought us things. Sometimes we have helped our friends. The people were always coming—"

"Shut up and open the rest of your secret larders."

"I swear you see everything. We are loyal to Hitler. This is all we have."

"Go out to the barn. Stay there until I tell you to come back. I will make my own search. You will wish you were dead if you are lying."

"Ja. You will see we have told you the truth. Please be easy with us this one time," the farmer pleaded as he and his wife hurried out.

"You will Heil Hitler from your heart from now on," the Obersturmführer called after them.

He removed his black leather coat, looked at Paula, and, smiling, said, "Take off your coat. I am not going to do any searching. First, we will refresh ourselves with this fine cognac. Then you will put a good meal on the table for us. We have ham and bread and who knows what other delectables."

"Will you report them?"

The Obersturmführer chuckled. "I won't need to. We SS have a magic for making trash into good Germans. Is my magic sufficient for you, Frau Schmidt?"

"Ja," Paula answered.

"I will still the hunger that brought you out here," he said.

Paula stood silently beside the table without removing her coat.

He placed two fresh glasses on the table and filled them with the cognac. "Sit down. We will begin with a fiery treat, thanks to the French."

Paula still did not move. He went to her, unbuttoned her overcoat, removed it, and hung it on the wall beside his. She sat down. He joined her and lifted his glass. In search of words that would win his favor, she said, "I toast our Führer and the honor shown him by a soldier like you. I admire you. I am sad for you in your sorrow of losing your wife."

"You can't know my loss when you still have a living husband. It kills my only—"

Herman cleared his throat. Abruptly he toasted, "To victory." He began to talk about meat, his knowledge of smoked hams, his preferences in beef, and his favorite sausages. Occasionally he asked Paula questions such as, "Do you know what goes into making the carnival veal sausage of Munich?" she obliged with answers that kept him talking until they had finished two glasses of cognac.

Then he said, "We will see what we have in this cache that has been revealed to us."

He selected items from the floor larder and put them on the table. He drew his dagger and ran its razor sharp blade across a huge ham, carving off thick, pink slices. Paula cut fresh brown slices of bread. He opened a package and discovered it was sugar. "It is a strange time of day for a feast," he said, "but eat."

Paula ate falteringly. She felt so tense that at times her body would not accept food. But when she registered his scrutinizing gaze and his black uniform with its emblazoned lightning flashes, she ate ardently.

After a while he refilled the cognac glasses and toasted, "To the pleasure that is now to come."

Paula emptied her glass and returned it to the table. Without looking at him, she rose from her chair as if she were about to leave.

He stood up and studied her, with his smiling face noticeably musing a statement, but he said nothing. Instead, he went to her, put his arm around her shoulder and took her with him down a hallway and through a doorway to a room in which drawn curtains allowed only a dim light to reveal a dark frame bed with a walnut cast and a matching dresser.

When they reached the bed, he released his arm from her shoulder. She stood still, not daring to move. He took off his tunic and hung it neatly on a chair. Looking at her, he sat down and pulled off his boots. Then he stood up and with careful deliberation pulled his belt from his trousers, and laid it across the bed.

"Undress," he ordered. She still stood motionless by the bed as he removed his shirt. She looked into his ice blue eyes and instantly retreated from his penetrating stare by lowering her eyes to his muscular chest. She saw how light reflecting from the top of the walnut dresser accentuated his SS eagle tattoo and gave his chest the amber cast of cognac.

He reached over and unbuttoned her blouse. She was bewildered by her submission in allowing him to undress her. He pulled her blouse from her body. He unbuttoned her skirt and let it slide to the floor. She could feel her heart throbbing as her body relented, allowing him to pull up her petticoat that brushed the skin of her neck and face moving upwards . . . until he dropped it to the floor. She was too overwhelmed to be able to plot how to break free from him. He slipped off her panties. All the while, not a word was spoken.

Her hands trembled as he touched her hair, moved his fingers along her eyebrows, down her cheeks, her neck, and slowly and deliberately to her breasts which he cupped firmly, deliberately, before reaching for his belt. A cold current of terror shot through her as he wrapped the belt around her left upper arm. With involuntary contortion, her body recoiled from him and her arms flailed against his chest. He struggled against her, bringing the belt around her back, around her other arm, pulling it tight, and buckling it in a manner that denied her the use of her arms.

As she felt the cinch of his belt, she gave up trying to resist him. She shivered as if a draft had caught her. With her mind racing she ignored the registration of her senses. He lifted her into the bed and took off her shoes and stockings. She could see perspiration on his forehead and a new intensity in his eyes as he drew himself upon her. Sitting astride her, breathing in deep rhythm, he looked down upon her imprisoned, naked body. "Beautiful cat with your scheming lies, you are caught now," he mused.

"Please, unbind me. Please," she pleaded.

"You want to claw my eyes out, maybe, lying and scheming cat."

"I beg you, free me, please. You have me helpless."

"You will learn to like it, cat," he laughed as he shifted his body over one of her legs leaving his knee against her crotch.

He began to caress her damp belly with his palms. She trembled in occasional shivers as his fingers reached up to fondle the nipples of her breasts. Taking hold of her shoulders and squeezing hard, he smiled down to her eyes. "You need not fear me, because at this time it pleases me not to hurt you."

He moved his face down to hers and touched his lips teasingly to her eyelids then across her forehead and down to her cheeks, circling her face with teasing kisses.

"Please free me, dear Herr Offizier. I will be good. I will not fight you," she pleaded.

"I must be sure my magic has taken hold of you." He brought his tongue to her body and ran it along her breasts, lingering to suckle the nipples transiently before he said, "First, you must lose your fear of me. A cat in terror is treacherous. I will unbind you only as you give up to me."

His hands became more purposeful as he stroked her thighs. She breathed deeply, and lay still trying to calm herself, so he would free her.

"I will tame you, my cat, Paula."

She was damp with perspiration from her agitation—certain now that no escape was possible. "I give up to you . . . I have no power to resist you," she mumbled as she felt the body sensations of his tongue on her thighs as electric shock passing along her skin.

"For certain I have you now, Frau Schmidt," he gloated.

He pressed his lips to hers. She received them indifferently, scheming how indifference to his sensuality might be her best chance against him. Still, at the sensation of his hands thrust between her legs, she squirmed in uncontrollable reflex that he interpreted as lust for him.

"I will free you now."

He removed his belt from her arms and brought his face close to hers. Repulsed by his course lips, she implored, "As you are honorable, please stop."

"Ja-Ja . . ." Herman groaned, probing her pubic hair to thrust his penis between her vulva lips.

"I want in," he howled as he shoved his weight down.

"Ohhh—" she screamed as he rammed into her dry vagina to take total control of her.

He raised himself and stroked deep into her again. The pain made her throw her arms around him.

"Ohhh—" she moaned as he thrust again. "Ohhh. Please, please, dear Offizier," she gasped as he again read her agony as lust for him.

"Keep your arms away," she heard, but her arms stayed locked around him to hold him from thrusting as he hunched faster and harder, driving into her—now moaning and gasping with her until with guttural groans he reached climax. . . .

He lifted his hips from her and with recovered calm, he said, "I want no woman's arms around me. I am no baby." With this he broke her arms free from him and tried to pin them to the bed. Paula, mindlessly savage in her misery, thrashed and kicked to get away from him.

"I should not have untied you," he protested. "It was foolish of me. I have had my pleasure. You need not act so stupid."

Her mind was caught in a vortex. She could see his limp and dripping penis as he lifted himself from her. She wanted to scream hysterically, but her fear kept her silent.

He swung his legs to the floor, as he lifted himself from the bed, he said, "Dress yourself."

She lay on the bed and tried to regain her composure. She got up and started to dress.

He cleaned his body, dressed deliberately, and primped before the mirror, smartly smoothing his uniform into place.

As she was dressing, she began to feel dizzy and sat down on the edge of the bed. He turned from the mirror and looked down to her. Facing up to him, she said, "I give up to you. Let me go home. My child needs me."

"You think I will arrest you, don't you," he teased. "I will not turn you in. That's what you want to hear, isn't it?"

"Yes."

"Only do not ever forget to whom you owe your loyalty."

"Yes."

"Come, I am through with this farm house. It is time to go back to the city. First, you must clean the kitchen. We will take nothing with us. The SS code of honesty and decency will show here today along with the loyalty I have fired. I want everything left in good order."

1153 HOURS, 29 JANUARY, FRANKFURT, GERMANY: The water train nearing Frankfurt screeched to a standstill, flagged down by a man in a black leather coat. After a brief exchange, the train started again with Obersturmführer Mehlhoff and Paula Schmidt in the engine cab with the engineer.

Paula's heart was pounding and she was trembling, but she could not sort out her agitation. She took hope from the rhythmic clanking of the wheels and the staccato of the steam engine that promised escape from the SS rapist still holding control of her. He now smiled at her in what she read as smug enjoyment of his power to commandeer the train. She returned his smile with a nervous grin and then stuck her head into the cold air to clear her mind.

Looking ahead, she saw the silhouette of Katharinenkirche above the outline of Frankfurt-Altstadt, the thousand-year-old core of the city. Frankfurt was the home of her family for many generations before her. Her country's antiquity back to the time of Christ spoke from the buildings and art of Altstadt, reassuring her she belonged to a world beyond this diabolic morning.

Obersturmführer Mehlhoff moved closer and asked, "Do you hear sirens?"

"What?"

"Do you hear sirens?"

Sirens! She clutched the steel window frame of the engine cab in panic as the air-raid sirens wailed.

"Easy!" Mehlhoff shouted. "Look at the clouds covering the city. It could only be nuisance strafing planes flying low."

The train veered onto a side track.

"Air Raid Control has side-tracked us here for now," the engineer shouted. Steel screamed against steel until the train was stopped.

It is a warning of bombers nearby, not overhead, Paula noted of the wail starkly clear in the country quiet. "You are right about the clouds hiding us. I didn't panic like this when the bombings first started. It is obvious they are not coming here."

Then she remembered the comment about strafing planes. They were on a favorite target, a train. Low on the horizon she saw an airplane.

"Look! I'm getting off," she screamed.

Mehlhoff held her.

"Let me go," she pleaded.

He had seen the plane before she had. He had decided that he would leave the train if the plane swung its nose in their direction, but the plane turned away.

54

Steam blew from the engine safety cock making further conversation impossible. Mehlhoff jumped from the train and motioned for Paula to receive the support of his arms as she jumped, which she did. They started into a field that took them away from the railroad tracks. He grabbed Paula's arm. "There is no need to run. Be calm," he directed.

She felt safety in his authority now.

"Yes, I am foolish. I can't control myself anymore when the bombers come," she told him.

For a moment they stood still, looking for indications of what was happening. The train crew was running toward a cluster of houses. The siren wail ended. The locomotive stopped hissing steam. The stillness of open fields in winter prevailed.

"Look at the train crew run," Paula said. "There must be a shelter there."

"Yes. There must be a shelter there," Mehlhoff agreed.

"I must get back to my Karl. Tante Hilda may have gone up to the apartment with him. Let's run."

"We will walk," Mehlhoff ordered.

They started across the field. Paula half ran, while he strode beside her, silent, with his eyes upon the horizon. Presently, he grasped Paula's arm, bringing her to a stop.

They stood still, listening. Paula heard nothing, but like an animal before an earthquake, she sensed an impending horror. Then she registered a familiar perception so slight it was almost intuition. A sensation like a biting army of ants raced along her flesh—she had recognized the sound that was not a whisper, not a hum, not a rumble, yet a change in the quiet. She knew that this change would progress into a vibration that could be felt as much as heard. Suddenly the notes of a starling broke shrill across the field as the bird took flight into a thicket of trees.

"I've got to get home!"

"No. We will wait here for now."

The disturbance grew into a faint, all-pervading murmur. The murmur intensified until it was an earth-trembling rumble that rustled the leafless trees.

Paula no longer denied the message from the sky. Once initiated to this prophetic sound, one never forgot. Paula

Schmidt and Herman Mehlhoff both now knew—from high in the sky, heavy bombers were moving upon them.

"We must keep our heads," he said. "Look at the sky. I tell you they are not coming here. Above the clouds where they are, they have no idea they are over Frankfurt. You think they would bomb a sea of clouds? They are on their way to a place where there is clear sky today. Those pig dogs do not frighten me with the mere sound of their engines. We are going to calmly walk to your home."

Paula pointed toward the Katharinenkirche steeple. "It's that direction," she said. They started walking. As they walked the rumble grew louder.

"If they were coming here," Mehlhoff said, "the flak batteries would know it from their course and they would open fire. As a professional officer I know these things. Why do you think the anti-aircraft cannon are not firing? We have a thousand 88-mm cannon around this city. Do you hear one cannon fire? No. I will tell you why. As long as we do not fire they do not know that they are above Frankfurt." He laughed in appreciation of this wisdom, yet the rumble of bombers grew louder.

1213 HOURS, 29 JANUARY, FRANKFURT, GERMANY: Paula looked up to the overcast from which the sky noise came. Obersturmführer Mehlhoff held her arm, quickening her pace toward the air-raid shelter of an apartment complex about a quarter mile distant. As he hurried, he kept talking. ". . . we can be sure we are safe, because the flak batteries are not firing. The enemy has no way of knowing there is a city under them if the flak does not fire. We have secret weapons for knowing where the bombers are, how high they are flying, and what direction they are going, even through the clouds. The shells are fired to go precisely where the bombers are and explode precisely there. Just one shell explodes into thousands of pieces that rip into the enemy. These bombers are debris before they get here because they must fly straight and level when they come in to bomb."

His voice was drowned by the sudden thunder of the thousand 88-mm Air Defense cannon of Frankfurt joining the rumble of the bombers.

Mehlhoff turned in bewilderment. His eyes searched for something to fight. His muscles flexed. The sky-noise was unworldly. *Who can know our city is under the clouds?*

They began to run toward the first apartment house. They were running when a salvo of about a hundred bombs struck a sunshine flare into the gray sky. Paula cried out and fell to the ground sobbing, counting, to measure her distance from the multiple strike. "One. Two. Three." Each number she counted meant that the bombs had missed her by eleven hundred feet, the speed at which the concussion traveled. "Four. Five."—a warning breeze, then the blast slapped across her.

She was hardly aware of Mehlhoff's arm pressing her down to the earth. "Dirty bastards!" he cursed. "They're not human. Filthy pigs. Murderers of women and children. Damn Jew Terrorfliegers."

A rain of money-size spent shrapnel from the exploding anti-aircraft shells began to fall. The opening salvo of bombs had landed in a line almost a mile away, but Paula and Mehlhoff knew that this was only the beginning of the hell to come.

They were still a quarter mile from the apartment house where there was promise of an air-raid shelter. Herman considered making a run for it. Two more salvos blossomed behind Frankfurt-Altstadt, silhouetting the Katharinenkirche spire for an instant. White bubbles of pulverized stone rose from Altstadt. In one place a column of smoke and flames shot skyward above the stone-cloud.

"My boy," Paula sobbed. "Oh, God. Oh, please. . . ."

Hugging Paula down to the ground, Mehlhoff snapped himself into combat discipline. They were in the middle of a pasture some six hundred feet long. Beyond this was a similar pasture and beyond this the first house that would have an air-raid shelter.

"Get up. We are going to run for a shelter," he ordered.

A three-foot stone wall separated the two pastures. They ran to the stone wall where leafless branches of a birch tree spread over a wooden shed-roof that leaned against the wall. Herman's mind registered that here they could at least get the protection of the stone wall and the wooden roof. The lean-to was three feet high on its tallest side where it lay against the wall. He took in every possibility for getting below ground. There was no ditch. He looked under the roof and saw that there was no hollowed-out ground here. There was only the frozen ground and the wooden roof leaning against the rock wall.

Paula was crying. He slapped her face. "Control yourself," he ordered.

He again weighed the distance to the apartment house, and he weighed the closeness of the advancing curtain of death.

Paula kept crying.

He began to cross the wall. Again a bomb-curtain flashed. He quickly grabbed Paula and hit the ground next to the stone wall that could shield them against the arriving concussion. The impact rushed past, sparing them. Lying flat, he studied the death dust lifting to join the pulverized aftermath becoming a vivid crown over the city. The death dust was nearing.

From the houses ahead, they heard screams and saw people running. In the pasture ahead, two chestnut draft horses galloped along the stone wall enclosing them. One horse abruptly changed direction, dug at the ground, reared back, snorted, shook its mane, and galloped on aimlessly. The other horse tried to jump the wall, failed, scrambled to its feet, and galloped back along the wall unsteadily, neighing and tossing its head.

"Get under the shed roof," Mehlhoff ordered.

They crawled under the protection of the inch of wood to the top and the foot of stone to the side of them. Herman pushed Paula next to the wall. Seconds dragged as they lay waiting for the next salvo.

"I shouldn't have left Karl. Hilda surely took him upstairs with her. Oh loving God, why am I out here?"

Mehlhoff lay on his stomach and raised his head to look across the city. He saw jagged columns of fire and smoke reaching into the clouds. The fires were not only to the left but also to the right—here, under the lean-to roof, they were centered in the death sweep coming closer. One of his hands clutched Paula's shoulder and the other gripped his dagger. His mind was filled with anticipation of the bombs coming. *These pig dog bastards got my wife this way. This isn't war. This is filthy murder. Killing women and children. This isn't war anymore. This is shitty, Jewish terror. This is waiting for filthy cold-blooded murder.*

The bomb bursts stopped. The cannon and the engine rumble still constituted ear-torturing sound, but the lack of bombs bursting made a relative quiet. They knew that the respite meant only that the next wave of bombers was moving in.

The bomb bursts started again. Herman saw the bursts a mile to the north. A few seconds later he saw a multiple salvo burst closer. He counted to two before the concussion jolted the earth. He observed that this division was missing the city. The bombs were falling in fields. They were missing. He gloated, *these goddamn super pigs are missing.* The bombs were advancing across the fields to where they lay.

He began to tremble. His body convulsed in shivering rhythm that he could not control. Abruptly he twisted sideways to stare up through the roof and storm to confront the bombers. With frustrated rage he shouted, "Waste your bombs on the fields. Come on. Kill me. You'll pay for it. We Germans will remember. Every one of you will hang by your balls if it takes us three generations!"

1228 HOURS, 29 JANUARY, FRANKFURT, GERMANY: SS Obersturmführer Mehlhoff cursed and Paula Schmidt prayed . . . waiting for death to strike. The bombs carried in from yet another direction. Then there was a welling of sound, as if from a fast-moving train bearing upon them. Paula gripped her face to the ground. Mehlhoff clutched his hands over his eyes. The air was alive with fire. In the next instant the roof was gone and the tree was a grotesque skeleton.

They are still alive. Again the bombs come. This time the house they could not reach is gone. Again and again the bombs burst around them. There is a giant flash and a rumbling concussion from the railroad yards they came from.

Again Altstadt blossoms with bomb clouds. When the clouds settle, only gray sky is left where the steeple of Katharinenkirche had shown on the horizon.

After an hour the bombing ends. The guns grow silent. The sirens wail All Clear.

Time bombs still burst sporadically. But for survivors the fiery aftermath of the heavy-bomber raid—the Grossangriff—is just beginning.

Shock has erased expression from Paula's face. Blood runs from a gash in her cheek. She rises, falteringly.

"My arm?" Mehlhoff asks. One side of his uniform is in shreds. The arm is at an angle between the wrist and elbow. "Cut away my uniform," he directs.

Paula wields his dagger. "I will make a support from wood splinters."

"First, your forehead," he orders. He examines her wounds. "We must stop the bleeding. Take my handkerchief and tie it across . . ."

After tending to each other, they start toward Paula's house. "I am afraid of what I will find," Paula says.

"We will go together."

They move unconscious of time and distance. Walking into a city of living rubble.

They move on, deeper into the misery, with eyes that wanted to deny vision.

Chains of people handing water from the river Main to the flames.

Canyons of broken stone and twisted steel.

The torso of a woman.

A stretcher, abandoned, on fire.

An explosion. Screaming. Running forms. Fire hoses.

Tangled masses of hoses from the river Main.

Poisonous smoke billowing down.

Hanging walls.

Hallways leading into nowhere.

Feet protruding from the ruins.

Pungent flames.

Running, fleeing, gasping forms.

"Hilfe! Hilfe!" from under rubble.

Women armies digging into ruins.

Men screaming under fallen walls.

A blind man tapping in a fiery street.
Stretchers borne by little boys.
Barefoot feet on broken glass.
Gutter graves. Street rivers. Crater walls. Volcano sky.
Now clearing debris.
Water running into cellars.
Fire, splashing, crying, wailing below.
One arm in a sling, the other moving stone.
Fingernails torn wrestling tangled steel.
On, into rubble-blocked streets. Searching toward home.
Heavy feet. Knotted stomachs. Cold hands.
Until it is evening.
They are almost at Paula's home. No flames here.
They walk in the middle of the street, across rubble.
Then Paula sees. She stands, looks, and begins to run.
A gaunt wall stands alone.
The staircase to Paula's apartment is still intact.
The door, splintered, hangs open to emptiness.
"Karl! Hilda! Where is my boy?" Paula calls to the ruins.
A shawl-clad neighbor comes to her.
She wraps her shawl around Paula's shoulders.
She embraces Paula.
"You call to the dead.
We tried to get them to the bunker, but too late."
Paula tears herself from the shawl about her.
She climbs upon the ruins.
She collapses on the broken stone.
She has no tears now. Her hands grip debris.
The rubble grates her lips as she cries, "Why?
God in heaven, I ask you, Why?"

Document A, **The Key Point System**, following, establishes the existence of **an air offensive to destroy German homes** at the time of the Frankfurt raid of 29 January, 1944. The Key Point Factor determines the target priority of possible target cities.

Document B, following, is a **record of the official denial of the existence of this air offensive to destroy German homes**. The Under-Secretary for Air declares to the House of Commons, "We are not bombing the women and children of Germany wantonly."

DOCUMENT A

THE KEY POINT SYSTEM

Economic Effects of Air Offensive on German Cities

Appendix A

In January 1943 a method was devised for appraising the economic value of German cities. This appraisal, known as the "key point system" was to determine the most profitable economic targets for strategic effect by concentrated night attack against the built-up area of the city.

Frankfurt/Main:

Population	Key Point Rating	Key Point Factor*
570,000	153	27.0

The two most important economic effects of general devastation produced by night bombing of built-up areas (**apart from casualties, the economic effects of which are negligible**) were thought to be:

Direct: Destruction of dwellings and de-housing

Indirect: The expenditure of manpower and materials on rehabilitation

*U.S. Strategic Bombing Survey, European Theatre, Area Studies Division Report, 1st Edition, 29 October, 1945. Government Printing Office, Washington, D.C.

DOCUMENT <u>B</u>

EXCERPT FROM BOMBING VINDICATED

. . .they are misinformed people. They have not studied all the facts. They have formed their conclusions on ex parte evidence. A good example of the arguments which they rely upon is to be found in the pamphlet **Stop Bombing Civilians!** published by the 'Bombing Restriction Committee' whose address is 49 Parliament Hill, London, N.W. 3, and whose purpose is thus set forth at the beginning of the pamphlet:

"To urge the Government to stop violating their declared policy of bombing only military objectives and particularly to cease causing the death of many thousands of civilians in their homes."

The indictment is incorrectly drawn. The Government are not violating their declared policy. It was definitely stated by Captain Harold Balfour, the Under-Secretary of State for Air, in the House of Commons on 11 March, 1943, that we were still bombing only military objectives. **"I can give the assurance,"** he told the House, **"that we are not bombing the women and children of Germany wantonly.** If in the pursuit of our objective the German civilian population have to suffer, it is not our fault." **This, it will be seen, was a specific denial of the assertion that we were no longer aiming at military objectives and that we were attacking towns indiscriminately.** I believe that denial to be correct, and I have at my disposal information which could not be available to the Bombing Restriction Committee.

J.S. Spaight, C.B., C.B.E., Late Principal Assistant Secretary, Air Ministry, Great Britain, Bombing Vindicated, G. Bles, London, 1944.

This report was written primarily for the use of the U.S. Strategic Bombing Survey in preparation for further reports of a more comprehensive nature. . . .

ECONOMIC EFFECTS OF AIR OFFENSIVE
ON GERMAN CITIES

PREFACE

1. **The major cities of Germany present a spectacle of destruction** so appalling as to suggest a complete breakdown of all aspects of urban activity. <u>On the first impression it would appear that the area attacks which laid waste these cities must have substantially eliminated the industrial capacity of Germany. Yet this was not the case.</u> **<u>The attacks did not so reduce German war production as to have a decisive effect on the outcome of the war.</u>**

U.S. Strategic Bombing Survey, 1945, U.S. Gov. Printing Office, Washington D.C.

THE WAR: CHAPTER THREE

ENGLAND, 100TH BOMB GROUP, WING HOSPITAL: Captain Randi Scott strode into the hospital ward where Captain Buck Pierce was recuperating. Her purpose was to keep her promise to inform Captain Pierce that Colonel Raymond wanted to visit with him about his son's fatal flight. To both sides of her were white iron beds occupied by combat-wounded airmen whom she pitied and cherished.

Bed 17: Right leg missing, the other held by cables with arms and leg dangling free.

Bed 18: Eyes showing from a gauze cocoon.

Bed 19: A body propped up with chest and an arm in an angular cast pointing skyward and held by a steel frame.

Bed 20: The thin form of what seemed to be a teen age boy lying flat, strapped to a board platform with eyes looking to the ceiling.

Bed 21: "Captain Buck Pierce. It's temperature time, my hero."

Bewildered hazel eyes of a bandaged face looked up to her as she inserted a thermometer between his lips, sealing his ability to reply.

"I'm Captain Scott, the supervising nurse. Your nurses say wild things about you. Your chart looks good. The doctor says he'll release you for barracks recuperation if all looks well today."

From three beds away came, "I'm nerval in the serval. Help me! I'm nerval in the serval."

"All right, Dan. Your medication's coming," Randi answered. Then to Buck she continued, "I've come to see you specially, to, ah, first, learn how you're feeling and how you're healing."

Buck removed the thermometer and said, "Maybe I'm not quite awake. I'm looking up to sexy brown eyes and cinnamon-black hair, and I'm hearing this is the head nurse calling me her hero and saying she's come to see me special.

66

You even know my handle, 'Buck.' What do you want?"

"I'm checking on you. Do you need help in washing up?"

"A bath?"

"Yes, that. I want to talk to you, too."

"I can walk to the shower. If you'll go with me, while you're talking, I'll wash down as far as possible and up as far as possible—"

"Yes, Buck. Then I can wash possible, right? Tell me a new joke."

"You got me. I'm short on jokes. I was trying to bounce back from you putting on I was special. I'm only special here as a pilot hauling bombs. Why are you looking at me with those watery eyes?"

"I want to talk to you because you were the pilot when my friend Dean Raymond's son was killed."

"You're a friend of the inspector general! God, that's how I'm special."

"Not just that, we're both from Wyoming. We're both a long way . . . I live in that part of the West, too. I've spent a lot of time in the Big Horns near Buffalo where your records say you're from."

"That's a lot of special! I mean, coming from my part of the country and all. I shouldn't have been so edgy. Call me flak-happy. Two missions in a row my co-pilot's been killed sitting beside me. I'm not looking to be called a hero."

"That was the war, not you, Buck."

"I guess, but you just said you're a friend of my last co-pilot's dad. That wouldn't make me a hero to you. What do you want from me?"

"There is something I want, Buck. I'm sure you can understand that Tom's dad would like to visit with you about how it happened. He asked me to look into when you'd feel up to seeing him."

"You're talking about the big shot that came from Washington to nail us for not making headlines because we're waiting for clear sky bombing. The inside scoop is that his being here is why we were ordered to take off in the snow storm. My buddy Marks blew up with his crew, trying to get off the ground in that storm. Now he's asking me to—"

"Colonel Raymond's being here had nothing to do with that mission. He's here to—it's too complicated, and this isn't the place to talk about it. Trust me, if you knew him—"

"You're talking like a really good friend of his, Captain."

"My name is Randi."

"Whatever. I've got word he's looking to court martial somebody. It could be me, since I didn't challenge the orders that put Tom on my crew, green as he was. He didn't even have combat gear until an hour before take off. His head was so crowded he came on board without an oxygen mask. I just played along, because he was sent to me by the brass, and I knew who he was. Now the brass will be looking for a scapegoat, and that could be me. It's an old story, whitewashing asses by putting the blame on pilot error. I don't want to see him—that's for sure. He's on the prowl for revenge."

"I'm nerval in the serval. Help me! I'm nerval in the serval."

"It's okay, Dan. This is Buck. I'll come sit with you 'til you're feeling better." To Randi, Buck said, "We knew each other before he flew one mission too many. He trusts me, so I've been keeping him company."

"It's not yet time for his shot to relax him. He's trying to tell us he's nervous in the service. He must bother you. We're waiting for a bed to transfer him."

"Move him next to me. He likes me near him."

"Nice thought, Buck, but he'll still be here when you're back to the world. I've got to go. I would like to visit with you some more, away from the hospital. You'll have a different attitude toward Colonel Raymond when I tell you more about him."

"When you let me out, I'm heading for London while I'm off combat. Wouldn't you?"

"I don't know. I haven't had the chance to get further away than Norwich. Would you meet me in Norwich?"

"You plan to soften me up, don't you?" Buck paused, connecting his gaze firmly with her damp dark eyes fixed upon him. "Whatever. I'm not going to say no to you, Randi."

"I'm nerval in the serval. Help me! I'm nerval in the serval."

Randi started away. "We'll talk about it when you get released," her voiced trailed.

FRANKFURT, GERMANY, WITH WALTER PLANK: After thirty hours in the arm chair of the old woman's kitchen, Walt was moved into the back seat of a sedan and taken into the city of Frankfurt. Since he could not open his eyes, he depended on sound for knowledge of his surroundings. As the sedan penetrated rubble-filled streets, he registered voices of panic, moans of mourning, and screams of commands. The sounds mixed with smells of chemicals and burnt flesh. It was a haunting, foreboding darkness punctuated by delayed-action bomb flashes that carried pink brightness through his sealed eyelids. In this nightmare he fought to keep calm.

I've got to remember who I am, where I came from . . . who cares about me. I am a 100th Bomb Group Lead Bombardier. I've got to remember. I may be a father by now. My wife may be hugging our baby and wishing I were with her. I've got to armor my brain. I've got to remember.

What seemed like an eternity later, he was placed in a bed. "Medizin fur Schmerzen, bitte," he pleaded.

A woman's voice said in English, "Don't think we will use our precious medicine to relieve your pain. Think of the thousands you have murdered. You don't deserve comfort."

He heard a key turn. He judged by the quiet that he was alone. He lay on his back with his arms stretched to his sides so that his burned hands would hang free of the bed. Sleep would not come. He wanted to turn on his side, but he had to remain in this one position. It occurred to him that this was the position of Christ on the cross, and he remembered the scripture, "Father, forgive them; for they know not what they do."

He prayed, assuring himself that there was still God's love. Hours passed. Biblical verses long forgotten came to his mind. Then with a shiver he recalled the words of the cross, "My God, my God, why has thou forsaken me?"

The woman said I should think of the thousands I have murdered. That was telling me that they aren't going to help

*me. I always knew that if I got shot down it would be like
this. I have to escape. If I stay here I'll die. I need a miracle. I can't escape with my eyes swollen and my knee torn
open. Marg's Gypsy ring is killing me. God is punishing me
for not staying loyal to Cathy.*

Finally he fell asleep. He was back in red-rock country in
Oak Creek Canyon. His wife and child were with him.
Everyone but him was seated on the flat, smooth stone floor of
Slide Rock. The canyon walls rose straight up. He was high
up on the red cliff with his hands stuck in a crevice. Cathy
was gazing up at him with her hands clasped, crying, "Oh God,
he's dying!" Suddenly he awoke to his misery. He remembered again that something had to be done about the rings on
his swollen fingers. Again he fell asleep. Then he was awakened by a gruff voice saying, "For you the war is over."

LONDON, ENGLAND, WITH SAM O'BRIEN: The *Bare Lass* crew,
lacking pilot and co-pilot, was put on combat fatigue leave.
Bombardier Sam, after visiting Buck in the hospital, left for
London. He was now enjoying the purchased hospitality of
Sandra, his mystery lover recently discovered at the
Grosvenor House U.S.O. dance.

Sandra was watching Sam melt a cream chocolate into
his mouth. "They came from Switzerland. Don't ask me
how I got them."

She moved over to a white, gilt-edged vanity where mirrored glass wings reflected her image into illusory depth in
which she was Sandra, again, again, and again, on to infin-
ity. With Sam enraptured by her multiple presence, she
unpinned her hair and let it fall. She picked up a brush and
combed the bristles slowly along the black strands. Sam
reflected that her eyes were the blue of a glacier lake as he
studied the woman echoing into the looking glass.

"You're an Oriental beauty, Sandra, with your high
cheekbones and olive skin. But I never saw an Oriental
with blue eyes and long legs. Open your robe so I can feast
my eyes on all of you. Maybe you're Mongolian. You're from
Outer Mongolia. Hairy brutes brought you in from the

frozen wilds on a sled because you were the most beautiful thing that had ever happened out there, and the men were all fighting over who could have you. They sold you in Ankara to a sheik with a hundred wives, and you were his favorite. You stole his heart and cut his throat and made off with his jewels in the dark of the night on a white stallion."

Sandra enjoyed Sam's eyes and his sensual smile as she slid her glistening black robe from her shoulders and rose to reveal her nude breasts and thighs.

"You've traveled the world and you're still on your way with your beauty a treasure men would kill for. The jewels aren't important to you. You live for the lust that you excite in men's souls—"

"My dreaming red-headed Sammy from Chicago, where do you get your stories? Everything you say is true. The generals crazy with lust for me pay with their souls. Your fantastic stories tell me who I really am."

"That doesn't fit with you choosing me, a second lieutenant bombardier."

"I like your smile and your wings. Ever since the bombing I love wings—we were saved by men with wings. We all said, 'Never have so many owed so much to so few.'"

"That was Churchill talking about the pilots who saved London. I just trigger bombs over Germany."

"You flyers are all exciting."

"Yeah, we have fun and rant and rave, 'cause we're headed for an early grave."

Sandra, suddenly serious, said, "I hate my life in London. That's why I love you. I live in your dream stories."

Sam said, "I just want to smell your perfume and snuggle into your hot crotch. I want the groaning and laughing while we're making love."

"You are under my spell, aren't you Sammy? You are my bird man. You are my dove who will always return from the sky to me."

"When the shells are exploding I can call on your spell to bring me back to you."

"You alone, Sammy, lift me out of London. You're so trusting. You would do anything for me, wouldn't you, Sammy?"

"I'd rather be something besides your Sammy. Can you love me as your Danny? I am half Irish, you know."

"Danny? My lamb Danny?"

"For me, you are my Sandra Lavore. Lavore floats better than Pirusambi. Really, I need a better name than Danny, too. Give me a bird name, but not your dove. I'd like to be a more soaring bird, not an eagle, but something breathtaking, free of human-problems."

"We'll dream up a name for you, and I'll be your Sandra Lavore. Anything you want: Sandra Lavore's cream chocolates, her Four Star Hennessy, her kisses, her pussy."

"For now, serve your Hennessy," Sam proposed from Pirusambi's gold velvet divan.

Sandra went to a glass cabinet and poured Four Star Hennessy while Sam expounded, "There's a kind of gadget that hangs from the ceiling with metal birds flying in a circle. Have you seen flying birds like that in London?"

"You want birds for over your bed, Sammy—Danny—soaring bird, whoever you are?"

"No. Before I came to London we learned that our bombardier friend Walt, his wife, had a baby. He doesn't know, 'cause he was sent on a special mission. He's in Russia now, or Mongolia, I think outer Mongolia. I want these birds for his baby girl lying in her crib."

"I'll help you look for them. Then will you help me? Mine is a big, big wish."

Sam raised his glass, "We'll click our glasses, and our wishes will come true."

They sealed their wishes with a sip of cognac. Then she put down her glass and, after kissing him passionately, said, "I would like to go back to the air base with you."

"That's a shocker! There's too much secret going on there. I could hide you in my bombsight bag if you were smaller, but the bombsight's so secret they keep it in the vault—"

"Not on the bomber base, just close by so I can be near my soaring bird."

"I need more cognac. The English are awfully suspicious.

They got rules. I don't think I could rent you a place. They're so nervous about invaders and spies they've even taken down all the road signs."

"We could pretend that I'm your wife."

"If we do that," Sam said, "it might get to be so real that you would come back with me to Chicago when I finish my missions."

"We could visit the places where you grew up. I could meet your family. We could find a cottage along the big lake you told me about."

"I wouldn't take you to Fuller Park where I grew up. It's a war zone of Irish, Germans, Lithuanians, Jews, Italians, and Austrians. With my dad Catholic Irish and my mother Orthodox Jewish, I fought my world war there before I was fourteen. Now I've moved my mother to Lawndale. But I'd take you to see the steel mills where fire shoots geysers into the night, and iron runs in red rivers as thin as water—"

Abruptly, Sandra injected, "Why did you leave America to fight the Germans?"

"I didn't join to fight. There was a parade. The sun was shining. Then a crazy rain storm blew in. The paraders all got soaked, but people were laughing. There were yellow tulips. I'm not making sense. It was a happy time. I was standing dry in the doorway of an army recruiting office. Soaked sailors carrying duffel bags passed by me. It put me in a mood. I felt like I wasn't part of the action. I didn't want to join the navy, so I went in and signed up with the army. After that, the rest just happened."

"So they trust you with the secret Norden Bombsight. Do they also trust you with the new Magic Eye bombsight that can see through clouds?"

"I just sit up in the sky and look down on the world so far away it looks like nobody lives there. No, I really fly on a broom stick, sometimes on a pitch fork, and I aim my bombs with a forked stick called a sling shot."

"I believe you, and I won't ask any more questions," Sandra laughed.

"I won't ask questions either. We'll just love each other and dream together, my Sandra Lavore. Let's move into the bedroom."

"And when you go back to the base you will try to find a place for me? Just a small place—-near the base, so we can be together more."

"It won't be easy—"

There was a loud knock on the apartment door.

Sandra reacted with shock. "Could that be for you? I don't tell anyone where I live. Go to the door and see who it is."

Sam went to the door.

The knock repeated.

"What do you want?"

"I have a government letter for Miss Pirusambi. Duty calls," came through the door.

"You're at the wrong door. This is the residence of ballerina Lavore," Sam shouted.

"Stop, Sam. I'll take care of this."

Sandra called out, "I am Miss Pirusambi. Give me a minute." She pulled her robe tightly about her. To Sam, she said, "I know what this is about. It would be better if you returned to your hotel for now. Leave through the back door. No questions. I'll join you as soon as I can."

NORWICH, ENGLAND, WITH BUCK AND RANDI: Buck was drinking a half-and-half with the owner of the Lord Raglan as he waited for Randi. In two hours he planned to be on the train to London to join Sam. His doctors had ordered "barracks recuperation," not a London leave, but he was on his way to London.

A white dressing showed on his neck. His right hand was bandaged, and his face and hands showed scars of newly healed skin. In his gas mask bag he carried two bottles of bourbon whiskey.

Presently he took his half-and-half to a table in the family room, a more respectable place to meet Randi. *Her uniform doesn't change the fact that she's a woman. I like the way her blouse fills out even when she is standing tall and straight. I like the brown of her eyes, too. She's got a hurt look in her eyes, like she's trying not to cry, even when she's smiling. When she locks those eyes on me, I can't think. She spooks me, like she's someone from my past. Her hair is not cinnamon-black like I told her. It's pure black.*

I've heard how nurses are free-spirited when it comes to sex. Is her colonel sleeping with her? I've seen some pretty measly characters bring in good-lookers with their colonel's eagles. She is probably feeling herself a part of his big shot world. To her I'm a nobody, not a romantic date. Then why am I here? Maybe because of my part in Tom getting killed, but it was a shell that had his name on it—fate, not me. Whatever. I ought to admit I'm here, too, because I want to see Randi.

Tom was a game greenhorn, and I was hard on him, I hope not because I was mad at his dad. Anyway, how combat-ready he was didn't make a difference to the shell that hit him. Let the brass who assigned him to fly with me tell that to the inspector general. I'm not talking. I'm not forgetting that Marks and his crew died on that take-off.

When Randi comes I'll take charge and get us to someplace where we're really alone. Where can we go? How can I still catch my train? . . .

Randi was crossing a bridge of the blacked-out street leading to the Lord Raglan. Hearing water running in the cold February night, she stopped and listened. Above her, a slight breeze stirred in the leafless trees, and below her, as she listened intently, she heard the murmur of water sliding over sandy loam. The water was less lazy than creek water of the High Plains, but not as lively as Spearfish Canyon water that rattled pebbles.

She turned back and felt her way to a path that led down to the stream. High in the sky a full moon glistened between clouds that hid the stars. The moonlight shimmered silver on the water and lit her passage. At the stream's edge she cupped her hands into a chalice and lifted water of the running brook to her face to renew her connection with Nature. She consciously exhaled her steaming breath and watched the vapors dissolve into the night. From a thicket along the stream she picked up sounds of what she felt was a small animal also taking nurture from the stream.

Oh how good it is to be alone with nature. Only two hours ago I was holding the hand of an airman as he died. Think of something else. Get back on the street and finish your walk to the Lord Raglan. Buck will be leaving for London. I'm going to crawl into my robe and settle in with my gin and orange. I'm going to sink into myself until I don't give a damn.

Returned to the street, she thought as she walked . . . *Buck . . . Dean . . . what a sorry circumstance. Human decencies . . . father-son feelings . . . I want to be the peacemaker, but I'm caught in a warrior world.*

Dean again. But here it's no dancing in the tropical moonlight and midnight champagne on the beach. I'm not the freshman nurse I was in Manila. I'm not awestruck by rank anymore, but he still overwhelms me. It's all his world when we are together because I want to get away from the blood and syringes. He's always the hero. I'm his nurse. Is there a streak of my mother in me that enjoys being taken over by a man?

When his head is in the war, I should be angry, but I only admire him. Here I am on my night off being the good nurse for him again. Am I? I am drawn to Buck. He's so young, so lacking in the authority Dean carries. He's more like me, in ways, yet he's so innocent-cocky I want to hit him and hug him both.

Buck, waiting, was separated from his thoughts by the owner asking, "Are you Captain Pierce?"

"To some people."

"Captain Scott informs that she is expecting you. She is like royalty to us. I admire nurses. There is no glory in their duty, only heart. Take the stairway across from the bar room. Her room is the second door to the left."

Buck was suddenly confronted with flipped circumstances. Instead of needing to take charge to get Randi alone, he needed only to accept her invitation. He was still trying to re-frame his thinking when he knocked on her door.

When she opened the door he was surprised again, for instead of her Captain's uniform she was wearing a beaded

76

robe with colorful geometric designs. The robe hung across her left shoulder, covering her left arm and held to her body with leather thongs tied at her waist. Her right shoulder was uncovered, leaving her right arm bare and free.

"Hey? Where did you get the antelope skin robe?" Buck asked.

"It was my grandmother's. Come in. You're on your way to London, and I'm settled in for a night away from the hospital."

As she closed the door she continued, "Would you like a gin and orange? I'm having a tall one to wind down. The Wing got hit hard today."

"I know. We lost a crew from our squadron. I'm carrying some Old Crow bourbon if you'd rather start into that."

"I'll stay with the gin. Save your bourbon for London—not that I approve of you going to London. You need rest, and you need to be careful to prevent hemorrhaging. Don't tell anybody that I know of your plans."

As Buck mixed drinks he answered, "If the doctors only had two sure days before going back to combat that had already claimed ninety percent of them, they would probably head out for a last fling even if they had their heads in slings."

He passed a drink to Randi and dropped into a soft chair. His eyes took in the rose ambiance of the room and the hypnotic flame of a coal fire in the hearth.

Randi sank into stacked pillows on her bed, took a drink of gin and orange, and said, "Don't worry, Big Buck. I'll put you out in time to catch your train to London, wise or not."

"How did you learn that handle, 'big Buck'?"

"From the nurses—and all about the wild things you've been telling them."

"Yeah? Like what?"

"For a start, they said you're friends with Indians who taught you to hunt with a bow and arrow and fish with a spear. Is it true, Big Buck?"

"I thought you meant wild stories about women."

Randi observed Buck moving to the edge of his chair and leaning toward her. With a smile that anticipated his reaction to her words to come, she continued, "Did you tell them wild love stories, Buck? I wouldn't expect wild love stories from living alone out in ranch country. The ranch boys in Spearfish where I went to high school were so far out of town they were more horny loners than red hot lovers."

"You're from Spearfish? In high plains distance that's almost neighbors!"

Randi smiled, enjoying Buck's excitement under her teasing foray.

Buck was thinking. *There are only two steps from this chair to her bed . . . but those are two very long steps. How can I get from here to there?* "I like your robe," he said, "the way it's loose around your neck, hiding some mighty tempting territory—barely," and he grinned. "It reminds me of Indian friends back home."

"So you are a Wyoming white man who has Indian girlfriends?"

"I didn't say girlfriends. I said Indian friends. I meant the robe, not what's underneath it. Besides, if you were my Indian girlfriend I'd be a lucky cowboy."

"That's enticing, but what makes you sure I'm Indian?"

"I'm not sure, but since I first saw you I've had a haunting feeling you were someone from my past. Now I realize your eyes have a mood I remember from a sad and lonely Sioux. Maybe that's the tie—you were right about ranch life. I missed out on a lot of the town dancing and romancing, and we were Quaker. There aren't many of them in Wyoming for Sunday socializing. But ranch life was good— God, you do have tempting territory, Randi."

"Let's keep the subject Wyoming. What was good about ranch life?"

"I have my own cattle, my own horses. I hunt and trap. In the summer I backpack into the lake country above Clear Creek—the Big Horns—where there's elk, deer, bear, mountain lion—you name it. I've done some rodeo riding, too, mainly bronc riding. A Cheyenne-tribe friend taught me hunting with a bow and arrow. After that, shooting a deer with a gun was too easy, like slaughter."

"The Seven Brothers Lakes above Clear Creek are a favorite place for me. Sometimes I imagine myself there when I want to get away from here."

"Randi, I remember looking down into the water there and seeing big trout swimming around in what looked like forty feet down. I've cussed a blue streak trying to get those lake trout to take bait."

Randi settled into her pillows and envisioned herself basking on a lakeside and looking up to the mountains. "I like seeing the huge boulders stacked up above the timber line as big as houses and reaching from the lakes clear up to Cloud Peak. Have you ever climbed Cloud Peak?"

"I've been up as far as the snow line in July."

"I have been clear to the top, over forests and mountains as far as I could see. It was a powerful spiritual experience."

"I've brought in two fish at a time fly fishing below the Peak at the headwaters of Clear Creek," Buck countered.

"Wouldn't it have been something if we had met up there, Buck?"

"Yeah. I've been up there a long time without seeing one human being."

Randi was imagining herself with Buck on a lakeside under the lodgepole pines.

"Do you have a girl waiting for you back home?"

"Lots of girls back home, and in London, too."

"Oh? You'd answer different if you were really in love. Fix us another drink. I asked you here because of Tom, and we're talking about home instead. Tom was Colonel Raymond's only child. Your attitude when we talked at the hospital baffled me."

Buck only smiled and with exploring eyes savored Randi settled into her pillows.

"Say something! You're smiling at me like you can't hear me."

"I'll mix the drinks," Buck answered. "I don't have to rush away. I can order a taxi to save the time of walking to the station."

Randi turned onto her side with one knee raised and a shoulder further cradled into her pillows. She studied Buck as he rose. Seeing him stand six-feet-plus, she pictured the lean body and muscular chest that she recalled from his hospital stay. She followed his movement as he walked across the room. Tonight, in his uniform, his presence was more formidable. "Buck, I can see you riding a bronc and flying a bomber, but you're fresh off the ranch in the people world—sap green," she taunted.

"Ranch sap green? I'm damn sure no colonel city slicker, and I don't want to be."

"I'm not saying I want you to be, but there is an education you don't get from riding a horse. I've learned a lot, fighting the casualty war since the tunnels of Corregidor. You don't need to hear about it. I only want to get through to you that the killing can rob you of your sympathy for the suffering."

Buck handed Randi a gin and orange. "You look too lonely. Move over so I can relax beside you while we talk. I want to learn more about you. I admire your spirit of caring. I saw it in the hospital. I know I've a lot to learn from you."

"Stand beside me. I'm not moving."

"Why? You're just the Colonel's messenger, is that it?"

"No. That's not it."

"Am I too much a ranch animal for you?"

"If I need to be blunt—your mind is too much on going to bed with me."

"Too much, Randi? I like every part of you I can see. Hell, I'm about to go out the door and out of your life. Let's get close together for a little while and pretend we're back home. I'll put my arm around you, and we'll talk about how Tom was killed and how his dad is suffering—like you're my Indian girlfriend."

Randi tried to organize her frustration. Buck's toying with the despair of Tom's death made her angry. When she finally spoke, her anger was turned to despair. "Yes, I'm part Indian. My grandmother is Sioux. Dean would think less of me if he knew. Maybe I shouldn't be trusting you—"

"Why? We're High Plains neighbors—"

"Let me finish. Since I was little I've heard talk of women's tears and wails when their men went off to war,

Indian wars before white-man came. Fighting people was more daring to our men than hunting buffalo. Sioux warriors decorated their horses and put on war outfits like you. You, with your weird flying gear. You decorate like they did, too. Naked women and bombs on your planes. They had eagle feathers and scalps. But you're the same in what you expect from a woman because you're on your way to the killing."

"I'm not—"

"Bring your pillow to my bed, if we're going to talk serious, but I'm not inviting you for special warriors' privileges from your woman."

"I'm supposed to think serious about suffering and sympathy when you're lying in bed with your knee up in a way that's showing me almost all your territory?"

Randi lowered her knee. "I shouldn't have changed out of my uniform. I didn't expect that wearing my robe would drive you loco."

Buck brought his pillow to the bed and said, "I know that heading back to combat, my mind's not working like yours. I've had too many narrow misses. The only chance I've got to live through this war is to make it through the needle's eye alive when my turn comes."

Randi moved over, and Buck reclined beside her.

"Should we switch jobs, Buck? My hell is trying to work miracles on the war's human debris. I have my gin to black out thinking about it. You've got your bourbon. You got out of the hospital easy this time. The ugliest wars are fought in hospitals."

"You're fighting the good war, Randi."

"You're risking your life. Your courage deserves more honor than mine. If you get through your needle's eye, keep in touch. Maybe one day we'll climb Cloud Peak together."

"How can I keep in touch?"

"If the Germans get you, I'll keep in touch . . . if letters can get to you."

"If they don't, and I'm alive, I'll find you."

"If you're going to catch your train, you'd better go tell the owner to order your taxi. Take a breather in the cold air while you're downstairs. When you get back I want to talk serious about Tom's dad and you visiting him."

"There's another train in the morning. I could stay with you tonight and take that," Buck proposed.

"That wasn't the plan."

"Whatever. After I call the taxi we'll still have time for a drink of my Old Crow . . . special smuggled to England in my flight boots."

Alone, Randi wondered if this really would be the last time she would ever see Buck. . . . *How do I want to spend my last half hour with him? It could be longer. It would be better for him not to be up all night traveling and hitting after-hours bars. Maybe I should let him stay, not to make love, just to be together. But it's more than time together that he wants. Damn, I should be thinking about what I want!—*

Buck sauntered in. He passed the chair and went to the bed where he propped himself closer to Randi. "They'll knock when the taxi gets here," he told her.

Randi regarded him intently. "Are we going to talk, or are you moving closer for a better way to say good-bye?"

Buck put an arm around her and said, "I'm listening."

"We've got to talk about why we're meeting. You've got to believe that Dean had nothing to do with the mission you're mad about. It's not his fault that Tom and your friends were killed. His work is so secret he can't say much, but I know he's blaming the English for us starting to bomb in bad weather."

"Randi, you're asking me to believe that it's just a coincidence that we started to wipe out German cities instead of just factories and oil refineries just at the time that this inspector general got here from Washington?"

"Buck, his idol is Billy Mitchell, the general who first fought for air power to win wars. As long as I've known Dean, he's been fighting for air power as a way to win war. You'd know more about how that could be done than me, but he's been outspoken about keeping bombers on the ground until they have clear weather to bomb military targets."

"To let your colonel friend off the hook, you're asking me to believe that the English, not our country, is now running our U.S. Air Force?"

"I don't know what's happening, Buck. Dean can't talk about it, but whatever it is, that's why he's here. I'm your Indian friend telling you not to blame Dean for politics of war we don't know anything about. See him, for me."

"It's not that simple, Randi. A captain does not visit an inspector general without orders coming down through channels ordering him to."

"This is different. He's asked me to—God, Buck, can't you understand?"

"Hey, my sad-eyes sweetheart, there are no regulations for skipping chain of command for heart-to-heart talks. The word is out that the inspector general is looking for vengeance. I'm in a nutcracker. There are too many un-answered questions."

"Will you dare see him, for your sad-eyes sweetheart? Not as military. As human!"

"I'll do next best. I'll tell you, and you can tell him. Tom did a great job of flying on that mission. His dad can be proud of him. What happened is that we lost an engine and had to abort. On the way home a fighter nailed us with a 20-mm that exploded in the cockpit, on Tom's side. You know how it messed me up. If you saw Tom after they brought him in, you know that he couldn't have known what hit him. That's the whole story. Short, being as sad as it is, right?"

Buck wiped tears from Randi's eyes and held her close, with only the crackle of the coal fire invading the quiet. After a while he confided, "Waiting for you tonight I was thinking about how even your long black hair spooks me." He moved his lips to hers.

"I don't wanna—" Randi was saying as he silenced her with his kiss.

Randi resisted tentatively, then, in spite of her inten-tions, she melted her lips upon his and relented in his embrace. She shivered as he slid a hand under her robe, cupping a breast tentatively and brushing across the nipple in reaching down to part her robe. As he snuggled his blouse against her bare breasts, she wrapped her free arm around him.

Buck reached down to her waist and pulled open the thongs that held the two sides together. Randi suddenly pushed herself free. With her robe pinned down by his body she scrambled from the bed and across the room to where the coal fire burned.

Buck was left in bed alone with her robe. His eyes reached to her suddenly distant presence. The flame-light shimmered on her bronze nude body.

"Damn you!" she stammered. "I'm mad as hell at you and me both! I need more gin, Old Crow, coffee or something!"

Buck got up.

"Stay away from me!"

He started toward her.

The emotion in her eyes fixed into defiance as he stepped closer.

"Jesus, Randi. You're so beautiful. I've never seen a beautiful woman like you. I've had my heart on my sleeve for you ever since I first saw you."

"Your heart is between your legs!"

"Come to me and I'll show you you're wrong."

"You better b'lieve I'll make you human the hard way if you come closer."

"Randi, let's have a drink and talk. What's come over you? I'm just haywire crazy about you. I just wanna get on with how things were goin'. Forget your Colonel and be my Indian girlfriend."

"Dean's too far into his brain, and you're too far between your legs."

"What about you?"

"I'm into bodies. What you're looking at. Minds, too— nerval in the serval, that's me! Throw me my robe. No, don't. I'm going to get back into uniform."

"I'm not going to touch you."

Buck picked up the empty glasses. As he crossed the room to the bourbon bottle, Randi moved away from him and took the blouse of her uniform from the wardrobe. She buttoned her military blouse over her breasts and sat down on the edge of the bed. Buck poured drinks and went back to the soft chair, from where he reached a drink to her.

She took her drink and returned to her seat on the edge of the bed. "When you were out of uniform in your hospital bed, you were different. I think you get screwed up by your military uniform with your wings and captain's bars," she said.

"I'm in a tornado. You talk about Cloud Peak bein' powerful spiritual. That's what you are for me, Randi."

"Your humanity is locked up by your war outfit."

"You're the one who's saying, 'stay away from me!' The nurses told me about you in the Philippines taking hell from the Japs, and being a loner who doesn't talk about it!"

"I don't talk about myself because I'm hurting. You're too much a big-shot pilot to admit you're hurting. You expect me to love you; you need me because you're going to the killing, right? It doesn't have to be me. That's why you're going to London, right?"

"You're shoving me out the door!"

"You don't need to catch the train. You can spend the night here, not making love, staying only to be together. We can fall asleep finishing your Old Crow. Sleeping here would be best for you."

"Do you expect I could stay here without trying to love you?"

"What makes you lovable is that I see through you trying to be a tough, wild man. Big Buck, I don't think you've ever been a red hot lover all the way."

"You're crazy. We may never see each other again, and you're tearing me apart. I've gotta catch my train."

"Would you want to see a crazy woman like me again?"

"I don't know. Why should I want more of this? Are you like this with your colonel?"

"No. I'm his angel nurse, especially with Tom gone, but I can't get close enough to him to not feel lonely. With you, I want to knock your head off, but I don't feel lonely. Which is worse?"

"Randi, do you want to see me again, if I manage to stay alive?"

"I'm too weathered for you. You need a nice, innocent girl for your first love. If you don't find her, let me know."

"If I manage to stay alive, I'll find you. Wish me luck."

"You are still a virgin, aren't you?"

"Go to hell. It was you who said ranch guys were horny loners. I'll say that girls I went with in America always stopped at the brink. I haven't stomached buying a Piccadilly Lil, and I'm not going to London to buy one now. Make what you want of that."

"You're going to London to find your first red hot love!"

"If that taxi doesn't get here quick, I'm going to get my first red-hot love here, regardless. I can still nearly see your tempting territory."

"You can sit beside me and look at the fire with me, instead, if you want."

"If I do, blame yourself if I don't stay civil—I'm gonna pour us a last bourbon."

Returning with the whiskey, Buck sat down beside Randi. As he handed her a bourbon, he said, "I see you've got a silver star on your blouse. That's a mighty high decoration for a nurse. How did you get that?"

"As soon as you see my blouse, you start measuring my decorations. You do get carried away by war outfits. Maybe I should have stayed in my robe, but that drove you another kind of crazy."

She tipped her glass to Buck's and toasted, "I drink to you having a romantic first love before you fly again. If you must leave, I won't forget you, Big Buck."

"I'm going to drink to you and me talking skin-to-skin some day, and I'm going to think about everything you've said. I'll admit I don't really know what assholes are running this war. I'm going to try to be less pissed off at your colonel friend. In case it helps you understand me, I'll tell you I came into this war from being a pacifist. Most of the guys following our orders don't take killing as serious as me."

Randi and Buck, sitting together on the edge of the bed, sipped their Old Crow quietly until Buck said, "I don't even know your Indian name."

"My spiritual name is Singing River."

"Do you think we'll ever climb Cloud Peak together, Singing River?"

"Do you think we'll ever climb Cloud Peak together, Big Buck?" Randi echoed.

"Time will tell."

"Time will tell."

For now, their time ran out with a knock on the door.

FRANKFURT HOSPITAL, WITH WALTER PLANK: "For you the war is over," an intruding voice repeated. "For me goes on and on. I come feed you."

Working his facial muscles, Walt's pain told him that his helmet and oxygen mask had confined his facial burns to a goggle-like shape surrounding his eyes. *Eating! . . . Mush with a rancid odor . . . too soon the meal is over.*

He communicated that he was still hungry. The German laughed. Walt regretted having admitted his hunger to the enemy.

A while later the door opened again.

"Achtung!"

Conversation. Then the voices started to fade away.

Walt called, "Bitte, Geehrter Herr, meine Hande—die Ringen!—"

A sterile voice answered, "Talk to me in English."

"Are you the doctor?"

"Correct."

"I need help for my burns. My rings are stopping circulation."

The voice sliced back, "Your bombing makes higher priorities on me now. You wait."

The door closed. The key turned. All was quiet again.

This is the German arrogance. I will keep strong.

The words, "He who doubts is lost," crept into his mind. *God saved me from the burning bomber. He brought me sleep last night. I must trust in Him.*

The sirens started.

"Oh, God! No bombers now!" he prayed. *They call me Terrorflieger and Chicago gangster. They ignore how they bombed England. Hitler bragged on the radio: "Wir werden ihre Stadte ausradieren!" We're going to wipe out your cities!*

"The Germans are getting back what they started!" he said to the room.

The door opened. Someone came in and began to apply a solution to his eyes.

"Air raid coming?"

In German, came back, "If Grossangriff comes I go bomb shelter. You stay locked here. You learn what heavy raid is!"

Walt moved his eyelids that were coming free under the solution. As his vision sharpened he saw a soldier, no older than himself, with a long, jagged scar running across his forehead and down under and past his left ear.

The soldier cleaned and dressed Walt's knee where a two-inch chunk of muscle was torn out. He did not treat Walt's hands.

"My fingers! Please get off the rings," Walt pleaded.

"Doctor do that. Sit up. I take you surgery."

After the long time of waiting, . . . onto a surgery table.

Blinking his eyes, he looked up and saw bright lights and white-gowned men. The lights swam and he closed his eyes again. As he concentrated, the lights and figures came into clearer focus once more. He realized that time had elapsed. He looked down to his hands and saw that they were in white gauze bandages. He felt confused . . . disconnected from the activity around him. He was wheeled back to his room and placed back in bed. Soon he was unsure that he had been away, until he again saw the bandages.

The scar-faced German said, "We give wedding ring you later. Ring on finger cut off we keep. Government keep jewelry."

"Finger cut off?" Walt asked, but the German was gone.

He looked down to the different shape of the bandage on his right hand and groaned. *It's not your fault, Marg. I shouldn't have—it's God's punishment. He closed his eyes.*

Later, his eyes roamed the room in which he lay. He saw that the room was barely wide enough to walk beside his one bed. He was facing the window and could see the shadows of bars beyond frosted glass. *Frosted glass to hide the outside world from a sick person is a very German touch.*

"I'll make a window of the ceiling," he plotted.

Nevertheless, in the days that followed he found his attention focused more on his hands than on his intended ceiling escape. He would stare for hours at the peculiar bandage on his right hand that concealed his missing finger. He would envision himself after the war with his wife, Cathy, always with his right hand ring finger missing . . . marking his transgression.

He began the habit of moaning. The scar-faced German warned that he was making too much noise.

He imagined luxury meals: fried potatoes, beef stew, apple pie, bacon and eggs. His actual menu was a repetition of grits, cauliflower soup, potatoes, and black bread. He was always hungry.

He could call for help for "Pissen" and "Scheiszen." He began to look forward to these body imperatives as relief from his solitude.

At times he would be in the *Lucky Lady*, reliving the last panic-stricken moments of the bomber's fatal flight. At other times he would escape into formless meandering—hanging as one hundred fifty pounds of flesh mired in unending space. Then he would pull himself back to his room and recite his catechism he had worked out to keep sane.

I am an American Lead Bombardier.

I was shot down bombing Frankfurt.

I'm healing so I can break out.

Back to my wife and my life.

Then he would concentrate on needing to urinate, thinking that he might get a drink of water if someone would come to help him urinate, and plotting that after that he would concentrate on thinking of a next event to wait for.

ESCAPE TO LONDON, WITH BUCK AND SAM: The train-track staccato of the L.N.E.R., London bound, carried across the English landscape. A full moon thwarted the black-out with glow that occasionally broke through the clouds, exposing the moving train to searching eyes of German bombers. Inside, slouched in a compartment shared with an elderly gentlemen in a tweed suit, was Buck.

"Sir, is there food on this train?" Buck asked. "I haven't stopped to eat."

"Regretfully, no, Captain. You're a bomber flyer, I'll venture."

"Yeah. How did you know?"

"You're bandaged a bit. I speculated battle damage. I see hordes of your bombers flying out to give Jerry what he's got coming."

"I'm a pilot. One of those birds is mine. It's as banged up as a buzzard-bait nag, but it's always brought us back. I've got a damn good crew."

"I've lived through the blitz with thousands of incendiaries burning up London. Now it looks like it's starting all over again, a baby blitz of three years ago, a bad time to be in London. Jerry's got the full moon tonight he loves."

"I can't worry. I've only got this night. Right now I need something to eat."

"I've got food. You share the glory of our English pilots. Be my guest."

A box came out of a travel bag as Buck heard, "Going to London makes me jittery. I'm really not hungry. I hope you like lamb."

"Lamb is fine—but it's your meal. Sharing is as far as I'll go," Buck said.

"If you insist, I'll nibble a bit."

After the meal Buck fell asleep. The steel wheels continued their clickety clack rhythm down the track to London and the women of London.

The blitz had killed more than fifteen thousand Londoners and rendered more than thirty-five times that many homeless. In Buck's time of 1944, hundreds of thousands of former homemakers were living lives barren of family treasures that had given them a sense of connection. Few had been able to establish a new home life. Also, bombing, not being a clean killer, had yielded many maimed bodies and maimed minds.

Most of the children had been evacuated to safer areas. Some had been brought back tentatively, but most London mothers lived without their children and without their husbands. They lived with loneliness and longing. Tender passions were stifled "until the war is over," but the days held too many empty hours and the waiting was too long.

An alternative was National Service—England was conscripting women. About half of the women between eighteen and forty were in the military services or in industry. Most wages barely covered necessities. Food rationing denied luxurious dining. Only a very few women were untouched by the war. Most women suffered vastly disrupted lives.

Into this circumstance, thousands of anonymous soldiers came lusting for instant, intense love to rescue their morale. They had the money for binges of buying, eating, and drinking. The GI with silk stockings as his entrée became as famous as a Yank with chewing gum. Combat flyers were especially famous as generous lovers eager to spend their money before they faced death again. The ultimate catalyst for sudden love was the black-out. In the black-out, what occurred promised to be unaccountable. The hypnotic power of total darkness blotted out thought.

"London!" sounded in Buck's ears as his benefactor of the lamb feast awoke him. "We're in Waterloo Station, Captain. I'll be on my way. Enjoy yourself, but go to an air raid shelter if you hear the sirens."

Buck left the train and entered a tea room. His eyes took in the movement of a waitress wearing green and white. Her blond hair had the same reddish cast as the hair of Lena Doubert, the homecoming queen of Buffalo. Wyoming was far away . . . the world of green and white was very close as the waitress leaned across his table.

"I'll give five pounds to reach down to where I can see," he offered.

"You Americans treat every girl like a street walker."

"I'm sorry. I'm not good at telling a girl how luscious she is. I've just got today and tonight in town. I'd like your company to do the best there is to do."

"You'll not get company this way. Go to the dance at the Covent Garden and ask more gentle. That's my advice."

"Would you meet me there?"

The waitress in green and white only smiled.

"I hope that means, yes. I'll be looking for you."

"I'll think about it."

Buck left a big tip and in parting said, "If you'll meet me, I'll be gentle."

He left trying to fathom her smile. *Does it mean she'll meet me?*

At the hotel, he had a message from Sam: "Wait for me. I'll be back."

"I'll take a room."

"Sorry, we're filled up. We only have a three-room suite."

"I'll take the suite, and write this message for Sam O'Brien: 'I'm here, taking a break 'til the pubs open.'"

Later, lying on the great bed of his luxurious suite, Buck whispered, "Randi, my Singing River, look at me! I'm resting like you said I should." Then he reflected . . . *One night left. Ten more missions to go. The big shots running this war have the odds figured out. There's no beating them. They've got a ring through my nose. My folks' pacifist talk was dumb, was it?*

Inside the green and white. Five pounds to touch what I see. Tender white, soft sweet, white breasts. She could never know the glow . . . God if she were lying here with me! . . . Why am I so dumb in what I say to a girl? Give me the words to get a girl before I fly again.

Sam woke him hours later with, "Sandra's waiting downstairs to meet you. They wouldn't let her come up. We've been shopping for the flying birds toy for Walt's baby. Sandra says for the right price she can get you a classy girl."

"I'm not interested in a whore."

"It's more fun if you have a girl, Buck."

"I was with a nurse girl-friend in Norwich. I left her because we had plans to celebrate. Now what?"

"I'm just having fun like we came to do."

"Yeah? Well, I've got a girl who's going to meet me at the Covent Garden."

"Maybe Sandra would like to go there. I'll find out and leave a message. We'll definitely get together somewhere."

"We'll see. Just get on back to your Sandra."

Sam left. Buck got up, bathed, nursed his bandages,

shaved, shined his shoes, and tidied his captain's uniform with its silver pilot's wings. Finally, having passed his self-inspection, he went down to the hotel pub, and afterwards to other pubs and up and down the streets of Piccadilly Circus, all the time not touching his gas mask reserve of bourbon. He was saving this for sharing.

When the timing advised by bartenders was right, he went to the Covent Garden and searched for his waitress of green and white. No luck. *I'll sit this one out.* He went up to the balcony that overlooked the dance floor and took a table, still searching. *No alcohol here. Is that an air raid siren? It's in the music. My imagination.*

A girl approached. *Nice shape. A twinkle in her eyes. A cheery smile.*

"Do you want to dance, Captain?"

"I'm sitting. Let me get you a chair."

"I want to dance."

"I'm all left feet, but if you want a wild ride, I'll try."

She laughed, "I'm Emily. You talk funny."

They went down to the dance floor and stumbled about in an obvious effort to keep in rhythm with the music.

"Let's sit out the next one," Emily said.

"Would you like a drink of whatever they're selling here?"

"Lovely."

Three drinks later, after a lot of "funny talk," and Emily laughter, Buck asked, "Could I get away with spiking our drinks with whiskey here?"

"No, but my parents are at the Barley Sheaf. The drinks have zip there. You'd like my parents. They like Americans and flyers, too. I know they'd like you."

At that point Buck saw Sam at the head of the stairway, searching the tables.

"Hey, Buck, I knew I'd find you!"

"We're on our way to the Barley Sheaf. Emily, this is my bombardier, Sam."

"Is it okay for me to go with you? Sandra's gone home."

Together, they went to the Barley Sheaf. . . .

Glasses of dark and pale beer on the tables . . . Buck, Sam, Emily, and Emily's parents crowded around . . . Singing . . .

Here's to Richard, he's true blue.

He's a rounder through and through,

He's a failure, so they say,

If you can't get to heaven, go the other way.

So drink, chug-a-lug, chug-a-lug—

Emily's dad protested, "We English drink our porter slow. We sip it." Then he relented and emptied his mug to the chant of chug-a-lug, chug-a-lug.

"In Chicago we say, the faster it goes in, the faster it comes out," Sam said.

Later, at the urinal, Emily's dad asked Buck, "Do you like my Emily?"

"She's cheery. She gets you laughing when you're with her."

"That's Emily. She keeps it all inside. Her home was bombed out three years ago along with ours. Her husband and boy were killed. She's not one to feel sorry for herself, but she's never gone out alone until tonight. I talked her into going to the dance. 'Go meet an American flyer, I said. Get your mind off England.'"

Back to the beer and the singing.

Again at the urinal.

"Captain, you'll be going back to the war tomorrow, but you come home with us tonight. It's the least we can do for you. Emily says I should ask you. You come along and share her room with her, like decent people. In the morning we'll fix you fresh eggs and let you go bomb the Germans with all of us proud of you."

"Richard, you're a gentleman. That's some offer. I gotta think about it."

With Emily's father gone, Buck said to Sam, "When a man asks you to sleep with his daughter, it's time to regroup. This deal is getting too sticky for me."

"They've got a lot of heart, Buck. They've suffered from this war like you and I don't know. This is their way of saying they care about you."

"Care, hell! He wants a ranch in Wyoming!"

"Buck, you can't turn down their hospitality!"

"Oh? I'm going to pick up my coat and liquor and tell them they are great people, but we've got to leave. I'll ask for her address for next time I'm in town."

"They're not pure enough for you, are they Buck? So, off we go. Where to from here?"

Sam didn't return to the table for the good-bye scene.

Afterwards, when they were waiting outside for a taxi, Buck agonized, "I hope I left them feeling okay. I like Emily . . . and her parents, too."

"Taxi!"

"Where to?"

"Anywhere."

"You must tell me where you want to go, Captain."

"Buckingham Palace."

The moon broke through the clouds as they traversed the blacked-out streets, passing shadowy forms of people walking.

Sam said, "People are afraid that the Germans may bomb tonight."

"I've heard that, too, Sam, but this is our only night. We have to think positive."

Suddenly the driver announced, "Buckingham Palace."

"Pull up and wait. We'll take a look around and then go on."

They approached the gate. Buck led the way to where two girls were standing. Then he called to the guard strutting back and forth, "We are desirous of an audience with the King. Would you kindly arrange for us to enter?"

"You're Americans, aren't you," one of the girls said.

"How'd you know?" Buck asked.

"By the way you're rude about the Royal Family. We missed our train. We're from Brompton, in the Brendon Hills, Somerset County. The next train doesn't leave until morning. We can't find a room."

"I've got a room. Actually, I've got a suite. You can have it. We're celebrating."

"What are you celebrating?"

"Escape from the war. Tomorrow we go back to combat."

"Thank you, but we couldn't take your suite."

"I won't be near the joint. This is our last night to live it up."

Sam went to the girls and introduced, "I'm Sam. This is my pilot, Buck."

"Hello. I'm Patricia. She's Jennifer."

"Patricia, I like the way you're friendly. I'm sorry if I was rude. I was just trying to spark things up. Do you understand, Jennifer?"

Speaking for the first time, Jennifer said softly, "Yes. I'm shivering out here, Patricia. I think we should accept his generous offer to sleep in his suite."

The four entered the taxi and rode to Buck's hotel.

When they picked up the key, the clerk informed, "We don't allow women guests."

"They're not guests. They've missed their train. I'm giving them my suite."

"The suite is registered in your name, not in the name of these, ah, friends."

"Then change the registration."

"Under the circumstances that is impossible."

"Do you understand what I'm trying to do?"

"I understand perfectly."

"This damn hotel. You English don't know what hospitality is!"

Buck turned around and in the light of the lobby saw how pale Jennifer was. She bore a weak smile, and her eyes looked troubled.

They returned to the street. When close to Buck, Sam confided, "Patricia says Jennifer just got out of the hospital."

"For a fact?" Buck put his arms around the girls and assured them, "We'll find you a room. Let's go to Sadie's. That's a gin-mill where we can talk things over. I've got some bourbon to warm us up."

At Sadie's, a bourbon later, with the hammered strains of "Anne Boleyn" banging from a piano with a knocked-out front, the crowd sang, "Long live Anne Boleyn!"

"She holds her head up with a wild war whoop—
WHOO—WHOO—"
And Henry cries 'don't drop it in the soup!'
THE SOO—OO—OUP.
With her head tucked underneath her arm,
She walks the bloody tower. . . ."
Two bourbons later, with the four seated at a table, Sadie's crowd, packed at the tables and jammed along the twenty-foot length of bar, sang, ". . . Roll me over—in the clover—-roll me over, lay me down, and do it again. . . ."

Buck poured another whiskey for Patricia. *She is bright and cheery like a yellow flower!* But across the table Jennifer sat in silence. He felt challenged by her restraint.

"Are you hungry, Jennifer?" he asked.

"You're very kind, but I don't think so."

Buck hoped that the two bourbons Jenny had sipped would boost her spirits. *She'll smile and glow. We've got to find them a place to sleep.*

Sam was missing Sandra. He was seeing her desert-sky eyes and dark hair flowing over sheer black silk . . . and he was puzzling the mystery of the voice behind the door with the message, "duty calls." *I'm lucky she asked me to come back after midnight. I'm glad she's not here. She's for candlelight and wine, not this noisy gin joint.*

Patricia asked, "What do you do on the airplane, Sam?"

"I'm a washed-out pilot, better known as a bombardier. What is a bombardier—the gaunt gray ghost of a long lost race—"

"Cut the poetry, Sam. You're a bombardier volunteer. You're no wash-out."

Sam lifted his glass and continued, "The glass to his lips and they heard him say, 'Bomb Bays open. Bombs Away.' Then this ancient relic of the Second World War passed through the door and was seen no more."

Sam emptied his glass. The girls, even Jennifer, laughed.

"Bombing is not funny to me," Buck said.

"Not to me neither, Buck," Jennifer said. "I don't know why I laughed."

Sam interjected, "There's blood running out of your neck bandage, Buck. We'd better get you to some first aid."

"Randi warned me. Let's get to where we can see what's happening."

"We'll go with you, if we can help," Patricia offered.

"You stay here and keep warm," Buck instructed as he placed his handkerchief on his neck. Sam, get out my billfold and leave them some money for drinks to hold the table 'til we get back."

"I want to help," Jennifer said. "I'm trained in first aid."

Sam hurried out and promptly came back. "I got a taxi that knows a place with a medic and stuff for bomb victims. They got rooms to rent there, too."

"Let's get some bandages and get me into a room with some light. Jennifer says she can patch me up."

The four went to a second class hotel that provided bandages and rented them two rooms. Jennifer soon stopped Buck's bleeding. Meanwhile, Sam kept the taxi waiting. Now he said, "I've got to leave. Sandra is waiting for me."

When Sam was gone, Buck told Patricia and Jennifer, "I'm getting ready to call it a night. If you'll share a room, I'll take the other one and not go back to my suite. But you must want to get something to eat before you go to bed."

At that moment, the moan of air raid sirens rose to a wail that filled the room.

Patricia pleaded, "Get us to a shelter!" She started to sob.

They hurried down to the Underground station marked as the air-raid shelter for their hotel. Once they were below ground, Patricia calmed down.

Jennifer explained, "Patti's had a bad time with the bombs. The government sent her to live with us after she'd lost her family. I've never been caught in a raid. We live in a small village. I guess the Germans think we aren't worth the bother."

"Don't depend on it. It isn't much bother to dump a belly full of dynamite when someone's shooting at you. I've seen more than one village go poof, poof, like popping corn. I didn't see people frying. I just saw corn popping."

"Have you ever been caught on the ground in a bombing?" Patricia asked.

"No. But it's sure no fun in the sky. I don't know what it's like below."

A thunder of anti-aircraft cannon rumbled down to the shelter. Buck surveyed the long stretch of multi-deck bunks lining the wall side of the subway platform. The bunks were occupied by people of all ages.

Buck said, "This isn't going to be a big deal. The krauts haven't got a thousand four-engine bombers like we go in with. They've barely got a hundred left and they ain't going to risk many of them fertilizing London free-style."

Suddenly the floor jarred with the concussion of three large explosions. Buck looked up to the exit and announced with firm decision, "I'm doing you no good down here. I'll see you back at the hotel when this is over."

Patricia looked at him with disbelief. Jennifer asked, "What's the point of going out there and risking your life?"

"Because it's happening up there, Jennifer. The bombing . . . the ass backwards, bottom end, baby version of what we're delivering. I want to see it."

"Don't go," Jennifer said. "Stay safe with us." Buck was already climbing the stairs.

"Patricia, you'll be all right here on your own. You're totally safe here. I'm going with him." With that, Jennifer ran after Buck. "Wait, I'm coming with you."

"Don't be silly, Jennifer. There's no reason for you to come with me."

"I know what I'm doing more than you do. I'm more sober. I'm coming with you."

Buck and Jennifer left the shelter together and walked to a vantage point to watch the action. The anti-aircraft guns quit firing. The only indication that the night was not normal was some thirty white shafts of searchlights combing the sky.

The murmur of bomber engines high in the sky steadily grew louder.

"Let's get a roof over us to keep the falling flak from hitting us when they start shooting again," Buck proposed as he wrapped an arm about Jennifer and drew her with him into the passage of a store entrance.

"How many are up there?" Jennifer asked.

"Not many, but they're bombers, and they don't sound like ours or yours."

The pom-poms opened fire with their rhythmic, thunderous cannon-belches that mutated the quiet of the London night to the din of a battleground. Buck was not ready for the conversion. He had expected to experience the raid as a spectator, but the familiar combat dread at once pumped through him. His heart thumped. "This is too familiar. I'm seeing myself flying one of those birds up there. It's getting to me."

Jennifer pressed close to him. "I'm cold."

He wrapped his arms around her.

"Put me inside your coat."

Buck opened his coat and wrapped it around her. She held the great wool coat around the two of them.

"It almost reaches around both of us," she said.

"Nice. I wouldn't believe it was big enough."

"I'm small."

"You're thin, not small, but there's a lot of steel running through you."

The night flashed bright about two hundred yards away. A moment later a crash of concussion jolted them against the closed steel shutters of the shop entrance.

"Are you okay?" he asked.

"Yes."

"I'm glad he dropped only one bomb," Buck said.

The near pom-poms went quiet. The bomber rumble tracked toward where the more distant cannon were now firing. The searchlights still probed the sky with their shafts.

"That near bomb barely missed us. You shouldn't have come along."

"I know," she said.

"Then why did you come?"

"Because you wanted to go."

"That's no reason."

"I was afraid you wouldn't come back."

"What?" Buck asked in a whisper pressed close to her ear.

"I didn't want to lose you. What if you started bleeding again or got hurt?"

"Jenny, you're plumb amazing! I didn't have any idea you went for me."

"I wanted you for me, but I didn't know how to show you. When you started to leave though, I had to go with you."

"Into the goddamn air raid?"

"Wherever—"

"Look! They caught one in the lights! See how those lights hang onto him. That could be me caught up there . . . not in the lights. I fly in daytime, but in the flak. Look! He's catching it!"

"I can't feel sorry for him. Think of the people he's killing."

"I wonder if in Germany somebody's thinking when we're upstairs, 'I feel sorry for those guys getting nailed up there.' I had a friend say when he got home he'd never shoot birds again—but he never got home."

"It's weird, watching people killing each other. It's like a dream. I feel that it's not really happening."

"You feel it, Jenny, when it just cuts holes in you—not when it kills you."

"Maybe we should pray for all the people getting killed or already dead."

"My parents would do that. I'm too deep into the war to be able to."

The pom-poms started to pound nearby again.

Jennifer trembled, and Buck held her closer.

"My knees feel rubbery," Buck said. "Maybe I'm needing food, but I'm not hungry now. I've got a finger of bourbon left, when we get back to the hotel."

"Let's go back to the shelter—"

"They've got one in the lights again. Did you see that bright burst?"

The light shafts abandoned the fiery burst and began to probe for other prey.

"Those poor bastards are dead."

"God forgive us. We know killing is wrong, but we do it," Jennifer prayed.

"Amen," Buck finished.

The bombers departed. The pom-pom staccato stopped. Even the distant guns turned quiet. The searchlights began to shut down, one by one, until only the moonlight and three fires far away fractured the black-out. Buck and Jennifer stood in their passageway, wrapped in the great coat, in the blackness of oblivion.

"It's all over. The Luftwaffe isn't what it used to be."

"I know it's over, but my heart is still pounding. I still feel like I'm afraid, but I'm not. I guess I'm just still excited, Buck."

"I know. It's the same way in combat. It's hard to let loose when the action is over. The blood keeps rushing."

"Hold me tighter," Jennifer said.

"Turn around. Face me."

She turned and pressed close to him. He cupped her head in his hands and held her.

"Yes," she whispered with softness that caressed him. "I'm still excited!"

He kissed her eyelids and brought his lips to hers with tender eagerness.

"Buck . . . love me," she whispered, pressing tighter against him.

"I want to, Jenny."

"I've been starved too long."

"Me too, Jenny. I want to love you." He caressed her face and kissed her again.

"I've been waiting for you in my dreams," she whispered as she wrapped her arms around him.

He held her so close she could feel his heart thumping and his chest's deep rhythm.

"Oh, God, Jenny . . . I want to love you now! . . ."

She could feel his breath quicken. As they passionately kissed, he opened his trousers and he lifted her dress, and nuzzled his crotch between her legs, against her panties.

She lowered her panties and sobbed between quick, short breaths, "I want you inside me!"

He snuggled his bare crotch against the soft damp skin of her groin. . . .

"Push it into me, Buck . . . I want you inside me!"

"I'm trying . . . It ain't easy standing up. . . ."

"Love me, Buck. . . ."

He took her buttocks in his hands and held her fast.

She arched her back and pushed her groin to him as he pushed into her.

She tightened her arms around his waist. "All the way in . . . I won't get a baby standing up. . . ."

"I'm all the way, Jenny. . . ."

"Ooh . . . I'm feeling it nice now!"

"Oh . . . Oh!" Buck groaned as he pumped and pushed harder into her. "Oh! . . .

We're doing it, Jenny! I love you!"

"Oh! Yes, Buck! Yes! Oh!"

"Ah . . . Ah . . . God, Jenny! Wow! Oh! Wow!"

She grasped her hands into a knot on Buck's waist and shuddered, "Ooh-ah! Yes! Yes! Keep it in me." She kissed him wildly on his cheeks and chin and eyes as they held together without moving. "Oh, I love you! I love you! I love you!"

Buck cupped her head and brought her lips to his. They held there in a long nuzzling kiss. She lifted her arms to surround his chest again.

Buck breathed, "I've been turned upside down and can't quite find my feet again."

"I feel like I've been far away, and now I'm back again," Jenny sighed.

"I'm so spent I'm wobbly."

"I'll always feel different after this. I'll never forget you, Buck."

They reluctantly separated and re-arranged their clothing.

The sirens wailed an all clear message. They left their secluded passage and walked back to the hotel. Patricia was already back and in her room. Jennifer went to her and said, "I'll be sleeping in Buck's room. I've asked the hotel clerk to wake us in the morning in time to catch our train. . . ."

When she entered Buck's room he asked, "Do you want the last drink? I haven't got food, but at least you can have the last bourbon. I've had enough."

"It will keep. My head is swimming, and I want to lie down," she answered, and she began to remove her clothing.

"I'll get out of my uniform. We can go to bed skin-to-skin."

"Yes. Nice."

When they were both nude, Jennifer said, "Your body is a work of art, even with your bandages. We're lucky you didn't start bleeding again."

"Yours is a special kind of beauty, Jenny. Thin like a dancing star, with a steel spirit—thin and strong. One in a million, the way you came with me into the bombing."

She turned back the covers and climbed into bed; then she pulled the covers open for him to slip in beside her. "Buck, I want to wrap us together under the quilts and hear all about you, not the war. About your home and family."

"You first," Buck insisted as they cuddled.

"I feel so close to you it's mysterious . . ." Jennifer said. "Anyway, we came to London for my first art show here. I guess I worked too hard to get the show together. The opening was too much for me. I got so exhausted they took me to the hospital. I got released this morning. I'm all right now. I just need rest."

"I feel awful, keeping you up. I didn't know . . . still, I was told . . . I'm sorry."

"It wasn't you. You were trying to help us. The air raid wasn't your fault. I chose to go with you. It was fate. I'm glad. You're just out of the hospital, too. I'm happy for both of us, hugging each other in this warm bed. Hold me tight."

He turned on his side to face her and pull her against him. "I wish you'd talked about yourself sooner. I had no idea you're an artist."

"I paint children . . . their faces in the war . . . among the ruins, away from home—happy pictures, too. My show in London is running three more weeks."

"I'll come to see it, if I get back to London."

"If you come to visit me at home, I could show you other work I do. I'm also working to help refugee children . . . enough about me. I want to know about you."

"I'm done in," Buck said. "I can't put together any sense. I'm finished in a way that can't be helped. I'll tell you about me in the morning. . . ."

He drifted off to sleep, and soon she, too, was asleep.

When he awoke hours later the room was empty. With an aching throb of memory, he recalled his arms around Jennifer. His eyes searched the room for her. On the bedstand he saw a note:

> *You were sleeping when I had to leave. I hate to go this way, but it's easier for me than waking you and saying good-bye. With all my heart I hope that this is not good-bye.*
>
> > *I love you,*
> > *Jenny*
> > *Jennifer Devenshire*
> > *3 Store Passage*
> > *Brompton, Somerset.*

He looked at his watch. 10:43. He hurried to catch his train. He and Sam had a compartment to themselves on the Norwich-bound London North Eastern Railway. They sat quietly for a long while, each in his own thoughts, looking out to the ever-receding gray landscape being punished by a pelting slush that was half rain and half snow.

Presently Sam said, "I've been thinking about Emily, trying to see things through her eyes. I can see myself in my own home, married, with a little kid hanging on to me, and my grandparents down the street where I grew up, and then . . . nothing. No husband, no kid, everything I got together in my life . . . gone. Not even my folks' home to go back to, 'cause they're bombed out, too. Can you imagine what that would be like? There's sure a lot of love between those people."

"I have to tell you, Sam, I know it was wrong, the way I treated her—and her parents—but their brand of giving their hearts was too strange for me to take."

Sam said, "You don't understand that they're solid together in a hell we don't know. They went along drinking chug-a-lug style, which is not their English way. They know too many of us are getting shot down. They care so much they're crazy to do all they can for us."

"I'm lost. It was all good fun, then, whambo, he's acting like I'm Emily's husband!"

"Buck, you were giving Emily the signals that she was peaches and cream. To her that added up to going to bed together since you only had one night."

"I'll write to her. Yeah . . . she was peaches and cream."

Their thoughts turned inward again as the wheels clickity-clacked back to combat.

Buck broke the silence—"Sam, we didn't get a present for Walt's baby."

"Sandra got me to realizing that a personal letter to his wife was more important. She helped me write it."

"Her?"

"She doesn't understand you either. She says you were raped in Sunday school."

"What does that mean?"

"It's something for you to figure out."

"I've got a lot to figure out, Sam."

"What came of your meeting with Randi? Was she the nurse you were with?"

"She's one hell of a woman. I'm not meaning in bed. I mean, as a human being. That's something for you to figure out."

"I don't worry about mysteries, Buck. I live with what life deals me."

"Well, Sam, on this leave, life's been dealing me stars. I love them, all of them, especially one of them. This was supposed to be a celebration for me, but it's been more of an education. I've sure learned a lot about women. I don't understand them."

FRANKFURT, GERMANY, OF PARCELS AND RINGS: To have a secret weapon, Walt was still using the crutch he had been given to help him walk. It was easier to endure Corporal Schwenk with the jagged scar across his head when he pictured him receiving death blows from the crutch. Wearing Schwenk's uniform, he hoped to pass as a German long enough to get away. Yesterday Schwenk had removed Walt's water pitcher and drinking glass. Now Walt wanted a drink of water very badly.

Locked alone in his room, he was focusing on the empty space between two fingers where he had once worn Marg's ring. He pictured the gold band with the narrow setting of rubies surrounded by tiny diamonds. Marg had told him that many generations ago her mother's family had bought this ring from roving Gypsies. He turned his eyes to the ceiling and drifted back to Marg in England. Her eyes sparkled in his memory as he recalled taking the train north with her. He had told her that he was married. She had not told him that she was married. He had spent his week's leave with her. . . .

"I am Nurse Johanna, a Catholic Sister. I assisted in surgery with your finger."

He turned and saw, on this Friday morning of 11 February, a nurse in a nun's habit, with blue eyes and a warm smile. "When I heard you talking in English, I thought my mind had flipped. Where did you come from?"

"I slipped in. When I saw you in surgery, you brought back memory of an American I miss very much. We were about to be married when the war made me return to Germany. I knew you couldn't be him, but I had to check your records to clear my mind. I saw on the charts that your bandages are to be taken off today. I decided to do this personally."

"Where did you learn such good English?"

"When I was studying medicine in America before I took my vows. I wanted to live the rest of my life in San Francisco."

"I've been wanting a drink of water all day. My mouth is caked."

Sister Johanna got him a glass of water.

He drank in gulps. "Thank you!"

"I gave up San Francisco dreams when the war started. I was called to serve in my homeland by my church. Now I am here, wedded to Christ and nursing the wounded. I don't argue with God's will . . . Put your hands on the table where I can work on them."

"How can you say it was God's will to come back to help Hitler?"

"I have gained much, spiritually. I came to battle the beast. Your own leaders call for service to God and country. I came back to serve. With the dying, God is more important than country. But the beast is here, too. You likely don't know as much as I do about the beast who brought the Nazis to power."

"By the beast, you mean Hitler?"

"Yes—I mean the beast in each of us—the devil."

Walt said, "I know how Hitler screams that Germany's destiny is to take over the world. I came to stop him. You came to help him?"

"Deliver us from self-righteousness, the Bible says. I need to give you a Bible. Do you know how many leaders of the Catholic Church have been killed resisting the Nazis? . . . Forget I asked . . . if you ever get back to San Francisco, tell William Turner that Sister Johanna Wagner was your nurse and she still misses him."

"Write down the name. Help me to escape. Escape with me. Sister, you don't belong here as a nun."

"I am needed here. That is all you need to know."

"Would you help me escape? I need a map and a compass."

"The civilians you have bombed are waiting outside to kill you. Appreciate that even I must find medical reasons to come to you. Here you are scum, a criminal, a murderer. Still, I come to you. Use your hospital time to pray for forgiveness. Hold your hands still. I will trim the burnt skin."

"Preach to your Corporal Schwenk about criminals. The Geneva Convention guarantees war prisoners humane treatment. Schwenk doesn't even allow me water."

"Schwenk removed your water pitcher to stop you from breaking the glass to commit suicide. The Intelligence people want you alive. If Schwenk is heartless, know that he left part of his brain on the Russian Front. He has a steel plate for a skull. Don't expect kindness from him. Ask what the war has done to you. Has it brought you closer to God? I will pray for you."

"Your nun's outfit and all could be a sneaky way to get information out of me. You have my name, rank, and serial number. That's all you'll get. If you are a Catholic, tell me about the Catholic Gypsies. Do they have a patron saint? I want to know because I was told the ring you took from me in surgery carried a Gypsy blessing."

"I know that you claimed the ring was religious. I helped cut off that finger. I've seen a ring like that before. It bears the blessing of Saint Sara, but you lost it."

"No! The doctors kept the ring when they cut off my finger!"

"Walter Plank with William Turner's brown eyes, I know much more about you than you think. You are an adopted son of a Methodist missionary who works with American Indians in Arizona. You are a decorated Lead Bombardier who has bombed Germany twenty-three times, two less than enough to be sent home. You are married, and your wife is expecting your first child. . . ."

"How can you know all that?" he interrupted. "I can't believe you're a nun!"

"You needn't know how. I have to leave now. I'll be back. When I locked your cell door coming in, I felt I had locked off Germany. I told myself that no one will know what I do in this room. With you I can touch back to the life I will never again have. I smile as a nun, but inside I am tormented by anger."

"Why are you here? If you're a nun, escape and go back to America."

"I am not wanted in America. When I was in California my friends wouldn't let me forget I was German. If I had been Jewish, they would have loved me as a refugee. As it was, they came to hate me. Finally I changed my direction backwards. With you I can let loose the war inside of me. A mere scream from me would have the guards kill you."

She bent over and kissed Walt on the cheek. "I have more than anger warring inside of me. I miss my William Turner.

Until later. At best, I will have too little time with you."

"How you feel free with me stands my hair on end!"

"I'm in a battle with myself. I love Americans, but I now live with your bombing brutality. I want to scream at you, but instead I kiss you. I will leave now—until later."

"Don't leave yet. Listen to me. I'm due the protection of the Geneva Convention!"

Johanna put a finger to his lips as a signal for him to be quiet. "Spend your time praying to be able to swear you will never bomb civilians again if you escape."

When the room was empty, Walt thought: *I know she came to me for reasons I don't know yet. Has she got some kind of love-hate torture in mind for me? Is she some kind of maniac? Maybe she's setting me up for her scream game to get me killed. Yet once she sounded like she was tied in with the Resistance. She could be setting me up for an escape. I don't know whether I'm going to be loved, tortured, or killed. This will drive me crazy if I can't stay calm. This is a madhouse.*

A heightened sense of helplessness, confusion, and panic layered over the boredom, hunger, and loneliness he had been enduring. *What happened in my life to bring me to this? I've read about Hitler's secret weapons of rockets, jet airplanes, new kinds of bombs, and poison gas he's getting ready. Maybe Hitler can still win the war. If I can't escape, maybe I really should kill myself. Maybe the Nazis will end things for me by starving me or God knows what. Maybe Johanna's surprise for me is to kill me as a kind way out.*

As Friday dragged into the afternoon he contemplated how he could kill himself. . . . *Walter Plank is only a few years of memory. It doesn't matter that I don't know who my real parents are. Tracing back many generations still doesn't span a grain of sand. I have no loss in not knowing even my nationality. Nothing would be lost if I would die now rather than sixty years from now. To the people who would miss me, I am already gone.*

"Johanna!" . . . the memory of her morning visit rescued him from his melancholy. She had said she would come back. He feared her return, yet he wanted her back to rescue the wandering of his mind.

Suddenly he was convinced, as she had wanted him to be, that she was not one of the enemy. Her talk of battling the beast, he reasoned, told that she was struggling to keep the gentle part of herself in charge of her life. *Whatever she has in mind for me, it will be better than the emptiness and dread that goes on and on.*

The day wore into evening without the hoped-for return of Johanna. On Saturday the cauliflower soup had no taste. He wondered how he could have been eating it all of this time. He had to defecate so he pushed the button, and as usual he had to wait. In the past he had waited as long as two hours for Schwenk to arrive. But today the waiting was too much for him. He defecated in his bed. To teach him a lesson, Schwenk did not change the sheets, and, to avoid presence in the foul air of the room, he did not feed Walt that night.

Walt thought about the many prisoners who would be treated like this by Schwenk if somebody didn't kill him. He saw himself leaning on his crutches as he sneaked near Schwenk, pretending to be very lame, and then, like lightning, shifting and swinging the crutch with a killing blow that would crush Schwenk's metal skull into his brain. The picture of Schwenk dead gave him power to endure the excrement in which he lay and the foul air he was breathing.

Then he heard the key turn in his cell door. Johanna, neat and smiling in her nun's habit, entered. "I heard Schwenk bragging about the predicament he left you in. I shouldn't have come, but I'm going to take care of your problem."

She unlocked the window and raised the frosted glass to allow fresh air to enter. "Get out of bed and take off your bed garments. I'll wash you since your hands are still too tender to wash yourself. I'll soon have you clean and between fresh sheets."

"Let me help you undress," she added as Walt rose and tried to obey her instructions.

Soon he was standing in the middle of his cell, naked, and Johanna was cleaning the excrement from his buttocks and crotch. She changed the water twice before she more carefully lifted his testicles and penis and wiped all of him meticulously clean with clinical calmness. It seemed to Walt that the final rinse was given with deliberate tenderness beyond sanitary needs, but Johanna's face registered only her characteristic smile.

When she had finished, she said, "Stand here until I put fresh linens on your bed. Let me look at you. By God's grace the war has left your body almost untouched. You are healing nicely. You are not scarred so deeply that you will be ugly. I hope that you are sufficiently reverent to thank God that you can still see."

As she made up the bed she continued to talk. "In this visit the nun-nurse rules me. Your wife and lover have opened their hearts to you with different kinds of passion. My privilege tonight is less romantic, is it not, Walter? Love has many dimensions. I expect that you will be learning more of that as you stay a prisoner in this land of gore."

"You helping me is a miracle. Saying 'thank you' is not enough. I'm going to think about you—about your dedication to serving the wounded—about the beast in all of us you teach about and all that."

Johanna said, "Do not thank me. I am with those who battle the beast, and we do not always win. Do you understand me?"

"I don't know, Sister Johanna."

"I had planned to stay away until I come to pray with you for our preparedness to die. I have learned that you are about to be transferred. I had a plan for us, but it can't happen now. In my war, I love you spiritually as William Turner, and there is more to why I am drawn to you . . . I must have time to tell you the whole story, but I must go now. If I don't see you again, know that I will carry Saint Sara's blessing for you. I don't intend riddles. I will come back and tell you more if I can."

After midnight a new sergeant came on duty. He was scheduled for a shift of fourteen hours instead of the usual twelve because of extra Red Cross duty. "Good Sunday morning," he said to Walt as he put on the light.

"This new job. You first prisoner. I speak English. I back the Russian Front . . . I no speak English. I no training hospital. I tank commander. I hurt by head. Makes nothing. I safer less brains. This good job. No kill."

Whatever expression the sergeant's face could have offered was hidden under a mask of burn scab. As he ladled barley soup to Walt's mouth, he said, "It's odd time eat, but Sister Johanna say, 'Feed Plank.' You lucky soldier. Clean bed. No Russian Front."

The sergeant left. *Sunday . . . Church . . . Don't think back. Think ahead to survive. Sister Johanna says I'm self-righteous. Still, I have only her to wait for. Pray for forgiveness? Pray to change maybe—to survive.*

He yearned for the spiritual world Johanna spoke from. In church he had seen people in agony, praying to be saved. He felt that agony now. I will have much time in prison to pray to become a better person. He shifted sideways and saw the sergeant come back with a box about a foot square and five inches deep. He placed the box on the table beside Walt's bed.

"Red Cross box," the sergeant said. "Out Switzerland. Box today . . . every prisoner. I read English. I give you, and read what is:

"Spam . . . Corned beef . . . Salmon . . . Paté . . . Klim . . . is powder milk . . . Jam . . . Margarine . . . Sugar . . . D-Bar . . . is chocolate. Walt did not want to show emotion to the German, but his eyes filled with tears . . . Nescafe . . . is powder coffee . . . Raisin . . . Cheese . . . Crackers . . . Old Gold—three packs . . . is American cigarettes . . . More chocolate . . . A card, write home. Das ist Alles. I put in box. You wait. I come give you. Much work now. Ask one thing now?"

"Give me the chocolate." Walt said. "You take the cigarettes with you."

"Ja wohl," the sergeant said. He tore the wrapper from a D-bar to expose the brown, coarse ground chocolate that was mixed with meal as a ration for troops. After holding the chocolate while Walt ate from it, he asked, "Want write home? I print English."

Dear Cathy, Mother and Dad.
Thank God I am alive. I am slight wounded, but o.k. Is
baby born? I hope you well. Don't worry. Write me by Red Cross.
Love, Walter

"So. I write English. Speak me more English."

"I will always remember this," Walt said.

"Must have Geduld," the sergeant said as he squarely engaged Walt's eyes.

"Ja. I know," Walt said. "Must have Geduld. In English that's patience, but more."

The sergeant's lips were formed into a smile that turned up one corner of his scarred mouth, allowing Walt to see him, for the first time, showing feelings.

"Ja," the sergeant said, as he drew out his handkerchief and blew his nose.

"What is your name?" Walt asked.

"I Feldwebel Heisler. Go now. I much work." He blew his nose again and hurried from the room with the cigarettes.

Walt heard the lock click into place. "Geduld," he pondered. *In English, patience, but here courage half way between patience and crazy.*

The sirens started. There was a commotion in the hallway. Then his door opened abruptly and Schwenk came in.

"So, is true! Your room clean and you clean, too! Guilty pay! I boss here, not Sisters Jesus! You terror bombers get me out bed, but Germans go shelter. You lay here, shit, pray. Terror Flieger, I lock you here now."

"Geduld," Walt told himself in the darkness left after Schwenk turned off the light and locked the cell. *I have my Parcel to tell me I am part of a world that cares about me.* A quiet took over that was so complete it seemed there was no one left in the building, no one above ground but himself.

I should be hearing the incoming bombers. Where are they? In the middle of the night they will be the English. They come in from all directions all at once.

He lifted an arm and found the D-bar Heisler had left within his reach. He brought it to his mouth and sucked on the sweet chocolate as he prayed: *Jesus, bless the Red Cross, and kill all the Germans making this war. Forgive me for doubting you. Get me home again, and I promise I will be a missionary for you as long as I live.*

He began to hum the song, "Jesus Loves Me." Suddenly the click of the door being unlocked broke into his humming. The door opened, but the hall, too, was totally dark, so he did not know what was occurring until he heard Sister Johanna.

"The air raid has given me the opportunity to get back to you. Everyone else is in the underground shelter. I am in trouble. I am not allowed to attend to you anymore. They have stripped me of my nun's habit and put me into the uniform of an army nurse. Walter, are you hearing me?"

"That's terrible. They can't make you dress like a German soldier! If you're in that kind of trouble you shouldn't be risking your life to come see me."

"Listen. I have brought you a Bible and your wedding ring laid between the pages. I have written Heil Hitler on the first page to give you a chance to lie about how you got it, if it is found. Your Gypsy ring I have taken from the surgery and will wear for you on my rosary. It will be a spiritual tie between us, for your blessing. Do you hear me?"

"I do."

"I will sit close to you so I can speak softly. I want you to believe that I am truly the Catholic Sister I say I am, but more, too. I risked coming to you because I want you to know that I, myself, have been to Saintes-Maries-de-la-Mer to worship Saint Sara. The Gypsy worship of her takes place in the south of France in the village Saintes-Maries-de-la-Mer on the Mediterranean. The Gypsies have made their pilgrimage there since the fourteen hundreds when emissaries of King René found a crypt and a Christian altar there under an ancient church. Hear me, Walter . . . in the crypt are bones of the persecuted Holy-Land Marys. When a black statue was placed in the crypt with the faith that it was the likeness of Saint Sara, a new church was built above it."

115

"Who are the Holy-Land Marys?"

"Sisters of Mary, the Mother of Jesus. In persecution they were put to sea in a boat without oars—I must finish—I need to tell you I have touched the statue of Saint Sara myself for her blessing. And afterwards, I followed as her black statue was carried down to the shore where it is said she saw a boat sinking in a horrible storm and threw her cloak onto the waves and by a miracle it floated and carried her safely to the boat with the two persecuted Marys: Mary, the mother of James and Joseph, and Mary Salome, the mother of James and John. She carried the two Marys to shore on her cloak. They blessed and baptized her. In years that followed, the two Marys preached the story of Jesus while Sara went from door to door begging gifts for a church to the gentle spirit of the Holy Marys."

"Sister Johanna, your religious miracles are all new to me. Since I was shot down I can't keep up with what's happening. It's crazy that you are risking your life to tell me about Saint Sara and the Holy Marys."

"Since we can't see each other, I hold my hands to your chest to know you are with me. . . . Hear how still it is. It is never so quiet as when one is waiting for the bombers. Do you understand that?"

"You are always too deep for me."

"It is never so quiet as when one is waiting to die. Is that easier for you?"

"Since I've been shot down, I can't keep up with what's happening. Why is it so quiet? The bombers are past due to be here. We could die any minute."

"You don't know how true it is that we could die at any minute. Since the bombers have not come, the soldiers will come back. If they find me here, they will arrest me. I have a scalpel with me to be sure they will not take me alive. If we are caught, I must die in protection of those who still fight the beast, and you can die with me."

"Oh, no! How am I to wait for that and stay calm enough to listen to you?"

"I have finished. I waded the shoreline with the Gypsies when they dipped the black statue of Sara into the sea. The

Archbishop of Aix was there, and he passed Sara's blessing to the water and in that way to the joining streams and the land from which the water flowed. I had to tell you that we share this blessing. If we survive, you need to know what I carry for you in your ring blessed by Saint Sara."

"I hear the All-Clear siren. How can you keep talking? It's so dangerous!"

"My life is in God's hands, but it is time to leave. Tell me and I will go—do you believe now that we have a secret spiritual connection, you and me?"

"I believe, Sister Johanna. Wear the ring for both of us." Walt felt her hands leave his chest.

"Remember where I live. I hope to be a missionary. If we live through the war, Sister Johanna, you can lead our mission!"

When the lights came on, there was no Johanna. But the pounding of his heart made him sure her visit had not been a dream.

In the afternoon of that Sunday, 13 February 1944, he was, as Sister Johanna had predicted, escorted to the Luftwaffe Interrogation Center at Oberursel.

THE HUNDREDTH BOMB GROUP, ENGLAND: WITH THE GHOST OF MUNSTER: As Sam and Buck rode their bicycles away from the flight line after a pinpoint target raid on a factory on 13 February, Sam said, "It's Sunday. Let's do something special."

As they were switching out of their flight gear, the First Sergeant came into Hut 23 and informed them that the Group had been put on Combat Alert for the coming day. He also reminded them that the award ceremony for medals was tonight. "This time you'd better show up, Captain," he told Buck.

"Sure, Sergeant, every five missions we get our automatic "air medal," and if we last through twenty-five we get our Distinguished Flying Cross, but I'm not here for the ceremonies."

"Also, Captain Pierce, Colonel Raymond told me to inform you he will be at the Officers Club tonight."

"What does that mean? Is that an order to see him? I've got to have orders to break channels to see the inspector general."

"That's all I was told to tell you."

"Thank you, sergeant."

Celebration plans were canceled to get some sleep before the early morning Alert wake-up. But first Buck and Sam went to the mess hall for a main course of spam. After the meal, Buck agreed to join Sam and attend the award ceremony. "I'll get a message to the Colonel that I can't see him because of the ceremony."

Four lieutenants in dress uniform approached the table of Sam and Buck and sat down with the caution of newcomers feeling their way into strange territory. One of them explained, "We just arrived. We're replacements trying to learn what life is like here."

"I'm Sam, or Hatch. This is my pilot, Buck. So you're replacements. All of the crews that got here with us have been shot down except for Minor's and Radky's. One crew made it through the twenty-five missions you need to go home."

"I take it that you've been here quite a while."

"Three months," Sam said.

"Has one of you been assigned to bed 17 of Hut 23?" Buck asked with sudden interest in the conversation.

"I've got bed 17. I'm Edward Briggs. Why do you ask?"

Buck answered, "It's the damnedest thing. Three guys have come and gone out of that sack, and they've all had the same nightmare. The last guy got shot down just three days ago. The way he told it, he used to wake up and there was this guy standing at the foot of his bed, about nine feet tall, wearing full flying gear including an oxygen mask. He would just stand there looking, like it was his bed and he wanted to get in. Then he would turn around and walk out through the wall. We call him the 'ghost of Munster' because it started the night after the guy owning that bed got killed on the mission to Munster."

One of the lieutenants smiled. Briggs and the others did not.

Buck continued, "Maybe he won't bother you, but you might keep your forty-five handy just in case. . . ."

Sam interrupted, "Buck's humor is suffering from flying in too much flak today. He's just trying to welcome you, and wish you good luck. Right Buck?"

"Are you having a lot of losses?" Briggs asked.

Sam answered, "The insignias of some of our bombers are painted on the walls. I'll tell you about them, and you can decide. There's the *Lucky Lady* over there—her luck ran out two weeks ago. Next to her is the *Messie Bessie*—she just keeps flying—she's still around. Next is the *Piccadil Lil*—she's been gone a couple of months. *Mark's Marvel* never made it off the ground, taking off in a blizzard. Then there's the *Laden Maiden*—she went down last Thursday. We've lost five ships in the last two weeks before we could get their pictures on the wall. *Horny*, that's her picture on the end wall—-she isn't any more—I saw her go down."

"Come on, Sam, they don't want to hear our history. It's your first night here, lieutenants. Don't panic. You've heard us tell that we've been here three months. Well, we're still flying. Wish for our luck, and enjoy your meal."

"I didn't mean to be grim. I was just telling it honest. Welcome to the Bloody 100th, guys. Come on Buck, let's get on to the ceremony."

Next morning, after a pre-dawn briefing, but before take off, the mission was scrubbed. In the next ten days Buck's crew was Alerted as a possible lead crew almost every day, but all the missions that were not scrubbed had other lead crews. On 24 February the *Bare Lass* finally invaded enemy skies as Group Lead for the 100th. The target was an aircraft factory near Posen, beyond Berlin. It was Sam's first combat duty as the Group Lead Bombardier. He made all his calculations twice and performed calmly, but black smoke hiding the target prevented him from knowing if he had scored a hit. The 100th Group did not lose a single ship on this flight, in spite of the great depth of penetration and in spite of the many enemy fighters that attacked other groups.

On the evening after the mission, the new pilot occupying the Ghost of Munster's bed, Lieutenant Briggs, attempted to compliment Buck for his skill in leading the Group.

Buck laughed. "I call it luck, Briggs. Has the ghost given you a bad time?"

"No, I like him. He's promised I'm not going to get shot down."

"Trump card, Briggs. Your crew's lucky to have you as their pilot!" . . .

The very next day, Buck led the Group again, this time with the Group Air Executive as co-pilot, more precisely, Command Pilot. The target was an aircraft factory in Regensburg, heavily defended and deep in Germany.

Buck boasted to his crew before take-off, "If I get so much as a misfire on any engine, I'm going to shut off the fan and head for Switzerland—it's practically on course. You'd better start practicing your yodeling."

"We believe you," various members of the crew came back, having heard Buck's plans to divert to neutral territory many times before.

"Should I tell your plan to Major Reddick since he's going with us?" Sam teased.

Buck laughed, "No. Let's surprise him!"

The inbound trip went well, but at the target the flak was extremely heavy. The Second Element Lead of the Low Squadron went down while Sam was screwing the bomb-sight dials. When the run was over and the Group was out of the flak, Buck interphoned, "Sam, I don't know what you hit down there, but that run was short enough to rate a promotion. That leaves seven more to go, if we finish this one."

Sam thought he had hit the target, but he couldn't be sure until he saw the strike pictures. The engines purred homeward without missing one stroke to assist Buck's threat to divert to Switzerland. Debriefing confirmed that the Group had lost only one ship under Buck's leadership. Sam checked the strike report that went forward to Headquarters and was frustrated by the conclusion imposed by smoke: "results unknown."

The combined Eighth Air Force-Royal Air Force offensive launched in late January was now keeping Germany under attack night and day, in good weather and bad. To keep the offensive going the Eighth had begun flying crews with so little sleep at times that crew fatigue was factored in as an expected cause of losses.

The duties of one day were at times not finished before near-midnight, and wake up for the next day might be as early as three or four in the morning. No time or energy was left for personal plans, but this was immaterial, for leaves and passes were not given to combat crews during the offensive. March arrived with Buck's crew on Alert on most nights and always restricted to the Base.

Early in March the offensive was directed to Berlin. The *Bare Lass* was getting battle-damage repair on 6 March when the Eighth again penetrated to Berlin.

Buck's crew, grounded for the day, joined the many on the flight line at 1715, the estimated time of return, to wait for the bombers. The 100th had sent out twenty-one ships. Two had aborted. Nineteen were still out.

Five minutes passed. Three ships came over the field— one with a feathered propeller—another shooting red flares to get ambulance help for wounded. These ships landed.

Five more minutes passed. Another ship appeared, barely above the tree-tops, wobbling as it stretched its glide to reach the field—inboard engines dead—outboard engines moaning sickeningly under emergency power—until it landed on the runway.

Then there was a lull, with everyone waiting . . . everyone still waiting. After a while no one understood why everyone was still waiting. It was obvious that there were no more ships to wait for.

Sam turned away from the runway with his voice breaking, "They were all just boys like us. We watch a parade and all the marchers and can't let honor pass us by. There's got to be a better world."

Noting that Minor's crew and Radky's crew did not return, Buck said, "That leaves just us still here from the guys we came with. We're riding in a slaughterhouse boxcar."

The Red Cross gathered shillings in the Post Exchange for sending Parcels to survivors captured by the enemy. The newsmen wired copy, ". . . and men died in their ships.

. . . Men were blasted out of their ships. . . . And men floated down through sky-strewn wreckage."

At breakfast a day later, the mess hall had many newly arrived second lieutenants. Sitting beside Buck was the pilot, Edward Briggs, whose ship was among the few that had returned.

"I see that the Ghost of Munster is looking after you like he promised." Buck said to Briggs, loud enough for new arrivals to hear.

"He came again last night—nine feet tall at the foot of my bed—promising again I would not get shot down," Briggs responded soberly. The listening replacements wrinkled their brows and lifted their eyebrows in bewilderment.

"That's good news," Buck continued with feigned grimness. The humor was a melancholy privacy between Buck and Briggs who had outlived their friends. . . . In the following days the Eighth concentrated on airfields and the top-secret coastal rocket-launch targets. Then a new category of top-secret targets was added, the "no ball" list: coastal defense fortifications. When the "invasion proof" Cherbourg coastline was targeted, the flyers began to expect an invasion soon.

Buck's ten, now an elite lead crew, was kept in reserve for the time when the Group would lead the Wing. Meanwhile, crew members were kept busy with briefing and training of new replacements. On March 16, when the 100th was designated to lead the Wing to an aircraft factory near Augsburg, their time had come. The briefing informed that this was a raid to help the coming invasion by destroying air power.

Leaving the meeting, Phillips, the *Bare Lass* navigator, in a rare gesture, approached Buck. Phillips and Buck had long ago decided they could best tolerate each other by keeping their exchanges limited to flight duty talk when in the sky. Now Phillips said, "Captain, did you discern the significance of what we just heard? I joined the air force to win this war through air power. Now they're sending us out to destroy the Luftwaffe to help the invasion. We've become the army's lackeys to help their invasion when we're supposed to be bombing targets that will put them out of a job."

"Why are you telling me, Phillips? I'm not running the show."

"I've got to say it to someone. You were the only person I thought might be interested in what I see happening."

"I am interested, Phillips, but we've just got the job of delivering the bombs. I'm the driver. You've got the map. So let's get started."

Airborne, at mission altitude, and with the Command Pilot, Major Reddick, relieving him at the controls, Buck reviewed what he might do if the *Bare Lass* got hit. *The easiest out will be Switzerland. Maybe even Reddick will be ready to sit out the war, if we have an excuse. But, leading eighty-one bombers, it will have to be a damn good excuse.*

The heavily defended Augsburg aircraft factory was targeted today because of the clear-sky bombing opportunity. Due to the deep penetration in clear sky, fighter attacks were expected. Gunners nervously searched the sky with slow, deliberate motion, moving, stopping, and moving again. Had a soaring bird been able to fly to that altitude, it would have been riddled by a thousand fifty-caliber machine guns.

By the time the 100th arrived at the target, the sky was dirty with flak smoke. Far below was a lake of the black, smudge-pot smoke used by the Germans to conceal targets. Sam had studied the target folder until he knew it by heart. As he now studied the black smoke he saw gray blossoms popping through the black. Direct hits? Something was wrong. Then he discovered it. Three roads came together a certain way on the map. He saw the intersection now on the ground, but instead of the factory being to the right, there was a big field there with a farm. *The Germans have laid camouflage netting over the factory to make it look like a field and a farm. They've laid the smoke screen over open fields to the north. The First and Second Divisions have bombed the smoke over an empty field!*

Bombardier to Command Pilot: The smoke screen's a decoy. Signal the trailing Groups to watch where I bomb in the field."

Buck saw an ashen sky ahead dancing with hundreds of scarlet flashes changing to black. To fly on was to pass into a live furnace of spraying steel.

Sam had a dial in each hand, and he was synchronizing the crosshairs to make them lie dead center and still across the target. He felt a jolt that told him the ship had been hit, but he could not stop now. Then he felt Phillips, the navigator, pounding him on the head.

"Get away from me!"—but Phillips kept pounding.

"Get away!"

The ship jarred again. The bombsight went black.

"Oh, no!" Sam yelled. "Now I'll never know!"

Phillips hit the bomb release switch that dumped the bombs.

Sam heard, "Your interphone and oxygen's been shot out!" He grabbed the large walk-around oxygen bottle. It was punctured by a dollar-size hole. The oxygen refill line was knocked out. He scrambled up to the cockpit. Buck was on a small walk-around bottle, refilling it from Reddick's supply line. Feeling woozy, he rushed through the bomb bay to hook up to oxygen and interphone in the radio room—succeeding in time to hear, "Okay, you gold brickers, get out the emergency oxygen bottles. Our main supply's been shot out. I'm starting a minute-to-minute "oxygen check." Go easy on your ammo—we may need it—we'll be peeling off soon for a lone trip home on the deck."

Messerschmitts were coming in from one o'clock high. They dodged the 100th and attacked the Low Group. One bomber went down in a gradual, straight descent with no chutes coming out. Another went into a twisting, steep dive, wing on fire, with no chutes for a long while, then two chutes, then a ball of flame.

Reddick interphoned, "Since we're leading the Wing we'll have to hang on as long as we can. The fighters will hit our Group when they see the Lead peel off."

Reddick saw the Low Group un-jell. Reserve ships from its High Squadron slid down to fill the slots vacated by ships going down. Then the Group formation began to re-form and tighten to be ready for the next wave of fighters.

More Messerschmitts showed at three o'clock level—about fifty of them. They seemed to be poised to again attack the Low Group of the Wing led by the 100th. A parachute bloomed from one of these fighters. Its different color gave it a foreign look in the German sky.

On the interphone: "Crisis. No time for talk. Hang on for peel off." Buck wobbled his wings as a signal for the Deputy Lead on his right to take over. Then he hit emergency power to break away clean, keeping ahead of the Group as he slid into a vertical bank and dove until the air speed reached the red line. He was in a life-saving race now to reach the precious oxygen of lower altitude.

When he had reached down to where the ground was almost level with his eyes, he began a treetop race to escape fighters looking for lone prey. He was too busy now to dream of flying to Switzerland. Flying at tree-top level required his total concentration.

They reached France, still skimming the ground—with no friendly-fighter escort. The four-engine *Bare Lass* was hurdling buildings and almost touching the grass of open fields—driving down French roads a few feet above the ground.

Phillips was trying to navigate, but he couldn't get visual check points flying so close to the ground. He could only furnish Buck a homeward course based on compass guesses. He finally predicted that they would soon arrive at the English Channel. Then a flak tower picked them up. The 88-mm cannon got off several bursts. Missed.

Minutes later three F. W. 190's came in—drew up behind—out of range—about five hundred feet above. The *Bare Lass* gunners stabbed at them—hoping that the fire of the tracers would scare them away.

We're dead with them out of range, cued up to drive in for the kill. Bite the dust soft horns—I'm going to beat you to the draw! Buck interphoned, "Pilot to Crew: Hang on and get ready to shoot. I'm going to haul up and skid left. These krauts will fly into our range before they know what happened. Here goes—"

The *Bare Lass* lifted, twisted, and shuddered under Buck's violent leverage. The airframe quivered as the machine guns came alive, spewing out hundreds of 50-calibers, filling the interior with pungent smoke.

One F.W. plowed into the ground and tumbled somersaults across a field. Another pulled away trailing smoke. The third hauled up with the bomber's maneuver, then chandelled with a vertical twist and aimed back into attack.

Buck raced down for the protection of sweet earth, but there was no hiding from the fighter coming in from ten o'clock high. With four *Bare Lass* machine guns spearing into the fighter, Buck skimmed the ground and was suddenly dodging between buildings of a village.

The fighter's shellfire skipped across a garden ahead and rose to the *Bare Lass*. With a black belch, Number One burst into flame.

"Feather Number One."

The propeller spun dead—but still the fire!

Reddick pushed the remaining three engines to emergency power to stay airborne. Buck skidded and twisted between buildings. "I gotta have more power. Kick Number One back on quick!"

Reddick set the burning One spinning again.

"We've got to get enough altitude to bail out before she blows up. Get ready for bail out, pards. You too, Major Reddick. But wait for the order . . . Bail out now!"

Parachutes blossomed. The right seat was empty. Sam dropped into it. "It's just us left."

"Get your ass out!"

"Are you giving up?"

"No questions. Get your ass out so I can leave!"

Sam left. His chute blossomed.

Buck put the *Bare Lass* into a dive with full emergency power on, airspeed passing the redline—further and further—to blow out the fire. Nearing the ground, Buck pulled back on the wheel—with the *Bare Lass* mushing—clipping tree leaves but still flying. Number One was now blazing across the wing and fuel tanks.

Buck pulled back into the sky. Number three propeller started running away. Number 3 was screaming. Buck was pulling for more altitude. Three hundred feet. Four hundred feet. He clicked on the Autopilot to continue the climb.

The flames were still spreading. He left the cockpit and ran through the bomb bay to get to the Waist exit. Out. Pawing for the ripcord—still pawing. Chute opening— ground coming. Ground here! Hit! Hard!

PART II

The Earth

THE EARTH: CHAPTER ONE

"Moooooo."

Close by. But not loud.

"Moooooo."

Where was he? In a pasture. His face in matted, moist grass. Yes. He had jumped. Now he was plastered to the grass. He turned his head. There was a big dumb cow. Standing. Looking. Sniffing.

Air! He needed air. His throat was clogged. He coughed. Saliva and blood. He couldn't get up. *I'm alive. Thank you, God. Thank you . . . Thank you . . . Thank you. Again he coughed blood.*

Am I dying?

"Monsieur."

"Monsieur."

Who was calling? Now he saw. She stood beyond the hedgerow. She was dressed in pink. She wanted to help him.

"Allons!"

"Allons!"

She called to him, but she would not come near him. Have to go to her. Unbuckle parachute. Pain. Stiff all over. Heart racing. *I need a doctor. I have to get up. Now or never.*

"Allons!"

The Germans will get me if I don't get up. Now or never.

"Plut a Dieu! Au secours! Qu'est-ce qu'il y a, Monsieur?"

I can't just lie here.

He unbuckled his parachute. He raised on an elbow. Then a knee. To his feet. He staggered forward.

Two rifle shots. Bullets whisting. He dropped to the ground. His left knee wouldn't bend. Pushing with his good leg he snaked forward. Finally, he pushed through the hedge.

The woman had moved up the hill toward a house. Beside him were cows eating grass. They were slowly chewing grass.

131

"Moooooo."

Got to get up. Got to follow her. Got to have help. On his feet. Following her.

"Hande Hoch!"

Two soldiers were on a knoll in front of him. Their rifles were pointed straight at him. His knees sagged. He collapsed.

"Fur you der war is ofer."

"Thank you."

The lady dressed in pink swatted the cows' rumps furiously, as if she were there to chase the cows home. The soldiers in gray watched as she drove the cows up the hill.

The soldiers took Buck's money from his billfold. They placed the billfold back into his pocket. They took his escape kit with its wad of French francs. Then they looked for injuries but found no visual wounds. They lifted him by his shoulders and carried him to a motorcycle then lowered him into a side car. The motorcycle bounced along a cobblestone road to a stone bridge. They crossed a stream swollen with spring rain and entered a village. They pulled up before a building with a swastika flag.

One guard was old, lean, and sallow. The other—*he looks like Goldstein from Buffalo.* The gray uniforms looked like posters of "the enemy." Stabbing pain—as they carried him inside. They laid him on a bed.

His top turret gunner was sitting on a cot across the room.

"So they got you," Buck said.

"I sprained my ankle," Clair answered.

"I barely pulled the rip cord. My chute . . . I made it . . . but I'm bad off. Get me the morphine from your parachute."

"The Germans got it. I'll get it," Clair said.

"Thank you."

Clair made signs to a soldier with wire-rimmed glasses who had the first aid kit from Clair's parachute harness. Clair tried to show that something in the kit was needed.

The soldier wearing glasses said, "Nein. Kein Selbstmord. Aber ich hab was."

"I can't understand him," Clair said.

The soldier wearing glasses brought out a bottle of cognac and some glasses.

Buck could not reach the glass to his mouth. The soldier with the wire-rimmed glasses held the glass as he drank.

"Thank you."

The two soldiers who had brought Buck in saw the cognac. They started to argue with the soldier wearing glasses. The lean, sallow soldier tried to take the bottle. The soldier with the wire-rimmed glasses had more stripes on his uniform. He took back the bottle. He poured Buck a second drink. Buck felt sick. He put his head over the side of the bed and vomited cognac, blood, and bile.

The soldier with the glasses whined orders to the lean, sallow soldier. The sallow soldier got a bucket and rag and cleaned up Buck's vomit.

The soldier with the glasses got the morphine. Clair reached for it.

"Nein."

"He needs it for pain."

The soldier gave Clair a look that made him retreat to his cot. No one spoke for a long while. The soldier examined Buck again and said, "Go Doktor."

"Thank you," Buck said.

Buck could not move his legs anymore. His left knee pained badly—and his back—his back pain was a sickness that reached out of his guts. The pain ran up into his neck to a hot knot in his skull.

His heart did not pound as before. Yet he was still in the shattering shock of hitting the earth. The room and the soldiers were like a movie. The calmness of everyone around him was like play-acting. Ever since landing, there was this great contradiction between the simple, slow pace around him and the raging excitement within him. His only bridge to the strange calm outside was "thank you."

After a long while, the noise of a car carried into the room. Clair could walk, and he was escorted out. Buck couldn't move his arms or legs. *Am I all stiff? Or am I paralyzed?* The soldiers carried him out.

Buck and Clair were put in the rear seat of an open car. The driver was a freckled-faced soldier no more than sixteen.

The soldier that looked like Goldstein of Buffalo got in beside the driver and faced backwards with a pistol. They started away. In half an hour they were slowly driving along the cobbled street of a French town. The driver periodically blew the horn to clear the road of French pedestrians. The pedestrians seemed disinterested in making way for the car. As the car passed, the people stopped. The people regarded Buck and Clair facing the soldier with the pistol in the front seat. Occasionally a hand shot above a head with fingers forked in a V for Victory sign. The V symbol for allied victory appeared and disappeared in flashes above the shabbily-clothed civilians. Buck and Clair were heroes parading in the open car. This was an ovation. There were no cheers—because they were prisoners.

The car came to a stop at a cross street filled with people. A sign on the side of a shop told that the town was Cherbourg. The driver began to ask directions. Clair and Buck listened to the German struggling for French words. Then they heard the Frenchman rolling the music of his native language from his tongue. Two French girls about their age came up to the car. A half dozen candy bars and several full paper bags fell into Clair's and Buck's lap. The two girls waved good-bye and ran into the crowd.

Goldstein started shouting. He grabbed candy bars and paper sacks and threw them out of the car. Clair shifted his hips to hide some of the candy under himself. One of the bags tore open as it hit the street. Two cookies fell out. One rolled erratically along the cobblestones for a few feet before settling to rest.

The German driver swung the door open and ran after the girls. Then he stopped and looked around. Then he looked around some more. The street showed nothing but disinterested, slowly-walking people. The driver came back to the car. The Frenchman who had given the driver directions still stood by the car. The driver got into the car and worked the accelerator nervously. Goldstein shouted at the French people. The car began to move. Buck saw the girls come running. They threw more candy into the car. At the same time, Buck saw a brown-uniformed man with polished boots step in front of the car.

"Nimm sie mit!" the brown-uniformed man shouted.

The driver jammed on the brakes and jumped from the car. He ran into the crowd. Presently he came back holding one of the girls. He put the girl between Buck and Clair.

She had dark hair, blue eyes, and glowing cheeks. Her hair was swept back carelessly. Buck could see that she was frightened and that she was beautiful.

The driver entered the car again.   People crowded around the car. The brown-uniformed German with the polished boots stood erect on the sidewalk on the opposite side of the street and watched. The driver worked the accelerator nervously, raced the motor, and blew the horn for the crowd to clear the road ahead of the car.

Buck and Clair again saw the one girl who had escaped. She was near the car again. They saw her reach down and pick up the cookie that still lay on the street. She backed away to the sidewalk across from the brown soldier with the polished boots. They saw her raise the cookie high above her head. They could see that she wanted desperately to throw it. The driver saw her, too. He watched her expectantly. She watched him. It was a wordless challenge. Her face was tense. Her arm was twisted to throw.

The car started to move. Her arm dropped. She dropped the cookie. She clutched her eyes. A little boy's eyes followed the cookie as it rolled. He picked it up.

The car moved away with Goldstein turned backwards to guard his prisoners. The arrested girl looked at Buck and smiled. Buck smiled back.

The girl showed a string of beads, clasped them in her hands, and asked, "rosaire?"

"No," Buck said. He wanted to lie, "Yes."

Clair pulled open his flying suit and showed a rosary chain around his neck.

Buck closed his eyes over tears. "Thank you," he said to her. *Oh, God, stop the pain.* "Thank you," he told her again.

The car turned through a gate in an eight-foot stone wall. Buck blinked his eyes. The building looked like the county courthouse of the town where he had trained his flight crew in Nebraska. They lifted him from the car and took him into a large, high-ceilinged room. A desk was diagonally set across a corner. Straight, wooden chairs lined two walls. To the right of the desk sat four unfamiliar American air crew. One had a bandaged head and one had a leg heavily wrapped.

Where is the rest of the Bare Lass crew? Have they all escaped?

On the top of the desk, two worn shoe soles showed with a bored face between them looking into the room. Buck was placed on a couch in the opposite corner from the desk showing the worn shoe soles. Someone brought in Buck's and Clair's parachutes and Clair's escape kit. The official roused himself and searched through the parachutes. A blue uniformed man with a doctor's satchel came in.

"Heil Hitler."

"Heil Hitler."

There was a lot of talk in German. Then the doctor turned to the air crew. When he had finished with Buck, he said in English, "I can not say how things are with you. Until you get X-rayed you must not move."

"Thank you, doctor. I can't move. I'm either stiff or paralyzed."

"When will the war be over?"

"You tell me," Buck answered.

"Why do you fight the Germans? We are like brothers. The girl we just released said she threw you candy because she thought you were Germans in the car. Why do we fight each other?" The doctor questioned.

Buck did not answer.

"I must ask you, Captain, was anything taken away from you after you were captured? This is purely a question to prevent criminal action. We must keep our soldiers' behavior honorable."

The soldiers that stole my escape kit and my money must have lied to save the French girl. These small-fry krauts have got their own game against the big shots. Aloud Buck said, "I wasn't carrying an escape kit or any money, if that's the question. I did have morphine on my parachute harness. I sure could use it."

"No. It's against orders to allow this."

"Thank you, anyway."

The doctor reached into his pocket and drew out a clean, folded handkerchief. "I wish you well," he said, and he put the handkerchief into Buck's hand.

Buck could not move his hands any more, but he could still move his fingers enough to hold the handkerchief.

"Thank you, doctor. You're okay."

After the doctor left, five blue-uniformed soldiers arrived. Their wing insignia told that they were Luftwaffe. Buck was placed on a stretcher. Along with the five other prisoners, he was loaded into the straw-strewn bed of an open truck. The warm day was ending. There was a chill in the air. Clair wrapped a parachute around Buck. The rough road made Buck's pain worse. The truck started through countryside half green with summer and half gray with winter. An evening-air sadness prevailed. The prisoners were silent. The sadness defied words.

The English Channel coastline showed briefly upon the horizon. Then the truck turned down a newly cut trail into a woods and stopped before several new, long, and low buildings. The truck motor was shut off. This imposed a finality to the stillness, but a faint murmur of ocean waves meeting shoreline tempered the silence. The sun had deadened to blood-red as it descended.

Buck's stretcher was lifted from the truck. As the darkness deepened, he felt increasingly isolated. Overwhelming events that had kept him frantic were receding. The sadness of the open truck still prevailed. Now he observed absurd patterns of camouflage paint and camouflage burlap.

He was carried into a room so low that all but the one pudgy guard who now accompanied the stretcher bearers could have reached up and touched the gray ceiling. He was laid onto the straw covered lower half of a double-decker bunk. The prisoner with the head wounds was helped into the upper bunk. The four other prisoners were kept standing against the wall near a crude plank table.

The pudgy guard laughed as he said in English, "Mit uns gits no chicken und pie."

Each of the prisoners was given a slice of coarse, muddy-gray bread that was smeared with gray cheese. Seven Luftwaffe soldiers sat at the table and ate thicker slices of the same bread.

As the prisoners and soldiers ate, the room got darker. One of the guards closed the black-out shutters and turned on a dim electric light that hung above the table. The soldiers offered Buck a drink of water and a piece of the bread. He refused both. The prisoner above him with his head wrapped in gauze took the water but no food.

The prisoners who could walk were ushered out to another room. On the way out, Clair asked if Buck wanted one of the French candy bars that he had concealed.

"No, thank you," Buck said.

Buck could now only move his toes and fingers. His left knee had swollen badly during the day and had become extremely sensitive. The bowel-knotting back pain had eased. When he was not being moved, and when he completely gave up trying to move, his pain would reduce to aching. The biggest discomfort now came from the pressure of the board bunk on his injured back. The straw was no help. It was bunched in knots under him. He could not move to rid the pain of the knots.

Maybe this is as far as they will take me. What about the guy above me? Why have they brought us here? he asked himself.

Vaguely, he heard the ocean. Only a few miles across the English Channel was his bed in Hut 23. He remembered the Cherbourg coast on the map. How close it had looked to England. But where he was now, the war was an infinite distance from breakfast in England. His head was to one side far enough to see the top half of the room. He could see the dim electric light and the faces of the Germans gathered around it. *They must feel numb when they hear the ocean and think of the invasion that's due to come from there.*

He could not see the top of the table, but he could see the bottles on the table. *Are they trying to drink away their jitters?* A late-arriving guard was eating. Buck watched the guard's jaws work upon the bread. He remembered bitching at breakfast about the bread not being really white. He was gone from that world forever. Now the telegram would go home ". . . missing in action . . ."

To his dad, the worst had happened when his son had enlisted to kill people. But his mother—she had never given up with him. "If you ever need God, remember, His forgiveness is great," she had reminded him.

I need God tonight.

What pulled me into the war? I could have avoided it as a son of pacifist parents. Was it that life on the ranch bored me? A need to be a hero? To help my country's fight?

Again he was an overgrown eighth grader coming home from school. The world was good in those days. In those days he had liked living on the ranch. It was different when he got older. The ranch was dull, once it kept him away from the high school sports and girls of Buffalo.

He respected his parents' religion then. Was it not having a girl that made him want to leave? The guys were joining the service. And his dad was preaching that he shouldn't sign up for the war.

Maybe I joined in protest. In church they prayed for a just world. My friends were putting their lives on the line to make it happen. I couldn't sit through the words that said it was better to only pray to get things right.

If I could decide now, would I join again? Were my parents right? Is war evil? Big shots using small fry for politics through killing?

The *Bare Lass* was still in the sky in his memory. He wanted to keep it up there. It had been a good ship and crew. When he thought of the guys of the 100th who had been killed, and the guys still flying, he felt proud even in his misery.

Here you lay, you big bastard. Am I ready to die? If I've done wrong, forgive me, God. Did I join up of my own free will?

No. It was not that simple.

"Mother!"

What was that? He distinctly heard the word again . . . "mother!" . . . It came from the bunk above. Now all was quiet again.

Thank God I got that last letter off to my mother. Any fool could know that shells couldn't keep missing us right, left, rear, ahead . . . forever. Mother kept asking in her letters . . . was I praying to God? So I wrote, "I know God is still up there." When I'm disgusted with the mess the world is in, it's not enough for me to pray. With this Hitler maniac loose, we've got to hang him. He hadn't mentioned in that letter that some of his thoughts had come out of a drinking session at the officer's club the night before. One of the pilots had read something that he had memorized. *Humans are mainly distinguished from other animals by . . .* He couldn't remember.

A surge of laughter came from the guards at the table. *Why didn't I study German in school instead of Spanish? All I can understand are "Cognac, Hitler, and SS."*

Missing in Action . . . my parents will read. In a world covered with telephone wires and radio stations it seems crazy that there is no way to tell them more.

Three of the Germans came over to his bunk. The pudgy guard was flanked by a heavy-boned, thin guard carrying a bottle. Another frail-bodied guard carried a lit candle. They came in close to Buck. The guard with the bottle knelt on the floor. The pudgy guard bent over Buck. The guard with the lit candle wrapped himself around the corner post and brought the smoking flame down close to Buck's face.

"We want to know what for you bomb us, you Schweinhund?" the pudgy guard said. The other guards spoke in German and he translated, "Why you come over here to make war? Is America not rich enough?"

Buck decided not to answer.

"You want to make much money. The Jews pay you a thousand dollars every time you bomb us, Ja? We know about you Chicago gangsters. You murderer."

The pudgy guard leaned closer. Buck looked into glassy eyes set in a red face. With the sick-sweet fumes of his alcohol breath came, "Tell us, why bomb our women and children? Where is your manhoodkeit? You do anything that Rosenvelt pays you. You Terrorflieger!"

Sick with his silence, Buck said, "Leave me alone. Ask Hitler. He started it."

He knew he shouldn't argue, but he couldn't listen to their ignorance. The Nazis were calling him a gangster. The Nazis! He was here in all this foulness because of them, and they were blaming him!

"What for you bomb women and children?"

"We're giving you what you did to women and children in England."

The pudgy guard said that the bombing of England was retaliation for the bombing of German cities which began in May and went on through most of June before the Germans started bombing England.

"If you're such nice guys you wouldn't be treating Jews like you do."

"What you know about Jews? There are many ways to make suffer. What you know about how Jews made German suffer?"

"All you know is propaganda," Buck said.

"What you know, Herr Hauptmann? All you know is propaganda!" Buck heard with a spray of saliva coming with the vehemence. He felt too sick to reply. He closed his eyes.

"What does the one up above have to say?"

The candle light went up to the bandaged head of the bunk above. "Speak up!" The German made no further demand, for there was a glaze in the open eyes that told him that this person would no longer answer for his acts on earth.

"Er is todt," Buck heard from a voice that told in its tone: He is dead.

My God, that was him calling "mother."

The discovery of the death sent the Germans back to the table where they drank some more. After a while all the guards except the pudgy guard left.

Buck couldn't sleep. He watched the German sitting stupidly under the dim electric light with eyes looking toward the darkness where death lay. Did he feel safe from the night under his electric light? Beyond the Germans were the windows with the black-out shutters closed against the night sky. The soldier had a look of self-satisfaction that recalled the saying Ignorance is bliss. Had he grown up reading a newspaper every day? Was he a regular church-goer? Did he have a Bible? Did he have an answer for everything? Sure. He looked like that kind of guy. He was a filthy, self-satisfied patriot. *Too bad for you, honorable patriot. Too bad for me; I'm your prisoner.*

Buck, looking at the dim electric light, could feel the invasion of night into the room. The stranger above had died calling for his mother. What had happened to the bright world he had grown up in? Had he been stupid in his eighth-grade gladness? Had he lost his head like a light-crazy moth when the war had come? Again he was with the sadness of the prisoners in the twilight of the open truck, and from there he felt joined in sick sadness with his parents and his combat compatriots, his friends who had died, and all other victims of the war.

Eventually he fell asleep. When he awoke, the guard was opening the black-out shutters. The sky beyond the window was clear. His eyes ran down his big, bulky frame that he could not move, and his thoughts of the night came back to him.

The prisoners were given another slice of the muddy-gray bread smeared with gray cheese. And they were given ersatz tea. With Clair's help Buck drank some tea, but he did not try to eat. The prisoners who could walk were ushered outside to relieve themselves. The door was left open. He could hear the chatter of birds outside. He could remember the newly plowed fields out there. He could feel the warmth of the sun coming in.

What was it about the morning? It was not an odor. It was something else. It was a definite communication—a significance of some kind that made a difference in the world. "I brought you something," Clair said when he came back. He tucked a dandelion blossom into a crack where Buck could regard it against the dark bottom side of the dead prisoner's bunk.

Buck studied the yellow circle of sunshine of the dandelion. The blossom was so tender it appeared to have opened for the first time just minutes before. The yellow, slender petals were rays of sunshine velvet with dew. The flower was sunshine fire from heaven that lifted from the ground outside. And the stem that reached the earth's life to this cup was beautifully nude, as if, in having the life borne through it, it carried an inner splendor complete in itself.

He smiled up to the flower. "Did you ever see anything so innocent?" he said aloud.

He recalled how as kids they used to hold dandelions to their chins to have the sun reflect rich yellow upon them in answer to the question, "Do you like butter?" Now he studied the curves of the petals and the sensitive symmetry with which the heart opened its face to the world. He took in the tender texture of the sun yellow. There was no evil here.

He wanted to reach up and touch the flower, but he could not move. Again he felt the morning air. And it came to him that the difference he couldn't identify was that the earth outside was alive, living so powerfully that it made the fighting of humans insignificant. The war had not made the slightest change in springtime's schedule. The earth, the sun, and God were all working together in the energy of the spring morning.

He thought of Randi. He pictured the Buffalo ranch hills, green and clean with deep, cool grass. He wished that he could be in the young, deep, green grass, running his fingers through Randi's hair.

Was his longing only the cry of his sick heart for home? Why was it Randi?

"It's the springtime," he murmured. Nature was giving his lost self a new hold on life. The dandelion was an invitation to share in the holy orgy of budding and spawning of the earth that was, beyond reach of the war, God's heartbeat.

A Gypsy song has a timeless connection with Buck's experience and sings for him in a grander dimension. It is particularly appropriate here because the Gypsies in Europe were under persecution by Hitler at the very time Buck, lying wounded and helpless, was uplifted by the gift of a dandelion. The Gypsies have a long history of poetry and song of persecution and solace, and in this song they voice their grander dimension of Buck's experience.

Bavaria was grand

Decked with gold pieces

Würzburg was grand

Decked with flowers

When they carried me off

Decked with chains

Translation from a Gypsy song: First recorded from Ungri dialect of German Romani in 1934. Translated from German by Dorothy M. and H. Gordon. Published by Hanns Weltzel, "The Gypsies of Central Germany," Journal of the Gypsy Lore Society, XVII, Part 1 (January, 1938), 23.

THE EARTH: CHAPTER TWO

Early in the afternoon the Germans took away the prisoner who had died. Later Buck was carried out by two guards he had not seen before. Clair gave a final wave as his pilot went out the door.

"Thanks, Clair. I'll see you after the war."

Buck was taken to Le Havre to await a train. For a while he closed his eyes. When he opened them a boy was staring at his stretched-out, death-like form. He winked at the boy, and the youngster ran away.

When the train arrived his guards could not swing the stretcher into the narrow passage of the third class coach. Finally they took the stretcher to the first class section. The guards were visibly happy in being forced to ride in first-class cushioned comfort.

When the Train Master came by and saw that a prisoner of war was riding first class, he reacted with extreme rage. The guards decided that it would be best to try again to get into the third-class section. They got Buck out of the train.

Eventually they hauled the stretcher into a third-class compartment through a window, and the train started away. The guards sat down on the third-class wooden benches and cursed the Train Master as they gave Buck drags of their German cigarettes. They managed to explain to Buck that they were taking him to Paris to Clichy hospital. Buck felt that they were being nice to him in alliance against the Train Master.

The guards kept looking up to the sky. Once, the train almost stopped as it passed the twisted, smoldering wreckage of a locomotive. One guard went into a play-act for Buck, to communicate a dive-bomber swooping down on the train. He pointed imaginary bullets across the compartment, and he rocked with the imaginary concussion of bombs. In the middle of the night they arrived at Clichy Lazarett. Buck looked into a star-filled heaven as he was carried toward the entrance of a multi-story building. From the night sky came the strange sound of French air raid sirens wailing an alarm. As the stretcher bore forward the hospital increasingly blocked his sky vision until it wiped out the last of the stars.

He moved through a low-ceilinged entrance. Then he looked up into a softly lit entrance lobby five stories high. On one side, across the entire wall and five stories tall, hung a silk red, white, and black flag bearing gigantic Hitler eagles up to the eternal ceiling. Upon the opposite wall was a flag of the same vast width and five-story height, displaying a swastika. The red, white, and black of the mind-shattering huge flags carried a silken glow of luminescent brilliance.

"Christ!" Buck muttered, tyrannized by the display of Nazi power.

He was carried through this dim-lit entrance vault to the bright lights of a receiving section. An hour later he was taken up to the eighth floor. There a gate of steel bars was opened. He was routed through the open gate, and he heard the steel bars close behind him.

He was taken to a room with two beds and lifted into one of the beds. He lay between clean, white sheets on a spring supported mattress.

"Danke Schoen," he said in the German he had learned for thank you.

Sirens wailed the long steady tone he had learned meant All Clear. He slept soundly.

Next day he was X-rayed. When the doctors looked at the X-rays, they ordered the job to be repeated. But days passed with no new X-rays. By the end of the week he could use his arms enough to feed himself. His left knee was still as big as a watermelon and extremely sensitive. The prison-ward nurse kept towels propped under the knee to ease the pain. There was only one prison ward nurse, Stella. She worked seven days a week.

Though still plagued by back pain, he was gaining some ability to move his body, but his headaches, centered where the back of his neck joined his skull, were getting worse.

He could not turn from his back to his side. But he could now lift his head from the pillow and feed himself.

Each day there were three to six air raid alarms, but bombs seldom fell close to the hospital. Yet, the gnawing of hunger weakened his will to not dread the air raids.

Doctors came by once each day. They looked at the blackboard chart that hung on his bed. They talked in German. They then went away again. No pills were given, no preparations were given to drink. No one even brought him water to drink, except when the French maid came through each day to clean the floor. He always looked forward to her coming, and he always thanked her profusely for taking time to bring him water.

He had never had so much time to think. His thoughts went back to the ranch beyond Buffalo. He would think about the planting going on. About Goldy, his horse, and Rex, his mongrel dog. About the house and the pot-bellied stove. His mother and his father. And mingled through all of these thoughts was Randi and now Jennifer and Emily and Lena Doubert, his Buffalo girlfriend who had never answered his letters.

Sometimes he would think back to the missions he had flown. He would refly the last mission. The fire. The bail out. The French village with the girls and the cookies. And finally he would come to the dandelion.

Clair had thought to bring him a stupid little dandelion bundle of sunshine. Now, remembering that dandelion for what it spoke, helped him remember that it was springtime outside as he lay in the hospital.

As the days went by in a succession of cauliflower soup, he visualized T-bone steak, corn on the cob, apple pie, smoked ham, mashed potatoes and gravy, and cold white milk. There was always enough beef and venison on the ranch. There were so many good meals he had enjoyed, like feasts of Thanksgiving turkey and cranberry sauce. A lot of good tastes haunted him beyond words to describe them. *I will have to think more about how to describe these good smells and tastes.*

On the first day of the second week, the prison-ward sergeant, Walter, wheeled him to a ward adjoining a surgery. While he waited, he noted that the nurses here were attractively French. Two in particular wore their French most invitingly. Walter had his back framed by a doorway. The nurses took turns in crossing behind Walter's vision to fork their fingers into V signs for Victory over the German's head. When a golden-haired nurse threw Buck a kiss, it took great concentration to continue to look past Walter with a dead-pan stare. He then decided that he would have to escape while in Paris. He imagined himself a fugitive in Paris. Then he was wheeled into surgery.

A heavy needle was pushed into his knee and a lot of blood was drawn out. After this treatment the knee improved rapidly. He began to work up escape plans for when he could move better. He still could not manage to turn from his back onto his side. He had never realized how many muscles were needed to turn from his back onto his side.

One night he was awakened by someone being wheeled into his room. His roommate had one leg in a plaster cast and the other fixed into a pulley arrangement with hanging weights pulling on it. With a British accent, he told how he had gone down in his Spitfire pumping for fuel for his dead engine all the way to the ground. He and fifteen other Belgian pilots among the troops interned in Corsica had escaped to England and vowed to fight the Germans unto death. All but three of the sixteen had met the terms of their oath.

"Kickie," the name the Belgian offered, would sometimes lay with a grimaced face and issue an occasional moan. During the better times the two would visit.

"Hum, almost nine o'clock. Still no raid. The guys must be having a second helping of bacon and eggs," Buck enjoyed saying.

One night a raid got started with the usual sound of Germans hurrying to the shelters, then lights out, and stillness—that quiet before the bombers come. Finally a hum, growing louder, until the sky rumbled and flak rattled windows. Then the bombs, exploding, close, shaking the room.

"Go away. For me the war is supposed to be over," Buck protested.

"I hope they hit this place," Kickie said.

"Kickie, we're here."

"So are a lot of Germans."

When the lights came on again, Buck looked at Kickie and thought, *Americans are different. The look of war from the underside in Europe gives me a lot of questions I never thought to ask.*

"What are you doing?" Buck asked as Kickie began to massage and press the side of his cheek.

"I keep moving it so it won't heal," Kickie said.

"Your whole cheek bone is moving around! It makes me sick to watch it."

"When the Germans start to ship me out of here, I'll show them my cheek bone. If I stay here until the invasion, I may have a chance to get back to the war."

Buck shook his head in puzzlement.

Next day was marked by the victory of Buck being able to turn onto his side.

The nurse Stella, who understood English, came by and he told her, "You work too hard. You ought to go soak up some spring sunshine."

"How? I work fourteen-hour day, seven-day week. Americans no know war."

In following days he often saw a pajama-clad figure pacing in the hallway. Though the man limped, he kept his carriage erect. Buck looked forward to being able to walk in the hallway beside him to put his body in shape to escape.

His body seemed to be on a schedule of improvement that defied the lack of medical attention. In two more days he was able to lift himself to his elbows.

Shortly before lunch Walter came in with two Parcels. "The Red Cross looks after you. What looks after Germans?"

"God, Kickie, can you believe it? Look at this stuff. Real spam!"

Lunch was a banquet of K-2 crackers, jelly, cheese, spam, and chocolate. Later Buck wrote the post card back to the other world.

Buck began to ration himself the Red Cross food. He allowed himself a little liver pâté this time, a little corned beef the next, and so on, to supplement the black bread, cauliflower, and potatoes of the meager German ration. His stomach had adjusted to his new life so well that a small amount of food would make him feel full.

Kickie became more talkative telling of England, ". . . and when we got to her place she gave me a pair of her husband's pajamas, but I never wore them.

"In the morning, it was grand until her husband called from the stairway."

"She went out, and then came back and said, 'He's making breakfast.' We ate together, the three of us, in their lovely cottage. He fell over himself praising how we Spitfire fighter pilots had saved England. He said he had to get back to London, but I could see by his valises he'd come to stay."

At another time Kickie talked about flying. ". . . in the Spitfire when I got restless I would head for the ground and start the guns going. Trains. Troops. Farmers. Even shot a cow or two. When you're near the ground with your finger on the trigger, anything that moves gets it. C'est la guerre. The Germans like war so I give it to them."

"Why the hell would you want to shoot a poor cow who never even heard of Hitler?"

"She was a German cow."

In the next days Buck suffered pain that was worse than any he had ever endured. The pain ran from the fingers of his left hand, along the bone of his arm, into the shoulder socket. It felt as if the nerves had been wrapped into a turnscrew. He asked the doctors for drugs to ease the pain but was given nothing.

Kickie's pain also got worse. One of his compound fractures had become infected under the cast. When Buck's pain would let up, he would sympathize with Kickie's suffering. Then the tables would turn. Eventually the two made a mutual "no sympathy" pact. But it didn't work.

During this time, Buck got stronger in spite of the pain. Walter gave him a cane and informed him that from now on he was to use the Abort at the end of the hall.

On his way back from the Abort he encountered the pajama-clad marcher he had been watching. "I'm Captain Pierce. Are you American? It's been a long time since I talked to an American."

"Lieutenant Colonel Burtram B. Fanning," the small, wiry man answered.

"You sound like you're from the South," Buck said.

"Refresh your memory, soldier. Name, rank, and serial number are only while under the enemy."

The marcher reversed his direcetion. *There's a brass monkey.*

Buck counted the many doors. It was verboten to even look into any room. He estimated that at least thirty patients were being cared for by Stella and Walter. Some of the doors had windows like his, but most doors were solid.

In the next days of walking back and forth to the Abort, he encountered a walker with no ears and no nose. The rest of the face was scar tissue. The hands were also scar tissue. The fingers were like twisted rope. This person giggled a lot and poked at the French maid and pulled at her dress, like a child might. The maid put up with him to a point. Then she splashed water at him from her scrub bucket. This would drive him to retreat.

Buck could walk wobbly without the cane now, but he kept using it to fool the doctors. Like Kickie, he wanted to still be in Paris when the invasion got there. While walking one day, he opened one of the solid doors. Inside he saw a patient with his face puffed into a ball. Both his arms and face were covered with a brown salve. The patient lay on his back and moved his arms back and forth as if he were trying to clap his hands. A peculiar whimpering noise came from his mouth. Buck quickly closed the door.

Holy Jesus Christ. Why don't they kill him?

He went back to bed. The nerve pain started again. When Stella came by he asked, "Why don't you give pain medicine to prisoners? You don't care if we get well, die, or go crazy. I've been here over a month with my X-rays ruined. The doctor ordered new X-rays but nobody did them. What good are the doctors if nobody pays attention to them? What about the guys behind the solid doors?" . . . Stella had gone.

"Now you've done it," Kickie told him. "You Americans speak to educate. Germans can't be told anything. They have to be shown. As their prisoner you have to learn to be silent."

Walter came in. "I understand that our American is making complaints here."

Silence.

"I will notify the authorities."

In the morning a doctor in a white coat came in and told Buck he would be transferred to another hospital. At 3:00 P.M., Buck was escorted away. He took along his last Red Cross food and a chunk of moldy bread Stella gave him as a parting gift.

A forty-passenger bus wound through Paris streets with Buck alone and two guards as escorts. He had expected the Paris streets to be empty, in a gaunt wait for liberation. It was true there were no cars on the streets, but Paris was busy. Instead of cars there were bicycles and all kinds of other foot-pedaled vehicles—even four-wheeled, car-like contraptions. The afternoon was warm, and the tables of sidewalk cafes were crowded.

A walking marathon was coursing down the street. People along the street were clapping and cheering as the contestants passed. Assistants were riding bicycles beside the walkers and dousing them with water. *What crazy, wonderful people. They're as stubborn as spring when it comes to changing their ways because of the war.*

The bus drew near a high brick wall and stopped by a huge, rusty gate. The branches of an old vine system spread over the crumbling bricks of the wall. Young leaves of the spring season were growing over the dead branches. The gate opened and someone in workman's clothing was escorted into the bus.

"I'm Bill Johnson from Texas. I drove my B-26 into a cloud of buckshot and I came out heading for the ground. I've still got some of the crap in my neck."

After hearing from Buck, the Texan continued, "You've been in a hospital. I've been in a dungeon—seventeen days. They snatched me out of a bistro on Place De La Bastille. I thought I was with the Maquis until my girl rolled her eyes at the Nazi that nabbed me. The Huns figured I was a spy 'cause I ditched my uniform. I've been all this time convincing them I was a shot-down pilot. All I got to eat was a piece of bread a day. From the gas it gave me, I'd swear it was petrified wind."

When they had been transferred to a train Buck gave Bill a K-2 cracker smeared with liver pâté and some of his moldy bread. Only one guard had gone aboard with them. The three were alone in the compartment. The guard sat next to the door with a submachine gun on his lap as he carved and ate fresh black bread. He did not share bread with Buck and Bill.

As the trip lasted into the night the air in the room got warmer and staler, but the guard would not open the window or the door to the hallway. Bill and Buck sat at opposite sides of the window and mumbled to one another.

Presently the guard's eyes closed and his head nodded.

Buck leaned closer to Bill. "Texas, I've been thinking we can escape."

"How? This train's full of troops carrying guns."

"We could grab our guard's machine gun and head through the window."

"What do we do if we make it out through the window?" Bill questioned.

"Run for it, with the krauts shooting, I'll admit."

"After the dungeon I'm a sack of bones. I'm too weak to outrun a hatrack tonight."

"With the train full of soldiers, I figure our only chance is through the window."

"Could we unlock it?" Bill asked.

The black-out curtains were fully drawn. Buck peaked through them to study the window lock. As he looked, he saw a train wreck that had been cleared from the line of traffic. Several of the cars were still smoldering.

"It would take too long to get this window open. We'll have to crash through it. Trouble is, Tex, I'm still not up to running, myself."

"If we knew they're going to kill us anyway, I'd say, let's risk it. What the hell."

Buck said, "It's risky staying here, too, with our dive-bombers shooting up trains."

"They're not going to keep me once I get some strength back. After what I've learned in France, I could get back to the Maquis and be smarter this time."

"But now we're still in France," Buck reminded.

"Are you saying we should go for it?" Bill asked.

"Our freedom is clicking away on those rails."

"You're getting me nervous, Buck. Let's go for it."

A commotion awoke the guard to life. Three soldiers entered and took vacant seats.

"We either missed our chance or our coffins," Buck muttered.

The train crossed into Germany and arrived at Frankfurt at 1:15 of the following afternoon. The Frankfurt West-Bahnhof, where the train stopped, had been hit earlier in the day. Russian slave-labor battalions had already repaired most of the damaged track, but the Kasselerstrasse train they were on was still not able to get to the Hauptbahnhof. Instead, it had stopped here. Buck and Bill were ushered past the bomb craters and wreckage that were the center of activity of the swarm of workers.

"We blow it up, Tex, and our Allies' slave laborers repair it. It doesn't make sense."

They were taken to a lower level of the station. There, in a corner of what was serving as a lobby, were some twenty unsmiling POWs with an array of torn, blood-smeared clothing, dirty bandages, wrapped heads, limbs in plaster-casts, burns, bruises, and open wounds. The crude first aid of some told that they had just been shot down. The casts and professional bandages of others told that they had been brought in from hospitals. A few were leaning on crutches. Most were standing unsupported. Though one of the prisoners spoke German, he had learned nothing of why they were being held here.

Civilians coursed by the POWs. Certain people—the inevitable few—stopped. These few held fast, as if they were drawn by a power they could not resist. In all his life, Buck had never seen hatred such as he read in these faces. When someone stepped closer and spit at him, he said, "Texas, if they don't get us out of here fast, we're in for big trouble."

There were now three guards, one with the submachine gun and two with rifles. Bill took account of the weapons and said, "Our guards will protect us."

"Our guards? Whose side do you think they're on?"

"We'd better hope they'll protect us, Buck."

The prisoner who could speak German learned that they were being held in wait for a bus. In the past, civilians of the city had thrown bomb rubble at POWs as they marched to the prison. So now a bus had been ordered for them. But there were few buses. So the wait.

A quarrel started between the civilians and the guards. Suddenly a big German with a limp and a big mustache confronted Bill. He started shouting. A guard came over and tried to motion the man away, but the man would not leave. He remained before Bill and pointed and shouted. He then turned to the guard. Other Germans closed in.

"What the hell's going on?" Bill asked the German speaking prisoner.

"Don't worry. Since you're in civilian clothes, this guy is claiming you're a German deserter. He swears you're his neighbor's boy who deserted."

"That's crazy!"

Bill faced the crowd. "Me American. Texan." The guard reached to Bill's neck and showed Bill's dog tags. "That won't help me. I've gone through that before," Bill said.

"They say we were bombing the German people to make big money. They want the guards to let us all try to escape so they can catch us and hang us."

More people stopped, not knowing what was occurring, but joining the protest.

"Luftwaffe protect Terrorfliegers?"

155

"I shouldn't have taken off my uniform," Bill anguished in his workman's clothes.

A boy barely in his teens brought a burlap rope. One of the guards raised his rifle to hold off the crowd. A Luftwaffe soldier came through the door and shouted in German.

The prisoner who could understand German shouted, "Our bus is here."

The POWs were ushered out, while the guards leveled their guns on the crowd.

Suddenly Bill was grabbed by three people of the crowd. Buck held on to Bill, but his grasp was futile. The guards seemed confused about what to do. They shouted, but this changed nothing. The guard with the submachine gun was the closest to Bill. For a moment it looked as if he might fire as the people dragged Bill away, but he did not fire. No one fired. The guards only hurried the rest of the prisoners out and into the bus.

"I'm American. Texan," were the last words Buck heard above the crowd noise. The prisoners stampeded into the bus with Buck last to enter. When he had first been shot down, his mind had been so muddled that everything had happened like in a nightmare. Now his mind registered clearly and with alertness and in its helpless torture fastened upon the dumb, crazy words. *The condemned man ate a hearty meal. It isn't true. I was trying to stretch out my food. At least I gave him a cracker and some bread.*

They started away, not down a street, but through a passage cut through rubble. Traveling down Bockenheimer Landstrasse, Buck's mind was still with the horror of Bill. But as they traveled on and on through the ruins, the grotesque devastation that had once been a city impacted more and more upon Buck as endless mayhem. The bus continued everlastingly through the passage between rubble, through canyons of hanging walls. They passed a cathedral with its spire half chewed away, its cross tilted over empty sky. Block after block, mile after mile, were ruins, ruins, ruins, where people had once lived.

Finally, Buck could see open country beyond the city. A few bomb craters scarred the vacant lots, but a spirit of life came from plots of grass. Once he saw a dandelion blossom lifted through the green grass of springtime, contrasting the horror of Frankfurt. Again he told himself that the world of the dandelion was God's world.

The destination of the bus turned out to be the Oberursel, Luftwaffe Interrogation Center. Upon arrival prisoners separated. Some were sent to a hospital others to the interrogation center. Buck was soon before the desk of an interrogation officer.

"You were seen parachuting so we have your identity. Next, you've been in the hospital so long your news is stale. You can go. What Group were you with, Captain?"

"You tell me."

"I will not play with you. You were in the 100th Group. You were a Lead Crew pilot. You come from Buffalo, Wyoming. Your father and mother are pacifists, and on the night before you left the United States you attempted to call your parents in Buffalo, Wyoming."

"How in the hell do you know all that?"

The officer smiled, "We are the Intelligence of the Third German Reich. We know these things because we are efficient. Because we are efficient, we will win the war."

The officer looked into the file again, "On January twenty-ninth your ship aborted from a raid on Frankfurt. Your co-pilot was killed. He was Tom Raymond, and he was the son of a colonel who was an inspector general from the High Command of your air war. We have interrogated this colonel. You see, Captain, sooner or later we get all of you."

Buck was ushered out to a processing line. He still carried his Parcel with four K-2 crackers, 1/3 can of spam, 1/4 can of jelly, 1/4 pound of powdered milk, and 17 sugar cubes.

"Government property all is confiscated," the guard barked.

His watch and all other government-issue items were taken from him. He was allowed to walk away wearing his personally purchased uniform which, by the advice of older crews, he had worn under his issued flight gear.

Suddenly his Parcel was taken away. "You can't take that! That's Red Cross food!"

Laughter. "You have a lot to learn. Next."

The next guard took away his billfold.

From the end of the line he heard, "Off with all of your clothes. Everything."

When Buck was naked, the man who had taken the Red Cross food said, "Do you still think we cannot take away your food? Maybe already you do not feel so important. Naked you are only an animal, eh? Oink. Oink. Can you grunt? Fort mit ihm."

Buck was headed down a long hallway that had many narrower hallways leading from it. There were hundreds of doors regularly spaced like a line of troops. Steel pipes stood out above the doors with control valves by each entrance. Next to each door was a six- inch metal flag contraption. Some of the flags were in the up position and some in the down position. After a while Buck was steered into one of the doorways. The guard closed the door. There was no door handle on the inside.

Buck surveyed the cell. It was four-feet wide and eight-feet long. It had a board bed with a straw mattress and one blanket. On the floor was a brown stained glass jug that Buck figured was either for pee or for tea. Under a steel-barred, frosted window was a steam radiator. Now he knew why the control valves were in the hallway. The only thing he could control was a handle that lowered the metal flag on the wall outside of his door.

For Texas Bill, the war is for sure over. The thought ran through his mind again and again.

He decided he could lie on the board bed a long while before the isolation would begin to bother him. He pushed the lumps of straw in the mattress to one side and lay down. Pain stabbed from his neck through his shoulders and down his arms to his hands.

"If this isn't a Nazi sweat box, I haven't heard of one," he said.

It sounded strange to hear his voice break the silence of the room.

"C'est la guerre, Bill and Kickie and Clair and Walt and Sam and Marks and my co-pilot Tom Raymond and all you other gangsters living and dead. We've been shit on."

The juices of his empty stomach and the depraved world burned in his throat.

"At least we know, where shit falls, flowers will grow."

THE EARTH: CHAPTER THREE

Sam, Samuel O'Brien, had lowered the flag to signal a guard. After thirty-one days in solitary confinement he was not sure of what he would say when the guard arrived, but he had lowered the flag. This made the waiting bearable.

He had no paper or pencil. He had only his mind to write with. *My first day as an aviation cadet . . . Hundreds of acres of barracks and thousands of close-cropped heads. I stood by the latrine mirror and studied my short stubble of copper-red hair. I put on the cap with the military crown and saw my face under the cap's giant silver propeller between gold wings. It was not me. I walked out of the latrine feeling I wasn't myself.*

In London, Sandra was finishing her bath. Rubbing herself dry with a pink Turkish towel. Powdering her crotch with April Showers talc. Dabbing herself with Springtime in Paris. Running her fingers through her under-things. Roast chicken for dinner or tender roast beef with mashed potatoes and butter. Afterwards, green peas. Big, juicy, round, green peas with melted butter.

What was that? The guard was stopping! No, he had not stopped.

Military training? The blue vase lecture! There was this soldier. He was ordered to get a certain blue vase. He went out and went through hell to get it. Damn near killed himself, damn near starved, damn near went crazy, but he did not give up. That was the point. He was ordered to get that blue vase, and he came back with it.

In my third grade school fights one day I had to give up or get killed. Only after I gave up did I realize I was wrong. Losing taught me. . . .

He got up and rattled the handle of the flag lowered in the hallway. He said aloud, "By now a guard should be here. I should have talked the first day. Third Grader Sam."

Back to Los Angeles, back to the apartment of the girl my Ma told me to see. She was dressed in yellow gingham tied

159

*tight to the waist and ruffled at the neck and knees. I was in
my new uniform like an actor in a play. She had a bottle of
wine. I lit a candle.*

"We might as well go all the way," *I said, and I pulled
down the shades to make the noon day night, to help the candle light. I held her chair as she sat down. I wish I could
remember what we ate.*

She listened closely as I lied about my military life.

"Just like I made my street stories better for my mother,"
he told his empty cell.

I tried to sit down on the bed with her.

*She threw herself onto the bed and started to cry big
tears.* "Go away. Please go away."

*I sat on the bed and put a hand to her face to draw her
hair away from her eyes.*

"Don't touch me."

"Gosh, I want to love you."

"You have to leave. I'll write to you."

"I don't want to leave."

"I don't want you to go, but you have to leave." *With a big sob.*

*I walked down to the street corner. I was on my first
pass. Standing on the street corner half drunk from a half
bottle of wine in the middle of the day, I didn't know where
to go.*

*I crossed the street to a drug store and phoned my ma in
Chicago.*

"It's Sammy. How is everything in Lawndale?"

*Lawndale—heartache Lawndale. She's living in
Lawndale now, and I am going to keep her there with the
allotment from my pay.*

"No, I am not lonesome," *I told her.* "I'm on pass, having
a good time in Los Angeles. I've gained weight. Muscle. I
like being a soldier. I'm going to go to bombardier school."

*Then I went back to the Biltmore Hotel. I found Cook,
Kotler, and little Hap Hennessee at a table in the hotel bar.
They had all three been chosen for pilot training.*

*Kotler and Hap were drinking crushed ice concoctions.
Cook was sipping a pink drink through a straw. The bartender*

looked at the straw in the pink drink and the crushed ice and lime concoctions, and he came to our table and asked, "Are you going to be pilots?"

"We three are. He's going to be a bombardier."

"You're all going to be air force officers?"

"Yeah."

"This round is on me," he said.

Sam said aloud to the empty cell, "They are all dead now."

Here comes a guard.

He swung his feet to the floor and went to the door as it swung open.

"What gibts? You vant tu speak tu der Offizier?"

"Ah—I got to schiessen."

"Come."

Sam started toward the Abort. The trip to the toilet always gave him a chance to break out of his memory universe, to re-find himself in the real world.

Back to the cell again. *Again I changed my mind about telling all I know. My only secret is the Norden bombsight, and they have it from shot-down planes. Is it the Jew in me saying no?*

They turned up the radiator again. *I can take the heat. I'm from Chicago. Hot Chicago nights. With the window open you get the sour smell of the alley and the racket of the Dew Drop Inn where Pa is drinking until his tongue tangles. The red glow of the steel-mill furnaces is hanging in the sky and the soot of cinders is drifting darker than the night.*

"Are you from Fuller Park?" *That sounds good. Ugly things sometimes have a nice name.*

"I've come to visit your ma. Here's a penny to get some gum. Don't come back 'til I leave."

Down the street I go with my pal Joe taking ergot to the Palace Rooms. "Honey, when you're on the street, I'll give you a nickel every time you send the men to me."

"Let's move to Lawndale, Ma."

"It takes money, son."

"Pimping for the Palace rooms, that's what Sam's up to."

"Sam, go get some ice"...

"Go with your son. He's afraid."

"An Irish lad is not afraid" . . .

Off I go alone. I come back with my wagon smashed. "They told me no kike can walk their street."

"You're Irish! Go back and get that ice!" Blue ice?

Nine Polaks were waiting when I went back. Sammy, the Irish-Jew didn't have a chance.

"Ha! Your daddy's got the pox!"

I didn't see my dad after that. He was "away."

Somebody calls up from the alley, "You want to play church, Sammy?"

"Sure. I'll be right down."

"Sammy, you kneel down and close your eyes. Say, 'I am in church praying to God.'"

"Church on fire!" The piss from their circle of hoses hits me.

"If you go to work, Ma, maybe the kids will quit talking about how you make your money."

"Sammy, everything I do is for you."

From the noise of the street: "Sammy, a German kid moved in. We're going to teach him to play court." They found fresh horse manure on the street and wrapped it in newspaper . . .

"Guilty or innocent?"

"Guilty," came their verdict. *"Let her fly!"* And the manure flew.

They brought Pa home in an iron box. I was twelve. I stood by the grave at St. Mary's and held my arm around Ma.

"Are you Jew or Irish?"

"Neither. I was hatched from a bird egg."

"Here comes dinner!"

He grabbed the tarnished glass jug. In his mind's eye he saw the food coming. There was the wheelbarrow heaped with sliced bread. Behind that was the man with the jar of smear. And last was the hand truck with the yellow water called tea.

The double rap. The door top is opened. Sam holds the jug in his left hand. He reaches the right hand into the hall.

One. The bread is slapped into the right hand. Two. The smear is wiped across it. Three. The tea is poured. Four. The door is closed. Double rap. Next door. Open. Feed. Close up. On down the hall in a train receding to silence.

Eat. Enjoy. All day you've had the growls of hunger. Now for the orgy of the slice of bread. Too soon it is gone. The beast of the belly. What to do? The tea. That will help fill the emptiness. Gastric lust for stomach bulk.

Then the tea is gone, and again he is on the bunk. Chicago ... *The Loop, with the buildings reaching into the sky so high you feel swallowed up . . . The Loop is Chicago. I hate it.*

State and Madison. That's the place from where the town divides into east and west and north and south. Maybe Chicago is a jungle, but it's got a center. It was there that I watched the parade. The cops were holding the people back and saluting every time the flag went by. It was Springtime. There were a lot of sailors in blues carrying heavy sea bags up the sidewalks, against the crowd. One guy was having a real rough time. His face was white and his eyes were feverish. I wanted to help him, but I knew he had to do it alone.

Then it thundered and started to rain hard, but nobody would leave the parade. Like there was no way out for the sailor.

The stores lowered their canvas awnings. We on-lookers jammed underneath the canvas to watch from there. A band came by dressed in red and gold, playing "The Stars and Stripes Forever" right through the rain. Then came a float of lavender, pink, and blue and a crest of yellow tulips. A hundred girls arrived with batons swinging and blouses clinging wet to their skin, each coming with big, proud smiles and dance-like skips like from fairyland.

Suddenly, a trumpet player fled from the parade to join us on-lookers under the canvas. That started a paraders' panic to escape the rain.—Go! Go! Go! Scatter! From up and down the street came happy shrieks of women, children, grandpas, fathers, mothers, everyone caught up in the excitement of escape from the pouring water.

Only some boys and girls in bathing suits kept parading. They were dancing circles with a wide banner that read Fun Buds or Sun Buds. Dancing in that rain!

After that parade I walked into the recruiting office and joined up. It was not enough to just watch from under canvas. Heading home to Lawndale on the Douglas Street L I wondered where my life was going now.

Lawndale. The Chicago bosses use it for the Cook County Jail, the Criminal Court, the Municipal Pound, the Contagious Diseases Hospital. They set aside Lawndale for dogs and people they don't care about. But on 46th Street is a library to get books, and nearby is the International Harvester Company where Ma got a job.

I walked past the high brick walls of the Pilsen Brewery and past the high stone walls of the Cook County Jail. Even then I didn't like the walls that separated the in-people from the out-people. Farragut High had its "ins" and "outs," too. There were the walls between the Poles, the Austrians, the Germans, the Irish, the Italians, the Lithuanians . . . and there were the walls between the different Protestants, and between the Protestants and the Catholics and the Jews. Negroes didn't dare leave South Chicago. Everywhere in Chicago there were walls between people.

I turned down Fuller Street and took the stairway to our second floor apartment to tell Ma.

She cried.

"You did right, Sammy. This is a war against our people."

I told her, "I'll send you money to buy a house."

"No big dreams, Sammy. You just kill those Hitler people and come back to me safe."

"Out!" A guard shouted.

He was escorted up the hallway and taken to the counter where his clothes had been taken away to leave him naked. He was ordered to take off his dog tags. He thought he was being readied for execution. Then one dog tag was returned.

"One goes to Red Cross to show you prisoner," he was told.

He got his shoes back, his socks, his long-john underwear, his billfold—nothing else. All else he had carried or worn was military-issue, under Geneva Convention rules, subject to confiscation. He walked away dressed in his long-johns. The guards pushed him into a big room filled with dozens of prisoners in various states of dress and undress. Standing in the crowd, he searched his long-johns for a place to tuck away his billfold.

"Sam!" he heard.

He looked up, and before him he saw his pilot, Buck, dressed in uniform with wings and captain's bars but looking strangely different with many pounds of weight loss.

"Gosh. You. I can't figure out where to carry my billfold."

"There'll be no money for it here, but give it to me. At least I still got pockets."

"I've been in here thirty-one days, Buck."

"I got locked in here only three hours ago. I guess I've been in the hospital so long my secrets are too stale to count."

"I've been in Solitary here for thirty-one days."

"You told me. Why so long?"

"I don't know. I wouldn't talk."

"Never mind, Sam. We're on our way out of here."

THE EARTH: CHAPTER FOUR

"Captain Brewster Pierce," the soldier called who had directed pig noises at his naked body three hours before.

"Here," Buck spoke up.

The German approached Buck and saluted. In perfect English he announced, "As the highest ranking Allied officer of this shipment you are in command of the prisoners. We will relate to you as directed by the Geneva Convention on rules of warfare. You will be responsible for discipline, food, and all other prisoner problems."

Buck returned the salute carelessly. "Is this a joke? Where is the food?"

"Herr Hauptmann will bring the food directly. Now we have some papers for you to sign."

Buck read the document handed to him:

We give our word of honour as America and British officers and non-commissioned officers that we shall not
make any atempt to escape nor
get in touch with the civilian population nor
make any preparations for future escape
during our trip from Oberursel to the point of our destination i.e. the camp in Wetzlar.
This is signed by one of us for all POW's who take part in this trip.
Any man who will break his parole will be put to death.

Frankfurt a.M. Oberursel.

"I can't sign this. If anybody wants to escape that's their privilege."

"You must sign. We can not leave until you sign."

Silence from Buck.

"I will report you to my superiors at once if you do not sign!"

"That won't be necessary, Corporal. You start us on our trip, and I promise to give the matter serious consideration."

"I shall depend on it."

"You have my word as an officer."

"Aufmachen," the German ordered. The prisoners moved out. Sam inhaled the outdoor air made splendorous by the very expanse of space. The group was herded into a barbed wire enclosure next to the Interrogation Center. The enclosure contained a building about fifty feet long and thirty feet wide and another building about half that size. Guard towers on timber stilts were interspersed above the barbed wire.

Buck's shoulder joints, neck, and arms were paining and he was weak, but being in charge he felt he had to look the place over. The smaller building had a troop kitchen with a twenty-five-gallon steel vat. He told Sam, "We've got kitchen enough to cook a banquet."

In the bigger building Buck found many small rooms, each with four triple-deck bunks crowded into it. The bunks were all occupied and half of the prisoners were crowded onto the floor for lack of another place to rest. The bunks had lumpy straw mattresses and no blankets. Many of the prisoners who had no bunks milled from room to room in unreasoning search for a berth.

In the room next to the entrance, Buck said, "This room is our headquarters. I'll need these two beds for me and my adjutant."

"We've been shot down, Captain. It's every man for himself here. You find your own fart sack," one of the occupants of the bunks in question said.

"Oh? Then you stay where you are and see what you get to eat."

"Don't move for me. I'll sleep on the floor," Sam said.

"You will not," Buck said. "This is our headquarters. I need two beds."

The occupants now smiled, got up, and each gave Buck a "yes, sir."

"Do you need any help in the kitchen, sir?" one of them asked.

"Don't get any ideas. This ship is going to fly fair and square. Equal for everybody."

"Captain Pierce, the Hauptmann's at the gate to see you."

Buck went out to where a Luftwaffe captain stood with a fiber basket under one arm.

"I bring food for tomorrow, Captain. We would give bread and potatoes but the bombing has disrupted our transportation. We have only Red Cross food this time."

"Hauptmann," Buck said, "we have each had only a piece of bread today. I can't believe that you bring tomorrow's food for two hundred men in a basket like a man brings lunch for a family picnic."

"We have detained only 189 prisoners in this compound."

Buck felt his anger well as on the day when he had talked too much in the hospital, but he remembered Kickie's advice, remained silent, and took the food to the kitchen. He found that he had been given several cans of corned beef, powdered milk, jelly, and spam along with some packages of K-2 crackers and what remained of Stella's gift of moldy bread.

"Can you use some kitchen help, sir?" came from beyond the closed kitchen door.

"Keep them out of here, Sam."

Sam called, "Go back to your bunks. The only food we got is for tomorrow."

From outside came, "That food's for us. We've got a right to come in and see it."

"Write to your congressman," Buck yelled. Then to Sam he said, "Part of what I see they took away from me, personally. I saved it by going hungry. I have a right to it, but I'm going to put it all into the big pot when we cook. We'd better sleep right here just in case anybody gets ideas about helping themselves."

Buck went to the many crowded rooms to acquaint himself with the problems of the prisoners. It was dark by the time he started back to the kitchen. He stopped to regard the barbed wire and the guard towers. He could hear snatches of conversation coming from the prisoners: ". . . we were crippled from the flak and fighters were coming in . . ." ". . . three guys were hanging from the rafters of the railroad station . . . civilians had hung them there for all to see . . ."

The sky was quiet. All of his life the sky had carried an open, free feeling for him. Tonight he looked up to the sky from which he had been shipwrecked and was struck by his infinite separation from this heaven. Overwhelmed by the feeling that he was trapped, he hurried back to Sam in the kitchen.

Sam said, "Coming out of solitary is like coming out of a fog. I haven't even found out what happened to you since we bailed out."

"We've been too busy, Sam. I haven't even had time to feel sick, and those kraut bastards just kicked me out of the hospital 'cause I talked too much, not because I was fit."

Sam and Buck stretched out on the floor, and in the darkness they talked of the past days and weeks and beyond this the past world. Presently Sam said, "It would be just like the Germans to have this whole place wired to hear what we're saying."

Buck commented, "Our Intelligence would go mad if they knew how our guys are jabbering with microphones maybe planted in here, but it's all personal talk, and I'm beginning to see life as too big a deal to be bothered with all the military orders."

"When I was in solitary," Sam said, "I figured the Germans wanted me to talk to prove I wasn't a Frenchman playing POW, since they caught me on a French farm. But I gave only my name, rank, and serial number like Intelligence ordered me to. I guess that was stupid."

"When did the pencil pushers care about us? They only care about rules."

"A guy could go crazy here. Sometimes I get so carried away with dreaming I forget where I am. Maybe that's bad, but it makes being here easier."

"What's ahead for us, Sam? I've thought back to what Sandra told you in London about me being raped in Sunday School. Maybe she meant I was robbed of my power to hate. A Belgian named Kickie had the bed next to me in the hospital. He could hate. For me Hitler has got the krauts so crazy they don't deserve hating."

"I'm worried about the Germans finding out I'm half Jewish. Keep calling me Hatch. Don't call me Sam anymore."

"Right. Hatch." Buck paused. "I'm too soft like my old man. I figured leaving would change me, but I don't know."

"Maybe what's ahead for us will change you."

Buck answered, "I see us Americans being here as vigilantes, just temporary, until the world sheriffs take over. We're supposed to get world law and order from fighting this war. If the League of Nations would have put a world sheriff in after the last war, he would have hung Hitler right off and spared us being here. There's got to be a world posse to string up villians like Hitler like we used to in the early West."

"I've been in solitary so long the war has got me half crazy."

"To God the war is just a little pile of shit in a pasture, Sam. Our trouble is we got ourselves stuck in that shit."

"If we ever get freed, I'll be looking for something better than Chicago," Sam declared.

Conversation gave way to sleep.

Next morning at 11:00, Buck and Sam served twenty-five gallons of salt water flavored with the basket of Red Cross food the Hauptmann had brought for the 189 prisoners. Buck spiced the soup with the lump of moldy bread.

Sam's final gourmet suggestion was, "Put in more salt."

There was a large sack of salt in the cookhouse, so Buck obliged. The salt masked the lack of food in the water.

"It's pretty salty, but it sure hits the spot," was a standard comment as prisoners filed by for seconds. On the following morning a ration of potatoes arrived. Buck and Sam boiled the potatoes and weighed out a seven-ounce ration to each prisoner. They tasted the potatoes as they boiled them, but to keep discipline over their hunger, they kept reminding each other, "It's going to be equal for everyone."

After the meal the Luftwaffe Hauptmann (Captain) came in and ordered Buck to fall in the prisoners for Appell.

"Appell?"

"Ja. Appell. You must be counted before we ship you to Dulagluft on the other side of Frankfurt to wait for the train to permanent prison."

After the count they were marched to a public railroad station. There they waited dressed in what clothing they still had after their military-issue garb had been confiscated. Sam, standing with his head barely reaching above Buck's shoulders, cut a dashing figure with his red beard and his off-white, long-john underwear. Buck, with his forewarned preparedness of flying with his personally-purchased uniform under his flight gear, was now among the few in full military dress. Yet he did not look dashing with his stubble of mud-brown beard and his soiled gray trousers gathered in on his shrunken waistline.

Soon a train came and took them to the Wetzlar rail station from where they were marched to the nearby Dulagluft prison camp. Beyond the Dulagluft gate was a cluster of buildings and to one side were several large tents. Prisoners stood near the gate, waiting for the new purge, that is, the new group of prisoners. Once inside the barbed wire, Buck and Sam collapsed, exhausted from the march from the rail station. Sitting on the ground, in half stupor, waiting for energy to return, Buck saw someone approach and look down at him.

"Are you the ghost of Switzerland?" he heard.

"Who the hell—oh—Christ! It's bed 17! The ghost of Munster got you!"

"No. A black cloud of fighters got me, like in the nightmare—"

"Gosh, Briggs, at least you're alive. How are things here? Is there anything to eat?"

"The old timers say it's better than it used to be."

"Old timers? The krauts said they were sending us here only temporary. How old timers?—You bastard. Now I get it. Now we're the newcomers, eh? Glad to see you, ghost of Munster," Buck fumbled.

"Likewise, ghost of Switzerland who came here instead. We've got a big stew cooked for you. But you'll have to shower and get deloused before you can get in here to get it."

"Shower?" Sam asked, unbelieving.

"Yeah. And with hot water. Believe it. And with soap, too! Then you'll get a Red Cross suitcase full of stuff—a razor, soap, towels, socks, and stuff like that. You'll each get a set of long-johns, too. Sam, you'll have a spare for Sundays."

"Briggs, you'd better be telling us the truth about all this fancy stuff we're going to get," Buck said.

"Line up," someone ordered.

Soon they were under the promised hot showers, scrubbing themselves clean.

"When I was in Solitary, all sticky with sweat, I used to dream about water pouring over me. This is like another dream," Sam said.

Then they were issued a fiber suitcase called a Red Cross Capture Parcel. It contained the various items Briggs had said they would get.

"Briggs leveled with us all the way, Hatch. I can smell that stew!"

The stew, made from Red Cross Parcels sent from neutral Sweden, was served in quart-sized klim cans—the milk-spelled-backwards cans of Red Cross powdered milk. It was a stew of potatoes, spam, liver paste, corned beef, powdered milk, sugar, and K-2 crackers. With full stomachs, Buck and Sam sank into blissful sleep on the straw-covered floor of one of the big tents.

In the afternoon of the second day at Wetzlar Dulagluft, Buck and Sam relaxed in their tent and watched POWs play a ball game. The ball had been sewn together from a shredded flying jacket. The bat had been shaped from a tree limb.

"Batter up!" someone shouted.

The ball game evoked a mood for Sam that brought back his last Chicago parade. *Why do Americans like a ball game? Why do I like to watch?*

Watching the game, Sam heard conversation of POWs nearby—"Where do the krauts get the idea we're Chicago gangsters? . . . One kraut said we were paid a thousand dollars a raid by the Jews. . . . It's not only the Jews they're against. I'm no kike, and they let me lay for two days without even bothering to bandage me."

From the ball diamond came, "Blast out!   Clean the bases!"

"This is like being back home," Sam said.

"Why did you join up?" a prisoner beside Sam asked.

Sam said, "There was a parade and there was a rainstorm.   There were some sailors carrying duffel bags right through the rain. Afterwards, I went into the recruiting station and signed up."

"I'm supposed to know from that?"

Ignoring the question, Sam said, "Look at them out there. It doesn't matter what nationality you are. It's how you play ball that counts.   Listen to the laughing.   Ever since I've been shot down I've been noticing the lack of smiles on the Germans—"

"Hatch," Buck broke in, with a nudge of his elbow, "we're happy because we're still alive."

"It's more than that. We know the Germans could kill us right now without blinking an eye.   We're happy because we're playing ball."

From the field came, "Bang out a beaut—Go Home! Go! Go! Go!"

"Playing ball is like being kids again.   Watching the game brings back my last Chicago parade with yellow tulips and kids dancing in the rain."

"Dandelions are my flower. They'll take over a lawn or field of weeds if you'll let them, and I say let them. A field of dandelions is like the sun shining up at you."

Sam wrote with his mind: *Throwing flowers through the air. Little children do you dare? We who watch from under canvas . . .*

That evening there was again enough food to satisfy everyone's hunger.   During the night Buck awoke and looked out through the open tent to the night heaven rich with embers like a faraway field rich with dandelions.

Next morning he and Sam were included with a trainload of prisoners shipped out of Wetzlar.   For three days they sweated out air raids targeted against trains attempting to travel in Germany.

Early on Sunday morning the train was sidetracked in a small town, Sagan, about a hundred miles southeast of Berlin. A perimeter of some fifty wooden shacks lined the far side of the railroad yard as housing for slave laborers kept on hand to repair bomb-damaged tracks. In other marshaling yards Sam had seen hundreds of laborers urgently repairing damaged tracks, but here on this morning, as he looked out of the compartment window, all was quiet.

The sidetracked POWs waited for whatever would come next. The stillness gave Sam the feeling that the journey that was his life had come to an end.

Suddenly, a girl tapped on the compartment window. Her face and smile reminded him of Sandra. A rag shawl was wrapped around her head and brought down into a tattered coat. He cracked the window open far enough to allow conversation. She spoke in a language only he could understand. In a moment he instructed in English, "Russ. No good. Want soap."

Sam gave her half of his only bar of soap. She jumped up and down with glee, then ran back to the perimeter of shacks.

After more waiting the prisoners were herded into a column and moved down a roadway. Buck said, "I hope we're not getting marched into a Nazi hell-hole like they have for the Jews."

There was only barren ground along the road, but on the far-off horizon, beyond countless walls of barbed wire, there was a forest. As they approached the barbed wire they saw hundreds of drab one-story wooden buildings. They were brought to a halt before a ten-foot-high barbed wire wall.

Beyond the first barbed wire were eight feet of entangled coils of more barbed wire, and beyond this was another ten-foot-high barbed wire wal—in all, an impenetrable barrier. The barrier stretched into the distance, punctuated by tall guard towers on timber frameworks in monotonous repetition.

A huge double gate was opened. The in-coming purge was ushered into a forward enclosure of a vast prison camp with several separate compounds.

Sam said, "This is the graveyard end of the U.S.A. "bean patch" camp we started from. We've come from the beginning and made it through the war to be buried here."

"Pick up your spirits, Hatch. We're going to last through to freedom here."

They moved through another gateway to where prisoners were waiting to spot friends among the new arrivals.

"At ease," a U.S. Air Force major sounded as the gates grated shut. "You are in the West Compound of Stalag Luft Three. I'm Major Peyser, the prisoner of war in charge of rations. We have seventeen barracks, called blocks, and we have a cookhouse, three outdoor toilet buildings, some other buildings, and a meeting hall where we'll take you soon to hear from your Senior Officer. You'll notice a wooden guard rail about a foot off the ground about thirty feet from the barbed wire. Cross that rail and machine guns will open up at you. A kriegie's life here is a cheap commodity. So watch yourselves.

"By Geneva Convention rules, enlisted men and officers are held in separate camps, and officers cannot be put to work. This is an officer's camp, but we do have a few enlisted airmen here for the work, like distributing food. All rations, both German and Red Cross, are issued to the Senior Officer for distribution. The camp is run with military order under his command. Blocks are shut up at night, with police dogs roving the compound looking for someone to bite, so stay inside after the guards close the doors. That's all for now."

After the new POWs were showered and deloused they were herded to the meeting hall. The interior had no furniture. The new prisoners sat on the floor.

"Attention!"

An eagle rank colonel entered. His neat uniform distinguished him from the many prisoners wearing makeshift garb.

"As you were. I'll be brief, since a church service is scheduled to start here. I'm Colonel Dean Raymond, your prisoner of war Senior Officer. You've had the bad luck of joining us in this barbed wire trap where we are challenged to keep honorable military discipline under the enemy. We will have inspection every Saturday. Rooms and person will be kept immaculate. I see faces that need shaving. Mustaches are permitted but no beards. As captives of the enemy, a soldier here who does not follow his Senior Officer's orders is subject to court-martial as a traitor when the war is over. I'll be giving you more information and orders from day to day through your block commanders. On your way out you will be assigned to blocks and rooms."

"This can't be," Buck said. "The war is supposed to be over for us, and now we've got the same inspector general that was on our back before we were shot down. Inspection every Saturday? Where does he think he is—West Point?"

Sam said, "I'll bet you wish now you would have visited with him when his son got killed as your co-pilot."

A thin prisoner, walking with a twisted motion, limped forward on a cane and approached Sam and Buck. His eyes were surrounded by pink scar tissue that was common to airmen who had been caught in a burning ship without goggles above their oxygen masks. The prisoner's hands also bore the disfigurement of fire.

"Hi, Sam and Buck!"

"Walter Plank?" Sam fumbled.

"Go away. You're supposed to be dead," Buck blurted.

"It's me all right."

"My God!" Sam exclaimed.

"I see they finally got you, too," Walt said.

"Hey, you got a baby girl!" Buck exclaimed.

"Was it a girl?"

"Yeah. Everything went fine," Sam said.

A kriegie put a hand on Walt's shoulder. "Please carry on outside. We'd like to begin the church service."

"Your navigator made it. He got here two weeks ago."

"Clifford Sheridan Phillips the Third! What about Reddick—the Command Pilot flying my right seat?"

"Major Reddick? Yeah. He's here, too. He's on Colonel Raymond's staff."

"Christ, Reddick and Phillips!" Buck exclaimed. It was a wild time bailing out!"

"Well, Phillips is here, six feet tall with his big hands and feet," Walt said.

"Hey, you guys. We want to start church. Outside, please!"

As they crushed their way through kriegies, Walt continued, "Sooner or later they get us all. But we're the lucky ones who are still alive. We're just trapped in this barbed wire hell."

PART III

The Prison

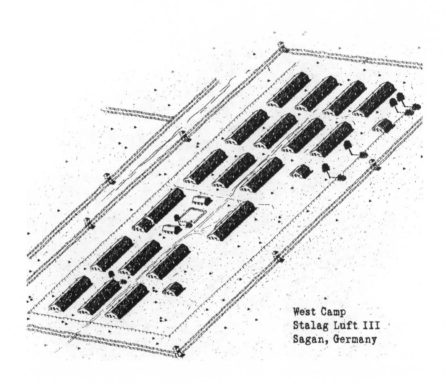

West Camp
Stalag Luft III
Sagan, Germany

THE PRISON: CHAPTER ONE

STALAG LUFT III, GERMANY: Stalag Luft III (Camp Air III) was about one hundred miles southeast of Berlin in land cleared from a forest in lower Silesia. As Allied air-war casualties increased, the camp had been extended until it contained a population of about fifteen thousand former combat flyers held in five separate compounds. The newest, West Compound, was opened in April 1944 to hold fifteen hundred. Now, to absorb more *Kriegsgefangenen*, a name shortened to kriegies by the captives, twenty-three-hundred were being crowded into this compound.

The weekly German food ration per prisoner was 4 lb. 10 oz. of potatoes; 3 lb. 13 oz. of bread; 7 oz. of blood sausage and meat; 5 1/2 oz. of hardtack; 1 oz. of barley flour; 5 oz. of sugar; 1 1/2 oz. of limburger cheese; 4 oz. of unspecified cheese; and 6 oz. of margarine. The total calorie count came to 677 per day. Lt. Col. Sneed, the medical officer, a flight surgeon who had been captured in Italy, maintained that 2500 calories per day were needed to adequately sustain life over prolonged captivity.

Red Cross Parcels were the only source from which the needed additional food might be obtained. These came primarily from the U.S., but some came from Canada, England, Argentina, and New Zealand. As they arrived by train from Sweden or Switzerland, they were stored in the *vorlager* for distribution by the highest ranking prisoner, the Senior Officer in West Compound, Colonel Dean Raymond. German rations, calculated on a population basis, were delivered directly to the senior officer for immediate distribution.

To aid survival, kriegies organized into "combines" and received rations as a unit. A combine varied in size from three to fifteen persons. It usually consisted of the kriegies who shared a room. A standard block held one hundred forty kriegies in thirteen rooms of various sizes with triple-

181

deck bunks. The Senior Officer assigned the supervisors and workers who distributed the food to the Block Commanders who then supervised the distribution within the blocks. The arrival of sufficient Red Cross Parcels to prevent starvation was always in question, forcing a no-win guessing game in which the Senior Officer had to weigh the risk of starvation later against the desire to feed the hungry now. One Red Cross Parcel per week per prisoner as supplement to the German rations was called "full rations." In the present week, although the reserve was low, Colonel Raymond still had the compound on full rations. The enlisted men received the rations for the Senior Officer's staff and prepared their meals. These enlisted men worked with the other enlisted men who were doing the work of food handling for the entire compound. This situation invited the corruption which was soon to come.

Kriegies found uses for almost everything. The plywood Red Cross shipping crates were transformed into chairs. Empty tins from rations were reworked into eating platters with seamed edges, cooking pans, light fixtures, miniature cook-stoves called *klim can burners*, and countless other innovations.

The klim can burner was a small can punctured with hundreds of nail holes and encased in a larger can with air holes cut at the lower circumference. Air came in through the lower holes and flowed into the fire-can with a draft that burned about anything that could be cut into matchstick-size slivers. Some models boasted a forced air draft obtained from a hand cranked blower. These marvels of fire magic were the most prized possessions of every compound.

For news the Germans provided the newspaper *O.K.*, for Overseas Kid, in English, and, in front of the cookhouse, from a loudspeaker, the news in German. Each block had a newsman, the kriegie who could best understand the German news to translate it.

There was also a secret news source under strict control. The penalty for this activity—contact with the enemy—was death. Colonel Raymond, under secret orders, was organizing an Intelligence-gathering system to feed information back to this channel.

On this day, when Buck Pierce, Sam O'Brien, and Edward Briggs arrived, a Y.M.C.A. donation of seven musical instruments and a Red Cross shipment of shirts, trousers, and shoes also arrived. Sam jubilantly received a shirt and trousers to cover his underwear suit.

Buck, Sam, and Briggs were quartered with Walt in Room 7 of Block 169 that was surrounded by rows of somber, one-story wooden blocks on treeless and grassless flat land. Some thirty feet from the room window, a building called the "abort" issued odors of human waste. The view from the room faced west, showing a barbed wire barrier and guard towers, and beyond this bare land, and further away a scrubby forest of pine trees. Within the twelve-by-fourteen-foot interior were two three-deck bunks facing each other with a table and benches in between, directly before the door. In the near left corner was an eighteen-inch-square stove three feet tall. Beside the door were two shallow clothes cabinets. Beyond the table, under the window, a clothes cabinet was laid on its side to serve as a work table and food locker.

Buck studied the room and quipped, "There's only space to walk lock step."

"It takes a while to settle in, coming from freedom," said Walt. "It was easier for me since I was in the hospital and Interrogation Solitary six weeks before getting here. The way to get privacy is to walk the perimeter."

"What do you mean, the perimeter?" Briggs asked.

"You don't know? That's the track we've beat around the camp inside the guard rail. It's a place to pace for guys still fighting being caged. We try to help the newcomers. They've all got to tell their story of how they got here— 'There I was at twenty thousand feet with fighters and flak to all sides of me.' We try to listen to them. We've all got a lot to get out of our system, so we've got to listen even though we're sick of hearing the stories."

"I'll take the lower bunk on the right," Buck said after surveying the room.

"Cliff's got that bunk. He's out walking the perimeter," Walt informed.

"Clifford S. Phillips, the Third? He's with us in this room?" Buck asked.

"Yeah. Since I knew him, we lined up together to get the same room—"

Sam interrupted, "We'd better decide who's in charge here. Since Buck and Walt are both Captains, it gets down to their date of rank. Let us know so we can start out smooth."

"We were promoted on the same day," Walt said.

Buck answered, "Then we go by who comes first in the alphabet, Pierce or Plank? So I'm in charge. Clifford Sheridan Phillips can find himself another bunk."

"Buck, you said you were through with the military shit," Sam interjected. "Cliff is settled in. I think it should be first come first served."

"Me, too," Walt said.

"Okay, we'll start out smooth. Everybody stays where they are, but this is just the beginning of me being locked up with his majesty from Princeton."

"What am I walking into?" the *Bare Lass* navigator, Phillips, broke in. "Buck! Briggs! And Sam the bird man! You look like hell, especially you, Buck. What happened to you? Where have you been? They caught me as soon as my parachute hit ground. I came through the bail-out fine— with only the cut I got in my leg. I'll fire up my klim can burner and brew some ersatz—that's German for artificial— coffee. It will be weak and awful, but hot. I want to shut up and just listen to what's happened to you guys."

"Pilot to Navigator: It will be a treat to see you just listen. Is this going to be for as long as we're stuck in the same room?"

"Hey, Buck, you said we were going to start out smooth."

"Right, Sam. Being in charge, I'm going to run a loose crew, except for Phillips talking too much—hell, who am I kidding?—I'm damn glad to see you alive, Cliff Phillips!"

At this time, Dean Raymond was walking with his West Point classmate Henry Bellrage, who had been shot down one-and-a-half years ago on the coast of France. Dean was proclaiming, ". . . Officially, I was sent into combat as an inspector general, but I suspect now that I was duped. I should have realized I'd over-reached my protest when a key general asked, in my presence, 'Has Billy Mitchell risen from the dead? Do we need more than a Billy Mitchell court-martial to quiet the "victory through air power" fanatics?' I see now that I was sent out to troubleshoot as a way to get rid of me in Washington."

"So, Dean, we've still got the old generals and admirals trying to fight this war like another World War One. Understandable. That's how they got their fame. That's all they know. They truly believe war can only be won with sea battles and land invasions."

"Henry, as air force planners we sold our country the strategy that we could win the war from the sky. To win this way, our country locked-in on our promise and is building the thousands of aircraft we asked for. We are under honor now to deliver."

"We both went down in honor."

"Don't speak for me. I didn't get shot down knocking out a critical target. Henry, the air force has lost control of when and where we bomb. We know from the bombing of England that bombing civilians only strengthens a country's will to fight, but that's what we're doing. I'm seeing our promised way to victory twisted into massacre for vengeance. It's a disgrace."

"I went down bombing submarine pens. That was definitely a worthy target."

"Right. But that was on a clear day. That's our problem. We need clear days, but the weather won't cooperate. We want to wait for clear sky targets like Oil. Since the English gave up daylight bombing as too dangerous, they have insisted we should abandon our daylight, pin-point bombing strategy. But we know that as of January, bombing at night, they were only getting half of their bombs within three miles of their aiming point."

"So, you were not only fighting the old guard army and navy, but also the weather and the English."

"It was a dragon with many heads, Henry. At Stanmore Headquarters General Butler kept trying to get American officers with higher rank than the British so we could outrank them in decision-making. But Leigh-Mallory managed to keep the British dominating. It was a bureaucratic hell that drove me to combat and delivered me here."

"There I was at twenty thousand feet with fighters and flak to all sides of me," Henry commented.

"What?"

"Nothing. It's just a little prison song we sing."

Dean continued, "I'm down. The brass is rid of me. But the top priority for this war is still to knock out Oil. In a modern war the enemy can't fight without—"

"I see the Hauptmann, you know, Captain Eiler," Henry interrupted. "Ask him why we got shorted on potatoes yesterday. He wouldn't short us without orders. I don't know what's going on. It's a bad sign—"

"He left word I'm to meet him—I don't want to leave you with the impression that I don't respect the need for ground forces for mop-up occupation after the enemy is helpless—"

"It's a bad sign. We're in trouble if they keep shorting us on potatoes."

"But in the last months we've been bombing targets to prepare for a huge invasion of Europe. General Spaatz kept telling the Combined Chiefs that there would be no need for a bloody invasion if they would just allow the air force to concentrate on the targets that would force Hitler to surrender." . . .

At this time, Buck, Sam, and Cliff were walking to the Staff Officers' quarters to visit the Command Pilot who had been shot down with them.

"I'll be damned!" Major Reddick called when he saw them. "You all lived through our fiery bail-out! What about the rest of the crew?"

"Clair, the Ball Turret, made it. The krauts caught him with me," Buck said. "Then they hauled me away on a stretcher."

Phillips speculated, "Maybe the rest of the crew escaped and got back to England."

"Pierce, when I saw the ship pull up on fire, I thought—'stupid cowboy, he's riding that fire to put it out.' I kept yelling, 'bail out!' until the goons knocked me into the dirt. You deserve the Silver Star for how you flew to save your bomber."

"I hated to desert that patched-up crate."

"You're looking good, Major," Sam said. "You've got yourself a good deal here. I hear you've got a staff mess with enlisted men to fix your meals."

"Lieutenant O'Brien, if you are chiding me, complain to your room commander and let him go up through channels. We're still military here. I knew Colonel Raymond at headquarters. He asked me to serve on his staff. I didn't seek command responsibility."

Phillips interceded, "We didn't come to argue. We've got a special tie with you. We're the *Bare Lass* survivors, all glad we're still alive."

"Let's not ass kiss, Phillips," Buck said. "The Major wants to hear from us through channels. You field grade officers with your staff mess haven't caught on yet that we're all just kriegies—all coyote rank to the goons. Pass that up through channels."

Sam said, "I was just kidding you, Reddick."

"Buck is just ornery from being hungry," Phillips said. "Can we all leave friendly?"

Buck said, "I'll be more friendly if you drop by Room 7 of Block 169—as a kriegie."

"Your attitude, Captain Pierce, is a threat. We are still in the air force, even if we won't get paid 'til we get freed."

Raymond and Bellrage, still walking, crossed the open area where the count of prisoners, Appell, was held twice a day. Raymond was still chattering, ". . . ground generals ordered us to destroy Hitler's air force as preparation for a ground invasion, planned for—I won't say when."

"Let's talk about what's happening here, Dean."

"In a moment . . . Let me finish. We saw no need to take out Hitler's air force. It was going to be useless without oil anyway. But we were ordered to destroy it to prepare for the invasion. We were also ordered to destroy railroad yards to prepare for the invasion before we could go for Oil. Then Leigh-Mallory gave us priority assignment to destroy rocket launchers aimed at England before we could go for Oil— in spite of the fact that our Eglin Field tests showed that the rocket launchers could best be knocked out by minimum altitude attacks of fighter bombers."

"Dean, I know we had to knock out Oil. But what about the potatoes?"

"We were being pulled further and further away from our promise to achieve victory through air power. So, Henry, we are going to have an invasion. With horrendous ground fighting. General Billy Mitchell, if you could only rise from the dead and champion our—"

"Leave the war behind you, Dean! Your war talk is frying in my head, and you still haven't told me what you're going to do about the potato shortage."

"I'm going to see Hauptmann Eiler right now."

"I'm going to hit my sack and rest my brain."

Next day, April 23, 1944, an eighteen-year-old 2nd Lt. bombardier, José Cabrera, from Bodega Bay, California, occupied the empty bunk of Room 7, Block 169. Cabrera was broad-chested and muscular with rusty brown hair, darker than Sam's red hair. His brown eyes roamed the room of his new world anxiously. He had left the U.S. only three weeks ago. As he lay in his bunk he kept talking. ". . . I haven't even written home since I left. This can't be real. Coming across Germany with our fighters blasting the trains, I was sure we would never make it. I saw five wrecked locomotives, two of them still smoking."

Then he jumped down from his bunk and looked through the window, as if he were expecting someone. Then he circled the table several times, and finally he lifted himself back up to his third tier bunk and asked, "What do you do to pass the time here?—It was my first mission. There were holes of clear sky but mostly big heavy clouds, and the enemy fighters were queuing up where we had to look into the sun to see them—"

"Come on, José," Briggs interrupted, "let's take a walk and talk about it."

Next day, Dean Raymond and Henry Bellrage visited while they sat on tree stumps in the sun. "Henry, I want you on my staff to head food distribution and get your meals prepared for you. It's not right for you to be a one-man combine."

"I headed rations once. The cheating demoralized me. I like my way better."

"You're not talking like a major. It's your duty to assume command when asked."

"I've been down so long that maybe I'm 'around the bend,' to your eyes. We old timers have each found our own way to make the best of being here. You'll understand better in time. I'm trying to earn my pay. For one thing, I've organized courses that may get college credit when we get home."

"Henry, have I loaded too much talk on you? I've been so intent on sharing the news of how our integrity has been violated, I haven't considered you."

"It's been rough, listening to you tell how our plans got twisted into vengeance killing and our crews got killed for generals of World War One mentality. Why did you pick me to talk about it? Why not Major Reddick? He served with you in Headquarters."

"Reddick doesn't care. When General Spaatz fanatically bucked his superiors to save our strategy I was with those who backed him. Reddick was kissing ass to get a promotion. Reddick is a career officer, a lock-step thinker."

"But you put him on your staff."

"Yes. To follow orders, not to visit."

"Why not put him in charge of food distribution?"

"No, he's better to help with discipline."

"And I'm better for visiting?"

"Obviously."

"Then tell me what's been bringing us so many kriegies lately."

"I told you we were ordered to destroy the Luftwaffe to prepare for the invasion. We got clear skies a few weeks ago, and we had what's become known as the "big week." We shot down 600 German aircraft. But it cost us thirty-three valiant fighters and 240 four-engine bombers. That's 2433 crew. There's where your most recent flood of kriegies has been coming from, Henry."

"I've been seeing the guys come in, and the things you've been telling me are still frying in my head. But please tell me what you've done about the potato problem."

"I'll tell you what I've done. I've put my West Point classmate Major Henry Bellrage in charge of that problem."

"Not me. I've been down too long and you're the Senior Officer. It's past time for you to drop the war and take up the fight for our survival here."

By May 1, Colonel Raymond had learned that he had only empty talking power against Luftwaffe decisions. The Red Cross Parcel reserve had decreased, and he had weighed the need to put the compound on half rations—thirty-five percent below the minimum calorie count.

At 9:30 A.M. of May 1, the combine of Room 7, Block 169, was on the assembly field awaiting Appell. Each block was in a separate five-man-deep formation. The seventeen block formations, totaling about twenty-five hundred prisoners, were arranged in a U-shape around the center of the field. Colonel Raymond stood at the center of the U, and each kriegie block commander stood in front of his block. While awaiting the arrival of the Germans, the kriegie Block Commanders were making announcements.

Lt. Col. Burtram B. Fanning, commander of Block 169, announced, "This week we will begin half rations, because no Red Cross Parcels have arrived. Parcels have to cross Germany to get here, and our offensive against trains is building. You can add that up. A combine of six will get only three Parcels this week.

"Your Senior Officer will conduct an inspection on Saturday. Few of you have full uniforms and none of you has a change of clothes, but we're going to tidy up as best we can. If your shaving water is cold and your razor is dull, get used to it. We will have clean-shaven faces."

In the background, Hauptmann Eiler approached with two of his staff and a contingent of six guards. Eiler saluted

Raymond and received a return salute. This was the formality prescribed by the POW Articles of the Geneva Convention of 1929. The Luftwaffe did not salute with the Nazi party's upward thrust of a stiff arm but with their own one hand movement that was much the same as the American salute.

Next, Eiler proceeded to the nearest formation and exchanged salutes with the kriegie Block Commander. Then the count began with the Germans pacing briskly, always exchanging salutes before beginning to count the next block. If the number of the count did not match with the number in the Luftwaffe register, or if the Germans intended to do quarters or tunnel-work investigation somewhere, the kriegies would be kept in formation, perhaps for hours. Today the dismissal order came promptly.

When back in their room, Combine 7 gathered around the table. Walt said, "I have to leave pretty soon to catch the German news on the loudspeaker."

"We've got to talk about how to keep going on half rations," Briggs pleaded.

"Talking won't help," said Sam. "We've got to escape, but we can't dig a tunnel when all the buildings are on concrete pillars with space underneath for the ferrets to poke with steel rods. Anyway, the North Compound tunnel got fifty poor sons of bitches shot six weeks ago. Who wants to try a tunnel?"

"The kriegies transferred in from other compounds say there hasn't been an escape that worked since Stalag Luft III was started," said Briggs. "If we're going to escape, it's going to have to be with some bright new angle."

"I hear you volunteering to come up with a 'bright new angle,'" Buck told Briggs.

"I'll take the job, but don't expect miracles."

"I figure our best chance to last with less food," Sam reckoned, "is to slow down, like bears in winter, and wait for the invasion to free us."

"You're awfully quiet, Phillips. What are you thinking?" Buck asked.

"Several things. First, we get five packages of cigarettes in each Red Cross Parcel. I abhor cigarettes being sent in place of food, but the cigarettes are coming, and I propose to trade my share at the Acco for food."

"That's a good idea," Buck responded. "We'll give each man his share of the cigarettes. Those who don't smoke can trade them at the Acco."

"What is this Acco?" José asked.

"I'll take you by on the way to the cookhouse, Joe," Walt said. "It's a place for trading that we kriegies have set up. Everything has a price in points kept in a record book. The points vary according to the demand for what you want."

"As of now, I've just quit smoking," Briggs announced.

"Let's plant a garden," José suggested. "The Red Cross has sent seeds. I know we've only got our table forks and knives and spoons to work the ground, but I'm willing to try. There's some empty ground outside our window, and I've got experience."

Phillips interjected, "I got cut off. I have another idea. If we're not going to get enough food, the least we can do is drink hot water. We get a four-ounce can of powdered coffee in every American Red Cross Parcel. If we just put a pinch of it on the handle end of a spoon and add it to hot water, we can stretch it out for a long time. We can have a coffee session to give us a lift every afternoon at four, like the British with their tea."

"Great plan!" Walt approved as various voices joined him.

Phillips continued, "Whittling up stumps the goons left in the ground, we have fuel for firing up our klim can burner. I volunteer to be stump whittler, fire master, and coffee maker."

"I'll take on the job of keeping check on how the Colonel's staff is dividing the food that comes in," Buck promised. "I'll check, too, on how the enlisted men of our block are splitting up the food for our different rooms, including their own. Okay, Walt, go get the news. We'll talk about the Saturday inspection later."

Buck went out to walk the perimeter. Up ahead he saw Colonel Raymond walking alone. His heart pumped faster as he debated whether to walk faster, catch up with him and introduce himself. *What would happen then? Should I go straight into giving him details of Tom's last flight? How much has Randi told him about the bedroom stuff at the Lord Raglan? If Randi broke up with him, is he blaming me?* While he pondered, he saw Raymond turn and start walking toward him. *I'm going to talk with him, but not today. Walking the perimeter with him is not the right way.*

Buck reversed his direction and walked away.

Dean Raymond's mind was back in McLean, Virginia. He was home with his wife, Katherine. Now there were just the two of them in a home with too many bedrooms. *By September the trees will be golden. By Christmas I may be there.* He could see red and green Christmas lights sparkling on the windows under the snow of the roof edged with icicles.

"How is my friend of West Point?" he heard.

"Pushing my legs to get into better shape, Henry."

"I'll join you for one lap. I'm not as ambitious as you."

"I'm older than the prisoners I command. I've got to work harder to be physically fit for whatever is ahead for us. When our troops get here, we may have to help in the battle for liberation. I'm secretly going to organize the camp to be ready if needed."

"I used to be more eager like you, but I've been worn down, transformed, liberated, say it as you will. I'll have been a prisoner two years come October 21."

"Did I hear you use the word 'liberated' for what's happened to you caged up here?"

"Up is down, and down is up and prison can be freedom. Here, all is a paradox in my 'around the bend' vision."

"As you keep talking I'm beginning to think you really are around the bend."

"Then let me listen, Dean. After all your talking you still haven't said how things are with Katherine and how she and you are healing from the loss of Tom."

"That's true. I'm beginning to realize how much the war has consumed me. My private life's been all knotted up inside, lost to me, while I've lived in the war of brass and krauts. When I was Inspector General I felt too many lives hung on my work. I couldn't afford private feelings. You know my history, Henry. My eagles could be stars if I'd been less ruled by my convictions."

"You've made enemies by not being meek, but so what? Look at me. I'm only a major."

"That's because you were shot down."

"It doesn't matter. I've got new dreams. Non-military."

"Don't say that, Henry. The peacetime air force is going to need you."

"You think that now. But you're the new man down."

"Right. I carry a lonely feeling being here as the leader of shot-down flyers who could have won the war but weren't given the chance. I can't tell them either."

"You don't need to. Their challenge here is to forgive the past and find God's love for their future. You may not understand what I'm saying now, Dean, but you will."

"I resent your self-righteous attitude. I am not going to allow myself to go around the bend."

"Friend, let's go make a cup of coffee. Do you have a klim can burner?"

"I'm not finished."

"I know you're not finished. You've only been here two weeks. If you don't have a klim can burner, I'll help you make one."

"I'll have my staff make us some coffee. We've got a couple of chairs there. I still need your view on the food situation. I'm weighing the wisdom of putting the compound on quarter rations."

"I can't help you with that decision. But we'll do the coffee your way today. Next time it's my turn. You've got to make a klim can burner. You've got to be able to make out on your own, do your own good work. You haven't asked me, but when we're sipping coffee, I want to tell you about the college courses. I'm hoping to offer actual college credit."

"That's good. I want to hear more about that. I don't want to get into talking about the war again, Henry. I've got to keep my mind on my new life here."

On Wednesday, May 3, Buck put on his uniform blouse with his wings and captain's bars. His uniform trousers carried the press of being laid under his mattress overnight. He was clean-shaven and his shoes were shined. At 2:00 P.M. of this warm day, he knocked on the door to the quarters of the West Compound's Senior Officer.

"What is it, Captain?" he heard as Raymond opened the door.

"I'm Brewster Pierce. Your son was my co-pilot on the day he got killed. I've been wanting to talk to you for a long time, about him, and how it happened. I hope Captain Scott gave you my message at least."

"Come in. It's been three months since you sent me an excuse instead of meeting me. A lot's changed. It's a different world for us. I hope you've changed."

"You were investigating why Tom was flying that day. I was the pilot who flew him. You could have blamed me. You know the old scapegoat, 'pilot error.' You were investigating down through channels. It wasn't for me to go to the Inspector General. It would have been easy for you to come to me."

"There was more to your problem than that, Captain. You were angry because a friend of yours was killed on that takeoff. If you had come to see me, I could have explained that I was against that mission, too."

"It's hard to believe that, Colonel. You had us in an offensive. I'll admit I wasn't doing things right. I didn't even write home. I was bushed, but it's true I was mad. You were from Washington where our orders came from. But I still intended to see you. I'd promised Randi I would, and I wanted to."

"You promised who? Are you referring to Captain Scott by her first name?"

"She's a special friend to me, but I didn't come to talk about her. The war is over for you and me, and I thought it was past time to talk to you."

195

"The Captain Scott you mention has told me some things about Tom's last flight. I hear that it happened so fast he couldn't have suffered."

"Colonel, I came to tell you he was a damn good pilot. You can be proud of him. The way he flew, you'd never know it was his first mission. He showed a lot of courage. I gave him a thumbs up once for how good he was flying. We were in a slot where he had to fly a lot of formation, and he held us tucked in close like an expert. I didn't get to visit with him before the flight, so I haven't got any personal talk to give you."

"To you it may not seem like much, your coming to tell me. But your coming means a lot to me. You were with him to the last. It gives me a personal connection. He was so young."

"I didn't mean to upset you, mentioning Randi. I didn't know you still . . ."

"Captain, you can't be as naive as you sound. You're taunting me. You can't expect me to believe you're a special friend of Randi Scott. You're just a ranch-hand boy to her."

"I came here to talk decent, not to be horse-whipped. As for Randi, if you and her are so close, she would have told you her grandmother is a full-blood Sioux. She told me, because she knows I've got Indian friends. We live in the same part of the West." Buck stood up. "I'm going to leave," he said as he walked away.

"Come back, Captain. That's an order."

"You can't order me to be friendly. I came here friendly, and you laid into me like I was a scalawag—I say you're too old for Randi."

"Be careful, Captain. I'm the Senior Officer here."

"I'm not looking for trouble. I just want to be left alone."

For the next few days Buck was left alone, but he felt his independence was not as secure as the temporary peace indicated.

Saturday, May 6, arrived and with it, the impending inspection. Walt, Cliff, and José had worked hardest to tidy up the room and their personal appearance. Nobody had used the Red Cross shoe polish until today.

Ed Briggs, feeling the stubble left after his shave with a dull razor, said, "If you can sharpen a razor by rubbing it back and forth inside a glass, I haven't got the knack yet."

Cliff said, "Toilet paper. That's my dream. My GIs finished my last roll."

"I'm saying again, I'm not pressuring any of you to dandy up for this inspection," Buck emphasized. "The brass figures we would live like pigs if they didn't inspect us. If I ever slack off being as clean as I can be with no way to take a bath, let me know."

"Buck, it's easier to go along with the inspection than fight it," Walt said.

"I'm saying things are bad enough here without getting pressure from our Brass."

"I believe there isn't one of us that isn't helped by pressure coming from the top," Walt replied. "Take me. I haven't shined my shoes until today, and I feel better for it."

"Oh?" Buck replied acidly. "Maybe I should order an inspection every day so we can all feel better more often."

Cliff sought mischief . . . "I'm looking at this inspection as theater. 'All the world's a stage. And all the men and women only players.' It's been a good first act, but God knows how I'll feel by the time the curtain falls if Buck is going to keep playing the Lone Ranger."

Buck shot back, "Sign up for a play if you're so damned eager for theater."

Cliff grinned. "I already have."

"What happened to Hatch, our peacemaker?" José asked.

Sam said, "We're living peaceful, considering how we're crowded in with each other day and night all the time. I'm not hearing arguing, I'm hearing different ideas. Some of us are living with pain from being torn up and burned and all the rest, including getting skinnier, but nobody's complaining. I want to write a poem about what I'm not hearing, except when I wake up at night and hear the groaning."

"Attention!" Walt called.

Lt. Col. Fanning entered. "At ease. Your Senior Officer has asked the block commanders to conduct the inspection.

I'm not going to be a hard ass this time. I'm checking for the basics. I expect beds to be made up tight enough to bounce a coin, and I expect room and person to be clean and everyone to be clean-shaven."

He looked at the bunks and said, "Your beds are not up to standard. As for cleanliness—mediocre. I see that your room commander is not clean-shaven. Report to my room with an explanation before Appell tonight, Captain Pierce."

"That won't be necessary. I can explain now. I shave on Wednesdays."

"You will shave every day from now on, Captain."

"I've only got one sharp blade left and sharpening blades with a glass does not work for me. Once a week is enough."

"All of you should know that you can be court-martialed for your conduct while in the hands of the enemy."

"Hang your court-martial on a tree, Fanning. I'm a shot-down pilot with a body knocked out of whack. Nobody's going to lock me up because I didn't shave every day. While we're at it, remember when you wouldn't be friendly with me back at Clichy hospital? You were chicken shit already then. My size will be worth more than your rank before we get freed."

Lt. Col. Fanning faced Buck with stiff posture and contained vehemence. The combine remained tensely frozen until the Lt. Col. faced away and left the room.

Buck closed the door.

"It wouldn't have been that tough to shave, Buck," Walt said. "Do you want a mob here with lice and diseases and God knows what?"

"You've got a chip on your shoulder, Buck," Briggs said, "and you're getting us involved. They should have taught us more about what's expected of us if we got shot down. Now there are all these questions."

"There's more involved here than a shave," Buck said. "There's a sick attitude here that the best brains have the highest rank. Everyone forgets who got us here, locked up and hungry, with machine guns pinning us in. But even here the highest rank is still pushing us. I've got memories of buddies who were killed following stupid orders."

Sam smiled, "I think you are an ornery bastard, Buck, with nerve pains running from your neck down through your arms and making you spoil for a fight. I've come through too much with you to be mad at you now."

"If it weren't for your orneriness, the Focke-Wulfes would have me in the grave," Phillips said. "Let's hang together. That's all we've got going for us."

"Don't speak for me," Walt protested. "I think your Christian parents didn't teach you enough, Buck, but I need to be a better Christian myself. So I'll be forgiving."

Buck answered, "Walt, with the future we're facing, I hope we can get beyond just forgiving each other. What do you say, Joe?"

"I don't know what you're fussing about. I could use more help in the garden, though. I'll never get it ready to plant in time if I have to do it myself."

Buck ended the conversation with, "Let's go walk a lap."

By June 1, the secret news system was working smoothly. A kriegie would enter a block and proceed down the hallway, saying *soup's on*. One person from each room would then drift into the wash room. The news was written on paper thin enough to be quickly eaten if an alarm came that a German had intruded the security net. The source was such a closely guarded secret that no kriegie ever admitted knowing it. After the news was read, the representative of each room would go back and tell the news to his combine. It was a strict rule that the secret news should never be talked about after it was heard.

On June 6, Ed Briggs came back from soup's on and told the gathered Combine 7, "I'm going to tell you once. Hear it, and forget it. Early today the Allies landed in the Normandy section of the northwest coast of France. It's one hell of a big invasion."

"There can't be a rule against singing, 'I'll Be Home for Christmas,'" Buck rejoiced.

"Let's celebrate by bashing some of our food store," José Cabrera proposed.

Briggs intervened, "Not yet. We've got to all pretend this is just another dreary day until we get the news from the Germans."

Next day Hauptmann Eiler brought in a copy of *Volkischer Beobachter*. The headlines read, "Die Invasion Hat Begonnen." Release of joy spread like wild fire.

But the invasion advanced less fast than anticipated. A more immediate anticipation was the "Barrel of Fun" that was to open July 24. The theater had been created from cans, crates, and diverse junk and cloth. Cliff was an innovative genius of the theater team.

Even more immediate was the Fourth of July. A day of sports was planned—boxing, gymnastics, volley ball, and a softball game. A crowd of twenty-five hundred was assured.

Saturday, June 17, Fanning announced: "We are going to quarter rations." . . .

On this day, the number of guards at Appell was doubled, and after the count, they surrounded the formations. Minutes of waiting gave way to hours. Kriegies suspected that the secret radio was being hunted. After four hours of standing, they were dismissed.

After Combine 7 had returned to the room, Briggs said cryptically, "I hope we can get some soup out of our pantry today." But soup's on did not come. At noon Briggs said, "I am not going to serve any lunch. That will give us more food for dinner."

"I'm for that," José said. "It's easier to be hungry if I can look forward to dinner."

The lunch that would not be served was a toasted one-fourth-inch slice of margarine-smeared barley bread—a generator of gas regardless, but better toasted.

"We'll have our coffee session at four just the same," Cliff announced.

"We'll have a big dinner," Briggs informed. "A cubic inch of spam, fried potatoes, ersatz coffee, and chocolate-coated barley mush. We'll cut back starting tomorrow to make our food stretch."

Sam, speaking from his own world, said, "Maybe one day the goons are going to call out all the Jewish kriegies and have them line up to get shipped out to a special place."

Walt said, "They wouldn't dare, Hatch. Since the invasion, we've got German prisoners—we could get back at them to get even."

Buck assured, "Hatch, I'm so sure that won't happen I'd go out with you."

"Did anyone see the Germans bring in potatoes and bread today?" José asked.

"Let's get a grip on ourselves," Buck ordered. "We'll pull in our belts and make it on quarter rations. The garden is growing, and we've got our cigarettes to trade at the Acco. Walt, you can help, too. We know some guards will risk bringing in food to trade for American cigarettes. Work on your ferret friend Smitty. I'm going to work on beating the cheating in the food dividing. If there's going to be a shortage from cheating, let it come off the belly fat of the Colonel's mess. Joe, I'm going to help you more with the garden, too."

"That's good. I can't get enough water on it, carrying it with small cans."

"I'll seam some cans together," Buck said. "I'll help you dig, too."

At four o'clock Cliff had coffee ready. The combine took places around the burner flaming under the coffee pot in the table center. After a while, Walt said, "You know I'm missing a finger, but I haven't told you the ring I wore on it got me close to the Catholic Sister Johanna, my German nurse. In England, Marg had told me that ring carried a blessing from a Gypsy Saint Sara. Sister Johanna had been to southern France to worship Saint Sara with the Gypsies. She told me that Gypsies from all over the world gather there every year to wade in the water where Saint Sara rescued the two persecuted holy Marys. They come to receive her blessed powers, like for healing. The Catholic Church even sends a bishop to lead the worship, so that ring was not just a make-believe charm."

"Who got it, Walt? A German Catholic?" asked José.

"Sister Johanna got hold of that ring, and she promised to wear it on her rosary to keep the power working for me. I'm telling you because I want it to work for all of us. If you think I'm crazy, don't laugh. Keep it to yourself."

José said. "I'm Catholic. I wouldn't laugh at a thing like that."

"I'm half Catholic. Who's to say how God works?" Sam took a piece of paper out of his shirt. "Like Walt, I've got something I don't want people to laugh at. I wrote it out:

> We want the garden to grow
> From the dry soil.
> We want our minds not to slow
> From the turmoil.
> We are six combined for survival
> And still each alone
> When we argue and laugh
> To not think of home."

"Nobody's laughing, Sam," Cliff reassured.

Buck said, "I see kriegies moving out for 4:30 Appell. We'd better be on our way."

On the following day, it was obvious that the Germans had not located the secret radio, for soup's on came in on schedule.

In the afternoon, Colonel Raymond asked Walt to walk the perimeter with him, and when they were out of ear-shot, he said, "Captain Plank, because you speak German, we've got work for you in Intelligence. If you volunteer and then violate the secrecy, you will be court-martialed. Before I go further, do you volunteer?"

"Certainly, sir."

"We want you to work at establishing friendships and trust with the Germans. Concentrate on guards and ferrets you feel might give you information on subjects we'll inform you about. You must be able to take pressure from your friends without confiding your reasons for being friendly with the goons. Think about it."

"I don't need to think about it. I am a Christian, and I joined the war to end Hitler's evil, as service to God. That's deeper than any friendship. You can trust me."

"Sign up for Major Bellrage's course to improve your German. Come to me only in an emergency. I'm closely watched. Be walking the perimeter tomorrow at three.

Your contact will join you. His code word is 'Free Trade.' Drift away now."

"Wilco," Walt said, and he started away. As he passed the combine garden he asked Briggs and José, "Where are the other guys? We're supposed to work on this together."

"Cliff is at the theater," Briggs replied. "We told him to go. They need him."

"Buck is working in the shoe shop," José said, "but he made the bucket. He seamed the cans together like a real tinsmith. It hardly leaks. We can carry more water now, but we still need rain. I've got carrots, beets, spinach, corn, onions, turnips, tomatoes, peas, cabbage, and radishes planted. Walt, have your Gypsy Saint bring us rain."

"Are you going to help?" Briggs asked Walt.

"I've got to get the news for Appell. Where's Hatch?"

"He's in the sack," José said. "To make up for not doing more in the garden, he drew me Donald Duck with my kriegie number and me looking through prison bars and holding a sign, 'I Wanted Wings.'"

Briggs said, "He moons too much. He needs something to get him out of his sack."

"How are you doing with escape plans?" Walt asked.

"I'm no miracle worker. If you manage to dig a tunnel the goons wait with rifles as you crawl out like they killed the fifty from North Compound. Our best bet is the invasion."

Walt said, "The day the bullets will be flying here is getting closer. One day the guards will be falling out of the towers dead. Thinking of that keeps my spirits up."

Briggs commented, "Your ideas are getting too big for me to concentrate on digging dirt an inch at a time. Go get the news."

With Walt gone, José said, "I've traded my cigarettes at the Acco for points to gamble on the Fourth of July soft ball game. I won a trophy playing at Bodega Bay, and I think we've got a winning team here."

"Let's lean back on a couple of stumps for a bit," Briggs said.

When they were resting, José reminisced, "My dad fishes for a living. My great-grandfather came from Mexico in the early 1800s, and our family has lived in Bodega Bay ever since. Francisco Bodega y Cuadra sailed in there in 1775. I didn't know any other place until I joined the service, and if I ever get back I'll never leave again. Ed, you come visit me and we'll go out on the ocean and bring in some fish. I can see us with a bottle of beer after a big meal of fish and rice, talking about the days we spent here."

"You gotta come to Nashville. My folks have a fish restaurant along the river, and our home has a porch over-looking boats going by, and some docking at our restaurant."

"No wonder we hit it off, Ed. You and I have both got fishing in our blood."

"Yeah," Briggs said, "but I got married to a girl whose family is into horse farming. I had a fall from a horse when I was a kid, and I haven't been interested in horses since. I'd rather run a fish restaurant if I can't be a pilot."

"What's your wife's name?"

"Joyce. We went through the wedding and off I went. All my life is back in Nashville just getting started, and I'm on the other side of the world."

"What made you join up?"

"I was thinking I'd be drafted anyway, and I wanted to be a pilot. Joe, getting chosen to be a four-engine bomber commander was the biggest honor I ever had."

"I joined to help fight the Japs. After the Japs attacked Pearl Harbor, we were under blackout on the California coast, worried the Japs might even invade. The Army was so scared they even moved all the Japs out to a holding camp near Sacramento."

"Joe, do you think we'd have signed up for the air force if we'd known flying was going to get us here, digging dirt this way in Germany?"

"I don't know that I hit one target," José said. "I am at least going to get a garden out of this crappy Nazi dirt. Growing a garden to fill an empty stomach is not new to me, but it's the first time without my family—Here comes Hatch. We better take his help while we have a chance."

"We're too late. It's time to quit for Appell," Briggs said.

On June 23, five thousand Red Cross Parcels arrived, but after weighing the bombing hazards of rail transportation, Raymond decided to continue quarter rations at least until July.

THE PRISON: CHAPTER TWO

In early July, a package of cigarettes got twenty points at the Acco. A D-bar got 150 points. A twelve-ounce can of spam (chopped pork) brought 85 points. A one-pound can of klim (powdered whole milk) got 100 points. These prices were skewed by the approach of the Fourth of July, because luxury goods were wanted for a celebration bash.

The eight-ounce chocolate D-bar was a prize trade item. The D-bar was only surpassed in price by a can of sweet condensed milk, a rare item coming only in New Zealand Parcels. Shipwrecked flyers, who once may have tossed in bed in longing for their girlfriend now lay awake in longing for the carnal pleasure of a D-bar.

To prevent food from being saved for escape, the Germans punched a pencil-size hole in each can. The cans, received once a week, were immediately resealed with margarine, but in the hot weather of July, careful planning was needed to keep food from spoiling. Canned fish had the shortest life span—three days at very most. Spam was longer lasting and more fatty and appetite-satisfying and so was more valued. But the D-bar reigned supreme.

Even when food shortage left kriegies hungry, it was common practice to save food for an orgy of feasting, days or even weeks ahead. Paradoxically, meals were more delicious here than in the former world with its steak and apple pie for stomachs not as hungry. Time was measured by distance from mealtimes. Whereas, in the world of home, sex talk was publicly taboo, here food talk was taboo.

The big day, the Fourth of July, dawned bright and warm. José said, "God must have loved celebrations when he gave our church so many saints to celebrate."

"This beats any saint's day," Buck replied. "Today we told the King and Queen of England to go to hell. The only place we've still got the British system is in the military with its officers and men like knights and serfs."

"Aren't you enjoying your rank, Captain Pierce?" Cliff challenged.

Buck answered, I'm not saying every-man-for-himself is always best. To get ten guys to be a team in a bomber crew, you need a pilot. But if you haven't noticed, I'm not wearing my rank anymore. Being a kriegie of the German heel-click-ing military is turning my stomach against that crap."

Sam said, "I want to hear about the ball game. I know Joe has two D-bars bet so he must be pretty sure we've got a good team. You'd better be right, Joe. I've gambled all my Acco points on your say-so."

"Me, too," Briggs said, "and so have the rest of us."

"You guys are all betting along with me?"

The combine made a tally and discovered that they had a total of ten D-bars wagered on Jose's team.

"I hope I didn't brag too much. Walt, you and Briggs ought to run the three-legged race. With your right leg bad, you've probably built up your left leg to where you could win."

"Thanks, Joe, but I'm too bent out of shape and wobbly. I know you're only kidding to make me feel good, but I'm feeling good about things I can't tell you about."

"Joe," Buck said, "the garden's coming up, so you're a hero win or lose the game. If it weren't for my arms not working right yet, I'd be in the gymnastic bar competition."

Briggs offered, "Today we'll have a double meat serv-ing—a half inch of spam and some beef stew, plus a potato, and a surprise that Walt can tell you about."

Walt revealed, "I got Smitty to smuggle us a couple of onions strapped to his legs in trade for cigarettes. He said he'd try to bring in a couple of apples today, too."

Briggs added, "We're having barley mush with sugar and the apples if we get them."

"I'll be performing today in a preview of "Barrel of Fun" opening on the 24th," Cliff announced. "It's double-talk planned to go over the goons' heads. Uncle Joe is Stalin. The East is Russia. Hitler is Berlin. Blood sausage is what the Russians are doing to the Germans. You'll figure out the rest. If it works the goons will be wild trying to figure out why we're laughing. The big joke will be if the goons join us in laughing, out of ignorance."

Sam said, "I'm going to make notes for a poem and maybe do a sketch."

"Walt, you should end this coffee-time with a prayer to Saint Sara telling her we need those D-bars!"

"My religion is nothing to joke about."

"That's right, it's nothing to make fun of," José agreed.

"I'm not joking," Clifford said. "I'm Unitarian. We say, 'When in doubt, try it out.'"

Buck said, "Let's go. I heard first call for Appell five minutes ago."

When Appell ended, the twelve-piece-band, Flying Syncopators, paraded at double fortissimo. A kriegie with a shaved head and handlebar mustache led the frolickers following in startling designs of shorts fashioned from linings of Red Cross overcoats.

After the parade, kriegies who had not had a bath or a shower for months of the warm summer splashed furiously in the stagnant water of the fire pool. Beside the pool, boxing matches and gymnastic competition proceeded with a few lapses when over-earnest competitors collapsed from surpassing quarter-ration energy.

In softball, Block 169 faced off against Block 158 at 2:00 P.M. José had been given an extra slice of toast for lunch with an extra smear of butter and liver pâté. He started the game as catcher. At the end of the third of the five-inning game, Block 169 led by a score of four to three. José had brought in two of his team's four scores. In the fourth inning, José went in as pitcher.

"Strike 'em out. You can do it, Joe!" Sam shouted with gusto that broke through his melancholy—the pitch went wide, seemingly ominous. Yet, on Joe's next pitch the batter fanned the air in vain search of the ball. But when 169 got back to bat they were still losing. With the last chance to bat looming for Joe's team, Combine 7 went wild.

When José came up to bat, 169 still trailed five to six, with runners on first and second. Even Walt got excited. "Come through Joe!" he shouted.

Poised by the plate, José rocked his five-foot-eleven sinewy frame back and forth. He held his bat ready in defiant challenge.

Wham! He swung and the ball started a long trip through the sky beyond the furthest fielder. The runner on second rounded the bases and crossed home plate. The man on first rounded second, third, and went home. Behind them came José, pounding the dirt around the bases. Home run! The score was now eight to six.

"You did it!" Walt sang out.

"The game's not over," Buck cautioned. "Block 158 still has another inning to bat."

Another batter came up for 169 and struck out. That retired the team.

"It's up to you, Joe!" Sam shouted. "Three strike-outs and it's over. Pitch it to them dirt-ball dirty!"

The 169 team huddled and then a new pitcher came out. He pitched balls straight and easy to hit. The game was suddenly over with a score of eight to nine. Block 169 had lost.

José came off the field so empty of energy he could barely walk.

"You played one hell of a good game, Joe," Briggs said. "It just wasn't our day to win. Let's get you some hot coffee and sugar cubes."

Buck and Sam walked beside José and gave him support as he stumbled toward their room, dejected and exhausted.

"Why didn't you stay in as pitcher?" Buck asked.

"We were ahead. I was afraid I would lose the game."

Sam said, "You played great! We just lost, that's all."

Briggs added, "It's still the Fourth of July. We've still got the show and the bash."

After the show, Combine 7 went back to their room to prepare for their bash.

Walt brought out three apples and three onions. "If you won't talk about us having these, I may be able to get more," he informed.

Sam complimented Cliff, "You were a big hit, Clifford Sheridan Phillips."

Cliff reflected, "We had people laughing in spite of themselves and where they were. That is theater."

As they started eating, José told Walt, "Thank the guard Smitty for the onion flavor."

"After the spam we still have the biscuit pâté that's got lots of bulk and the powdered-egg-custard apple pie with butter in the crust," Briggs informed.

After the meal, José, lifted from brooding, "My theater is the garden. It needs rain."

Cliff added, in a message that spoke for others, "I ate too much."

At 10 P.M., the guards locked the block for the night. The vicious dogs, now loose outside, barked sporadically. The only contact with the outside world was now the switch that triggered the emergency-light signal on the roof—the light that was to be used only in life-threatening circumstances. For excretory emergencies at night, a ten-gallon vat sat at the end of the hallway. Before midnight, many kriegies were urgently rushing to the vat. They had eaten too much for their starved stomachs to hold. Of Combine 7, Buck, Cliff, and Briggs were among those who lost their dinner.

At the following evening Appell, Fanning announced, "We will have an inspection this Saturday at eleven. Also, your Senior Officer will address you about military discipline and organizing for an emergency."

Later, Buck commented, "Seems like our Independence Day was too free-spirited for Raymond. He's got to get us into lock-step."

"He's got to get us ready to fight," Walt corrected.

Sam offered, "We can't fight without guns."

Briggs said, "If the Nazis try to kill us, we had better be ready to fight."

Buck registered, "I'm hearing that you believe Raymond's organizing is more than chicken-shit military. Okay. I'll compromise with you temporarily."

In the war, Germany continued to retreat from previously won territory. The Russians advanced, often up to fifteen miles a day, and crossed into Poland. Minsk fell with the loss of one hundred thousand German troops. To the West, the build-up of Allied forces continued on the Normandy beachhead. The Atlantic Wall was breached, and a counter-attack by four SS Panzer divisions was contained. After Caen was taken and U.S. forces captured St. Ló, General Patton's Third Army broke through the beachhead and moved into Brittany.

To the South, the Allied advance approached the German Gothic Line on the Arno and across to Rimini. Polish troops captured Ancona on the Adriatic Coast, and U. S. troops took Livorno on the west coast of Italy.

In West Compound, a news room was started in which maps of all fronts were kept current with German news and posted on the walls. Two kriegie newspapers, published weekly, were also posted. *The Stalag Stump*, named after the rapidly disappearing stumps, boasted type-written copy. *The Kriegie Klarion* was printed with pencil.

The Salvation Army's donated library grew to several hundred books. The classes started by Major Bellrage gained a volunteer faculty of seventeen instructors. Among the courses now offered were German, algebra, geometry, litera-ture, French, Spanish, chemistry, geology, and sociology.

On Saturday, July 8, Lt. Col. Fanning issued an "unsat-isfactory" inspection report for Combine 7, even though Buck had shaved and shined his shoes. Buck told the com-bine, "I'm collecting my own court-martial points on how our Senior Officer's staff is cheating on food rationing."

In Jose's garden two stalks of corn were eighteen inches tall and still growing. The rest of the garden offered only a frail promise of delivering a harvest. José took to looking out of the window of Room 7 to his planting and on to the guard rail, barbed wire walls, and guard towers with machine guns pointing at him. He would watch transfixed by his relation-ship with the plants, and he would pray for rain.

When Walt came by one day, Joe said, "I've even been praying to your Saint Sara. How come you've got a Catholic saint, anyhow, when you're Methodist?"

"I don't know. It doesn't make sense, but I'm not giving up Saint Sara."

"Maybe you'll turn Catholic, Walt. Right now I'm going to carry more water."

July problems were aggravated by worry about the fanatic Nazis going crazy as they continued to suffer defeat. In this circumstance, Cliff tried to focus on the July 24 opening of "Barrel of Fun." Sam continued with his occasional drawing and writing and, more and more, his sleepy, dreamy sack-time. Buck used his shoe shop work tools to make a table knife into a razor-sharp weapon with a handle for a firm grip. He confided to the combine, "I'm going to hide it in the fire sand-pail in the hallway. If it comes to a showdown, I can't match the goons with their guns, but I can give them trouble on my way down."

Walt translated news, studied German, and visited with guards. Briggs now was the cook. Also, he began a course in Spanish. Yet he told Cliff, "I'm ready to climb the barbed wire and let the goon machine guns liberate me."

Cliff said, "On the Fourth you were singing 'hubba hubba'. What's happened?"

"Hubba hubba," Briggs replied.

"I'm glad that's settled," Cliff concluded.

But Briggs was still walking a tight-wire, tense about enduring captivity.

On Friday, July 21, a German radio bulletin so stunned Walt that it was difficult for him to tear himself away from the loudspeaker to get to 4:30 Appell. At Appell he read his hastily translated report: "The news of the murder-attempt on the Führer and his fortunate escape has bound the German people together in determination to place all their efforts and faith in obtaining a final victory." To this Walt added, "They're talking about Hitler's miraculous escape as if it came from God. It's obvious there's a lot they're not telling."

At the morning Appell of July 21, Hauptmann Eiler stood firm for a moment before Colonel Raymond, as if to make his usual Luftwaffe salute. Colonel Raymond was about to raise his arm in answer. But Hauptmann Eiler, instead, jabbed his arm into the air with the stiff arm salute of the Nazi Party.

Raymond pulled himself to rigid stature and did not answer. Hauptmann Eiler continued to hold his Nazi thrust. When he was sure that Colonel Raymond was not going to return the Nazi Party salute, he lowered his arm, turned on his heels, and proceeded with the counting of the prisoners. At each block he encountered the same rejection of his Nazi Party salute. By the time he had saluted and not been answered at each of the seventeen blocks, the morning was electric with tension.

When the dismissal order came, the tension continued. The assassination attempt of July 21 had obviously brought a radical change. It appeared that the Nazis had taken control of the Luftwaffe.

Colonel Raymond was ordered to report immediately to Hauptmann Eiler. He entered Eiler's office expecting a polite encounter.

"Remain standing," Eiler snapped. "Be reminded that I speak English only because I have personally studied it, not because my duty requires me to talk in English. Major reorganization has taken place in Germany in the last three days. The Nazi Party salute is now our official salute and must be answered. You can decide if you will cooperate to help me keep my command or risk getting an SS commander. This is a critical time. Germans despise you. In Germany you are terror monsters who deserve firing squads. I advise you to provide no excuse for those who would usurp the Luftwaffe role of protecting you. At evening Appell you will answer the Nazi Party salute."

"Let me talk," Colonel Raymond insisted.

"No. I have finished with you."

By afternoon Raymond had passed down new orders to his block commanders.

Inside Room 7, Cliff Phillips lay in his bunk, covered with his blanket in spite of the warm day. It was the opening day for "Barrel of Fun."

"I've got to make it to the show. Get me excused from Appell so I can get some rest before showtime," Cliff appealed to Buck in a scratchy voice.

"I'll report you sick in bed to Fanning," Buck told him.

But when Buck reported to Fanning, he got the answer, "If Cliff can make the show tonight, he can stand Appell."

"I'm not asking you, Colonel. I'm telling you. I'm in charge of Room 7, and I am reporting that Clifford Phillips of Room 7 is sick and will not stand Appell."

"I'm commanding Block 169 where Phillips is quartered, and I am telling you, Captain Pierce, that Phillips will stand Appell," Fanning retorted.

Buck went back to Cliff and said, "Fanning was an ass, but you stay in bed under my orders. The goons will count you in your bed. If you're not feeling better by six, rethink doing the show."

The sky turned darker as kriegies assembled. Everyone was anxious to get the count over before it started to rain. Everyone was also anxious to see what would happen when the Nazi straight-arm salute demanded recognition by the kriegie commanders.

The Germans approached in cadence that spoke march music, not with their usual casual striding. In contrast to the patchy clothing in which the kriegies were vulnerable to the storm's whimsy, the Germans were all uniformed in smart rain gear, ready for the storm if it should break.

The rain started with big drops as Hauptmann Eiler strode up to Colonel Raymond and thrust an arm up and forward. Colonel Raymond responded with his usual U.S. Air Force salute, and with that the kriegies knew that the confrontation had been resolved. As the count proceeded each block commander in turn answered the Nazi salute. When the Germans reached 169, Buck sang out from the ranks, "We have a sick prisoner in Room 7, Block 169." The Germans broke step at this unexpected interruption; then they continued on.

Meanwhile, rain poured down and soaked into the caps, shirts, trousers, and shoes of the kriegies. When the dismissal order came, Room 7 kriegies scrambled to their room, wrung out their clothes, hung them up to dry, and retreated to their beds to get warm.

Suddenly, after a brief knock, the door opened. Lt. Col. Fanning stood framed in the doorway still dripping water from his soaking. "You'll not get away with openly defying my orders, Captain Pierce."

Buck got out of bed and walked his six-foot-two naked body to the doorway where he stopped an arm's reach from the five-foot-seven Burtram B.

"You're breaking the privacy of our room. Step in here and I'll wring the chicken shit out of you along with the water you're dripping," Buck said.

With that Buck raised an arm toward Fanning. The Lt. Col. stepped back and was gone before it could be known whether Buck intended to touch him.

"What was that all about?" Walt asked.

"Politics," Buck said. "The South against the West. He doesn't know I still can't use my arms at shoulder height. I've got to start working out my arms on the high bar."

Cliff had reserved space for Combine 7 to attend the opening of "Barrel of Fun." So everyone got into their still-wet clothes to leave for the grand occasion. Briggs went over to Cliff and said, "We've voted five to zero for you to stay in bed. There is talent enough to get by without you."

"It's more than my act. It's the opening. We've put a lot into this."

Cliff got up and began to dress. "I don't know if my voice will last, but I'll do my best."

The theater was a marvel of transformation from the once bleak hall. The exit doors even had electric exit signs. The stage curtains of sewn-together blankets were pulled open on schedule. Colonel Raymond was in the front row.

"Good day, gentlemen . . . sorry no ladies. I give you the grand opening of 'Barrel of Fun!'"

The Flying Syncopators struck a chord then broke into a medley that shattered the solemn air of the audience in wet clothes. A while later Cliff came on with an updated version of 'Flying Home.' . . . "Take the blood sausage and shove it up!". . . As the skit continued his voice got scratchy and weaker. Buck got up and went out to the door that led to the stage area. He was waiting when Cliff came off stage.

"It was dismal," Cliff said. "My legs are limp. I've got to get back to bed."

"I can tell that, Cliff. That's why I'm here. I'll help you back."

During the night Cliff's breathing became wheezing gasps. In the pre-dawn night, Buck awoke, got up, and sat by the open window while he listened to Cliff's breathing. The rainstorm had washed the landscape, and the night air coming in from the window carried a pine smell from the forest beyond the barbed wire. Buck watched the search light sweeping past the window with its arc. Once the light fixed on him. To be sure that bullets would not be fired, he sat very still until the light moved on to the West. As the light moved, for a moment he was sure he saw a rabbit caught in its beam. *That would be the end if a rabbit is eating our garden as fast as it's coming up!*

In the morning, Cliff was no better. It was obvious to the combine that Cliff would not make today's performance.

"What do we do if he gets worse tonight?" Briggs asked.

"I found a guy that made a wooden tube for a smoking-pipe stem. I borrowed it, just in case," Buck answered.

"For what?" Briggs asked.

"Don't ask."

After ten o'clock lockup, with the outside doors barred and police dogs on patrol, the combine discussed getting through the night and decided to take turns sitting up with Phillips. At half past midnight, when Sam was on watch, he woke Buck. "He's worse. I don't know what to do."

"I've never seen a sore throat so bad you couldn't breathe," Buck said. "I'm going to get my knife and heat it red hot on the burner to sterilize it. I know where to cut a hole so he can breathe through his neck with the tube I got. I saw a guy breathing like that once. I don't want to do it, but I'm not going to sit by while he chokes to death."

While Buck sterilized his knife, Cliff continued his gasping breathing.

"I'm not looking to play doctor unless I have to. We'd better hit the emergency light to get the guards. Maybe they'll take him to the infirmary in the vorlager."

Sam pushed the hallway button that lit the signal above the block to signal a life-threatening emergency. In fear that Cliff might start to choke, Buck sat ready with his knife and breathing tube.

"If I have to cut his throat, I'm going to turn on the light whether the guard in the tower shoots in here or not," Buck said.

After a quarter hour a guard appeared, observed Cliff, and left. By now everyone in the room was awake. In a little while two guards, lighting their way with flashlights, brought in a stretcher.

"We've got to report this before they take him away. This has to be done officially," Walt emphasized.

"I'll wake Fanning and tell him," José volunteered.

"Do that, Joe," Buck said. "You can tell him more politely than I would."

When the Germans left with Cliff on the stretcher, Fanning stood in his doorway and watched. All of the combine followed as the guards carried the stretcher down the dimly lit hallway to the outside door. The event carried an air of foreboding. For Combine 7, the enemy was taking "one of us" away. It was an uncertain parting, halfway between rescue and final good-bye.

Next day, Buck asked the medical officer, Lt. Col. Sneed how Cliff was doing.

"I don't know. I'm not allowed in the vorlager," Sneed reported. "I sent three other suspicious cases of bad sore throat out there yesterday."

"What happens in the vorlager?" Walt asked the medical officer.

"They haven't let me inspect. I am told the Germans have a doctor who comes as needed. Slave laborers with dubious medical backgrounds are assigned there by the krauts. They have some medical supplies, but as the Germans keep losing, the shortages get worse. A POW infirmary is lowest in priority. The place is being enlarged to sixty beds for the twenty five thousand of us in all the compound of Stalag III. It would be disastrous if we had an epidemic."

"How can we learn how he's doing?" Buck asked.

"If they assign another prisoner to his bunk, you'll know the worst. If you see him again, you'll know the best."

At 4:30 Appell Fanning read: "The Germans report that four cases of diphtheria have been diagnosed today from patients sent to the infirmary from this compound. This is a highly contagious and deadly disease. Anyone with a sore throat and fever is ordered to remain in bed henceforth until examined by our medical officer. All compound activities are canceled as of this reading. This includes the theater production."

The following day Fanning announced: "The Germans report three new cases of diphtheria today. Stay in your rooms, and keep the flies away from your food. The flies are our worst disease carriers. . . ."

Next day, July 28, a very hot day, Sam took over Cliff's coffee-time. "I figure if I can't know how he's doing, I can at least keep his coffee-time going. If it makes us hotter on the inside than we are on the outside, it may make these days seem cooler." The combine gathered around the table.

"Does anyone have a scratchy throat?" José asked. "I'm okay. I'm just asking."

It was a poor opening for the "something special" Cliff aspired to for coffee-time. The talk today was about how to control disease. Should they boil the tin plate dishes? Or maybe try to heat them red hot? What about the flies?

Walt said, "I wish people would send screens and toilet paper instead of sports and music gear. With the toilet thirty feet from our window, no wonder we get the GIs all the time." For about three days of every two weeks, all in the room except José regularly suffered the dysentery Walt referred to. The cure was not to eat until appetite returned.

Buck continued, "Don't forget—Fanning ordered us to keep the flies away. José, will you tell Fanning we've already ordered the flies to stay away, but the critters won't listen."

Sam said, "I want us to agree that tomorrow at coffee-time we're not going to go on like today. We've got to do something special to give us a lift. I could talk about a dream banquet if you'll let me. Or read you a poem. Or tell you some jokes."

218

Next day, July 29, the count of new diphtheria cases was down to one, but the activity restrictions were continued.

Sam again held coffee-time. At the end, Walt read part of his first letter from his wife:

> *". . . Sometimes it helps to think of the masterpieces of music, literature, etc., and the courageous, unselfish humanitarians who have given so much to try to make this a better world. Idealists are for the most part, like you and me, the ones who will be needed most when it's over, to think straight, and help build straight, and up."*

On July 30 there were no new cases of diphtheria. Sam continued Cliff's coffee-time. Today, Briggs talked about the river life of his Nashville home and some of the popular fish menus their family restaurant served.

Sam ended the coffee session with what he called a short poem. "I've titled it, 'We're Not Talking.' . . . What we're not saying . . . We're thinking . . . What we're not thinking. . . We're dreaming . . . What we're not dreaming . . . We're wishing . . . We're not talking.. . . That's what we have in common."

Next day, the last day of July, there were again no new cases of diphtheria. At the coffee session, José talked about going fishing for salmon and some of the meals he was going to serve if he started a restaurant. Then he asked Sam, "Would you explain what we were supposed to get from that poem you read yesterday?"

"What I meant was . . . I know we're all waiting for a new kriegie to be assigned to Cliff's empty bunk, but none of us is talking about it. Each of us has got a lot more eating on us, but we're not talking about it. What we are talking about is the stuff we say because we'd rather not talk about what we're feeling and thinking. But we all know what we're not talking about, and this gives us a kinship."

In the first weeks of August, fierce fighting in the French coastal area of Avranches, Caen, and Falaise resulted in tens of thousands of German losses. After Avranches, U.S. forces advanced along the coast westward. The rest of the

Allied invasion force fanned into France. But kriegies of Stalag Luft III in the heart of Germany realized by now that the invasion of June 6 would bring them no quick liberation.

To the South, on August 15, ten divisions of Allied ground troops and an airborne division landed on the French Riviera. In Italy the British took Florence, but departure of French mountain troops for the Riviera landings prevented a follow-up through the Gothic Line.

To the East, the Polish Resistance gained control of much of Warsaw, but the Russians, within sight of the city, halted their advance and would not assist them. Hitler then sent in his cruelest SS troops and began to destroy the city with determined brutality. The Russians to the South moved through Moldavia and into Rumania.

In West Compound, Combine 7 waited to learn if Clifford Phillips was still alive. Walt tried to get information from his ferret friend, Smitty, but this did not work.

Briggs called on Raymond, and learned that two people had died—no names given.

Buck tried to contact Hauptmann Eiler directly, but he was referred back to his Senior Officer, and Briggs had already tried that.

August 6 was a special Sunday for joy: The diphtheria restriction was ended.

For José, this Sunday was special because it allowed him to begin his new project of collecting fertilizer for the garden. He stood at the gate with his empty Parcel box when the bread wagon came through pulled by a team of dray horses. At times the collection process got pushy as a cluster of garden-growers sought to lay claim to whatever warm pellets the horses dropped, but José was lucky enough to get a full parcel of horse manure.

"Mail man," Briggs announced as he saw José approach with the horse manure.

José replied, "That's right. We're going to mix up a potion with some oomph for these garden goodies. And today we're going to have fresh radishes for dinner, Ed. One fresh radish for each of us and one left in the ground for Cliff. We'll see what we can save. I've lost the tomatoes. The other stuff is living but not coming past the ground. Buck says he spotted a rabbit out here. That could explain what I'm seeing."

In another part of the compound, Walt was talking with Smitty, in German. . . . "Since we talked last, Smitty, I got a letter from my wife telling about my new baby girl."

"You're lucky to have a girl. She won't have to go to war."

"Have you heard from your wife?"

"Nothing. I got only the one letter saying our boy was killed when our house was bombed. She wrote that she was sent out of Frankfurt for housing in Pellheim. I have written to her in Pellheim, but without a street address that didn't work."

"You should ask for an emergency leave to go find her," Walt advised.

"What is the emergency when her story is happening all over Germany? You flyers do not realize . . ."

To switch the subject, with a trade in mind for apples to make pie, Walt said, "I admire how you come in hiding trade goods. I know the penalties are forbidding."

"I am in a world I can't change except for what I can do for myself. Leave now. It's not wise to talk long where we can be seen. Tomorrow I will bring apples."

Raymond was taking advantage of "freedom" Sunday by visiting his friend Bellrage. They sat in the shade of Henry's block. "Can we start courses again?" Henry asked.

"Perhaps. We're not out of danger. We could still have an epidemic that could wipe out the camp."

"Dean, the power of God needs to be recognized in sparing us from an epidemic."

"If your Christian Science readings achieve healing, you should get followers here, since we have nothing else to fight disease."

"Our Mother Church provides us Science and Health Readings, the Quarterly, other books, and the Bible. The Nazis closed the Christian Science Church in Germany and confiscated all its property in July 1941. What we do here is banned beyond the barbed wire, but the Luftwaffe hasn't interfered with us here—so far."

Dean replied, "Maybe they're easy on you because they offer us no alternatives."

"I personally have benefited. We began our readings in my first prison at Schubin by the Polish Corridor a year and a half ago. My faith has helped me survive tough times."

"Tell me that you haven't had the GIs."

"I can't say that, but God's love is a healing power."

"For starvation?"

"I'm still alive and without the extra food of your Staff Mess."

"That's a dig! I admit I have found no power to control the cheating in rationing."

"Nor anything else, I venture. I've learned to accept my lack of power. You're settling in."

"I've been down four months, but I still boil when we hear of the abuse of air power—"

"Abuse?" Bellrage interrupted.

"Yes. Take Ploesti as the most crucial case."

"Dean, Ploesti is behind us. Focus on how to survive here. What keeps me going is organizing kriegie education."

"What is this—wisdom from around the bend again? I didn't drop by to get preached to. It's time I left, Henry."

"You brought up Ploesti."

"True. And you reacted like the millions who don't know the true history of that raid. It was a repeat of the Billy Mitchell challenge to prove what air power could do. It was imperative that we succeed in that mission and they stacked the cards against us once again like the navy did in our bombing test of 1921. Churchill, through Marshall, fore-doomed the mission."

"How foredoomed?"

"By assigning Brereton to run the mission for one thing."

"Wasn't Brereton the general who ignored warnings of a Jap attack on Luzon and left his B-17s lined up on the ground where the Japs pulverized them."

"Precisely. I served under him in the Philippines. You named his record, and he had no European high-altitude bombing experience. Yet, they chose him to head that most critical mission. Strange, isn't it?"

"Now you've caught me. Tell me more."

"With the ground invasion already launched, it shatters one's mind to add up the clues. Brereton was given full tactical freedom to plan the Ploesti raid. General Ent flew it with the daredevil eccentrics Killer Kane and Hot Foot Looey, among other great Group leaders. Brereton knew from the beginning that he would stay safe on the ground. Still, he took total authority to plan the flying. He wouldn't take advice from any of the operation leaders chosen to fly the mission."

"I know the amount of effort taken to keep that mission a deep, deep secret, Dean."

"Henry, all the flyers assigned to that mission, the bombardiers, the navigators, the pilots, the Group commanders, everybody including the Command Pilot General Ent, fought the stupidity of his plan. They rebelled with a plea for a high-altitude mission using the Norden bombsight. One group commander even wrote a letter of appeal. General Ent signed it. You'd think the collective judgment of these hand-picked, highly-seasoned heavy bomber crews would have been respected, but Brereton refused their advice."

"Why didn't higher command intercede?"

"Ah! That's the strange part. Brereton's plan went up to Eisenhower, whose staff criticized it. But, get this—Eisenhower approved it. Why? Nobody dares to accuse that world hero of a decision that was self-serving—but it was. I'd like to think it was innocent, but Ike was determined to divert the air force from Oil to direct support of his ground armies—this was his World War One tank commander mentality. Air force failure in Ploesti would get Ike what he wanted—proof that the air force could not win the war by trying to knock out Oil—proof that his planned ground invasion was needed to win the war. So Ike had a motive to approve Brereton's plan, even if he was advised it was crazy."

"What about Marshall? He could have stopped it."

"Marshall? His staff took the easy way out, passing the decision back to Brereton—in spite of full knowledge that the Operation Commander, General Ent, who was assigned to fly the mission and the Group Commanders assigned to fly the mission had appealed against Brereton's plan. So the catastrophe in Ploesti was dictated before the mission was flown."

"Unbelievable."

"It gets worse. Henry, hear this. Brereton didn't start the bombers flying on the deck 'to surprise the enemy.' He had the 160 four-engine bombers make their long haul in at altitudes from twenty-five hundred to twelve thousand feet, like blowing his horn all the way to warn the enemy the bombers were coming. Then, after parading their arrival all the way, he had them go down to the deck 'to hide' for the final miles to the target. Flying a few feet above the ground, ordered to keep radio silence, they obviously got lost. General Ent had the good sense to eventually disobey Brereton's orders, cancel radio silence, and release the Groups to bomb 'targets of opportunity.' By then, bedlam reigned, with bombers flying blind through smoke and fire, crashing into each other, skimming the ground so close that machine guns were downing them. We lost thirty-four percent of our bombers—"

"I've heard from the men who flew—"

"Then our enemies used the Ploesti debacle as evidence that we could not deliver victory through air power, that we had to shift our priority to support of ground troops."

"Maybe you should let yourself go around the bend, Dean."

"Maybe you should, too. For us the war is over. Here we can learn of justice, prudence, temperance, and fortitude, and we can cleanse our lives of the evils of pride, covetousness, lust, anger, gluttony, envy, and sloth—"

"Christ, Henry, how can you drop me from Ploesti to a sermon about the cardinal virtues and deadly sins. It is truly time I left. There's a gap between us I can't bridge."

"The longer I am down the more I realize that God is giving us the chance here to—"

"Shut up! This camp is down to almost no reserve Parcels. At 4:30 I have to tell half-starved prisoners in danger of an epidemic that I'm starting them on one-tenth rations—"

"I've listened. Listen to me now, Dean. As soon as I talk, you get angry."

"Thank you for your coffee, Henry—"

"Don't leave me without telling me about Katherine. Have you had a letter from her? I've been wondering how she's coped with the loss of Tom?"

"I've been down since March 30, but not one letter yet. I'll see you."

Next day Combine 7 received an estimate of six-tenths of a Parcel, based on the premise that Phillips was still alive. The garden was now even more significant as a hope for food, and the threat of a marauding rabbit was even more disturbing.

The combine started an all night watch for the rabbit. The kriegie sentry sat by the open window and followed the searchlight as it roved in rhythmic sweeps. After a while the guard in the tower took to directing the light into the window occasionally to frame the kriegie on watch. Then, as if he had deduced the reason for the watch, he occasionally centered the light on the garden. Nevertheless, for three nights no rabbit was sighted.

Shortly before dawn of the third night, when Sam was on watch, the light suddenly locked on the garden. He focused on a big, long-eared rabbit in the center of the light. He jolted awake and with instinctive reflex jumped up and shouted, "Haaah! Raus! Raus!"

"Sam! The machine gun's going to kill you standing there yelling!" Buck hollered.

"The rabbit! He was right there in the garden!"

Everyone joined Sam.

"He was right there in the middle of the light," Sam exclaimed.

"Why did you yell in German?" Walt asked.

"It was a German rabbit."

Buck proclaimed, "We have to figure out a way to kill that rabbit."

After morning Appell, the rabbit talk continued.

"If I was out there trying to escape there would probably be three police dogs chewing up my ass, but a rabbit can come and go without rousing one."

Briggs switched the subject: "I went to Colonel Raymond again about Cliff. It's been over two weeks. He told me there were two more deaths, but no names yet. But I learned something else. The goons have brought in wagon loads of what they call kohlrabi."

"Kohlrabi? We've got to get in on this . . ." Buck headed out the door. By noon a dozen soft ball size kohlrabi were on the table.

"Hey, I know what these are. They're like turnips," Walt grinned. "We used to eat them raw, but they were a lot smaller. They're really good eating."

"We can use one every day for our big meal," Briggs proposed.

Buck suggested, "We could use one to knock out the rabbit. Joe's a pitcher, right?"

"I'd better throw a strike the first time. He wouldn't stay for—"

"What's this talk about throwing strikes?" Clifford Phillips intervened as he came through the doorway.

"You're alive!" Buck shouted.

"Gosh!" Sam exclaimed.

"I had you figured for dead!" Briggs blurted.

"I'm not much alive—ready to faint from walking—I need to rest. I'll talk later."

"Do you want to eat first?" Briggs asked.

"Later, Briggs."

"Hit your sack," Buck ordered. "We'll get out and leave you alone."

"I've been doing your coffee thing for you," Sam offered triumphantly.

"I've kept a radish in the garden for you," José joined.

"We'll have a coffee-time outside," Buck told the combine.

Once outside, Walt remarked, "His eyes are hollow, and he's so skinny and pale, I can't see how he lived through it."

José said, "I prayed for him every day."

"To be honest, he used to get on my nerves," Buck confessed, "but when he was gone I came to realize how smart he is in special ways and how he works to lift our spirits."

"Me being from Nashville and him a Yankee from Princeton, I used to figure we had nothing in common, but now I think we do. I want to tune in better to how he's thinking."

Sam reflected, "I wish I could be more like him. We've both got an art itch, but he has the talent to bring it out. Mine's stuck inside me."

Walt said, "By God's mercy he didn't die, but that doesn't make him a hero. He's not a believer in my religious beliefs, and he treats Joe like a Mexican who isn't as up to—"

José cut in. "He is a hero. He ain't perfect, but who is?"

After Appell Briggs served the expected pièce de résistance— soup of kohlrabi. But with the meal barely begun, faces twisted with chewing effort. "This is eating shredded wood," José blurted, with all concurring. But all continued to chew the bulk. It was precious on one-tenth rations. Cliff got up and consumed some soup, then went back to bed to try and sleep in the stale, hot air of the August night. Sam went to bed, too. The remaining four played pinochle with the worn-out deck long ago donated by a U.S. charity.

By *lights out*, a plan for the night's rabbit war had been finalized. Kohlrabi would be the weapon. At the critical moment, José would be mobilized to throw the critical pitch. . . . But the watching of that night was in vain.

It was now Friday, a day in which the kriegies had to stand under the hot sun for five hours while guards searched the compound. Cliff, who had been spared this ordeal by his illness status, informed that guards had spent a lot of time searching Room 7. "What do you think they were looking for?"

"Did they find your knife?" José asked softly as Buck shook his head to say, "No."

After the 4:30 Appell, which was brief, Briggs again served kohlrabi soup. And again, after lights out the rabbit war re-commenced. This time José was scheduled for the hour in which the rabbit had been discovered two nights before. All night long the searchlight roved back and forth with no target sighting.

On the following night, with José on watch and Buck standing beside him, the light suddenly centered on the rabbit.

The light stopped roving, telling that the guard in the tower had locked on the target. José pitched a fast ball kohlrabi with all his might. And he missed. Yet the rabbit did not move. José raised a back-up kohlrabi and was about to throw when the machine gun in the tower fired three shells. The rabbit flipped into the air then plunged to earth and lay in the circle of light.

Buck jumped through the window and ran to where he, too, was centered in the light. He grabbed the still-quivering rabbit, bounded back to the window and jumped into the room.

"Close the window! A dog's after me!" he called to José.

"You're crazy, Buck, running out into that light! I was sure the guard was going to riddle you!"

"He killed the rabbit for us. Man-to-man, I was sure he wouldn't shoot me going out to get it," Buck said.

Sunday, August 13, at two in the afternoon, Combine 7 served a bash behind closed doors to keep the aroma of fried rabbit from revealing their exploit. But the news of Buck's defiance of the machine guns to get a rabbit for dinner spread through the compound, making Buck famous for his daring.

At 4 P.M. next day, Sam served a coffee-time outside in the August breeze to celebrate Cliff's recovery.

"Don't ask me about the infirmary. I got well in spite of being sure I was dying."

"Nobody asked you," José said. "I just want you to know I was praying for you."

"My religion sure helped me when I was laid up," Walt offered. "I got a new hold on what Christ's blessing can do."

"I came out different than when I went in. I'll say that," Cliff said.

"How?" Buck asked. "Never mind—I can understand your not wanting to talk about it. I went through hell in a bed myself. I saw guys you could only help by killing them."

Still, Cliff pressed on. "I kept asking, 'What in life is worth this suffering?'" . . .

The combine pondered Cliff's words in silence until Sam confided, "I get questions like that in my head about the whole people world. That's when I get stuck for words."

"You're talking poems," Walt contested. "Cliff's talking about what we're asking God when we're facing dying. Cliff, did you come out different, finding faith in God?"

Cliff replied, "I was reaching—for—what in life was worth living for?"

"That's what I mean," Walt said. "It brought you closer to wanting to serve God."

Cliff shook his head. "I came out closer to theater. What kept me going was the memory of me getting people to laugh in Barrel of Fun."

"I'm sorry for you, if you've found nothing better in life than laughing," Walt reacted.

Sam said, "With my parents pulling me to both Catholic and Jewish, I found my answer in make-believe—sort of like your theater, Cliff."

"I'd like to hear more about that when I'm feeling better, Sam."

The daily German rations per person remained one medium size potato, eight ounces of bread, one ounce of hard tack, one-seventh ounce of barley flour, one ounce of sugar, three-fourth ounce of cheese, one ounce of margarine, and, once a week, officially, but actually less often, an ounce of blood sausage. To improve this circumstance, the garden received indulgent baptism with "horse pellet elixer."

On Tuesday, August 15, Buck received a letter from Randi. He read the thirty-seven lines on War Department Form 111. Then he read the letter again, reflected, and read it again. Finally, he folded it into his breast pocket.

Cliff also received a letter—from his mother. After reading it, with tears in his eyes, he told Sam, "I haven't heard from home in almost six months. This is medicine for me."

Sam shared, "I'm waiting for a letter from my mother. She must be awfully worried that the Nazis have killed me, especially after Hitler's crackdown three weeks ago."

"The Nazis won't get you. Your dog tags list you as Catholic and your name is O'Brien," Buck insisted.

Cliff said, "Hatch, you stuck up for me when Walt knocked me at coffee-time. You said your world of make-believe was what you found, like I found theater, to live for. Walt doesn't know how make-believe, like Greek tragedy, sent the Greeks home crying but feeling better about being human."

"I know, Cliff. The Greeks had lots of religion, but they still needed theater to get those deep feelings."

"In two days we're going to open 'The Happy Hour.' That will label us as nuts."

"Cliff, I understand what you were trying to do with your coffee-time theater, too. That's why I tried to fill in for you."

"I'm through with the coffee-time. It's every man for himself now. Coming back, I hate our small room with the same six of us twenty-four hours a day."

"We all hung in with you, Cliff. Buck even got ready to operate to save your life."

"I know. I appreciate all of you. You're trying to find a higher plane in this kriegie trap with your make-believe like I'm trying to do with theater. Briggs acts like he wants to try, but doesn't know how. And José is certainly trying, wearing blisters on his hands in the clay dirt for his dream garden."

"I think Joe thinks you're looking down on him, calling him José."

"He is José. Not calling him José is not respecting that he's Mexican. I'll have to tell him—"

"What about Walt?" Sam interrupted.

"Look, I'm not blaming any of you. Walt's busy with the Germans, getting news and trading for us. But we can't get away from each other. We're locked together in the same room every night. That's the hell of it."

"You're not criticizing how I'm spending my time?"

"No, Sam, not if staying in the sack doesn't drive you crazy. You're looking for the heroic, like in Greek tragedy."

Sam said, "If everybody in our room thought like you, I'd probably start doing more. I don't want to go crazy. I don't know what's going to happen."

"Unknown to Washington and London, the enemy was at the crossroads in 1943 because of gigantic oil expenditures on the Russian Front, far out of line with expectations
. . . The fighting in North Africa was also a heavy drain on petroleum resources. Already, Albert Speer, Minister of Arms and Munitions, was warning Hitler of the increasing tightness of oil; such admonitions were to reach a crescendo and drive his chief to a distraction in time. America and Britain knew the German stocks were low, but they did not realize how exceedingly low; therefore, oil was not given priority in the strategic bombing program. . . an error that temporarily saved the day for Germany." [1]

"When interviewed after the war, Goering stated flatly that the greatest effect on the defeat of Germany was caused by, ". . .precision bombing, because it was decisive. Destroyed cities could be evacuated, but destroyed industries were difficult to replace." [2]

[1] *Low Level Mission*, Leon Wolff, Doubleday and Company, New York, New York, 1957.

[2] *Global Mission*, Henry Arnold, Harper, New York, New York, 1949.

THE PRISON: CHAPTER THREE

The day after Buck received Randi's letter, he stood before Colonel Raymond, shaved, with shoes shined and in uniform, minus wings and captain's bars. "I came because I got some news yesterday I thought you might want to hear. I waited too long to see you about Tom, so I've come right away this time."

"What is your news?"

"I got a letter from Randi Scott. She wrote that she's heard from you. I thought you would want to hear she knows you're alive—in case you haven't heard from her."

"Did you bring her letter?"

Buck took the letter from his breast pocket. Dean took the letter.

"I didn't mean for you to read it. It's my private mail."

Dean returned the letter to Buck. "This is the first news I've had that my letters have reached anyone. I haven't received any mail. If you're being genuinely considerate, I owe you thanks, but I'm suspicious since you have the reputation of needling senior officers."

"As I told you, Randi and I feel close because we're both from the High Plains and the Big Horn Wilderness."

"You've let me know that I don't own her, Pierce. I won't apologize for being suspicious of your motives."

"Our difference is that I'm thinking civilian not military while I'm waiting to get freed. I've quit being suckered by the crap that I'm a hero. Being military got me to hauling bombs to kill civilians. Now I'm shot down and seeing what I did, and I'm hating my part in it. I've quit trusting the military. That's why I don't have a good record here."

"Under the enemy, we need military discipline here. But thank you for coming by, Pierce."

"I'm hearing that it's time to leave, but considering the barbed wire wall, I won't be able to get far away, will I?"

On Thursday, August 18, West Compound received enough Parcels to bring the total reserve to 2 1/2 Parcels per man.

Before evening Appell, in the empty time that was once Cliff's coffee-time, Briggs asked, "Walt, what's the latest reading on how close the Allies are?"

"As the crow flies we are about six hundred miles from the new invasion in southern France. We're about that far from our troops in the Normandy invasion, too. To the south it's again about six hundred miles to our troops. The closest front is Warsaw. That's two hundred fifty miles away. If the Russians start our way we could be home by Christmas."

"Hitler will kill us before he lets the Russians free us," Buck predicted. "The only way we're going to get freed is to escape and get to friendly territory."

Walt responded, "Since Hitler's crackdown, if we get caught escaping, we'll be shot as spies. The Nazis are getting so fanatic that our prison is actually a fortress saving us. Even ordinary Germans are plain terrified of the SS since the crackdown. We'll be hearing from Colonel Raymond. I'm sure he's got plans for us."

Buck asserted, "It's our leaders' planning that got us here in the first place. If we want smart planning, we'd better do it ourselves."

The discussion ended with the call for Appell where Fanning announced: "More Parcels have arrived, but we'll stay on one-tenth rations to save reserves for the winter." Through all the next day Raymond's decision to continue one-tenth rations was criticized as inhumane.

On Sunday, soup's-on reported a revolt in Paris and bands of civilians fighting the German garrison. Combine 7 decided that the good war news was cause to plan for a bash in spite of one tenth rations. Friday, September 1, twelve days ahead, was chosen.

Under a sky of low-lying, dark clouds that promised a long, slow rain for the garden, Buck talked about his hospital stay in Paris, "I'll bet my Belgian friend Kickie's happy along with the French nurses I wished would have kidnapped me."

"I wonder if Sandra has ever been to Paris?" Sam pondered.

"You're a puzzle, Sam. Few guys have been talking about wanting a woman—maybe nature has dried up our balls. You don't fit the picture, dreaming about Sandra. I've read about guys in prison having sex with each other. That's not the way it's been here."

Later in the morning, Buck, Briggs, and Walt attended Protestant services. José was leaving the Catholic service as they entered the theater. "I'm going to water the garden," José said. "We can't gamble on the rain. We've got twelve days until the bash. We've got to get a good harvest. It's a war I've got to win."

In the afternoon Walt met Smitty and made a cigarette trade for apples and onions. As always, they talked in German. "Any news from your wife?"

"Nothing. The war can't last much longer even though for fear of the SS nobody is saying we are losing. I get bored crawling around underneath your blocks looking for tunnels, but being here saves me from being sent to the Russian Front. I trade to get money for Paula and me when the war is over, which could be soon."

"Could it be? The Russians may soon take Warsaw. That's very close to us."

"Stalin will let the Poles be butchered in Warsaw to be rid of them and will never invade Germany. He knows that Germans want America to take Germany and will fight ten times as hard to keep the Russians out. You will get no liberation from Russia."

On Tuesday, Walt met Oberfeldwebel, master sergeant, Krauss, who had been a Heinkel bomber pilot. Krauss had revealed that he kept a war diary and offered to let Walt read it if Walt would write his diary into German for him to read in exchange, as a secret between them. Today Walt was visiting to learn more about the diary exchange scheme.

"Our German scientists have traced our ancestry back to a super Aryan race in India," Walt was told as he waited for a chance to turn the conversation.

Krauss spent the next half hour informing Walt of the unique characteristics of true Aryans that made him proud to be German. Walt couldn't get in one question to learn more about what Intelligence value Krauss's diary might have.

Krauss continued, "Our Führer has a team of scientists completely devoted to tracing the thirteenth century migration of the Aryans from the Punjab area of India where long before the Greeks they had a flourishing civilization."

Walt walked away. He had decided to ask Colonel Raymond about the diary scheme.

On Wednesday, soup's-on reported fighting in Paris and allied invasion forces moving closer. In his mind's eye, Buck saw Kickie pushing his broken cheekbone around to keep it from healing so he could be in Paris when it was liberated. . . .

In a meeting with his staff, Dean Raymond reported, ". . . With the east and south fronts moving toward us and the Germans taking major losses, I'm going to move to one-fourth Parcel rations for now. I'm still planning for survival in the coming winter, nevertheless. Our latitude is 200 miles north of the U.S.-Canadian border so we can be sure it will get cold here. If we don't get liberated we'll need more food and fuel to survive. With Germans getting squeezed in more every day our lives here are going to get rougher, and we'll have to get more military. We will not become an every-man-for-himself jungle. We'll need more food to survive and more fuel to keep from freezing."

Fanning volunteered, "We've got to clamp down on rebels."

Dean faced Fanning and asked, "How do you propose to clamp down on rebels?"

Fanning answered, "Old-timers have told me commanders have sometimes resorted to unconventional methods such as getting volunteers to plain beat the shit out of them."

Sneed, the medical officer, added, "Forced dunking of them in the fire pool has been employed, too, but each situation requires its special solution."

Raymond weighed what he had heard before he answered, "I know that textbook military methods don't apply here. Our challenge is to achieve leadership by other means than the tactics I have heard today."

Peyser, the rations officer, reported, "Our Intelligence network has been endangered by poor security with soup's-on. Needless to say, this endangers our agents' lives."

Raymond responded, "I'll draft an order to be read at the next soup's-on. If that fails, I'll consider soup's-on to be an unacceptable risk and end it."

While Dean's staff was discussing discipline, Sam was lying in the combine garden. He was watching a gray spider weave a web between the two still-standing corn stalks. Under the comforting warmth of the sun, he watched the disciplined web-weaving with hypnotic fascination. He decided that he would keep observing the progress of this spider's work over the next days if rain did not wash the web away.

Friday, August 25: After Sam had finished his lunch of a one-eighth-inch slice of toast and, today, a German ration of pea soup with black bugs, he went to the garden to again observe the world of his spider. After getting comfortably situated he saw that a fat little green caterpillar had gotten caught in the web. It twisted and turned violently to free itself. Meanwhile, the spider advanced until it was on the back of the caterpillar. While the worm writhed in convulsive twists, the spider jabbed then backed away and jabbed again and again. The caterpillar was trying to twist around as if to bite the spider. *What is the spider doing? Is it torturing its victim with stings? Or is it probing for the exact target that will bring a quick end to the battle?*

His interest welled to excitement—*I'm not going to get involved. This is nature at work. No matter what happens, I'm not going to take sides.* The caterpillar struggled desperately to get free but seemed to be irrevocably ensnared. As Sam watched he could hear Buck calling to him from the window. His eyes left the battle to regard Buck waving to him.

"Come on, Hatch, you've missed the news," Buck called. "Paris is free."

Sam glanced back to the web. The caterpillar was not moving. The kill had been finalized. In violation of his intended neutrality, Sam freed the caterpillar and lifted it from the web to the top of a stump. He was studying the caterpillar for signs of life as Colonel Raymond approached the window where Buck was standing.

"It had to be you!" Colonel Raymond snapped. "Captain Pierce, shouting a secret report puts you in a different category."

"I checked every direction for goons before I opened my mouth. I knew it was safe."

"Did you see me within earshot?"

"I could see someone walking this way, but I could tell you weren't a kraut."

"I am charging you with breach of top secret security in a battle setting."

Raymond continued westward. Sam, taken aback, got up as he took a last glance of the battle scene and saw the spider curled into a ball. With contempt he smashed the spider into a smear of spindly legs and creamy slime as he left the scene to hurry to Buck.

Buck told Sam, "In the hospital in Paris Kickie told me I'd have to learn to keep my mouth shut under the enemy. I guess I'm too slow at learning. I'd like you to keep the hassle between me and Pa Raymond to yourself."

"I won't tell anyone."

Buck continued, "If Kickie's still in Paris today, I'll bet he's one happy Spitfire pilot."

Next day, instead of soup's-on, there was an announcement: "Due to security violations the Senior Officer has canceled soup's-on."

On the following day, the only news was Walt's German translation: "The SS is defeating the insurrectionists in Warsaw, with fighting now in the city sewers. In France further strategic advances to the rear are inflicting severe casualties. At bridgeheads across the Seine disastrous Allied losses are being inflicted by heroic German troops."

Afterwards, Fanning announced the return to one-fourth Parcel rations.

Kriegies puzzled about the return to one-fourth rations on the same day of Raymond's gut blow canceling soup's-on, their only connection with rescuing forces. Some said he'd increased rations as a pay-off for stopping soups-on for no good reason. Others blamed Buck, the rebel who had jumped into the searchlight to get a rabbit. Rumor had it

Buck had done something wild again—this time something that broke secrecy rules.

Buck answered probers with, "I'm top-secret educated to say nothing."

Combine 7 handled the unrest by focusing on their coming September 1 bash. They kept the garden growing to save it for the big day.

September 1: Raymond braced his shoulders and began three laps in the morning chill that spoke of winter coming. Like most kriegies, he had traveled this path so often his reality was more in the migrations of his mind than in what was happening around him.

To the West he saw the ground armies pounding toward Germany. . . . *Hitler's commander-in-chief in the West has committed suicide. Since we've broken the beachhead we are gathering speed, even moving beyond Paris on the way here . . . 200,000 Germans dead or wounded . . . 200,000 taken prisoner . . . 20,000 vehicles destroyed. If Hitler keeps fighting, what about us? In the East, the Russians are coming, twice as close as our troops. If they would help the Poles take Warsaw, they could be here in two weeks. We have to be ready to fight if the SS tries to stop the Russians from freeing us. But if we form into combat units too soon, our secret organizing will get us massacred. We'll be free or dead by Christmas.*

He looked up to the nearest guard tower and saw the guard idly following him with his machine gun as he walked. *Hitler is promising victory with secret weapons. We know his flying bombs work because they're already hitting England. Worse—his promised V-2 rockets come straight down from space—unstoppable. We can't say his jet and rocket airplanes are propaganda because they are already flying. They can knock out every airplane we've got when he gets enough of them. What about the heavy water mystery? Why are our scientists in such a panic? A super bomb? A new kind of bomb that could win the war? We've got to end this war soon.*

He was passing Henry Bellrage. "Do you want company, Dean?"

"Not today, Henry. I'll drop by soon." *Randi? Part Indian? I should have guessed. She has the high cheek bones and the tan that doesn't need sun—don't think about her. Think about the armies coming. Oil—the blood of the Nazi war machine. The gore of needless ground fighting is going to stink in the history books when the truth comes out. If merciless killing makes the Nazis criminal, let's try the eighty-drinks-a-week, cigar-smoking drunk who ordered the area bombing of German cities. After the war the guilty generals will have good excuses for their conduct. Even mother-killers on death row have good excuses—*"What's on your mind, Captain Plank?"

"I saw you walking. You said I should see you if I had a special reason."

"Walk with me. Don't slow me down."

"I've got a friendship going with an ex-Heinkel pilot, Krauss—I mean a fake friendship. I think I can get his diary if Intelligence wants it—"

"I know of Krauss. I can't see the Luftwaffe transferring a combat pilot here if his brain was dealing a full deck. Go on."

"I could fake a diary of a B-17 bombardier. He said he would trade diaries so we could read each other's. I could organize to copy his quickly."

"Highly ambitious. You're a zealous soldier. Kriegies are reporting you to be a goon-lover. That's the label we want for you. We want the Germans to believe you love them, so you can work as a counter-agent for us. I'll ask Intelligence about your idea."

"Thank you, sir. I want to help in any way I can. Most kriegies expect other guys to do the dirty work and killing to get them home."

"That's it for today, Plank. You'll be contacted." *If Krauss's diary has any military information, which I doubt, it's too stale by now to interest Intelligence. But if we make this exchange, the Germans may think Plank is a goofball collaborator. Intelligence-sparring busywork—busywork to avoid the horror of thinking in this time trap.*

Food? Until now, it's meant nothing to me that most people in the world don't have enough to eat. Why men kill is better learned from the pit of an empty belly than from the military history books.

Fear? I once admired the furtive bolts of deer for their quickness. Now I know better, but with no place to bolt to. Peace will be going to bed without fear of being jolted awake — "*Raus!*"

Boredom? Marooned in my own brain. When the boredom bug used to bite me, I would busy myself with work, go to the officers' club, take in some night life—with favorite people—favorite women—indulge myself with alcohol to mellow the itch of passing time. A bottle of scotch here every day would help me escape this forced monk-tank thinking.

Flying? The freedom lift of pulling your wings into the sky. Did I write the words, "I basked in golden down of sun-blessed clouds; I fought the black turbulence of tornado-wrought darkness."

He was now passing the office of the Luftwaffe Commander of the West Compound. *Was Hauptmann Eiler ever a pilot? I will have to ask him. There is a special bond between men who fly. I'll try sky talk with him—Wagnerian sky talk . . .* "Ground war stupidities defile the honor the Luftwaffe has earned in its sky battles. Using war to decide what is just defiles our bond further. Do you agree, Hauptmann?" *If he was ever a pilot, that might help us.*

In Room 7 the combine was preparing to eat the garden crop. José had harvested the entire beet crop of two beets and the entire corn crop of four ears. Plus, he had pulled eight carrots. He had left seven carrots in the ground. This was the entire reward for all the digging, planting, watering, guarding, and fertilizing of their dreams.

Buck returned from the enlisted men's room with the news, "Sergeant Dawson was also raised as a Quaker Friend. He's going to watch that we get our fair share of rations."

As the pièce de résistance of the harvest meal, Briggs made "kriegie whip," the famed dessert of powdered milk, sugar, and water beat into froth with infinite patience.

When the combine gathered at the table, Walt said, "I'll say a prayer before we start."

"No one prayer would speak for all of us," Sam cautioned.

"For crying out loud, start eating," Briggs urged.

After the meal Briggs abruptly stood up and proclaimed, "I've waited until after the bash to tell you: I'm quitting being the combine cook. I've got to try more reading to fight the barbed-wire blues."

"Ed!" Cliff exclaimed, "Try theater. I know you flew your bomber almost back to England with two engines dead and with your crew bailed out. You're a hero and you keep it all inside you. Theater would bring you alive—"

Buck interrupted, "We pilots know amongst us who is a hero. You're just a navigator, Phillips. Quit this theater talk. We'll share the cooking from now on, Briggs."

José said, "With the garden gone I'm feeling like you, Briggs—I'm going to take a walk." Jose's leaving started everyone out of the room to escape each other.

On September 5 morale was lifted by the arrival of enough Parcels to shift from one-fourth to half rations. There was still no soup"s-on, but even the German news evoked new hope.

On September 9 Buck called on Colonel Raymond and told him, "I realize I didn't keep my mouth shut like the rules said I should. Straight out—I've come to see if you'd give the soup back to the kriegies and just keep me off of it. I don't deserve it, since I caused losing it. With the war heating up everybody is starved for soup—you know what I mean."

"So you've come to sacrifice yourself to be a hero. War is not that simple, soldier. Your breach of security was only the straw that broke the camel's back."

"I'm sure you're getting soup—along with your extra potatoes."

"You're dismissed, Captain."

"Not Captain—kriegie. We were all one rank to the flak and it's the same here with the goons. Size, muscle, and guts are what will count here as the going gets rougher. I'm going to be watching to see how you rank on that score."

"Is that a challenge?"

"I'm saying it respectful. All of us are looking to you as our leader and asking how you can handle real trouble."

"You're out of order, Captain Pierce."

"You can say that now, but if you ever need me you'll talk different. I'm no slacker."

"If you're looking to me as your leader, start showing it."

"I will, if you'll lead us right."

At evening Appell, Walt's translation of the German news included: "Another of Hitler's secret weapons is in action. Huge rocket bombs are already falling in Paris and London straight from space with such speed that there is no warning before they burst. This is only the beginning of the secret weapons that will bring victory for Germany."

September 17 brought electrifying news of a huge airborne Allied landing at Eindhoven, Nijmegen, and Arnhem. The Germans called the offensive "an enemy debacle."

German updates over the next days claimed that many thousands of Allied troops were being taken prisoner every day, and more had already been killed, and more were trapped and were being annihilated. Morale was shattered.

On the September 21 Raymond briefed his staff then went to visit his friend Bellrage.

"Have you gotten any new mail, Henry?" he asked after opening cordiality.

"I'm wishing I had. Margot's letters revive me. That might sound mushy to you, Dean. I know Kathy hasn't meant that much to you in recent years."

"I got a 'dear john' letter from Katherine," Raymond replied.

"Oh, Dean. Why did she write you that kind of letter here?"

"I'm sure she figured it wouldn't upset me, or she wouldn't have written it. But it does upset me. Tom is gone. Now she is, too. It leaves me all alone. We were separated too much, but you were separated from Margot, too. I have no good excuses. You know my weaknesses. I did get a beautiful letter from Gayle of my Hawaii days. In England, I briefly got together with Randi, my nurse-friend of my Philippines days, and she was a great solace when Tom was killed. But I envy the love between you and Margot."

"Stop. You'll get a new grab on life when we get back. Tell me about Arnhem."

"Arnhem? Cause for despair. The Allies executed a radical maneuver to short-cut the war. But British paratroopers who were supposed to take the bridges were dropped in the wrong place—the middle of SS tank forces—and the weather's closed in—no help from air power. We're surrounded and getting butchered. It's goddamned ground gore at its worst. The invasion is in big trouble."

"So we are here to face the winter?"

"Correct . . . if the Russians don't get here."

"What's our food situation? It's rumored that your staff is eating well."

"My small staff's amount of ration little affects what one kriegie gets when divided by twenty-five hundred. Being older, we have to exercise more to match the fitness of kriegies barely out of their teens. I'm forty-two, Henry. We are of another generation here."

"I didn't mean to start an argument."

"I've told you, you should be on my staff, too."

"I don't intend to aggravate you, Dean. I was in your situation before you got shot down. I had to turn my thinking to the grace of Jesus to keep from going to pieces. That's why I'm organizing education and doing Christian Science reading now."

"Henry, you can't really believe that the brain-warped Nazis anxious to kill us are going to wither away if we just turn our heads to education and healing? I just came from alerting my staff to the crisis building here. We're facing starvation, the winter, the enemy, anarchy, and our own brain vulnerabilities. As the Senior Officer, I have no military power to enforce my leadership, and you talk of—"

"By anarchy, do you include me?"

"Yes, if your independence and preaching of love sabotages the discipline we need."

"Dean, I'm worried about you. You get too agitated. You should be setting an example of us helping each other to get through whatever is coming for us."

243

"To hell with your wisdom of free-spirited helping each other. We have all types of kriegies here. Who do you think would take over if I stood aside like you do, Henry? You and I are in this goon cage because people stood aside and let the bad guys take over in Germany."

"By standards of might, Dean, remind yourself."

"Weren't we educated in West Point to the reality that might decides what is right? What else wins wars? Please, Henry, I came to see you to get away from my troubles, not to save you from loopy thinking."

"Let's quit this and drink some coffee. I've got a new jar of Nescafe."

"All right. I'll calm down, but you calm down, too."

"I only want to remind you of the cardinal virtues and deadly sins before you leave. We have a blessed opportunity here."

"Shut up!" Dean roared as he strode away.

"Dean, I haven't seen one kriegie lose his temper with the Germans. Doesn't that prove that anger is a sin we are free of here?—Don't leave angry!"

Storming back to his quarters, Dean continued to process the conditions he could not escape . . . *I've got to learn new ways to improve discipline—What are the secrets of charismatics like Aimee McPherson? There are ways to win leadership that I've never tried. I know about getting power through fear—fear of hell—fear of firing squads—but even sparkling mirrors can hypnotize men into obedience. I only want to learn enough to get the discipline we will need here to fight, if we need to.*

Across the compound Buck was propped up in his bunk, re-reading Randi's letter with its censored omissions.

Dear Buck:

So, the caterpillar has taken you through the needle's eye. D. R., too, has qualified for the caterpillar club. I've had a letter from him. ███████████████████████████

██

I'm waiting.

I went through the Red Cross to keep my promise to keep in touch. I am still working in the factory rebuilding machines as best we can from the H. D. we're getting in big shipments. █████████

██

██

I received your letter, Big Buck, signed, 'your lover,' as you warned you would. When you said that, I thought it was the bourbon talking. I was driven by warring feelings and I was woosy. I still feel different ways about you, but I'm going to be as daring as you in how I sign. ██████████████████████████

██

██

██

I missed your Old Crow and thought of you.

Your letter didn't say anything about London. Was it as crazy as your time with me? I felt lonesome after you left. Our night was crazy things coming together as they never could again. I wondered why you didn't keep in touch. Then I got the bad news.

I know you must be yearning to be back home. Keep looking up and you will find the flights of eagles in the sky. They are on the wing for all of us. When I get home, I will look you up. I want to climb Cloud Peak with you all the way.

Love,

Randi Scott S.R.

Buck puzzled: "*Randi Scott Singing River. . . rebuilding machines the best we can from the H. D. we're getting in big shipments? Rebuilding machines*"—*I figure she means she's nursing wounded back to health, and big shipments means a lot of wounded are coming in, but who or what does she mean by H.D.? I'm going to work on that puzzle until I figure it out.*

September 24: It was raining. Steady drips of water had formed pools on the floor. Buck, Briggs, and Cliff were playing three-handed pinochle. Walt was propped up in his bunk, writing. Sam had chosen bunk-travel over pinochle. . . . *Hitler has his power reaching out from Berlin like a spider web . . . It's been a month since the day of the spider. . . .*

Joe came in. Seeing the water on the floor, he called, "Dinghy drill in Room 7."

"Join us, Joe. We'll make the next game four-handed," Cliff invited.

"I'm heading back to Room 14. We're swapping yarns."

"Since the garden's kaput, you're mixing like an insurance salesman," Buck quipped.

"Sure . . . over two hundred prospects here. I hope the goons will crowd in more."

"Get out of here. You're not funny," Cliff teased.

The conversation attempted more humor than usual because a trainload of Parcels had arrived. Combine 7 was looking forward to six full Red Cross Parcels tomorrow.

Between deals Buck chattered, "The days of the wild West were the best time to live in. Trouble was settled man-to-man with no book work. The West went backwards when easterners brought in their ways of doing things. They called that progress, but it wasn't."

Cliff contested, "From Wyoming to Princeton is going backwards?"

"S-s-e-r-g-o-r-p to you, Cliff, if I'm spelling it right backwards."

"Come on guys. Play cards," Briggs protested.

Cliff persisted, "Bringing in our East way of law courts to decide between right and wrong was a better way than deciding by who draws fastest. It wasn't s-s-e-r-g-o-r-p."

"Cliff, I'm saying if we were Zane Grey's heroes we wouldn't be here jailed on the other side of the world. We got sent here by the big shots from your part of the country . . . I don't mean to hassle you, Cliff. I'm cutting up, kidding. I'll shut up."

"E-r-u-t-a-n. I'll agree to that difference going from West to East," Cliff came back. "If you seriously want to argue this stuff, come to our Unitarian meeting. That's what we do there, argue friendly-like, to learn from each other."

Deal me an erutan hand or a ssergorp hand, whatever, it couldn't be worse than what I've got," Briggs complained.

From across the room, Sam called, "Walt, I checked out a journal on Gypsies. Do you want to read it before I take it back?"

"I'm busy. Ask me later."

I can still see that caterpillar twisting to get free. Next thing I knew it was dead. Then I smashed the spider into a smear. Me and the spider are both killers. The spider killed for its dinner— Why did I kill the spider? Sam turned over and adjusted his lumpy pillow. *Killing the spider was the same as me with my bombsight killing . . . Did I do the bombing for my mother? Hatch does take sides after all . . . actually. I've got to think more about why I signed up—*

"Sam, hit the deck. We got a parcel for you."

Sam crawled out of his bunk with disbelief. He was handed a parcel that was from his mother. Opening it, he found powdered soup, pancake flour, and canned sardines.

"My mother knows I'm alive! I got a parcel from her before a letter. Let's throw a bash!"

By combine policy Sam had the choice of keeping any or all of his private parcel. Cliff told him, "We're going to get six full Parcels tomorrow. Keep your stuff for private snacks."

"My mother would want us to share it. You're cooking today, Cliff. Use it. That way we can bash today yet. I'm going to buy my Ma a home in her favorite part of Chicago."

"Heis wasser time, Hatch," Cliff reminded. The combine had voted Sam the job of getting the hot water each day from the cookhouse where it was heated in big boilers.

"I'll go with you," Walt said. "I have to catch the news."

A short time later, waiting for the news report to start, Sam and Walt heard the loudspeaker playing the haunting song of soldiering, romance, and loneliness, "Lilli Marlene." This was the song of German troops that had been heard across the no-man's-land of the Italian Front and was now sung throughout the world.

247

"When I hear 'Lilli Marlene,' it reminds me of Sandra," Sam said.

"You'd better queue up in the water line. I'll join you when I've got the news."

Sam moved into the line of kriegies waiting with tin pitchers to receive heis wasser. A gust of chilling wind caused him to pull his wool stocking cap over his ears. *Where did the Red Cross get the wonderful thousands of khaki stocking caps with the little bills on front? Too bad they ran out of wool overcoats but lucky our combine all got wool overcoats before they ran out.*

When Walt approached he told Sam, "Reading between the lines it seems that some of the trapped Arnhem troops got out. In Warsaw, the Resistance surrendered, so there goes the hope of liberation coming from there. The Germans brag that three hundred thousand Poles were killed in Warsaw in what the news calls a great victory for Hitler's SS."

While Walt waited with him, Sam asked, "What was it like for you as a bombardier—knowing you were sending tons of dynamite down on people?"

"That's a dumb question."

"How did it feel, pressing the button? Did it feel like, maybe, squashing a spider?"

"You're talking crazy. Too much sack time, Hatch. You need to keep busy."

"Why? I'm thinking about what to do. I'm not like you, always fired up and busy."

Water not hot enough to steam had been poured into the combine's dented tin pitcher. With news and heis wasser in hand, Walt and Sam started back for a bash of Sam's parcel.

At this time, in the vorlager, a silver pitcher of steaming hot ersatz coffee was on the white table cloth of Hauptmann Eiler's luncheon offered for Colonel Raymond.

"Wine?" Eiler asked as he raised a bottle of vintage Mosel.

"I'll refrain on the wine, in respect for the starvation diet you have us on. I accept the hospitality of your food in deference for us both being pilots."

"You know I am a pilot? I am only a civilian pilot, not a military pilot like you."

"Flying gets into your blood, doesn't it, Hauptmann? Looking down from the cathedral of space an army is as insignificant as a hill of ants. We are enemies by politics, but I never forget that we are, firstly, both flyers, whether Luftwaffe or Air Force."

"I never forget the thousands of women and children your air force has murdered. I am firstly devoted to our Führer, not to the pleasure of flying."

"Can you get me books in English to educate me on why you are so devoted to your Führer? His genius for rallying Germans is a mystery to me."

"I will try."

Eiler turned on the radio. March music filled the room.

"I wish to listen for the cuckoo bird that is the warning of bomber attack."

Raymond decided: *He has put on the radio to keep our conversation from being picked up.*

"Colonel, why are you organizing to train commandos?"

"My question is will we have coal to keep us from freezing in the coming winter?"

"You will get what coal we have for you. Our women and children come first."

"What about the Geneva rules that call for equal treatment for POWs?"

"Colonel, you are being belligerent. Will you provide coal for my daughters and wife?"

"If we don't get coal we will start tearing apart your buildings for fuel."

"Get back to why you want to train commandos. Do you expect the SS to replace me?"

"If your Intelligence discovers that I am giving a few prisoners extra physical training, you need not report that as training commandos. What is the problem?"

"You assure me that is all that you are planning?"

"Of course. If I intended to train commandos, it would be to help the Luftwaffe protect us from the SS. But I only intend physical health training."

249

"Physical health training. You may train one hundred. After that I will report."

"One hundred, as you allow. By our honor as officers," Dean promised.

On October 2, the enlisted men of Block 169 received powdered coal compressed into bricks about three inches wide, six inches long, and two inches thick. Room 7 received thirty-five bricks to last the week. This was hopefully enough to cook the evening meal each day.

On October 4, Raymond met with five trusted officers to organize the secret training of one hundred commandos. An English prisoner who was a special forces expert was put in charge and told to include training to inflict death without weapons.

With no coal to heat his room, Raymond went to bed to get warm and read about Aimee McPherson: *How did she rise from an unknown preacher in her twenties to world fame in her thirties? She was in stage central of a grand show pointing the way—the star with the message, the sparkling mirror. From her I learn the power of joyful promise. "Follow me to liberation." And from the book idealizing anarchy, I read bullshit for achieving voluntary cooperation. . . .*

He fell asleep and faded back to his Mercury Targa, driving the Pali pass with rain crashing against the windshield. Then to he and Gayle stripping off clothes on a beach and running as far as their feet could carry them into the deepening water. Swimming out to where the surf churned and beyond to quiet water under a diamond sprinkled sky. Basking in the tropical water phosphorescent with moonlight and earthbound stars of ships gliding across the sea. Riding the surf shoreward, rolling and tumbling with the foaming white water bright in the moonlight—lying on the warm sand of Oahu's north shore beach.

Coasting the Targa into the aroma of steaming ti leaves, tropical spices, golden yams, roasted corn, exuding smoke, and pineapple slices of a luau. Drinking scotch with Gayle sipping piná colada. Voluptuous hula dancers and haunting ukulele serenades.

Then the wine. "Portuguese Lancers," Gayle suggested. The rapture with which her blue eyes studied possibilities! Onion soup—*La Soupe ol'oignon gratine'e.* A pink miniature rose in a water glass flagged the "independent territory of Gayle-Dean." A main course of lobster in cognac sauce. Flaming brandy dessert . . . and then the wading through black-mirrored surf to the laughter, ukulele music, and flaming torches of the Royal Hotel.

Gayle, naked, coming toward him from across the bedroom suite. "You are classic art happening with every step you take."

Fondling her strawberry-blonde hair and stroking her freshly-scented body. Her whispering . . . "Uhmmm, that feels good . . . rub a little lower. Right there. Uhmmm . . . I wish it could be like this forever."

"Oh . . . Yes . . . It's nicer with you on top!"

"I love you."

Kissing with sensual craving and their bodies wrapped together . . . the surging tropical surf and the scent of jasmine pulsed together in their passionate wilderness—

Dean Raymond in Stalag Luft III suddenly realized he had climaxed in the wilderness of Hawaii, but Gayle was not with him as he reached for her. He could not bridge back to her from the loneliness in which he heard police dogs snarling by his door.

In the half-light of dawn, a guard entered and told him that a new purge of kriegies was at the gate. He dressed quickly and went out to meet them. It was a group of thirty prisoners whom the SS had refused to turn over to the Luftwaffe until now. SS troops with fixed bayonets escorted the limping and shuffling newcomers through the gate. They were clothed in garbage collections of civilian and military remnants, and they were shivering in the freezing cold. Some had shoes. Others had only rags wrapped around their feet.

Dean led the way to the cookhouse and steaming vegetable soup. They told how the SS had forced them to work in a mine with only a bowl of watery slop called soup once a day. They ate with no concern for the dead worms cooked in with the moldy vegetables.

October 5: In the morning cold, all of Combine 7 were in bed to keep warm except for Buck, who was sharpening his secret knife. *Old timers tell me weird things have happened to guys on the shit list like me.*

Sam, reading, called, "Walt, I found something here that I can't believe. You have to come here. I've got to show you."

Walt went over to Sam's bunk and Buck followed him.

"This is the translation of a story told by a twenty-year-old Gypsy of I-h-t-i-m-a-n with a dialect of the "v-l-a-c-h group," whatever that means. The story is called 'The Vixen and Pirusambi.' The vixen is a female fox, but Pirusambi is a Gypsy name. My Sandra's last name is Pirusambi! Listen. The story is going along and then right here it says, 'Stop! Don't kill me! I'll get the king's daughter for you. Pirusambi let her go.'— Pirusambi. That's my Sandra's name! Sandra's a Gypsy!"

"Sandra's got blue eyes . . . a Gypsy with blue eyes?" Walt challenged.

"It's right here in the book, Walt. That's her name."

Walt said, "She's not my kind of Gypsy. Saint Sarah was a missionary Gypsy."

"And you've got a missing finger because of her," Buck reminded.

The followers of Hitler called themselves Aryans, forgetting that the Gypsies were the first Aryans in the world, tens of centuries ago in the north of India, where their emblem was perhaps the swastika—that crooked cross which the Nazis have stolen with all the rest!

From "Germany and the Gypsies," by Mateo Maximoff, pages 106 of Journal of the Gypsy Lore Society, Vol. XXV, parts 3-4, issue of July-October, 1946, T. and A. Constable Ltd., printers to the University of Edinburgh. Obtainable from Bernard Quaritch, 11 Grafton St., New Bond St., London, W.1, England.

WAR PRISONERS LOOK TOWARD PEACE

Time to stop and think has been given to few Americans of Army age in these times. . . . Most of our time is given to thinking of and preparing for peace. The American contribution to the European peace interests some of us and in a discussion last night we found many reasons to believe that it can and should be more significant than it was after the last war. . . .

From articles in __The Christian Science Monitor,__ by Lieutenant Robert R. Brunn, a prisoner of war in Germany.

THE PRISON: CHAPTER FOUR

Wednesday, November 1: In Italy, counter-attacks and very heavy rainfall had brought the Allied campaign to a stalemate. In the East, the Russians had halted their forward thrust. In the West, increasing resistance had stopped the Allies. Kriegies hoped the Western Front would advance again as soon as Antwerp was opened as a supply port.

Red Cross food, reduced to half rations in October, was about to be reduced to one-fourth rations. Coal rations were meager. The Room 7 stove was only warm at 6:00 P.M. when the Combine used all their coal for cooking. Coal had become cherished as much as food.

It was now 6:00 P.M. but today Buck was in the cookhouse with the co-pilot of his fatal flight, Major Reddick. ". . . Buck, it's good you got your arm strength back because we've selected you to try out for special physical health training. It's secret, strictly for volunteers."

"It's strange you trusting me if it's secret."

"Buck, your history made for a stormy session. I argued for you because I know you're an ace in action."

"I'm not buying into the line that I'm being offered something without strings attached. I'll come once to see what it's about."

By the stove of Room 7 the subject was last night's hallway concert in which "I'll Be Home for Christmas" had been played several times on the compound phonograph. Today the combine talked about what to do in Stalag Luft III if they would not be home for Christmas.

José proposed, "We should start saving food for a bash, regardless."

Cliff said, "Walt, get us more food from your goon-buddying."

Walt shot back, "Accusing me of goon-buddying is no way to get my help."

José said, "The trades and the news we like, but why all the extra visiting with the goons, and why are you writing up your life in German? I'm asking you friendly."

"I'm keeping busy. It's my nature. When it comes to Christmas, I'll work to get us food smuggled in, but don't accuse me of goon-buddying."

Sam cut in, "Thanksgiving calls for a bash before Christmas, but going on quarter rations in this cold weather to save for a bash, we'd have to eat shoe leather."

Briggs asked Walt, "Is it true that Raymond is studying Nazi propaganda?"

"Instead of chasing rumors, you're supposed to be working up an escape plan."

"If I'm not in my bunk one day, you'll know I got one. Why shouldn't I ask if our Senior Officer is studying Nazi propaganda? I'm no blind believer like you."

"A lot going on here can't be talked about. We have to trust our leaders," Walt said.

Sam said, "They said on my radio we're not going to get any potatoes next week."

"Hatch, you don't have a radio. You're imagining things," Cliff politely instructed.

"I'm picking up the signal from the fillings in my teeth. The voice talks in English. He gives me announcements . . . whether you believe it or not."

"Hatch, you're going to go to the library with me in the morning and check out another book to read instead of listening to your radio," Walt asserted.

"I'm reading a book. It's about birds," Sam replied. "There's a country where there was nothing but birds until man got there. I'm reading up on what it would be like to live there."

"Come with me when I make my rounds visiting, Hatch," José invited.

"You've got your ways. I've got mine," Sam said. "What I dream of is nicer places than being here cooped up together all the time in the same room."

"Write a poem about it, Hatch," Cliff recommended. "We all know the feeling."

"Yeah," others joined.

Cliff broke the train of thought with, "I've set up a Unitarian meeting for Sunday even if only three people

showed up last time. I've especially invited Colonel
Raymond."

"Our stove's gone cold. Let's go to bed to get warm,"
Briggs suggested.

On Sunday, seven people, including Briggs and Sam,
showed up for Cliff's Unitarian meeting. As Cliff was reading from Sir Edwin Arnold's translation of *Light of Asia*,
Colonel Raymond entered and took a rear seat.

"... The blue doves cooed from every well, far off
The village drums beat from some marriage-feast;
All things spoke peace and plenty, and the Prince
Saw and rejoiced. But, looking deep, he saw
The thorns that grow upon the rose of life:
How the swart peasant sweated for his wage,
Toiling for leave to live; and how he urged
The great-eyed oxen through the flaming hours,
Goading their velvet flanks: then marked he, too,
How lizard fed on ant, and snake on him,
And kite on both; and how the fish-hawk robbed
The fish-tiger of that which it had seized;
The shrike chasing the bulbul, which did hunt
The jewelled butterflies; till everywhere
Each slew a slayer and in turn was slain,
Life living upon death. So the fair show
Veiled one vast, savage, grim conspiracy
Of mutual murder, from the worm to man,
Who himself kills his fellow; seeing which ..."

Raymond's mind drifted from the words he was hearing
... *That's what my life is all about: policing the strife. After
the reading, I'll speak on this and the need to organize to
police the peace as a reward of this war. I'll point the reading's message into my campaign for discipline.*

"... So saying the good Lord Buddha seated him
Under a jambu-tree, with ankles crossed—
As holy statues sit—and first began
To meditate this deep disease of life,
What its far source and whence its remedy.
So vast a pity filled him, such wide love
For living things, such passion to heal pain,
That by their stress his princely spirit passed
To ecstasy, ... "

Raising his eyes, Cliff said, "I read this for us to talk about because it says there's no escape from killing things. This hits home to what we did in getting here and what we should do about it when the war is over. The book says Buddha sat down and crossed his legs and said this pain and stress of all living things puts me into ecstasy. He's still sitting that way in statues of the East like that's the answer, but is it?"

A discussion began. Briggs, Sam, and Raymond remained quiet. Then Sam abruptly offered, "I wrote a poem about what Cliff's talking about:

Yellow tulips glisten in the sunshine after rain.
Dancers sing into the sky from which rain came.
I am caught within the eye of the storm.
Beyond my prison, soldiers swarm.

A long silence followed Sam's contribution. He decided that this meant the message intended by his poem remained his private vision. While he lamented his lack of talent to reach people with his poetry, Colonel Raymond stood up—

"Most Americans know only the first part of that reading—life as friendly—peace-loving. So when an enemy stabs us in the back like the Japs did at Pearl Harbor, we haven't got a strong military to fight them. Enemies will surprise us again if we don't get the second part of that reading—that life is strife. Defense has been a need of man since the days of stone hatchets. The War College reports that in only eight percent of known history was there peace. Our weakness for killing each other comes from our human brain, not our animal instincts. Honey bees, not humans, have the most harmonious society. After today's reading, it should be clear why we need discipline here to be fighting-ready for whatever comes. Thank you for inviting me, Lt. Phillips. I have to leave now."

The discussion faltered after the speech of the senior officer. Presently Cliff said, "That's it for today. We'll have a candle burning up front next week—our light reaching up."

The next day Buck met his physical-health-training teacher, Pitt, a Royal Air Force kriegie. After exercises that were explained to be tests of Buck's physical condition, Pitt said, "I'm going to teach ways to kill without weapons. I'll start with a demonstration. Act like you are leveling a pistol at me and see what happens."

Buck reached out with an imaginary pistol. At that moment he was struck on the neck, twisted around, and struck again with such speed and force that he was on the floor half-conscious and throbbing with pain before he could react.

"Christ!" he yelled, "This is crazy. No more for me!"

"I could have killed you. I hit light, as training. If I were a Nazi pulling a pistol, would you like to be able to do what I did?"

"If it takes getting killed to learn, leave me out."

"Be back tomorrow. Same time."

"We'll see," Buck said as he limped away. *What's going on here? That bastard hit me way beyond training. I should have had my knife, but that would really set him off. I'm in trouble.*

On the following day Walt delivered his diary to Colonel Raymond.

"An ambitious accomplishment," Raymond praised. "I'll clear it with Intelligence for censoring. This will help get the Germans to trust you."—*If they don't know your diary is fake, which most likely they do. We play this intelligence game of always presuming we are outsmarting the enemy though we know we likely are not.*

"I'm working as hard as I can to get them to trust me," Walt assured as Raymond walked away with the product of the many days of his tedious writing in German.

In the afternoon, Buck came into the room with a bruise on a cheekbone.

He answered quizzical looks with, "I was doing a little wrestling with a Limey, and he got me with a surprise. But I had a piece of rope along, and I taught him some rodeo work on how to bulldog a steer and knot him up quick with a four-string tie. I think he came off better respecting American ranching."

Walt and Buck shared a walk-and-talk to the south side of the cookhouse.

"I can talk German so good now I can pass as a kraut when I escape," Walt boasted.

"That's a laugh. If you got out alive, how would you walk hundreds of miles in winter without being spotted getting food, crossing bridges, and heading what you'd be guessing was the right direction? God, have you forgotten that the civilians are eager to hang you, Walt? I can still hear their cheering when they got Bill—from right beside me."

"Buck, lay off. Don't be so realistic. I'm cold and hungry. I need to keep hoping I'm going to escape. Let's just sit back and dream of better times."

When they were propped against the south wall, Buck said, "I've been thinking a lot about getting back home and into the Crow Peak wilderness. When my mind is wandering, I can see my spread reaching into the mountains and my ranch lay-out with the barns and corrals—but the house is foggy to me—that needs a woman's ideas."

"Cathy and I were going to work with my folks as missionaries in Arizona. My dad was so nice to Cathy my mother was jealous. Now Cathy wrote she is back in Nebraska with our baby. You know my folks aren't my real parents. My mother wanted to have her own baby, but my dad couldn't do his part—I mean to make a baby. He has a powerful way of taking over people. Cathy hasn't written about what went on after I left—why she went back to her folks. I still want us to be missionaries. The Arizona Indians are in terrible need of Christianity."

"Walt, Indians were getting along without us for longer than we've been badgering them. The Arizona Indians probably wouldn't miss you going to Nebraska."

"The Indians I'm talking about live in round mud huts, like animals. They've got all kinds of diseases and no religion. Cathy and I felt it was God's call for us to save them. Now with her gone back to Nebraska, I don't know what to think."

"Be happy we got potatoes today. Look at the bright side. We're getting more used to being hungry and cold. I'm feeling closer in touch with my horse Goldy out in the winter with just her horse hair skin to keep her warm. We've at least got Red Cross overcoats."

"Buck, when I was in the hospital what saved me was an American Red Cross Parcel. I got it just when my brain was twisting me into giving up, losing my faith in God."

Buck closed his eyes and lifted his face to the sun. "I love this warm yellow dandelion. My nurse friend in England called hospital time the bed war. I learned what she meant the hard way. Suffering is hell, but it's an education you don't get in school. My dad used to say, 'suffering is not enough.' That used to leave me scratchin' my head. Enough for what? Progress? My hospital time was progress."

"Mine wasn't progress, Buck. In spite of all the horrible things the Germans are doing, in the hospital I was beginning to feel guilty about what I had done to them."

"I'm still feeling guilty, myself, in spite of the Nazi sons-of-bitches. Killing is something my Friends-to-everybody religion taught me to be against. When I joined the war I was mixed up and I still am. How do you stop sons-of-bitches like the Nazis?"

"You kill them and all those, too, who put 'em into power. But let's not argue. I've just finished an awful tough writing duty. I just want to sit here and enjoy the sun."

"Since my arms are working better, I'm going to start training myself in self-defense. If you hear of anybody who's got a book on that let me know."

"Briggs has been snooping in the library a lot. Ask him."

"Has it occurred to you, Walt, that we call all the rest of our combine by their first name, but Ed we all call Briggs? I got started off with him wrong way back in England by ribbing him about the 'ghost of Munster.' It was a bad joke. He was the goat, and I was the smart ass, but I can't go back and start over. We're in the same room and still, I can't figure him. It's like he wants to scream and doesn't know how. He worries me."

"What's come of his hubba hubba push? He's got a look between sad and glad that doesn't change. Cliff wants him to try theater work. I can't see how that would help."

At the theater Briggs was asking Cliff, "How could you guys make all of these special lights and stuff out of tin cans? I envy your talent."

"It's not talent. It's love of what we're doing. I can get you into it."

"I haven't got the talent."

"All the world's a stage, all the people merely players, Ed. Before you climb the barbed wire to let the machine guns end your misery, try it. Let yourself go. Write a song. Fart or whistle. Do something to lift your spirits!"

"I'd like to, if I had the talent."

"I'll make a deal with you. You come up with an idea. Silly. Dumb. Dull. Who cares? We'll jazz it up to make it play. Not for the theater for a start—for the combine."

"I couldn't lose on that. I'll work on something and let you know."

The next day, Wednesday, November 8, a chilling wind brought news of freezing weather coming. In a corner of the cookhouse, Raymond convened his staff. After the soups-on news, now only coming to his staff, he listened to Block Commander reports and responded with orders he deemed appropriate. Then he reported, "Now that Eisenhower has his invasion to show history books how World War Two had to be won, High Command is belatedly giving us chances to knock out Oil. It's too late for us to make the invasion a mere mop-up of Hitler's paralyzed war machine. But our air force is hitting oil depots and refineries by day, and the Royal Air Force is trying to hit them by night. We're still handicapped by higher priorities we're forced to honor—raids in support of the invasion and to bomb rocket launch pads spooking England. Yet, in spite of being screwed, we will still win the victory through air power—by bombing Germany out of Oil. But at this time, ground armies are still getting heavy resistance. We still haven't had enough chance to achieve the amount of oil shortage we need.

"Now about our situation here. We've started training commandos. We're going to organize in military units, squads of eight, with squad leaders for a chain of command, I'll give the block commanders more details later."

As the meeting ended Raymond asked Sneed and Peyser to wait. "Colonel Sneed, I'm writing a formal protest reporting violations of Geneva Convention rules. I need a medical evaluation of the danger of an epidemic deriving from our food and fuel shortage."

"Also, emphasize the crisis of no drugs to treat disease. I'll write up a report."

"In another vein, Dr. Sneed, I'd like you to visit Major Bellrage. See if you think he would qualify for repatriation as a psychiatric emergency."

"I hear you. I know Bellrage has been down a long time. I'll visit with him."

"Now, Major Peyser, I need to talk to you, my Rations Officer. On quarter rations we will run out of Red Cross Parcels by the end of January—in the middle of winter. I'm planning to lower—"

"Colonel, we can't lower to less than quarter rations. The Germans give less than a potato a day, a couple of slices of bread, and a cup of wormy soup. We've got to gamble on the front getting here, the war ending, or more Parcels arriving before we run out."

"My plan, Peyser, is to go to one-tenth rations until the weather gets colder."

"The weather is already too cold to get by on one-tenth rations."

"Thank you, Peyser, I'll make the decision after meeting with Hauptmann Eiler."

"I assume you'll push Eiler about the coal-ration shortage. We're not even in the ball park of rations equal to German troops' like the Geneva Convention requires."

"Peyser, the Germans are running out of food, fuel, and everything else. As their shot-down terrorfliegers, we are lowest on the list for what is left, but I will push."

The meeting with Eiler began without a lunch ceremony. When Raymond complained about the coal, Eiler replied, "Everyone in Germany is sacrificing as we prepare for our victory offensive."

This Hauptmann is scared to death of the SS. I've got to convince him that I care about his and his family's personal welfare. "Hauptmann, with generals like Rommel committing suicide, you know that your war situation is not nearing a victory offensive. Neither your Luftwaffe command nor your family's personal welfare is served by patriotic bullshit."

"I will not tolerate such disrespect!" With no explanation, Eiler turned on the radio. Then he asserted, "I must be convinced that your organizing activity is strictly for physical health. I must never hear of prisoners training to fight. And I must warn you personally, Colonel Raymond, for your own safety, guard your tongue when you speak to me."

"Turn off the radio. I will guard my tongue. I will talk about the books you gave me." When the room was quiet, Raymond continued, "I was impressed by the twenty-five demands of National Socialism set forth in Munich. Hitler's demands must have had great appeal for Germans impoverished by the Allies after the First World War. Also, I picked up the attitude of Germans who felt impoverished by the wealth and power of the Jews. Hitler came as their savior—their Führer, literally. Your books helped me understand."

"Colonel, to understand you must have lived in Germany and suffered with us. Now I must end this meeting. Henceforth, put your complaints into writing, officially, but expect no changes. Be grateful that we still have the mercy to let you live."

The meeting with Eiler was on Friday. On Sunday, Raymond began one-tenth rations.

At the morning Appell of the following Wednesday, November 15, the Germans announced an identity check. In the hallway of one of the blocks, they had set up a table which held boxes of identity cards that included pictures. The question of whether race was listed on the card was of particular concern to Sam as he waited. When he finally stood before the table, he was directed to show the prisoner-of-war tags that the Germans had issued to be hung around each prisoner's neck.

"Stimmt," the guard called to signify that the number Sam was wearing agreed with the number in his record. "Stimmt," he called again as he checked the picture against the person he was viewing. The guard then asked, "What is the name you use here?"

"Lieutenant O'Brien."

"Your card read Samuel O'Brien. Samuel is Jew name. O'Brien is Irish. Have you change name to hide that you Jew?"

"You have my name, rank, and serial number. According to the Geneva Convention that is all I have to—"

"Enough. We know you from Chicago. We know you Chicago gangsters the Jews have hire to bomb us. I put your card in special file. Next."

When the identity check was over and the combine was gathered around the stove, Sam asked, "Were any of you told your card was going into a special file?"

No one answered.

Finally Buck reassured, "Sam, whatever they told you doesn't mean a thing. You're Air Force. That's all that counts. The old timers tell me the Luftwaffe has never separated prisoners by race. You just got a chicken-shit guard who was trying to scare you."

Sam wanted to believe Buck, but doubt lingered.

"I got another radio report on the potatoes. We're not going to get any," Sam advised.

Walt said again, "There is no radio. Quit talking about it."

"Suits me. I'd rather talk about the restaurant I'm going to start. I'm going to serve fried rabbit with hot, crumbly, cheese-filled baked potatoes. First, a glass of sweet port wine. Then a big bowl of shrimp cocktail. After that, assorted cold meats served on fresh green lettuce and roasted nuts to munch on between mouthfuls of cold cuts—"

"Stop!" Walt exclaimed. "What happened to the rule forbidding food talk?"

"I was talking about my future business," Sam protested.

Buck said, "I didn't stop him 'cause it was sounding too good to stop."

"Okay, you dreamers," José announced, "I have your feast of the day. One half cup of cooked crackers, a quarter-inch slice of toast, one half of a hot potato, and a quarter-inch slice of blood sausage."

Three days later a Red Cross shipment arrived. Half rations began immediately. On Monday Cliff served rations of spam for dinner.

"My spam today is going to taste better than T-bone steak," Buck remarked.

"Einstein said it first . . . all is relative," Cliff said.

"Hubba hubba," Briggs chanted.

Buck put another brick of coal into the stove and explained, "It helps to be the block coal officer. My friend Jack Dawson slipped us two extra bricks today."

"We shouldn't be taking more than our share," Walt admonished.

To change the subject José said, "How about you starting coffee-time again, Phillips?"

"I've used my cigarettes to trade coffee for Unitarian meetings. Come to the meeting next Sunday for coffee-time. Colonel Raymond's going to speak," Cliff informed.

"The word's gotten around," Buck said. "I'll be there."

"I'm thinking we should talk about why we're here," Walt proposed.

Briggs joked, "Tell us, Walt. Why are we here?"

Walt said, "I don't know if you're teasing, but we never talk about how we're trying to make the world better by whipping the Japs and goons."

"That's old news. We're fighting to make the world safe

for democracy," José said with feigned seriousness.

"That was the first World War," Walt corrected. "My idea is the Allies should organize the world like we organized the United States to keep peace between countries like we keep it between the states. That's worth talking about."

"Why?" Briggs asked. "If I live through this, I'll ask for no more."

"Listen to me," Sam began. "About this country where there are only birds. Hundreds of different kinds of ferns and flowers and trees are there that are nowhere else in the world. No snakes, flies or mosquitoes or any other ugly things either— not even poison ivy. This place is two big islands and it never gets too cold or too hot. It's all palm trees and luscious plants and ferns with no mean animals, or things to cause you harm."

"Heaven!" José beamed. "Tell me too it's got more fish than you can catch, and I'll never miss another day of church."

"You're not far off, calling it heaven, Joe. The people who live there call it Godzone. When we get freed, I'm going to live there with Sandra. There's a place called Lonely Bay where a beautiful princess once lived alone. The fishermen used to sail by there on their way to sea— to wave to her naked on the beach. Now she's passed on and the trees are there growing fruit wanting to be picked, and the fish are still flashing silver in that bay waiting to be brought in for baking with butter and potatoes. I'm thinking I might start my restaurant there. I might just serve fish and frog legs if they haven't got rabbits there—"

"Hatch, that's enough for today," Buck advised. "The coal's burned out."

At morning Appell of Wednesday, November 22, Fanning announced that regardless of weather everyone from now on would be required to walk the perimeter at least two laps a day as part of a new health program. He explained that the block had been divided into teams of eight kriegies each with team leaders named to head the training.

When the count was over, Hauptmann Eiler ordered the formations to hold fast. Guards circled the kriegies, and for four hours they could not escape the cold wind that was blowing that day.

When finally released, Combine 7 hurried back to their room for shelter. They found chaos. All the mattresses were dumped on the floor and slashed with knife jabs that exposed their innards of wood shavings. The contents of lockers and stored food were scattered on the floor between the slashed mattresses. The table was overturned. The bunks were pulled away from the walls. The lockers, too, were twisted out of place. Nothing was untouched. Other rooms of the block were not in disarray.

"Let's look through the other blocks to see who else they hit," Buck proposed.

The broader survey revealed that two rooms in other blocks had some dislocation of contents, but no room was close to being the disheveled mess of Room 7 of Block 169.

"Why us?" Buck puzzled.

"Obviously they think we've got something we shouldn't have," Walt said.

"They're hot to find weapons," José noted. "Have you thought about that, Buck?"

Buck muttered in a low, toneless voice, "I've checked. My knife is still there."

"Maybe they think we've started a tunnel," Briggs speculated.

"With our floor built on stilts, it couldn't be that," Cliff reasoned.

"Maybe they're looking for sand from the digging? I don't know. They're sure as hell looking for something in this room," Buck pressed.

Sam reflected, "Maybe that guard who told me he put me in a special file is behind this. Maybe this is because I'm in this room."

"We can guess our way around the bend trying to figure out these goons. Whatever it is, maybe this is the end of it. Let's get this mess cleaned up and think about something else," Buck appealed. "Tomorrow's Thanksgiving day. I made a deal with my friend Jack to give us some extra coal and weigh us a bit heavy on the German food, since it's a special day. Did you make a trade with Smitty, Walt?"

"A trade? We were out of cigarettes until today, but he promised to bring in some onions and apples for us on credit—can you believe that—for our holiday."

By half-ration standards, the resulting Thanksgiving was a feast in a warm room. After the meal, Buck confided, "We got a break from the enlisted men today because I agreed as coal officer to turn my head when they measured out their coal. Their room's warm today, too."

"I told you I don't want to hear this kind of talk," Walt said.

Cliff broke into the increasing tension with, "Edward Briggs of Nashville, Tennessee, has an original song to premiere at this time."

Briggs insisted, "This is Cliff's thing, too. We worked it up together."

"Well, we're going to sing it together," Cliff said.

"Let's stand by the window, Cliff, where I can read the words."

In a voice cracking between bass and baritone, Briggs joined Cliff's tenor resonance:

CRIPPILY OLD CRUD

"Sing it again!" Sam appealed,

"Not on your life," Briggs said in full retreat.

"Who's next?" José asked.

"I'll tell you more about birds," Sam began. "In America, we wiped out all the passenger pigeons—hundreds of millions of them. There used to be so many they made a pink cloud a mile wide and eighty miles long flying over Kentucky before civilization got to them. Now there isn't one left. Civilization does horrible things destroying God's wonders. I'm anxious to get to my bird land. That place is so far away from any other country that it's a whole different world. I haven't told you about—"

"Hatch, it's been a good Thanksgiving meal, but I see everyone's starting to leave the table," José apologized. "Maybe you could tell us some other time."

"Come with me, Hatch," Buck suggested. "We'll work out on the bar . . . build our arm strength."

On Sunday the ground was white with a two-inch cover of snow. Colonel Raymond crunched his way to the room intended for a small Unitarian meeting. So many kriegies were there that he moved the meeting to the theater. Cliff kept the curtains closed, and on the edge of the stage floor he placed a tin can holding his promised flaming candle which was the only warmth in the cold hall. Raymond stood at audience level before the gathered group with the candle flame lifting beside him at shoulder height. Ten minutes into his talk, Buck entered carrying a book and took a seat in the front row.

After glancing at the German sergeant monitoring his speech, Raymond continued, ". . . so we are not just organizing health teams to survive to liberation. Our program of physical health training will give us self-confidence and athletic prowess for future success in life and love. The victor in lower animal romance usually allows the defeated a merciful retreat. With humans, the struggle is less physical but also less moral. According to Wolfgang von Buddenbrock, as I have copied the conclusion of his studies, 'We have here the astonishing fact that amongst animals, matters are considerably more moral than amongst humans.' In other words, in our human struggle we must win to survive.

"In a previous meeting I was reminded of our God-given nature to kill or be killed. We politely call this the food chain. It means we need to be ready to defend our lives in all places including here. Creatures like the Brazilian fire ants and some human beings are aggressive out of sheer malice as if they enjoy inflicting torture on others. We need to train here to be ready to fight the Brazilian fire-ant-types—when we get home.

"Even hyenas don't kill their own species. In that way they're more moral than people around us who kill their own kind for no reason other than politics. Germans have organized their military might so effectively because they understand that physical health preparedness is vital when challenged by killers. The Germans demonstrate that physical health includes military discipline. We need to train hard to be equally as healthy as the Germans, for our self defense. . . . The meeting is now open for discussion."

Buck immediately rose. "I apologize for being late. I was waiting at the wrong place. I brought this book from the library to read something. Being late, I decided not to— but hearing the Colonel say people are worse than hyenas, I decided to read a small part that made me feel good about people. It comes from Modern Political Theory:

"Governments from their very nature use force, force to separate men who are naturally friends into different and hostile nationalities, force to separate men who are naturally brothers into different and hostile classes. . . . Government means compulsion, exclusion, distraction, separation; while anarchy is freedom, union, and love. . . . Anarchy is not the absence of order; it is the absence of force. . . . Men's natural friendliness will grow and deepen until, instead of seeing each alien other group a rival to be feared, or an enemy to be overcome, they will regard it as a friendly society."

"I had to read that at least. The Colonel is very educated, so I know I missed a lot of important things, but I couldn't let stand what I did hear. Cliff told us arguing polite here was what his church was all about, their way to find God's way. That's why I read that."

"We return to discussion," Raymond said.

After waiting for further response that no one offered, Cliff thanked Raymond for coming and concluded the meeting.

Buck went back to Room 7 and climbed into bed to get warm. When others returned, no one talked about the meeting. It was as if the meeting had no significance in this day's reality of the coming meal, the stale air, the snow outside, and the room so cold that even bed offered no comfortable warmth. That night, when all were trying to find sleep, the discomfort of the cold was wordlessly communicated by the stirring that told all were awake.

On Tuesday Walt gave his Intelligence contact the copy he had made before returning Krauss's diary. Then he called on Raymond with some notes and told him, "He was mighty cocky when he was flying combat. After he crashed and was grounded, he smarted off to his superior officer. That's when they transferred him. He reminded me of Buck. Here he wrote, 'Most Germans would die for their Fatherland, but I am a rebel.'"

"He says he is a rebel?"

"He couldn't have meant he was in a real revolt against Hitler."

"A rebel is a rebel."

"I don't think Buck's trying to drum up a real revolt."

"Get on with the diary, without your comments."

"Here he wrote, 'The sky is a privileged battleground reigned by those who fly.'"

"I am laughing—as a Colonel in our air force. That's a fantasy from World War I."

"Here's another note I copied. 'The other night when I brought up the boxer Schmeling, Walters got red in the face with anger, because Schmeling gave up to a Negro.' Then he wrote about bombing Coventry, only the sky part, nothing different, but here is something I thought worth copying. 'We are having a shot down English pilot at our pilot's mess for dinner tonight. After all, though we are enemies we are still both pilots.'"

"Our guard Krauss wrote that? You have to keep trying to get friendlier with him."

"Hear this: 'General Göring is sterilized, so his children couldn't be his—'"

"Let Intelligence sift through that rubbish. What else?"

"He had some poems a pilot named Seymour wrote. I sent them on untranslated."

"Right. They'll translate the poems for codes. Did he write about German bombers?"

"Not exactly. But at the end he wrote this: 'I thought I was a hero when I was a bomber pilot. Now that they sacked me I am wiser.'"

Raymond went to the window from where he could see an arriving purge of patriots waiting for the barbed wire gates to open. "At least the end is not drivel," he mumbled.

"Sir, before I leave, I'd like a favor for my friend, Lieutenant O'Brien. He stays in bed most of the time, and now he's says he's picking up radio news from his teeth. He recites poetry that nobody understands. He talks about a far off country where there are only birds. He says he was born from an egg that hatched in the sun. He wants us to call him Hatch. If you gave him a job to keep him busy, his mind might get to working better."

"Leave it to me. I'll take care of it."

On Tuesday, November 28, Raymond met with his staff and block commanders for what he called a November wrap-up. . . . "In the West, unexpected German resistance, heavy rains, and supply troubles have stalled the advance. The Allies have been clearing mines all month to open the port of Antwerp. Antwerp and London are both now getting flying bombs. The front is stalled a few miles from the Rhine. Our bombing has continued to hit oil depots and refineries, but we still have competing orders to hit communication targets. The Oil bombing is good news too late to save us from the invasion, but it will still shorten the war.

"Three hundred miles away to the east we're still waiting for the Russians to move. To the south in Italy, our offensive of November 21 is stalled by wet weather."

"So, we're here to face the winter if the Russians won't free us. Our reserve is six and two-thirds Parcels per POW.

274

German potato and bread rations may be cut further.

"We are now training one hundred commandos. We must train no more than precisely one hundred. This is a deadly risk. I've been talking to groups to build morale. I intend a precarious balance between keeping reserve food and rationing enough to keep training. With the air offensive hitting marshaling yards, I expect no more Red Cross—"

"Guards approaching. Four of them," the security kriegie called.

Raymond continued, ". . . Red Cross magazines tell that we are in a model prison, and we must be sure to write—"

"What is going on here? You have no request for this meeting!" a guard challenged.

"We only got together to talk about mail and what we should write in letters."

"You know that you must have approval and monitoring for a meeting of this size!"

"We will disband at once."

"I order you to! Next time file a request!"

The guards left and took a direction toward Block 169.

In Room 7, Buck, propped in his bunk to keep warm, was listening to Cliff, also in his bunk. ". . . I was disappointed by both of you. Pa Raymond didn't come with a Unitarian attitude, and you came armed with a book—ammunition to get him. Pa Raymond's brain-dancing might have fooled the snooping kraut, but it didn't fool me. Neither of you—"

The four guards entered the room.

"Stand up! All you! Which one is Samuel O'Brien?"

Buck, Cliff, Briggs, José, and Sam got out of their bunks.

"I'm Captain Pierce, the room commander. Direct your questions to me."

"One is missing. Who is it?"

"Captain Plank. He's walking the perimeter," Buck answered.

"We get orders pick up Samuel O'Brien. If we need check identity tags, we do."

"Until we know what this is about, we're not going to cooperate," Buck asserted.

"I'm Lieutenant O'Brien," Sam said.

"You come with us."

"Wait a while," Buck protested. "You've got to tell us what this is about."

The spokesman guard answered, "We no generals tell you what is about. We get orders pick up Samuel O'Brien. Come. Out with you."

Sam put on his overcoat and said, "Look after my scrapbook, guys. I've got some poems and drawings in there I would like my mother to have."

Those were his last words as he was ushered through the doorway. Briggs, Cliff, José, and Buck followed down the hallway and watched as he was escorted toward the monstrous barbed wired gates that opened to the hostile German world.

A drawing by Lester N. Smith, a World War II prisoner of war of Stalag Luft III.

THE PRISON: CHAPTER FIVE

Walt returned from his walk in time to see Sam being taken away. Buck told Walt, "Since you talk German, you take this up through channels and stick with our brass all the way to Hauptmann Eiler—and talk to him yourself! The goons have got to bring Sam back."

Gossip about Sam spread with various speculation. Raymond got a meeting with Hauptmann Eiler next day. Afterwards, he went to Room 7 and told the combine, "Eiler said he could only tell me that Lieutenant O'Brien is being interrogated at the Headquarters of the five compounds. He pointed out that he had no authority beyond West Compound. I demanded more information at once, but he told me to come back tomorrow at two."

By the time Combine 7 had lived with Sam's empty bunk for two days, the mystery of why he had been taken away and what was happening to him made his absence doubly difficult to endure. Everyone of the compound was trying to guess what kind of new, morbid policy had been signaled by this abduction. The minds of Combine 7 sought other directions to escape agonizing about the unsolvable puzzle.

Buck joined José in visiting, and once while they were walking he asked, "Have you run into anyone who knows Judo or any of those other weird ways of laying somebody low?"

"That's a funny question. I've been looking for that, too. Why do you want to know?"

"I can't tell you, but believe me, I've got my reasons. A couple of times lately I got to tussling and by god, Joe, I swear I was marked to get killed."

"Were you tussling with a Royal Air Force bloke by chance?"

José came to a stop and looked squarely at Buck while he waited for his answer.

"Yeah. How did you know, Joe?"

"Because I got the same message from that bloke."

"I'll be damned. Then I wasn't marked for the ax. They wouldn't be out to get you."

"No, but it's a damn mean game."

"Game? It's way beyond that, Joe. We'll come out ugly son-of-bitchin killers."

"We're both of the chosen damned, Buck."

"Good name for it. We're marked for suicide shit-work."

"Okay, Buck. Let's practice on each other and give that Limey some education.

"Yeah. We'll have him singing 'Piss on the King.'"

In Room 7, Briggs was telling Cliff, ". . . Joyce is from a rich family of Tennessee horse country. Having lots of time to think here, I'm mixed up one whether that's the kind of life I want. The one thing I know I'm good at is being a pilot. Maybe I could get into airline piloting. I'm looking for kriegies to talk to about what it's like to spend your time raising horses, not like out west, the Tennessee kind of horse raising. One guy told me General Mitchell, our air force hero, gave up flying to go into horse raising in Virginia."

Walt came in clapping his gloved hands. "At least it's warmer in here than outside. I couldn't learn a thing. Smitty claims he doesn't know anything, which is probably true, since he's only a ferret. All day I've been thinking about Sam—how he did things we didn't appreciate, like drawing keepsake pictures. The one I like best that he did for me was the nose of my B-17 with the rest of the plane blown off. I've got my head glued to the bombsight, and I'm saying, 'I wish the pilot would keep this damn plane level.'"

Cliff said, "Until now, we talked more about how Sam was messed up from too much sack time. How did you talk about me when they took me away with diphtheria?"

"We had you in a robe with a halo, talking about your coffee-times."

"What's for lunch?" José interjected as he entered the room.

Buck, entering with him, asked, "Any news about Hatch?"

"None," Walt answered, "but call him Sam. It's clear the goons know he's Jewish."

Buck said to Walt, "You know that name is more than hiding he's part Jew. When we squabbled, Hatch always tried to stop us. With a Jewish mother and a Catholic father, his fighting was in his own home as much as on the street with the Polish, Irish, Germans—hell I can't even remember them all. Did you know his dad was a drunk—shoving him out on the street to fight? There's more, too—stuff I won't even mention. The story about the sun hatching him on a stump wasn't so crazy when it told him he was from a better place."

Cliff added, "He doesn't want to see himself as a fighter."

"Give Sam at least three days before you start doing his funeral speeches," José said.

At that moment, "Hatch" O'Brien opened the door and walked in.

"Hi. You won't believe what I've been through."

"Jesus Christ!" Buck exclaimed.

"I'm starved," Sam said. "All they fed me was barley soup."

"Go to bed and cover up. No questions until you're warm and fed," Buck ordered.

"I've got to report that he's back," Walt said, and he hurried from the room.

Sam, when covered with blankets, kept talking. ". . . They kept insisting I had a secret radio. I was totally honest. I told them I was picking up radio news in English from the fillings of my teeth, and that was all. Instead of believing me, they got madder and madder as I kept telling the same story. They slapped me around, kept me in a chair, and wouldn't let me sleep. They kept switching the guards pestering me. They kept screaming I was trying make a fool of them telling them I was getting the radio signals from the fillings of my teeth. Finally I got so sleepy I couldn't talk sense anymore. Then they let me sleep, sitting in the chair, and when they woke me up a real mean looking lieutenant was staring at me like he was going to get the truth from me or kill me. We went through radio questions all over again with me so sleepy my mind wandered into talking about iwas."

"What are iwas?" Buck asked.

"Those are a kind of real ornery birds. Maybe I thought of them because of how ornery the goons were treating me. I told the goons the iwas probably had no idea of how ornery they were. I'm trying to remember just how I said it because it turned everything around. I think I said the iwas probably felt like me when I smashed the spider.

"They stopped me there, and the lieutenant looked over to the corporal. I said I was no better than the iwas because I knew the spider was just killing to get something to eat, but watching him doing it made me mad, so I killed him, for no reason, just for the kick of wiping out his life.

"The lieutenant and the corporal started to exchange more looks. I knew I should shut up, but I was so groggy I couldn't stop talking. The lieutenant started yelling at me in German so I started talking nice stuff about birds and ferns and other luscious plants with not even one animal around—that paradise country called Godzone I've told you about. I told them they shouldn't think I was making it up because it was a real country right here on earth that I was going to live in if they would give me a chance to.

"The lieutenant smiled then, and he looked at the corporal with his eye brows raised and started making circles around his ear. The corporal nodded like he'd picked up a signal, and he lifted a finger and started to make circles around his ear, too. The lieutenant patted me on the shoulder and said, 'Be at peace, lieutenant. We will let you live to go to your paradise. While you are our prisoner, enjoy your radio, but you must never again smash any spiders. That is an order! Such cruelty will not be tolerated in the German Reich!'"

"'Yes, sir.' I told him."

"They laughed, and the lieutenant called in the other guards. He braced them all to attention and gave them that cold, Nazi kind of screaming dressing-down that knots your stomach. The next I knew there was a lot of 'Heil Hitler' saluting and they threw my overcoat at me and marched me back to the West Compound. When the gate opened, they pushed me in so hard I fell on my face. Then I got up and walked on in here. That's all there is to it."

Fanning had entered the room while Sam was talking. Having heard the last of Sam's story he now said, "Welcome back, Samuel O'Brien. Colonel Raymond has talked to me about the report Eiler gave him on you. We're going to keep you busier. I am assigning you to be the "block coal officer." Since Pierce has held that job until now, he can give you the details of your duties. First, take a day of bed rest to recover."

Hatch had returned to Room 7 on Friday, December 1. On Saturday he began an earnest study of the block's coal situation. He knew all of the stumps in the camp had been torn out, chipped up, and burned. Now, coal was the only source of heat, so he saw his job as a very serious responsibility. To him, the coal was just as crucial to survival now as food. He counted the seven bricks stacked neatly beside the stove of Room 7. He recorded that each of the bricks was seven inches long, two and one-half inches wide, and one and one-half inches thick.

Next, he went down the hall and knocked on the enlisted men's door. When the door opened, he noted that, though it was still morning, the room was comfortably warm.

"I'm the new coal officer," he announced. "I've come by to take inventory."

"We haven't counted up exactly. We've got the coal heaped in the store room."

"Which one of you is in charge of the coal?"

"We all work at it."

"I'm going to need one of you to be in charge. Jack Dawson, let's make it you."

The door to the store room was open. Sam looked inside and asked, "Why is there so much coal here that you haven't rationed to the rooms?"

"We just got it yesterday. We're going to get it out to the rooms today," Dawson said.

"I notice your room is warm. Are you burning some of the coal before you divide it?"

"Not at all. We're burning coal from our share."

"Never mind. From now on we're going to count the bricks like they were bricks of gold. We'll stack them as we count them so we'll know exactly what we have. Then we'll figure what each room has coming, exactly. I want all of us to work together friendly."

"I think you're getting carried away, talking about this coal like it was gold. We've been doing this job with Captain Pierce with no complaints."

"I didn't ask for this job, but this is the only way I can see to run it."

When Sam left the storeroom, he carried a tally of exactly how many bricks were on hand. When the distribution was made later in the day, he accompanied the coal to each room and checked off the number of bricks delivered.

On Friday, December 8, Combine 7 had a meeting to start planning a Christmas bash. The talk centered on saving food and coal to have a big Christmas meal in a warm room, accepting by now that they would not be "home for Christmas."

After several hints, another topic was brought up openly by Buck. "What we're trying to tell you, Hatch, without making you feel bad, is that the way you're running the coal job is getting us shorted on food. Since the enlisted men giving out the coal are also giving out the German food, we figure they're telling us something."

"That's right," Walt said.

Briggs explained, "We're not saying you shouldn't run the coal job honest, but you ought to know we're all paying for it."

Sam, after pondering the problem, responded, "Someone should tell Colonel Raymond. There's no point in telling Fanning because he's been pressuring me to give him extra coal, and I haven't listened."

"Come on, Hatch," Buck said. "You know the whole Command staff is tied in with getting favors from the rations handlers. Complaining to them is asking the foxes to lock up the chicken coop."

Hatch answered, "I'll talk to the enlisted men."

"Good luck," Buck said cynically.

José tried to support Sam by saying, "It's right how you're handling the coal job. We're just letting you know it's hurting our saving food for Christmas."

Over the next week Hatch talked with Jack alone and with the enlisted men as a group, to convince them not to short Room 7 on food rations. "After all, what I'm doing has nothing to do with them," he appealed.

A week passed without anyone of Combine 7 mentioning a rationing problem in Hatch's presence. By this time it was only a week and two days until Christmas. Sam asked Buck to tell him, honestly, if the combine still felt they were getting shorted.

"Hatch, if you're asking for the truth, our bellies have been too empty and our bodies too cold to save more than a can of spam and some crackers. We've talked the situation over, and we've decided we're not going to hassle you."

"Thanks for letting me know."

On December 16, Colonel Raymond called a crisis assembly of his staff to report that the Germans had launched what they were calling "the long-prepared-for German counter-offensive." They were smashing through the Allied lines. They were claiming this bold surprise would bring German victory.

With demeanor that betrayed his bewilderment, he went on, "With total surprise, Hitler has attacked the thinly protected center of our line along the Ardennes with two hundred fifty thousand troops and more tanks than we thought they had. The Germans have gone for broke. If we defeat this offensive the war will be over soon. If we don't, we're in very deep trouble."

Three days later soup's on reported that a fifty-mile-wide breach and fifteen miles deep had been cut in the Allied front and pockets of allied resistance had been bypassed. The whole town of Bastogne had been isolated by Rundstedt's tank armies. Allied air power couldn't help because the weather was un-flyable soup clear to the ground. In Raymond's words, "If we get some clear weather our beautiful Air Force will have a chance to help our ground gripping generals who got us into this mess. If the weather doesn't change soon, I frankly don't see what will rescue our ground war from this disaster called the Battle of the Bulge—unless the Germans run out of oil."

West Compound, getting only the German news, sank into deeper despair with each news report as Christmas approached. By Christmas Eve the German news had the blitzkrieg sixty-five miles into allied territory. In this circumstance Combine 7 gathered to talk about how to celebrate Christmas.

"I've got a Christmas present to cheer you up," Sam said. "I'm going to give the coal job back to Buck to handle his way. We'll keep it in my name, so Fanning won't appoint an officer in my place that would treat him special and maybe short us. Buck's friend Dawson has already promised me he'd give Buck a break to get us a warm room tomorrow and a heavier food ration for Christmas—to make up for things. I'm going to walk a lap now to get away from any talk to argue me out of this."

When Sam returned, Buck told him, "We've been talking good things about you. I've had a talk with Dawson, too. I'm going to run the work for you, but I'm not going to sell out on you, Hatch. I'm going to be as honest as I can without getting us shorted."

Nature was generous on Christmas morn. The sky was clear and the sun was strong. By noon the outside temperature was fifty-degrees Fahrenheit. José opened the window to let outside air replace the foul air of the night. At 1:30 in the afternoon, with the room air-fresh, Briggs closed the window and heated up the stove to prepare the Christmas meal and warm the room. The Christmas meal was twice a normal half rations menu.

As a concession, Cliff hosted a coffee-time program after the meal, including a chorus of "Jingle Bells," with José adding an encore in Spanish. Sam apologized for not being able to get the right words together for a poem telling how he felt.

Suddenly Buck got up and said, "In my family's religion we have Meetings in which we all sit quiet until someone has the urge to say something. If everybody's for doing that today on Christmas, I'd like us to sit quiet and see if anyone has something to say."

The combine grew silent, sitting around the flame of Cliff's klim can burner heating the coffee. After several minutes Briggs broke the silence with, "We've been sharing our bread-farts in this room for going on nine months, and at times putting up with each other has been rough. But at other times, like when Cliff was sick and Hatch was taken away, it was different being a combine—more like what it's like here now."

Buck got up and said, "I'm not bitching. I'm giving thanks for our luck on this Christmas when you add up the scores of guys getting killed today in the fighting."

Without getting up, Walt added, "Amen. Blessed be those who are dying for "honor, God, and country." I'm sorry Smitty couldn't come through with apples for a pie, but I'm thankful he at least came through with the onions."

Cliff rose to say, "What I'm thinking right now is I'm never going to forget how you cared for me when I had diphtheria and almost died. Saying thank you isn't much of a Christmas present, but I'm giving you that."

"Me, too," Hatch said. "Cliff's talking for me, too, for when I was sick afraid."

José got up and stepped away from the table before he said, "We're missing the sunshine. It must be seventy degrees on the south side. I'm volunteering to clean up and wash the dishes as my present. Don't argue, 'cause I'm planning my own present of washing my long-johns in the leftover hot dishwater."

The good-news Christmas gift had not yet arrived. On Christmas the skies had cleared and an unending air attack had begun that was devastating the German troops and tanks of the Battle of the Bulge. Eisenhower brought up extra divisions for counter-attack. Bastogne was reinforced by a U.S. airborne division. Patton's Third Army pushed north to relieve the attack on Bastogne.

By New Year's Day the German news was rich with "strategic advances to the rear." Raymond gathered his staff for a war review and with it he announced that shortage of oil—gasoline—for the advancing German tanks had been a major factor in defeating Hitler's stunning war-victory gamble. With a larger perspective, he informed that from May to January, air power had reduced German oil production by more than half.

Raymond's most arresting report of the New Year's Day was that the Russians, only two hundred fifty miles away, were now ready in strength and supply lines to launch their promised final offensive against Germany. A vast attack was expected within days.

After the meeting, Raymond told Sneed and Peyser, "Since the Russians could be here within weeks, I'm ordering each kriegie to increase his walking, in stages over the next two weeks, until he is walking eight miles a day. I have to push our training this hard, but I can't move to higher than half rations. Moving to full rations would risk starving in February if the Russians don't get here."

"Kriegies are losing weight on half rations without more exercise," Sneed protested.

Peyser advised, "We need to move to full rations for at least two weeks while we're into this training push."

"I'm hearing both of you. We flew our combat crews without enough sleep, expecting casualties from pushing beyond medical limits, for the greater good of an offensive. I have to proceed likewise here, for the greater good. In our more critical food situation, I'm going to take personal control of Parcel distribution. Eiler will allow us to inspect the vorlager Parcel warehouse tomorrow at two o'clock."

After the inspection of Parcel reserves Raymond spoke to his medical officer: "You haven't given me your diagnosis of Major Bellrage. Do you think he might qualify for emergency repatriation as a mental case?"

"Henry's been down a long time, and he's been through a lot. He's changed. By the time you and I get out of here, we may have changed as much. He's no danger to himself or other people so let him be. Loosen up, Dean, for your own mental health."

Three days later, on Saturday, January 6, Room 7 was scheduled to get a visit from their block commander between 10:00 A.M. and noon. While waiting, the combine was surprised by an uncommon visitor, the kriegie mail clerk. "Did you guys hit the jackpot! You got four letters. Stay in your bunks and keep warm. I'll bring your mail to you: Brewster Pierce . . . Samuel O'Brien . . . Walter Plank . . . Ed Briggs."

After reading part of his letter, Walt exclaimed, "Wow! You guys remember me telling about Sister Johanna? My wife got a letter from a Sister Johanna in San Francisco who wrote she was my nurse in Germany, and I'm okay. Cathy writes, 'She wants me to tell you she's back in the U.S., and she's wearing the Gypsy ring of Saint Sara for you.'"

Briggs said, "Joyce's father passed away. She's inherited money to build our own place, and now she has the horses of her father's place to start our own farm."

"My letter's from my mother," Sam said. "She's working in a factory making things that the censor blacked out. She doesn't mention Sandra. I gave Sandra my home address and told her if I don't come back someday, she should write to my mother to keep in touch. Maybe she wrote and my mother didn't mention it, or maybe that part got blacked out."

Buck said, "I got another letter from my nurse friend, Randi, and she writes again that the H.D. keeps coming in. What in hell is H.D.? I've been wracking my brain on that for months. Does anybody know?—"

At that moment Lt. Col. Fanning knocked on the door and entered, saying, "We've got lookouts posted for secrecy, so gather around and I'll get started. The war's heating up in ways you wouldn't know, not getting the allied news. We've got to move fast to get ourselves ready for action. We're organized into squads of eight. North, South, Center, and East compounds are also organized. You six will be joined in your squad by two kriegies from Room 14. Captain Pierce is your squad leader, with Captain Plank next in line.

Pierce and Cabrera have been getting special training as part of one hundred commandos. If we call them out for a special assignment, that will leave your squad short.

"To get in shape each of you is to lap the perimeter a mile and a half starting today and an extra half mile every day from now on until you get in eight miles a day. If trouble strikes, our alarm is a bugle blowing *adjutant's call*. If you ever hear adjutant's call, get to your room at once and get a runner to me for further instructions. That's all for now."

"Wait a minute," Buck said. "While you're here, I'm telling my squad to follow your orders, so don't put me on the court-martial list if some of my squad do what they think best for themselves in spite of what you're ordering. We've got no magic to keep us going like our leaders eating at the senior officers' mess—okay, leave, Lieutenant Colonel Fanning. I know you don't want to hear about us having our own brains."

The next five days were a suspense of ambiguous German news reports. Meanwhile, the perimeter path became a line of walkers, and Buck wondered how far kriegies would overtax themselves to comply with orders.

Saturday, January 13, was twenty degrees below freezing. As Sam waited in line for heis wasser, with his breath steaming contrails and his mind in London, he was abruptly alerted by shouting. Walt ran toward him, blaring, "The Russians have started their offensive! Yesterday at 10:00 A.M.! The news just said, 'At 10:00 A.M. yesterday the guns of the Russian armies roared the resumption of battle.' Sam, Uncle Joe's coming to get us!"

Sunday, January 14: Walt, finishing his translation for 9:00 A.M. Appell, said, "I'll give you the highlights. There is major fighting along the whole six-hundred-mile Eastern Front. The news calls the fighting on the roads to Germany 'unheard of fury.' Berlin admits the Russians have taken a town ten miles from the Warsaw-Kracow rail line that connects Hitler's armies. There's too much—I can't write it down fast enough. It's unbelievable!"

"It's great!" José rejoiced. "When will they get here?"

"They're coming awfully fast. At ten miles a day, they'll be here before three weeks."

Cliff gleefully rubbed his hands. "I've got coffee saved for my church meetings that I've quit having. I'm going to have coffee-time today in honor of the Russkies."

"I say we use our coal ration to get the room warm for coffee-time," Briggs proposed.

"We've got three apples from Smitty for an apple-like pie as a bonus," Walt added.

The combine left for morning Appell anticipating their coming liberation.

In the afternoon, when the apple pie was served, Cliff said, "Don't give me any. I'm on the no-eat prescription for the GIs again. I'm too weak to walk my laps today."

"Moving up a half mile a day, what are we supposed to be walking now?" Sam asked.

"Five and a half miles today," Walt answered.

"Who's doing it?" Buck asked.

"I am," Walt said.

"And you're limping worse. You ought to get a medical release. I'll apply for you," Buck volunteered. "I'll apply for you, too, Cliff, while I'm at it."

"I am walking as much as I can," Cliff said.

Buck noted, "If the Russians get here, the Nazis may do something crazy to keep the Russians from getting us. Do what you can to be in shape."

Cliff said, "I'm a reacher. I was meaning for this time to be something more than problem-talk—something loftier. Do you have a poem, Sam?"

"Me? I was hoping you'd come up with a song or skit, Cliff." . . .

Walt broke in, "I'll get apples for next time. Smitty knows his wife, Paula, is alive now. He's asking me to get him and Paula to America. That gives me an edge in trading with him."

Monday, January 15: Walt reported: "We're in the center of an arc two hundred miles away with the Russians coming in on a front two hundred miles across. Berlin says six hundred thousand Soviet troops are attacking from Warsaw to Krakow. They warn that the Red Army is not simply aiming to gain ground, it intends to end the war. In Poland Marshal Koneff's troops gained seventeen miles today to split the German armies."

Walt now said, "I told the war news first, but I've got other news. In the vorlager right now are five thousand Parcels still on wagons that came in early this morning!"

There was high praise for Walt's reporting as the combine hurried to Appell. In the afternoon, Briggs asked Buck to join him for a few laps. As they walked, Briggs asked Buck some questions about his life.

"You've talked about your saddle horse, Goldy, but have you ever raised horses?"

"Does a mare have colts? Why do you ask? Does your wife want you to horse farm?"

"Yes, and it's not what I want to do, but I'd like to learn more about it before giving her a flat . . . no. I'm feeling I want to keep being a pilot, flying, free in the sky, not tied down to breeding Tennessee walking horses."

"You got the wrong wrangler for advice on your kind of high brow horse raising. My life is more mountain-combing and open sage brush cow-chasing. I think we've got less rules for doing things where I live than you have in your blue-blood horse country. If my friend Singing River and me would hitch up, it would be no problem staying together for life 'cause we'd be too busy whipping the winters and living the summers to think of what we're missing."

"Maybe after the war they'll be looking for pilots with four-engine time to fly airliners. If I can't be a pilot, rather than raise horses, I'd like to start a restaurant with fish baked with lemon and butter, or cornmeal batter-fried. A white-meat fish fried right will almost melt in your mouth—"

"You're cheating, Ed. You've got me drooling for food we ain't got. I want to hear when we'll start getting full rations now that we got five thousand more Parcels. Pa Raymond's probably thinking he's extra smart saving food in case the Russians stop coming. He's not seeing that walking is taking us backwards—forward Ssergorp."

"What?"

"Progress backwards."

"He'll start full rations. Wait and see," Briggs predicted.

Tuesday, January 16: Cliff wrote in his kriegie diary: *I'm weak, but I'm hungry again. I had a package from home with cookies, candy, and toilet paper. Today I ate my mother's cookies.*

Wednesday, January 17: Two million Russian troops were now on the offensive in the East. Some were only forty miles from Germany. . . .

The snow of the perimeter path was beaten flat from the many feet of kriegies. Sam and José were among the walkers. "Hatch, I've been thinking about you being Catholic. We've got that in common. How come you never go to church with me?" José asked.

"Are you saying, because of what might happen, I ought to get right with God, Joe?"

"Honestly, that's what I think. I like you. I know you come from parents with different religions, but with your name O'Brien I see you as Irish and needing to make your peace with the Church."

"The church meaning Catholic?"

"Yeah."

"My Jewish mother is the best part of me, Joe. She's all heart. My dad made me cross myself, but I could never be Catholic, not meaning to knock you, Joe. When I think of my mother, I'm all Jew for what she's been through—but I'm not going back to being Jew, either. Before I got shot down, I took out lots of insurance for my ma, just in case. Now I'm looking to be a new person, where the albatross land after circling the world."

"Hatch, you talk bullshit about moving to your birdland, and you talk about getting mistreated as a Jew. You think me as a Mexican in Bodega Bay didn't get shit on? We Mexicans were in California long before the newcomers there today who treat us like foreigners. I've got my war stories about growing up just like you, but I'm never going to leave Bodega Bay. I'm going home to get my own fishing rig."

"Cliff says I'm a reacher, more than a Catholic or a Jew—reaching for a better place."

Thursday, January 18: Raymond and Sneed were visiting by the warmth of a stove boiling the day's potato ration. When they began to discuss their different professions, Raymond asked, "Sneed, how did you get from gynecology to being a military M.D.? What would make a man specialize in probing women's organs of reproduction?"

"I ask you, Dean, what would make a man specialize in the job of killing people?"

"It's the military's job to kill the no-good products of your profession. The Russian military is doing a good job of that today—twenty-five miles past Warsaw and still coming. From the southwest they're only one hundred and seventy-five miles away."

"Dean, Stalin parked next to Warsaw and let the Nazis slaughter hundreds of thousands of Poles. He might stop at the German border and tell the Allies, 'If you want Germany, spill your blood, capitalists.'"

"At tomorrow's staff meeting I'll report on how I'm planning for any contingency. I need to get your medical outlook."

"I've already told you. You're pushing our training beyond what is possible."

"I've ignored what you told me, because it's only one factor of my command crisis."

"You've ordered walking eight miles a day. I've run calculations, and by my figures the miles walked yesterday averaged three."

"I didn't expect total compliance. I ordered eight to put on pressure."

"We got five thousand new Parcels on Sunday. You could have used a quarter of them to bring us to full rations, if only for this week, but you didn't. Kriegies aren't complying as a consequence of your decision—"

"Stop it, Sneed. Wait for my analysis tomorrow. I can't base decisions on unfounded optimism. It's still a long time until Spring."

Friday, January 19: The Russians, with a fast-moving tank spearhead, had reached the German Silesia border one hundred sixty miles from Stalag Luft III.

Dean briefed his staff, "I'm watching to see if they further extend their supply lines and continue into Germany. For now I'm staying with half rations. I must plan for being here months from now, even though we could get adjutant's call at any time."

Major Peyser rose. "Colonel, kriegies can't walk eight miles a day without more to eat. We're getting a lot of heavy complaining. What can we tell them?"

"My command judgment will not be ruled by popularity."

A tense quiet pervaded. Raymond left the briefing to meet block commanders.

Saturday, January 20: Before Appell Walt told the combine, "The news says they've reached the German border at Praszka, which is only one hundred forty miles from here, but, of course, the news is always late. They could be closer. It's hard to believe that Hitler would let it be told, but the news says three million Soviet troops are on the march on a six-hundred-and-fifty-mile front from East Prussia to Czechoslovakia."

"I see the red flag, hammer and sickle and all, flying over Eiler's office," Sam said.

"They'll have to let us stay here until our air force can fly us home," Walt reasoned.

"We'll have our reserve of Parcels to keep us eating—three good meals a day and a warm room from the coal the *krauts* have stored," Briggs added.

Sunday, January 21: The loudspeaker reported the Russians were six miles inside the German border, one hundred twenty-five miles away. At morning Appell, Fanning announced, "Full rations distribution, one Parcel per kriegie, will begin this week, staggered on Thursday, Friday, and Saturday. Also, your senior officer advises that you use your ingenuity to put together a back pack from clothes you can spare, in case we're ordered to evacuate."

Later, Combine 7 talked about the latest developments. . . .

"They can't move us . . . we're in no shape to march," Walt decided.

"They couldn't move us in the middle of the winter . . ."

"To carry our stuff we're supposed to make packs out of "ingenuity" . . . whatever the hell that is . . . Raymond's got his head up his ass."

" . . . out of this Thursday-Friday-Saturday stagger, we got scheduled for Saturday. That's almost a week from now. There are plenty of people here to get out all the Parcels to everybody today yet . . ."

"You're good at talking to our big shot in camp, Walt. Ask him why he's so crazy," Buck proposed.

"I've already been told he's thought things through and won't change anything."

"Who's walking eight miles a day?" Cliff asked.

"I did yesterday," Walt said.

"And that's why you're limping worse than I've ever seen you," Buck responded.

"My knee that got the flak hit is acting up."

"Walt,"I applied for medical releases for you through channels, and they've ignored me. Now as room commander, I'm ordering you to rest."

"I don't want a release—"

"Hey," Cliff intruded, "Let's lighten up. I've got some good news. I've lined up our Melodiers trio of violin, bass violin, and banjo for a hallway concert Saturday night. They're good. Really good. You're going to glow when you hear them—"

"It's no use trying, Cliff," Sam said. "Too many heavy questions are stirring."

Monday, January 22: Buck put an arm to Walt's shoulder and steered him away from perimeter path. "I ordered you to rest. The stove's hot. Let's get a warm sit."

"That's a good idea."

Once in the room, Buck pulled a bench up to the stove, and he and Sam sat down. Walt picked up a shirt and a needle with thread and joined them.

"What's that?" Sam asked.

"I'm sewing together a pack with a needle I made from a klim can opener."

"Wherever you got your thread, it's too light for a pack," Buck advised.

"I traded for it at the Acco. It's all I could get."

Buck said, "Stop and think, Walt. If we're ordered to leave, there will be gobs of stuff left here to scavenge for making packs then."

"Are you going to ignore the order to make a pack now?" Walt asked.

"Stupid orders make fertilizer for white crosses. You follow my order to rest today."

"Big things are happening. The block's depending on me. I've got to get the news."

"The news will happen without you, Walt. You spend two days in your sack."

Tuesday, January 23: At morning Appell, Lt. Colonel Fanning announced to Block 169, "Captain Plank is in bed with a medical problem. We're going to have to go to the library and get our news from the map board."

1. Russians drive to 165 miles from Berlin.
2. Soviet Forces capture Karlsruhe 115 miles from Stalag Luft III.
3. German attack breaks through allied lines at Hagenau.

Adapted from New York Times Map of January 23, 1945.

Wednesday, January 24: Walt, back to news gathering, told Sam in the hot water line, "They're on a thirty-seven-mile front near Breslau. That's eighty miles away. They can get as close as thirty-five miles without crossing the Oder. Crossing that river is the key to our freedom."

"I give them three days to get here, Walt. See you in the room if I last through this freezing weather," Sam shivered, shuffling his feet and slapping his arms to keep warm.

After morning Appell Sam fell into trail with the line of walkers training for the unknown expected soon, but his mind was elsewhere . . . *parrots, eagles, and ravens that have only one love for all their lives. They all look alike to me but they must not to each other. The violet and bronze pigeons show off to their lovers with swoops up into the sky until they hang still and then they fall swishing like a plane chandelling until they pull up into a tree. I want to go see that when I'm free.*

The albatross . . . living on the water and circling around the whole world for five years until coming in to nest on land on the same place they came from. That can't be true, but it is. I can't say anything about that. The guys would laugh at me. I hope their kids come back, too, . . . a family reunion. No wonder the ancient mariner was cursed for killing an albatross. . . .

Thursday, January 25: The Russians had advanced thirty-eight miles on the previous day. The nearest front line was moving northwest along the east bank of the Oder, the next natural German defense barrier. Raymond knew that the Lublin Poles spoke of the Oder as the future western boundary for Poland. Thus he had decided that the Russian offensive would stop at the Oder. He now re-thought this forecast for he had just learned that the Russians had crossed the frozen Oder River by Oppeln.

Should I have started full rations earlier? He discussed his policy with Major Reddick.

"You've been like an athletic coach," Reddick told him. "You've carried the self-discipline and put the pressure on for those who needed it."

"I hope so," Raymond replied. "That's why we need officers in the military. Most people are followers. I don't expect to be admired for being the hard ass I've had to be— 'putting on the pressure,' as you call it."

"The leader who needs to be popular belongs in politics, not war," Reddick told him.

"After the war, maybe I should quit the military and take up politics," Dean answered. "Our country needs leaders who put the good of the country above popularity."

That night Dean lay awake a long while. *If we get freed, I'm going to make my vacation a jungle big-game hunt— that will be a challenge to recharge my spirit. My liberation medicine will be Scotch whiskey and with it the hunt. What then? I can't think that far. Maybe I'll want to settle down. My luck in love has never lasted. Maybe the answer is to go back to my marriage, but Katherine has closed that door.*

Friday, January 26: In an emergency visit to Colonel Raymond's room, Hauptmann Eiler rattled, "I have no orders about what I should do if the Russians suddenly arrive here. I expect this is because Berlin plans to hold at the Oder. I ask you, Colonel, what is the news from your source? It is best for all of us to know what the situation really is."

"I agree. My source contradicts yours. Allied news reports that the Russians have crossed the Oder and established a bridgehead at Steinau."

"Steinau? Only eighty kilometers from us? Why didn't I hear through my channels?"

"Perhaps it's not true, Hauptmann."

"What do you think?"

"I used to think your forces would hold at the Oder. Now I don't know."

"Another question. I don't expect you to tell your secrets, but can you assure me that you can pass down orders quickly to all our prisoners in case of emergency?" Eiler asked.

"What kind of emergency?"

"I don't know. What if the Russians suddenly arrive, attacking, with our thousands of prisoners in the middle of the battle? What then, Colonel?"

"If you would surrender immediately it would save needless killing, Hauptmann."

"An expected answer. As I see it, if the worst comes, the most probable order will be for us to retreat with you. I do not believe Hitler will allow the Russians to free thousands of flyers to bomb us again."

"This I will tell you. We have a signal to announce an emergency. We will council then and decide what we will do. Since we have no weapons, our options are limited."

"It is good that you have thought ahead and planned. Panic would be disastrous."

"I agree."

"Colonel, I give you my word that I will personally notify you at once of orders I get. My guards will not start to kill prisoners if you do not attack first."

"I will make no promises. When you inform me of your orders, I will decide what we will do. You can be sure that your trouble will not be prisoners in panic."

"I respect that we are on different sides in this crisis. I have my wife and daughters in Sagan, and I am in horror of what will happen to them if the Russians get here."

"If we have finished our military exchange, I prefer to hear no more, Hauptmann."

"Of course." Eiler unthinkingly clicked his heels as he about-faced and left.

Saturday, January 27: Today, Combine 7 was to finally get their full Parcel per man. Added to this promise was the hallway concert of the Melodiers to be performed in the hallway. Beyond these expectations was the excitement of the Eastern Front getting closer.

Walt got up at 8:35 A.M. and walked to the cookhouse with Sam. Reading the centigrade thermometer, Sam transposed to twenty-degrees below freezing, fahrenheit.

A kriegie asked Walt, "What's the latest on Uncle Joe's Cossacks?"

"Give me a chance to hear—" But when the report ended, Walt did not stop to talk. He hurried back to Room 7. "The news said the Russians crossed the Oder at Steinau but were driven back. That's less than fifty miles from here. We'll have to wait for the four o'clock *Wehrmacht Bericht* to get more on it. If they get across the Oder there's nothing to stop them from coming straight to us."

"Walt," Buck asked, "did you ever get Pa Raymond to tell you why he held up giving us our Red Cross Parcels?"

"Yes, I did. He said that a Parcel before Saturday would have given us a Parcel and a half, since we'd already been rationed half a Parcel for the week. He told me we still have only five weeks of reserve on full rations and war is never predictable."

"Whose side are you on, Walt?"

"I'm not saying he was right. I think maybe he was planning ahead too far."

"This is another case of out-of-touch leaders ruling the small fry whose asses are in the wringer."

At 9:30 A.M. Appell the block commanders put their kriegies through calisthenics while they waited for the count to begin. When the count was finished, Walt hurried back to the room and went back to bed with all his clothes on.

He reviewed his planned routine for the day. From under his blankets, he weighed the possible consequences of the Russians crossing the Oder fifty miles away. He decided to skip the trip to the map room and instead work at sewing up his pack. *I'm not in shape to march. In this weather I wouldn't stand a chance, but I'm going to be ready to try.*

He got up and shaved, and after that he worked on his pack. Then he went to bed again to get warm. At 11:30 A.M., Smitty came by, motioned Walt into the hall, and began to talk in German, "You have ways of getting news we don't get. How close are the Russians?"

"I don't know any more than you."

"You must know more. You have no idea what beasts the Russians are. For you they mean freedom, but for me—God knows what. I want to give you Paula's address. She is in a town near Dachau in Bavaria. In case I'm captured or killed by the Russians, I want you to tell her what happened."

"I'll do that for you," Walt promised.

Smitty passed Walt Paula's address. "I brought some bread for you. I couldn't get anything else. I don't want anything for the bread. If the Russians get me, tell Paula I said we must both trust in God that we will be together again." He hurried out the door.

Walt went back to bed until his lunch of two cups of ersatz tea and two one-eighth-inch slices of toasted black bread, barren of the margarine or jam of better times.

At 12:30 P.M. he went to the map room and library. First, he studied the Eastern Front drawn on the map on the wall. Then he checked out the book he was supposed to receive today. *I can't know. Maybe the front will hold. I don't want to lose my turn with the book.*

Limping across the compound, he decided he should walk the perimeter while he waited for the *Wehrmacht Bericht* at four o'clock. On the way, he passed Colonel Raymond.

"Sir, if I can do anything to help, I mean, if you need an interpreter or anything—"

"I have my Staff, but I'll keep you in mind, Captain Plank."

"I'm sorry to bother you. I just wanted you to know—" Raymond had walked away.

Walt started to walk the perimeter path, but after one lap he decided the walking was doing more harm than good. He went back to the room and worked on his pack.

At 3:45 P.M. he started to the cookhouse loudspeaker. On the way he passed the recently assigned guard, Schumann, who was a small man of about sixty. In spite of his uniform, Schumann still looked like a farmer. He had a wrinkled face and his mouth was turned down in a frozen, sour expression. A rifle with an extremely long barrel was slung from his shoulder. The butt of the rifle almost touched the ground. To Walt, Schumann was a bizarre example of how Hitler's war of "supermen" had gone awry. Walt had been rebuffed by Schumann every time he had tried to be friendly, yet, wanting to locate Krauss, he hesitantly asked, "Can you tell me where Oberfeldwebel Krauss is?"

"It is no business of the prisoners to know where their

guards keep themselves. Move along!" Walt noted again that Schumann could not be approached.

At 4:00 P.M. Walt had his pencil and pad ready as the announcer began the official report which said the Russians had been held at the Oder at a point that he knew from the map was thirty-five miles away. *Who can say how old this news is? Can I believe this?*

At 4:30 Appell he read his translated report. After Appell he ran to catch up with Krauss. "Do you think the Russians have crossed the Oder? If they manage to cross the river, will you march us away?"

"How should I know? Ask me nothing! You have only to hope you will be freed. For me a breakthrough could be the start of a fight unto death."

Walt went back to the room to wait for dinner. It was 5:00 P.M. Then 5:30 P.M. and the Red Cross Parcels had still not arrived.

José complained, "What the hell is wrong? We usually get them by noon. I was figuring we'd have the Parcel food for a big dinner."

"They say they're slowed up because Pa Raymond's making them keep a record of every Parcel they hand out," Buck said. "It's a phony excuse to me."

Cliff asserted, "Let's not wait. Let's eat what food we've got left and settle for that."

All agreed. They each ate one-fourth cup of boiled K-2 crackers flavored with cheese, a toasted one-fourth-inch slice of Smitty's gift of bread, and one half a boiled potato.

Cliff interrupted his eating to comment, "Colonel Raymond should have to answer for his food handling when this war is over."

After the meal, Walt washed the dishes and then his long-john underwear, which he hung above the stove to dry.

At 7:30 P.M. the six Red Cross Parcels arrived.

"Let's have dinner all over again," Buck proposed.

José said, "We had dinner. The Parcels we just got have to last us a week. We should wait and have a big meal in the morning."

"I'm with you, Joe," Briggs said.

"Me, too." Walt agreed. "We only have five Parcels each left in reserve."

"How do you vote, Sam?" Buck asked.

"I know you tell me not to pay attention to my private radio, but from what I'm hearing, I think we should hold off until tomorrow."

Cliff said, "I'm with you on this one, Buck. We should eat now, for the energy, just in case."

"We're out-voted, Cliff, by the belly-blind. We've been scared of starving for so long, we're afraid to eat a meal when we've got one."

At 8:30 P.M. the Melodiers began their concert in the hallway. When the trio had finished three variations of "On the Sunny Side of the Street," whistling and clapping filled the block.

Sam got out of bed and came over to Walt. "Let's go watch," he suggested.

"I'd rather rest," Walt said.

"You're worrying too much."

"Sam, if the Russians cross the Oder, they'll probably be here before the news can tell us."

"If there's shooting, I'm for getting under the block and digging a hole," Sam proposed.

"In the frozen ground with no pick and shovel?"

"We'll figure something out."

"We've got our organization. Maybe we'll take over the guard towers and help kill the Germans," Walt speculated.

"I wouldn't be any help at that. I'm still for trying to dig a hole."

"We'll all do what we're told. We'll fall into our squads and take our orders from our squad leaders. That's what we'll do," Walt declared.

"I don't think they'll let the Russians free us," Sam said.

"Sam, I can feel freedom real close tonight. I can see our guards getting crushed under Stalin's tanks."

"Whatever happens, let's stick together," Sam proposed.

"I'm not in good enough shape to be much help to you, Sam. You'd better stick with Buck. He's got a knife."

"Buck's in the commandos. The same with Joe. I didn't

mean just two of us stick together. I meant the whole combine. I'm going out to the concert, Walt."

The Melodiers started into "Home on the Range." Sam
squeezed a place to sit on floor. The kriegies, packed together, hummed along while the violin, banjo, and bass violin
music lifted them from the hallway to the wide open range
of America.

ADJUTANT'S CALL!

Everything stopped. All was totally quiet except for the
sound of a trumpet carrying faint but clear through the
north door closed against the winter night. In the silence
following the end of the trumpet message, a murmur of conversation slowly rose to a crescendo.

Lt. Colonel Fanning shouted, "At ease. Stand by for
orders." And with that, he hurried from the building.

The kriegies in the hallway pushed their way back into
their own rooms. For five minutes they shuffled nervously,
conversed tensely, and waited. Then someone shouted, "Here
he comes," and everyone pushed back into the hallway.

Fanning, breathless from running, stepped onto a stool.

"At ease. Orders are that we march in one hour. The
Germans have released this property for salvage. They say
the Russians are going to get it, so it doesn't matter, but
they warn us not to let the place catch fire. That would
make a landmark that could draw shellfire. Arsonists will
be shot."

A mix of uneasy talk and groans broke from the listeners.

"You're free to use anything here to build packs or sleds
or whatever you can figure out to haul your stuff out of here.
The Germans report the Russians thirty miles away. Their
orders are to get us out of here before the Russians arrive."

Fanning paused to catch his breath, then continued,
"We'll each get a Red Cross Parcel as we pass through the
vorlager on our way out."

Now Fanning drew another deep breath and for a
moment stood quiet before he said, "Well, goddamn it,
whether you live through this or not is up to you.
Hauptmann Eiler says orders came from Berlin to shoot any

prisoners who can't keep the pace of the march.

"Colonel Raymond orders, if you can't keep up, throw away your food first, your blankets last. I'm telling you, I'm sure not dropping back to help anyone who can't keep up. Each of you is on your own. If you're crippled, check with me. I've got a list of prisoners the Germans are going to let stay here. That's all. We are to be in front of the block in our emergency formation and ready to march in about an hour—ten o'clock."

Combine 7 went back to their room. Walt thanked God for the foresight to make a pack. He opened his locker and began to remove his personal things—soup, tooth brush, memory pad, and house plans he'd been working on. Buck had opened the Parcels and everyone else was taking food to carry with them. When Walt looked up and saw the Parcels being emptied, he crossed the room and saw that the sugar cubes and the D-bar chocolate bars were already gone. He got a can of liver pâté, corned beef, klim, and butter, and stuffed these into his pack above his one cotton blanket and one wool blanket. Over all of this he put his damp long-john underwear.

Everyone was so busy getting a pack together for survival that they paid little attention to each other. Beds were being broken apart and mattresses were being ripped open for materials to make sleds and packs. All were frantically working to gather and pack their belongings and food.

A runner came by and barked, "Be ready to fall out in ten minutes."

It seemed impossible that so much time had passed. Perhaps the fall-out time had been changed, Walt thought. He slipped into the harness of his pack and leaned his weight into the straps. A ripping sound told him that the pack was tearing apart. All his supplies clumped and clattered to the floor, and the cans rolled away. He gathered up his scattered cans and supplies and heaped them onto the remains of his bunk . . . *I can't give up, but I'm whipped. . . .* In desperation he rushed to Fanning's room and asked if he could be put on the medic's list of those who would be left behind.

"Get serious, Plank. You're walking out of here."

The other combine members all now had packs of various kinds ready.

As Walt returned to the room, Buck was coming toward the door with a huge sack-like pack slung over his shoulders.

"Where's your pack?" Buck asked.

"It came apart," Walt replied.

"I tried to tell you," Buck said. "We're out of time, but where's your stuff?"

"On my bunk."

Buck un-slung his pack and called to Walt, "Get your stuff off your mattress."

Wielding his razor-sharp knife he ripped Walt's mattress in half and pulled off the cover. He doubled back the ends of the cover, brought out some wire he had stashed under his own bunk, and pierced the wire through the cover as thread to secure the loops. "This may cut your shoulders, but it sure as hell won't come apart. Put your arms through the holes and I'll throw your crap into it. Come on. We're due outside. I fixed up Sam with the same deal. I've checked the whole combine and we're all set to go."

"I'll never forget this, Buck. You're saving my life."

"Don't crow yet. We're just getting started. It's thirty degrees below freezing. I'll stay with you to kick some speed into your ass as long as I can."

Outside, some other kriegies were working to get their belongings onto sleds they had somehow managed to put together from the wood of their bunks.

Combine 7 took its assigned place in their squad formation. Sam leaned forward to counterbalance the heavy pack Buck had made for him, and he watched the building of sleds going on around him.

Buck went to the doorway and called, "Come in here, Squad 7. There's no point in standing outside freezing while we're waiting to move out."

"Everybody stay where you are. That means you, too, Captain Pierce. Get out here," Lt. Col. Fanning countermanded. "We're due to march."

Buck and Walt took their places as a leader and deputy leader of Squad 7.

"Where's Joe?" Buck asked. He approached Fanning and saw that José was with him. "Come on, Joe. Join our formation."

"He'll be marching with me," Fanning said.

"By whose orders? He's in my squad," Buck objected.

"By my orders. He's a commando, and I say he's marching with me."

"Its okay, Buck," José said. "What's the difference? He asked me, and I said it was okay with me if that's what he wants."

"Fanning, you're starting my squad with a man short. After your speech about every man for himself, you're pulling out big Joe for your partner. You're the Block Commander, but that doesn't stop me from keeping track of what you're up to."

From the northeast, light occasionally flashed on the horizon and rumbles carried to the waiting formation. With a light snow cover on the ground, the freezing night had now turned clear. The kriegies stomped their feet to try to keep warm as they waited. No guards were in sight. Kriegies began to wonder if the Germans had deserted the camp.

After twenty minutes, Oberfeldwebel Krauss came running. He spoke hurriedly to Fanning then ran to the next formation standing in front of the adjoining block.

Fanning announced, "I am informed that the Germans are having trouble getting organized to move out. We are dismissed to go back to our rooms until further notice."

The kriegies of Block 169 scurried back into the building they knew so well. The unexpected reprieve brought optimistic speculation that the Russians might arrive before the forced march could begin.

The stove was red hot from the excess of reserve coal that had been fed to the fire. The entire building was warm for the first time that winter.

The promise of a second Red Cross Parcel coming as they left camp would be a bonanza of food beyond what their already full packs could hold.

An orgy of feasting began. It was a bash to outdo all bashes—not an organized orgy but a chaos of indulgence working against time running out. José made pancakes from flour long hoarded from his package from home. Cans were opened and abandoned still half full as kriegies moved on to indulge the contents of other cans just opened. A pan of salmon stood neglected as the combine members gorged themselves on spam—the precious pork loaf that had been rationed in miserably thin slices for the past many months. K-2 crackers with thick layers of jelly were eaten with the pork loaf. It was not a competitive scramble. There was more than enough for all.

Only Walt was not caught up in the bash. He ate some bread and spam. Then he sat down on his bunk and with a long cloth he had torn from a remaining mattress cover, he tediously and tightly wrapped his right knee. Several times he caught Buck, Cliff, Briggs, José, and Sam looking at him, and he wondered what they were thinking. *I don't need anyone to help me, and I think they all know that. Maybe this is the beginning of what Fanning announced as each of you is on your own. We'll sure be learning who is more than on his own.*

Sam came over, "I'll hang with you, Walt."

"Other way 'round, Sam. You're going to have to step lively to keep up with me."

"Either way. We'll stick together. Deal?"

"It's a deal."

"Everybody out! We're due to march," a voice yelled from the hallway.

It was 11:00 P.M. Saturday, January 27, 1945.

As the combine walked away from the bedlam of food and trash of their final hour, Sam said, "Boy, is this place going to stink in three days."

As Walt walked down the hallway to the exit door, he jabbed his good leg through the abandoned bass violin. Minutes later, the kriegies of Block 169 headed toward the road, passing through the vorlager enroute. On one side, they were guarded by Smitty, now carrying a rifle, and on the other side by the sour Schumann, slouching with his long rifle hanging from his shoulder.

The kriegies moved through the great gates to the vorlager where more guards were waiting to flank their march.

The column then headed toward the outer gates that opened to the German world.

Some of the makeshift sleds were long and thin, some were short and thick, and some were so high they balanced like towers. Some of the packs were buttoned-up shirts, some were trousers wired shut at the big end, some were fiber Red Cross Capture suitcases tied to backs with rags, others were burlap sacks tied to overcoats, and yet others were cardboard boxes strapped on backs with rags.

As Block 169 moved past the open doors of the warehouse, lights showed vast stacks of Red Cross Parcels. Breaths were steaming as Parcels were thrown from man to man in fire brigade fashion until each landed in a passing kriegie's arms. The stream of kriegies moved on, into the darkness beyond the last of the great gates—now standing open.

When Walt was close to Smitty, he said, "I see that tonight you have a rifle."

"Who knows where this night will lead?" Smitty answered.

Buck said to Walt, "Ask him what he'll do if Uncle Joe catches up with us?"

Walt ignored Buck.

The column stopped.

"Why have we stopped?" Walt asked Smitty.

"Look ahead and you will see."

Walt then saw that the road ahead was packed with running figures.

"We are the last compound to move out," Smitty explained. "Eight thousand prisoners from other compounds are ahead of us."

"Why are they running?"

Smitty shrugged his shoulders and moved away.

Sam said, "This is death. We ought to try to break free right now before we get started."

"Break free to where? How long could you hide from a bullet in this weather?" Buck asked. "They've got to have a place in mind that they're taking us to. Our only chance for now is to stay with the march."

Block 169 moved onto the road and began to run.

PART IV

The Road

Against the Wehrmacht.

Upon learning that a prisoner camp of 10,000 Allied airmen was in danger of being overrun by the Red Army, he called it a disgraceful situation which might give the Russians 10,000 volunteer soldiers. Goering suggested that 15 trains be made up for their evacuation. Hitler angrily said: no, strip them of shoes and trousers and march them back through the January snow and mud and to kill those who dropped out.

Excerpt from article in <u>*Stars and Stripes*</u> *newspaper, 1945*

THE ROAD: CHAPTER ONE

To prevent liberation by advancing Russians, on the night of 27 January 1945, the approximately ten thousand prisoners of war of Stalag Luft III at Sagan, Germany, were started on a forced march. Many of their hurriedly improvised packs and sleds came apart under the running pace of the first mile. In advance of the march, the prisoners were informed that anyone who could not keep the pace would be shot. Because prisoners could not stop, they had to abandon what they could not push, pull, or carry with them as they ran. The roadside of the first mile was littered with clothing, blankets, cans of food, torn packs, and broken sleds.

By the time 2344 prisoners of the West Compound joined the west-directed thousands, German civilians were outside despite the cold, gathering a winter harvest of wool blankets and diverse Red Cross food with treasures of chocolate, cigarettes, and coffee that were priceless in bomb-stricken Germany. Block 169 passed between countless stacks of these critical life supplies standing stark and bizarre upon the white, frozen land.

After a mile of running, the pace slowed to a fast walk. But the ditches already rich with precious supplies kept receiving more and more priceless provisions as kriegies continued to lighten their loads. The prisoners added mile to mile, laboring, perspiring in the freezing night under a moonless sky of cold stars that glistened with icy light. After many miles someone ahead shouted back, "Rest stop. Stay on your feet. If you sit down, you may never get up."

The march came to a halt.

Sam rubbed his face to get some feeling back into his skin. He said to Walt, "The way you're limping, I don't see how you keep going. I'm beat."

Buck leaned over to shift the weight of his pack and with effort encouraged his squad. "At least all seven of us are still here. Have you had to throw away much stuff?"

"I had to get rid of most of the extra Parcel I got at the gate, but I managed to get the sugar cubes and a D-bar into my pockets," Briggs said. "I've still got everything else I started with."

Buck turned to Walt. "Ask a goon where we're headed."

Walt moved ahead to Smitty, tonight on duty as a rifle-carrying guard. He asked in German, "Where are we going?"

"God knows. Nobody has told me anything. It's a terrible situation. I'm in no health for this kind of treatment."

Walt relayed Smitty's comments to Buck and added, "Thanks to your wire sew-job, my pack's still got everything."

"I gotta get rid of some weight," Buck said. Anyone want some stuff?"

No one answered.

"Damn it. I'm not going to throw my stuff away after carrying it this far," he said.

"Jesus, I'm cold," Cliff said in a hoarse whisper. "I'm giving out. I'm going to freeze if they don't get us inside."

"I've seen it fifty-six below at home, but this feels worse with the wind blowing," Buck said.

"Have they shot any guys falling back?" Briggs asked.

"Who knows?" Buck responded. "I'm not falling back to find out. These goons are scared shitless tonight. They aren't playing around. You've been hearing the police dogs at the rear, yelping for a butt to chew on and then changing their tune. You fall back and the best you'll get is chewed up and left to freeze."

"The only chance we got is to escape," Cliff said. "A guy can only take so much.

When we get to a good place, I'm going to head into the woods."

"And then what?" Briggs asked. "Freeze?—if you don't get a bullet."

Sam said, "Look over there at Fanning putting stuff into Joe's pack. Didn't he say it was going to be every man for himself?"

"I see it," Buck said, "if Joe's dupe enough to carry it, it's his problem."

Colonel Raymond was at the head of the column talking with Hauptmann Eiler, who had just ridden up on a bicycle. A horse-drawn wagon stood next to them, and guards were putting their packs into the wagon.

"You gave me your word that the wagon would be used to carry exhausted prisoners to shelter," Raymond protested.

"Conditions have changed. I am now ordered to shoot those who cannot keep up."

"To hell with orders. You gave me your personal word."

"The West must keep pace with this march. That means my guards must keep the pace, too, and some are not young men in good health. I must use the wagon to carry the packs of my guards. There will be no wagon for the prisoners. Now keep still."

"I'll keep still, but you'd better do some deep thinking about who is winning the war tonight, Hauptmann Eiler. Before you break your personal promises, remind yourself that the Allies will be punishing war criminals."

"Colonel Raymond, as a professional soldier, you certainly must understand that I am not responsible for what I am ordered to do." Eiler turned away and wheeled ahead on his bicycle.

Raymond was left with foreboding concern for what would happen as the march continued. Eiler had earlier told him that the Luftwaffe had made no plans for evacuation and that the order to march had come directly from Hitler. So, now the Major in charge of all Stalag Luft III had gone ahead by car to try to arrange emergency evacuation quarters for the ten thousand prisoners marching. The Major had promised to send back information. Meanwhile, the thousands of kriegies were being herded aimlessly westward in the freezing night.

During the running pace of the first mile, Raymond had struggled to stay at the head of the West column. When the pace had slowed, his energy had not returned. Stiff and weak, in no condition to continue the ordeal of this night, he now saw the column ahead already moving away.

The West kriegies began planting one foot before the other on the white glaze of icy road glistening in the starlit darkness. Ahead someone slowed, the change evoked no comment. In the numbing cold of the nightmare marathon, each prisoner was reduced to the effort of keeping up with the man ahead of him. They plodded on and on, with a five-minute rest stop every hour, until the horizon began to show the light of coming dawn, and on, further, to a frigid sunrise.

In the morning light the road showed an endless stream of humanity stretched backwards and forwards on a white desolation of snow trampled into ice. As the cold sun climbed the sky, the guards continued to urge the kriegies onward. The seven of Squad 7 were still together, stumbling forward, until the village of Freiwaldau came into sight.

The column of another compound continued on through the village. The West formation of some two thousand krie-gies was marched into the village and brought to a halt on the central street.

Smitty had Schumann take over his guard post. He told Walt he was going to walk ahead to see what he could learn. When he returned he said, "Herr Hauptmann is trying to get us into the village hall to get warm and rest."

"It's too good to believe," Walt said.

Kriegies stomped their feet to keep from freezing. Most heeded the warning not to sit down. In spite of their misery, they were desperate for something to eat. Briggs, Walt, and Buck each got out a can of spam. Buck drew out his knife and cut the cans open.

As Smitty watched, Walt told him, "After all these months we've got plenty of spam, but now we've got no bread."

Smitty said, "Wait, I'll get you bread and you give me spam." He walked to the nearest house. In a little while he came back with something under his coat. When Schumann wasn't looking, he gave Walt a loaf of dark bread.

Walt made a spam sandwich and passed it to Smitty. Then he made sandwiches for the squad. Squad 7 and Smitty all ate ravenously. Adam and James, the two assignees to the squad from Room 14, each brought out a can of corned beef. A second round of sandwiches was made and eaten, shared with Smitty.

An hour passed with nothing happening. Smitty went forward again. When he came back he said nobody knew anything. By now the sun was high in the sky; yet the temperature was still below freezing. The endless waiting made the air seem colder. After two more hours of waiting, Cliff said, "I feel like I'm soaked in ice water."

Finally a voice shouted, "Prepare to move."

The column moved ahead a quarter mile and then was herded into the central square of Freiwaldau. There, in the large open area of the square that surrounded a small one-story building, the kriegies became a mob trying to gain entry to the building. By the time Squad 7 got near, a thousand kriegies were jammed in front of the open door, unable to get inside. Cliff estimated that two hundred may have managed to squeeze into the building.

The almost two thousand who could not get shelter milled about in the square. Several groups broke up their sleds and built fires with the wood. A few kriegies wrapped up in their blankets and buried themselves in the snow, huddled together.

Squad 7 had no sled to burn. Sam said that if nothing else could be done he was going to bury himself in the snow. Cliff insisted with chattering teeth, "Don't. When you lay down in the snow, it's the end."

"We've got to do something," Buck said. Slowly, anxiously, purposefully, he began to circle the square that was ringed with guards standing their posts numb with cold and half asleep. As Buck walked, he passed Raymond, indifferent to the Colonel's presence.

The Colonel, standing alone, observing the miserable confusion of the West kriegies, felt himself an old man. His struggle of the past months to perfect an organization to deal with a crisis like this had come to nothing. In staying with the pace over the miles of last night, he had come to realize how old he was as a man in his forties.

As Senior Officer, he had expected Hauptmann Eiler to give him priority in providing him shelter. He had rehearsed in his mind how he would inform Eiler that he would not accept shelter as long as any of his men were left outside. But Eiler had not offered him shelter or any other special privilege.

He observed how the prisoners were clustered in combines. In dream-memory weariness he visualized himself in a combine of school classmates. Then his mind focused on how he had trained himself to be aloof to effect greater authority. *There's my staff over there, together but apart from me. Why do I feel ignored? Is it because I have no power here in the square? I'm needed now more than ever. I goddamn must find the strength to head the column when we move out. With me up front they'll keep following. If they don't, they'll wind up at the rear of the column being chewed up and shot. These kriegies need their Senior Officer leading.*

Across the square, Buck saw some guards aggressively compelling prisoners to move away from an alley.

"They're making a big fuss about keeping us away from the Polish slave laborers' quarters," one of the kriegies commented.

"Polish?" Buck asked, suddenly interested.

"That's how I understood it."

Buck immediately began to circulate through the crowd, until he found a Polish-speaking prisoner. They talked briefly. Then, taking this prisoner with him, he went back and gathered Squad 7 near the alley. "Where are Adam and James?" he asked.

"Gone back to their own combine," Walt reported. "Their combine is burning their sled to get warm. They've deserted our squad."

"Their tough luck. I've got a plan. I'm going to assign each of you to watch different guards. We'll use 'not yet' and 'clear' to signal when the guards' eyes aren't on us. If we get a clear from all of you, I'll give the 'go,' and we'll dash like lightning down the alley and into the first doorway."

A little later there was a sudden surge of activity by the

central building and with that Buck got a chorus of clear.

"Go!" Buck called. The squad ran down the alley and disappeared into the room of a Polish woman. Other prisoners joined the escape. When the alley was clear, sixteen kriegies were crowded into the tiny room that had a double-deck bunk.

Buck's interpreter explained, "She says to be very quiet. If the Germans catch us here, she'll be in bad trouble."

Dark, sparkling eyes and high cheek bones gave the woman an oriental look. She was young and attractive. She cradled a baby in her arms and withdrew to a lower corner of the double-deck bunk. The bunk took up a third of the floor space.

"I know what you're going through," she began with the translator talking for her.

The knot of humanity tried to squirm into comfortable positions in the little room.

"Here, sit on the bed, up above, too," she said.

She looked into the weary eyes of huddled prisoners and started into the story of her past. "We marched here from Warsaw. It took twenty-one days. It was the hardest for the children. I was pregnant then. What filth. We were full of lice. Not once did we have a chance to wash. It was hot, and there was little water. Many played out. I saw people die and people get shot."

"What will we do now? We can't stay here," Cliff mumbled to Buck as she spoke.

"We'll get warm first and think this out," Buck mumbled back.

"Put more coal on the fire," she said. "It's my ration for the week, but you must get warm. It was something in Warsaw with the Ukrainian soldiers. They would grab a girl right off the street. We all put dirt in our hair and made ourselves ugly so the soldiers wouldn't want us." She laughed. "I tell you, we were a mess to look at in those days."

She opened her blouse and put her child to her breast. "My brother-in-law lives with us, too," she informed as she began to nurse her child. "You would think they would give

319

five slave workers a bigger room."

Kriegie eyes that had not seen a woman in many months tenderly took in the sight of the child sucking the nipple of her breast. The presence of the woman and the sound of her voice carried warmth through the room with the growing warmth of the fire. One by one, the kriegies fell asleep.

After an hour of nervously darting back and forth to the alley, the brother-in-law announced, "The Germans are moving the prisoners back to the street. It looks like they're about to march on. You've got to get out there. There's no other way. They'll kill us if they find you here."

The kriegies jolted each other awake. They agreed that they could not impose on the Polish slave laborers any further. No one could think of anything to do other than rejoin the kriegies waiting to march further. They began to lighten their packs. Each item was judged and then replaced or put aside. Those who carried kriegie record books tore off the covers and ripped out empty pages to cut down on weight. As the lower bunk was heaped with discarded clothing, blankets, and food, the mother radiated thanks.

The brother-in-law went out first. They waited for his signal, then scrambled back to the square. The Germans were calling for blocks to reform. There was such confusion that their re-entry from the alley was ignored. Prisoners were trying to cooperate, hoping that marching on would take them to shelter. But coordinated obedience was unattainable. The lucky kriegies who had temporarily gained shelter once again began to pound their feet to keep warm. The many who had spent the afternoon outside were so numb that they no longer bothered to keep exercising.

About 6:00 P.M. the column began to move. Buck looked out to the squalid sight of bedraggled kriegies shuffling along the road before him. Squad 7, now five kriegies of Combine 7, joined the march with strangers around them. They had given up trying to find Block 169.

The re-start of the march was uneventful, tedious trodding under the load of makeshift packs with straps cutting into shoulders. For those whose sleds had not come apart or been burned, walking was the easier work of pulling and pushing along the ice and beaten-down snow of the road.

As the formation started across an open, flat stretch of land, Smitty came close to Walt and said, "We've got eighteen kilometers to march. There's shelter there for us."

Walt interpreted the news to the men around him.

"That's eleven miles," Sam said. "Thank God that Polish woman let us in to rest."

"Too bad Joe missed out," Buck said. "I wonder how he's doing?"

"I saw him and Fanning. Joe's pack is bigger and Fanning's is smaller. Figure that out," Briggs said.

Sam answered, "I talked with him back at the square, and he said, 'The Lieutenant Colonel is being real nice to me.'"

"Yeah? I never thought Joe would be such a sucker for being used by the Brass," Cliff confessed.

"Forget Joe," Walt said. "We've got us to worry about. How about your feet, Buck?"

"Blistered. I think they'll be better now that I've lightened my load."

"You're still carrying more than any of us," Sam said. "You got to lighten up more."

"I'm on my way now," Buck said. "I'm not lightening up any more. We're going to need to eat, wherever we're going. I don't like starving."

"Don't worry about Big Buck," Walt advised. "Nothing's going to stop him."

"I don't know how you keep going, Walt," Sam said. "Leaning into that cane, nothing's going to stop you." It was not so much confidence as concern that prompted Sam to encourage Walt.

"Sure. You'll make it," Briggs agreed from his position directly behind Walt.

Cliff said, "I'm getting wobbly. We better get to shelter before eleven miles. I can't make it that far."

"We're all going to make it, Navigator," Buck assured. "We're on our way to the target. No stopping us now. A step at a time."

As darkness deepened, the eastern horizon began to

tremble with light. An occasional faint rumble came from where the light trembled. Once a star shell blossomed, blue-white, far away in the eastern blackness.

The column proceeded into the rolling hills of Silesia. The road channeled through a deep forest that now blocked the view of the horizon shell-fire. Smitty moved in close to Walt and said, "Tonight I would rather be in your shoes than mine."

"Have you heard any war news?" Walt asked.

"Bad. Berlin admits the Russians have a bridgehead across the Oder. I figure they will be crossing in strength tonight." Smitty fell silent and moved away.

The moon was down and the sky was clear as the second night of sleepless, forced marching continued in the freezing cold. Again the star-light reflecting from the snow bestowed what light was offered by the night.

About 10:00 P.M. a multi-engine drone broke the silence of the hills as an aircraft flew over very low. From ahead came, loudly, *clear right! clear right!*

Kriegies pushed and bumped one another to get to the side of the road. Galloping horses pulling a wagon came racing down the road from the front of the column. The driver was screaming German gibberish.

The wagon had barely passed when a rifle shot rang out. A heavy volley of rifle fire followed.

"Hit the ditch," someone yelled.

The road emptied in an instant.

Rifle fire sounded from all sides. Schumann planted himself on his knees right in the middle of where Combine 7 was lying in the snow.

"Was ist das?" Schumann shrieked as he fanned his rifle at the blackness of forest around him. A high pipe-organ-note bullet whined by. Schumann fired blindly into the trees. Kriegies squirmed to burrow themselves deeper into the snow.

"Was zum Teufel!" Schumann screamed. He dropped prone in the middle of Combine 7 as he continued to fan his rifle at the night.

Buck lay beside Schumann. He gave thought to stealing Schumann's rifle. *Taking the gun would begin worse trouble.*

Better to squirm deeper into the snow, be still and wait.

The firing ended as mysteriously as it had started. From the rear of the column the sinister barking and howling of the attack dogs penetrated the quiet of the forest and hills.

From far ahead came the command, "Get back on the road."

The prisoners cautiously began to lift themselves out of the snow. A rifle shot cracked. Then another. Suddenly the wild firing began all over again. The shooting continued for several minutes. Then, gradually, quiet returned. The stillness again was marred only by the howling and barking of the attack dogs at the rear of the column.

"We're moving out," someone yelled. Kriegies scurried onto the road and briskly followed the pace that had quickened to escape the rifle fire. Men, so exhausted they had been ready to fall before the shooting started, now hurried along with new energy.

"What's this all about?" Walt asked Smitty.

"I don't know. Maybe Communist partisans, or maybe trouble at the rear of the column. Bad duty back there. Everyone jumpy. Bad."

"What are they doing with the guys that can't keep up?" Walt asked.

"Thank God I am not on duty back there," Smitty said.

"You must have learned something back at Freiwaldau."

"Keep moving. Don't fall back. That's all I can say."

The formation passed a guard standing over a prisoner lying beside the road.

Smitty moved close to the guard and exchanged a few words with him.

"What was that about?" Walt asked.

"Nothing we can help with. For him the war is over."

"We must have come fifty miles since we left Sagan," Sam said.

"According to what I've been told, thirty miles," Walt replied.

"It's a hell of a long thirty miles," Buck said.

"If it just weren't so cold," Cliff said. "I'm giving out. I can't go further. I can't keep up. I'm going to slow down."

"Phillips, you bastard. Shut up. I'm giving out, too, but we're all going to keep up. No dropping back," Buck decreed.

"I'm freezing," Briggs said. "But I'm following Walt, limping ahead of me with his cane. I'm saying, if he can do it, I can."

"I'm going to slow up," Sam said. "I'll catch up later."

"Damn it, Sam. Don't fall back. Hang on," Walt said. Then he lied, as if he knew from talking to Smitty, "We're almost there."

Buck grew silent. With each step, his weight pushed into his blistered feet. Every few minutes now, prisoners tentatively joined Buck's squad as they slowly lost ground toward the rear of the column.

Finally the houses of a village came into view silhouetted against the sky to the sides of the road. This brought hope that the march was about to end. The column was brought to a halt. Everyone waited for Colonel Raymond to pass word back that now they would get out of the cold.

Buck, now ignoring advice to stay on his feet, plunked himself down against a stone wall. There he felt the relief of being freed of the weight pressing into his blistered feet.

The horse-drawn wagon Hauptmann Eiler had promised for prisoner emergencies now passed up the road loaded with packs of the guards.

Sam said, "I heard on the news that each squad is going to get a wagon and a horse."

Buck kicked Sam on the shin. "Don't start that, birdman. We're going to get no wagons or horses either for this trip."

A thin moon lifted into the night. Walt saw the moonglow behind the silhouette of a large house. At the gateway of the house he saw the silhouette of a woman. She stood in the gateway and looked out to the river of humanity choked to stillness in the street before her home on this winter night.

She walked to the street edge. Walt crossed over to her. "Guten Abend," he greeted.

"Your night is not good," she returned in German.

He guessed that she was about sixteen years old.

"I can pay in cigarettes for something hot to drink," he told her.

"That much I can do," she answered, and she turned and ran back to the house.

After a while she came back with a three-gallon pail full of steaming ersatz coffee.

Kriegies swarmed about her, holding up cigarettes and empty klim cans.

"Keep your cigarettes. At least I can do this for you," she told Walt.

When the coffee was gone, she said, "We can never stop the Russians now. You'll be on your way home in a few weeks."

"A few weeks is too long when you're freezing," Walt told her.

"Have hope. The war will soon be over," she answered.

After an hour, word was passed back that Raymond was protesting an order to move on to the next town.

"It's good to know Colonel Raymond is up front," Walt said.

"Colonel Raymond will get us all wagons," Sam said.

"He's probably riding in one," Buck replied with cynical humor.

Colonel Raymond was miserably exhausted, but he had pulled himself together to argue with Hauptmann Eiler. "If you force us further, I'm going to hold you personally responsible for every life that is lost. Where are the others? Have they been given shelter? Are we the only ones still marching? You are making a war crimes case against yourself, Hauptmann Eiler."

"Colonel, there are no buildings here to hold two thousand prisoners. I am ordered to march until we find shelter."

"Where? How far? I need to know!"

"I was to be told, but no word has come. There is a town ahead, but in this night and with no road signs, we may be on the wrong road. The Major may have returned on a different road. If we have casualties, that is war. I can give one hundred emergency cases shelter in a barn I have commandeered. The rest of you will march on."

A runner came back to where Combine 7 was waiting. "Listen," he called out. "Those who absolutely can't make six more miles to shelter can hold up as you pass the village fountain. We have just one barn, so we can only take the worst cases. Keep going if you can stay on your feet."

When the runner had gone, Cliff went forward to ask Raymond for a place in the barn, but when he got to the Colonel he saw kriegies lying on the ground. Some were moaning and some were sobbing. Some were still . . . too exhausted to move. Cliff decided to go back to the combine and try to march on another six miles. On the way back to Squad 7, he passed José and Fanning. "How are you doing, Joe?" he asked.

"I've got a bad foot," José said, "but we're going on. Colonel Fanning and I have pooled our stuff, so we've got to stay together."

"Pooled your stuff?"

"Sort of. I've got the heaviest part. He's smaller and older."

"You're an asshole," Cliff told Fanning who received the message with silence seemingly commanded by a body too fatigued for response. "Fanning, you said at the start this was going to be every man for himself."

"I don't mind," José said.

"Joe, tell him to got to hell. Get your stuff and come back to our squad."

José ignored Cliff's pleading.

"Well, Fanning, I'm telling you to go to hell," Cliff said. Then he returned to the squad. As the formation reformed, he told Walt how Fanning was using Joe.

"Fanning's our block commander, and Joe is helping him because he was asked to. It's not for us to judge him or Fanning," Walt remarked.

"No? Is judging people only God's job? If so, he's got his work cut out for him tonight. We're learning about people we thought we knew, what they really are, what we are, counting me too," Cliff proclaimed.

Combine 7 moved up the road, passing the village square with the fountain, where eyes turned upon casualty kriegies lying under a huge statue. Buck hobbled up to the emergency cases and dropped a bundle of his food. "Here's something for breakfast," he said, and he moved on up the road.

The sky was clouding up and it was getting windier. Blowing snow added to the freezing temperature that guarded against escape. The blue-suited guards flanking the column understood that the true guard tonight was the winter more than their threat of gunfire. In the prisoners' minds there was nothing to do but keep moving toward shelter.

A German officer came along side of the column on a bicycle.

"Halt an!" he shrieked in German. "I have ridden one thousand meters out of town, and I have only seen three guards. Where are the guards?"

Schumann stopped and stood at terrified attention. "I think the rest of the guards will soon be coming," he faltered.

The officer spewed vindictive as he started wheeling back to the town.

In a short while Smitty came running, gasping for breath.

"Let the Leutnant scream. That hurts nothing," Smitty said. "We were having coffee, trying to get warm. Two guards are already dead. We had to get out of the cold. If we pass a house I can sneak into, he may wonder a long time where I am."

Walt warmed himself with these messages of trouble in the German ranks, but outwardly he offered sympathy to Smitty to keep his valuable friendship.

Clouds slithered over the moon. Not one star remained to light the night. Not one light showed anywhere. As the kriegies marched on, only the spectral glow of snow relieved the darkness.

The wind carried a lethal sting. The cold was bone-aching. The marchers began to bob and wobble on the glaze of road. The weight of the packs made the make-shift rag shoulder straps cut into flesh like wire.

Briggs kept his eyes on Walt's shoulder straps as his markers for the direction of his steps. Before the shooting he had been ready to give up. But now the sensations of his body seemed to matter less. The rhythm of Walt's foot-cane movement had locked itself into a cadence commanding his feet to move. Walt, adding mile to mile in numb stupor, felt he was getting stronger. Several times in the last half hour he had found himself crowding against the kriegie in front of him, once getting his feet tangled.

"Goddamn it," Briggs finally called. "Settle down, Walt."

At the next rest stop, Briggs said, "Following you, Walt, it doesn't look like you can make another ten steps. But you keep going, and keep going, and keep going. At this point you've got me mad, you bastard. You're not getting away from me."

"I am praying to Saint Sara," Walt said. "I'm saying, 'Give me strength now, and I will live for you the rest of my life.'"

"It's my blisters and the goddamned cold," Buck said. "I've been in hellish Wyoming cold, but nothing like this."

At the head of the column, Colonel Raymond was again protesting to Hauptmann Eiler. "We've covered six miles. Where is our shelter?"

"We have six more kilometers to go."

"That's over three more miles! We move on and on, and always we have further to go. I beseech you, Hauptmann, in the name of—"

"Don't beseech me when you know I am under orders. We can only move on until we get to shelter."

"You can say that. You are riding a bicycle."

"Perhaps we are lost. It's so dark. I don't know."

"Eiler, I plead with you personally. Stop this march, for the sake of all of us."

"Shut up, Colonel. If I stop you here you will all freeze. I will give you a ten-minute rest stop. I have commandeered a barn at the next farm. Separate out your worst 250 men. The rest will have to move on."

"Move on to where?"

"We are bound for Muskau. It cannot be more than six kilometers away."

Raymond told his runner, "Pass word back that we're going to get shelter for 250 prisoners. This shelter is for kriegies who absolutely can't keep going. It's up to each to decide if he can go a little further." *I have to lead this march. I've got to keep going for six more kilometers. Have*

I fallen asleep? I've lost track of time. Have I only missed two nights of sleep? It seems like endless time has passed since I began this march.

In contrast to the feelings of isolation Raymond had suffered in the Freiwaldau square, he now felt connection with the marchers he was leading and triumph in his perseverance that had kept him at the head of the column. Like a pendulum ever returning to the beginning of its arc, life had him back to his destiny—leadership. In his leadership he had now chosen to rely on individual human honor to decide who was most needy as his kriegies passed the available barn.

Everybody from Combine 7 decided to leave the emergency barn space for kriegies they saw were done for. About seventeen hundred moved on. When they had covered the six kilometers, Eiler could not be found. Oberfeldwebel Krauss, now marching at the head of the column, complained, "We have lost our way, for certain. We must have taken a wrong turn."

In the last three miles, Buck, against his strongest intentions, had lost ground toward the rear. He was no longer with Combine 7. Of the four still marching together, Walt and Sam walked in front, and Briggs and Cliff followed.

"Why are we still walking? We'll never make it. I'm not going further," Sam said.

"We're headed for that light up ahead," Walt said.

"I can't see a light."

"I see it. Believe me and keep moving."

"I think that the goons will march us until we're all dead," Sam protested.

"Don't think. Believe. Saint Sara is saving us. I see the light."

Packs began to fall again. Walt began to study the side of the road. He told himself that if they were almost there he should be thinking of how he would survive once he got there. Occasionally he saw abandoned fiber cases, Red Cross Capture Cases, that had served as packs. *These slick cases will slide easily on the icy road.* He had a piece of rope and now he got the idea that he could tie such a case to his waist and have it slide behind him effortlessly on the icy road. He saw another abandoned case ahead, and he abruptly shifted to the ditch and brought the case with him. Sam helped tie the case to his waist, and it began to slide behind him.

"You're going crazy," Briggs said. "Get that thing out from under my feet."

"I'll walk to the side of you," Walt said.

"Stay in front of me. I'll fall back a little. I'm following you."

"Only six more kilometers," the guards relayed back in German.

Walt now truly believed that the march would end in six more kilometers. For him the land of promise was near. He could see the light—a small white, bright light, too big for a star, low in the sky ahead, as if it were shining from a hillside. Intuitively, he was sure the light came from the place of refuge where they would soon arrive.

But the nightmare of forced marching continued. Marchers, one by one, continued to fall back toward the rear of the column or suddenly collapse to a final resting place in the snow Each prisoner endured again and again his promised last mile. Forty miles. But still driven on. Forty-one miles. Still further to go. Forty-two miles. Now under sheer spell of will-to-live. Forty-three miles. Driven on step-by-step. Forty-four miles. Urged on by fantasies of relief with a few more steps. Forty-five miles. Mind-promises were no longer rousing the waning will-to-live. Forty-six miles. Tramping mindlessly now with will-power gone, yet feet still moving. Forty-seven miles. Always the guards still promising that shelter is close ahead.

A murmur passed through the column as kriegies began to pass another man, an all important man, losing ground toward the rear of the column.

"It's Colonel Raymond, Sam."

"I see him, Cliff."

"It's Pa Raymond for sure."

"It's the Old Man."

"It's the C.O."

Each house passed, each hope of shelter, drew a crowd that

broke up only under the attack of dogs and gunfire driving the kriegies back to the road.

Forty-eight. Forty-nine. Fifty. Fifty-one. Fifty-two. Fifty-three. The column was shorter now. Less than half of the men were still marching.

Walt was still dragging the extra suitcase, occasionally saying, "We're headed for the light. We're almost there."

Sam, Briggs, and Cliff were still with him.

Raymond was now one step ahead of two police dogs that were held in leash by a guard. When he was unable to command further movement from his legs, the dogs chewed at his ankles. Twice he had been urged forward by bayonet jabs to his buttocks. Now he was no longer in command of himself. His body was performing apart from his will. What thinking powers he still had were locked to the animal Dean Raymond reacting to the torture of his senses. "Easy way out. Easy way out," he kept saying in a litany grown out of the past hour.

"I'm dumping a blanket. Want it?" someone beside him asked.

"No."

"You can roll up. Play dead."

"Can't quit. Want to. Can't. I'm leading."

"Yeah. Leading the heelers."

"Can't. I'm leading."

"Me, too. Goddamn can't."

"Tom got the easy way."

"No easy way tonight."

"Singing River. Buck's learned too late."

"Tom's pilot?"

"Raymond. Yeah. Head honcho. You can't quit."

"You too. Keep going, rebel."

"Yeah. Beat the heelers, Colonel."

"I'd help, but I can't."

"Yeah. Me too. Gotta take the spurs. Keep going."

"Hubba hubba."

"Hubba hubba."

The faint glow of dawn carried an eerie lightness to the road in which the kriegies were reeling ever forward. A murmur of wailing voices carried from the column.

From where four kriegies of Combine 7 were still walking, a babble arose: "Wake up, Cliff. Wake up, Cliff. Wake up, Cliff."

"We're almost there."

"Give him some sugar."

"Six more kilometers."

"Keep going."

"Watch Walt."

And then, like the shriek of a hyena, a plea: "Rest stop!"

But there was no stopping. There was not even the slightest slowing of the pace.

Then Sam was by the side of the road weeping as he rubbed snow into Cliff's face, slapping him. Sam prayed, "Please, God, help him! Come to! God, please! Hang on!"

Walt and Briggs helped hold Cliff upright as the column moved on, but Cliff dropped back to the snow, lifeless.

A guard approached with bayonet drawn, and Sam, Walt, and Briggs rejoined the column, reeling onward. Briggs now lifted the case that Walt, leaning on his cane and stumbling erratically, was still dragging. Briggs carried the case in his arms as the three stumbled forward until they crossed over a bridge. They marched into a dead-end street. No place to go. Nothing to do but stop. The kriegies behind them kept coming. With sleds and packs they jammed into the square, jamming against each other in the dead-end square of Muskau.

A burble rose to a din of men calling for friends, for shelter, for help.

There was no leadership now. There was only panic.

Sam was holding out his empty klim can. "A German girl gave me a cup of coffee. I figure she'll be back."

Walt said, "That was last night, towns ago. We're now in the light."

Briggs, in pity of the fanatic fire consuming Walt, was still holding the case that Walt would not give up.

There was no one to take command. There was only the mob and the winter.

Then a voice shouted from a balcony, again and again. "At ease! At ease! At ease!"

It was Major Henry Bellrage. As the mob quieted, he shouted, "Clear the sidewalks. Use them to help bring up the exhausted. Regroup into blocks. Start with one-sixty in front of me. The Germans insist we must get into block formations to be counted before they will take us to shelter. While we are forming up to be counted, stay on your feet and keep moving. Eiler is trying to get churches and other shelters for us. We must get organized."

The prisoners were too exhausted to obey. Block numbers were shouted from all directions. Confusion ruled, but Bellrage kept calling into the street. Finally, response began. About fifty prisoners, including Sam, Walt, and Briggs, formed a column-of-fours they called Block 169. They were counted. Then they were escorted away—backtracking down the street from which they had entered the square. As they reeled on, in the dawn light, they could see prisoners huddled, still, along side the street, in the freezing cold, as if lifeless. Block 169 crossed back over the bridge from which they had come.

"Buck?"

"Pa Raymond?"

Dean and Buck were huddled against the stone wall of the bridge. Sam, Walt, and Briggs broke from the column and went to them. Their breaths told that they were alive.

"We're at the light. We've got shelter. We'll take you with us."

"A girl has hot coffee for us."

"No, Sam. That was last night. Walt's right. It's now light."

They were herded into the column and led down a side street lined with stone houses.

"I know this street. I know every house. I've been here in a dream," Briggs said.

They were brought to a halt before a pottery factory.

"Where is the Block 169 commander, Lieutenant Colonel Fanning?" a guard shouted.

A kriegie volunteered, "He didn't make it. We passed him laying in the snow with José Cabrera."

"We've got to have someone in charge. Who is the senior officer here?"

"He is. Colonel Raymond," Walt said.

"Inside then."

The kriegies entered the warmth given off by blazing pottery furnaces. They stretched out on the concrete floor and slept.

THE ROAD: CHAPTER TWO

While the fires of the Muskau pottery furnaces provided warmth to the sleeping kriegies, the fire of opposing armies raged along the Oder. Wehrmacht Berichts of January 29 reported that the Germans were pushing the Russians back across the river, thus re-establishing their Oder defense line. By the time the West kriegies had slept away the day of the 29th and been left in shelter through the following night, their forced retreat had become less panic-driven.

The kriegies enjoying the warmth of the Muskau pottery furnaces were contained by a steel fence that surrounded the factory. Civilians of Muskau gathered outside this fence to barter.

In German: I have bread to trade. I have a four-year-old who has never tasted chocolate . . . five pounds of potatoes for the soap I see.

In kriegie German, learned to trade for bread: Haben Sie Brot für prima Amerikanische Zigaretten?

The stay extended through the next day. Food obtained was shared by the survivors of Combine 7 and others in need. No one was left hungry. Another night passed with the surviving prisoners in the pottery factory still recuperating.

Muskau had not been bombed so the hate-charged emotions of bombed cities were less present here. You'll be home soon . . . Geduld . . . The war will soon be over . . . words of encouragement offered to the frazzled survivors.

When Walt opened the case he had dragged, he found only ragged clothing of little worth when measured against his fanatic effort.

Buck, Sam, Briggs and Walt used January 30 to build a sled with materials they acquired through trade with the civilians. Buck was especially intent on having little weight on his back when he left Muskau.

On that evening Buck saw Dean Raymond standing with his back to the fire of a pottery furnace. He went over to him and said, "I never did throw away that blanket you wouldn't take."

"Aren't you glad? You'll need it now."

"It's the only blanket I've got. As much stuff as we all dropped, we haven't got much left."

"I realize that. We're headed into the unknown, Buck. I feel the weight of being the leader with no way to help us."

"I've come to respect the load you're carrying," Buck said. "I can't feel different about you as part of the Brass, and about other things going back to England, you know. But I see now I handled things wrong. I shouldn't have let your haywire power that was badgering our Brass dingbats stop me from being decent to you as Tom's father."

"You've been the haywire one out of plain ignorance of what I was trying to do. But your rebel ways have taught me something. My head was into our fucked-up air war so far I wasn't interested in what pilots like you were thinking—until it got personal. Then I wanted to hear from you."

"Randi tried to educate me, but what we've been through side-by-side wised me up."

"Do you feel wiser, Buck? What we went through . . . I'm undone. My gyro's tumbled. Where do I go from here?"

"You're not alone on that. If it weren't for my Combine, we'd both be goners. Who was the guy who took over in the square? Without him nobody would have saved us."

"Henry Bellrage, my around-the-bend classmate took over."

"How come? He wasn't on your staff."

"I don't understand that myself, Buck. My staff was too pooped to care. All I know is, he was the man who took charge when there was no one else to do it."

"I want to tell you again that your son was a fine pilot. Worth being proud of. He was sitting beside me, and as quick as that he was gone. He didn't suffer."

Dean grew silent. After a while Buck continued, "He was a damn good pilot."

"Thanks for saying it, but that's not enough to put me at peace. What I can't forgive is that he died for a senseless raid to bomb civilians, not a military target."

"What are you saying? I've been told that you being there as inspector general is what jacked our Brass into flying

that raid. Stupid orders made us take off in a snow storm
to kill women and children. That's Hitler's kind of war, not
mine. That's what's pissed me off about you. Now are you
telling it honest, saying you were against it, too?"

"It's more damn true than you'll ever know. Washington
sent me into the war to inspect as a way to get rid of me. I
was a Billy Mitchell . . . too noisy."

"Who's Billy Mitchell?"

"You don't know? Well, it's time you learned. It's about
the power politics between the army, navy, and air force and
a lot more ruling this war, but it's too big a story for telling
today. Today I'm worrying about getting what's left of us
through to wherever they're taking us."

"Hubba hubba to that. I'll leave you be and get back to
what's left of Combine 7."

When Buck returned, Sam, Walt, and Briggs, lying on
their blankets, were talking about the march.

"I was brought closer to Christ by Saint Sara in a wonderful way," Walt said.

"I'm hoping that somehow both Cliff and Joe got picked
up by somebody and rescued," Sam said.

"We can hope for Joe, because we don't know. But Cliff
was dead when we left him," Briggs leveled.

"I remember Cliff saying once that me and him were both
reachers. Well, he reached once too far when he gave up the
place he could have had in the last barn," Sam reflected.

"Adam and James didn't make it," Buck informed.
"They missed out on our getting warm and resting with the
Polish woman. It might have made the difference. They
marched out with their own Combine 14, but they couldn't
keep up. I hope they got into one of the barns or got into a
German house or something."

"It won't help to talk about who didn't make it. We should
be talking about what's coming next," Sam pointed out.

"Who knows what's coming next?" Briggs asked as he
raised his arms in a gesture of despair.

Walt was still in the past. "It was strange. At first, I
wasn't sure I saw a light, but I said I saw a light to keep us

all going. Then, as we kept going, I began to really see it, and I began to really feel stronger," Walt said.

"Don't forget that in the end Briggs kept you going by carrying the case you'd been dragging. You were beyond good sense, crazy," Sam said.

"Weren't we all?" Briggs asked. "I was thinking I was in a street I knew, and you, Sam, were saying we were about to get hot coffee."

"However crazy I was, it got me here," Walt declared. "From the start, I didn't think I'd ever make it, but I did. I knew Sister Johanna was wearing my ring—it made the difference."

"The ring? Whatever power it gave you, it got me through, too," Briggs said. "I was believing you, telling us we were headed for the light, even though I couldn't see a light. I thought you knew from talking to the guards. I followed you like I was glued to you. I kept saying, 'If he can make it, I can.'"

"I lost a finger, but it's saved my life."

Buck relaxed onto his blanket and turned to Walt, "That sounds like you're feeling your English love Marg saved your life with the ring she gave you. Your blood must still be warm for your Marg, even though you're married. You do have a wild side, Walt. It's not all religion. Admit it."

"More than ever I want to be a missionary against the wild side, like Saint Sara," Walt answered.

"I like the wild side," Sam asserted. "Albatross lovers. Birds flying free. That's for me—Sandra and me." He got up and wandered away.

The survivors of the march not sheltered in the pottery factory had been sheltered in churches. Other kriegies had been marched in during the past two days. After German regrouping, there were now some fifteen hundred kriegies in Muskau. Shortly after noon, they were ordered onto the road again. Colonel Raymond, now walking with a decided limp, was at the head of the column.

It was a warm day for winter. After the two days of rest, the prisoners shuffled up the road with an air of stoic indifference toward the hardship of their shabby lives.

"Hubba hubba," they called again and again to the children, old people, girls, and mothers lining the streets to watch them pass by.

Buck, thinking of Randi as he regarded the stream of war's human wreckage shuffling up the road, sang to himself, with confounding yet comforting paradox, *Singing River*. And again he puzzled . . . H.D.? *What is she trying to tell me with that?*

Smitty and Schumann were back at their guard positions with Block 169. Schumann was his old sullen self, but Smitty was calm, in marked contrast to his mood when they left Stalag Luft III. As he walked his post, Walt asked, "Smitty, how many of us who started made it here? We had to get counted before you would assign us to shelter. You must know how many were counted."

"The count was over five hundred, but that didn't include prisoners left in the barns."

"What happened to the rest?"

"The rest I can't talk about. I was not on duty at the rear of the column. I'm just a Gemeiner. I know nothing. Hitler's orders were to shoot all who could not keep up. What actually was done was not told to me. Nobody is talking."

"What about all the shooting when we hit the ditches? What was that about?"

"I don't know. Somebody must know, but they're not talking. Hitler is clamping down on the Luftwaffe these days. Everyone is too afraid to talk. You are still alive. Be satisfied with that. I am talking with you too long. I'm going to move away from you."

Every few minutes a wagon loaded with refugees overtook and passed the column. The wagon beds were loaded with belongings and heaped with straw from which the heads of women and children protruded. The men of the families rode up front; their heavy fur coats and stovepipe fur hats told of eastern origin. Occasionally an army truck, heading east, would cause a call of "clear right!" as the truck labored against the stream of refugees and kriegies westbound. The sober faces of the soldiers on the trucks bespoke their feelings in heading into battle. The reality of the Russian offensive was starkly manifest today in the refugees fleeing westward in panic.

A drizzle began that was half snow and half rain, and, slowly, the icy roadway, upon which kriegie sleds depended, began to melt. Then the sun came out. For a while tall trees to the sides of the road sufficiently held off the afternoon sun to allow the sleds to continue. The cold rain had soaked into clothing. Alternating interludes of sun and rain advanced the possibility of another miserable night.

At sunset the column arrived at Graustein. To the welcome surprise of the kriegies, the Germans dispatched the various blocks to pre-arranged shelter. Buck, Sam, Walt and Briggs made their bed in the hay of a barn and slept while rain pattered on the roof.

In the morning Walt busied himself with friendliness toward the woman in charge of the farm. He learned that many refugees had stopped here. There was little food for the horses, but she had managed to help all who had come to her. What did she think of Hitler? "Politics are for men," she had said. "Women's place is to look after the needs of people and care for the animals. These cares men do not involve themselves with in war."

Sam and Buck spent the next morning in preparing a spam-potato-a-la-cheese stew. Sam held the klim can pot and stirred the stew while Buck whittled match-size slivers of wood and fed the klim can burner to keep it flaming. Walt and Briggs brought two apples that the farm woman had given them. The four seated themselves around the klim can burner while water heated for coffee. But when the meal was served, Briggs did not eat. He explained that he had the GIs bad and no appetite. Afterwards the apples were shared, but Briggs gave his portion to Sam.

"This is living," Buck said.

"Yeah, we never had it so good," Sam added.

Walt boasted, "Wait until you see what I connived for a place to sleep tonight. We got a private room in what used to be a chicken coop. We've even got an electric light . . . and

I've asked Krauss about the roads. He says we'll be heading through a forest when we leave here and that there's still plenty of snow on the road there for our sled."

"There'd better be," Buck replied.

"Any news on where we're headed?" Briggs asked.

"If the guards know, they're not talking," Walt said.

At 3:45 in the afternoon the order came to march in fifteen minutes. Buck, Sam, Briggs and Walt quickly packed their sled for the move order, all the while complaining to each other about being cheated out of their connived private, chicken-coop room.

As the prisoners formed up to leave, Walt started a conversation with a pretty German girl. She followed along and continued to visit with him as the column moved away. Her blue eyes, long blonde braids, and fair skin were made lovelier by the many months away from girls.

Oberfeldwebel Krauss had been caught by surprise by the sudden order to move. He arrived wobbly drunk. As he caught up with the block, he put an arm around the German girl who was still walking beside Walt.

"Ah, our life is getting better," he said to Walt. "We must take her with us, eh?" Then switching to German he continued, "How about it? Will you come with us? We will see that you always have lots of chocolate and sugar and all sorts of fine food from the Red Cross, won't we Walter?" He now put his other arm to Walt's shoulder and continued to talk to the girl in German, "Really, you must come with us, you lovely girl. We have a good life, we wanderers."

To all this the girl only laughed.

"Sure, you must come along," Walt agreed to keep with Krauss's mood, "and when the war is over, we will all go to America."

"A good idea," Krauss said. "I have loved girls in Germany, France, and Italy. It is time I loved the girls in America."

"When the war is over you can visit me here," the girl said to Walt. Then she stopped and waved good-bye.

Krauss called back to her, "Do not worry. The Russians will not get this far."

Schumann, guarding the left flank where Walt was walking, ignored Krauss. Buck and Sam had been pulling the sled while Briggs pushed, and Walt now traded places with Briggs to allow him a rest.

"You, Hauptmann Buck, are you French?" Krauss asked in English.

"If you say so," Buck said.

"I like the French," Krauss flourished, throwing an arm to Buck's shoulder. "Paris is a good, good city. Girls outstanding! I had a girl there as beautiful as a Strauss Waltz. She was wild like a tiger when we made love. I have never had another girl like her. Jeannine, she was. Mon petit champignon . . . my little mushroom . . . but like a tiger. That was my Jeannine."

The formation had re-entered the town of Graustein. "Herr Oberfeldwebel," Schumann called as he moved close to Krauss. "You have drunk too much and are hugging a prisoner. Our countrymen are watching. I am sure you do not want to give them the wrong impression of their Luftwaffe."

"Mind how you speak to a soldier of higher rank, Gemeiner," Krauss growled. Schumann's rebuke nevertheless sobered Krauss. He took his arm from Buck's shoulder and moved away from the column.

The some fifteen hundred kriegies of the previous day's march had been re-gathered from their various assigned shelters. Colonel Raymond was again at the head of the column. Eiler was not now the German in command. In his place was a newly assigned leutnant, distant and curt.

"Where is Hauptmann Eiler?" Colonel Raymond asked.

"Herr Hauptmann is with his family," the Leutnant coldly reported. "You must remember that our families are not safely on the other side of the world like yours. Our homeland is being overrun by Eastern hordes. The war is more serious to us today than this march of prisoners is."

"If you are in charge, I would remind you that the Geneva Rules of War stipulate that prisoners of war are to be marched no more than ten miles a day. Obviously that rule has been criminally violated these last days. I expect it to be respected in the march we are starting."

"We are on our way to Spremberg, and we will not stop until we get there, no matter how many kilometers that is. If all goes well, we will be there by morning. Marching at night is a precaution for your benefit as much as ours. To enemy bombers a column looks the same whether it is prisoners of war or German troops."

The march proceeded with a five-minute rest stop every hour. The night was so warm that the snow was melting. By midnight the Combine 7 four had pushed and pulled their sled over three short sections of bare dirt road. Briggs was too weak to be of much help in getting through the sections of rough going. Where the road was still snow covered, the sled-pack travel was easy going.

During a rest stop, Walt reviewed their problem. "This snow melting is getting scary. None of us is in shape to pull a plow. I weighed myself at the farm, and I only weigh forty-five kilos. That's ninety-nine pounds. I weighed 145 before I was shot down. What will we do if we lose the snow?"

Sam said, "We should have packed our stuff in our backpacks and loaded them on the sled, so if things went wrong we could take off our packs and keep going."

"Hind sight," Buck commented. "As things are, we've got to get through with this sled, regardless. It's carrying everything we need to survive."

When the march started again, sour Schumann marched behind them with his long-barreled, World War One rifle. At 2:00 A.M. the formation passed into a clearing. Suddenly Buck, Walt, Briggs, and Sam were in panic—there was no more snow. The ditches showed nothing but dark, wet dirt. The road itself was a bed of sticky mud. Walt and Buck pulled with all their strength while Briggs and Sam pushed as hard as they could. Tremendous effort was required to plow the sled through the mud.

The situation was hopeless. Then the sled started moving easier. They looked back and saw that Schumann had lowered the butt of his rifle to the rear of the sled and was helping them push. Everyone kept struggling to defeat the impending disaster, until the road changed back to the slick snow base of a Spremberg street. Schumann slung his rifle back on his shoulder and returned to his post and to his usual sullen self.

The march ended next to warehouses. At 3:00 A.M. the Luftwaffe served hot, thick barley soup. The guards borrowed kriegie klim cans and joined the bash. Again, Briggs did not eat. He felt weak from not eating, but he could not hold food down.

During a five-hour rest stop inside one of the warehouses, Buck, Walt, Briggs and Sam took advantage of the warehouse light to put their belongings back into their makeshift packs. While they were working a kriegie dressed in blue walked by, and Sam heard him say, "He's as timid as a kiwi bird."

Sam called out, "Did you say kiwi bird? Where are you from?"

"I'm not a limey. I'm from New Zealand."

"Godzone?"

"Where did you hear that?"

"I read it in a book about a country where there are only birds."

The New Zealander laughed. "There once were only birds. Now we're more known for sheep."

"I want to live in your country when we get freed. Here, tell my combine about the birds. They think I'm around the bend because I've been telling how your country is like living in heaven."

"Heaven is reaching a bit, but we do call it Godzone. I'll tell you, believe him when he says my country was a land of only birds, and it's still a good place like none else on earth. It would be heaven for me today if I were there. I've got to get on, mates. If I ever get home, and you ever get there, look me up at Russell in the Bay of Islands. I'm Russ . . . so that's easy. Russ of Russell."

"You're going to see me, Russ—Russ of Russell," Sam called after the sudden visitor from his land of dreams.

"This is crazy," Walt reacted. "All along the place you were dreaming about was real."

"This is going to take some talking. We've no time for it now. Let's keep concentrating on getting our stuff into our packs," Buck ordered.

At 9:00 A.M. the kriegies were formed into a single file and marched along a trail that wound into the hills. The guard Smitty was flanking the column next to Walt. His preference for this post seemed to tell that he remembered that he had given Walt Paula's address and might soon need Walt in a special way. Both understood that continuing their communicating carried mutual advantage. At the moment Smitty told Walt that the trail they were following led to a railroad station.

"This is a hell of a funny route to be taking to a railroad station," Buck said as he hobbled along on feet too tender for the weight he was carrying. The single-file train reminded Buck of a stream of ants winding its way in blind succession.

Up ahead, around the next hill, a machine gun began to chatter.

"Who said we were going to a railroad station?" Sam asked.

"If you're worried, you're not alone," Briggs said.

No one dared say what they were thinking. Sam reminded himself that the Germans had never said where the marching was taking them. *Is there a plan that would make another prison camp unneeded?*

Briggs said half aloud, "For you the war is over." *Is this the garden of peace?*

Then they rounded the hill and saw that the machine gun fire was coming from a tank maneuvering across the field while gunners fired upon a practice target.

The trail gave way to a street. After a march down the street for a half mile, the railroad station that Smitty had promised Walt came into sight. A column-of-fours was formed. The formation was marched to a siding where a freight train waited. The box cars were the infamous type of World War I boxcars known as the "40 & 8s,"—for 40 men or 8 horses.

A runner approached. "Count your prisoners for a Red Cross Parcel issue."

"This must be a dream," Sam exclaimed. "A train to ride in. Food to eat. Wow!"

The Parcels had been side-tracked here by a priority shipment for the front. There were three Parcels for every four men. After the food had been rationed, the kriegies were loaded into the boxcars. One guard and fifty-four prisoners were put into each car.

Briggs, Sam, Buck, and Walt were loaded into the boxcar guarded by Schumann. As they waited for the train to depart, Hauptmann Eiler passed by, escorting a woman in furs and two girls. The arms of all were heavy with belongings. They entered a boxcar of the prison train.

"It looks like Eiler managed to save his family. I'll bet the guards were not so lucky," Buck said.

Walt was suddenly curious. "What about your family, Schumann?" he asked in German of the guard standing his post at the open door of the boxcar.

Schumann, who spoke only German, returned, "Don't pretend to me. You do not care about my family. When I want to discuss my life with you, I will let you know."

In a short while the door was pulled shut and locked from the outside with Schumann locked in with his fifty-four prisoners. No one could say why the Germans had chosen to lock a guard into each boxcar.

What seemed like hours later, the train started to move toward a destination still unknown. Schumann was left to share the discomfort of the prisoners. For the time being he was, in effect, a kriegie with a gun. As a German soldier, he was alone.

In the interior with illumination coming only from the cracks around the door, kriegies opened Parcels and put together something to eat. Combine 7 with three Parcels ate K-2 crackers and liver pâté. Briggs tried to eat, but he could not hold down food. The combine made him a special dish of crackers, raisins, and jam. When he tried to eat, he couldn't fully swallow before the food came back up.

In addition to the klim can each carried tied to his waist, extra klim cans, with tops included, had been saved since the march began. All of Combine 7 had such an extra can now. They had filled these cans with water at Spremberg before being loaded into the boxcar. Walt now played doctor by dissolving sugar cubes into Briggs's water, to give Briggs energy, but Briggs couldn't even hold down this sweet water. There was no further medical assistance that the combine could think of, other than the kriegie cure for the GIs, not eating. So Briggs was left to rest.

There was not space enough for the fifty-four kriegies to sit or lie down at one time. By taking turns in standing up, space was made for some people to sit down and some to lie down in the twenty-five by eight-foot boxcar. Everyone occasionally gained a chance to stretch out.

As the day wore on . . . with the wheels clanking, grinding, and squealing . . . body elimination became a problem. More kriegies than Briggs had acquired the GIs since they left Sagan. Those who could no longer contain themselves made use of the klim cans they were carrying for cooking and eating. Briggs's elimination was scant but bloody.

The only ventilation in the car was that which seeped through cracks. The lack of fresh air provided some protection against the cold. The fifty-five had the advantage of the body heat they were generating in the confined space. But after a while odors of human waste loading the stagnant air constituted a putrid atmosphere.

Near sundown the train was side-tracked in a small town. The doors were opened for the prisoners to go out and relieve themselves. Townspeople lined the tracks and watched as hundreds of kriegies squatted with pants down and eliminated. Since there had been no issue of bread and other German rations in the past days, kriegies eagerly sought trade. Some people offered bread for cigarettes and chocolate. During this time, Schumann disappeared. When he returned he had a three-gallon pail.

"Fur scheisserei," Schumann explained with obvious pride in his acquisition of a can for elimination. The signal to reload came while prisoners were still waiting at water faucets for their turn to wash feces from their klim cans and

fill them with water for the next lock up. The waiting kriegies shouted protests against moving on. Guards shouted
with them and delayed the loading long enough to allow
almost everyone to wash out and fill their klim cans. When
the doors were bolted shut again, Sam, Walt, and Buck took
advantage of the waning light offered by the cracks to eat a
sound meal. It was going to be a long night, but, at least, it
promised the comfort of a full stomach.

Briggs still could not hold food down. He murmured that he
was feeling cold, and Walt and Sam wrapped him in their wool
blankets. This left Buck's blanket for them to use alternately.
Walt, Buck, and Sam gave up their turns to lie down so that
Briggs could continue in his lying-rest at the back of the car.

As night deepened, the glow of live cigarettes became
orange stars in a black cosmos. By taking lights from the
glowing cigarettes from person to person, on into the night,
the kriegies kept the stars alive.

Schumann maintained his station next to a crack by the
door. Here he could breathe the fresh air coming in, and here
he could see outside into the cold heaven of white glowing
stars that contrasted to the gold-star heaven of humanity
within the boxcar. He often roved his eyes across the indoor
starlight as if in envy of those smoking, but he never asked for
a cigarette. Now he shifted his place to allow a prisoner the
privilege of a few minutes of fresh air by the crack of the door.
Afterwards, the prisoner offered him a cigarette.

"Wo sind wir?" a prisoner called as Schumann drew a
light from a glowing ember.

"Wo gehen wir?" another prisoner asked. Since the
beginning of the trip the kriegies had pestered him with
such questions. He did not know where they were going, but
he did know where the train was. Yet he never answered.
Once he told inquisitive prisoners, he was here as their
guard not their travel guide.

"Wo sind wir?" someone called again.

In the blackout it was hard for Schumann to know where
he was. But this was his part of Germany. He recognized
the station. Yet he did not tell the name of the town.

A half hour later Schumann shouted, "Offendorf!" as they passed through a town.

The kriegies didn't know what to make of Schumann's sudden outburst. Then they understood that he had finally decided to be more than their guard.

Hands clapped and calls of "Hurrah" and "Eh, Schumann" filled the boxcar. From then on Schumann called out towns until he was too far away from his home territory to recognize the stations.

Briggs lay on the floor, wrapped in two Red Cross wool blankets, not eating or drinking, but resting, with eyes closed most of the time. More kriegies came down with the GI's as the train moved on through a second day. By nightfall many kriegies wished they could start walking again. Bodies jammed together for more than thirty hours cried for space. The aches, illness, odor and lack of fresh air, yielded a disease of spirit.

"Chemnitz!" Schumann called out as he recognized the city just before midnight.

The train stopped. After a long while the door was opened. An air raid siren began a series of wails of four seconds each. Schumann, suddenly extremely nervous, spoke hurriedly to a passing guard. Then he told in German that the air raid warning was for approaching heavy bombers. He said that the railroad yards would certainly be their target and that an ammunition train was on the next track. He said that he had seen the signs posted on the cars, warning of explosives. He clarified that it was not totally certain yet that this city was the target, but the Grossangriff warning that had meant great attack of heavy bombers had been given.

The door was closed and locked again, but the train did not move.

"Here we go," Buck said. *For you the war is over.* "If we live to be liberated, we'll probably slip on a banana peel and kill ourselves going up the front steps to home."

For twenty minutes it was very quiet as everyone listened for the sound of the first bomber, the first of a thousand, the message that ten thousand tons of terror would soon rain from the sky. Then the sirens gave a long continuous wail.

"Entwarnung," Schumann said with obvious relief. He did not have to explain that this meant, all clear.

The door opened again. Outside, German women in Red Cross uniforms ladled soup and water for prisoners, who were allowed out one boxcar at a time, to receive this benevolence ladled into their klim cans.

Then the train again started into the darkness of the German blackout. Finally, it got light. In the middle of the morning there was a rest stop with a repeat of line-up for elimination along the tracks.

In the evening there was a similar rest stop. Afterwards, kriegies ate food from their packs before dark. But food was less important now. The combination of dysentery, boxcar confinement, and the stench of body waste had stilled appetite.

All but a very few of those who smoked were out of cigarettes. There were not enough smokers now to keep the chain of fire going, and there were no more matches. So on this third night the boxcar world was starless. Black bleak with gloom.

Around midnight blue-white lightning began to flash through the boxcar cracks. At least, it seemed as if the flashes were lightning. Schumann studied the sky through the doorway crack and told Walt that it was definitely lightning. The light coming through the cracks fleetingly illuminated the dark knot of humanity in the car. The fireworks of light and dark patterns playing upon the interior roused even those who were having their turn at lying down.

But Briggs did not react to the wild light display. Walt talked to him but he did not answer. Walt tried to lift Briggs to a sitting position to see if he might take some water, but he felt dead weight in his arms so he let him lie down again, and he felt for his pulse. "Sam, see if you can find Ed's pulse. I can't, and I can't feel him breathing either."

"Let me to him," Buck said. "He's got to be okay. He'll be better by morning."

After a while Buck said, "Would you take over, Sam? I can't find his pulse either, and I can't feel him breathing."

Sam pulled away the blankets and lay his head on Briggs's chest. "He's not breathing."

"Keep the blankets over him just the same . . . let him rest," Buck said.

Walt prayed. "God, he is yours. We loved his gentle spirit. He was too good to last on this earth. Help us accept your will."

The lightning ended, and the unrelieved darkness took over again in the boxcar.

Sam thought how little light it takes to see, once darkness has fully opened your eyes.

In one corner, a group of kriegies started to sing, "Home on the Range":

> Oh give me a home,
> Where the buffalo roam,
> Where the deer and the antelope play.
> Where seldom is heard,
> A discouraging word,
> And the skies are not cloudy all day.
> Home, home on the range,
> Where the deer and the antelope play.
> Where seldom is heard,
> A discouraging word,
> And the skies are not cloudy all day.

When this ended, someone said, "Schumann, you sing. You sing for us."

"Sing for us, Schumann," another kriegie called.

"Sing, Schumann."

Unexpectedly, Schumann began to sing:

> Pater noster,
> Qui es in,
> Sanctificetur nomen tuum. . . .

"What's he singing?" someone asked.

"I'm Catholic. It's the 'Our Father,'" someone said, "from the Mass."

. . . Libera nos a malo. Amen.

Clapping greeted his Amen. A stir that was not quite laughter passed over the kriegies.

Schumann continued with another song:

> Libera me, Domine, demorte aeterna, in die illa tremenda:

He's singing the Libera, for the dead," a prisoner said. Deliver me, O Lord, from everlasting death on that day of terror:

> Quando coeli movendi sunt et terra:
> When the heavens and the earth will be shaken.
> Dum veneris judicare saeculum per ignem.
> As Thou dost come to judge the world by fire.
> Tremens factus sum ego, et timeo, dum dis
> cussio venerit—
> I am in fear and trembling at the coming
> judgment—
> Atque ventura ira.
> And the wrath to come.
> Quando coeli movendi sunt et terra.
> When the heavens and the earth will be shaken.
> Dies irea, dies illa, calamitatis et miseriae:
> That day will be a day of wrath, of misery,
> and of ruin:
> Dies magna et amara valde:
> Dum veneris judicare saeculm per ignnem.
> As Thou dost come to judge the world by fire.

Schumann kept singing until he had sung every song he had learned in church. Then he fell silent and receded into his old self, and the train clanked on with its indifferent clickity-clack of the steel road leading to the unknown.

PART V

The Crucible

THE CRUCIBLE: CHAPTER ONE

FROM THE JOURNAL OF DEAN RAYMOND: After three days of fifty-four of us being locked in with vomit and excrement in a twenty-five-by-eight-foot boxcar, yesterday we were side-tracked in a vast rail yard. The guard locked in with us said we were in Nuremberg. Out of concern for our safety, I at once asked, "For how long?" He only shrugged his shoulders.

I was anxious, because of the offensive against rail transportation. During my work with rating German targets I had learned that Nuremberg is one of three main railroad centers that feed the lower Western Front. It is the junction between Stuttgart and Munich, the other centers, and it can handle three thousand cars a day. Bombing Nuremberg jams east-west and north-south rail traffic to southern Germany. I hoped we would leave quickly.

After an hour, I heard the screeching sounds of boxcar doors sliding open. Then, our door screeched open. The fresh air, though cold, was heaven-sent.

We were ordered to form a column along the north side of the railroad yard, which at this point was only four tracks wide. But the demand of nature had me first squat bare ass and relieve myself before I took my place at the head of the column.

About five hundred to eight hundred yards to my right I saw a stretched-out wall of barbed wire with many guard towers. Behind this I saw many one-story buildings.

"This is the end," a guard shouted. "You are at Langwasser prison."

I was shocked that we were to be imprisoned so close to Nuremberg. I looked back to the train we had left, and I saw a body being carried out and then another and another. I knew that some of us had not survived the trip, but that didn't make it easier to watch the bodies coming out. I told myself that I should keep watching and take a count, but I needed to face away from the past, and I did.

Going into Langwasser, I saw many compounds separated by double barbed wire walls like at Sagan. Compounds are called camps here. I was informed that what used to be West Compound of Stalag Luft III was to be put with fifteen hundred POWs that would be Camp 5, and I was again the senior officer. I was assigned quarters in a communal kitchen. There are about ten thousand prisoners in total here.

In Spremberg, my medical officer, Sneed, and my friend, Bellrage, were put on a train going somewhere else. Peyser is here, and will again be my rations officer. If I live to do it, I will recommend Bellrage for the Silver Star for how he rescued vital order by taking command in Muskau.

In Spremberg we also lost the highest ranking prisoner of Stalag Luft III. Through a mysterious arrangement with the Germans, he and a few of his high-ranking staff were driven away in a car for immediate repatriation. This general did not ask me to join those getting a quick way home. For this I am glad. He spared me the temptation to escape my leadership responsibility.

I was rescued, personally, by an abandoned capture Parcel that a guard gave me. I had thrown away all my belongings, but I now have a wool blanket, a cotton blanket, winter underwear, and the contents of a food Parcel—minus the cigarettes and D-Bar. I also have the bonus of a tooth brush, a razor blade, a razor, and the notebook I am using to start this journal. I ask myself who abandoned the Parcel, and what happened to him.

I have arranged for majors and higher rank to be quartered in the kitchen with me. It is freezing cold here, and we get coal rations only for the communal kitchen. The kitchen stoves will provide some warmth for us, and we again have enlisted crew for work duty. They will run the kitchen and prepare the meals for the senior officer staff as in Sagan.

From this place, I see Sagan as a model POW camp. Here POWs receive no mail. There are no books. No means for sports or other group activity. Most indoor space is filled by three-deck sleeping frames. Once kriegies leave their beds there is no place to spend time indoors. Living a day here is living with fleas, hunger, cold, and worst of all, the constant dread of bomber attack. I have been here less than twenty-four hours, and already I am appalled—more later.

WITH BUCK, WALT, AND SAM: "Goldy never wanted the barn as much as I want the bunk I'm going to get tonight."

"I'm dreaming of the hot shower we'll get to delouse us, like in Sagan," Sam said.

"Hatch, a guard has told me that we won't get showers going into this camp."

"At least we'll get dry. Rain falling with snow on the ground is crazy like Chicago."

They were marched past a big brick furnace that was half in ruins from a bomb strike. "Stay close, so we'll be put into the same building," Buck said.

The camp was long and narrow with no open area, only a road between rows of barracks. At each barracks, 175 prisoners were counted into the building.

An air raid alarm sounded. The prisoners were told this was the warning of enemy planes in the vicinity, but not overhead. Assignment to barracks continued.

It was dark before Buck, Walt, and Sam were put into Barracks 92 of Camp 5. In the lighted interior, they saw a long bay with a center aisle and with one side divided by walls, to form six open-ended compartments. Each compartment had a very narrow aisle between two, huge triple-deck bed frames that each had narrow board dividers between twelve mattresses. This construction provided berths for twenty-four kriegies in each compartment. On the other side of the barracks, opposite from each compartment, was a space filled by a table, two benches, and a smaller table. In some spaces there was also a heating stove. There was not enough room for all twenty-four kriegies to be out of bed and yet inside at the same time.

Three triple-deck bunks stood along the far end of the building to total 153 berths, but 175 kriegies had been assigned to the barracks. In the ensuing scramble for beds,

Sam and Walt obtained adjoining mattresses, but Buck got no berth. He quickly claimed the floor at the end of the aisle where Walt and Sam held bottom tier mattresses.

The sirens began to wail the alarm that meant enemy planes overhead. All lights went out. From voices in the dark came:

"Lucky we got bunks before the lights went out."

"I saw slit trenches on the way in. I'm heading out to get below ground."

"Think again. I just now drew machine gun fire trying that."

"Trying to go outside after dark? Don't you know better?"

"As near as we are to the railroad yard, this is no place to be above ground."

"If I'm going to get killed, I'd rather it would be from our bombs than kraut bullets."

"I don't hear anti-aircraft guns. I'm sticking where I am. We've got no choice."

"I figure it's not heavy bombers. I think they've got a special warning for them."

"I'm too wet and cold to care. I'm wrapping up in my blanket and going to sleep."

"Something's biting me."

"You too? Something's biting the piss out of me."

"I heard they moved out Italians to make room for us. Those Italians sure left a lot of sharp-biting something behind."

"My bunk only has nine slats holding up a one-inch mattress."

"If you're bitching, I'll trade you for my spot on the floor."

"Shut up. I want to listen to what's happening."

"Don't worry. You'll know if it starts happening."

"There's nothing we can do about it."

"Would you rather be back in the boxcar?"

"Kill him for asking."

The talk in the dark slowly diminished with the Overhead Alert still on and the biting of vermin continuing. Exhaustion brought sleep at least for the moment, until exploding bombs could reawaken alertness. But on this night no bombs fell.

FROM THE JOURNAL OF DEAN RAYMOND: I haven't made an entry in eleven days. Today is Saturday, 17 February 1945. I have met with Hauptmann Eiler who remains in charge of what is now called Stalag Luft III, Camp 5. The other compounds of Stalag Luft III were sent elsewhere. This place was Stalag XIII-D holding Italian officer POWs until it was emptied for us. There is a camp of Russians here, too, but they are not subject to the rules of the Geneva Convention.

Our camp at Sagan is still not liberated. My judgment in keeping several weeks of food reserve is vindicated by the fact that the Oder River has held as a defense line, in spite of the panic that resulted in our nightmare death march. If the Germans had not panicked, we would still be POWs in Sagan, now thankful for the food reserve I kept.

Except for an hour or two in the morning and again in the evening we are under constant alert for enemy planes in the vicinity. At times, we get the overhead alert, but there has been no Grossangriff alert yet. I am certain the heavy bombers will come soon.

Bombs dropped up to now have come from Mosquito bombers during the few all clear periods between American daylight bombing and British night bombing. The Mosquitoes come in so low and fast that sometimes they drop their huge bombs before the sirens sound a breech of all clear. This unnerves the bomb-wary, for even during the all clear periods, we cannot be sure a bomb isn't heading our way. Some of our windows have been broken by blasts so huge they are preceded by a rush of wind before the concussion strikes. We now leave windows ajar to help absorb explosions.

A loudspeaker provides us air-raid warnings and war reports. Heavy bombers bring a special "cuckoo bird" radio call when a four-engine-bomber sky train is advancing in the stratosphere nearby. It feels strange that, after my days of decision-making anguish in sending bombers out, I am now in anguish waiting to learn if the decision-makers have chosen us to receive the bombs today.

The Chemnitz rail yard, where our boxcars were sidetracked next to the ammunition train, was hit by over a thousand heavy bombers three days after we left there. Magdeburg and Leipzig also got bombed that day. Three days later, our heavies hit Lutzkendorf. That, sadly, was the only Oil target. The heavies also hit the railroad yard at Magdeburg again. Just three days ago they hit Magdeburg another time, but the big event has been Dresden.

The Germans report that the RAF bombed Dresden twice during the night of February 13 and that the city was already on fire when our heavies got there on February 14 and then returned to bomb it again on February 15. Between the two air forces enough concussion and incendiary bombs were piled onto that city to cause an unprecedented fire storm. Berlin claims that hundreds of thousands of evacuees, refugees and prisoners of war were in Dresden at the time, because the city had been recognized as a safe haven—a city with no military targets, few air defenses, and no previous bombing attacks. By German reports, more than one hundred thousand people were killed there. Reports say fire swept through the city with hurricane force that sucked the air out of the shelters, suffocating the people inside.

We got news that over one thousand heavies struck still burning Dresden again and also pounded Magdeburg again two days ago. Chemnitz, too, again caught hell with two successive night bombings by RAF heavies. It seems that once a city is picked, there is no escape from the cauldron. We are in the crucible, being tempered for the coming cauldron. Our chances of being picked next have increased with the news that the Western Front offensive is heating up. Nuremberg is the key southern rail junction.

Yesterday over one thousand heavies hit places I recognize as Oil targets, but in addition they bombed the rail yards at Hamm, Osnabrueck, and Rheine—-vain effort, which slave laborers have no doubt already repaired. German news is predicting failure of the massive air offensive to cut off train traffic to the Western Front, but that doesn't spare us here.

Hitler has proclaimed martial law. Eiler defended Hitler's action as needed to control refugees from the East scrounging for food and shelter. He said he himself had been ordered to use martial law to eliminate troublesome POWs and foreign workers.

Authority and resources are shifting to greater Nazi control as Germany is being taken over by fanatics. Eiler is losing power to get what we need, but as required by the Geneva Convention, he has granted me access to an English edition of the rules for treatment of prisoners of war. I am compiling a report of violations, an urgent protest to the International Red Cross. I will deliver it in eleven days, 28 February, when the Representative from Switzerland is scheduled to visit our camp.

February 19: Yesterday Berlin reported that Sagan had fallen to the Russians—three weeks after we left. Today's news said the offensive against railroads has intensified. Osnabrueck, Rheine, Muenster, Siegen, Vienna, Graz, and Klagenfurt were bombed—the first two for the second time in four days. Some raids were joint efforts, with the Fifteenth Air Force from Italy that together made up a force of two thousand heavy bombers.

It is now evening. The RAF will no doubt bomb tonight.

February 20: Last night the RAF bombed Dortmund, the Ruhr transport center. Prisoners here take hope from the fact that only five buildings of Camp 5 have been leveled by bombs, and those before we got here. No one talks about it, but as few as five percent of bombs slightly off target when the nearby rail center gets bombed could level this camp.

The Germans won't let us use the slit trenches the Italians dug. They say the Italians used them to start escape tunnels. The guards have orders to shoot any prisoner trying to use a slit-trench. During overhead alerts we all have to go to our barracks.

Rescue from the ill fate likely here can only come from arrival of our troops before Nuremberg gets a Grossangriff. In English, Grossangriff means vast assault—referring to a massive raid of 4-engine bombers.

Since our troops are far away, the odds are against us. The rail yard is too close.

We could try to escape. But Hitler's martial law makes an escape attempt almost certain death. Just being seen without a guard is enough to be shot without questioning.

—We just got a Grossangriff alert—

WITH SAM, BUCK, AND WALT: Near Barracks 92, Sam, Buck, and Walt looked up to an overcast covering the whole sky ten thousand feet above. They listened for the drone of the four-engine-bombers so familiar to them, but the sky was totally quiet.

A guard came running, waving his rifle and shouting, "Inside! Inside! Alle inside Kaserne. Grossangriff kommt."

Pushed back into the barracks they retreated to their compartments. Today Buck had a bunk because one of the twenty-four kriegies of the compartment was in the "hospital."

Buck said, "There's no room for anything but go to bed. There's nothing to see anyway. The bombers are coming in above the clouds. Trouble is, having bombed from above the clouds, we know that means they'll be scattering their loads, which means we are a part of the target."

"With a lot of alerts, nothing's happened. Maybe it's a false alarm," Walt speculated.

"You heard how nervous the guard was," Sam noted. "I think they're up there, coming in. I can see myself sitting in the nose, flying over the peaceful clouds like I was on a tourist trip."

"This is no tourist trip, if they're up there," Buck stressed.

"I know," Sam commented, "if we were up there we'd soon be having flak making a black wall full of cherry blossoms we've got to fly through."

"You'd better get your minds down from upstairs," Walt said. This is going to be a different story, being underneath the bombs."

"I don't hear anything," Sam said. "Maybe I was wrong about it being a real raid."

"How can we hear them with all this talk in here," Buck said. Then he shouted, "Why don't you all hit your sacks and quiet down."

Those who were still up took to their bunks.

John Howell, lying in the bunk between Buck and Walt, said, "We know they can't pinpoint the railroad yard from above the clouds so it's certain they'll be dropping a bomb every five hundred feet in Wing formation two miles wide . . . and that includes us."

"Did you just figure that out?" Buck asked. "I'm picturing at least ten Wings up there of one hundred ships each. Figure what that means."

"They'll be bombing by the signal from the Pathfinder's Magic Eye," Walt said.

"Yeah," John agreed. "And by the Pathfinder method we're a part of the target!"

"Stop burying us before they get here!" the kriegie next to Sam said angrily.

"There are craters in the woods next to us, and buildings gone in camp. Lots of Italians must have got killed," Buck continued.

"The Italians were in the air-raid trenches," Walt reminded.

"Those slit trenches wouldn't help against five-hundred-pounders exploding here," Sam said. Then, feigning calmness, he added, "This camp will probably still be here when the war is over."

"Right, Sam. Let's be optimistic," Walt joined.

"Listen. Feel that. I'm getting a vibration in my bunk," John said.

"That's them," Walt spoke softly.

The mumble of conversation of the kriegies now occupying the three tiers of mattresses subsided to silence with total concentration on the alien earth-rumbling.

With unrelenting progression the rumble augmented.

Walt broke through the kriegie listening with, "If we could see them, we could know what direction they're headed—"

Walt's voice was drowned by the sudden din of two thousand 88-millimeter anti-aircraft cannon firing. The makeshift tin chimney of the unused heating stove tumbled to the floor.

For a few minutes there was only the flak noise and the trembling and rattling of the barracks while the bomber rumble got stronger. Then the compartment flashed bright with rampant bursts of light. The bomb-wise at once began to count the distance-time before the concussion would strike. The first jolts hit, locked-in immeasurably close to the next, and the next, and the next. Unending for endless minutes the bursting bombs twisted the building, bouncing kriegies in their bunks, and knocking the open windows to and fro.

Most of that bunch was nearer than a mile away, Sam calculated.

With words spoken aloud, but lost in the noise, Buck said, "That's the first salvo. We'll soon know if this Wing is headed toward us."

The light flashed again. Then the concussion. From farther away.

Being the first Wing in, maybe that's setting the pattern, starting closest to us and moving away, Walt reasoned with the bombs still bursting.

The bombing ceased. The cannon sending up the barrage stopped. The rumble of the bombers faded away.

"It sounds like the next Wing is a little behind schedule," John observed. "I hate this goddamn waiting."

"The waiting is the terror the krauts talk about," Buck said. "When the bombs are bouncing me, I'm so much into it, I'm frozen."

"Jesus, Saint Sara, spare us," Walt whispered in private prayer.

"When I was guessing there are ten Wings coming, I hope I'm wrong. I'm not ready for more of this," Buck said.

"Each time will be different," Sam guessed. "Better or worse . . . we know they're not even trying to drop in the same place."

"Yes, but you don't need to say it," Walt said.

The flak opened up again. Then came the light flashes and then the concussion.

Walt thought . . . these bombs are closer, but only a little closer, maybe a half mile away. They may be taking out some railway track with these. This Wing must be on a different heading or the lead bombardier is screwed up. They've passed us. We got missed again.

Then all was quiet again.

John said, "The way things are going, the next Wing may start laying their eggs through the woods and bring their carpet straight across us."

"If you think that, keep it to yourself," Buck said. "We don't need to hear your pants-pissing worries."

Buck got up and rushed to the window. "You've got to see this. There is fire and smoke coming up from the opposite side of the city, way far away from the railroad yard."

No one left his bunk to check Buck's report. Buck returned to his mattress.

The sequence of flak going up and bombs coming down began all over again. This time the bombs were more than three miles away.

Now Walt was shivering. He looked over to Sam who was wrapped up in his blankets, lying on his back, and looking up to the bed slats of the bunk above him, looking calm as he waited for the bombs to burst again.

"I'm shivering because I'm cold," Walt excused himself to Sam. Then he rolled over and saw that Buck and John were shivering too.

"I'm not shivering because of the cold," Buck said. "I'm shaking from waiting for the next Wing. The next salvo may hit us. Oh, hell, I should keep my mouth shut."

John said, "Yeah. If we were in the slit trenches we'd have a chance, but laying here flat and facing up to it helpless—anybody in their right mind would be shaking."

The waves of bombing continued for one and a half hours. Finally, the quiet lasted.

The long wail of the all clear sounded. Kriegies lifted

themselves out of their bunks weak from lack of enough to eat but weak even more from the trauma of the raid.

Walt said in a faltering voice, "This place is the hell of Job, but this has been the worst of being here. Not having enough to eat robs me of my nerve to take the bombing."

Kriegies hurried out to see what havoc had been wrought by the raid. Columns of fire and smoke were rising across the miles of city to the East and South of the rail yard.

The ground was littered with steel fragments of flak shells that had exploded in the stratosphere. Kriegies who a short while ago lay helpless in dread of death now picked up shell fragments as souvenirs of their ordeal.

Buck, looking at the city, ignored the spent flak and said, "What's this? I've got to find out what this fertilizing freestyle is all about. I'm going to look up the head man." He hastened to the communal kitchen and asked to speak to Colonel Raymond.

Raymond came to the door, shaking his head. "Wild situation! With the delayed-action bombs we know they've dropped, it will be twenty-four hours before the fire-fight can get to the flames. Bombs fell to both sides of us. This camp is going to get leveled. It's only by sweet luck we didn't get leveled today."

"You can see by the smoke and fires they didn't even hit the railroad yard!" Buck blurted.

"No. They didn't."

"That's why I've come to you. Why this raid? Since they didn't touch the target, they'll be back, and soon. Am I right? We've used up our sweet luck. I'm not looking to die for this horseshit. Colonel, back at Muskau you told me you knew things about the air war—too much to go into. I want to hear what you have to say. Now. Our asses are on the line. I'm pissed off about being set up to go through this again."

"Come out of the cold, Pierce."

When Buck was inside he faced Raymond. His voice was now half an octave higher. "What's going on here? We know the big priority here is the railroad yard. Still, our air force just damn near killed us to fertilize the city freestyle. So now the target is still there, and we're here sweating. We know our air force is going to come back to blast it. Goddamn it, what's going on?"

"You know. You've had the pilot briefings for missions like today's. Remind yourself. The curtain has just been pulled back showing the red target X on Nuremberg. Now what did the briefing tell you? You tell me. I want you to show me you know why a lot of honorable young American patriots flew here today and deliberately killed women and children instead of bombing the railway yard. What did the briefing officer say?"

Calmed somewhat by the role-playing, Buck recited: "'The target for today is the railway yard of Nuremberg. We've got to knock it out because—yak, yak, yak. Wings will break into Groups as they approach the I.P., and our lead bombardier will get on our Norden bombsight and score a shack in the middle of the goddamn railway yard.'"

"And if the target is obscured by cloud cover?"

"Oh. That. 'If the target is obscured we will remain in Wing formation and toggle our bombs to fertilize the city freestyle.'"

"Fertilize the city freestyle?"

"Yeah. Erutan talk. Nature spelled backwards. The air force calls bombs pigs. Bringing them home live is aborting them. To kill with them is to deliver them. All Nature backwards. So to bomb a city is to fertilize it freestyle."

"To scatter bombs over a hundred square miles of population if you couldn't see the military target?"

"Right."

"Then why are you asking me? You know the answer."

"That answer, yeah. But why? Why wouldn't the briefer say: 'If the target is obscured, bring your bombs back and we'll try again another day'? I'd a hell of a lot rather land my plane with a load of live bombs than fly through the wall of fire of two thousand cannon aiming at me like our guys had to fly through today. I've brought live bombs back and landed with them when I had to abort. What's different that couldn't let the pilots today take their bombs back home and save them for a military target?"

"It's the difference that lost Hitler the chance to invade England and maybe win the war. Hitler didn't stay with the plan to wipe out the RAF and get control of the sky for an invasion. He switched to bombing civilians. That gave the RAF the breather they needed to win the Battle of Britain. Churchill himself said that Hitler's bombing of civilians rallied the English will to never surrender. Now Churchill is pushing the bombing of German civilians, which he calls "de-housing" them—to get the Germans to surrender. Contradictory? Yes! Let's go outside. I want to see what's happening."

As they walked out to where they could see the city burning, Buck said, "I'm pissed off, too, about all of our air crews getting shot down doing this."

"What we've lived through today is the strategy of a brain loaded with eighty shots of whiskey," Raymond answered. Then, listening to the delayed-action bombs sporadically bursting and surveying the flames flaring across the broad expanse of city horizon, he said, "I've talked too much. For your ears only. Never to be talked about. Historians will have to penetrate a mountain of official cover-up to document the warped brain-work ruling our World War Two. You and I have a short cut to the truth through our personal bombing experience . . . both over and under the bombs."

"About what you've said . . . I'm not going to shoot my mouth like in Sagan. You can trust me," Buck declared.

Standing in the cold air of the February afternoon, Raymond closed further discussion of the raid with, "You'd think the weather would warm up enough to at least melt the snow."

"I had you figured wrong, Colonel. I'm realizing how dumb I was, blaming you."

"You have to understand, Pierce, that when you are less fussy about where you drop your bombs, you get better tonnage figures for headlines. The Brits get big headlines with their huge tonnage figures of night bombing. When we had problems flying daylight raids, they fought us to make us fly at night, like they do. using their key-system ratings to de-house Germans."

Buck broke in, "I've got to admit that at times I felt like it was suicide to take a B-17 into Germany in daytime before we got the fighters to stay with us all the way to the target."

"That is one of the problems we licked. Right?"

"You'd better believe it. The first time we had P-38s with us all the way we called them 'friendlies from heaven.'"

"We put American ingenuity to work at breakneck speed to make our daylight, pinpoint bombing work. But we lost in the power struggle, in lots of ways. It's too long a story for young pilots like you. You have to have lived it as I have, way back to the court-martial of Billy Mitchell. Buck, study air force history, if we survive this place. You were right if you came to verify that we would soon be hit again."

"That question was the last straw that drove me to come to see you."

"Bloody doom is our prospect, it would appear. But we don't need to advertise it, do we? There is no point in preaching bleak fate to those who can't do anything about it."

"Colonel, a lot of kriegies here have figured out we're in deep trouble, but we're not talking about it."

Moving an arm across the horizon, Dean spoke, "Carnage without purpose, like the day my son was killed sitting beside you."

"I wish I would have listened to Randi. She tried to tell me about you."

"I have to end this. I've got to look up Hauptmann Eiler. I'm going to advise him that I am ordering kriegies of Camp 5 to use the slit trenches for air raids. We'll see how he handles a fait accompli."

"That's good. Tough-talk him. I'll leave you to get on with it. What you've told me will stay between us."

"Pierce, before you leave, one warning. Don't bring up Randi. There are limits."

"The same goes for me, Colonel. It's a long way from Wyoming to Washington."

"Agreed, but I'm glad we've found some common ground."

WITH DEAN RAYMOND: Raymond waited in the German headquarters for two hours, but Hauptmann Eiler did not appear. Eventually, he talked to Oberleutnant Kruger, Eiler's newly assigned deputy. Before he could declare his intention to use the trenches, Kruger told him in perfect English, "Look to what you have done to our city. Look to the fires, and tell me why we should not kill all you. Whatever you want, the answer is no."

Time to reverse. Agree with him. Hold out to see Eiler.

"It is not us who orders how the war is fought. I only ask to talk to Hauptmann Eiler. The Geneva rules—"

"Geneva rules be damned," Kruger interposed caustically. "Hauptmann Eiler is trying to learn if his wife and family are still alive, and you come to me with the Geneva rules. You have killed thousands here today! Was that according to the Geneva rules?"

"I only ask to be allowed to wait for the Hauptmann."

"Wait if you will."

Eventually Raymond had to leave to stand the 4:30 Appell. Afterwards he returned to Eiler's headquarters to wait some more. An ominous air prevailed. Since, in his thinking, Nuremberg had been chosen, he envisioned the RAF getting briefed for a visit tonight.

Finally Eiler appeared, and Raymond risked saying, "Though we are on opposing sides, may I, nevertheless, ask how your family fared?"

"The roads are blocked. I tried different routes, but I can't get through. They were housed in the suburbs. I believed they would be safe there, but I heard that their district has many fires. I will try again in the morning. Why are you waiting to see me?"

"Hauptmann, I recognize how anxious you must be, but I need your cooperation to save lives here. I insist on using the air raid trenches the Italians dug. I promise with my life we will not use them to start escape tunnels. We expect our troops to liberate us here."

"This meeting is unnecessary. I have informed you of higher orders on this subject. Your timing is bad to expect my help to save the lives of terrorfliegers."

"By the Geneva rules we have the right to use those trenches, and I am informing you that we are going to start using them. If you wish to use your machine guns, aim them at my door when the next Grossangriff arrives."

"You are defying me. That is very dangerous under the present climate here."

"I have taken steps to have the Allies informed of why, if I am shot. You will soon be under war crimes scrutiny. Your personal crisis has arrived in this war. Are you going to follow orders that make you a war criminal?"

"Herr Oberst Raymond, are you asking me to get myself killed by disobeying orders?"

"You do have to walk a fine line, I understand. I want a solution that does not get you shot and still gets us use of the trenches."

"Well then, at night, you must remain in your barracks. Why is obvious. On day raids, as always, you will go to your barracks and remain there for overhead alerts, except for Grossangriff alerts. I hold to my orders rigidly on this. However, I will add an order that demands clearance from me before firing on prisoners using trenches during a daylight Grossangriff. The order to fire on anyone outside at night still stands. Is that clear?"

"That is clear. But a RAF Grossangriff would be at night. I might risk getting shot."

"There is nothing I can do about that."

"Thank you, Hauptmann."

"One moment. Don't think our agreement means I forgive the crime of your country on this day. My private worries are so big that I don't wish to concern myself with punishment plots for prisoners now. I could change my mind."

"I'm leaving before you do."

Dean at once relayed the new air-raid rules to all kriegies. The news somewhat eased the gloom and apprehension.

WITH WALT, SAM, AND BUCK: Delivery of soup and ersatz coffee from the camp kitchens was denied by an overhead alert. Since the Grossangriff had denied boiled potato distribution, the evening meal for Combine 7 was only what bread they had saved. Red Cross food was nonexistent. Without lights, because of the overhead alert, kriegies groped about in the blackness, bumping into each other, until they retreated to their bunks to escape each other. In their barracks, the fleas, waiting for them, began to feed.

Walt was covered with more flea bites than Sam and Buck. Or, perhaps his body was less tolerant of the bites. He was covered with big welts from head to toe. If there had been medical help in the "hospital," he would have gone there. As things were, he stayed where he was. He didn't want to risk losing his bed to someone sleeping on the floor.

The sporadic explosion of bombs of the noon raid continued into the night and fires occasionally plumed into awesome clouds of flame that swelled orange light into the barracks. The night turned clear, but stars beyond the windows were blocked by smoke lifting from the city. The temperature turned warmer, making sleep easier for kriegies cold from insufficient covering. Yet the murmur of voices in the darkness told that few were asleep. The past day had awakened fear that was still alive, alerting ears to listen for bombers. Logic told that anti-aircraft fire would precede any bombers coming on this night, but the fear did not hinge on logic. It hinged on the one-and-one-half hours of bombing lived through only hours before. However, no special warning came, and as midnight passed, voices stilled until morning.

"I've got one more day blacked out," Sam said as he awoke and rubbed a pencil lead through February 20 of the calendar he had made. "I've made the goal of something to live for, the blacking out of Black February. First thing each morning I black out yesterday on my calendar."

"To give me the will to live through this, I've got the help of my Bible," Walt added.

Buck asked, "Does God know you stole it?"

"I didn't steal it. I got it from an enemy farm woman when she wasn't looking."

Buck said, "She was a kind person the way she helped all of the refugees coming through and fed the horses of people who couldn't pay. She put over a hundred of us up in her barn, too. She let you come into her house 'cause she trusted you."

"It's only a small Bible. She had a big one. I needed it. Me taking the Bible from a German isn't half as bad as you taking the scissors from another combine, Buck."

"Okay, we'll change the subject, Walt."

"The sun is shining and the snow is melting. Let's go outside," Sam suggested.

Buck said, "I'm not sure a clear sky is good news today, but I won't say more."

They went out and waited for the morning Appell, here held on the road between the barracks of the camp. With no library, no theater, no newsroom, or any of the other Sagan options for mind use, boredom, loaded with fear and misery, weighed heavier. The barbed-wire walls were more hideous from the heavier misery their presence imposed. The abort buildings were adjoined to the no-man's-land perimeter. This made an irregular boundary which made perimeter walking difficult, leaving only the road for exercise roaming.

Walking while waiting, Walt remarked to Buck, "I've been reading the book of Job. When I read about Job in the ditch, covered with boils, I thought it's like me full of welts from flea-bites. As much as Job was hurting, I'll bet he wasn't itching like me. I wish I had his ashes. They could cool down the burning."

"I know the Job story from Quaker Meeting," Buck said. "God was so bored that one day he started a gambling game with the devil. God bet on how much suffering he could put on his innocent and super-loyal Job before Job would tell him, 'Piss on you.'"

"That's not in the Bible," Walt snipped.

"You'd better believe it is. I can't read your German Bible to prove it, but you read chapter three of Job where he finally tells God off."

Buck and Walt stopped walking and faced each other as Buck continued, "There is a verse there that I read at Meeting when I didn't know if I should be a conscientious objector or join the army. 'Why is light given to a man whose way is hid, and whom God hath hedged in?' I was trying to tell the Meeting, especially my parents, that I couldn't know the right thing to do when God purposely hid the way and hedged me in. I just had to break out and start blazing my own way."

"The sunshine is too nice for you guys to be arguing religion," Sam interjected. "I'll bet before the day's over the snow will all be melted. Besides, we'd better get to Appell."

About noon, Walt walked to the center of the camp where the loudspeaker gave reports on bomber activity. Sam and Buck walked to the center of the nearby area where Barracks 93 had stood before it was destroyed by a bomb. Sam had explored the place, even though most kriegies avoided it for the stigma it carried. He had found a twelve-foot square of concrete floor and, on the west side, some loose bricks and a hole filled with garbage. "Look," he pointed out. "The guys running Raymond's mess have been dumping their garbage here. It's frozen. I wanted to show it to you because it has potato peelings that might be good to cook up."

"The stuff looks pretty rotten to me, Hatch. But let's keep watching for when they throw out fresh peelings."

"Think of it, Buck. The Brass is having their potatoes peeled, and we're dreaming of getting the peelings out of their garbage. They're sure living better than us."

"It's always been that way. It just wasn't as obvious in Sagan. If we ever get Red Cross Parcels here so we won't be starving so bad—"

"Inside! Alles inside! Grossangriff coming!" A guard yelled as he ran past.

"Oh no! Not again!" Sam agonized.

"Erutan! But at least today they've got clear sky. They won't be fertilizing freestyle, and we'll be in a trench. Hurrah to Pa Raymond."

Walt had not returned when the Overhead sounded. Buck ran to a Barracks 92 window and detached a shutter. "For over our heads to protect us from falling flak," he explained as the two hurried to a trench that was quickly filling.

"I don't want to talk about it. I just want it to be over. God, the city is still burning. Why wouldn't they wait at least until the fires are out?" Sam brooded.

"War, Hatch. Bombing while it's still burning is uglier. You kill more people this way. Anyway, we know what the big prize is today with a clear sky for pinpoint bombing. The railroad yard. I hope every Group bombardier will land his bombs in target center."

"Hey, Buck, bombardiers are human. What do you expect? They're aiming from five miles up from the middle of a flak barrage. They're going to land bombs all over this part of town if they're going for the railroad yard."

"Cross your fingers. Do you hear them? It's like their sound is coming from the ground. There is no sound like a thousand B-17's coming in from the high sky."

"Yeah. But I can barely hear them."

Buck said, "We hear enough to know they're coming."

Sam looked up to the sky. "All of you better hit your bombs dead on. Not too early. Not to the side. Dead on, or we're done for."

As the bomber rumble got louder the kriegies looked and saw the incoming ships so dwarfed by their altitude that they were barely visible silver pinpoints in the blue. By the illusion of distance the dots were moving very slowly as they advanced toward their Initial Point from which they would begin to fly straight and level on their bomb run.

The anti-aircraft cannon opened fire from all sides. In twenty seconds the eighty-eight-mm shells traveled to the altitude of the bombers and began to explode in a barrage before the intruders. The bombers flew into the black sky of the exploding shellfire. The black sky moved with the bombers, engulfing them as they advanced. Beneath the blackness, a downward scribing, jagged trail of gray smoke wrote its way earthward with the message that a Flying Fortress was fatally hit and going down.

If I were up there being the pilot of my Bare Lass, I'd have a chance to fight my way home. Here I can't do a damn thing but wait. The barrage is reaching clear to the railroad yard now. The krauts were sure ready for this one. It must be murder up there. Wait until it starts down here. It can't be much longer now—

With ear-torturing crescendo some three hundred blockbusters exploded in succession so rapid their earthquake concussion was combined with the flashing sky, eruption of flame, and welling of pulverized debris. The bursts were so close to the camp that kriegies could not know if the camp had been hit. They could only know if they, personally, had escaped.

Some thirty-five more crescendos were yet to come. In the trenches of Langwasser prison, B-17 bombardier veterans knew that no two Groups would land their bombs in the exact same place. The Norden bombsight, even when employed with the skill of the best of bombardiers, still had its accuracy limited by the many variables affecting the course of its bombs to their intended target miles below.

The next Group hit their payloads further to the left, in the forest, with the closest bombs landing at least a half mile away from the camp. The following Group delivered their earthquake crescendo straight ahead, with a count from flash time to concussion that gave a one and a half mile distance— the rail yard, dead on—a "shack" in bombardier talk.

Cannon fire continued from all sides and bombs continued to explode with as little as a minute of interlude between the massive salvos as Group after Group followed in train to drop its bombs. Bombs hit the tracks where the West Compound had arrived sixteen days before. Bombs hit behind the camp, so short in their aim that they missed the camp. And, from the plumes rising from new fires in the city, news came that not only the rail center but the larger expanse of Nuremberg was being hit again today.

Finally the repeating terror-wait of where the next Group would drop was over. The delayed-action bombs kept bursting sporadically, but the raid was over. Buck and Sam came out of the trench where they had outlived the February 21, 1945, Grossangriff.

Walt returned. He was still so nervous his voice cracked when he said, "I got into a trench with Pa Raymond and his staff. I was thinking they wouldn't be as nervous as me, but it was terrible being with them. Pa Raymond was calm like a rock no matter where the bombs blew, but some of the others were worse than me. I'd gone through too much before I was shot down. My nerves are wrecked. I'm still shaking, and I know it's over."

"Was anything hit in camp that you could see?" Buck asked "Not where I was."

"The guys coming from the other side say we got missed over there, too."

"It's a miracle they missed us. Look at the city now. It's burning worse than yesterday!" Sam chattered.

"Sam takes the prize for staying calm," Buck said. "I was ready to piss my pants, and he looked out to the show like he'd paid a ticket to watch."

"Don't fool yourself," Sam said. "After the barrages we've flown through with the *Bare Lass*, I thought I knew what being scared was, but waiting for the bombs is more like torture than being scared. There weren't any shells popping ahead of me to tell me how close I was to getting hit. I didn't know anything except that any second I might be dead without knowing what hit me."

"Yeah," Buck said. "In the movies they've got bombs whistling as they come down like in the first world war. Somebody ought to get the word out that there is no whistling warning these days. If anything it's something like a locomotive tumbling. But if it's coming down on top of you there isn't even the sound of St. Peter opening the gate."

"What's going to happen for something to eat?" Sam asked.

"The German rations are held up because of the raids," Walt said. "Looking at the city burning I'm expecting the Germans to come in here and kill us because we're from the air force that's causing this. With no Red Cross food, I'm feeling panicky."

Buck said, "Maybe it's all in my head, but I can smell flesh burning. Something horrible is burning."

Sam pondered, "The city's been burning for twenty-four hours, and now it's starting all over again. You know thousands of people are dead in there, and those left are fighting to save what they can. If it's them we're looking to for something to eat, I don't know why they'd give it to us, knowing who we are. What are they doing for their own food and water, those that are still alive? I want to wake up and see it was all a nightmare, and I'm really on Lonely Bay in Godzone."

Walt suggested, "Let's get in line and fill up everything we've got that will hold water. The spigot is still running, but who knows for how long."

When the three were waiting in line for the one spigot available for Barracks 92, Sam asked, "Walt, how come you've started to call Colonel Raymond . . . Pa Raymond?"

"I'm seeing him different than I used to," Walt explained. "In Sagan he had everything organized and I was even working for the organization. I can tell you now I was so friendly with the goons because it was my job to get information from them. It was even more complicated. I was ready to do anything he wanted. When this unknown major had to take over in Muskau—"

"You mean Bellrage?" Sam interrupted.

"Yeah. That was an eye-opener for me. Raymond's just an old man trying to be the young man he once was. Ever since we left Sagan he's come apart. Here he's got the high-ranking officers sharing the cookhouse, but he's got no real staff because here he's got no power over anything. We're all just kriegies here, him too. I don't think of him as the Colonel in charge anymore. He's just the guy trying to help us. That's why I call him Pa."

"The war ain't over yet, Walt," Buck said. "He may turn out to be more of a leader than you give him credit for. He's keeping a lot to himself, for your sake—not for you alone, Walt—for all he's the head honcho for."

"Am I hearing right?" Sam asked. "Am I hearing Walt knocking the Colonel and Buck defending him? Things have gotten turned ass backwards if I'm hearing right."

"I'm not knocking him," Walt said.

"I'm not defending him," Buck said. "I'm just laying out what I've come to know. He's got a lot of chicken-shit faults, but he's not the only one of us showing faults as the frosting of better times comes off."

"Frosting?" Sam asked.

"You know what I mean. As things get tougher we're showing our real side more, for better or worse," Buck said.

"Okay," Sam said. "Drop the subject. Just tell me the RAF is not going to bomb us tonight."

Bomb thunder continued to come in from Nuremberg all through the night, but the RAF heavies did not appear. Next day the fires were still sending plumes of flames into the sky. A cloud of smoke many miles across drifted to the south from the city. That night, again, the RAF heavies did not show, yet on the following day, with only an occasional explosion now, the city was still burning.

On the third day following the February 21 day raid, the Germans brought in a ration of orange cheese so large that there was a quarter pound for each prisoner of war. Word of the cheese ration spread in advance of the cheese actually arriving.

"This is perfect timing," Sam told Walt and Buck. "Let's check the garbage hole for some potato peelings to add to the cheese."

Sam, Buck, and Walt went to the garbage hole, and to their elation, they found what appeared to be freshly discarded potato peelings. They filled a klim can with the peelings. When the cheese arrived they had their klim can burner already fired up. They immediately began to cook a potato-cheese soufflé.

When they sat down to eat, they found that the potatoes, in spite of their best efforts of selection, carried a sour, putrid taste. But, in addition, the cheese had a chemical, metallic and bitter taste. Nevertheless, their soufflé was warm, and it was filling. They ate their plates clean without stopping.

Just as they finished, a kriegie major came into the barracks and shouted, "At ease!"

Everyone was quiet.

"I have an important announcement. Do not, I repeat, do not eat the cheese you were just rationed. We think it is poisoned. We are in the process of retrieving it, but until the enlisted men get here to get it back, do not eat any of it."

"We've already eaten it," Buck said.

"We've eaten ours, too," a spokesman for another combine lied.

"So have we," another spokesman lied.

"Hit the abort and throw it up if you've eaten it. It's been contaminated by poisonous chemicals in the process of putting out a fire in a cheese factory. We don't know whether it was issued to us innocently or not, but the order from your Senior Officer is, 'Do not eat it.'"

When the major had gone, Buck, Sam, and Walt agreed that whatever they had done, they would live with. For better or worse, they did not intend to undo the satisfied full feeling they were enjoying. The other combines of the barracks decided not to return the cheese, but instead to wait and see what happened to Sam, Buck, and Walt—if they survived, a cheese meal was promised for all.

The watch began, with the three also watching for the first signs that might give them a chance to reverse their intentions. When no symptoms developed within the next hour, everyone began to sense victory. Kriegies who had not yet eaten the cheese downed their quarter pound to quiet their hunger before the enlisted men could arrive with the major to confiscate it. Though the cheese was a taste disaster, no one got sick.

On the following day, when Walt was listening to the loudspeaker, he was approached by Oberleutnant Kruger.

"You understand German, correct?" Kruger asked in German, in a tone that was assertive, not questioning.

Walt answered in German, and Kruger continued, "Have you noticed the trains running on the tracks that pass the camp? Have you seen how the trains are moving to and from the front as much as before your air force tried to destroy this rail center?"

"Yes, I have," Walt returned in conciliatory tones. He had heard about this newcomer to Eiler's staff, and he had been advised not to converse with him.

"You have killed thousands of civilians here, but you have not won a victory over the German transportation system.

We were prepared for you. You saw that from our defense, but you did not see the thousands of workers we had waiting to undo your tactics. You Chicago gangsters are criminals but you are not capable of defeating the Deutsche Reich. Translate that for your comrades to memorize. Look at me when I talk to you. Tell me you understand me!"

"I understand Oberleutnant Kruger, and I will translate your message."

"Good. You know my name already, too. Very good. I will be paying attention to how you translate the news here."

FROM THE JOURNAL OF DEAN RAYMOND: February 27: I have not made a journal entry for ten eventful days. Nuremberg was bombed on February 20 and 21, but chance saved us—our camp was not hit. Our odds for escaping doom here have improved since the rail yard was knocked out. Smoke quit rising from burning Nuremberg only two days ago.

Berlin reports that other mainline rail yard cities were bombed—Krailsheim, Kitzingen, Ansbach, Neumarkt—and about a dozen more—yesterday Munich.

An offensive has opened on the Western Front. The Allies are sweeping into Germany with such success that we could get liberated before we get bombed again. As of today, our troops are one hundred fifty miles away and still coming.

The Western Front needs bomber support and a lot of other targets, mainly Oil, need bombing. Nevertheless, the Allies are continuing to bomb Berlin, which is now practically in Russian hands. Yesterday our Eighth Air Force went to Berlin with what the Germans report were three thousand tons of explosives and incendiaries—"dropped to kill women and children and burn the city to ashes," the German news reported. Then, the RAF bombed Berlin again last night. Why?

I am baffled. I'm not asking a moral question. I don't expect morality in war. Why not let the Russians get Berlin as a live city rather than a dead pile of rubble? The decision to bomb Dresden has become infamous but is only one instance of the carnage without purpose.

Months ago I got my mind free of High Command deci-sion-battles, but now that I'm under their bombs, I find myself again furious about the perverse mentality ruling target selection. Will we ever be free of the onward-with-yesterday-planners, the power-greedy-strategists, and the revenge-mad-drunks raping air force ability to win this war? Tomorrow the Swiss Red Cross Representative is due to visit here. I have my protest report ready. It is my only hope of getting improvement of our conditions.

ARRIVAL OF THE RED CROSS REPRESENTATIVE: At 1:00 P.M. of February 28 the gates of Langwasser, Camp 5, opened to allow the entrance of a sleek gray sedan. A young man stepped out who was wearing an immaculate tan camel-hair overcoat, a brown felt hat, and matching kidskin gloves.

Hauptmann Eiler and Colonel Raymond approached, and introductions were exchanged that established that this was the Red Cross Representative from Switzerland.

Shabbily clad, unwashed, skinny, hungry, and cold krie-gies stood by in shocking contrast to the impeccably dressed representative from the outside world. Raymond felt deeply grateful for this visit, yet he felt contempt for the dis-parity of circumstance between the visitor and the visited. He was ill at ease in his own shabby uniform that he had worn every day for the past eleven months until the seat of his trousers was now worn through. Words were inadequate to express his grievance. What could he say to a man who was only a few hours away from the normal world where no one knew life as it was suffered here?

Dean learned that four days ago an agreement had been reached to allow Red Cross supplies for prisoners of war to be trucked into Germany from Switzerland.

"Can you give me a date on which we can expect emer-gency supplies?" Dean asked. "Our situation is desperate."

"Colonel, prisoners of war are being marched back from the front all over Germany. Tens of thousands of POWs are on the road or in temporary encampments along with tens of thousands of refugees, all needing food. Need I say that your desperate situation is widespread? You are in a country increasingly destitute for food for its own people. The Red Cross is further burdened by lack of transportation, since the Allies have an air offensive to destroy Germany's transportation capability. Of course, I will try to help you."

Hauptmann Eiler carefully listened to the needs and supply conversation.

Raymond added, "I have a protest report for your urgent attention. Also, if the Hauptmann will allow us a minute away from our meeting, I would like you to make a quick observation of how I am personally quartered."

"Yes. That would be appropriate. Excuse us for a moment, Hauptmann." The representative spoke with authority that came from wanting an opportunity to speak to the Senior Officer prisoner privately.

When the two were out of earshot, Raymond said, "I fear the Nazis have sinister plans to kill us before we can be liberated. I have nothing specific to put on paper, but a few days ago, for example, we were given a cheese ration that contained poison. It turned out to be survivable poison from fire-fighting chemicals. But I remain suspicious."

"Colonel, you have cause to be suspicious. After the bombing of Dresden, Hitler issued an order to liquidate all American and English air force prisoners. You are in grave danger—Yes, Hauptmann, I suppose you are joining us to proceed with our tour of the camp?"

URGENT PROTEST TO THE
INTERNATIONAL RED CROSS:

1. I protest under provisions of the International Convention relative to treatment of prisoners of war published at Geneva, Switzerland, July 27, 1929, of which the United States and German Reich are signatory powers, Part III, Section V, Chapter I, Article 42.1.

Subject: Complaints of prisoners of war respecting the conditions of captivity. The senior American officer of Stalag Luft III, Nuremberg, Germany, presents in writing those basic requirements violated by the detaining power at this camp, citing the authority as contained in the Convention and by subject. Violations are as follows:*

A. Prisoner of War Camps (Part III, Section II, Article 9)

Proximity to Military Targets:

Stalag Luft III is within approximately three (3) kilometers of a major railroad choke point and marshaling yard. During the past two weeks, the local area has been bombed by heavy aerial main efforts with apparent attention to railroad targets. The dispersion of bombs both by day and night has been close to this Camp. There are no slit trenches or shelters which prisoners of war are permitted to use during air raids. Prisoners of war are kept in over-crowded huts at the point of guns. The location of this Camp and local air-raid precaution policy is unjust and untenable and a protest of strongest nature is hereby registered for present and future consideration.

B. Food and Clothing:

1. Inadequate Diet:

(Part III, Section II, Chapter II, Articles 11 & 12), The present German rations of prisoners of war according to medical opinion is less than that required for basic metabolism and will inevitably lead to loss of weight and starvation. Under the present unhygienic and unhealthy conditions, resistance of men will become so lowered as to render them highly susceptible to any disease.

2. German Issues:

Dehydrated vegetables are consistently wormy. No ersatz jam or honey is issued. As closely as can be figured, the present ration totals under 1218 calories per man, per day, which to sustain existence for a protracted period. It is impossible even with an inflated imagination to consider the present German issue as a depot troop ration.

3. Communal Issues:

Permission is requested to distribute food from kitchens during air raids in order that such preparations as are possible may be served warm.

4. Clothing Replacement and Repair Facilities:

There is no stock of clothing nor are there replacement or repair facilities provided as required of the detaining powers. The majority of the men from Sagan arrived here with only the clothing in which they stand. New purges from the Italian Theater are destitute. Clothing and shoes now being worn are rapidly wearing out. Boots, overcoats and trousers are suggested.

C. Installation of Camp: (Part III, Section II, Article 10)

1. Overcrowding of Barracks:

At the present time there is only nineteen (19) square feet of barracks floor space and 119 cubic feet of air space per man. In this minuscule area men must live, eat, and sleep. This is a serious condition of overcrowding which may lead to respiratory-borne epidemics such as Abelo-spinal meningitis, pneumonia, influenza, etc., aggravated by malnutrition, no heat, and filth as our present conditions apparently condoned by responsible authority.

2. Lack of Heat:

No coal is provided for the barracks. Shortage exists in Communal Kitchens. Present ration is used in the Hospital and seven Kitchens. Two Kitchens have been closed and still only 180 kilograms per day per kitchen are available. A minimum of 400 kilograms is required. This condition enhances the unhealthfulness of the barracks, dirtiness of food utensils and the containers and means cold or lukewarm food.

3. Shortage of Bedding:

Many men do not have the depot troop issue of blankets. Many have no bed of any kind and must sleep on cold, damp floors. At present there are over 1246 men sleeping on the floor in Camps 5, 6, and 7. Stuffing and pillowcases are vermin-ridden with no replacement nor opportunity to clean those in use. It is felt that no depot troops of the detaining power are subject to this treatment. . . .

Excerpt from official protest to the Red Cross from a U.S. Senior Officer, Langwasser Prison, February, 1945.

WITH BUCK, WALT, AND SAM: Thursday, March 1—Sam's first job of the morning was about to be performed. With Walt and Buck sharing his triumph, he blacked out the last day of his Black February calendar.

"Victory!"

"What are you going to live for now?" Buck asked.

"Springtime."

"For twenty-one more days it's officially winter," Walt pointed out. "I'm still living for ashes to rub the itch out of my flea bites."

"You and Job. You're reading too much Bible," Buck said.

"Job, I am. He had boils. I've got flea welts. And I'm asking God why."

"Are you really asking?" Buck questioned. "You must think you've got the answers in the Bible or you wouldn't be reading it so much. Have you been thinking about that verse, 'Why is light given to a man whose way is hid, and whom God hath hedged in?'"

Sam intervened, "I'm thinking we should all empty the shredded paper out of our mattresses. A lot of guys have been doing that to rob the fleas of a place to live."

Walt agreed and added, "We can burn the paper in the burner to warm up the "black death" soup the goons are giving us."

"Suits me, if it will end how I'm getting bit every night," Buck said.

"Three of my slats are slivered into bits for our kriegie burner, but I'll balance on the five left if it will stop me from getting bit from my toes to my eyeballs," Sam said.

"Let's sew our blankets into sleeping bags, too," Buck proposed. "Get us protection against any fleas still looking around for a victim. We can turn the bags inside out once in a while and hunt down any fleas that got inside. We'll get rid of those bastards yet. Right?"

"Let's get with it," Walt said.

That night the three went to bed with mattress covers empty of straw and with blankets sewn into sleeping bags. The blankets had been turned inside out and minutely searched under sunlight until it was certain they had been sanitized of all fleas.

Within a minute after Walt had gone to bed, he cried, "I just got bit!"

"Me too!" Buck howled. "Where shit falls, flowers will grow."

"Me too. I'm out of ideas. You'd better call on Saint Sara, Walt."

FROM THE JOURNAL OF DEAN RAYMOND: March 2: I delivered my protest on February 28 and learned of a Hitler order not here recordable. On the same day, Propaganda Minister Goebbels announced new food cuts: two pounds of bread less a week in adult rations and a drastic curtailment of fats, meats, and other rationed articles. We have had no Red Cross food since we arrived here. Even before Goebbels' message, our German rations were too meager to sustain life. To survive we need the Red Cross—I'll write more when I'm feeling better—

March 11: No Red Cross help has come. I have taken personal control of food rationing to be sure that each of us, from myself to the lowest in rank, is equally treated. Also, I continue to press Eiler for fumigation to rid us of vermin. Each day and night, always, I wait for the bombers, for the rail center is busy again. On the bright side, each day's news of the Western Front gives us new hope.

Great gains have been made. Our forces north of Coblenz have established a vital bridgehead east of the Rhine by winning the Ludendorff Bridge intact at Remagen. Where the front is only one hundred fifty miles away, there hasn't been much change. I sweat out each High Command bombing decision. When will our railroad yard be chosen again?

The offensive will include leveling of our rail yard. But, against the odds, our camp has been missed until now.

The news tells of more Oil targets being bombed—finally, bleeding Hitler's war machine dry. But these past days Berlin was again and again and again, the big target.

Because of its significance to us as air-war prisoners, I refer back to the March 4 bombing of Dresden. The German news referred to Dresden as the Reich's most ancient and cherished city. Why was this particular city so fanatically exterminated when it was about to be taken by the Russians? And now the Berlin bombing under similar conditions? I expect that the truth will forever be buried in phony cover-up. The news said that more that one million people were in Dresden at the time of the unrelenting, repeating Grossangriffs of both English and American heavy bombers. According to the report, some six-hundred-thousand bombed-out evacuees, refugees, and Allied and Russian prisoners of war were there. The report said the English and Americans are claiming Dresden was a communications center and a base for the defense of eastern Germany and they attacked only industrial and transportation targets there. The Dresden carnage may impact on us prisoners of war very directly . . . More later.

WITH WALT, SAM, AND BUCK: Sam came back from his trip for hot ersatz coffee with news that there was no hot water for coffee. Buck came back with three cups of cold, black-death soup. After the meal Buck said, "Jack Dawson, my Quaker friend, is working in Raymond's kitchen. I'm going to go check out why there's no hot water today."

"Check on the potato peelings, too," Sam said. "I'm watching for a fresh batch."

"I'll go with you to get the news," Walt said.

"When we get back, I'd like you and Sam to stand watch while I do my shelter work."

To get an air raid shelter for use against the RAF night bombers, Buck was digging a hole under the concrete where the potato peelings were dumped, an area that could not be seen from the guard towers. But walking guards could discover his activity, so he needed Walt and Sam to stand watch for him. He had hidden the entrance with loose bricks and a broken slab of concrete. He referred to the project as "my shelter" because Walt and Sam had decided not to risk getting shot going outside at night to reach it.

"Okay, I'm going to dig it small then, for me alone," Buck had told them. "I figure my chances are better against the bullets than against the bombs."

When Buck returned from his information-gathering, he went straight to the concrete slab. It was a clear-sky day with no breeze. The sun bore down strong, warming him as he waited for Sam and Walt, so he could continue his klim-can digging work. He was surprised when Sam approached running.

"What's the matter?"

"A kriegie just told me Walt passed out by the loud-speaker. He's on the ground and wants us to come get him."

They hurried to the loudspeaker. There they found Walt, sitting on the ground.

"What's wrong?" they asked in unison.

"I blacked out. I'll have to cut down on walking until we get more to eat."

"You're making too many trips to the loudspeaker. When the news is ready to get us out of here, we'll get it from the gunfire," Buck advised.

They helped Walt back to the barracks, and they all three took to their beds.

"I've got news from my friend Jack about today's lack of coffee, but keep it to yourselves. I don't want to get Jack in trouble for telling me. Get this, the staff officers used the hot water to take a bath."

Walt said, "I don't believe it. I used to fall all over myself to support Pa Raymond's orders. I'm learning he's no better than guys like you, Buck."

"So I'm as low as they come, and if Raymond was in on this, he's not God's chosen son like you expected him to be. I'll admit I might have a low-down lapse and keep the hot water for a hot bath—damn sinner that I am, if I had the chance. Like when you stole the Bible. The trouble is the Brass is a bunch of sinners like us, but people expect better of them. That's why they get away with so much. You've got to keep chewing their ass, and people like you won't do it. I will. Wait and see."

"You make noise, Buck, but I haven't seen any good come from your rebel ways."

"In Sagan? Run by court-martial lock-step? Times are

changing. More toward every man for himself. That's not all good, like with the hot water. Fighting back when you're shit on is the only answer. That's why I'm saying I'm going to see Raymond about this."

Sam said, "Not to change the subject, but I yelled across the fence to the Russian camp today. A Russian yelled back and waved. Since the krauts take the Russians out to work, they get more to eat than us. Maybe we could get them to throw us some food?"

"Sam, the dreamer. What happened to your land of birds and your princess Sandra?" Walt asked.

"These days have been sparking poetry for me. When I get to where I can look back, I may find the words to write about us guys and our life here."

"Write about the furnace ruins we saw coming in here," Buck suggested. "A guard told me it was once used to burn people. He laughed when he said it . . . like he was joking, but it was built to do something. There's a mystery for a poem for you, Hatch."

At 2:10 P.M. of March 14 a wave of shouting rolled across the camp.

"What's up?" Raymond asked a kriegie who was running toward the gate.

"Three white trucks with red crosses on them are waiting at the gate!"

Colonel Raymond joined the crowd that gathered to watch the trucks enter the camp.

"It's a glorious day," he said aloud to the sky.

FROM THE JOURNAL OF DEAN RAYMOND: In celebration of receiving food, I want to make a journal entry listing the contents of a Red Cross Food Parcel. There were enough Parcels to ration one for every three POWs. I learned from the Canadian drivers that kriegies are calling the trucks "white angels." Yes, the love words with which I once revered my nurse . . .

Spam (12-ounce can)
Corned beef (12-ounce can)
Salmon (7 3/4-ounce can)
Pâté (6-ounce can)
Milk (powdered, 1-pound can)
Margarine (1-pound can)
Jam (6-ounce can)
Sugar cubes (1/2-pound box)
Coffee (powdered, instant, 4-ounce can)
Wheat crackers (K-2 biscuits, 7-ounce box)
Raisins (15-ounce box)
Cheese (1/2-pound)
Cigarettes (5 packages, 20 cigarettes in each)
Chocolate (2 D-Bars)

WITH SAM, BUCK, AND WALT: On the night of March 16 the lights were still on and Sam, Buck, and Walt were taking advantage of the light to fix a pâté cracker snack before going to bed. Then the lights went out. "Field training on how to live blind," Buck complained.

A guard opened the barracks door and yelled: "Grossangriff!"

Quiet welled in the darkness. A distant siren was wailing the overhead alert. Then nearby sirens began the imminent attack warning.

A kriegie by an open window yelled, "Walt, come hear this. A loudspeaker is blaring something. What are they saying?"

A minute later Walt said, "They're calling out the position of the bombers as they come toward us from zone-to-zone, like they only do for the heavy bombers."

In a buzz of conversation, Buck told Sam and Walt, "I've heard enough. I'm heading for my shelter." With that he pushed his way through the dark interior to reach the open doorway. Once outside he ran blindly, falling into a bomb crater from a previous raid but regaining his direction and heading for his secret shelter.

Arriving safely, he pulled away the brick-and-concrete blind and squeezed himself into the hole that was large enough to fit comfortably below ground and under the armor of six-inches of concrete floor. He was still adjusting his body when he heard Walt, "Buck, can you fit me in?"

"Goddamn it! Get on top of me. You're lucky I dug it big enough to squeeze in two in case one of you changed your mind."

"I'm here, too," Sam said.

"I didn't build space for three! Get on top of Walt. We'll see how much we can squash down into here when the time comes. I'm going to be flatter than a penny on a train track."

"I can get low enough to get tucked under the concrete," Sam said. "When the bombs start coming, I'll push down harder."

"God," Buck complained. "Leave me a chance to breathe. Where flowers will grow! I knew the RAF would come sooner or later. Those sons-of-bitches come in from all directions all at once."

"Are you beginning to hear them?" Walt asked Sam whose ears were above ground.

"Let's not talk," Sam said. After a while he added, "Not yet. Wait. I hear something now—rumm—rumm—not like ours—like a Lancaster or a Halifax."

Walt said, "I hear they come in all at the same time to overload the air defense. Not in a sky train like us, for an hour or more. They're in and out quick."

"Keep talking. Maybe you'll convince yourself," Buck said.

Cannon fire drowned further conversation. The roar of approaching bombers welled an assault on ear drums. With the explosive suddenness of lightning, flares of various colors lit up the sky. Then the bomber noise unexpectedly faded away with the cannon still firing, but distant enough for talk.

Sam relayed, "They've got flares in the sky, high up, bright, blue-white, hundreds of them, like bunches of grapes, so many and so bright I could read a newspaper. Low to the ground they've got colored flares, blue and gold."

"'Markers Down,' they call those bottom ones. They're the secret colors to show the coming bombers where to bomb," Walt explained.

"You'd better be wrong. The krauts just shot up the same colors above our camp."

Anti-aircraft cannon again began pounding with an intensity that shook the ground alive with vibration.

Sam put his hands to the bottom of the concrete slab and yelled, "I'm pushing down. We're about to get—" A wall of flame erupted before him. He bent his head down and pushed his hands up against the concrete to squeeze himself under ground to beat the concussion on its way to him. With the sound blast, the ground jolted, shaking dirt into the hole. Bombs followed in such close succession that the ground convulsed relentlessly.

After the close misses, discordant impacts followed, in random bombing moving further into the city. For half an hour the bomb thunder continued ceaselessly. Then the intervals between bursts began to extend.

Buck said, "God, if it's over, lift out of the hole so I can breathe down here."

"They've got big fires burning all over the city, and flak, bursting cherries, all over, in the sky high above the flames. An orange streak's coming down—some poor crew got it. Searchlights reaching up. Holy hell! Wow! I'm squeezing down!"

A great ball of fire low on the horizon was welling toward Sam on a collision course, coming with whirring, whining, screaming attack of torturous roar. Sam, pushing down below ground, keeping his eyes facing forward, glimpsed, only a few feet above as it passed over, the ball of fire. Then crash! He pulled himself out of the hole and saw flames of wreckage rising from the forest just beyond the barbed wire wall.

Walt and Buck scrambled out. Buck said, "Let's get our asses back to the barracks if it's still standing. I don't want to get shot being out here."

At the barracks they found the door had been blown in, but the walls were still standing. They fumbled their way blindly to their bunks. Only delayed-action bomb-bursting in the city now broke the quiet. In mumbled exchange they agreed to tell no one about their shelter where they had spent the raid.

All through the night tongues of flame rose from the city on the east horizon. Near dawn the sky flared particularly bright, and a very loud and long rumbling explosion followed. Kriegies could only speculate what was happening, but they knew from what they could see and hear that more thousands of Germans were dying or dead tonight.

Next day smoke and fire kept rising across half the horizon. The city was still aflame in late afternoon when Walt responded to a note asking him to see Colonel Raymond.

"Plank, I remember how hard-working and trustworthy you were in your Intelligence duty at Sagan. I want you to head a news run for Camp 5. After last night's bombing and the city still burning, I have to be able to get news to all prisoners without delay. Also, I'm going to again provide BBC news, for POW ears only. You will carry the German news from barracks to barracks and with it the secret news and emergency news from me. For reasons you need not know, I believe your news run could save our lives."

"Yes, sir. But you need to know I'm not the worker for you I was at Sagan. The air raids have frazzled my nerves. I've got welts from flea bites all over me, like Job's boils. And I'm plain pooped from starving. I blacked out just walking across the camp four days ago. I'm not in shape for hard work."

"Plank, I could be saying what you're telling me. I've got every problem you've got, and my butt is still sore from getting bayoneted. I could check out sick and let the rank below me take over, but I'm still hanging in. I don't need to hear your problems. Just tell me if you will do this or not. I'm not ordering you. I'm asking you."

"Since you picked me and the job needs doing—"

"Good. Each day you'll have to get a piece of paper with the Allied news. At some point you'll say, *Sammy says*, and read the Allied news. If you get caught, eat the paper. Major Reddick will be in charge of the details."

"Wilco." Walt answered in his bombardier way of acknowledging his pilot's order.

When Walt crawled out of his bunk to begin his news-run on March 20, Sam requested, "Give us a preview like old times."

"This is old news, but new to us. The BBC says that a month ago the Germans had lost eighty percent of their oil supply. Along with railroad yards and trains, a top priority since then has been Oil. By now the Germans must be running out of oil."

"Where is the front?" Buck asked.

"About fifteen miles closer—about one hundred thirty-five miles away. We need a better map to locate the names I'm getting. Patton's Third Army has a thousand tanks tearing into Germany in what the Allies call a swift advance, but that's further north."

"We should put up a map board with all the names," Walt instructed.

"We'll make a map board when we do the fence project," Buck said.

The fence project Buck referred to was planned for the top of the hour to get needed fuel for klim can burners. All of the ceiling bracing they could risk removing had been secretly torn out. The sides of the washhouse had disappeared one day, vanished into tiny bits for burner use. The bed slats had been burned up until each bunk now only had five. A new source was to be the fence that stood as an L enclosing the entrance to the abort. This involved taking out three posts and burying them under the barracks and, while this was being done, breaking an eight-foot expanse of six-foot-long boards into match stick-size slivers that could be hidden within mattress covers. The project had to be completed in five minutes—the time it took for the guard to return on his beat past the building. The key to success was involvement of all kriegies of the barracks and superb coordination of effort.

When the execution signal was given, frantic work began. The boards were torn free and broken in half, then quarters, and so on, passing work out to more and more kriegies as the pieces became more numerous.

The success of the Barracks 92 mission of March 20 could be read from the quizzical look on the guard's face when he returned on his beat. He saw no barrier around the abort entrance. He stood for a minute in disbelief. He went to where the fence had been. He studied the ground where there was no trace of posts once being there. After a while, in seeming decision that his memory was wrong, he continued his surveillance walk.

WITH WALT ON HIS NEWS RUN: March 24: Beginning with the code for secret news, Walt read—"Sammy says: Our time has come. The American Third Army has opened a bridgehead on this side of the Rhine south of Mainz. That's the part of the front closest to us. They're about a hundred miles away. The Allies have got heavy censorship on, but they told the press the offensive starting on the Western Front has the biggest build-up since Normandy."

FROM THE JOURNAL OF DEAN RAYMOND: March 25: First, I want to enter that thirty-six thousand Red Cross Parcels arrived by train today from Switzerland, an unbelievable surprise. We will share these with other camps, but I have already started distributing a Parcel per POW. I am also going to release a Parcel for each of the two thousand Russians in the camp next to us. The food crisis is behind us, but the bombing crisis is still with us, ever more threatening.

Yesterday we got news of a massive offensive on the front closest to us. This great news is married to the certainty that the rail center serving this front will be destroyed. We have miraculously survived three massive raids of heavy bombers without casualties. I would quit the game if this were roulette, but this is no game. This is a battle plan in which bomber attacks always precede troop arrival. As of today, in defiance of Luftwaffe rules, I have ordered POWs of my camps to take to the trenches during night raids of heavy bombers. I've told Eiler I have done it. We will see what happens.

The heavies haven't returned for nine days now. After today's Red Cross Parcels we can at least say the condemned men ate a hearty meal.

I've been following the ground war, and I am witnessing the advantage of fighting an enemy who has no oil. After all the other jobs we flyers were forced to do, we were finally allowed to hit Oil. The consequence verifies what we promised long ago.

I specifically note that London has survived Hitler's stupid V-1 and V-2 campaigns that denied his fighting forces resources they need. However, the Allies sent thirteen hundred bombers to Berlin again on March 18, and the Germans are reporting many other city-wide raids. If I live to do it, I am going to document the chain of command behind pointless city-wide raids. Dresden is only the most infamous . . . more later.

WITH WALT ON HIS NEWS RUN: March 27: "Sammy says: Six Allied armies on the Western Front are engaged in the final phase of the war. Secrecy is shrouding the movements of the Third Army which may be headed for Würzburg and Nuremberg. The 4th Armored Division sped forward forty miles in eighteen hours and has captured an undamaged bridge across the Main River. The German radio has reported Patton's army near Fulda which is about ninety-five miles from here and approaching Würzburg which is sixty miles from here. The greatest concentration of armor in history is speeding toward Fulda."

WITH BUCK, WALT, AND SAM: The first day so warm that it promised summer was March 28. In the mid-afternoon Buck and Sam were lounging, propped against the south side of their barracks.

"I've got my pack ready," Buck said. "I don't think Hitler has in mind for us to get liberated."

"Who can say? If they do march us, it will be easier this time," Sam predicted. "We're tougher and the weather is warmer. Pretty soon the hills will be growing flowers. Getting out of here would be freedom all of its own—getting away from the bombs and bugs."

Buck said, "Thank God we got Parcels. We could start with Parcel food and Iron Rations to last a few days.

Getting thirty-six thousand Parcels, there was no reason for not giving us two Parcels apiece to help us catch up from starving. I'm pissed. It's too much like another Sagan—us being hungry when there is food to be eaten."

"The staff officers' garbage pit has got nice potato peelings again," Sam said.

"Their potato peelings can stay in their garbage," Buck declared. "One experience with poison cheese garbage-potato soufflé is enough to last me. I've still got to visit Raymond. I've got things on my mind that he's going to hear from me."

Walt walked up while Buck was talking and commented, "You've been saying you were going to visit Colonel Raymond for a long time. What's holding you back?"

"Maybe knowing you can't expect justice from a crocodile. I was taught that growing up. You can raise hell for justice or cave in like Job did. Read your Job story again— all the way to the end, sparing the cracker jack prizes. Some of us have to learn the hard way. I don't expect any change. I only want Raymond to know where I stand."

"Learn what the hard way?"

"Me talking couldn't get through to you, Walt. Keep scratching your flea bites—that's the way to learn."

Sam said, "Until I get rid of the fleas, I won't have mind for anything but scratching. What I'm asking, Walt, is how you let yourself get sucked in to doing so much work again. We're going to be picking you off of the ground for dead if you don't let up."

"I'm wondering how you've been lasting, Hatch," Walt came back. "At Sagan we had Joe, Briggs, and Cliff with us, and we had coffee-times, bashes, theater, a library—a good life next to how it is now. And still you were dreaming so much it got your mind loopy. You were writing poems and doing pictures for all of us then, too. Reading the Bible is helping me, but neither you or Buck have that. What keeps you going?"

"I'm going backwards since I beat Black February. I'm backing off from my dream to go to Godzone. I'm beginning to see that what's most important is never being cold or hungry again. I'm beginning to think I ought to enlist in the army if we get freed."

"You're the last person I'd believe would want a life in the army," Walt said.

"Yeah," Sam agreed, "but I've got a wife and family in my dreams. I want to be sure we're going to live without worries. In my Sagan dreams, I wasn't thinking enough."

Buck said, "Hatch is working on his future like a hydroelectric dam gathering water. Once he's freed he's going to start up the generator."

"I'm going inside to make Iron Rations," Walt said.

"We left your share of makings," Sam said. The "makings" of these compact bars of high energy food were sugar, crackers, raisins, chocolate, and margarine.

"How is the front doing?" Buck asked before Walt got away.

"There's a news black-out on Patton's tanks coming toward us. They're moving fast. I don't think the goons will march us though. They've got to know their war is lost."

"Then why make Iron Rations?" Sam asked.

"You know why. Because I'm guessing. Who knows what the fanatic Nazis are really going to do?"

"On edge here day and night waiting for bombers, I'm wanting to get marched out of here. The sooner the better," Buck said.

Sam broke the trend of conversation with, "I'm going to get down to the job of picking fleas out of my blankets."

"Me, too," Buck joined.

Sam and Buck turned their bed rolls inside out and laid them under the sunlight as Walt went inside.

"It's no wonder that people used to worship the sun," Buck said.

"Used to? I'm worshipping it right now."

They put their eyes close to their blankets and began to search for fleas.

FROM THE JOURNAL OF DEAN RAYMOND: March 30: Since my entry of March 25, bad weather grounded both the Eighth and the RAF on two days, perhaps lucky for us. The Eighth has bombed Brunswick, Hamburg, Plauen, Zeitz, Bremen, Wilhelmshaven, and Berlin. Zeitz, I recognize as an Oil target. The RAF has bombed Hanover, Osnabrueck, Muenster, and Berlin. Mosquitoes bombed Berlin for the thirty-fourth consecutive night on the March 25. The RAF has admitted the error of bombing the capital of Holland, The Hague, with apologies for the one thousand Hollanders killed and twenty thousand left homeless. After the Eighth's heavies pounded Berlin again on March 28, the Germans have ordered all "superfluous" residents to leave the city. Again today, an early German broadcast reported that a sixty-five-mile-long formation of four-engine bombers, extending back to Perleberg, was heading to Berlin.

WITH A RUSSIAN VISITOR: Shortly after dark of March 31, a raggedly-clad person entered Barracks 92 carrying a small burlap bag. The invader was a prisoner from the Russian Compound. In between sweeps of the searchlights he had wriggled his way through the barbed-wire barriers separating his camp from Camp 5. His purpose was to trade salt for cigarettes, coffee and chocolate. His plan was sound—Camp 5 had no salt. He quickly traded his salt and vanished into the darkness. After waiting and watching for some time without hearing a machine gun firing, the unanimous conclusion was that he had managed a safe return.

WITH WALT ON HIS NEWS RUN: Sunday, April 1: Walt read the news—"Sammy says: Happy Easter and good-bye fleas. A large quantity of American DDT insecticide powder has arrived by train from Switzerland. There are also khaki pants, barracks bags, razor blades, shaving soap, safety pins, and toothbrushes. We will ration these items today.

"Nine Allied armies are now on offensive behind three thousand tanks. Progress of the advance toward Nuremberg is under censorship.

"General Eisenhower has urged individual German soldiers to surrender. He declared that the German government had ceased 'to exercise effective control over wide areas.'"

"The BBC reports that there will be no postponement of the San Francisco Conference to organize a United Nations security force as agreed in Yalta.

"Approximately fifty seven hundred Allied planes closed the month of March with 165,000 tons of bombs dropped on railway yards, a synthetic oil factory, submarine pens, and other war installations of the Reich. Today Brandenburg, Halle, Brunswick, and Hamburg were bombed.

"Finally: Your Senior Officer informs that a food Parcel will be distributed to each POW today to keep our full ration schedule. We will issue more Parcels when the situation gets critical.

"That ends the news. Happy Easter from me, too."

WITH SAM, BUCK, AND WALT: "When the situation gets critical?" Buck sneered. "That did it. I'm going to go see the Head Honcho right now."

"Did you hear that? No more fleas. I can't believe it!" Sam exclaimed.

Buck agreed . . . "This is a great day."

Walt's news-run was followed by a meeting in each barracks led by a staff officer from Raymond's headquarters. The emergency organization set in place at Sagan was restructured, but this time to prepare for a march. The principal tactic this time, if ordered to march, would be to stall—to give advancing troops a chance to overtake the march. The Hitler order to kill all air force POWs was revealed. Under such a possibility, it was noted that good communications for immediate action would have to be maintained. How to act in a frontal area and how to help with special jobs such as airport construction for evacuation were also explained.

After the meeting Buck immediately went to Colonel Raymond's quarters. He had to wait in line, but when his turn came, Raymond greeted him courteously.

"I guess I picked a bad time, with people waiting to see you. I'll make it short."

"Relax, Pierce. We're not going anywhere. How have you been?"

"I don't need to tell you this place hasn't been a bed of roses. Can we move away a little so I can speak to you in private?"

"Of course. Over by the dead boiler. We're too short on fuel to fire all of them. How are your feet? Are you ready to walk if we need to?"

"My feet are as good as can be expected. I see you're using a cane these days. Are you up to walking?"

"Let's hope we don't need to. I shared some news with you before, for your ears only, relative to this place being our doom pit. If our luck holds out for another week, you can call me wrong on that. Now I've got other news, but there's a need-to-know factor, if you can respect that."

"Sounds like bad news, again. Why are you giving me this kind of special news privilege now, after wanting to court-martial me for not keeping secrets?"

"For need-to-know reasons, but maybe I enjoy you sharing the pressure I'm under."

"Whichever. I'm listening."

"It's this. If we head south, it may not be to another prison camp. The Germans are speeding work on a national Redoubt in the southern mountains. Our Intelligence has it that SS divisions and Nazi party officials plan to continue the war from there after the German field armies have surrendered. Eyewitness reports say that the Germans are pouring many hundreds of tons of supplies of all kinds into the Redoubt. It seems the SS is planning to march prisoners of war into this area to serve as hostages, human shields before their battle lines. Since Hitler's orders to kill us have not been carried out, there is a theory that this is why they are saving us."

"You figured I need to know that?"

"You're a commando. In a critical moment it might help you decide to lead an escape."

"I want to get my ass out of this camp before I worry about the next problem. What you said about getting bombed to shit here can still happen if we don't leave pronto."

"You think I don't know that? Is that what you came to tell me?"

"No. I came to talk about food. You can't hold back the food you've got for us, like you did at Sagan, sending us out to march half-starved. We've got to leave here in better shape. You've got the food we need, and we'd better get it this time. From what I heard this morning, you haven't learned from your mistakes. You say you're waiting for the situation to get critical? Come on. I know we're each getting a Parcel today, but it's been a week since we got a Parcel. Do you really know how little the Germans are giving us to eat? Maybe not, because I've seen nice potato peelings in your garbage. I've even eaten some of them. That ought to tell you something. Does it? Wise up. Each kriegie needs another Parcel, at least, that makes two, not one, just to catch up from starving and get our bodies ready for whatever's ahead for us."

"I've heard you, Pierce. I'll think about what you've said. I have to also think about how many kriegies would get sick from overeating if I suddenly doubled their rations. Is there anything else?"

"Yes. It's the news all around camp that your staff officers took a hot bath a while back with water that was supposed to be made into hot coffee for us. They say you took a bath yourself with it. In your place I might have done the same. Where you've got the power, I'm not going to fight you anymore when it's none of my business, but this water thing is my business. Still I'll let that pass 'cause we are none of us perfect. But you've got to give us two Parcels for each kriegie." With that Buck started to walk away.

"Who are you to load your concerns on me and then walk away?"

"I came to tell you, Colonel, because I figured you would hear me and not get mad after what we've been through. A lot of guys think these things but would never speak up to the man in charge."

"I've heard you, Pierce. Let's leave it there. I'll think about what you've said."

"I'll go. People are waiting."

In the afternoon during the day-long overhead alert of this day, nine P-47s came over camp at about seven thousand feet carrying bombs under their wings. The anti-aircraft fire did not open up. The planes flew overhead unmolested and went on to drop their bombs near enough to be heard when the bombs exploded.

By nightfall DDT flea killer had been generously sprinkled into every bunk and into all blankets. For the first time kriegies slept peacefully at Langwasser prison—-as peacefully as possible when waiting for a Grossangriff.

WITH WALT ON HIS NEWS RUN: April 2: "Sammy says: The Twelfth Armored Division of the United States Seventh Army on the southern flank is rolling across the Bavarian plains. Early today tank spearheads of this division were about forty-four miles from Nuremberg, the Nazi Mecca.

"The Germans have formed a guerrilla organization, the Werewolves, to wage suicide war on Allied soldiers and Germans who collaborate with Allied soldiers.

"U. S. bombers raided places in southeast Germany, especially Marburg on the Drava. "Finally: Your Senior Officer informs that there will be an issue of another food Parcel per POW today. Teams who helped with food distribution yesterday are asked to assist today to accomplish the issue of the second Parcel as soon as possible."

April 3: "Sammy says: *Special Notice*—The Germans have ordered the evacuation of this camp at 9:00 A.M. tomorrow, April 4. No German supply lines can be counted on for rations during the march. You are advised to use today to prepare your packs and your food supplies for departure in the morning."

WITH BUCK, WALT, AND SAM: "We sure are lucky to have received another food Parcel yesterday," Sam exclaimed.

"Is it luck?" Buck asked. "Who can say?"

"That's a strange answer. What did you talk about when you saw Pa Raymond?"

"Things not worth talking about, unless you have a need to know."

On the morning of April 4, Buck asked, "Are you happy with your packs?"

"Thanks to you helping us in reinforcing them, yes," Walt said.

"The supplies with the barracks bags came at a lucky time," Buck said. "It was easy with strong material to use. I could have used a pair of pants to replace my worn-out ones, but you can't have everything."

"We can thank God we got that second Parcel," Walt said. "With Iron Rations for six days and enough other food for four days, I'm content."

To the last minute, kriegies hoped that rescuing tanks would bring liberation. Getting everyone into the column to begin the march became a slow process. At the head of the column, Colonel Raymond asked Hauptmann Eiler, "What is the situation with your family?"

"They are safe. I have located them on a farm."

"Why are you moving us? You know the war is almost over."

"Herr Oberst, the generals do not confide in me. I only know we are to proceed south toward Munich."

The newly assigned Oberleutnant Kruger was with Eiler as his deputy. Smitty and Schumann had surfaced again among the guards at the side of the column. About noon the march got under way.

In Berlin grim officials were still issuing orders for their troops, but their authority was collapsing. Germany was becoming a land ruled at some times and places by Nazi orders and governmental laws and at other times and places by individual conscience.

The kriegies leaving the barbed wire of Nuremberg looked ahead to green hills and blue sky. Coming out of Langwasser Prison, entering the open landscape felt like stepping into freedom.

On the basis of data from the cross section survey, it has been estimated that the physical effects of strategic bombing were as follows:

TABLE 1. — Physical effects of bombing[1]

Killed 305,000

Wounded 780,000

Homes destroyed 1,865,000

Persons evacuated 4,885,000

Persons deprived of utilities 20,000,000

Chart III summarizes these results.

[1]All estimates include Russian-occupied Germany. The casualty estimates are based on interviews with civilians and do not include police officials, members of armed forces, displaced persons, people in concentration camps.

The United States Strategic Bombing Survey. The Effects of Strategic Bombing on German Morale, Vol. 1, Morale Division, May 1947, U.S. Government Printing Office, Washington, D.C., Page 7.

PART VI

Freedom

FREEDOM: CHAPTER ONE

When Colonel Raymond was a mile away from Langwasser prison camp, he told Walt, "I'm about to start a battle to control this march. I need you next to me to interpret."

Oberleutnant Kruger, walking ahead of Raymond with a contingent of guards, led the march south, bypassing Nuremburg, heading for a town called Feucht.

Kruger ordered a stop and came to Raymond. "You asked to talk to the officer in charge. For now that is me."

"You're only Eiler's deputy. I need to talk to the Hauptmann himself."

Luftwaffe Feldwebel (master sergeant) Bauer invaded the conversation. With his face close to Raymond's he barked, with Walt interpreting, "Quicken the pace! We have ten thousand prisoners following us, and the Waffen SS is retreating toward us. They have direct orders from Hitler to kill air force prisoners. Does that impress you?"

"Bauer, I'm the Senior Officer of the first fifteen hundred prisoners marching in this column. I am going to control the pace of this march by how fast I walk. We'll rebel en masse before we let this become another Sagan death march."

Kruger pulled himself erect, moved closer to Raymond, and said with authority, "Colonel, we have the guns, not you. I am in command, not you. When all our prisoners get on the road our column may be ten miles long, but at the rear we will still have our dogs to keep our prisoners walking lively."

"You don't speak of who is biting the asses of the SS. Our troops may beat the SS here. I tell you again. I need to speak to the Hauptmann."

"'The Hauptmann is still in camp in a command conference. He has a bicycle. He will be here. Enough talk. Now we march again."

As they started down the road, Buck edged close to Walt and asked, "What's the fuss?"

Walt told him, "Interpreters aren't newsmen. I can't tell you. You'll know soon."

"At least today is an easier start than at Sagan," Sam commented.

A half hour down the road, Buck nudged Sam to get his attention and said, "Notice how Kruger is slowing down when he sees he's getting ahead of Raymond. That's something new. His kraut temper must be building enough pressure to blow off his head."

Walt dropped back for a moment to visit. "Take a look at the carving on the Colonel's cane when you get a chance," he suggested to Buck and Sam. "A guard gave it to him."

"By privilege of rank?" Buck asked.

"No. For cigarettes. He's quit smoking."

"You should have a cane," Sam said to Walt.

"No. I'm walking on my two legs to strengthen them for my escape to Switzerland." The march moved through a countryside of dark soil being cultivated for Spring planting. The column stretched back as far as one could see. As some two-story stone houses were passed, children and old people hurried to the roadside to watch the flow of ragged, squalid, and bone-thin Kriegsgefangenen. The faces of the civilians were tense and hostile. Various voices shouted, "Murderers! Gangsters! Terrorfliegers! Schweinhunde!"

From the column came the answering calls now a ritual from previous marching . . . hubba hubba . . . hubba hubba.

Suddenly three fighters appeared ahead, flying barely thirty feet above the ground, racing down the road above the column, coming so fast it seemed certain they were about to machine gun the marchers. Guards, prisoners, and civilians bolted away from the road. For a wild few seconds, guards, prisoners, and civilians were tangled together, fleeing. With a roar the aircraft passed over, not firing. They were German FW 190s.

The mixture of friends and enemies untangled. Kriegies returned to the road, guards to their duty posts, and civilians to their roadside observer positions. The roles of war that had disintegrated momentarily under panic were quickly re-established: people again became guards, prisoners, civilians. More grossly: friends and enemies.

The march passed through Feucht where there were many gutted buildings and people watching and shouting while kriegies continued with hubba hubba. During a rest stop after Feucht, American fighters flew over low enough to be identified as P-47s. In a few seconds bomb-blasts reverberated. Raymond faced Reddick beside him.

"I know what you're thinking," Reddick said. "Those blasts came from the bridge we crossed about an hour ago and the column following us may have gotten hit."

Raymond nodded, "Let's hope not."

After ten more miles of walking, the Stalag Luft III contingent was separated from the march and assigned to barns, churches, and other buildings of a village. Raymond, with 150 other kriegies, got floor space in the huge attic of a hotel. He lay on his blankets next to a small window that had been opened for ventilation. From here he could listen for sounds of battle action of arriving SS or American forces.

From the road, three stories below, he heard the endless murmur of tramping kriegies as the column continued its forced march. Listening and thinking, he tried to guess what was going to happen as Hitler tried to force Germany to continue fighting beyond certain defeat. In the immediate days ahead he envisioned supply breakdown, chaos of conflicting authority, and danger of limitless brutality as government disintegrated to anarchy. He could not yet anticipate what to specifically expect as the march continued southward. *Are they marching us south to take us into the terminal Redoubt as hostages?*

"Colonel, I've come to escort you to Hauptmann Eiler," a guard broke into his thoughts.

He was led down to where Eiler was finishing his evening meal. Without rising as Raymond entered, Eiler asked, "Are you hungry, Colonel? I have more than I can eat."

"I have Red Cross food, thank you, but you must know we've had no rations today."

"The problem is transport. We have only the use of a truck that burns wood."

"A wood-burning truck?"

"Hitler's latest answer to our lack of gasoline. A furnace on the truck bed makes gas that is piped to the engine. With luck it will bring us bread tomorrow."

"It's more than food that I have to discuss," Raymond announced as he took a seat without being asked to sit down.

"Colonel, before you start, I want to tell you that your dive bombers killed two of your own countrymen today near Feucht and wounded several others. Too bad your country sacrifices its prisoners of war to bomb a bridge, isn't it? We are going to start marching you at night for your greater safety."

"We're getting mistaken for retreating Germans. I approve of the night marching."

Eiler refilled his wine glass and with smiling hospitality asked, "Wine?"

"Water for the one hundred and fifty prisoners locked in the attic will do."

"You need water?" The Hauptmann went to the door and ordered water to be taken up to the prisoners in the attic.

Raymond got up and poured a glass of water for himself. After a long drink, he said, "I have my own information to give you, but keep talking. You speak first."

"I will. I've just been briefed. We are marching you to a prison camp at Moosburg. That is about one hundred fifty kilometers south of here. We will march no more than seventeen kilometers a day, adjusted to stopping where there is shelter. We will have ten minutes of rest every hour. Once daily we will supply you bread and whatever other rations we have. Getting food to ten thousand prisoners moving down the road is a problem."

"What will happen if you don't get food to us? Will your guards stay if they aren't fed?"

"That is a Luftwaffe problem, not yours."

"Hold on. If your guards desert, we're no longer Luftwaffe prisoners. We're loose enemy airmen with a death sentence on us under Hitler's new orders. Sergeant Bauer says the Waffen SS is retreating toward us. If they overrun us and we're not Luftwaffe prisoners, they'll kill us. You say that's not my problem?"

"Your Luftwaffe guards will not desert. Remember that deserters are shot by the SS, too. Your guards need their duty guarding you as much as you need them."

"We are in a strange situation, needing each other, Hauptmann."

"It is good that you understand. You need to cooperate. Do have a glass of wine."

"Definitely, no, thank you."

"I expected I would have to educate you. I was told you were planning a mass escape."

"I have to educate you, Eiler. Kruger told me this morning that you've got dogs at the rear of the column to keep us marching lively. We won't submit to another Sagan march. We have a communication chain to reach all of the ten thousand of us within minutes."

"Don't believe Kruger. We will march by the Geneva rules as I just explained. We won't use the dogs. Why would you risk being killed in escape when you can simply wait to be liberated?"

"Your description of your plans does not match Kruger's. I expect that you're under orders you won't talk about, and I know about Hitler's terminal defense plan to get prisoners of war into his Redoubt. I goddamn will have to find out whether it's secret orders or our bizarre need behind your hospitality and promises tonight."

"Trust me."

"Your country is coming apart, Eiler. We can't trust any promises. Recognize we're near the day when you, not me, will be the prisoner."

"Be quiet! You are still a prisoner from the attic. You need to recognize that I am conferring with you as a privilege."

"Privilege? This meeting is a privilege for you. I'm here to get convinced that we have no need to revolt. We were leading the column today. With the column still marching, we'll be at the rear tomorrow. Are you going to have dogs to chew on our asses, Hauptmann Eiler?"

"Colonel, we will only have police dogs trailing to give an appearance of severity for spying Nazis. We will not use them. We will have other methods for dealing with stragglers."

"How will you deal with stragglers?"

"We will pick them up with horse-drawn wagons and move them back to the front of the column. Those who absolutely cannot walk any further will be given shelter."

"It sounds too perfect. You'd better be telling the truth. If you've got the dogs strictly to deceive the Nazis, that ploy is okay."

"I won't even speak of bayonets," Eiler added.

"If any ass gets a bayonet, that news will go through the column like a lightning strike."

"Colonel, you can trust me."

"Not yet. You're giving us the picture that your asses and our asses are frying in the same pan, but that could be a ruse to get us to cooperate with you marching us into the Redoubt. We've got grim implications brewing in this direction south. Tell me more."

"I am only a mere captain who is not told much. I have orders to march you to Moosburg. If I get orders to march you further we can plan together what we will do. I want to avoid the final battle unto death as much as you want to avoid being a human shield for it."

"We'll see. I'm ready to go back to the attic."

"Ask to see me any time you have a problem, Colonel Raymond."

"Likewise, Hauptmann Eiler."

Returned to his floor berth, Raymond again listened to the murmur of the march passing southward beneath his window. *I wonder what these thousands of tramping kriegies are thinking? They left home as heroes going out to fight for their country. Our secret news promises that they'll l be flown home within twenty-four hours after liberation. Return to home? How will these kriegies, toughened to live like wild animals, fit back into the caged life of their home towns?*

Tonight he was free of the doom-trap danger of RAF bombers, and tonight, thanks to insecticide, he could sleep without fleas biting him. *Tomorrow I'll be ready for new challenges.*

A few feet away, Walt, Sam, and Buck were absorbed in hushed conversation.

"I'm for staying with the march as long as it's headed toward Switzerland," Buck said.

Walt agreed.

Sam suggested, "We ought to ask John Howell along—he's got a compass."

"I'll talk to him about it," Buck said. "We still need a good map."

The column of fifteen hundred was re-formed at sunrise. The thousands who had passed during the night were out of sight. While waiting to march, Raymond told Buck, "I have to eat crow on Nuremberg being our doom-trap. Here we are, out of the place and still alive."

Buck grinned. "I'm not faulting your call. I'm glad we beat the odds."

"Why the guard dogs?" Sam asked, pointing to a dozen vicious dogs on leashes.

"It better be only for show," Raymond proclaimed.

Eiler and Kruger headed the march. Bauer, in charge of the guards, walked behind them with several guards ready for special assignment. One guard pushed a bicycle that was used for sorties up and down the line of march. Behind the Germans, Raymond marched with Walt beside him as interpreter and several of his staff including Reddick and Peyser.

The sky was clear and the air was cold. Colonel Raymond, walking with his cane, established a casual pace that the Germans, though in front, adjusted their walking to. No one kept step or tried to keep lines straight in what was mostly a three-abreast forced march.

Smoke rose from the chimneys of stone houses and a faint smell of wood smoke carried to the marchers. In the distance a church bell tolled, and from the hills to the west came the clanging of bells from cattle and goats. The road stretched ahead through flat fields and then to gentle rolling hills, green on this springtime morning.

Raymond reminded himself . . . *We have to stall as much as we can. The SS is behind us, but behind them is Patton's Third Army, or maybe Patch's Seventh Army.*

"Walt," Raymond said, "tell Eiler that when the sun gets high enough to warm us, we'll need an extra long rest. We have to have time to undo our packs and get something to eat, and we'll need water."

"Yes, sir," Walt answered, noting that he was now asked to be the spokesman to Germans who spoke English.

"The Hauptmann agrees with your request," Walt reported back a short time later.

When Eiler halted the column, Sam, Buck, and Walt rested where the road cut through a group of silver fir trees and shrubs of yellow broom, buck-thorn, and smoke-bush just beginning to leaf. As they relaxed, Buck risked taking out his knife. While Sam and Walt put together a breakfast of salmon, K-2 crackers, and jelly, he cut chips of wood from a dead branch for klim can use when water would be available to make hot coffee. Once a guard looked directly at Buck then turned away as if he had not seen the knife.

As he whittled, Buck said, "I talked to Howell. He's looking to team up with guys who each have something special to offer, like me with my knife and commando training."

To one side of the road kriegies arranged rocks into a giant POW sign as information for American fighters and dive bombers.

"Back on the road. We're pulling out," Walt relayed. To Raymond he said, "They told me we're going to rest in a forest this afternoon and start marching again tonight."

"That fits with Eiler's promise," Raymond told Walt.

The march continued at a slow pace. There were many new guards, older, some so much older that it was obvious Hitler was reaching deeper in drafting soldiers. But the trader Smitty and the singer Schumann were still among the guards flanking the column.

On this morning of April 5, villages passed through were all under Overhead Alert. At 10:30 A.M. fifteen miles from Nuremberg and five miles from Neumarkt, a woman waving her arms ran to the head of the column. Her behavior arrested the attention of all who saw her. She screamed, and her electric message, "Grossangriff!" swept through the column.

Bombers were still not in sight. The marching took a running pace to get to a grove of trees that was the only cover available. The road was still emptying when high, high above, tiny slivers of silver were discovered glistening in the sun. Formations were approaching from both the northwest and southeast.

Raymond weighed the significance of what he saw: *The sky-train in the northwest is the Eighth coming from England. The train from the southeast must be the Fifteenth coming from Italy. Nuremberg is going to get plastered today from both England and Italy . . . that would add up to over 2000 heavy bombers. The doom-trap is going to earn its name today. God help those who are still there.*

Contrails flowed rivers of cloud as the bombers advanced. Stratosphere winds dispersed the contrails into a cirrus veil of ice-dust across the blue. Kriegies stood under the trees at the edge of the forest and watched the ghastly spectacle of the air armada closing in on its prey.

Today the veterans of Langwasser prison camp grossan-griffs seemed to be outside of the doom-trap's danger zone. Yet, hearts were beating faster in expectation of the bombs that would soon begin the hell they knew.

When the first formations reached the city, sky-train contrails of bomber formations were still advancing in the distant stratosphere. The nearer high sky was filled with contrails streaming like a spider-web toward the chosen city center. The earth began to tremble. Bomb rumble shattered the country stillness with long rolls of thunder.

In a sky display that defied belief, the cirrus ice-dust veiling the blue sky pulsated in giant circular waves moving out from Nuremberg as circular shock waves move on water. For two hours repeated swells of earth-quake thunder and sky-veil pulsation generated across the fifteen-mile distance to the city. When it was over, kriegies looked at one another without words to express how they felt in escaping this raid by less than twenty-four hours.

"I'm going to bicycle back to Nuremberg to check on my family," Eiler told Raymond. "I have left orders to keep you off the road until dark. We will bring you water, but don't expect bread as I promised. After this bombing, we won't get food from there. Kruger will be in charge until I get back—"

"Instruct Kruger to honor my judgment in his decisions," Raymond interrupted.

"He has his instructions. I have arranged shelter for fifteen hundred prisoners in Berching. Rain is expected later tonight so you will march as soon as you are safe from air attack."

"I hope your family was spared, Hauptmann. Just one thing, call over Kruger and instruct him in my presence before you leave. He is unpredictable in his attitude toward us. We need to lock down what he is to do and how he is to work with me before you leave."

"You push me too far! The city is burning and my family is there! I am leaving!"

Toward evening, Buck fired the klim can burner with his wood chips and made hot stew for the three survivors of Combine 7.

Dean Raymond had no klim can burner and no empty klim can. Combine 7 had an empty klim can from their new Parcels. Walt gave this can to Raymond after punching a hole in it so the Colonel could tie it to his waist, kriegie fashion, for future use. Walt offered hot stew to Raymond. He accepted, and in return gave a chocolate D-bar that was shared by the combine. Afterwards each of the four had a hot cup of coffee from a new jar of Nescafe.

"To Phillips, Briggs, and Joe," Sam said as he raised his cup. "Coffee time is when I miss Phillips most. It was his reaching time. He said I was a reacher, too. He reached once too far when he gave up his chance to take shelter in a barn on the Sagan march. I hope we aren't pushed into that kind of reaching this time."

Oberleutnant Kruger approached Raymond and asked him to step aside, then told him, "After today's raid we will have no food for you. You prisoners with your Red Cross Parcels are eating better than the guards tonight, but things will change. When we get to the mountains, we will have access to the cache of food in place for Hitler's ultimate defense, but you will have no Red Cross Parcels."

"Kruger, how do you know where we are going and how we will be treated?"

"I know from my faith in our Führer. Now you are winning, but it is only a phase. Very soon our secret weapons will change this war in ways you can't imagine. We will reverse all your victories. Germany will never surrender. You will see."

"Beyond tomorrow is out of my range today. I've noticed we're getting more stragglers from the column ahead. Right here and now you've got the wagon filled and there are still more kriegies in no shape to keep up with us."

"I have everything under control. I am going to send the wagon ahead half way to Berching. There I will leave the stragglers and some guards to let them walk the rest of the way at a slower pace. I'll bring the wagon back for more stragglers."

Raymond said, "I assume that those who absolutely can't walk further will be held without bayonets or guard dogs to torture them."

"I find you arrogant, Colonel. I am in charge, not you. I do not need your approval of how I fulfill my duty!"

"We'll see about that as we go along. As of this time I won't give you my reaction to what you're saying. We will see what the next few days will tell." With that, Raymond turned his back on Kruger.

In the evening, kriegies built camp fires. After the months of winter in overcrowded barracks with no heat, being able to sit on the ground and take in the warmth of an open fire was a luxury to be savored. As darkness set in, Raymond had his staff officers circulate instructions to put out the fires to avoid attracting aircraft. At the same, his staff instructed that escape attempts were not encouraged as of today, but tomorrow could be different.

With the fires out, it was so dark that to escape one needed only to walk into the forest. When the order to get back on the road came at 9:00 P.M., there was no way of knowing if everyone returned to the march, for there was no count of the prisoners. Sam, Walt, and Buck were among those who started down the road again, since the march was taking them closer to Switzerland.

After an hour of walking, a cold drizzle began. Only the guards had raincoats. The water soaked through kriegie clothing clear to the skin and added weight to the makeshift packs burdening them.

Berching was still ten miles away. The route cut through a forest of tall trees. Between the overcast sky, the rain, and the tall trees, staying with the march became a challenge of seeing the road.

Sam said, "There is a poem about how little light it takes to see once the dark opens your eyes, but the dark's not opening my eyes tonight. If it weren't for last winter, I'd think this is as bad as things could get."

Around midnight it started to rain harder. The guards were getting wet now in spite of their rain coats. For the elderly recruits and other guards struggling to keep the pace, keeping prisoners from escaping became less important than finding shelter.

Prisoners began to vanish as underbrush was passed, a building was perceived, a large tree was seen . . . on and on. The urgency of escape on this night was focused on personally seeking the shelter the march was not affording.

Attempts to keep an orderly column were abandoned. At the head of the column, Kruger now walked beside Raymond who had Walt walking next to him.

About 1:00 A.M. the rain again eased to a drizzle. The line of travel was now through more open terrain where it was less dark.

Suddenly Raymond growled angrily, "How close are we to getting out of this, Kruger?"

"The Luftwaffe does not control the weather! We should be at Berching within the hour. Meanwhile, hold your temper, Colonel!"

"We should be at Berching? Don't you know? We've got to get out of this rain!"

"Hauptmann Eiler knows more about the plan. I expected him back by now. I'm going to commandeer a bicycle and ride ahead to find where we're supposed to find shelter."

Kruger left the sergeant, Feldwebel Bauer, in charge. The march continued for another two long, wet hours.

Then Kruger returned. "We are at the outskirts of Berching," he said. "We were supposed to have shelter here, but the thousands from Langwasser who got here before us have taken all the space. What extra space could be found was taken by British prisoners of war. The British have crammed into every possible other shelter."

Raymond was clammy cold and wet, and he was exhausted. He leaned on his cane and stared at Kruger. At a loss for words, he finally asked, "Where does that leave us?"

Gemeiner Schumann, the boxcar singer, moved close to the conversation. Not understanding the English being spoken, he turned to Walt to learn what the problem was. Meanwhile, Kruger responded to Raymond's question with, "I don't know what to do."

Schumann could not contain himself. He advanced squarely into the conversation. "Throw the British out! Throw them out!" he exploded.

"Get out of here, Gemeiner. This is a conference of command officers!" Oberleutnant Kruger barked at Schumann.

Schumann slunk away, and Raymond said, "As wet as we are, standing here is worse than walking. I suggest we keep walking and get into any buildings we come to, regardless."

At that point Eiler rode up. When he heard that Berching was already filled with prisoners, he said, "I was warned it might be this way. I arranged for shelter ten minutes beyond the town. Come, I will lead the way."

The march continued for another half hour with no sign of any buildings that could offer shelter.

Raymond abruptly stopped and said, "Goddamn it, Eiler, if this is command efficiency, Germany has reached bottom. We are chilled to the bone and ready to collapse. What you going to do about it?"

"I'll ride ahead," Eiler said. "Let the prisoners get under the trees to get what shelter they can until I get back."

Kruger offered to ride ahead and find shelter while Hauptmann Eiler waited with the column. Eiler responded in German.

Walt translated for Raymond, "He told him, no. This responsibility I will not delegate."

As Eiler started away, he called back in English, "I will quickly bring back good news."

After twenty minutes Raymond said to Kruger, "We're wasting time waiting here. Give me your Sergeant Bauer for some German authority and I'll walk ahead with my interpreter and scout for barns, any kind of buildings, myself."

"Feldwebel Bauer," Kruger called. Then he said to Raymond, "Go. Bauer will be your guard. You will not talk to civilians directly. Bauer will be the official authority. I am ordering him to be back within the hour."

Under these orders, Bauer, Raymond, and Walt started walking ahead, intently searching the darkness.

The immediate needs of the night had distanced discussion of the larger world. In all this time no one had asked Eiler what he had found in Nuremberg.

Raymond leaned on his cane and labored forward, searching the darkness, with Kruger and Walt beside him, searching. When they had walked about forty-five minutes, a horse-drawn wagon pulled up from a side road.

The driver stopped. After conversation in German, Walt interpreted, "The driver told Bauer the village where he lives has prisoners crowded into every possible place. We should try the next village, Plankstettin, three kilometers further on."

The Germans began to argue. Walt explained, "Bauer ordered the driver to take us to Plankstettin, but he won't do it. He says he is only a farmer trying to get to his work by the earliest light. Bauer ordered him again, saying fifteen hundred prisoners are soaking in the rain with no shelter, but the farmer argued we can easily walk."

The farmer whipped his reins across his horses and galloped away.

Breaking from his translation, Walt blurted, "How could he be so selfish?"

Raymond reacted, "We're seeing that Germans aren't taking orders from Hitler's military anymore. Too many leader's demands. His ears have simply gone deaf, Walter."

As they walked on, the rain stopped. Every trace of drizzle ended.

They had walked only a few minutes when they encountered Eiler.

Eiler, short of breath, spoke excitedly, "Herr Oberst, I have spoken to the Burgermeister of Plankstettin. I have organized six special rooms for the Colonel and his staff—"

"I don't give a damn about your special rooms! What have you organized for the fifteen hundred kriegies waiting for us to rescue them?"

"I have organized quarters in the hay barns of a big estate for eleven hundred troops."

"What about the others?"

"Colonel, from the report I got from Kruger, I believe that we do not have fifteen hundred prisoners in our column now. Space for eleven hundred should be sufficient."

"Point well taken, Hauptmann. Let's get back and start the march to Plankstettin."

"You don't need to double back, Colonel. I will ride back and start the march forward."

"Eiler, I'm going to walk back. I need to have your prisoners get their orders from me. If you ride ahead, get the news of shelter yelled out to draw in kriegies from the bushes."

Eiler began to ride back. Raymond, Walt, and Bauer began to walk back, back to the kriegies for whom Raymond assumed leadership tonight. *I could be out of my wet clothes and in a warm bed instead of staggering on this wet road, miserable and ready to drop. Am I reaching too far, like last winter? The offer of special rooms worries me. Is Eiler trying to buy me with a prize at the end of the day? I'm getting the Herr Oberst deference now—Sir Colonel—to set me up as the head leader, but in truth I may be the head follower. Am I his lead goat to get us into the Redoubt? Still, I need the leadership to save us from another march like last winter's. It's complicated. Tricky.*

To test the waters with Bauer, Raymond had Walt translate, "Bauer, as we get farther south, do you think the SS will take Luftwaffe soldiers like you with them into the Redoubt?"

Walt translated back, "Our Hauptmann has briefed us that our duty is guarding you, not fighting for the SS, but we aren't getting Luftwaffe food. We need food to stay with you."

My ace card is the Red Cross Parcels. If we are feeding the guards we'll be ahead in the power battle. White Angels, don't let us down. We need you more than ever now.

When they got back to Berching, Raymond told Reddick, "Pass the word that the Senior Officer promises shelter an hour ahead, and we're going to stay there at least two days."

Then Raymond asked Eiler, "How are you meeting your promises for the stragglers?"

"The wagon will come back as many times as needed to pick up all who can't walk."

"That satisfies me. Let's start walking."

When the march was under way, Eiler came to Raymond and said, "Walk with me to the side, Herr Oberst. I have terrible news to give you about Nuremberg."

The two commanders, officially enemies, moved far enough away from the column for their talk to be private. Eiler spoke with a broken voice, "Langwasser Prison is gone. Every building is destroyed. All the camps of the entire prison are leveled. Everyone who was there is dead."

"All the Americans who couldn't walk?"

"One hundred forty-seven."

"And the Russians?"

"The entire camp. Two thousand. And all Germans who were there, too. The slit trenches saved no one. Langwasser is a total field of rubble. The buildings, ground, and bodies are so plowed together that the incendiary bombs didn't more than scorch the rubble."

"How about your family, Eiler?"

"I will not discuss the situation of my family with you."

When his family was safe, he told me. Not talking is bad news. How bad? I dare not ask.

Raymond cleared his throat and said, "I confess that I was worried that you would not come back. I thought we were stuck with Kruger. It must have been tough to leave your family to return to military duty. I respect your discipline."

"To stay in Nuremberg would have been desertion. My choice was a bullet or this assignment. I didn't choose to be the commander holding prisoners that are murderers. I am only a patriotic German trapped into unchosen duty by war."

"My respect is only for your discipline."

"Knowing your bombing leadership, I have no respect for your discipline. Don't say you respect my discipline. Germany's collective discipline is your enemy. You and I are forced to duty with each other for a few more days. Don't pretend sentiment."

"As you say, Eiler. I regret that the war brings us to such indifference."

"Better that we keep our minds on getting to Plankstettin. As I told you, a private room with a bed is waiting for you."

Raymond chose not to answer.

Eiler went back to a cluster of Germans at the head of the column.

Should I take his room prize? Confirm the honor of my leadership? Leadership? No. I'm just a kriegie walking up front, maybe for better, maybe for worse. The puzzle's got me. Who is leading and who is following?

At dawn the column arrived at Plankstettin. In the dim light of morning an extensive six-foot wall enclosing several barns, barnyards, and houses showed on the right. Eiler led the way over a bridged moat entrance with a large gate opening to the walled estate.

As Raymond passed through the gate he told Reddick, "Get the word out that no one is to take a private room if it's offered. We will all sleep in the barns with the other kriegies."

Leading a stream of kriegies, Dean limped to a large barn. He found space on a dry earth floor and was soon asleep.

FREEDOM: CHAPTER TWO

APRIL 6, PLANKSTETTIN ESTATE: At four in the afternoon Raymond called a meeting of the four highest ranking POWs and told them, "I've got the sweats, my stomach's got butterflies, and I'm aching all over from coughing. I came in leaning heavy on my cane, and walking all night in the rain's made me worse. It's time I briefed you because you may be leading this march without me."

"I'm not able to march either," Lt. Colonel Hobson contended as the next in rank to be senior officer. "What I don't vomit runs straight through me. They brought me here in the stragglers' wagon."

"We have another day here, at least," Raymond informed. "If you can't march by then, Lt. Colonel Frye will be in charge."

"I've got blisters, but if we're going to get to rest here another night, maybe—"

"Did you come in on a wagon, Frye?" Raymond interrupted.

"No, sir. I managed to walk this far."

"You may have to walk farther then," Raymond said. "The Germans are going to sort out those who claim they can't walk. You're next in rank, Major Reddick, what about you?"

"I'm as fit as forty pounds underweight allows. You can count on me," Reddick replied.

Raymond coughed, took several deeps breaths, and shifted his roost in the hay of the loft meeting place before continuing, "Don't count me out yet. I want to inform all of you, regardless. I know soup is being served and we need to get in line so I'll get on with the briefing. We got news from our secret radio today, first time since we left Nuremberg, where, I can tell you now, our radio was in a hollowed-out bed post, being listened to every night. Today I learned more about the Redoubt. It begins only ten miles south of here, at Ingelstadt, where Eiler told me we're headed tomorrow night. Meanwhile we can't hope for rescue. Our troops still haven't reached Nuremberg. They're encountering heavy resistance."

Reddick asked, "When we get to the Redoubt, is the SS going to take command of us?"

"That's a riddle. Eiler swears his orders are to take us to a prison camp at Moosburg. That's thirty miles inside the Redoubt, but still thirty-eight miles north of the Inner Redoubt. Maybe the SS fanatics are only in charge in the Inner Redoubt."

"Inner Redoubt? What's this now?" Frye asked.

"Okay. The BBC reports that the Redoubt is 250 miles across and 150 miles deep. The Nazis are reported to be moving what forces they can gather into that area and stocking it for their final defense. But they've got an Inner Redoubt within that area for their ultimate defense. That's a stretched-out circle around Berchtesgaden—one hundred fifty miles wide and seventy-five miles deep. At Moosburg we would still be twenty-five miles north of the Inner Redoubt, seventy-five miles from its core, Hitler's Berchtesgaden retreat."

"If they're taking us there as hostages for the ultimate massacre, where are the first fortifications we dare not get sucked into?" Reddick interrupted.

"I don't know. That's why I'm bloody desperate to stay with the march. That's what one of you will have to decide if I'm not there."

"We've got nothing to decide," Frye said. "We've got no weapons for a stand off. The end of the war can't be more than a few weeks off. It would be wisest to do whatever we're ordered to do and just hope to be rescued."

"Frye, the German situation is changing so fast you can't know ahead of time what it would be wisest to do. I've decided for now we should keep letting them take us farther south, but as slow as we can move. If we get too difficult, our Luftwaffe guards will desert us and find other prisoners to guard. Keep in mind, if they get caught with prisoners refusing to march, the SS will shoot them and us both."

Hobson said, "They didn't get fed today. They won't stay. Eiler can't commandeer food when civilians don't have enough, either."

"I'm going to share our Parcels with them, if we're lucky enough to get a white angel visit," Raymond informed. "Our food may become our weapon to keep our Luftwaffe guards."

"Maybe the Plank family will feed them today. Herr Plank has 150 gallons of boiling soup in their pig-mash vat, measured out to give every kriegie a klim can full. The soup's got potatoes plus whatever else they feed their pigs. We've got to get in line or we'll miss out," Reddick emphasized.

"I'm going to end this. I need hot soup myself."

"Yeah. Maybe hot soup will stay with me," Hobson muttered.

Sam, Walt, and Buck were already in a line of several hundred kriegies. The survivors of Combine 7 had slept in the hayloft of the biggest barn and had awakened so hungry they had shared a full can of corned beef and the last of their K-2 crackers.

"We've still got our cigarettes to trade for food," Sam remarked as they waited in line. "We ate more of our Parcels in three days than we ever did in a week."

"Smitty told me—" Walt began.

"Smitty?" Buck interrupted. "I wonder if he's here. They're missing some guards."

"He's here, and he's offered to steal potatoes for us," Walt replied. "I took his wife's address with a promise to contact her, but I lost it. I haven't told him, so he's being real nice."

"If you promised, why don't you ask him for the address again?" Sam asked.

"When we're freed I don't plan to do favors for Germans."

Sam shook his head. "Then I'll ask him. He came through for us when we needed him, and we need his potatoes here now."

Walt smiled in assent. "When everyone's asleep we're supposed to sneak into the boiler shed where they're cooking the soup. He knows they'll have a coal fire stoked there all night. He'll bring us potatoes to roast in the hot coals."

"What's his angle?" Buck asked.

"He wants us to roast potatoes for him, too."

"Great idea all around," Sam said as he stepped ahead to close up the line.

"Hatch, don't forget to limp," Buck whispered.

Buck and Sam had decided to play lame in order to be left behind with those unfit to march on. With that in mind, Buck now said, "I'm feeling more pain with every step."

"You guys can't fake it," Walt insisted. "I heard only the guys they brought in on the wagons are going to get to stay. After all, everybody would like to stay. It's a great place to wait for our troops to catch us. I'm marching on, because Colonel Raymond needs me with him as interpreter, and I'm still planning the escape to Switzerland with John Howell."

"Without a map?" Buck asked.

"I've got a plan to get one," Walt answered. "Frau Plank has been real nice to me—maybe because we have the same last name. She let me come into their home and look at their atlas to see where we are. There's a map in there that shows all the way from here to Switzerland. I'll need your help to get it."

"If we help that gives us rights on the map, too," Buck contended.

"Yeah. But you and Hatch are staying here, you said."

"I mean, John should include us in the escape if we don't get to stay here," Buck said.

"He's already asked you to go along, Buck."

"What about Hatch?"

Walt replied, "It's a team project. Everybody has to have something special to offer. You've got the commando training and a knife. It's a two hundred-mile walk through enemy country with a lot of streams to cross. At the end there is the border to cross, maybe the toughest part. John hasn't said that Hatch has something to offer to help our chances."

Sam said, "I'm waiting here. It's a better bet to get freed here instead of getting killed."

"Our turn's coming for the soup," Walt mumbled excitedly.

When they had obtained their portions, they moved to the north wall to get away from the crowd.

"This is the best soup I ever ate," Walt said between swallows.

As he smacked his lips, Sam said, "There's got to be a place in heaven for people like the Planks. They're feeding over a thousand of us today, and, from how Smitty talks, they're going to have soup for us again tomorrow."

"I've been watching guys going around the back of the barn and wiping out their klim cans and getting into line again," Walt noted. "Everybody's been told the Planks only made enough for one klim can each. Somebody's going to miss out because of the guys cheating."

Buck commented, "Tomorrow the guys that missed out will probably be trying two trips to get even. I can see how this could snowball into a brawl if it kept up for a few days."

"Yeah. It's a lesson in why people need police," Walt observed. "A few greedy people take freedom away from all of us."

Sam suggested, "Let's head back to the barn and get some sleep if we're going to be up to roast potatoes tonight." The three went back to their berths in the hay.

Around midnight they stole their way to the boiler shed and squatted on the dirt floor by the long vat shaped like half of a barrel. When Smitty slipped through the doorway with twelve huge potatoes, their eyes were at the level of the fire alive with scarlet chunks of coal heating the soup for next day's serving.

Walt and Smitty conversed. Then Smitty left, and Walt translated, "He said three of the potatoes are for him. He'll be back."

They placed the potatoes between glowing embers and settled back on their haunches. For a long while they sat quietly with their eyes hypnotically fixed on the roasting potatoes.

Then Sam said, "A glowing fire sure can soak up your thoughts."

"What are you thinking about?" Buck asked.

"Me? About my mom. What she went through to support us. How getting liberated isn't going to be freedom if it takes me back to Chicago. After what we've been living through to keep alive, I'm feeling that my Godzone dream of making a living with a restaurant at Lonely Bay is too wild to risk. I've got to start thinking practical. I was dreaming of Sandra and our kids on the beach, without thinking practical."

"You've talked about staying a soldier. Maybe that's your answer," Walt said.

"Hatch, the last thing I can see you doing is being a soldier for the rest of your life," Buck said. "Phillips had it right when he said you're a reacher. You've got to get into something that needs your imagination. There'll be no use for bombardiers after the war. What the hell would you do in the army?"

Sam answered, "I don't know. It was easier when I was only dreaming. Now, getting hope of being freed, I'm asking what's really coming for me. I want the dreams of Godzone and Sandra. I'm going back to London for sure and try and find her."

"Are you still hearing the radio voices?" Walt asked.

"Not since Sagan. There must have been some peculiar radio waves coming in there."

Buck contributed, "My mind's been stuck back in England, running back and forth through time I've spent with women there, especially one of them."

"I'm thinking of my wife and our baby," Walt said. "Why did she move to Nebraska?"

Buck continued, "My nurse friend, Randi Scott, keeps filling my thoughts. I'm still trying to figure out her H.D. message. I'm not saying who used to call her his white angel. She's lived the hospital side of war, the human side, how it tears up people's minds and bodies. When I'm feeling low, thinking of her helps. She's a hero, Silver Star, for her nursing in the tunnels of Corregidor."

"I've got my plans for Catherine and me starting our mission with the Indians to fill my mind," Walt continued.

Sam asked, "What about Marg who gave you the Gypsy ring? Doesn't your mind go back to her sacrificing her heirloom ring to keep you safe in the war? That was powerful love. I'd think it would be hard to forget. There must be a part of you still in England."

Walt responded, "I lost my head, flying combat. I've erased Marg from my mind now. God works in strange ways. I paid for my sin by losing a finger, but through my weakness, I found Saint Sara. Now I want to save Indians like Saint Sara saved Gypsies."

"Sounds kind of mixed up to me," Buck remarked. "I've said before I don't think the Indians need you, but who knows? I'm not knocking your dream, if thinking so gives you a place to go. Hearing you two both nervous about being freed makes me realize it's scary. We've lived through a lot of shit, and I've said, 'Where shit falls flowers will grow.' Now we're looking for the flowers. I've been dreaming of having my own ranch, but, truth is, if I'd stayed home I'd be further along toward having it. Maybe the shit of war only grows dreams?"

The door cracked open and Smitty slipped in saying, "Potato ready? I speak English. After war I go America. Potato ready?"

"Sit down Smitty," Buck said. "We all want to go home. Yes?"

"Ich habe kein home. Alles kaput."

"Not alles. Your wife—she's safe. That's good. You start new after war," Sam said.

Smitty broke into German that only Walt could understand.

Walt translated, "These are good days for you, because you wait to get freed. I wait to be a prisoner, or worse, to fight unto death with the SS. The SS is going crazy. They killed seven of you who stopped during the march in the rain last night. I don't know what will happen to me. When you are freed, you must let my wife know about me."

Walt answered in English, "Ya. I will let her know."

"You give address me," Sam said. "I go see her."

Walt and Smitty conversed in German again. Then Walt translated, "He will write her name and address and give it to you, too, Sam, in case something happens to me."

"I'll stab you out a potato, Smitty," Buck said. "I like mine with the skin charred black. You maybe like yours paler."

Buck reached a potato over to Smitty. Smitty made a test thrust into it with his knife. "Is finished. I take."

"Wait," Sam said, "here are two more for you."

"Is hot. I put in pocket. I go."

Smitty left with the hot baked potatoes in his pockets, and Sam, Walt, and Buck again began to concentrate on their potatoes roasting in the scarlet coals.

"Nothing can match the beauty of a potato roasting in a bed of hot coals," Sam pondered. "Someday I'm going to write about this midnight supper."

Buck sliced open the white, moist meal within the black shell of a potato and said, "This is a bash like nothing I've had."

In the morning, April 7, Walt took Sam to the Plank home. At the kitchen door, he asked if his friend could see the map. Frau Plank, a thin woman with brown eyes and sallow complexion, rubbed her hands on her apron and gave them each a whole-wheat muffin. Walt asked for war news. She told him she did not know how close the Americans were, but the news said fifteen thousand wounded Germans had been captured in the hospitals of Goettingen, and the Americans had seized a gold cache in a salt mine worth more than a hundred million dollars.

Soon the three were in the parlor and were looking at the prize map that showed the terrain, roads, and streams from Nuremberg to Switzerland. After a brief look, Sam excused himself and left. Shortly afterwards, Buck rapped vigorously on the kitchen door.

Frau Plank rushed to answer the loud knock. Meanwhile, Walt tore the map out of the atlas containing it and returned the atlas to the book case. Then he hurried to the kitchen door where Buck was talking in English. "He wants to talk to your husband," he translated.

After more talk, Walt said to Buck, "She says her husband is conferring with the Luftwaffe officers. I told her I know where they are, and I will take you there, at once."

In German, Walt said, "I will come back. I want more of your family names to give to my father. Maybe we are related."

Once returned to the barn, Walt exclaimed, "I got the map! You both did your part great. Wait until I tell John. We're all set now. He's got the compass, and we've got iron rations for six days. If we stay with the column until we're one hundred and eighty miles from Switzerland, and if we walk thirty miles a day after we escape, we've got food enough to make it. We want you to come with us, Buck. You could be a big help if we get caught."

"If you're cutting out Sam, I'm staying here with him."

"Then give me my third of our food so I can make a combine with John Howell."

Buck said, "We'll divide what's left, as close as possible, but since you're going to break away from our combine, I can't see breaking open cans to give you a third of everything exactly."

"We've only got one can of jelly. Are you saying you're not going to give me my third?"

"That's what we're saying," Sam told Walt.

"Are you mad that John and I are going to escape?" Walt asked. "We need to form our own combine to plan our food. I want my third. That means my third of the jelly, too."

Buck snapped, "You're not going to get it."

The argument was interrupted by someone shouting, "A white angel's at the gate."

The Red Cross truck had come up from Switzerland with enough Parcels for a one-half Parcel per kriegie. Each Luftwaffe guard and officer, including Hauptmann Eiler, was also issued a one-half Parcel. The combine of Buck and Sam got one Parcel.

At noon Herr Plank again served one klim can of pig mash soup per kriegie. This time the German guards policed the line. In the afternoon, the Luftwaffe wagon for stragglers came to the gate carrying bread. Hauptmann Eiler did not say how he had obtained it. There was an issue of 1/7 of a loaf per kriegie—a slice 1 1/4 inches thick.

Toward evening Walt was called to a house where a young woman living on the first floor was shrieking while she held a prisoner at bay in her kitchen with an ax. After an exchange with Walt in German, she released the kriegie.

Walt explained to the crowd that had gathered, "Everything is settled. He was asking to sleep in her kitchen, and she thought he was talking French. According to her, the way he was saying 'Kueche' sounded like the word used in French for asking for sex."

"No loss, buddy," someone shouted from the crowd. "We won't be here for sex tonight.

I just got word we're marching at nine."

Colonel Raymond had not been seen during this entire second day at Plankstettin. Major Reddick had acted as his deputy in distributing the Red Cross Parcels and the bread ration. After getting the march orders, Reddick informed that one hundred fifty POWs would be allowed to remain and the sorting out of prisoners would be done by the Luftwaffe before marching time.

Over the previous two days, groups of kriegies had been passing down the road that ran along side the Plankstettin estate. The groups ranged from ten to several hundred flanked by as few as one or as many as twenty guards marching south in loose military formation.

At 8:00 P.M. Reddick called Hobson and Frye into a conference. "To bring you up to date, Colonel Raymond's still off his feet. Eiler told him he can stay here to recuperate. I think he should, but he's got a mind of his own. The Germans didn't approve either of you to stay here. So if Raymond stays, you'll be in charge, Hobson. Since you came in on the wagon, you can leave on it if you choose. Frye and you will have to work out who will march up front.

"We've been told we aren't marching to Ingolstadt tonight. We're marching to Neustadt, but that's on the Danube, too, opening to the Redoubt. Raymond says our tactic should be to stall. Try to make this a two-night march if possible."

Reddick paused.

"Anything new on what's going to happen when we get into the Redoubt?" Frye asked.

Reddick continued, "We got news about the Moosburg prison camp from the Canadian truck driver who brought the Red Cross Parcels. There are many thousands of kriegies there already. So, regardless of what the Nazis have in mind, we will have strength of numbers if we get there."

Hobson announced, "I can tell you now I'm going to have to ride in the wagon. So, Frye, you're in charge."

"That's no problem if my feet hold out," Frye said.

Reddick came back with, "I hope I've made clear that Raymond still hasn't conceded that he's going to relinquish command. As of now, he's trying his legs, as he puts it."

At this time, in a far corner of the hay loft of the largest barn, Buck and Sam were burying their packs and burrowing themselves into the hay to get totally out of sight.

"I'm glad we didn't ace out guys in bad shape and are trying hiding instead," Sam said.

"You saw how they were sorting out guys," Buck replied. "A kraut private decided that the two light colonels should march. That was his chance to put down high rank. If just one of the light colonels could have stood up, he would have put the other in a wheelbarrow and ordered the "stander" to push him."

"Let's stay quiet until everyone's gone," Sam proposed.

Buck answered, "If you hear me, it will be because a guard stuck me with a pitch fork."

The column formed up on schedule with Walt at the front as interpreter, but without Colonel Raymond. Frye, with Reddick beside him, headed the prisoners, and Hauptmann Eiler and Oberleutnant Kruger, plus four guards, headed the column. Other guards were waiting, ready to flank the column as it got under way. There were no guards with leashed police dogs.

The march was about to get under way when Colonel Raymond came up leaning on his cane, but with his head erect, and with his countenance announcing authority. "I'll be up front with Hauptmann Eiler, so, Frye, if your feet are hurting, you can join Hobson in the wagon. Reddick, I'm having you stay to command this stragglers' station. Walter, I want you to stay to interpret for Reddick. He needs a good interpreter. I've got a backup to translate for me. You've hung in with me on your own limping leg not complaining and coming through against odds, so wish me your luck. You're a good soldier. Excuse me. I need to start badgering Eiler to make this a short march tonight."

In the hay loft, Buck and Sam remained in hiding. When they got up in the morning, April 8, they made sure they were limping badly enough to fit in with the invalid stragglers. As they entered the barnyard, Sam nudged Buck and exclaimed, "My eyes must be tricking me—there's Walt and John!"

"Hey, what happened?" Buck called.

"Pa Raymond left Reddick behind and ordered me to stay to interpret for him. What about you guys?"

Sam said, "We didn't ace anybody out. We hid."

"What about you, John?" Buck asked. "I was picturing your eyes on your compass pointing for Switzerland like a bloodhound. Now you're holed up with the cripples."

"If it's any of your business, smart ass, I didn't ace anyone out. I marched for a couple of miles, then after I learned Walt stayed here, I slipped out in a dark stretch and came back."

Sam taunted, "I'm beginning to wonder if your fancy escape is just a lot of hot air."

"Wait until we've crossed the Danube, Sammy boy. You'll find out. That's the big river we've got to get past before we start hiking."

"Hatch, we don't need to waste our time listening to this," Buck said.

"You've still got a can of jelly that's a third mine," Walt reminded as they parted.

In the evening, Walt, Sam, and Buck conversed, but the subject of the jelly was avoided. The talk centered on the idea of trading in Schweigersdorf, a village to the east, above the valley. Since only two guards had been left to keep watch over the stragglers, Buck and Sam thought it would be easy to get away, do some good trading, and get back without trouble. Walt agreed, and an early morning time was struck to sneak over the wall.

Thus, on Monday morning, April 9, after a successful escape, Buck, Sam, Walt, and John Howell were hiking up a gentle slope that led to a forested plateau. John was along by invitation of Walt.

The strong sun rays cutting through the still morning gave promise that this would be the fairest day yet of Spring. They were walking free on a Bavarian hillside, free of the crowd of kriegies they had too long endured, free of the guards that had too long policed them.

They had left their packs buried in the hay. They planned to sneak back to their belongings in the coming night. Now as they walked the slope out of the valley, they carried only their own weight and their supply of cigarettes, coffee, chocolate, and soap for trading.

Buck said, "I know Walt's got cigarettes from the one half Parcel we each got yesterday, but since you smoke up your cigarettes, John, what are you furnishing for your share of trading?"

"That's between us not you," Walt answered before John could speak. "Since we're going to escape together, I'm using my cigarettes in trading for both of us."

John added, "He's saying keep your nose out of our business."

"Good. You've made it clear that what Sam and I trade belongs to us alone," Buck said.

They had reached a plateau where the road wound between pine trees. The area was rich with bird song. There were melodic progressions, bubbly notes, penetrating whistles, and fine trills of forest bird music.

Sam said, "I feel dumb. I read a lot about birds in Sagan, but the books don't help me know who's singing what."

"I'm hearing sparrows, larks, and warblers, and maybe finches," Buck said. Then he stopped and pointed to the side of the road. "Look, there are the first dandelions I've seen this spring. Reminds me of the day I was shot down, laid out flat, feeling like I was dying. Clair brought me a dandelion. That flower was a piece of sunshine to my spirits."

Buck went to the side of the road and picked one of the new blossoms. "Look at it, Hatch. How would you describe it?"

"I like your idea of sunshine. It's a bundle of sun fire."

Further up the road, where the sun reached down to a moist mat of dead leaves, Sam called attention to different looking yellow flowers. Nobody knew what they were.

"When I get liberated," Sam said, "I'm going to learn the names of flowers. Dreaming about things, I've gotten different ideas about what's important to know about, and flowers are one." Now he saw big groups of purple-red blossoms and with them vari-colored flowers lifting from the mat of dead leaves.

Buck said, "Those woolly leaves with the bell-like, red-brown flowers look like wild ginger to me."

After more lazy walking soaking up the morning's richness, they rested with their backs against tree trunks and the sun shining on their faces.

"I'm thinking back to our midnight potato supper. I'll never forget it," Walt said.

"Thanks to Smitty," Sam reminded. "He's gone on now, but I got his wife's address."

Rising from their sun basking, they walked to Schweigersdorf. The homes were two-story, stone structures. At the first home they were met by the snarls and vicious barking of a guard dog chained by the entrance. A swarthy middle-aged woman opened the door . . . then she drew back in shock at the sight of the bedraggled strangers before her—yet she quieted the dog.

As Walt talked to her she became excited. She went back into the house and came back with a half loaf of bread and some lard wrapped in newspaper.

When the trading was done, Walt retreated with her still talking. After she had closed the door and they were on their way to another home, Walt explained. "She said that everyone here is expecting American soldiers, but she was not expecting American prisoners of war. She was most excited about getting chocolate for her children."

At each home they visited, the villagers were friendly, and they were eager to trade. Where men came to the door the American cigarettes were the most prized trade item. As they left the village Walt said that everyone was anxious for the American army to arrive before the Russians.

They had acquired eggs, onions, lard, and bread, which for lack of back packs, they had tucked under their shirts. This gave them bulging bellies, as if their stomachs were bloated.

Sam said, "It's too soon to be going back to Plankstettin. Look at that other road going through the forest. Let's go back that way."

John objected, "For Christ's sake, we've got a good road back, why wander through the forest? You know the danger of being caught out here by the SS."

"Look who's talking," Buck commented. "I thought you were the escape hero, John, who is going to walk all the way to Switzerland, in spite of SS danger."

John, ignoring Buck, said, "Come on, Walt. If they've got a better road, let 'em take it."

Buck and Sam started into the forest in a direction that seemed to lead to the valley. Eventually they came to a fork and took the left road. After some time this road became an overgrown trail. They thought that by now they should be in the valley, near the road from Nuremberg to Plankstettin, but they were still on the plateau and in deep forest.

"I think I just saw someone," Sam remarked as he studied the forest beyond the moss-covered ruins of a washed-out bridge. They crossed the brook coursing over rocks where the bridge had once stood.

"I don't like this," Buck said. "I just got a glimpse of someone. We'd better turn back."

Starting back, they observed that to one side of the washed out bridge, about a hundred yards into the forest, were several wagons and some horses.

"It looks like we stumbled onto a camp of refugees," Sam said.

Suddenly they were surrounded by five people with clothing as ragged as theirs. Among them was a girl with a garland of dandelions in long black hair. Sam and Buck smiled but got only fierce, on-guard confrontation from the faces before them.

"Duntsi!" one of the men called.

An old man joined the circle that had formed around Sam and Buck. His face was angular and leathery-brown. His intense gaze registered mischief. "Are you from war prisoners marching south?" he asked in English with a British accent.

"Yes. We're American prisoners of war. American troops are right behind us. How is it that you speak such good English? Who are you?" Buck asked.

"I Duntsi Laubinger. This is Balo, Kalomar, Dadilla, Bana, and Gali. We refugees on way south France. We keep low here for little time. Wait for American army. I travel many countries. England nineteen hundred six first time. I learn language English."

"We saw refugee wagons like yours coming from the East when we were marching near the Russian Front northeast of here. Did you come from there?" Sam asked.

"I think no. We refugees from East, but we more south. Winter no time be north."

"We've learned that the hard way," Buck said.

"How long have you been on the road?" Sam asked.

"Long time," Duntsi said. "Much danger. Much bombs. Boom. Boom. Much trouble. Not much eat. We make trade. Trade horses. Germany not much horses now. Thanks to God, we still got horses, pull caravans."

"You speak good English," Sam complimented.

"Little English last years. I only bloke be talker when American army comes."

"We lost our way. Which way is Plankstettin?" Buck asked.

Duntsi pointed back in the direction they had come from.

"Thanks," Buck said. "We'll start back. We went the wrong way from Schweigersdorf."

"What you got under shirts? You like woman hold big child."

"We traded for food. We're on our way back to Plankstettin with our food," Sam said.

"You not now leave. You stay. Eat. Women cook meat. We make feast together. You bed down here. It good for us you here when American army comes."

Buck, ill at ease, turned to leave, saying, "The Luftwaffe only let us out to get food. We have to get back very soon."

"You stay, eat. We Ungri like Americans. I go you back Schweigersdorf when you want go. I give word."

Buck argued, "It is safe for you to wander free because you are refugees. But under Hitler's new laws, if we get caught free we get shot."

Sam's gaze had fixed upon Gali. Her fiery eyes met his in what he read as flirtation. Her bronze skin and high cheek bones reminded him of Sandra. The gold garland of dandelions in her midnight black hair crowned her beauty.

Duntsi said, "Hitler soldiers not come this place. They move south on fast road. Get behind Danube fast. We hitch horses, go south after they go. You safe here."

Buck mumbled softly for Sam's ears only, "Do you think they're planning to steal our food? It's been a long time since I had fresh meat. What do you think, Hatch?"

Sam's focus was on the messages coming from Gali's eyes. He answered aloud for Duntsi to hear, "It suits me to stay."

Duntsi led the way to the camp. "These bad times for Ungri people. Hitler's people kill many thousands. We alive and free through smart and blessing of Saint Sara. We celebrate come American soldiers. Eat. Music. Dance by fire."

Sam and Buck's eyes met in private reaction to the mention of Saint Sara.

At camp center, where iron pots and pans hung beside a blazing fire, Duntsi said, "We Ungri poor, but we feast. Ungri platter is big black diamond sky. Tonight full moon sky."

Beyond the camp the brook slithered across a sandy expanse and twisted on, vanishing into a grove of wild crabapple trees and hornbeam. Further along, the stream came into view again and ran through an open meadow before vanishing into gentle, forested hills. Beyond and above the forest a cumulo-nimbus thunderhead churned. From the dark upper regions of rolling, threatening clouds, a great gray smear of rain-flow swept down through the heavens until it tied to earth.

"I hope your rig rain proof," Buck said, unconsciously influenced by Duntsi's English.

Duntsi looked skyward and said with amusement, "We build so hot fire it put out rain."

Sam moved closer to Gali and felt Sandra's presence even though Gali's eyes were more brown and more intense, her forehead had more slope, and her nose was more angular than Sandra's. For him, Gali emanated Sandra's hypnotic aura. From the sun-fire flowers in her hair, his eyes moved up to the approaching storm. "I had a dream once in which life was a storm, and we were standing like this, watching," he told Gali, even though he knew she could not understand him. "I wrote about it, wishing for a time like right now."

She answered in a language he could not understand.

Duntsi remarked, "I tell her what you say," and he translated.

Buck spoke to Sam in almost a whisper, "Ask her if she's got a sister."

Duntsi reacted so quickly with hostile intonation it was obvious he had heard—"Gali only free woman in Kumpania."

Gali's eyes took on a sparkle of merriment. She took Sam's hand and pulled him with her as she ran toward the brook. At the water's edge she stopped, and, with a laugh, skipped ahead along a path that led downstream.

Sam guessed that she might be his age, but she moved with the carefree grace of a girl of twelve. He followed her, half-running. It was as if she were enticing him to into a childhood game like hide-and-go-seek.

As she arrived at the crabapple grove, a red bird winged upward and settled in the branches before her. She stopped and pointed to the bird. Then, moving on, she bent back branches for Sam to follow her more easily. As Sam came along side her, she moved a hand across a bed of leaves.

"Gali!" Duntsi's voice sounded from the campsite. She turned away and started back toward the camp. For a while she ran, then she stopped and started picking blue hyacinth and wild foxglove.

The thunderclouds moved across the sun, dulling the sky and land, transforming the flowers to richer radiance. Thunder broke the quiet. In the stillness that followed, a lark sang. From the camp, Duntsi called again, louder, "Gali!"

It started to rain big drops. Gali brushed the water from her forehead and looked up to the storm. Suddenly the rain came down in torrents.

"We're going to get drenched, Gali, if we don't take cover!"

Gali started laughing, and she started running back to the camp. Sam chased behind her, laughing with her. *We who watch from under canvas, can your sun-fun understand us?*

Then they were back in camp—soaked. Gali made for a nearby caravan. Duntsi called Sam into the cover of his caravan. As Sam entered he saw paintings of black birds, emblems, and flowers on the scuffed and worn wood of the dilapidated wagon.

Duntsi said, "Take off wet clothes. Wrap in eiderdown."

Sam stripped off his clothing and wrapped himself into the blanket. They sat huddled together under the canvas while the rain poured down. Through the open door they watched the storm cross the valley, cross the hills, and move across the horizon.

A blood-red sun slid through slivers of black storm remnant and coursed down beyond the distant hills. The scarlet of the sun was still glowing as the women put more wood on the fire and fanned the embers they had protected from the rain. In a short time the fire began to flame again. The wood smoke, after the rain, coming from the fire where the meal was being prepared, was a perfume that charged the air with expectation.

Wrapped in Duntsi's eiderdown, Sam went out to the fire and hung his wet clothing near the flames, next to where Gali had hung her wet clothing. Gali appeared in an amber calico dress that hung loosely on her shoulders and was held close to her body by a belt around her waist. She had replaced the sun-fire in her hair with blue hyacinth. He could not tell whether it was her change of flowers and dress, the evening, the fire, or a change of mood that made her different. Her merriment was replaced by an air of mystery, devilment.

Buck regarded Gali close to the fire, married to the undulating spirals of the flame.

He mumbled to Sam, "I'd forgot what it's like to be horny. She gets to me. I wish I would have had your chance with her alone in the woods."

"We had a good time in the woods," Sam smiled.

"She sure came back in high spirits," Buck reported.

"She's a free spirit. I want to be like her," Sam said.

Duntsi approached from his wagon. "Come, we leave cooking to women. My nephews want hear about America."

They left the fire to join Balo and Kalomar who had seated themselves in Duntsi's wagon. They began to converse with Duntsi translating.

"What will you do when the war is over?" Buck asked.

Duntsi shrugged his shoulders. "Travel good places, good people."

"Is that all?" Sam asked.

"I catch up with familia. Is enough. Horses pull load, cows give milk 'til they killed. We no farm animals. We Ungri. Live by spirit raven, not Nazi eagle. What we own we burn when we die. Is our way, not be greedy. Make good time. Not work get rich."

"Great attitude, Duntsi. If you've got the guts for it, to live that risky," Sam said. "After prisoner, I want a home with hot bath, clean clothes, and lots to eat always near."

"American, you live like us your body get tough. Hardship no damp fire in soul."

"Where is your home in peacetime?" Buck asked.

"You ask question I no answer. Eagle eyes hunt wanderers. We refugees. We travel, get away war. Ask no. Home where we alive. Peace familia gather south France."

Sam said, "I used to dream of living in a wonderful land with only birds, Now, if I'm freed, I'm afraid to go there. Too risky."

Duntsi translated to his nephews. They talked, then Duntsi said to Sam and Buck, "We say is God's will you be lost, come see us. Is meant be. Tonight Saint Sara bless us."

"Hatch is still a dreamer," Buck contended. "We call him our bird man. He says that birds don't gang up against each other like people and that's how he likes it."

445

"That's right. Growing up in Chicago, my father wanted me Catholic, my mother wanted me Jewish, the street kids beat me for not being Polish. It was war. I hated it."

"We know this people way," Duntsi said. "Hitler take away Poles, Russians, Jews, Gypsies, Ukrainians. We wait many year, save us. Now you come. Bloody miracle."

As a tantalizing aroma swept into the wagon, Duntsi abruptly shifted his conversation. "My nose tell me time we go fire."

All went out to where savory vapors rose from a black kettle surrounded by flames. Meat stew was ladled from the kettle into individual bowls and all began to eat. The stew had a wild, racy flavor.

"You eat hedgehog," Duntsi said. "Is wrapped in clay and bake in fire so we peel off prickly skin. Then we cook."

When the meal was finished, Kalomar brought out a violin. He began a haunting song in a minor key. The women clapped on slabs of wood and Gali created a tambourine accompaniment that crackled and rippled like wind rattling leaves.

Buck raised a hand and called, "Listen. We've got a big fire to see from the sky. I think I hear a bomber."

Duntsi motioned for silence. Only the crackling of the fire sounded in the stillness of the forest night. Sam looked up and saw the full moon as a lamplight in the endless expanse of star-studded oblivion.

"The sky is quiet to me," Sam said. His words sounded hollow to him, as if, in the reality of this moment, talk was out place.

"Stoke up fire," Duntsi said.

"Hey, Buck, dig out what we've got left of our coffee," Sam added awkwardly.

"You put the words in my mouth," Buck joined as he drew out a jar of Nescafe.

"Coffee? Many years only ersatz coffee roast from barley and rye. Dadilla, poke fire. How you make coffee from powder? Put in bloody pot and boil!"

"No. You will see," Sam said. "Heat water. I'll do rest."

Water was poured into a black pot and hung into the center

of the blaze. Everyone, watching the water heating, sat quiet, as if mesmerized by the flame radiance. For Sam the scene was once again a dream he had lived. The fire in the dark forest was an echo of the full moon above in the black sky.

Duntsi broke the spell with, "Come Gali! Dance for us. Tonight we one people. We be music—dance—real coffee!"

The violin began a plaintive strain. Gali danced toward the fire, then stopped. For a moment she stood motionless, but for her head lifting upward. Then a tremor ran through her body. She began to shift her feet in intricate patterns that with deliberate direction took her ever closer to the flame. She slowly reached her arms upward with undulating rhythm, as if her arms were weaving magic. Moving in rhythm with the music, she then reached forward and downward until her hands clasped flaming torches and drew them from the fire.

She twisted her hips and wheeled around with a burning torch in each hand, lifting her flaming torches as high as she could reach. Then she began to bring her hands down, moving the fire close to her body as she swayed forward and backward and from side to side. Her body trembled, sending fire-life into the folds of her dress until the amber danced with the radiant frenzy of the flames. Meanwhile, vibrant with the amber frenzy, she shifted into twirling fervor that swept her black hair free from her shoulders. Her limbs swayed and twirled as a current of flame. And all the while her face was impassive while her gaze was fervent, as if her body had been possessed by fire.

With the violin screaming she moved closer and closer to Sam, lowering herself as she danced until she was kneeling at Sam's feet with her body pulsating, her flaming torches blazing above her, her face still impassive. Then she rose, still swaying her thighs with the music, still shifting her feet in intricate patterns, slowly retreating toward the fire. Her swaying and twirling kept slowing until she abruptly stopped by the flames. With a hoarse cry she flung her torches back to the blaze and stood frozen, as if her surrender of the fire had left her lifeless.

The music stopped. No one spoke. No one moved. The world stood still.

Duntsi broke the silence with, "The water is boiling."

Sam said, "Make the coffee, Buck. I'm in a daze."

Buck took over. Everyone marveled at the power of the powder to make water into coffee, but the merriment of earlier in the evening was gone. Each drank their coffee quietly.

"You must tell Gali that her dance was—I don't know—beyond words," Sam said.

Duntsi translated, then told Sam, "She say, 'you stay, Gali dance for you every night.'"

"Tell her that in my dreams I will be here," Sam answered. When Duntsi had told her this, she smiled with her eyes firmly locked to Sam's.

The women took Gali with them as they retired to their caravans.

"Time we make shuteye," Duntsi said. "We stay with fire until die down, then we give you eiderdown for night. Morning, first light, I go with you Schweigersdorf. Like you ask."

Next morning, April 10, in the half-light of dawn, before anyone else was stirring, Duntsi woke Sam and Buck. When they had tucked their trades of the previous day inside their shirts again, the three walked together to where the village of Schweigersdorf could be seen ahead.

"You know road here. I go back," Duntsi said. "I no want German people see me. We lay low when stay here. When horses pull carts we see Germans. Trade. Go new place."

"Who are you escaping from?" Buck asked.

"Russians, understand? Dangerous say escape Hitler."

"You won't tell us where you come from?" Sam asked.

"Papers say Hungary refugees got caravans German government. Escape Russians. Was Gypsy caravans, but we Hungarians. We lay low. Cheerio mates."

"Wait, Duntsi," Buck pleaded. "Watch out you don't step on the eggs we left by the blankets. Eggs break too easy for us to carry. We left for you—Gali, Balo, Kalomar—to all you say."

"I get. We eat for you. You good mates."

"Tell Gali I say she is a gold raven with angel wings," Sam said.

"I tell Gali. You gold ravens, too. Cheerio mates."

They walked on alone. Buck, with his mind on Gali said, "You'll remember back and wish one day that when you were alone in the woods with her you'd loved her all the way."

Sam looked out to where the sun, lifting on the horizon, pierced javelins of light through the silver fir boughs and struck mirrors upon a pool before them. Finally he said, "Gali was so sexy wild because she belongs to no one. She is free."

"Yeah, and she was aching for you to get her," Buck said.

Sam did not answer. He had receded to his inner world. *The spider with the caterpillar trapped in its web—would I want Gali that way? I had people that way with my bombsight, but for killing. Loving has got to be different.*

"Here's where we start back down the road we didn't take yesterday," Buck said, bringing Sam back to his surroundings.

"I wish the world could be a place where Gali always stayed like she is," Sam reflected.

"You're into your dreams again," Buck said. "We've got to start thinking practical more, like you said. Being locked up in shit for over a year should bring us to more than our dreams. All the time we've had to think, should give us pay-off in how we live if we're freed."

When they had walked a few more minutes, Buck pointed to the side of road and said, "More dandelions. When I build my own home, instead of weeding the dandelions, I'm going to let them take over and make me a gold yard."

"Listen to the birds," Sam said. "They're singing up a storm again. What did you say they were?"

"Sparrows, finches, blackbirds, warblers—whatever," Buck said.

They rounded a turn. Directly before them were two German soldiers. One had a rifle pointed at them and the other had a pistol pointed at them. Between the soldiers and themselves were Walt and two other kriegies with their hands held above their heads.

"Hande Hoch!" the Germans shouted. Buck and Sam lifted their hands above their heads.

As the Germans closed in, Buck and Sam saw—between the elbow and the shoulder of their uniforms—the SS insignia of twin eagles extending from a swastika. Both Buck and Sam knew that these were the gray-green uniforms of a Waffen-SS Scharführer and Rottenführer, the equivalent of a staff sergeant and corporal, respectively.

"Looks like we've had it," Buck said as he and Sam were forced to turn and get in line with the other kriegies seized.

"How the hell did you get picked up?" Sam asked Walt.

"When you didn't come back, I figured you must be in trouble and me talking German might help you. I came back to find you. Next I knew they had me. I told them the Luftwaffe had run out of food and let us out to trade. The tall one in charge exploded. He screamed, "Things haven't come to the point that prisoners run around loose in the woods. If you're hungry get down in the gutter and eat dirt.' Then he said he was going to take us to the Volkssturm to hold until SS troops get here tomorrow."

"Still! Ganz Still Halten!" the Scharführer called. The seized kriegies marched on silently with the rifle and pistol pointed at their backs.

FREEDOM: CHAPTER THREE

TUESDAY, APRIL 10: The kriegies seized by the SS were taken to the courtyard of the town hall of Schwiegersdorf, next to an old stone church. Some twenty villagers—women of all ages and several old men—gathered to see what was happening. Because Schwiegerdorf was a settlement removed from a through-road and railway traveled by troops, the war here had only been news read about and talked about until today. Now the scene of ragged, skinny prisoners of war held by soldiers pointing guns at them carried the message that the war had arrived in their village.

The SS sergeant's voice rose in intensity and took more strident intensity as he continued to instruct the villagers. Three old men and a woman abruptly broke away and ran in different directions while the SS, with pistols drawn, intently guarded the kriegies.

Buck, not able to contain his concern, edged closer to Walt. "What's going—"

"Still Halten!" the sergeant yelled as he leveled his pistol at Buck.

With that, all the kriegies froze and kept silent.

Two old men in work clothes arrived, each carrying a very long-barreled rifle, recognized by the kriegies as World War One issue. The sergeant spoke to the old men with intense anger. He pointed to the kriegies and then to the women. One of the rifle-bearing workmen approached the kriegies and searched each carefully. Buck had left his knife hidden in the hay, and Walt had left his map there too. The search yielded only the food that Buck and Sam were carrying. The corporal, Rottenführer, gave this food to an old woman.

The sergeant, more precisely the staff sergeant, Scharführer, kept talking, ever louder and angrier. Two women turned away and ran down different roads until they disappeared. Another man in work clothes, about age sixty, came lumbering up. He had an ammunition belt slung over a shoulder and was carrying an ammunition box with one hand and a pistol with the other. A little later, a shorter man of about the same age hurried into the court yard with an ammunition box in each hand and the same kind of pistol in a holster.

The Scharführer looked at his watch, screamed something, and took a ledger from the breast pocket of his immaculate uniform. After directing more talk to the four men who had arrived with weapons, he advanced toward one of them. As he got near he received an awkward clicking together of heels and a sloppily raised stiff arm, a seeming attempt to give the Heil Hitler salute. The Scharführer spoke loud and sharp staccato words. The targeted villager nodded in assent.

The Scharführer now targeted each prisoner of war. With each, he lifted the metal tag that hung from the prisoner's neck and copied the number of the tag into his book. With each, he also copied the further designation of each tag, Krgfl. d. Lw. Nr. 3 Sagan. After further writing, he tore a copy of his notations from his ledger and gave it to the man who had given him the stiff arm salute.

Next, the Rottenführer talked to the men carrying weapons. Whatever he said brought them to inspect the load of their weapons and point them at the kriegies with such alertness that it appeared they were expecting an escape attempt at any moment.

Another woman arrived, frantically pushing a bicycle. The Scharführer took the bicycle then waved the woman away. At this time a tall, thin elderly man scurried into the courtyard. Moans of relief issued from the gathered civilians. The Scharführer went up to this last man to arrive. After a heated outburst directed at him, the two exchanged stiff-arm salutes. The Scharführer then turned away and mounted the bicycle.

The Rottenführer holstered his pistol and started walking away. The Scharführer followed, riding the bicycle. As he rode, he turned his head and yelled in German so strident and raging it was heard by the kriegies as gibberish.

At that precise moment the front wheel of his bicycle stuck in a crack between two cobblestones of the street. The Scharführer spilled into a puddle of watery sludge. He picked himself up and with a look of horror beheld his immaculate uniform fouled with the ooze of street dung.

The watching faces kept an emotionless mask. No one came forward to help him. Finally a woman went to him and motioned for him to follow her. They went into a near-by house. As soon as he was gone, the faces of watching villagers and kriegies alike broke into smiles. When he returned tidied up, he said no more. He wore his own emotionless mask now as he rode away.

When he was completely out of sight, the villagers relaxed into chuckles and conversation, as if they had been freed from a tyranny imposed upon their village. The armed men ushered the kriegies into a large room of the town hall and gave them chairs to sit on. All put their pistols back into their holsters and also sat down, with their rifles leaned against their chairs. They smiled toward their captives, showing embarrassment for what they were doing. Yet they kept their hands close enough to their weapons to make it clear that they intended to keep their prisoners from escaping.

Walt spoke to them, then translated, "They say they don't care if we talk. They're really ignorant about the military. They don't even know the ranks of the soldiers who gave them their orders. I don't think they know they're SS. But they know the war news. The guy in charge told me he had thought the commotion was the American army arriving."

"Tell us what the hell is going on now," Buck appealed.

"The sergeant gave them orders to deliver us for execution at nine in the morning. The orders have each of our kriegie numbers on them, so on paper we're dead. I've got to talk to them to get a feel of our chances of getting out of this."

After more talk in German, Walt came back with, "The guy in charge knows the orders are from the Waffen SS. He says the orders must be carried out. I heard the SS sergeant tell them he had all their names, and they would all be shot if any of us escape."

"Why didn't they shoot us now?" Sam asked.

"Proper military procedure I guess. They're scouts, in a hurry arranging quarters for their troops moving in. The sergeant was crazy mad because the people here were delaying him. The local Volkssturm was supposed to be ready for emergency mobilization. He screamed that the Führer was relying on them as his secret army and instead they were out in their fields."

"Cut the chatter. We've got to figure out how to escape," Buck interjected.

"Let me talk to them some more. I've got an idea."

In a while Walt reported, "I told them we are Luftwaffe prisoners who were allowed to come to their village to trade because the Luftwaffe supply had run out. I told them that we were ordered to be back in Plankstettin by dark. I told them the SS orders are illegal because we are Luftwaffe prisoners. And, I made it clear that when our Army gets here they will kill people who turned Luftwaffe prisoners over to the SS—"

Buck interrupted, "How is that going to save our ass? They're not going to turn us loose. There are five of them and five of us, but they've got the guns. Those aren't good odds, but we've got to take them."

"Not yet. It's still morning. We've got all day. Let me do more talking," Walt insisted.

Buck continued, "We can take out some of these guys before they can shoot, but not all of them. While you're talking I'm going to ask to go the john. If it's got a window I'll get through it and head for Plankstettin. Maybe a Luftwaffe guard will come back with me and take charge of us."

"Wait, Buck. If you try to escape and make it, we'll get guarded twice as close. If you get shot, we'll still get guarded twice as close. Let's try to work out a plan to escape together."

Sam proposed, "Let's give Walt a chance. We've got until nine tomorrow morning."

Buck relented.

Sam spoke to the other two kriegies who had been caught. "You're ahead of me in knowing who we are. I recognized you, but I didn't know your names. I've got them now—Ben Hearn and Carl Wilson, right?"

Walt conversed with the peasant guards again. Without understanding the words being spoken, the tension of the conversation carried to the nervous kriegies.

After a while Ben asked, "How are things going, Walt?"

"Not good. The guy in charge says he understands that we are Luftwaffe prisoners, but he has to carry out the orders from the SS, regardless."

Carl offered the opinion, "Talking isn't going to work. We're going to have to rush them or let Buck try his idea for escaping on his own and try to bring back Luftwaffe help."

"Slow down. All of you. I've got these Volkssturm guys nervous as hell about what the American Army will do to them if they turn us over to the SS."

"They're not alone being nervous," Sam said. "Walt's right. We've got to all act calm and friendly. Being fidgety is going to get them trigger-happy. To pull off an escape, we've got to first all act sleepy and bored, get them to relax and get careless."

"Yeah. Relax. I'll work on them some more," Walt said.

This time the conversation went on longer then ever. Finally Walt interpreted, "I think I sold them on the idea that they could get out of the SS orders by having the Luftwaffe write on their orders that they took us back into their command. But they're not sure I'm telling the truth. One of them is going to ride a bicycle down to Plankstettin and check out what I told them. We've got to hope that our Luftwaffe guards will sign for us, because we're really not their prisoners any more since the SS caught us."

One of the guards got up and left. After an hour of waiting for his return, two women brought in hot vegetable soup, black bread, and sausage. They gave each guard and each prisoner a bowl of soup, a piece of black bread, and a piece of sausage.

Finally, the guard-messenger returned. After conversation in German, Walt explained, "The Luftwaffe backed my story. The trouble is they've learned that the SS is moving in. They told the messenger they're going to start south to get away as soon as they can organize their prisoners to start marching. The messenger said they'll be gone before we could get there. But after more arguing I convinced them to at least try to get us back in time. So let's all cooperate to get us out of here and back to Plankstettin before they change their mind."

The trek back to Plankstettin began with the kriegies hurrying and the Volkssturm plodding at the rear, occasionally calling for the kriegies to slow down. When in sight of Plankstettin, Walt said, "If the Luftwaffe and kriegies have already gone we've got to get through the gate and back to our barn before the Volkssturm finds out. Let's get as far ahead as we can without drawing fire from their rifles."

"We've got to think further than that. We've got to plan quick how we'll whip these guys," Buck contended.

"I'm just worrying about getting that far," Walt said.

The leader of the Volkssturm now yelled, "Nicht so schnell!"

Walt advised, "He's calling for us to slow down, but walk faster. I'm betting they'll warn us again before they start shooting."

When the five kriegies reached the bridge before the gate, the Volkssturm recruits were about a hundred yards behind them. The gate was open. There was no sign of Luftwaffe guards or anyone else.

Walt instructed, "Head for the barn, but walk, don't run or we'll panic them. We know there's no one to sign for us but they still don't."

The five hurried to the biggest barn. Inside they found sixteen other kriegies with packs, bunched near the door. Recognizing Buck, someone called, "Hey, you're a commando. Tell us what to do. The SS is coming, and everybody's left while we were out trading."

Buck answered, "First off, there are five Krauts with guns coming in the front gate, and if we don't scram before they get here, we're dead. Get your asses out the back door of this barn and over the back wall."

"Lead out," Walt added. "We'll be with you."

Walt, Buck, and Sam grabbed for their packs.

Sam was the last to leave. He peeked through a crack and saw the five Volkssturm standing on the bridge before the open gate and looking into the emptiness of the walled Plank estate. Then he scurried to where the back barn door stood open. In a minute all the twenty-one stragglers who had missed the evacuation were over the back wall.

Walt called, "Don't scatter. I've got a plan for what to do next. Don't scatter. Keep together and do as I say. I know how the Germans think."

"You better believe him," Buck added. "He out-smarted the krauts to get us this far."

Walt led the way through a grove of trees. He circled around the estate, out of sight of the gate. He took a back street that led to the main road south. Once on the road, he called out, "Form into a column of fours. That's five rows with me out front. If I need to I'll shout orders in German. Whether you're lame or not, we've got to keep our lines straight. If we do this right, no German will look close enough to see we've got no guards."

Three hours later, after marching through a village and past many Germans, the formation of unguarded stragglers caught up with their Plankstettin contingent. Some one hundred thirty stragglers were enjoying a rest stop with three Luftwaffe guards giving them legal security.

Walt checked in with Major Reddick. "I hope you didn't need me. I went out to look for Buck and Sam and the SS caught us."

"How did you get away?"

"With good luck. It was scary. It got complicated, but we made it."

"I'm glad you got back. Some guys are still missing. I got by without you, but stick close from now on. Right now remind Kruger he's not marching healthy prisoners. We can't march further today. Tell him to camp us at the next farm."

"Is Kruger in charge?" Walt asked. "I thought he went on with the main column."

"No such luck, but he's quit bragging about victory in the Redoubt. He's eating our Red Cross food that he knows we control. Great equalizer—food."

"Who else is guarding us?"

"Only Krauss and a new guard, Werner, if you can call a guard new when he's so old and worn out he deserves a wheel chair."

"I learned today how much we need the Luftwaffe guarding us."

"They're learning they need us," Reddick responded.

Late in the afternoon the column camped for the night. As the day waned klim can burners heating coffee water flickered in the barnyard. For Buck and Sam, who had no coffee, there was the remembrance of Duntsi's "bloody miracle" joy of last night's coffee-time when powder and water suddenly became coffee.

Sam and Buck slept outside under the full moon and flickering stars. Buck reflected, "So much has happened today that it's hard to believe it was only last night that we were watching Gali's fire dance. We haven't even had a chance to tell Walt about Duntsi mentioning Saint Sara and southern France."

"I can still see her dancing with those torches," Sam said. "The further we get away from last night, the more I feel we're moving out to a world less in touch."

"In touch with what, Hatch?"

"I can't find words for it."

Buck reflected, "What I'm wondering is what did the Volkssturm do when they couldn't find any Luftwaffe to sign off for us?"

"Maybe they're hiding in attics, or maybe they're heading south like us," Sam said.

"I'm hoping they don't get shot. They're good people," Buck offered.

In the morning, April 11, Oberleutnant Kruger and Major Reddick discussed whether to wait for night before marching on. Walt stood by, though he was not needed, since Kruger spoke English. Kruger said that he knew

Reddick was getting Allied news. He proposed that they share German and Allied news in making plans. He said his sources reported that yesterday over a thousand American heavy bombers and hundreds of fighters had attacked the Munich area they were marching toward.

Reddick suggested that with so much air activity it might be wise to march at night.

Kruger reminded that waiting until night meant risking being overtaken by the SS.

Reddick and Walt exchanged looks of surprise when Kruger continued, "The SS might tear into the Luftwaffe for nursing along one hundred fifty invalid prisoners with the top heavy command of a first lieutenant and a staff sergeant and only one private. They might take radical measures to correct the problem."

"Radical measures? Do you mean, kill us and draft you for the Redoubt defense force?" Reddick asked.

"Extreme things are happening. It would be wise to keep clear of them."

"I'll agree with that," Walt volunteered.

Reddick and Kruger decided to march in the daytime.

Waiting to get under way, Walt passed Krauss and stopped to talk. Having endured Krauss's bragging in Sagan, he wanted to hear what Krauss had to say now that Germany was close to total defeat. Then he went over to Sam and Buck.

Sam held up a can of jelly as Walt approached. "After what you did yesterday, coming back for us and saving us, we want you to have the whole can of jelly," Sam greeted.

"That's right," Buck agreed.

Walt took the can and said, "I'll save it to share when we get bread to spread it on."

"Is your escape plan still on?" Sam asked.

"Yes, but we've both got the GIs. We'll have to be in shape when we make our break."

"Listen," Sam said. "The night we didn't get back, we were with a camp of refugees. They fed us hedgehog stew and we had music and dancing by their fire. The big thing

I've got to tell you is that these people worship Saint Sara! They claimed they're Hungarian, but they said they were heading for southern France. I think they are—"

Walt interrupted, "How do you know they worship Saint Sara?"

"One of them spoke English, and he told us," Sam said.

"That's true," Buck verified. "He said they were blessed by Saint Sara."

"I think they were Gypsies," Sam continued.

"Our Heinkel pilot guard, Krauss just told me some crazy stuff about Gypsies," Walt said. "Back in Sagan, he told me his brother was on Hitler's team proving that the Germans were Aryans who came from India and had the earliest record of being civilized. Today he told me this study team learned that Gypsies were the true Aryans, and nobody dares tell Hitler because he's killing Gypsies for being uncivilized."

Sam raised an arm for silence. "Do you hear that?" he asked.

From the empty road that at this stage of the war seldom carried gasoline powered cars, they heard the labored hum of a large vehicle approaching from the south. All eyes fastened on the hill. A giant white truck appeared. Huge red crosses were painted on it.

"White Angel!" rose as one voice.

The truck pulled into the barnyard.

Every kriegie and every guard received a Red Cross Parcel. With the Parcels came the cigarettes, D-bar chocolate, and instant coffee that were key items needed for trading.

Reddick and Kruger quickly decided to stop at the next village. Here new opportunity for trading was promised to extend the Red Cross food.

The kriegies gathered their meager belongings and newly won food into their makeshift packs and began to leave the barnyard. As Buck looked at the one hundred fifty limping and shuffling figures moving out to the road, he was reminded of Randi's description of her life with her hospital patients. *Here we are . . . your human debris . . . That's her message.* "We're getting a lot of H.D. Human Debris!" he blurted.

Sam, surprised by Buck's outburst, joined, "We're Briggs's crippily old cruds who want a discharge."

The contingent of stragglers moved to the village where an hour's rest stop was announced for trading. While making a trade, Buck was offered an old baby carriage for ten cigarettes plus some German money. Feeling the rawness of his blistered feet, he was very interested in this chance to get his pack off of his back. But he did not have German money. Krauss, hearing the negotiations, stepped forward.

"I pay the money. We'll be partners. You put in your pack, and I put in my pack. We'll take turns pushing," Krauss proposed.

The deal was closed. Buck pushed the carriage with a cargo of two packs to the village square.

Walt came by and said, "I traded for some bread. Let's open the can of jelly and bash."

"Great idea," Sam and Buck agreed.

"Things are looking up. We're bashing, and I'm traveling with wheels," Buck rejoiced.

The village square became a bazaar of kriegies having food celebrations on the cobblestone street. A weighing scale by a feed store at one end of the square gathered kriegies waiting to weigh themselves. When Sam got his turn on the scale, he said, "When you translate the kilo scale to pounds, I've lost forty-seven of the hundred and forty-five pounds I weighed before I was shot down."

"I'm down to one hundred and twenty," Buck said. "That makes me the winner over you, if pounds lost is the score."

"Hubba hubba!" Walt reacted. "I'm not worse off than you guys."

The voice of Major Reddick sounded over the conversation, "Let's start moving south."

Fluffy patches of fair-weather clouds were spread across the sky of the warm afternoon. As the march got under way, twelve fighters crossed the sky, flying northwest, low enough to be identified as U.S. P-51s and P-47s. They were flying steady, on course, seemingly not in search of a target, yet providing an air of uneasiness to the walkers exposed on the road.

After half an hour of walking, a rest stop was called. Using white items, kriegies made a sign next to the road—POWs.

As he rested, Walt saw a lone soldier coming up the road from the south.

"It's Smitty!" Walt shouted.

Smitty reported to Kruger. Stiff arm Nazi salutes were exchanged. Then Smitty walked over to Walt and talked until the rest stop was called to an end.

"What did he tell you?" Sam asked.

"He said he told Kruger he was ordered to come back to provide us another guard, but he confided that he had actually started to Pellheim to join Paula. After getting arrested as a deserter and escaping, he decided it was too dangerous, so he started back to Plankstettin. He said he had run out of food, and I told him he just missed getting a Red Cross Parcel."

"Tell him he won't go hungry as long as we've got food," Buck said.

"I go along with that," Sam added.

"I expect Reddick will say that, too," Walt said. "Having a guard like Smitty makes us safer. Since our two top guards talk English, the SS might take them away from us. I know how speaking the enemy's language makes people suspicious. Then we've got the old man they might take away as being too weak to guard us. Smitty is our best protection against getting massacred. He's ordinary solid Luftwaffe kraut."

"This is too crazy for me," Sam said. "You claimed my sack time was driving me crazy, but these days are more crazy than going around the bend. Everything's turned around. Raw for war. Who's friends and who's enemies?"

As the sun was setting, the march ended for the day in another barnyard. It was a fair weather night. Most of the kriegies slept outside under what Duntsi called the platter of big black diamond sky.

Next day, April 12, the march got under way in late morning. even though Allied fighters were periodically crossing overhead. Smitty now carried a long rifle of the World War One era. He flanked the stragglers limping and shuffling along where Sam was walking. Sam, bored by the endless tramping, asked Smitty, "You sing 'Lilli Marlene?'"

Sam knew that singing was forbidden on prisoner of war marches. Yet on this around-the-bend day of broken rules, he risked asking.

Without hesitation, Smitty began to sing:

> Vor der Kaserne, vor dem grossen Tor,
> Da steht eine Laterne, und steht sie noch davor.
> Da wollen wir uns wider sehen.
> Bei der Laterne werden wir stehen.
> Wie eins Lilli Marlene. Wie eins Lilli Marlene.

"I know the words in English," a kriegie next to Sam said, and he began to sing:

"Underneath the lamplight, by the village gate—Damn, I can't remember the rest of it."

"Learn it in German," Sam said. "You teach us, Smitty."

As the march continued, Smitty sang the German words over and over for those kriegies who wanted to learn this renowned song of love and war loneliness.

A half mile to the rear, Krauss and Buck were a solitary twosome, talking, as Buck pushed the baby carriage and Krauss walked beside him, carrying the rifle that gave Buck official Luftwaffe prisoner status and made himself an official Luftwaffe soldier on duty.

". . . You told us there was snow for our sled, you nincompoop. We believed you and ran into mud that damn near done us in."

"I told you what I was told. Why bring this up now? I know I was wrong."

"You better believe you were wrong! Schumann saved our ass that night by helping us push our sled with the butt of his rifle."

"Ja. It was bad mistake," Krauss admitted.

"A better time was when you showed up drunk at Graustein, bragging about girls you had loved in different countries. You walked with your arm on Walter Plank's shoulder like he was your buddy until another guard stopped you."

"If you have nothing else to talk about, it is better that you don't talk."

"Okay. We can talk about when you're going to push this goddamn baby carriage."

"Ja. We have two big babies. You push them now. I'll push later. Now I have to talk with Oberleutnant Kruger."

Krauss passed Smitty and his singing stragglers as he moved ahead to where Kruger, Reddick, and the old man guard were resting as they waited for stragglers.

When Krauss came near, Reddick called to him. "Where is Buck, the prisoner you're supposed to be guarding?"

"He's coming, slow. Way back. Too far to see, but he's coming," Krauss reported.

Reddick, who had been seated, now got up and went to Krauss. He faced Krauss with fierce eyes. "Don't bullshit me! He's coming so slow because he's pushing the baby carriage with your pack in it and you're walking with no load. I know the deal you made. You're supposed to push half the time."

Krauss said, "I'm going to take my turn."

"When?"

"After I speak with Oberleutnant Kruger."

"We don't know how close the SS is. You've left Buck at the tail end of our column without a guard. You get your ass back there as fast as you can and stay with him from now on if you want to eat."

Krauss turned to Kruger who had also gotten up, "Is that what you say, Oberleutnant?"

"Why do you ask? Why do you think you need to speak to me? I have nothing to say to you! You know we must keep all of our prisoners guarded at all times! Get back there at once and do your equal time of pushing since you made such agreement!"

"Ya wohl. Heil Hitler!" Krauss saluted as he turned and then started running back.

Around 5:00 P.M. seven P-51's, heading south, flew down the road at an altitude of about five hundred feet, but they did not fire. The fighters had come during a rest stop in which the POWs' sign of white belongings had been laid out beside the road. Kriegies debated whether it was their sign that had saved them.

Later in the evening the march arrived at the village of Sandersdorf below a magnificent castle. Oberleutnant Kruger went up to the castle to confer about getting quarters there. He returned more militant and agitated than he had been for many days. With brisk commands, he ordered the stragglers to form into precise military formation. He then circled the kriegies upward to the pig barns of the castle. During the walk uphill, he barked orders to his guards, demanding that they march smartly and to the stragglers he barked, "Straighten your lines. We must have order. Luftwaffe prisoners do not roam down the road like stray dogs under my command!"

It was obvious to the prisoners that something about this castle had made him anxious to display himself as a tough commander. He ordered Buck to move into the center of the column, seemingly to integrate the baby carriage as a mechanized part of the military order. The march was directed into an empty pig barn. By now the sun was down and the first stars were showing. The barn door was closed, bringing darkness until eyes adjusted.

"You will be locked in here," Kruger announced. "There will be no fires. Not one burner will be lit! Wehrmacht troops are housed in the castle. We are under strict rules here. I will arrange water and an abort. The floor is clean. It will stay as clean as when we arrived. If there is as much as one burner lit, you will all be shot."

In the morning the barn door, some six feet wide, was opened, but the prisoners were confined to the barn interior.

It was Friday, April 13. The view from the door showed the castle some one hundred yards away rising from a lower elevation to tower splendidly high above the barns. Near an entrance to the castle, several dozen troops with mirror-black boots and immaculate gray uniforms filed idly back and forth with the precise gait of mechanical soldiers.

Presently six of these troops filed up to the open barn door. "Chokolade? Amerikanishe Zigaretten?" they inquired.

The contrast between the immaculate exhibit of these tin soldiers inviting trade and the dirty conglomerate garb of the kriegies inside was so vast that it offered a logic for the kriegies being sheltered in the animal barns. A conversation began between the kriegies and the Wehrmacht soldiers. No trade items had yet changed hands when a German general appeared accompanied by a staff of three high ranking officers—"Achtung! Weg mit euch! Schnell machen!"

Hastily, the soldiers who had been visiting scattered.

"Who is the highest ranking prisoner here?" the general asked in English.

"I am, sir," Major Reddick said as he approached and saluted the rank before him.

The general returned the salute, then said, "I have come as a courtesy to inform you of the news that your President Roosevelt died yesterday afternoon."

"I respect your courtesy, but I can't give thanks for such news from the enemy," Reddick said. He saluted and turned his back on the general.

The general and his staff turned away and went back to the castle.

The kriegies were ordered to form up to march. They began the trek that circled them down to the road below the castle.

Unexpectedly, from a hedgerow a voice with a French accent sounded, "Roosevelt dead."

"That confirms it," Reddick stated with a cracked voice.

"Merci. God bless you," a kriegie replied to the hedgerow.

All the kriegies now accepted that their President was really dead. The news brought home close to them. Without their American flag waving or a funeral band playing the national anthem, the words of the French slave laborer had stunned them and united them in memorial awe. Their President was dead. No details were known. No details were needed.

"Who was the Vice President?" a voice near the rear of the formation eventually asked.

"Harry Truman," a another voice informed.

For the moment the news was not further discussed. Obviously, no one could find the right words to ask or to offer about what they had heard.

The march now headed toward Neustadt on the Danube River, the Blue Danube for those who knew it from the Strauss waltz. By noon, the day was very warm and walking up and down the hills was grueling labor even for those least suffering physical handicaps.

During an afternoon rest stop, Buck asked Walt, "How are you doing with the shits?"

"Bad. Same goes for John. We were going to break away as soon as we crossed the Danube, maybe tonight yet, but I'm so weak, I don't know."

"If the white angels keep coming we're going to be living good, Walt. You'd better think about staying with us," Sam advised.

As the rest stop ended a hot afternoon sun was shining in a cloudless sky. The old man took his guard post flanking the column near Reddick, next to Walt and John. Kruger led the march, walking ahead of everyone, alone, as if he were blazing a trail for soldiers following him. Smitty marched at the rear, staying with the stragglers that were struggling to keep the pace. Sam and Buck walked together, with Sam carrying his make-shift backpack and Buck pushing the baby carriage. Krauss, following his orders, now stayed close to Buck.

As the march started up a very long hill, Buck called to Krauss, "I'm not sure this hill is ever going to end. It's your turn to push this half-ass vehicle."

Krauss came over with his rifle still shouldered and took over the pushing of the baby carriage. As the weight of the cargo challenged his effort, he complained, "big babies."

Further forward, where the old man was walking guard, Reddick said, "Walt, it looks like your old Adolf is on his last leg. I saw him stumble and get up again. I'm betting he's not going to make it to the top of this hill. Go tell Kruger about him."

After getting Walt's information, Kruger fell back and talked with the old man. Then he went to Reddick and said, "I'm going to put his pack in the baby carriage. Don't object—Oberfeldwebel Krauss will push. If someone will volunteer to carry his gun and walk with him, I think we can get him to the top of the hill. From there the road goes down until we camp for the night."

John, hearing, volunteered, "I'll help him."

Walt asked, "Why you? You're sick. There are guys here in better shape than you."

"The old goon needs help. It's not his fucking war. He's trapped in it like us. I'm just going to help him to the top of the hill."

John went to the old man and shouldered his rifle while Kruger took off his pack and took it back to the baby carriage.

When Kruger was out of ear shot, Krauss complained to Buck, "Three's too many for this small carriage."

Up ahead, John continued up the hill with the old man's rifle shouldered and an arm wrapped about him to steady his gait. Then the hilltop was reached. Beyond and below the river Danube could be seen flowing a winding course, beautiful on this warm afternoon, but not blue.

A rest stop was called. Krauss took his pack from the baby carriage.

"Three is too many," Krauss said again. "Werner is too old to carry his pack. I'll carry my pack on my back. You share the carriage with Werner."

John returned the old man's rifle.

"Danke. Vielen danke," the old man said.

"You Adolf?" John asked.

"Me, Werner. Alles kaput."

"Hang in, Werner. Eat sugar from Red Cross. You know, sweet, sugar. Make strong. Hubba hubba." With these parting words John went back to where Walt was making a snack of cheese and K-2 crackers.

"Thought I'd try to cork us up," Walt explained. "I'm getting so fagged I just want to lay down and stay."

"Yeah. Cork us up, Walt. My legs are getting rubbery, too," John confessed.

By early evening the march was at the Danube. Guns were being set up along the banks of the river and along the road leading to the bridge.

After surveying the scene, Major Reddick told Walt, "This stretch of Redoubt isn't ready to hold off the Allies for long. In any event we're hardly a force to start a revolution. I'm going to let them lead us over the bridge, into their Redoubt, for better or worse."

As they crossed the bridge, they saw two bombs laid as mines on the roadway. The bombs were about the size of air force five-hundred pounders. The column then passed through Neustadt and detoured into a large field. Air raid sirens wailed and presently P-47 and P-51 fighters began strafing and dive bombing targets along the river. Again, the giant POWs sign was laid out.

Kruger went away for a while. When he came back he told Reddick he had arranged for a German food ration of some soup and potatoes. While the kriegies were waiting for the food to arrive, a Red Cross white angel truck appeared. The truck turned into the field. When it had stopped, Reddick asked the driver, "Did you bring food?"

"No, I'm empty—heading back to Switzerland for more Parcels. I stopped to see if any of you need help getting to Moosburg—that's where you're all being taken. I can take at least twenty."

"Hold on. I've got to talk this over with the Germans," Reddick said.

While Reddick talked with Kruger, Walt talked to the driver privately. "Could we ride with you to the Swiss border? A couple of us are planning to get across—I know you couldn't take us across, but if we could get that far—"

"Don't be foolish," the driver interrupted. "The Germans would shut down our whole operation if we started helping POWs escape. You couldn't get across the border anyway. It's too well guarded. I can haul you to Moosburg. Be patient. Freedom will come to you."

"Maybe not. Hitler's planning to take us with him as hostages in his final battle."

"I've heard that, but planning and pulling it off is a lot of difference. The Allies are hitting hard all along the front. You're life's at risk here, but you've got poor odds for getting home by trying to walk from here to Switzerland through country filled with SS and then trying to cross the border."

Reddick came back and said, "We can do it—for those in bad shape. How many did you say you can take?"

"Pile in until the truck's full. It's only an hour's drive away."

The news of an easy trip possibility back to barbed wire spread quickly. The price of taking the trip was the loss of open road freedom. But for the sick, the footsore, and those otherwise suffering the walking, this was a chance of rescue.

Walt went to Reddick and asked, "Could you manage without me interpreting for you? I'm getting so weak from diarrhea I'm wobbly."

"Take the ride, Walt. Kruger can do what interpreting I need."

Walt went over to Buck and Sam. "John and I have given up our escape plan. We're going to take the ride to Moosburg. What about you?"

"My feet are giving me a bad time," Buck said, "but we decided being on the road is better than being cooped up."

"Keep safe. I'll be watching for you, Walt said."

"If we get liberated and you don't, I'll write to you," Sam called as Walt pulled himself into the truck.

When the Red Cross truck arrived at Moosburg, it was too dark to see the size and nature of the prison camp. The gate was opened to admit the newly arrived human cargo.

The incoming were given a DDT delousing and a shower. They then found space amongst others on open ground. They would have to wait until morning to discover the wisdom of their decision to voluntarily be locked into this prison camp.

FREEDOM: CHAPTER FOUR

WEDNESDAY, APRIL 19: The column of Luft III, with Colonel Raymond still up front, had arrived at Moosburg on April 12. Five days had passed since the Stalag Luft III stragglers were known to be at Neustadt, less than thirty miles away. Walt and other kriegies were becoming concerned about what had happened to them.

Until a few weeks before, Moosburg had held thirty thousand prisoners. With the evacuation of POWs southward, this crowd had swollen to one hundred thousand with no increase in sanitary facilities. The sprawling, jam-packed camp had several compounds separated by barbed wire.

One compound held Russian prisoners who were taken out during the day to work as slave laborers. Often they returned with smuggled potatoes, bread, and other food, which they traded with Allied kriegies by using hand tosses across the barbed wire.

Aside from the separation of Russian prisoners, distinctions were no longer made between prisoners of different nations, different branches of the military, and different ranks. Colonels and privates from various nations slept next to each other and waited in the same lines to get water or a place on a toilet hole.

Lines a hundred yards long stretched back from every water faucet. The few toilet holes of the latrines were occupied all day and all night and always had waiting lines. To keep the toilets from running over, the Germans kept "honey wagons"—soldier-driven tank wagons pulled by horses—busy full time in pumping out waste matter and hauling it away. To cope with the critical conditions, some guards were assigned sanitation work and jobs such as escorting kriegies into the forest to get fuel. The wood obtained was rationed, but it was not sufficient. More wood was scavenged from the walls and frames of the barracks and latrines.

All floor space as well as bunk space was used for sleeping in the buildings holding Stalag Luft III POWs. In addition, five huge tents were set up to shelter prisoners. Yet, some arriving kriegies only had the platter of big blue diamond sky as their shelter.

On the afternoon of the fifteenth, while Walt was watching at the gate, the Stalag Luft III stragglers arrived, limping and hobbling. Buck was no longer pushing his baby carriage. He carried his pack on his back, in spite of blistered feet.

"What took you so long?"

"What was the hurry, considering?" Sam responded.

"Where's the baby carriage?"

"A wheel gave out a little ways back. Old man Werner wanted to come in carrying his pack anyway. I was hoping to use it all the way," Buck said.

Scanning the massive expanse of crowded camp, Buck observed, "This is a god awful big gathering of human debris. Are we getting Parcels enough here to feed everybody?"

"There's a full Parcel per week, thanks to the white angels, plus, believe it or not, once in a while, German rations of potatoes, black bread, soup, and cheese," Walt informed. "Your first problem is to stay dry. I got into a tent in a slough with three hundred of us packed together on the ground in four rows. There's hope for you, because when it rained last night we wound up in a pond of water, and a few guys deserted for higher ground outside."

"What's the big hope?" Sam asked. "I'm not a duck looking for water."

"We got the water thing licked. We're building a Venice. We've heaped dirt under our sleep space and dug trenches between us. We can build a couple of islands for you."

"Sounds good," Buck said, before being escorted away for showers and DDT delousing.

The Venice contouring provided Buck and Sam each a place of their own under canvas. However, a rainstorm during the weekend brought the water level to the brink of their sleeping platforms. A forecast of more rain made an offer from John Howell a chance for rescue. Some of John's combine, previous to his escape combine with Walt, crowded up more to allow space for Walt, Sam, and Buck beside them on their barracks floor.

MONDAY, APRIL 23: Colonel Raymond, again the senior officer of the compound, held special briefings in various locations. He explained that with no more appells, no more German news, and no more routine secret reports of Allied news, he needed to personally give prisoners some critical information.

He informed them that the Nazis were setting up an Inner Redoubt in the mountains thirty-five miles to the south. Hitler was claiming that the defense in this Redoubt, coupled with his launching of secret weapons, would turn the war around. Allied armies were racing to stop them. General Patch's Seventh Army had taken Nuremberg and was moving south towards Moosburg. General Patton's Third Army was moving south along Patch's flank, and was now, as best known, about thirty-five miles north of Moosburg. The Seventh Army had crossed the Danube at Dillingen, about thirty-five miles west of Moosburg. The French First Army had reached the Swiss frontier. All three armies were trying to block Nazi routes into the Redoubt.

In every briefing, Raymond then said, "That's the broad picture. Now the critical news that demanded these special briefings: I have been notified that within forty-eight hours thirty-five thousand of us will be ordered to march to the Inner Redoubt. Hitler wants Allied air force POWs with him as a bargaining chip, with the threat to execute us if his Inner Redoubt is penetrated. The senior officers of this camp have decided to buy time by complying with these march orders. We are hoping that we will be liberated before we reach the Inner Redoubt. Meanwhile, be ready to march on short notice."

TUESDAY, APRIL 24: Major Reddick circulated through camp with the announcement that Britain and the United States had reached an agreement with Germany whereby no more POWs would be moved from camps about to be liberated. In exchange no more German POWs would be shipped out of the European continent.

FROM THE JOURNAL OF DEAN RAYMOND, WEDNESDAY, APRIL 25:
With the news yesterday that we will not be marched from
this camp, my destiny as a leader is freed from the stinking
battle to keep the prisoners alive to be liberated. Although
life here is plagued by abominable overcrowding, the
Luftwaffe is working to keep this hell-hole livable, and we
are getting enough food to survive. I will gladly endure the
days we need to wait to be liberated here.

This is an historic day. Today the conference began in
San Francisco to write a United Nations charter. We who
fought this war were promised a United Nations world
peace and security force. Roosevelt started the process at
Dumbarton Oaks and advanced it at Yalta last February.
Then we lost him and got Harry Truman instead. Harry
Truman lacks the world vision to continue what Roosevelt
started. Harry announced that he would not attend the San
Francisco conference to form the United Nations. His
announcement reveals his indifference to what soldiers
were promised. In his myopic vision, he sees our military
muscle rather than a United Nations police force to keep
world peace. So we are back to where we were before World
War I with more wars ahead to fight, but not for me. I ask
myself, where do I go from here?

MOOSBURG PRISON CAMP, SUNDAY, APRIL 29: The prevailing
mood at eleven in the morning was dreariness. Dark clouds
threatening rain lent a menacing air to the day. Kriegies visited and exchanged questions about possible liberation soon but
whether it would rain or not was a more immediate question.

Conversation for the past months had most often centered on food, what it would be, when it would be eaten, who
would prepare it, and how it would be put together to best
quench hunger. The most exciting future was the next meal.
Conversation about liberation possibilities competed with
disadvantage at 11:00 A.M. with talk about the rain possibility and the noon meal experience only an hour away.

After rescue from the slough, Sam, Buck, Walt, and John
had joined their food into one combine and were taking

turns in preparing meals. Sam's specialty was a pudding made of black bread, raisins or prunes, a little margarine, and a little sugar, topped before serving with a cream made of powdered milk. On this Sunday morning, the combine was looking forward to Sam's bread pudding as the noon-time prize.

In the quiet of the past five nights, artillery fire in the northwest could be heard occasionally. Once in a while during the day an ME-109 or an FW-190 German fighter would be sighted flying at tree-top level to escape being discovered by the higher flying American fighters that were becoming more numerous. In the previous three days, the artillery fire was close enough at times to be heard during daytime. Whatever kriegies may have speculated privately from these events, they did not voice conclusions about the front.

In the reassignment of guards at Moosburg, Krauss had become a circulating Watch making unannounced visits to barracks, tents, and gatherings of kriegies outdoors. At 11:00 of this morning, Buck saw him walking alone and joined him to visit about their baby carriage journey and any news he might have.

Krauss told him, "All the guards are worrying about what the SS will expect of us if the battle comes here. You know that the Waffen SS is defending this territory I presume. Our Luftwaffe orders are to defend the prison camp, no more, but what will the SS order when they take command here?"

"Good luck, Krauss. If you wind up a prisoner, I'll check in on you, if I can. I'll see that you're okay and you're getting enough to eat."

"Ja. See me, but not to give extra food. It would look bad to the other Germans."

"Krauss, you used to brag about how efficient the Germans are. Look here," Buck said as he took out his wallet. He pulled out a flap that contained two pictures of himself in old clothes. "I've carried these secret escape pictures to make a false passport since I was shot down over a year ago. It's only a dime store secret flap. Your Intelligence went through this billfold more than once, but they never found the pictures to this day. How about that?"

"Put your pictures away," Krauss said. "I need not hear of such things."

Just then two U.S. fighters—P-51s—appeared with a high-pitched whining roar, flying not more than fifty feet above the ground. As they came over, Krauss ran for cover.

The two fighters circled back. Two more P-51s joined them. The four swept over camp with their whining roar rattling windows as they flew so low they barely cleared the guard towers. Kriegies poured from the barracks and tents in excitement and curiosity. They stood outside and watched as the fighters made another sweep over the camp.

Buck said, "They're giving us quite a show, but they're going to get themselves machine-gunned if they do it again."

One of the fighters went into a wide circle that brought him back again. As he came across the camp he laid his craft into a beautiful slow roll barely high enough above the ground to clear the buildings. Meanwhile, three fighters headed for the forest beyond the camp at tree-top level. Machine gun fire carried from the forest where the three planes were flying.

"Didn't I say so," Buck scolded. "They're playing around here too long. They're going to get shot down if they keep fooling around."

Light cannon fire rolled in from the tree tops. Two black shellfire puffs rose from the forest. The fighters vanished over the horizon of a hilltop. The sky was again empty.

But the machine gun fire and light cannon thuds continued.

"Isn't it like the krauts to keep shooting after the excitement is over?" Walt commented.

The machine gun noise did not diminish. Cannon fire thudded again, this time louder and nearer. Discordant crack of rifle fire nearby in the forest added to the cannon fire noise.

Kriegies outside waiting for the return of the fighters exchanged puzzled looks.

Someone said, "Get a load of that guard. He jumped into a hole. Then he came out. Then he went back in again. Now he's back up by the barbed wire again."

Eyes turned toward this guard now walking his beat along the outside of the barbed wire. Then the guard again ran back to the hole and jumped in. He tucked himself completely under ground.

"He's acting mighty strange," Buck commented. "It's clear he's afraid of catching a bullet. Whatever's going on, we're liable to pick up a bullet ourselves, standing out here. I'm going inside and lie on the floor until this quiets down."

Other kriegies started back into the tents and barracks, emptying the outside area. They did not hurry, but with deliberate direction they moved back into shelter. Whatever thoughts they harbored, they voiced no deductions about the strange fighter maneuvers, the puzzling gunfire, and the peculiar behavior of the guard.

After a while, from his prone position on the floor, Sam asked, generally, of kriegies near enough to hear, all now lying down, "Do you suppose we could be wrong?"

"If we're not convinced, the Krauts sure are. Something is going on," John said.

"You better believe it," Buck agreed.

All the firing stopped. Kriegies looked out the windows and saw that the guard they had watched was out of the hole again, standing by the fence, staying close to the hole. Another volley of machine gun fire opened, and he jumped back into the hole. The firing stopped, and he came back out, but he stood next to the hole, ready to jump back in. He unslung his rifle and held it ready to move into firing position. Or was he getting ready to throw it away?

The firing started again, this time rifle fire, cannon thuds, and machine gun fire mixed together. The guard jumped back into the hole.

"There are a lot of bullets flying around for you guys to be standing by the windows if you don't want to get hit," someone called out.

Kriegies took the advice and went back to their lying positions.

The gunfire persisted. After a while Sam said, "I have to take a piss," and he got up and went to the doorway. He saw that it had started to rain big drops that had already formed puddles. He thought of the distant cannon as the pounding of boots in loose overshoes. Or was it wet base drums? He felt that he had lived this scene before. There was a parade. Where were the bands today? Where were the laughing, splashing children? *We who watch from under canvas. . . .*

The surface of the rain puddles danced as they were struck by rain drops. Or was it bullets? How safe was it to cross the distance to the latrine? Raindrops or gunfire lead? He could not be sure what pellets were dancing before him. Yet he struck out for the latrine.

Wet, but safely arrived, he took a place by the brick wall urinal and allowed his urine to run warm from him. He fixed his eyes on the yellow stream fountaining against the red brickwork and directed the urine up and down into a V for victory sign.

This is a good place to stay until the shooting stops. Here I at least have the protection of the brick urinal on one side.

After a half hour of no change in the firing or raining, Walt came running in.

"What happened to you? It's past time for our noon meal," he said.

"I'm staying here by the brick piss wall for better protection until the shooting dies down," Sam replied.

"It's your turn to cook."

"Let's wait to eat," Sam suggested. "If we get liberated, we can bash."

"You were supposed to be making bread pudding!"

"Let's wait," Sam suggested again.

"This is ridiculous. If you won't do it, I'll make the noon meal myself," Walt declared. And he ran back through the rain and gunfire.

About half past twelve the gunfire diminished. The rain, too, all but ceased. Finally, all was quiet.

Sam left the latrine and walked to where he could see beyond the barbed wire. Other prisoners joined him. The guard got out of the hole, shouldered his rifle, and began to walk his post.

"Ist Stalag Moosburg gefallen?" a kriegie yelled across the barbed wire.

"Ja," the guard yelled back.

"How would he know if we've been freed?" another kriegie commented. "He's probably as confused as we are."

Another guard appeared at the south, along the outside of the barbed wire. He walked to the guard by the hole. The two talked. Then they turned in the direction the guard had come from and walked back along the outside of the barbed wire together. For a moment Sam guessed that the messenger guard was Smitty, but he looked closer and decided that this guard was too tall to be Smitty.

Shouts sounded from an area that afforded a view of the Moosburg city hall over a half mile away. Sam hurried over to the commotion.

"What's up?"

"It looks like they're taking down the Nazi flag."

Sam strained his eyes to make out what was happening above the city hall far away.

"There goes Old Glory. There she goes. Old Glory herself is going up!" someone yelled.

Sam could tell that a flag was being raised on the flag pole above the building, but it was too far away for him to make out what flag was being raised.

A few kriegies shouted. A few hooted. But Sam was not convinced that the American flag had been raised.

It started to rain again. The kriegies watching the flag drama scampered for shelter.

"Look!" someone yelled from a barracks doorway as he pointed toward the gate.

A giant gray Sherman tank slowly crawled through the open gate. The tank slowly moved toward the center of the compound.

Kriegies broke into the rainstorm from all directions. They swarmed to the tank and over the tank in gleeful splashing wonderment.

The tank stopped. A lid on top clanked open. A rain tarp appeared, and under the lifting canvas a blinking boy.

"Hi," he smiled.

"Hi," came back from all directions.

"Where you from?"

"California. Redwood, California. I'm Sam Hix."

The rain poured down, but the liberated prisoners did not care.

"How long have you been on the road?"

"How soon will we get out of here?"

There was no end to the questions.

After a while Sam Hix from Redwood lowered the tarp and disappeared back into the tank. The lid clanked shut, and the tank moved back through the gate. The gate was closed behind it. Each minute now was empty as the kriegies waited for freedom to change their lives in some specific way.

FREEDOM: CHAPTER FIVE

The unmatchable rumbling, clanking, and roaring of Patton's armored cavalry was already reverberating from the road as Sam Hix backed his tank into the traffic to carry out his next orders. General Patton's Third Army was pushing toward the heart of the Inner Redoubt—Hitler's Berchtesgaden. At Moosburg the challenge was to cross the German defense line of the Isar River.

On Patton's west flank, General Patch's Seventh Army was also heading for the Inner Redoubt and had already reached Munich, thirty miles further south. Patton was under pressure, determined to catch up with Patch and beat him in the race to Hitler's ultimate mountain defense Redoubt.

Patton's tanks armed with seventy-six-mm cannon were moved to battle stations for the Isar crossing. Interspersed between the tanks were half tracks—vehicles with the front wheels of a truck and tracks of a tank in the rear, each carrying an infantry squad or mortar crew. Two infantry platoons, being carried to the battle sight in half-tracks, had been cross-pollinated with a tank company to form a tank-infantry team to protect the tanks as they moved through the wooded area.

Jeeps, many jeeps, the smallest vehicles of the mobile force, were also in the traffic. They carried commanders and staff officers. Some had the MP markings of Military Police who directed traffic. Others were scout, messenger, and medical evacuation vehicles. The battalion and company commanders, who might soon move to the greater security of their tanks and armored personnel carriers, were still riding in jeeps.

Two-and-a-half-ton trucks, called deuce-and-a-halfs, most with canvas covering their cargo boxes, carried large boxes of ammunition and rectangular five-gallon cans of gasoline toward the expected action. Less often a deuce-and-a-half mess truck went by, carrying under its canvas B-ration capability with three aluminum cabinet field ranges—each with a gas burner that could be put inside to make an oven or put on top to make a griddle. Other deuce-and-a-halfs carried further chow possibilities—five-in-one rations used often by tank crews for a meal shared by five personnel—C-rations, for a quick individual meal—K-rations, a life-sustaining hunger cruncher with crackers—and D-rations, the chocolate bar so precious in the prisoner of war world.

And there were lighter trucks, three-quarter-ton weapons carriers, moving forward to be used, predictably, for carrying weapons, but also as telephone wire trucks and as general purpose kind of vehicles.

Some twenty Sherman tanks were parked on the far side of the road along with a one thousand-gallon tanker, refueling the tanks in the way preferred over refueling with five-gallon cans. Some of the waiting crews were chowing-down with five-in-one rations. Other crews waiting were doing maintenance—checking track tension—opening engine compartments and checking all the fluid levels—engine oil—transmission fluid—hydraulic systems of the cannon—on and on.

More deuce-and-a-halfs passed. They were the combat train crammed with the five-gallon gasoline cans for fuel resupply. Armored field artillery units followed with their deuce-and-a-half supply trucks.

Still arriving were heavy vehicles with the distinctive configurations of bridging equipment. If the good fortune of an opportunity crossing was realized—a crossing with minimal resistance on a bridge still existing when the tanks arrived—some of the units arriving would not be needed. But Patton's Third Army was advancing with capability to defeat whatever defense might be encountered.

The mortar units were deploying for short range smoke and high explosive firing across the river, and the artillery units were preparing to deploy further to the rear as allowed by their longer range capability.

Being caught in the middle of this complex battle activity, a stark realization came to those prisoners who were not too overwhelmed to register factual reality: their liberation had not been a rescue mission to free them, but a happenstance of battle action moving past them.

While the army moved by, within the Moosburg prison camp a detail of Patton's soldiers gathered the captured Luftwaffe officers and guards and confined them to the tents in the slough. The former kriegies of the slough were assigned to the Luftwaffe camp headquarters building. The rest of the kriegies were ordered to stay where they were.

The slough tent area was surrounded with rolls of barbed wire barricade, and troops were dispatched to police German prisoner construction of a slit trench latrine in the slough area. Military Police were posted to isolate the compound of German kriegies, thus allowing Patton's combat forces to quickly return to the battle to cross the Isar River.

A departing soldier said, "Blood and Guts Patton can't win battles with us playing caretakers to liberated POWs and captured Germans."

By late afternoon Patton's heavy artillery started preparatory fire over the prison camp to reach the enemy on the other side of the Isar. Colonel Raymond was told that the purpose of this fire was to prevent enemy movement of reserves, to inflict casualties, to damage equipment, and to degrade enemy combat effectiveness.

At this time two small, two-passenger Piper-Cub-type aircraft—L-5s—appeared flying close to the ground. Former air-war kriegies recognized this flying as artillery air-observation for adjusting the artillery fire into its targets. Veterans of high altitude flying commented that the flying of expendable aircraft in the frontal area was not duty they would choose.

The enemy soon began an answering artillery fire that crossed over the POW camp on its way to the American artillery. Seasoned war correspondents, seemingly indifferent to the artillery fire, entered the "no man's land" of the prison camp between friendly and enemy artillery fire. They interviewed RAMPs under the shellfire. RAMPs, the acronym for Repatriated Allied Military Personnel, was the new name for kriegies. Occasionally the correspondents identified the sounds of the shellfire to the RAMPs—woob-shoo—"that one's going out"—shoo-woob—"that one's coming in."

The artillery duel arcing over the camp continued through Sunday, Sunday night, Monday, and Monday night. On Tuesday morning May 1, after a bridgehead was gained across the Isar, the whining of shells and the thunder of artillery vibrating the camp buildings suddenly stopped. The RAMPs streamed into the silent glory of a warm, clear day.

Colonel Raymond's first intention of the morning was to call on the prisoner of war Eiler, now that their roles of prisoner and jailer were reversed. At the gate to the slough enclosure, he found a helmeted Military Police corporal standing guard. Buck Pierce and Sam O'Brien were also standing by the gate. The three exchanged "hellos" then Sam said, "I wanted to go in to see how Smitty made out in the liberation battle, but he won't let us in."

Colonel Raymond addressed the guard: "I'm the Senior Officer of this compound. I'm going in. They can come in with me."

"No RAMP is going in. Rank doesn't count with my MP orders. If there's somebody you want to knock the piss out of, take your complaint to the War Crimes Office."

Buck moved closer to the guard and said in a low voice, "Look, like I told you, I'll wait here. I'm asking for my bombardier and for the Colonel, too, now that he's here. I know you're the police with the orders, and what we want doesn't count. I'm just asking you as a favor, man-to-man. Forget your orders. These guys have got no way to hurt anybody. Let them in. I'll wait with you and you can arrest me if there's a problem. Hey—after what these guys have suffered under these goons,been through with these goons, if they want in, they've earned the right."

The guard went to Dean and Sam and checked each carefully to be sure neither was carrying a weapon. Then he said, "I'm not so perfect that I can see everything. You've got five minutes."

Dean and Sam hurried into the German Compound. Buck called to Sam, "Look up Krauss for me."

Dean began to walk the German Compound perimeter in his search for Hauptmann Eiler. Sam went in to the Venice of water aisles and island sleeping-berths that were familiar to him. On one island he spotted Krauss.

"I see you lived through the battle," Sam said. "Buck asked me to keep his promise to check on you."

Krauss got up hastily and saluted with the old Luftwaffe salute, not the Nazi thrust.

"Cut the saluting, Krauss," Sam said as he waved down Krauss's attempt at military courtesy. "I see we're both growing beards now. But we're still the same people we were two days ago. How are you?"

"I like the Red Cross. We get the same food as your soldiers. Mostly 5-in-1 rations, but we got no kriegie burners. No way to make coffee, but we eat good."

"There are lots of kriegie burners in the barracks. When we leave you can have ours. Are you getting enough water? Outside there are five hundred of us to one water spigot."

"The MPs bring us cans of water, but no way to shave. Is okay though. No complaint. I wait to go home."

"Where is Smitty—Gemeiner Robert Schmidt?"

"It's not good news to tell you. The SS fought us. Hauptmann Eiler told us, 'If the camp surrenders we all surrender. Our duty ends here.' But the SS said 'you must go with us, fight with us now.' Many of us fought to get away. Some didn't make it away. Oberleutnant Kruger . . . he missing. I think he go with them. Gemeiner Schmidt—I see SS kill him."

"You know that for sure?"

"I was there. I got away. He is for sure dead. I tried to help him, but he was dead."

"God! What a hell of a thing! After lasting through the whole war." Sam paused to register this shocking news. Then he continued, "I'll tell his wife . . . I have to go now. I hope you get home soon. The war can't last much longer."

"Thank Buck for telling you to come check on me. Americans good. Tell him all is okay. I wish you all home soon."

On the way out of the tent Sam again got the old Luftwaffe salute. This time from Gemeiner Schumann standing in water in his haste to get up from his island berth. Sam remembered how it felt to stand in the water, and deeper in his memory he remembered Schumann singing for them in the horrible winter night in which he was their guard in a cold and putrid boxcar. Sam fumbled, hoping his English would be understood, "Good see you alive, Schumann. No, no salutes. Hope you home soon. Sing Mass in church, home. Like in boxcar." Then he continued toward the tent entrance, jumping from island to island in the manner he had learned when he was living here.

Outside, Raymond had discovered Eiler standing by the rolled barbed wire enclosure and looking out to the larger prison compound. "Hauptmann Eiler," Raymond called.

The Hauptmann raised the old Luftwaffe salute that was forbidden by Hitler and Raymond returned it.

Eiler said, "So you are still here. Our worlds are upside down. The change is too sudden for me. I live and sleep with my soldiers. You treat us all as one rank. I have no way to keep clean and shave, but I am not hungry as you were so many days."

Raymond smiled, "You will learn from the difference of being a prisoner. I did—more than from my military education."

"I am now the Senior Officer like you were. Already I have a protest to the Red Cross."

"I would frame a protest myself, but I am no longer protected by the Red Cross. I don't have much time. I came to learn if you survived the battle. I got the report that the SS killed some of you."

"I survived, but for what good I do not know."

"I also have a question I can't forget. You have never told me how your family fared."

"I have no family. They all died horribly in the raid you flyers escaped by a few hours."

"Since our air force did the killing, it would not be appropriate to say I'm sorry," Dean said. He looked at Eiler and then continued, "At the same time, I don't want to hear you try to excuse Hitler's horrors by saying you're sorry."

"We are past apologies," Eiler said with his eyes squared back at Raymond.

"Where does that leave us?" Raymond asked.

"Each alone. Hopefully wiser," Eiler replied.

"My prisoner of war time made me wiser. I hope it will do the same for you."

"Perhaps I am already wiser than you. Your side won the war. My side lost. There is more to learn from losing. Beware, Colonel, of the leader who appeals to your patriotism. Have you learned that?"

"I will think about that."

Eiler continued, "What the Nazis got us to do was monstrous brutal, but you, too, were monstrous brutal. Hitler killed Jewish people with gas; your leaders killed German people with bombs. Guilt has no boundaries."

"Eiler, I was against what you condemn me for."

"Can you believe the same of me?"

"I don't know."

"There must be a defect in human brains to let our leaders take such power over us as they do," Eiler said.

Dean answered, "If you knew me better you would realize that my life reaches further than my country's victory. I, too, have learned from losing in this war."

Dean started to leave, then he hesitated and said to Eiler as parting words, "May you get to a better place."

Returning to the exit gate, Dean and Sam left the German POW Compound together, with the guard pretending not to notice them as he visited with Buck.

On this morning, with Patton's army across the river, the first RAMP processing personnel entered camp. These were three representatives of the Judge Advocate General's office. They set up an office in what had been the Red Cross Parcel distribution center. On the front of the building they hung a large sign that read, REPORT YOUR WAR CRIMES HERE.

Allied Command Headquarters had sent an order that put the English Senior Officer RAMP in charge of the camp. There were fewer English than American RAMPS but there was no explanation of why the English had been put in charge. Another order from Headquarters stated that no RAMPs were to be allowed contact with the outside world until after they had been released to their homes for "rehabilitation" for sixty days—presumably to re-civilize them.

In the afternoon, orders came that put Colonel Raymond in charge of a Repatriation Center to screen people turning themselves in to the Moosburg camp to gain RAMP status.

A Gasthaus—inn—across the road from the prison camp had been commandeered and scheduled to receive army supplies for this purpose.

Raymond had mixed feelings about the special orders. He did not want an assignment that might delay his evacuation. On the other hand, this gave him the chance to escape the barbed wire that was still hemming in the thousands of liberated prisoners. He immediately established himself in the gasthaus in a luxurious suite with a bed and white sheets and a bath with hot water. For his interpreter and mess officer, he remembered Walter Plank and arranged for his transfer to his staff. Walt, too, immediately moved into the gasthaus.

Since the front was now between Moosburg and Switzerland, the "white angels" could no longer get through with Red Cross Parcels. There was no reserve supply of Parcels, so RAMPs waiting for evacuation had to survive on what Red Cross food they had at the time of their liberation. Those who had bashed when liberated were back to a near-starvation diet.

General Patton had scheduled rations to supply his advance to the Inner Redoubt, not to feed prisoners he liberated. Appreciating the critical function of supply in determining the speed of his advance, he ordered his troops not to give food to RAMPS. Honoring the food needs of one hundred thousand liberated prisoners was not his mission.

The only hope for getting food was to beg from troops who could be contacted and might defy orders. If and when contact was made, many combat soldiers responded to the liberated prisoners' needs as best they could, in spite of their military orders.

The English Senior Officer had put English RAMPs in the guard towers to prevent escape—-now called violation of orders. Although there was no great fear that the English would shoot to kill, the prevailing attitude on this Tuesday was that the best way to get home soon was to follow orders. The compliant attitude was bolstered by the promise that evacuation would begin within twenty-four hours. Also, respect for the barbed wire walls had been established so firmly through captivity that it still persisted. For whatever reason, very few RAMPs tried to escape.

On this day, May 1, the first information on evacuation was released. RAMPs learned that the Air Transport Command was scheduled to fly in to an airfield near Moosburg and fly RAMPs out to staging areas in France. From there American RAMPs would be shipped by train to a base in France where they would await ocean transport to the U.S. But there was a problem—it was impossible at this time to get transport aircraft for this job. It would be several more days, possibly even a week or two, before transport aircraft could arrive.

In the afternoon, the post-battle quiet was suddenly broken. RAMPs rushing to the source of commotion discovered three petite girls in Red Cross uniforms. Each of the girls carried a basket containing oranges and donuts. Somehow the girls accomplished a retreat from the mob that closed upon them. Being in this camp of starving thousands with only three baskets of luxuries was a demonstration of how out of touch the outside world was with the kriegie (RAMP) reality.

Later in the afternoon, RAMPs shuffled past the REPORT YOUR WAR CRIMES HERE sign to study a caravan of vehicles that stood before the gate. The gate was opened, and soldiers got out of the vehicles, formed into a column of fours, and began to march into the compound. As the marchers got closer, the watching RAMPs discovered that the column was headed by a general with four stars on his shoulders and a pearl handled pistol swinging from his hip.

"It's 'Old Blood and Guts' Patton!" a RAMP announced awe struck.

The marchers stopped in the center of the compound. General Patton, accompanied by a one-star general and an eagle colonel, went into a prison barracks. In a short while he returned and stood on the landing, flanked by the one star general and the eagle colonel.

"At ease," the Colonel ordered to quiet the hum of voices sounding from the thousands that had gathered.

The compound surrounding the four-star General became as quiet as a Texas plain.

General Patton stood erect and silent, very much in command of the quiet. Then he said, "Gentlemen, after what I have seen, I want to compliment you on maintaining yourselves as soldiers should."

Next day, Wednesday, May 2, while Sam and Buck were standing in line to get to a water faucet, they talked about General Patton's visit. Buck commented, "Coming in here to H.D. kriegies and giving us bullshit compliments after he's ordered his troops not to feed us is showing more gall than guts to me."

"He freed us. Remember that. He's the hero," Sam replied.

"Hix in his Sherman tank is the hero for me," Buck said. "Patton makes a big show with his pearl-handled pistol, but he's riding back where it's safe when the shells are flying. It's like with us taking the flak and fighters while the generals wrote our orders from safe headquarters on the ground. His speech praising us while he's giving us the shaft is the last straw. We've got to get out of here, Sam. The krauts at least emptied the toilets."

"I've got to get to Pellheim to see Smitty's wife," Sam reminded.

"If we were out on a German farm, we could get stuff to eat and a way to clean up," Buck calculated. "With zero food coming in, we're getting in worse shape every day here. What made Walt so lucky? I wonder if he had bacon and eggs for breakfast this morning?"

"We should have asked Raymond to get us out of here when we had the chance yesterday."

"You're right, Sam."

"I'll write a message to the English," Sam said. "I'll write that we've got to see our American senior officer about somebody getting killed—I won't say it was Smitty."

Buck conjectured, "If we could get out, we could have the krauts cooking us good meals. With American troops here, I'll bet they're so scared we could get anything we want."

"We could hitchhike the thirty miles to Pellheim," Sam said. "But we'd have to check with Walt to be sure we don't miss getting flown out."

"Yeah. We've got to see Pa Raymond," Buck said.

Next morning, Thursday, May 3, Sam's message won a pass and an English RAMP escort to visit Colonel Raymond at the Repatriation Center. Approaching the gasthaus, Sam and Buck saw an especially attractive, blue-eyed girl standing near the entrance. As he passed her, Buck said playfully in his limited German vocabulary, "Ich liebe dich."

At the landing, the girl took the steps down to the cellar of the gasthaus while Buck, Sam, and the English escort started up the steps to the lounge. Buck observed the sway of her blonde hair on her sky blue dress and watched the grace of her hips shifting as she stepped down the stairway.

"Did you get a look of her, Sam? Wow!" Buck exclaimed.

"Sure did. She's beautiful. Her eyes are the color of blue sky on chrome steel. I wonder what she's doing here?"

"She looked like she'd been crying," Buck observed.

They entered a dining hall with some twenty places set on white tablecloths of four tables. Walt entered from the kitchen.

"You're in charge of all this?" Sam asked.

"Right. The good thing is that we're on troop rations. We get plenty of great food. How did you guys get out of camp?"

"We got a pass to see the Colonel," Sam explained.

"How about something to eat?" Buck asked.

"Sit down. Want some fresh white bread and ham and lima beans?"

"White bread?"

"Yeah. GI issue."

"Serve us a double order," Sam said.

"Include me," the English escort requested.

While they ate, Buck commented, "Looks like with food you get your pick of girls. We saw a blonde beauty on our way in."

"Her? She was the Freudenmadchen—the whore—of an SS general we took prisoner. They picked them young. The army kicked all the Germans out of their rooms, but they let her move down to the coal room, 'cause an American raped her when we took over and the officer in charge was shook up about it. Why do you want to see Raymond?"

"The SS killed Smitty, and, like I promised, I want to go see his wife and tell her about him," Sam said.

Walt put a hand to his head in astonishment. "After getting through the whole war? He was an okay kraut, had more spunk than most of them. I guess the SS took care of that."

"You're really feeling good, making fun of him being killed," Sam directed at Walt.

"We're free! The RAMPs in camp don't seem to realize it. We've been kriegies so long they can't believe it's over," Walt responded.

Buck scowled in reaction to Walt's words, "Is it over for the kriegies still behind the barbed wire and not getting food?" he asked. "Never mind. Thanks for the meal, Walt. Just take us to Pa Raymond."

"Before we go, since you're not getting food in camp, I want to give you my six days of Iron Rations I never used."

"Later," Sam said. "After we see Raymond. We're looking for a way to get out of camp. If we need to go back we'll sure take your Iron Rations."

Walt led the way to where Raymond had established his headquarters in the office of the president of an electrical insulator firm across the courtyard from the gasthaus. As Sam and Buck approached the Colonel's walnut desk he rose to shake hands and offer chairs.

"You can leave," Raymond told the English escort. "I'll see that they get back to camp."

The escort and Walt left, and Sam and Buck sat down.

"What's this crap about the English treating us like we're their prisoners?" Buck asked.

Raymond explained, "They didn't ask for the job. Headquarters is afraid RAMPs would go on a depraved orgy if they weren't kept under control until they're evacuated. Somebody upstairs decided the English would do a better job than Americans in keeping the lid on. Don't blame me. The Russians have been raping, murdering, and plundering here since they were freed, so Headquarters decided RAMPs should be kept in camp."

"I don't want to get sidetracked," Sam said, looking at Buck. "I want to tell you, Colonel, why we're here." He then explained the situation of Smitty's death and the promise to visit his wife who lived near Dachau.

Buck added, "I figure since Sam's half Jew, if he wants to do this for a German it's not for us to stand in his way. I want to back him by going along."

"The orders of restriction are emphatic," Colonel Raymond said. "No RAMPs are to be permitted to roam free in Germany. The Command Headquarters position is that you need time at home before they can release you degraded victims into open society."

"Since when aren't you one of us?" Buck asked.

"I didn't write my orders," Raymond said. "Obviously, Headquarters is trusting me to be civilized in releasing me for special duty."

"Because of your rank? Is the thinking that the higher the rank the better the person? Give this small fry captain and lieutenant some trust, too, Colonel. We were all one rank to the flak, bayonets, and the bombs. What's different now? We've got to get out of this stink-hole prison camp."

Sam added, "When it comes to orders from higher up, don't forget what would have happened if the kraut guards last winter would have followed their orders to shoot us."

"I didn't say I was going to follow orders without thinking," Dean said. "I haven't forgotten that our kriegie world got more humane as orders got ignored. Where, specifically, does Smitty's wife live, Sam?"

"In Pellheim, near Dachau."

"Dachau? A congressional committee is on its way to inspect Dachau. It's one of the worst—the news calls it an extermination camp. It was liberated the day we were. I'm to get a briefing on it and an emergency issue of a new uniform today to meet the committee there."

"If you're going there, could we ride that far with you?" Sam asked. "We could get the rest of the way on our own."

"It's not that simple. I'll have to get you assigned to the Repatriation Center first. I'll list you as procurement officers."

"I don't know what that is, but I'm sure we could handle it," Buck assured. "We've got to get out of that goddamn prison. It's getting worse every day. We were liberated Sunday and this is Thursday. You've got to go in there and see for yourself, Colonel."

"I'm going to do that. Now let me get on with what I'm going to do for you. Walt will have to see you back to camp to keep peace with the English. I'll get the transfer orders drawn up and have them delivered to you. You should be able to get a bath and a bed with white sheets by tomorrow. I'm going to Dachau on Saturday. I'll get a vehicle big enough to take you with me that far. We'll work out how to get you the rest of the way and back here."

"I really appreciate this," Sam said.

"I'm sticking my neck out," Dean said. "Be honest. Don't you agree that if all the RAMPs were freed with no police some of them would indulge in depraved celebration similar to the Russians?"

"I don't know," Sam said. "I think you can't judge Americans by the Russians."

Buck elaborated, "If you let the kriegies go free in this town, I'd expect all kinds of things good and bad to happen to the Germans. But the worst that they could do wouldn't match Hitler's record. Was there ever a leader the world locked up because he couldn't be trusted? Why pick on us small fry kriegies and keep us locked up?"

Dean smiled as he stared at Buck and tapped a pencil on his desk impatiently. "Still holding out for everyone running free, aren't you? It would have been easier for me as your senior officer to just let freedom ring—not pressure anyone into discipline and training for survival, just let everyone reign for himself for better or worse. Are you saying I would have saved more lives as your leader that way, Buck?"

Buck squirmed in his chair, shifted his body, and cleared his throat. "If you put it that way, I don't know. Some guys ain't got much pressure on their own. You were tough to put up with, but as tough on yourself, too. You helped me keep pigheaded enough to keep singing Hubba hubba. On the winter march, when we were both goners, we kept each other stepping one more step. You set the tone for that."

"I've got to say you set the tone for me, too, Buck. You were my rebel challenger."

Buck argued, "If you put it all together, it was a lot of things bigger than you or me that made the difference in our surviving, but you did set the bull-headed tone."

Sam said, "Who set the tone for helping other people? We lost two of our combine because they went too far in putting other people first."

With a hand wave, Buck rejected the attempt to broaden the conversation. "That's another matter, Sam. I'm not saying I'm not pissed off at the way the high-rankers put themselves above us, but the Colonel and I have had it out on that. I gotta say you were thinking of us above yourself, mostly. Which makes me ask, who's looking out for us now? I'm mad as hell about the way we kriegies are still locked up in that stink-hole camp after we're supposed to be freed."

"None of you are in chains, Buck. If it's such a hell in there, why are you staying?"

"If you're really asking me, Raymond, the whip that's holding us in there is we're scared as hell that if we escape we'll miss getting flown out."

"I can see that," Dean conceded. "You're still locked up because some people use freedom to run amok. A man deserves only as much freedom as he can handle civilized. I'm going to give you your chance to behave civilized."

Sam said, "I'd think you two would have had enough of fighting each other."

"We're not fighting each other," Buck corrected. "We're fighting something bigger than either of us."

"A lot of years separate us, Buck. You're of the generation of my lost son. Maybe that's what's confusing you, Sam. Buck's just discovering the world I'm too familiar with. We're both rebels, but in different worlds and in different ways. We're the same in that we're both among the few who are goddamn mad about what we find wrong in the world."

Buck added, "To me, we're sort of enemies—but we're sort of friends, too."

To redirect the conversation Sam asked, "As procurement officers, what are we going to be procuring?"

"We'll go into that, but not now," Dean said. "There is another matter I've been waiting to bring up. It is strange you came today. I'd sent a messenger to get you, Buck. My nurse friend, Captain Scott, sent a telegram through military channels that is also addressed to you. It reads, 'Colonel Raymond and Captain Pierce'—then the routing address—then, 'Learned Luft III West Compound Moosburg liberated. Are you safe? Reach me Third Division HQ. Going home. Waiting Cloud Peak all the way Buck. Captain Scott.'—That's it. I presume the words at the end got jumbled in transmission."

Buck was amazed. "How can I answer? I've got no authority to use military channels."

"I'll answer for us."

"For me sign—say, 'H. D. Buck to Randi. Yours from timberline up.'"

"More jumble, Buck? I'll sign for you as you want. My other thoughts I'll keep to myself."

Sam broke in with, "When should we be back here for the trip to Dachau?"

"We'll work that out after you're transferred."

"I appreciate what you're doing for us," Buck said.

Dean raised an arm in a waving gesture as they departed. Walt escorted them back to the prison camp gate where they signed in to keep their name on the evacuation list.

Once in camp, Buck sat down to ponder Randi's telegram. He recalled her telling of climbing Cloud Peak as a powerful spiritual experience. He got out her letter written to him in Sagan and ending . . . *When I get home, I will look you up. I want to climb Cloud Peak with you all the way.* After her telegram today, he was sure *all the way* meant more than mountain climbing. His heart pumped faster as it struck him that he might soon be seeing her.

Sam, meanwhile, was thinking about the big mistake he had made in not using the toilet when he was in the gasthaus. He walked to the latrine and stood in line for his turn to enter. When he got inside he found pools of urine and pasty puddles of feces covering the floor. He walked to another latrine. It, too, was running over. Countless flies invaded the stench. He walked on, only to find that all the toilets of the compound were overflowing. In distress, he squatted on a latrine floor and defecated. Then, after wiping his shoes on the dirt, he went back to their barracks and joined Buck where they would see Walt if he came. While they waited, one of the uniformed members of the war crimes team came by and posted a list of RAMPs ordered to meet at the Red Cross warehouse at 3:00 P.M.

"What's the meeting about?" Sam asked.

"The list is the shipment battalion you're assigned to. We drew lots and yours is the first group out once the airplanes get here. We have to meet with everyone before they fly out."

"We can't leave here at three. We're waiting here for transfer orders," Buck protested.

"We have a check-off list. You have to come to the meeting to get released to leave."

Walt had not arrived by three, but Sam and Buck went to the meeting.

Unlike the other prison buildings, the meeting-site warehouse was an old, well-built structure. Cracks in the interior walls showed coal dust that told of former use. Now only a few bales of peat were on the dirt floor. The odor of the peat gave the place the musty smell of a bog.

RAMPs sat on the dirt floor and speculated as to what the meeting was about. Sam ventured, "I think it's to tell us when the planes are coming, how we're to board, and all that."

At exactly three o'clock someone in a khaki uniform climbed onto a platform that had been made of the peat bales. He was dressed like a member of the military, but he had no insignia to indicate his rank.

"Greetings, RAMPs," he began. "I am a representative of the Judge Advocate General. You have seen our booth outside with the sign—REPORT YOUR WAR CRIMES HERE. We arrived as soon as the liberation battle ended. We have seen the inhuman conditions of captivity you endured. We are here to gather evidence on what you have suffered in violation of the Geneva Accords on the treatment of prisoners of war.

"We need your help to prosecute German war criminals. It is not only your privilege, it is your duty to help us find and punish the guilty."

"We never had it so good," a voice from behind Sam and Buck shouted up to the stage.

"Hubba hubba," another voice called out.

Some kriegies clapped, some laughed.

Above the din some yelled, "Give us something to eat!"

Another voice yelled, "Empty the toilets."

Other voices shouted, "Get us out of here."

The speaker's eyes were fire-bright in a face that jerked nervously as he waited for quiet to return. Finally he raised his arms to silence the crowd. Unable to bring his audience under control, he shouted, "RAMPs! Soldiers! We must bring the criminals to justice! Why won't you cooperate? We are only asking that you fill out a few forms."

"We never had it so good!" voices shouted again with an accompaniment of laughter and applause so loud that it carried from the building.

The audience began to leave. Sam and Buck moved out through a crowd of other kriegies waiting their turn to go into the warehouse.

"What's the big news in there?" someone waiting asked.

"You'll find out. The first thing they bring for us is not food but forms to fill out. It's not funny."

Sam and Buck went back to the barracks to learn if Walt had come by. No one had seen him. They went to the gate to check if he had signed in. He hadn't. They had started back to the barracks when Walt overtook them. "I got your orders. You can leave with me."

"Holy be! Hot diggidy dog!" they rejoiced.

They got their packs and followed Walt through the gate. At the gasthaus they were each assigned a room. Then they allowed Walt to serve them a banquet put together from five-and-one rations. Afterwards, they retired to the luxury of their private rooms, removed their ragged clothing, and took long, hot-water tub baths. Then they retired for the night.

Buck could not get comfortable on his soft mattress. His hips, callused from over a year of sleeping on hard surface, searched for support not available. Once he thought of moving to a blanket on the floor, but he decided to endure the bed rather than lose the feeling of lying between clean white sheets.

Sam had no problem with the softness of his bed. His difficulty was the private room—it felt like solitary confinement. The lack of noise, talking, snoring, and farting made him anxious. While his head told him he was free and in a wonderful room of his own, his feelings distrusted the quiet and had him listening intently for sounds. Occasional walking and talking in the hallway lulled him enough to allow his mind to meander through the past day.

The session with Colonel Raymond especially absorbed him. He had wanted to speak up but his thinking didn't fit in. He should have said . . . *I don't want to fill my brain with your kind of arguing. You have to get past people to find the good life. Nature and mysteries like the life of the albatross is more interesting. Rain falling from a stormy sky, sunrise sneaking over the mountains, sailboats going to sea, sea gulls flying a shoreline, ocean waves rolling in—those are things to talk about. God must be sad about the kind of arguing people do. Why don't people quit thinking about people and start enjoying the world worth fussing about? If I would have said that they would have told me I was around the bend.*

In the morning both Sam and Buck were still asleep when Walt knocked on their doors, "They've moved the

Colonel's trip up a day. We have to be ready to leave by eight. Get downstairs right away, and I'll serve you some ham and eggs before we go."

"Coming."

"Roger—Wilco."

It was a hasty breakfast, for the command car was already waiting. Colonel Raymond arrived in an immaculate new uniform complete with eagles on his shoulders and his command pilot wings and rows of ribbons on the left breast of his blouse. With neatly trimmed hair and a clean shave, the only indication that he was a newly liberated prisoner of war was his underweight condition and his limp.

The driver and Sam sat in the front seat. The Colonel sat in the back seat with Walt and Buck. As they started into the countryside, Raymond said, "A lot is happening. I expect an unconditional surrender any day. The Russians have taken Berlin . . . thanks to Eisenhower stopping the Allies so the Russians could have the honor of entering the capital first."

"If we got there first, why did we wait for the Russians to take the glory?" Walt asked.

"Politics, Walt. Read a lesson from it. Soldiers fight wars, but politicians run them."

For a while no one spoke, then Dean said, "This morning I got verification that Hitler committed suicide. He first named Admiral Doenitz to be the new Führer to continue the war. He had to bequeath his political leadership before he could kill himself—'The King is dead. Long live the King.'"

Looks of satisfaction were exchanged with this news.

"Why did he have to set things up for more people to get killed?" Buck asked. "The war must be a massacre by now."

"It is. Allied planes sunk or damaged sixty-four ships yesterday of a huge armada trying to get Germans to Scandinavia. In Italy the Germans surrendered unconditionally the day before yesterday. Since then Trieste was occupied by New Zealand and Yugoslav troops. Where German armies aren't surrendering they're getting massacred."

"Where is Trieste?" Sam asked.

"It doesn't matter," the Colonel said. "The point is, the war is over. All that remains is to get the new Führer to sign the papers."

"It matters to me," Sam said. Then he fell silent, taking the cue from Dean that his interest was in another dimension from the talk taking place. From the front seat, he ran his vision across the freshly plowed fields they were passing, and in his mind's eye he saw the refugee wagons of Gali's people on the road ahead on their way to southern France.

A giant, high voltage transmission line loomed into view. Under a great steel tower, a woman, lacking a horse, was urging a cow into the yoke of a plow to turn the ground for planting.

Buck said, "I think that cow wants a bucket under her with somebody milking. It's plain to see she's not understanding she supposed to be pulling the plow."

Raymond remarked, "That's a picture that tells where Hitler has taken Germany—from the age of electricity back ten thousand years to Egypt where a cow pulling a plow was the beginning of harnessed power."

"Maybe coming those ten thousand years since has been Ssergorp," Buck said.

"Meaning?" Raymond asked.

"Progress spelled backwards," Walt said before Buck could answer. "He thinks that's clever."

"Is that so?" Buck asked. "Maybe you should be saying something clever, Walt. Since you're going home to preach to Indians who you think need your religion, say something clever for us."

"Maybe you should both be less sarcastic," Sam intervened.

The Colonel looked at Buck and said, "I did inspect conditions in the prison camp after we talked yesterday. I found that the RAMPs are still not receiving food rations, and that they are trying to squeeze a few more days from food they had before they got liberated."

Buck nodded in agreement. "To me Patton made it clear with the artillery duel over our camp that he had his own game going. He wasn't going to let over-running a mere one hundred thousand prisoners of war slow his race to get to the Inner Redoubt. Why was he in such a hurry?"

"Wars aren't humanitarian relief projects," Raymond said. "Let's not let our feelings of self-importance confuse us. Patton liberated us by coincidence on the way to his military objective. He had an elaborate war plan that went well. There was plenty of gasoline for the tanks and a full array of vehicles. There was plenty of food for the soldiers. There was plenty of ammunition for the guns. There were plenty of tires for the wheels and repair supplies for the mobile equipment. There was just no food for hungry people he knew he would be liberating along the way. You can't win wars by concerning yourself with people other than the soldiers of your war machine."

Buck faced Dean and smiled as he said, "You tell it like you were talking to a West Point class. Did you inspect the shit and piss swimming on the floors of the toilets? Isn't there some level of pigsty nastiness that can get action from even a general like Patton?"

"I'm thinking like you on that, Buck," Dean responded. "The conditions of the latrines are untenable. We're not eligible to protest to the International Red Cross any more, but I did take a Red Cross worker representative with me, and he promised to have American army doctors inspect the latrines."

From his personal experience, Sam offered the prediction, "The Adjutant General's war crimes investigators aren't going to walk through what's inside for a close look."

Dean shifted the conversation. "We'll be driving into Dachau to deliver me to the congressional delegation. I was given a brief to prepare me. I want to share some of it, to prepare you.

"Thirty-two thousand survivors were liberated there last Sunday, three hundred and fifty of them were women. Our people are still working now on Friday to sort out the SS records and process care for the survivors.

"Among the prisoners held there were Stalin's son, Jacob; the former Austrian Chancellor and his wife; Prince Frederick Leopold of Prussia; Prince Xavier de Bourbon de

Parme; Rev. Martin Niemoeller, the German Lutheran who defied Nazi attempts to control his preaching; and many other notable enemies of Hitler—some now missing—probably transferred to a new hideout in the Tyrol. A French general was shot here just last week. One of the prisoners remaining said he is the son of Leon Blum, the former French premier. One American, a major from Chicago, from the Office of Strategic Forces, was a prisoner here. It's clear from the record that Dachau was more than a concentration camp for Jews. It was also a political prison.

"Nine thousand inmates died of hunger and disease or were shot over the past three months. Typhus was present in the camp, and fourteen thousand more died last winter. While the liberation battle was going on there was a train of thirty-nine coal cars on the siding. The cars were loaded with hundreds of victims, mostly Poles. Most had starved to death as the train stood there idle for several days.

"Colonel Cowling of Leavenworth, Kansas, was the first to slip the lock on the main gate of the camp. A flood of Russians, Poles, French, Czechs, and Austrians mobbed him and carried him on their shoulders until he was rescued by our troops.

"Inside the barracks were more than a thousand bodies of prisoners, some shot by the SS guards in a wild melee the night before. Most of the SS guards were killed in the liberation battle, the real SS executives of the camp have escaped.

"Look," Walt interceded, as he pointed ahead. "Do you think that's the camp?"

"We'll soon know," Dean said. "I expect we'll need tough stomachs to go in there. I have a feeling the congressional delegation is going to get more than they are prepared for."

As the car approached the gate, Dean instructed, "Drive in until you find the headquarters building. I'll get my schedule there."

After getting cleared through a gate, the car passed over a water moat and then crossed through a barbed wire barrier and entered the camp interior. The driver clamped his nose to block out the stench as they neared a stack of dead prisoners near the roadway. One corpse with shrunken eyes had an arm bent skyward pointing toward the car windows.

"God, have mercy," Walt mumbled.

Sam murmured, "God must be mourning the day he made human beings."

"I'm asking God to give me the chance to get my hands on just one of the bastards who caused this," Buck fumed.

Colonel Raymond was silent until the car stopped at a building where several other vehicles were parked. Then he said, "I feel like a dressed-up specimen, some kind of insect that will be looked upon today for clues of what happened here. Do our politicians really want to know? The U.S. isn't leading the way to organizing a world police to prevent this happening again. I'll be surprised if the congressmen who came here will go back fighting for a United Nations to prevent this kind of fiendish horror. If seeing this changes nothing, what will it take?"

The Colonel got out and went into the headquarters building. In a short while he returned. "Understandably, the delegation has decided to have its conference outside the walls of Dachau. Leave me here. I'll be driven to the region's occupation headquarters. You've got a map. Get directions from the guard at the gate for picking me up there. An elaborate lunch is planned at which I am supposed to pose for pictures with the politicians. I want to miss that. Be back no later than noon. I'm depending on you to rescue me. Walt, you go with Sam and Buck. The congressmen brought interpreters. You'll be needed in Pellheim more than here."

"Whatever you say, Colonel. I was hoping I could be of help here."

"Walter, after seeing how participants are dressed for the occasion, I think you would be embarrassed in your raunchy kriegie debris. I'm sure you don't want to serve as a showpiece."

The car turned around and started back to the gate. Suddenly a skin-and-bones prisoner waved them to a halt. In a feeble voice he asked in English with only a slight German accent, "Are you from the United States Congress?"

504

Sam answered, "No. We're just prisoners of war who were liberated from Moosburg."

The Dachau inmate informed that some people had come to the camp yesterday from the Judge Advocate General's office to collect information on war crimes. They had told him that United States Congressmen would be coming today to see how they could help them.

The inmate continued, "I know that with so many thousands of us here we cannot all get help at once, but what will they do with us now? Do you know? If I only knew what the plan is—"

Buck interrupted, "My advice is don't hold out for the plan. We'll hide you in our trunk and take you to a German farm. The Germans are so scared at this point they'll look after you in style until you get a better deal. Come on. Let's get you out of here."

"I can't leave. I have to wait for the plan for me. I think they are going to send me to a hospital."

"We understand," Sam comforted. "My friend was only trying to help."

"God bless you," Walt called back as they pulled away, leaving the Dachau victim smiling toward them in farewell.

After getting instructions at the gate on where to meet Colonel Raymond, they started toward Pellheim.

They spoke little, but after some time Sam opened conversation with, "Thank God we were under the Luftwaffe and not the SS."

"Thank God, too, for the Geneva Convention that gave us the help of the Red Cross," Buck added.

Walt reminded, "If we'd been political prisoners instead of military prisoners, we would not have come under the Geneva Convention rules. All of the horrible treatment of Dachau could have happened to us."

No one felt like talking further about Dachau. The driver filled the quiet with requests for directions from Sam, who was reading the maps.

When they arrived in Pellheim, they searched the streets until they found the address that Smitty had given

Sam. A large building with steep eaves stood before them. A faded mural of Christ in the manger decorated the expanse above the second floor windows. Walt went to the door while Buck and Sam waited in the car.

An old man answered Walt's knock. "Paula Schmidt, bitte," Walt requested.

From the second floor a woman called down in a tense voice, "Ein moment."

Walt waved for Sam and Buck to join him and went up the stairs to the second floor. A woman was entering the hallway. The door she had come from was still ajar.

Walt asked, "Paula Schmidt?"

"Ja, bitte."

Interpreting her reply as an invitation, Walt entered her apartment. Sam and Buck followed even though Paula never did fully open the door.

As they entered, Walt whispered into Sam's ear, "This was your idea. How do I break the bad news? She's nervous as a wet hen."

In German, he introduced Sam and Buck and then himself, and he told her that her husband had been one of their guards in their past year as prisoners of war. He explained that they were calling on her at his request.

Paula did not respond. She acted strangely distant and tense, and didn't ask any questions.

"Maybe we should give her the food we brought for her. That may break the ice," Walt said to Buck and Sam.

Walt talked further in German, and Sam went to the car and brought back a full knapsack of army rations. He handed the knapsack to Paula and told her, "For you. Essen."

Walt said, "I told her that we came to give her some important news. She said that it would be better if we talked somewhere else."

Buck admired Paula's shapely figure. He had not expected Smitty's wife to be so attractive. The top button of her blouse was undone. The flowered print pattern folded into the pale valley of her breasts. He stepped nearer to her and said, "Your husband Wache over us. Smitty, Robert Schmidt. He asked us . . . we see you."

"She can't understand you. Let Walt do the talking," Sam protested.

In frustration over his inability to communicate, Buck blurted the only full sentence of German he knew, "Haben sie Brot fuer prima Americanische Zigaretten?"

"Goddamn it, Buck, let Walt do the talking. Your words for trading cigarettes are out of place here."

"Yeah," Walt said. "Stand back and give me a chance to tell her."

Remembering that Walt had not intended to visit Paula, Buck said, "We'll tell you what to say. You stick to translating. I may be getting the words wrong, but don't pretend you're the big kind soul heading this visit."

Paula backed away and put the knapsack with food on a cabinet standing along a wall next to a cooking stove. On the wall across from the cabinet was a baby crib. On the wall opposite from the entrance door, a makeshift wardrobe and a double bed competed for space.

A pile of blankets was heaped on the bed.

Buck stepped closer to Paula once more, "Amerikanische Zigaretten for you," he said as he extended an unopened package of Lucky Strikes. To Walt he said, "Explain how to make coffee with the powder. We need to sit down to some coffee with her before we say more."

Walt translated Buck's message.

"Show her the chocolate bars, and tell her how to mix the powdered milk," Sam urged.

Walt conversed with Paula again, but as he talked she only became more nervous. He noticed that her hands were trembling. Again she said that they should talk somewhere else.

Walt told Buck and Sam, "She doesn't seem to be believe that we came here to be nice to her. She wants us to leave and talk to her somewhere else. Since I'm the only one who talks German, maybe it's time I told her why we've come. What do you think, Sam?"

"Gosh. I guess you'd better tell her," Sam agonized.

As Walt talked now, with a shrieking wail Paula covered her eyes. Simultaneously, a baby in the crib started screaming.

Buck patted Paula's shoulder to comfort her. "Smitty good man. Gut!" he consoled.

Sam said nothing. He wiped his eyes and turned his head to one side to give Paula privacy in her misery.

Walt spoke to her further. She dried her eyes, drew herself into disciplined calm, and turned toward the cabinet. She cut three thick slices from a half loaf of dark bread. In between slicing bread and drying her eyes, she spoke to Walt.

Walt translated, "She's apologizing for not having food to return our kindness."

Buck said, "Tell her to cut herself some of the white bread we brought. I'll open a can of spam to have with the bread and coffee if she has a can opener."

"Use your knife," Walt said.

"Not my knife," Buck said. "I'm saving my razor sharp edge."

"Forget it," Walt said. "We'll just have the bread and coffee. She's too upset."

The baby stopped screaming but continued crying. Paula went to the crib and lifted the child into her arms. She cuddled it, but the child only cried louder.

While this was happening, Sam noticed the blankets on the bed moving. He nudged Buck and pointed to the moving blankets. Buck motioned Sam to move behind him as he stepped over to the side of the bed and drew his knife from its sheath under his shirt. With his knife poised for attack, he signaled Sam to pull the blankets from the bed.

Sam took a firm grip and jerked back. As the blankets came off, a startled man raised a Luger toward Buck. Seeing the gun lifting toward him, Buck struck the arm savagely with a back hand. The pistol fired wild and tumbled to the floor. The bullet hit a glass vase with an explosive shatter. Buck lunged into the bed with his knife aimed at the man's chest.

Simultaneously, the trapped man kicked off of the bed and rolled onto the floor to retrieve his Luger as Sam and Walt dove to the floor to get it. Buck landed in the empty bed with his knife thrust into the mattress where the man had been a second before.

The floor was alive with wild scrambling to get the gun. Buck scrambled to get out of the bed. His feet hit the floor after the man had gotten hold of the gun and was now shifting against the wall to get into position for firing. As the Luger was lifting, Buck broad-jumped over Sam and Walt. With one leg forward and with his foot extended, he landed his shoe into the man's stomach. With his arms extended to cushion the impact he hit the wall, crushing against his assailant. He dropped to the floor over his doubled-up assailant and wrenched the gun from his hand.

"Okay, you son-of-a-bitch. Try something else and you're dead," he shouted. "Walt, find out who he is."

Paula, whose face was frozen as she watched, hugged her still-crying baby, and started babbling hysterically.

Walt translated, "She says be careful he's very dangerous. He's an SS officer who escaped from Dachau, and he's put on civilian clothes so he wouldn't be discovered. He is hiding here until dark when he has a way to get to relatives in Yugoslavia."

"Walt, tell him to get on his feet and stand against the wall with his hands over his head," Buck said.

The man rose, half doubled-up, holding his stomach, trying to catch his breath.

"Tell him I don't give a damn if his belly hurts. If he don't get his hands above his head, I'll kill him!"

Walt translated and with difficulty the man raised his hands.

Sam and Walt had gotten to their feet and were standing near the bed. Buck was standing just far enough from his target to be sure the pistol could not be grabbed away from him. Sam retrieved Buck's knife and joined Buck in a seeming backup for Buck in event of trouble.

"Ich Yugoslav," the man now whined, then he began speaking German to Walt.

Walt translated, "He says Paula is lying because she was living with an SS officer while her husband was in the war, and she is now afraid she will be arrested for it. He says he is really an ordinary soldier who escaped because he was ordered to fight with the SS. He says he only shot because he was afraid. He asks for mercy so he can go home to his family."

Sam said, "He's lying! Have Paula tell us more about him!"

Walt turned to Paula. After talking with her he said, "She will tell us his name for us to check his story."

Paula spoke slowly, "Obersturmführer Herman Mehlhoff."

"What else did she say?" Sam asked.

"She said he raped her and took her prisoner more than a year ago. He brought her here. Nobody dared help her because he is from the worst SS that arrests people as they please. She had his child and she never even dared tell her husband what happened to her. She had no way to get free from him—"

Paula interrupted Walt. Then he translated, "She says you can't know how an SS officer strikes terror in people. Obersturmführer Mehlhoff had favor with high people in the Party. He was transferred to Dachau from the Russian Front by Hitler himself as an honor for his fierce patriotism."

Paula now spoke directly to Herman Mehlhoff.

Walt translated, "She told him, now you snivel for mercy— for what? For kindness to let you be a beast again?"

Sam took a firmer grip on Buck's knife as he listened.

"I've got another idea for checking if he's SS," Walt said. With that he stepped forward, grabbed the lapel of the German's shirt, and ripped it as hard as he could.

Horrified, the German, still trying to catch his breath, tried to cover his SS tattoo.

With an explosion of rage buried for years, Sam lunged with Buck's knife. The razor sharp edge cut through flesh and pierced into Herman's heart. As Herman crumpled, Sam gave the knife a twist and pulled it free. Herman's pierced heart released a torrent of blood that gushed onto the floor as he fell face down.

Buck said, "I saw it, Sam. He was trying to escape."

"This isn't right," Walt protested awestruck. "We should have turned him in to the Military Police."

Buck retorted, "Turn him in to the MPs? Are you crazy? Regardless of who he is, they'd look for us for murdering him. God, have her do something with that baby. I can't stand it crying and crying and crying!"

As if of one mind with the words she could not understand, Paula opened her blouse and began to nurse her child.

"What a relief," Buck said. "Now we've got to get to work to save her from being arrested. First we've got to get rid of this buzzard-puke."

Sam's voice cracked, "That's right. If we leave him here the MPs will arrest her."

"Walt, you keep your mouth shut about this," Buck commanded. "And get through to Paula to not tell anyone what happened—especially not Americans—they'd fry her for hiding an escaped SS officer and say piss on who killed him."

Sam nodded as he said shakily, "You're right, Buck. To the MPs she's guilty because she was hiding him. We've got to get him out of here. I'll see to the burying he deserves."

Buck went to Paula who was now in tears. He held her close and told Walt, "Explain to her that we'll protect her. Everything will be all right if she says nothing. We'll clean up the blood and get rid of all signs of this varmint before we leave. And we'll give her our names and how to contact us if she needs us to prove she is no Nazi."

Walt told Paula. She nodded with a painful smile and tears still in her eyes. She sat down and continued to nurse her child as she stared at the body on the floor.

Buck said for translation, "Tell her I can't promise we can come back because we're due to get flown out of Germany, but she'll have our addresses."

"It wasn't your business to promise my address. I'm not coming back," Walt told Buck.

Sam and Buck wrote down their names and home addresses.

Sam emphasized to Walt, "Tell her I really want her to write to me. When I get back home, I'll send her things for her baby, if she'll write and tell me where to send them."

Sam's message started a new flow of tears.

Buck went down to the car and came back with a blanket. They wrapped the body in the blanket and took it down to the trunk of the car. Then they came back and wiped up all the blood, being sure to clean away every trace of the killing. Sam was the last to leave.

Unable to speak German, he pantomimed what he hoped would carry to Paula as, "I know we're leaving you feeling terrible, but there's nothing I can do."

Paula, weeping, nodded as if she understood.

Sam closed the door separating his world from hers.

From the car, as they left, they noticed that someone had hung a white sheet from a window next to the entrance.

"That wasn't there when we came," Walt observed. "I take it the people who heard the shot and racket decided to put up a white sheet to show they're not wanting trouble."

A safe distance away from Paula's place, Sam asked the driver to stop for a minute.

"Look straight ahead, and don't ask any questions," Buck instructed the driver. "This is private business. It's better you don't know about it."

Sam and Buck got out. "This is perfect for him," Sam eulogized. With that they lifted out Herman's body and dumped it into the sewer water of the roadside gutter.

"I hope we make it back by noon," Walt nagged as the car started away. "Colonel Raymond won't want to be kept waiting."

"Rest easy, Walt," Buck consoled. "We're still on schedule."

After traveling with no one talking for a long while, Buck commented, "To my mind, there are worse things than horse thieving when it comes to deserving a lynching."

Dean was waiting at the rendezvous site. The trip back to Moosburg started on schedule. The conversation centered on when the C-47 evacuation planes would arrive and what the plan was for RAMPs after that.

Upon return, Colonel Raymond asked for lunch to be served in the private dining room off of the dining hall. When they were alone, Raymond said, "It was obvious you had your lips buttoned on the way back. Why?"

What had happened on Paula's visit was confided to Dean. Paula's history and present circumstances were shared, too. The conversation was open, except that the killing of Herman was always referred to as "necessary" to prevent his escape.

Colonel Raymond said, "I told you that some of Dachau's top officers left the night before the liberation. Maybe he was one of them. It's good you stopped him from escaping, Sam. It took guts with only a knife."

Sam said, "It wasn't quite that way. Buck had a gun pointed at him. It was a big move for me. I didn't join the service to make it legal to kill people. As a bombardier I was above the killing, just pushing a button. I didn't want to kill anybody until today."

Walt admonished again, "We should have turned him in to the MPs, like I said."

"Stay on course. He tried to escape, so we turned him in to the gutter," Buck snapped.

Walt retorted, "He deserved to die, but not without a trial. That's the human rights we're fighting for!"

Buck contested, "He got his trial. Sam was the court."

Dean said, "Walt, you are entirely right. We won the war. We're now the world's MPs. We need soldiers like you who honor our MPs. As for me, even before Dachau, I was getting more interested in immediate people problems, like Paula's situation. Can you imagine Herman free and coming back to kill Paula and get his kid? If you think all these SS monsters are going to get killed by turning them in to the MPs, you're thinking different than me. I see them free faster than you can guess—but not Herman, thanks to Sam."

Walt came back, "Sir, but Dachau is what happens when people start taking the law into their own hands."

Dean responded, "People? Hitler, his government, was the law, not the German people. Let's get off this subject. I've had a hell of a day with the congressmen. I want to talk about procurement. Captain Pierce and Lieutenant O'Brien, hear me out. I've heard that there are wineries in this town and one, at least, has been axed by the Russians and has wine knee-deep in the cellar. My theory is that the plunder cannot be complete. I'm giving unofficial orders to liberate wine for us, without military transportation since the mission is unofficial."

"You mean carry it by hand?" Buck asked.

"Hardly. Walt has a crew to get a horse and wagon and the needed containers. The president whose office I'm using has said he'll help. These days he's most cooperative because he's scared to death, having worked with Hitler. He's even introduced his eighteen-year-old daughter to me with a glint in his eye. With his help, we might get some wine. I've had a dry palate for too long."

Sam and Buck acknowledged their assignment.

Dean went on, "Now I'm going to get the results of the doctors' inspection of the latrines. Then I've got to check in with my Repatriation Office. People are coming in who claim they're kriegies who were holed up outside the camp, waiting for the evacuation planes."

"I'd like to go with you when you check about the latrines," Buck requested.

"All right. Come along. Sam, you keep the wine project moving. I'm going into the camp personally."

At the Repatriation Center a sealed envelope from the medical inspection team was waiting. Raymond read the message enclosed, then said to Buck. "They ordered the latrines of our compound off-limits as a health hazard. They've posted MPs around them to keep kriegies out. Now they're inspecting the latrines of the rest of the camp."

"Meanwhile, where are kriegies supposed to piss and shit?" Buck asked.

"Let's get into the compound and see what's happening," Dean replied.

On their way through the compound they saw Major Reddick and stopped to get a first-hand report.

Reddick told them, "Come with me. On the way, flip your brain, because what you'll see you won't believe. After the doctors blocked off the latrines with MPs, some of us woke up.

We'd been numskulls waiting for our government to take care of us. We decided it might take weeks of paper work. It hit us that the German POWs had sanitary slit trenches because they had rights under the Geneva Convention. Since we were liberated, we were on our own to take care of ourselves. That is freedom."

"What did you do?" Dean asked.

"We got the English to let us send a detail of kriegies to town to liberate tools and get German volunteers. Being part of the victorious new power in control of people's fate here certainly encouraged them to volunteer. Some acted like they were glad to be asked."

Reddick stopped talking and pointed ahead to where RAMPS and German civilians were working together, digging slit trenches.

"Give us a couple more hours and we'll be open for business," Reddick said.

Raymond said, "I'm asking why my brain didn't come up with this answer sooner."

Buck was stunned. "Kriegies and krauts working together? This has got to be illegal."

Reddick continued, "We also found the honey wagons to empty the latrines, but no horses to pull them, or drivers either, since the German drivers are all now POWs or dead.

We got some farmers with horses to volunteer, and we've started pumping out the unholy crap we've been stuck with."

"I commend you, Reddick. You got us all to realize that we didn't have to wait for bureaucratic rescue. We took over."

When Dean and Buck left the compound, Dean headed for his office and Buck went to the kitchen.

"What's happening?" Buck asked Walt.

"I'm supervising, and our Fraulein Kristen Schultz is scrubbing the floor."

"I'm looking for Sam O'Brien."

"He's outside with the wagon we liberated. We're needing a horse and a harness to hitch it up."

Buck approached the German girl scrubbing the floor and said, "My name is Buck. Do you speak English, Kristen?"

Instead of answering, Kristen put down her scrub brush and ran out of the kitchen.

"What's wrong with her?"

"Soldiers trying to get friendly scare her after how she got mauled by a GI. When we got here we found her hiding in the cellar to keep from getting arrested with the general she was living with. Out of guilt, maybe, nobody's turned her in to the MPs up to now. I've been giving her food, but making her work for it."

"She looks so innocent. I can't see her making love with an old fart general. She can't be more than nineteen."

"She's twenty-two. From Berlin. There's a mystery about her. When they arrested the general his Luger wasn't in his holster. We're thinking she may have it. That Luger mystery is keeping her cellar room a safe retreat."

"She's safe from me, for sure. I'm only interested in flying out of here. I'm going outside to find Sam."

Buck did not search long before Sam called, "Come take a look at the wagon we liberated. The top is gone but it has the same kind of markings on the wood that Duntsi's caravan had."

Buck studied the wagon's wooden sideboards and discovered faded paintings of rosettes and trisula interspersed with flowers and ravens. "It's not Duntsi's," he said. "His caravan had a broken board on the front. But it's like his. This could be one of the other wagons of Dunsti's outfit. Any way you figure, it must have been headed for that beach in France where they go to worship Saint Sara."

"I'd like to go there some day," Sam reflected. "Remember my Sandra was a Gypsy—Pirusambi her name was. Walt is only interested in Gypsies because of the charm he thinks his ring carried. I want to know why Gypsies live so different. Can you imagine what it would be like on the beach with the Gypsy music and the girls like Gali and Sandra?"

"Dream on, Sam. I'm smelling that hedgehog stew, but let's get on with the wine job."

"We can't until they get here with the horse and harness. Do you know the reason Gypsies walk in the water on the beach in southern France with the statue of Saint Sara? It's because they believe God worked a miracle there to save two persecuted holy women from dying in a boat drifting off shore."

"Duntsi said they're Catholic. If Gypsies are Catholic, what you're saying doesn't tie in," Buck challenged.

"Buck, the Catholic Church made Sara a saint because these persecuted women in the boat were sisters of the mother of Jesus," Sam answered. "The miracle in Gypsy religion is God getting the persecuted women to shore like he took the persecuted man Jesus to heaven. It was God's miracle to tell us that in his Gypsy religion women are more important than men."

"Sam, are you making a big thing of God saving women to feel better about you saving Paula? You know, killing Herman, I mean? If God is trying to give us a message about saving persecuted women, he was sure speaking through you in Pellheim. I couldn't believe my eyes. It wasn't like you."

"Maybe what happened was bigger than me. What you're saying may be true. Maybe some power was working through me, like with Saint Sara."

"Don't let this Herman killing take you around the bend, Sam. Your Jewish mother would sure not want you talking a new religion."

"Gypsy religion isn't new. Hitler's own study team decided the Gypsies were the Aryans who started civilization. God's telling us through them that he's switched from the man Jesus to women."

"Settle down, Sam. When we get back home, if you can't stand Chicago, come to Wyoming and start your own ranch, like I'm going to do. That would help you get your mind back down to earth."

At this point some RAMPS of the wine crew showed up. "How do you like the wagon we liberated?" one of them asked.

"Where did you get it?" Sam inquired.

"You guess. We pointed a gun at a wagon full of Germans and told them to get out. They took off through the woods. It was that simple, but they got away with their horses."

"They weren't Germans; they were Gypsy refugees," Buck admonished. "We camped with people like them. They were about wiped out by Hitler, and they were eager for the Americans to get here to save them."

517

"Who said war is clean fun?" the spokesman came back. "They were grateful we didn't kill them Hitler-style. If we made a mistake, that's war. We goofed, but we needed a wagon. The news now is we found a horse in a pasture and have it tied up, but we still need a harness and some cans for the wine."

"You won't have to steal more stuff," Buck said. He led the way to the estate of the president of the electric company. There they were given a harness and a wine barrel large enough to hold twenty gallons. The search was ready to begin.

Sam's attention focused on the setting sun. "Your dandelion's going down, Buck. It's too late to start wine hunting today."

"Let's sit here and watch her set," Buck proposed. "Soon I'll be seeing her shining gold in Wyoming. I'm going to pack into the Big Horn wilderness, first off. I got a message to Randi about wanting to climb Cloud Peak with her. I told her I was hers from the timberline up, which probably doesn't make sense to anybody but us. If that climb ever happens I don't know where it will lead, but I'm sure going to try to get her to take that climb with me."

They went back to the kitchen, took chairs around a table, and while they sipped canned orange juice they talked about the night Buck and Sam had spent with the refugees whose wagon had the Gypsy artwork.

"Did Sister Johanna tell you anything about Saint Sara's teachings, Walt?"

"No, but there must be a book about her."

"I want to read it," Sam said.

"I want to study it," Walt said. "You know, Sister Johanna is in the States now."

Sam responded, "Walt, if you start asking deeper questions about the Gypsy religion, the answers might not fit with your Methodist preaching. What then?"

"Why are you asking, Sam?"

"I'm wondering if anything new you learn could change your life plans."

"Don't get smart," Walt reacted angrily. "With Sister Johanna in America . . . she may even work as a missionary with us. We're all Christians; that's what counts."

"But Christians don't roam around and take pride in not owning property, like Gypsies—"

Buck interrupted, "Lay off Walt, Hatch."

"Don't call me Hatch anymore. I'm Sam. I used to say I was hatched from an egg to get me free of the people-fighting I grew up in. Now I've learned that I'm into the fighting and I have to be. I'm glad I killed Herman. It's not right to make spiders the scapegoat for no-good people."

"Hatch, I mean, Sam, you're slipping back to your sack world. Goddamn it, brighten up. In a few days we'll be homeward bound to go our separate ways. We'll all have to sharpen up, 'cause it's going to be a big change to be free. There will be no one to stop us from going crazy, to say it blunt."

Walt got up and started to leave. "I've got a meeting with Colonel Raymond," he explained. His departure started Buck and Sam to their private rooms.

Walt went to the Repatriation Office where he was invited to sit in a brown leather chair opposite from Dean Raymond behind his walnut desk in his immaculate new uniform.

"I've come to see you about Kristen Schultz," Walt opened. "I need your advice. She tells a story about being kidnapped to live with an SS general, but what Nazi hasn't got a good story to save themselves? I don't know if she's lying or not. I'm asking if I should turn her in. I've checked with the war crimes office, and they don't have her name."

"You're saying she may be lying. If she isn't, we'd be putting her into a hell of a lot of trouble by turning her in. Is she friendly with you?"

"No, but she's friendlier with me than anyone else. Maybe because I talk German, but she talks pretty good English. She says she learned it where she was studying piano. She says her father is a conductor, and when she was twenty-one he took her to where an SS general saw her and asked to take her out. She says her father was afraid because the Nazis were suspicious of him. He told her it was too risky to say no."

"Is she saying her father forced his daughter to be a whore?"

"To him it sounded like innocent friendliness, she said, so she agreed. She says she hated the SS, and this general was thirty years older than her, but that was the beginning."

"The beginning of what?"

"She started to cry when I asked that. Then she said he took her to his apartment. She said in the morning he told her this would be her private apartment from now on, and he would bring her the finest piano for her to continue her study without leaving his place."

"How long ago does she say this happened?"

"When she was twenty-one . . . and according to her identity card she's almost twenty-three now."

"That would be more than a year ago. As you said, she could be lying, or she could really be a tragic victim of SS terror. Since, strangely, I'm quartered with a grand piano, I can check out if she's a pianist easy enough."

"Colonel, you're living in what was the general's quarters. If she's telling the truth, that would be her piano."

"Bring her to me tomorrow. I'll interrogate her. I've got to clear my desk now."

In the morning, Buck, Sam, and Walt hitched their liberated horse to the wine wagon and drove away to do the duty of Buck and Sam as Procurement Officers. By three o'clock in the afternoon the German civilians had convinced them that other soldiers had already emptied all the sources of wine. They returned and sat at a table in the lobby while they ate corned beef sandwiches and drank canned orange juice and planned for a better tomorrow. Suddenly the sound of airplanes welled above them.

They ran outside and counted twenty-five C-47s passing overhead.

"Our orders call for us to go out on the first trip!" Sam rejoiced. "I'm going to mark this day. Saturday, May 5, 1945—the day the big birds came to fly us away!"

"I'll be leaving, too," Walt said because our Repatriation Center is closing now that the planes are here."

As the exuberance quieted, Buck noticed storm clouds on the horizon and said, "It would be our luck to have bad weather coming when we're due to fly out."

"I've got a meeting with the Colonel," Walt said. "I'll see if he has news on the weather."

Walt found Kristen waiting for him as directed. She was dressed in immaculate white that she had somehow rescued from the dust of her coal room quarters. Together they went to Dean's office.

Dean dismissed Walt and asked Kristen to come in. He chose chairs that allowed him to face her without his desk protruding between them. "Captain Plank has shared some of your personal history, if what you told him is true, but I need to know more about you. Tell me about your family," he began.

"I have two brothers, but they lost—killed—in Russia. My mother ist noch—is still—in Berlin. She has—sugar sickness—I worry from her with the Grossangriff—bombing, in Berlin. If she is alive, there is little medicine now. I need go Berlin, for her, but the Russians would arrest me. They would know I lived with SS general. They kill me—no chance."

"What makes you think you are safe here?"

"Americans, too, not hear me. They call me Nazi whore. Rape and beat me. There can be no pity. I only wish back before the day the SS took over me."

"Wishing won't help you. You can't stay here. What are you going to do?"

"There is no hope. I know das kann nicht sein. I sing words of the refugee song, 'May I perish, may I die! For in God's name I have nowhere to go.'"

Dean cleared his throat before he answered, "No place to go? What can I say? You are not alone here today in that regard. At least you're still alive. Yesterday I saw horrors in Dachau that deaden my sympathy for what Germans have suffered under Hitler. But I'm going to give you the chance to convince me you are really a victim of the SS."

"I tell you only truth. I know not what to do. I have no place to go."

"I'm leaving Germany in less than three days. In all of the hell of the air war and my prison hell here I've witnessed horrors that I've been helpless to change. Rescuing you, if you're telling the truth, would be a personal victory to carry home with me. But, in the desperate plight you're in, I can't naively assume you are being honest. Come with me."

Dean led the way to his suite.

"Take a seat at the piano. First, I need to know if you are, in fact, a pianist. Play something to show your talent."

Kristen put her hands to the keyboard. Then . . . she suddenly pushed herself away and fled from the room sobbing audibly.

Dean went down to the kitchen. Walt asked him, "What happened? I saw her run back to the cellar. Should I go after her?"

"Leave her alone. She's a complicated person. I'll have to report her."

"I thought so. That's why I told you about her. Another thing," Walt continued, "We didn't find any wine, sir. I'm on my way to the president's place. You said he would help us so we're going to take him along with us tomorrow."

"Tomorrow? Ask him for some bottles from his private stock for a dinner celebration tonight. It's the end of our kriegie life and the beginning of wherever we're going from here."

Walt found the president eager to please them. Dinner was served with vintage wine.

Next morning, with Sunday church bells ringing from steeples touching storm clouds, notice was given that the airfield at Landschut was socked in. All flights were canceled. The evacuation was rescheduled to begin on Monday, weather permitting.

Dean instructed Buck that a successful wine mission was now imperative. On the Sunday morning, horse, harness, and wagon were put together. With Walt, Buck, and Sam on the driver's seat, the wine wagon was first driven to the home of the president. He boarded and perched on a wine barrel in the center of the wagon. From this station he directed the search party. As the wagon rattled through Moosburg, townspeople stopped and, with dazed looks, regarded the president of their local electric company seated on a wine barrel, being ferried in display by soldiers of their "liberators."

By early afternoon the search had yielded fifteen gallons of wine. Then it started to rain. The horse was urged to a trot on the wet cobblestone street until it returned to the gasthaus.

Meanwhile, Colonel Raymond was surprised by a visit from his West Point classmate, Major Bellrage. Bellrage explained that his train out of Spremberg had gone directly to Moosburg. After liberation he had squirmed through the barbed wire and gone to a German farm where he had worked for food and shelter. Now, to get evacuated, he had come to the Repatriation Center.

"Does Margot know you're still alive?" Dean asked.

"No. You surprise me, Dean. Your first question is about my wife. You've changed."

"I've been puzzling about you through the empty days we've had for thinking. I still hear your words of last August . . . 'Margot is what keeps me lasting here.' That was the day I got my 'Dear John' letter. I presume I didn't fool you with all my talk about the women I was waiting to get back to."

"I knew you were trying to convince me you didn't care about losing Katherine."

"Henry, I've also been asking myself what it was that gave you the strength to take command in Muskau when I couldn't. You hadn't trained as hard as I did."

"Come on, Dean, your leadership saved a lot of lives even though your body didn't always deliver what you wanted from it."

"I'm asking if your religion gives you an advantage. I'm still stuck with my two-foot ladder to heaven with no reward for being grounded with the enemy."

"We survived. We're going home. That's enough reward."

"I don't know where I'm going from here," Dean said.

"Strange you don't know, Dean, sitting in the new uniform of an eagle colonel. You have what it takes to move up to the highest ranks of the air force."

"You're baiting me. You're getting out. Why shouldn't I?"

"I was assuming you are still committed to the air force."

"Henry, I feel like I've been flying a very long mission and my ship hasn't landed. The war's not over for me. Maybe it never will be. But I'll have to find other challenges."

Bellrage fidgeted, hesitated, and then said, "Since Sagan I've decided love doesn't always defeat evil. I admit now that sometimes it takes force. I'm admitting it so you'll know I wasn't baiting you about staying in the military."

"Henry, how can you think, after all I've bitched about, I would want to stay in the military?"

"I apologize. I know you got exiled trying to be a Billy Mitchell of World War II."

"I got tricked away by the title—inspector general. Inspector of what? The decisions had already been made. All I accomplished was to get captured by the enemy."

"I know. I'll sum it up so you'll know I'm taking the picture home. As Billy Mitchell put it, the general staff again kept the air force in an auxiliary role to ground troops—and our Commanding General Spaatz still says the ground invasion was not necessary. Right, Dean?"

"Too right, but what has brought you to raise the flag in behalf of the air force now?"

"I've come to the question of what we should do about it what you've bitched about, Dean. The battle with the general staff started by Billy Mitchell has just begun. The answer is a stronger air force, stronger in control of what we do and I want to preach for it."

"I hear you, but you're getting out of the air force and suggesting I shouldn't get out. Be consistent."

"I've learned I'm better as a teacher. You're a leader, the kind the air force needs."

Dean leaned back, clasped his hands behind his neck, and vacantly said to the ceiling, "On the day they pinned on our wings we both sang, 'Nothing can stop the Army Air Corps.' Today we've been shot down too long for that song, classmate." He lowered his vision to eye contact with Henry and added, "It's time for me to pass the challenge to pilots with shinier wings. War strategy gets too mixed up with politics for me to stomach any more of the fight."

"We've come to a stand off, friend. Let's drop the subject."

"I agree, Henry, I've got a challenge right here today to puzzle about. There is a girl in the gasthaus whom I'm about to report to the War Crimes office. But the possibility still exists that she is a victim. I don't want to leave Germany feeling . . . this girl ended her interrogation today with the words of a song: 'In God's name I have no where to go.' Those words haunt me. They echo how I feel. I'm asking if my confusion—"

"Go the extra mile to be sure you are not making a cruel mistake. As for you—without Katherine and Tom—my advice is—a day at a time. Feeling lost is a scare to expect from suddenly being free."

"Good advice, Henry, maybe the around-the-bend vision we've picked up being kriegies deserves a scientific name as a special kind of sickness."

A knock on the door was followed by a voice calling, "Colonel, we got fifteen gallons of wine. I thought you'd like to know."

"We're going to have a freedom celebration tonight. Join us, Henry?"

"I'll decline. I've had too many years crowded in with too many people to fit in."

"I'll show you to a room to stay here until it's your turn to fly out."

When Bellrage was in his room, Dean searched out Walt. "I've given Kristen's case more thought. If she's lying, why is there a piano in the general's quarters? I need to see what we can learn from searching her retreat."

"It's a good time to search there now. She's working in the kitchen."

"Let's go. I don't want to report her without being sure."

Walt and Dean went down to the windowless cellar lit with dim bulbs hung from light cords. On the north side, a door was centered in a dark plank wall. Beyond this door, they found the gasthaus furnace to the left and a khaki canvas hung across an area to the right.

Walt pulled back the canvas. Dull lamp-glow cast deep shadows as it revealed a white bed standing on a dirt floor. Empty ammunition cases stood next to the bed. One held a suitcase with the lock broken off. "I figure somebody helped her hole-in here before we found her," Walt said.

"I'm looking for life signs—clues to who she truly is."

They searched the suitcase and ammunition cases and found a cloth coat, a rain coat, a pink satin lounging robe, satin slips trimmed with ribbons, skirts, sweaters, blouses, cotton stockings, an empty purse, shoes, gloves, handkerchiefs, five fine-cloth dresses carefully folded, and three pairs of silk stockings folded in a satin bag. Under the bed they found a hat box containing a lavender hat.

"This tells me only that she was not living in poverty. Who is she as a person? Let's keep looking," Dean reflected.

"I found something," Walt said as he pulled a cotton-lined container out of a pillow. Inside were sheer brassieres and lacy satin panties, and at the bottom was a family picture which included herself, two soldiers, and an older woman and man.

"Wow!" Walt reacted. "The general must have liked her wearing sexy dainties. Look. Some of the labels are French."

Dean looked at the picture and said, "She favors her mother. It appears we have verification of her family story. Let's look further."

"Get a load of this," Walt said as he inserted his hand into a double bottom in the hat box. "I'm touching metal. I think I found the general's missing Luger."

Dean pulled out a small round case and moved it close to the light bulb. "It's got a winder like a clock but it's not a clock."

Dean saw that the case was brass and that it had been recently polished, but it still revealed a long history with its dents, scratches, and nicks. He pulled on a pin beside the winder and the case began to play.

After he had listened until the music ended, he said softly, "It's Beethoven's 'Für Elise.'"

Walt had kept searching while the music played. "Ah! What have we here?" he beamed as he reached up to a ledge and brought down a box six inches deep.

Still with the spell of the music-box "Für Elise," Dean said, "Since we need to violate her privacy, empty what you have onto the bed."

"It's sheet music and piano music books. Chopin. Brahms. Beethoven. And one that says, 'Bach Preludes and Fugues.'"

"We've looked enough. Let's put everything neatly back and get out of here."

As they left, Walt asked, "Are you going to come and taste the wine?"

"I need to talk to Kristen. Get her to meet me in the private dining room at once."

"You know how edgy she is. I don't know what she'll do."

"Don't mention me. Ask her to make up a coffee service for two and bring it to the dining room. I'll wait there."

In fifteen minutes Kristen appeared with a silver tray carrying coffee. When she saw Dean she hesitated, then she placed the coffee urn, china cups, and silverware on the table and turned away with the tray.

Dean said, "Please don't leave before I can apologize."

From the doorway, she faced Dean in his uniform with its shiny American eagles, not SS eagles, but eagles.

"I am not going to report you. I was wrong in how I treated you. I know SS cruelty. I've been a prisoner in Germany. I have great sympathy for you."

"You soldier. How you feel what is for me? You prisoner? But now you carry eagles. How I believe you sympathy for me? I not show you I tell truth. Why you nice to me? What you want me? Tell me truth what you want so I know. I don't trust you tell me truth."

Dean turned his chair to face her squarely and told her, "I searched through your private belongings. Can you understand that I needed to? I tried to test your honesty by having you play the piano and that didn't work. I couldn't naively trust you."

"I could not play. You order me sit down to piano. Order me play. I much afraid."

"I knew you were very nervous. I regret putting you under pressure, but I had to. I only want to help you. If you can't believe that, it's your turn to test me."

Kristen smiled when she heard this.

"Please sit down."

Kristen put the tray on the table and took a chair.

"I have no test for you," she said.

Dean poured coffee as he said, "You will not have me to help you very long. The airplanes are waiting to fly us out. I may be gone in two days. I want to give you money to care of yourself for a little while after I've gone."

Kristen rose and started to leave.

"I am not trying to buy you. I want to help you for my own reasons. My giving you money is no crazier than the way you've been acting."

Hearing this she sat down again. They sipped their coffee, studying each other over the rims of their cups. Dean pushed some bills toward her from the partial-payment he had received.

When their cups were empty, she rose, picked up the money, and said, "You know I be much need. No hope. I need trust you. I go now."

Dean went to the kitchen. "Where is the wine? I'll try a glass. Then I have to check in on our evacuation schedule. I see it's still raining. We're supposed to be clearing out of here. The occupation forces want to headquarter MPs in this building."

Walt said, "It came on the news that the war's about over. We've taken over a million prisoners, and General Patch has captured Berchtesgaden—there's no more Inner Redoubt."

"Put a bash celebration together to go with our wine tonight," Dean ordered. "And go tell Reddick to join us and stay in a room here. If the weather clears, they'll start flying us out tomorrow. This may be the last night before we go our separate ways."

The bash Dean ordered was served on white tablecloths. The food, served in silver vessels, was the best that army field rations could offer. Dean enhanced the regal air with his new uniform. Others were still dressed in kriegie debris.

As the meal ended, Colonel Raymond and Major Reddick took a flask of wine and retreated to an alcove of the lounge. Buck, Walt, and Sam retired to a kitchen table that Walt had covered with a white tablecloth in keeping with the regal air of the bash.

After a while Dean and Reddick joined the wine drinking at the white clad table.

Sam went to the window. He studied the rain-drop rivulets running down the windowpane and remarked, "This rain looks like it will never stop."

"I got the forecast of clear weather tomorrow," Dean said.

"I'm packed for the ride to the airport," Buck laughed.

Walt commented, "While we're waiting, we're living in style."

"Happy day for you," Reddick leveled at Walt. "Across the street kriegies are living in filth and aching from empty bellies while we wait."

In an apparent move to break the tension, Dean said to Buck, "Tell us more about Wyoming. Does the free spirit of the Wild West still reign there, every man for himself?"

"Pretty much that's the spirit. Not lock step like our Senior Officer was when he left West Point. We'll never have a Hitler leading us by the nose in Wyoming."

Reddick interjected, "Buck, call it a free spirit or a pain in the ass, you've been bucking authority since the first day I knew you."

"Was I bucking authority when you were my Command Pilot, and I kept the Bare Lass flying for you to bail out?"

Reddick responded, "I haven't forgotten you saved my life. You were a good pilot and tough in action. But you're needling the Colonel for his trying to keep discipline under the enemy. You should be lifting your glass to him for getting us to this day alive."

"What the Colonel and I throw at each other is between us. You're not in on what we're talking about," Buck replied.

"I've been working with Colonel Raymond since we were both at Command Headquarters. You don't realize how little you know about him. There they called him the son of Billy Mitchell. I lift my glass to him."

"Stop this," Raymond insisted. "You're talking about me like I'm not here. I don't want any glasses lifted for me, Reddick. If I'm so worthy, why didn't you risk your promotion and hang in with us rebel pilots fighting for Oil targets?"—

Sam interrupted their conversation with, "I want to lift a glass to the kriegies who didn't luck out to make it through to be with us tonight."

"You're on the right course, Sam," Dean said. "Our missing are among the few, special champions. No, that's not right. They're among the many. All special. Too goddamn many."

Reddick's glass and Sam's glass were already lifted. Buck, Dean, and Walt joined them. All drank to the missing.

After a time in which no one found words, Buck squirmed in his chair and finally said, "In spite of what the Colonel's telling he doesn't want, I'm going to raise a glass for him."

Dean protested, "No. Buck and I are throwing stuff at each other that other people aren't in on, but it doesn't call for lifted glasses. Buck is a gut rebel and he's proud of it, but you don't know what I am, beyond your Senior Officer. Reddick touched on me a bit ago. The truth is I'm a brain rebel . . . a subject worth talking about fifty years from now, not on this last night in the land of the enemy. I would appreciate us changing the subject."

"I've got something to ask Reddick," Walt spoke cautiously. "As much as we've been through together, does anybody here call you anything but Major?"—

Buck interjected, "I've got something to say about that. Reddick's been trying to convince us he's hard as hardware, but he's let his soft side show. I remember how he helped save the old kraut who was trying to make it up the hill. We know you've got a soft heart in spite of you trying to hide it, Reddick."

Reddick sputtered, "Soft heart? I'm a soldier, not a nurse."

Buck came back, "Why did you order the guard Krauss back to guard me from the SS when I fell back with the baby carriage? That was caring about me. If you once were hard as hardware, you got human being a kriegie. . . ."

Two hours later, conversation was still flowing, but with less wine drinking. Sam, who had been scribbling on the tablecloth as others spoke, now said, "We ought to be talking about ways to make a living when we get home and ways to keep in touch."

Dean looked at Sam. "Hatch, many good things were said about you when the Nazis had you away—about your poetry, your imagination, your peace-making, and your dream to live in a land of paradise. You're special, among the few, a person needing a special place in life."

Sam said, "What I write and what I think doesn't connect with other people."

Dean said, "I got you the coal officer job to get you out of your sack world. You have gifts to be a writer or an artist if you don't go further into your sack world."

"He's been talking about staying in the army," Walt revealed. "I can't see him being a good soldier."

"Not so fast," Dean said. "He is more of a dreamer than a soldier, but with the years Sam has served, he could retire when he's forty with a paycheck to support his dreams. If you want me to, Sam, I'll recommend you."

Walt continued, "He had a girl he was paying to—and now—never mind—I just hope you can handle your freedom, Sam."

Sam came back, "Walt, you're the one who's out of touch. You plan to have a mission for Indians with a Catholic Sister and you're Methodist and this Sister is preaching a Gypsy religion you don't know anything about."

"Sister Johanna taught me."

Sam challenged, "Do you know Saint Sara was made a saint by the Catholic Church? She's the saint of persecuted women, not the man Jesus? Christianity doesn't worship persecuted women!"

"Let's not argue religion," Buck said.

Sam would not be stopped. "Considering how mothers sacrifice, I've got fine thoughts about how the world would change if women were in charge. Saint Sara and the two holy Marys she saved are a new Trinity—"

With vigor, Walt objected, "The Trinity is not two ship-wrecked women and the Gypsy who saved them! It's the Father, the Son and—"

Sam said, "No. Men are mostly killers. Women are the life-givers."

Reddick broke in, "Be agreeable or shut up."

Sam came back, "Okay. I thought I was saying something important."

Buck broke in, "Walt, I want to admit it was ornery to rib you about your flea bites coming from God playing a game like he did with Job— The wine's got to me, but I want to tell you, Walt, I ain't forgettin' you saved our lives by getting us away from the SS."

Dean raised his glass, "Gentlemen, I'm giving you my final hubba hubba. I'm heading for my bed." Colonel Raymond gained pin-straight stature with effort and labored to the doorway.

"Wait, Colonel," Sam begged, "I still have to pay respect to our special friends Phillips and José and Briggs who didn't make it."

Raymond faced back from the doorway. "Sam, I'm with you. There's no getting away from thinking about the missing. I'm leaving thinking of my son."

Walt got up and showed Major Reddick to his room. Buck and Sam still sat at the table. Buck's head was nodding and then coming back to alertness.

Sam, with no one listening, kept talking, "Without our airplanes, we're birds with our wings melting away in the rain. . . ."

Buck's head nodded down to the table and stayed there. Walt returned.

"So you're back. We're the only ones still lasting," Sam registered.

"We went easier on the wine. Buck's too big for me to get him to his room so I'm going to let him sleep where he is. Why don't you get to your room while you can still walk, Sam?"

"Good idea."

With Sam gone, Walt came around the table and read where Sam had been scribbling on the white table cloth: **Rain drops are the tears of God's love for us.**

He read it aloud. "Rain drops are the tears of God's love for us." "You're not for this world, Sam, but maybe you're not crazy," he told the empty room. "Buck gave me the Job story of God persecuting us as a game. Between Buck and Sam . . . I gotta choose what Sam's seeing in the rain."

Buck's head lifted a last time to see Walt leave before he rested in sleep.

In Kristen's retreat, disquiet within her would not let her sleep. She kept her Luger ready to protect herself. Both a dirge and a melody competed to dominate her spirit tonight.

Late in the night, when stillness told that the "celebration" had ended, her thoughts still stormed. She had proof in money received that she had been selected for special treatment. She kept asking why the Colonel had been so generous when she had not met his test. Even though she had panicked and fled, he trusted her—or did he really trust her?

She felt that she had been intimately exposed to him in his search of her few treasures of music and memories. He said that through this intimate search he had come to believe in her. But in the sinister reality of war, all of her private world could have been cleverly planted for his discovery to save herself.

In her sleepless night it became clear that true trust between them had to be locked solid for the melody to defeat the dirge in her struggle. Having arrived at this awareness, she knew she would have to go to him.

Twice she got up, put on her robe, and went out to the stairway. Each time she saw that it was still dark and still raining. On her third trip, pre-dawn light glowed on the horizon and she saw that the rain had stopped. She returned to her belongings and paged through her music until she found what she wanted. After this she went upstairs and bathed and then brushed her hair to smooth waves that hung to her shoulders.

Still wrapped in her robe, she went up to the suite where she had lived until the Americans arrived. She hesitated by the door until she found enough courage to gently knock. Getting no answer, she turned the knob and slipped into the room. The day had dawned bright enough for her to see Dean lying on the bed, propped against two pillows, fully dressed in his uniform with eagles and wings. He appeared to be sleeping. Her heart pounded as her memory explored him in the bed she had shared. She went to the side of the bed and stood quietly, studying him. Presently, he opened his eyes and regarded her with astonishment.

"I come for you. I need you lock trust in me. I come to you. So you know."

Dean fumbled, "I—don't know what you mean. I—don't know what you expect of me."

"I want to give music from me to you. I know it in my heart."

She stepped closer to him.

Not knowing why she had come to him, he decided to say no more.

She handed him sheets of music and said, "F. minor Fantasia, Opus 49: F. Chopin."

Leaving Dean holding the composition, she slid onto the piano bench and lifted her hands to the keyboard. Turning her head to face him, she said, "For you."

He swung his feet to the floor. Still seated on the bed, he waited.

She sat motionless, with both hands on the keyboard, breathing deeply, gathering in courage until she broke the silence with two bass notes in unison an octave apart, followed rhythmically by descending bass notes and a most brief echo back to the opening herald.

Again the herald sounded, now lower and more melancholy in tone, followed by a plunge downward. Lower still came the third herald, plunging even deeper, then briefly echoing back. Finally the progression rested in the deep reaches of the keyboard on a sustained pitch that floated between the uplifting echoes and the overpowering pull downward. With this descending progression of ten paired bass notes, Kristen had drawn Dean into sharing the provocative passion of Chopin's "Fantasia."

For Dean the bass descent of the opening passage was the war compacted into ten notes descending from opening fervor to closing woe. Now he was joined with her as she lifted into a world of melody—a melody of peace. But when only briefly connected with the melodic promise, the bass notes struck again as a duel between descending gloom and uplifting lyric.

Dean spoke to himself, "She's living in her music. How can she say, 'In God's name I have nowhere to go?'"

No lifting tones countered the descent. The music was imprisoned at a dissonant bass level—an imprisonment of hope in an inescapable sustained gloom of boundless melancholy.

Kristen, with her sleepless, distraught senses, suddenly dropped from the wild excitement of the treble rapture, was overcome by the boundless gloom consuming her. With a grieving sob she broke her hands from the keyboard, covered her face, and fled from the room.

It happened so suddenly that Dean could not react before she was gone.

"Kristen!" he called.

"What now?" he asked aloud with her music still in his hands.

He could still see her appealing to him as she sat at the piano and said, "For you."

He decided that he could only leave her to herself for now, leave her to calm her agony. He promised himself that he would not leave Germany before making certain that she would not be arrested.

A loud knock sounded on his door and Walt called, "Sir, I thought you would want to know. The unconditional surrender was signed at 2:40 this morning. The war in Germany is over."

Dean rushed down to the kitchen where a radio was broadcasting BBC news of the surrender details. Major Bellrage was there. "Don't leave, Henry. I need to talk with you," Dean appealed.

Walt entered and urgently sought Dean's attention to tell him, "I had the wagon and horse hitched to a post right by our front door, but someone managed to steal them."

Sam said, "They're probably on their way to southern France."

"You'd better get your head hitched in another direction," Dean advised. "All my officers below rank of major are due to leave at 10:30 A.M."

"Man, that doesn't give us much time," Walt said.

"Time for what?" Sam asked. "I'm ready."

Buck suggested, "Let's settle around a table for a last coffee time—Cliff-style—but with wine."

At 10:30, they were under the canvas of a deuce-and-a-half truck.

Sam said, "I feel like we're in England, in a truck bound for the flight line."

"Check your flight gear. Do you all have your oxygen masks?" Buck quipped.

"No, but I've got a German Bible I liberated," Walt said.

"To each his own," Sam philosophized. He felt the vibration telling him the truck had started to leave, and he continued, "I've been waiting 'til we start away to share what's happening in a poetry way. Here's what I see, 'In a field nearby a silver raven is waiting to lift us away from the prison world.'"

Buck, Walt, and Sam nodded in affirmation of the poetic vision, but on another level in affirmation of each other at the end of their days of "missing in action."

Dean at this time learned that he was listed to board for the airport. He insisted to Henry, "I can't leave with her in the cellar and the MPs taking over this building. Their minds don't read small print. Her tie-in with the SS will doom her."

"It's too late, Dean. We're scheduled to leave in five hours—3:30 P.M."

"Henry, I need to get both her and her piano out of here before we leave."

"Hold it, Dean. God knows I want to help. But face reality. We're leaving."

"God damn it, Henry, we've got to try!"

"All right, friend, I hear you. You're crazy, but you're right. We've got to try.

There's the farm where I stayed after I escaped. Good people live there, but we'd have to talk to them first. We don't have enough time, but—"

"How far a drive is it? We can have a jeep in fifteen minutes, whether by orders or liberation."

"Add another fifteen minutes and we could be there."

"All right. First we have to tell Kristen what we're trying to do. She's in such a panic she could do something crazy. I'll get the jeep. You tell Kristen I am working to get her to where

536

she will be safe before I leave. Tell her to gather her belongings and wait. I will be back in an hour."

"You better get that jeep fast," Henry said.

Dean rushed away. It took him longer than fifteen minutes, but he did obtain a jeep—commandeered for a "brief emergency."

"How did Kristen take my message?" he asked.

"She was considerably anxious, but she said she'd wait. She specifically used the words, 'I trust him.'"

Dean and Henry made up time racing down the narrow country roads. Eventually they came to the hillside farm where Henry had found harbor.

Dean said, "You know them, and I know your talent with people. I'll wait in the jeep. This needs to be done friendly."

"On that we agree," Henry said. He went to the field where his former hosts were working. Dean waited nervously.

Finally, Henry returned. Dean noted that he was not smiling and this worried him.

"Well?"

"Well, what do you say when God gives you everything you want and even more?"

"Be specific," Dean begged.

"Dean, have some faith in the power of love. They feel honored to have the chance to help her find her way back to her musical future."

Dean started the motor running as he asked, "What about the piano? It's a grand. That will hardly fit into their farmhouse."

"The barn you see ahead of you is really a warehouse. It was built to look like a barn and was used by the Luftwaffe to store aircraft parts where they wouldn't be bombed. Since I left, the place is empty, except for a bed. It would hold five grands with room to spare."

"Keep on, Henry! I'm going to turn believer in the power of God yet. I can't get back fast enough to gather a crew to get that son-of-bitchin' general's piano out here. Our next challenge is to get a truck to haul it. How's our time holding out?"

"We've got three hours," Henry said.

"Hold on while I burn up the road."

When they got back to the gasthaus, Dean and Henry went to the furnace room and explained the details of what was planned. Kristen, unnerved by her sleepless night and the strain of anxious waiting, wept with joy.

"Everything is going to work out. Really Kristen. Believe me. Don't leave your room. There will be a lot of things going on with us moving out and the Military Police moving in, so stay where you are. Hide behind the furnace if you must. We're going to find a truck and load the piano. We'll come back very soon."

"What you think best. I stay here. I ready to go when you say."

"Let's get going, Dean. Ask God to help us find a truck, get a crew, and load the piano in time. She'd better be waiting when we come for her. There'll be too many troops watching when and if we head out of here with a grand piano in a truck. We can't have her get eyed in the yard. Pray Dean."

The wait in the cellar was much longer than expected. With only an hour remaining to departure time, Dean and Henry finally returned.

"It wasn't easy. It was impossible, in fact, but we did it," Dean told Kristen. "There is a duece-and-half truck by the door that leads to the cellar and the piano is in it. We are ready to go as soon as we sneak you aboard."

They carried Kristen's few but treasured belongings to the truck. With a carefully timed dash Kristen was successfully boarded, and the escape mission to the farm started away.

After a half hour of rapid but careful travel to protect the delicate cargo, the deuce-and-a-half arrived at the farmyard. The hastily volunteered GI moving crew as well as Henry, Dean, and Kristen got out of the vehicle and reconnoitered the where-and-how of moving the piano from the truck to its new home.

When the piano was in place and Kristen's belongings were next to her bed that stood five yards from it, Henry asked, "Dean, what now? It's ten minutes to 3:30. We don't have enough time to get back to the gasthaus to catch our ride to the airport."

Dean said, "I've asked our driver to take us directly to the airfield. Get the truck ready to roll down the hill and wait for me. Give me a moment to say good bye. Come with me, Kristen. I brought the music you left in my room and a farewell gift you must not open until I am gone."

"The music pages are my gift for you to remember me," she told him.

"Your gift to me is my memory of you playing 'Fantasia.' All I want is you playing as I leave."

"Where can I write you?"

"I'll send you my address, but don't write to thank me. What I've done is for me as much as for you, as I leave the war, for wherever I'm going."

"I don't want us say good-bye like this, forever. Will I never see you again?"

"I promise I will not forget you. I want to keep hearing from you. I will see you again. I will be in the audience when you play your first concert."

"True? I believe you. Go now. I play, for you—for you to remember. Now I get past the much deep bass. I want you should hear melody and happiness in your remember me."

Kristen began with a melodic passage beyond the bass that had defeated her spirit. She continued playing, reaching higher, with new energy, uplifting with new hope.

As Dean listened, while the deuce-and-a-half coasted down hill, he heard the upward thrust intensify and dance in treble gloriously, bubbling "Fantasia's" triumph of hope . . . on his way to the waiting sky.